THE VICTORY

—PART TWO—

THE VICTORY

— PART TWO —

A GAUNT'S GHOSTS OMNIBUS

DAN ABNETT

BLACK LIBRARY

A BLACK LIBRARY PUBLICATION

The Warmaster first published in 2017.
Anarch first published in 2018.
'This is What Victory Feels Like (Forever The Same)' and
'From There to Here' first published in *Sabbat War* in 2021.
This edition published in Great Britain in 2022 by
Black Library, Games Workshop Ltd., Willow Road,
Nottingham, NG7 2WS, UK.

Represented by: Games Workshop Limited – Irish branch,
Unit 3, Lower Liffey Street, Dublin 1,
D01 K199, Ireland.

10 9 8 7 6 5 4 3 2 1

Produced by Games Workshop in Nottingham.
Cover illustration by Anna Lakisova.

See Black Library on the internet at

blacklibrary.com

Find out more about Games Workshop
and the worlds of Warhammer at

games-workshop.com

Printed and bound by CPI Group (UK) Ltd, Croydon, CR0 4YY

For more than a hundred centuries the Emperor has sat immobile on the Golden Throne of Earth. He is the Master of Mankind. By the might of His inexhaustible armies a million worlds stand against the dark.

Yet, He is a rotting carcass, the Carrion Lord of the Imperium held in life by marvels from the Dark Age of Technology and the thousand souls sacrificed each day so that His may continue to burn.

To be a man in such times is to be one amongst untold billions. It is to live in the cruellest and most bloody regime imaginable. It is to suffer an eternity of carnage and slaughter. It is to have cries of anguish and sorrow drowned by the thirsting laughter of dark gods.

This is a dark and terrible era where you will find little comfort or hope. Forget the power of technology and science. Forget the promise of progress and advancement. Forget any notion of common humanity or compassion.

There is no peace amongst the stars, for in the grim darkness of the far future,
there is only war.

CONTENTS

THE WARMASTER

For Isaac Eaglestone.

The King of the Knives!
The King of the Knives!
This is the song of the King of the Knives!

He sleeps in the woods and he hunts in the hives!
The King of the Knives!
The King of the Knives!
He dies where he doesn't and lives where he thrives!
The King of the Knives!
The King of the Knives!
He cuts all the husbands and preys on the wives!
The King of the Knives!
The King of the Knives!
His voice is as loud as a battleship's drives!
The King of the Knives!
The King of the Knives!
He comes in the darkness and he takes all our lives!

The King of the Knives!
The King of the Knives!
This is the song of the King of the Knives!

– Children's skipping chant, Tanith

'By the start of 791.M41, the thirty-sixth year of the Sabbat Worlds Crusade, the Imperial forces were stretched to breaking point. Warmaster Macaroth's scheme to create a schism between the archenemy Archon Gaur and his most potent lieutenant, the Anarch Sek, thus dividing his opponent's strength, had shown genuine signs of success over the preceding years. Macaroth had achieved this goal through select and specific military strikes, sabotage and propaganda, driving the tribal forces of Sek and the Archon into competition and sometimes open hostilities.

'Emboldened by the sense that a tide was turning, and that his foe was divided, Macaroth had moved rapidly to capitalise, extending the bulk of his huge Astra Militarum force across a midline front to prosecute both. But the ferocious legions of Archon Gaur had consolidated their hold on the Erinyes Group, and Sek's battle hosts were making a counter-push along the Archon's coreward flank through a series of vital systems that included the pivotal forge world of Urdesh.

'Further, Macaroth was facing increasing dissent from his own generals and lords militant. For over a decade, they had been urging that lasting success in the crusade could only be achieved through decisive focus on the warlord Archon, and that simultaneously campaigning against Sek spread the Imperial groups too thinly. Macaroth rejected this approach again and again, insisting that focusing on Gaur would allow Sek time to rebuild his strength, and that this would ultimately lead to an Imperial rout. Overruling objections, he tasked Lord Militant Eirik with the prosecution of Archon Gaur and the Erinyes Group, and drove the attack on Sek himself.

'He had, however, reckoned without two things: the manner of the Archenemy's defence of Urdesh, and the magnitude of a new threat revealed by the very operations designed to effect the schism between Gaur and Sek.'

– From *A History of the Later Imperial Crusades*

ONE

CORPSE

Human ship. *Imperial* human ship. Cold thing from which life-heat has bled. Nothing-thing. Corpse-wreck, broken, inert, adrift...

How long has it been dead? How long had it been alive? How long had it been brave? When and how had that bravery ended? Had the souls within it served their puppet-fool-god dutifully? Had they taken our blood before the void took them?

If they had been worthless fools, then this patch of space was their bone-yard. If they had been heroes to their kind, then this blackness was their sepulchre.

Just a hulk now, a sun-charred lump of chambered metal, rotating slowly through an airless darkness. At the current distance, it is visible only by auspex and sensoreflection. Drive core cold, like a perished star. Organics nil, just the trace residue of decomposition. But there are grave goods to be retrieved. Salvage potential is determined from the gathering meta-data. Good plating for reuse, hull panels, ceramite composites, fuel cells for trading, cabling, weapons systems – perhaps commodity loads too: promethium, small-arms, explosives, even food-packs...

Sixty thousand kilometres. Range and intercept is locked. The signal is given. Amber, the challenge screens blink awake like opening reptile eyes, bathing the command bridge with golden light. Ordnance automates from dormancy, rattling autoloaders and charging cells. Boarding arrays power up and extend, sliding hull-claws, mooring anchors and assault bridges from shuttered silos. The drives come up: a vibration and a hum, and the advance begins.

Forty thousand kilometres. The swarms assemble, tools and weapons poised, filling the ready-stations and the companionways behind the assault bridge hatches.

Twenty thousand kilometres. The corpse-ship becomes visible. A tumbling mass of metal, trailing debris clouds. A halo of immaterial energies shimmers around it, blood from the wound that spat the wreck out of the empyrean and into real space. Benedictions are murmured to ward against any daemonia or warp spawn that might have been left clinging to the dead thing's hull.

Ten thousand kilometres. The corpse-ship's name becomes legible, etched across the buckled steeple of its prow.

Highness Ser Armaduke.

TWO

GHOST

Silence.

Nothing but silence. A weightless emptiness. The pale yellow light of other stars shafted in through unshuttered window ports, and washed slowly and uniformly up the walls and across the ceiling.

The Ghost opened his eyes.

He was floating, bodiless, an outsider observing the life he had left behind through the fog of mortality's veil. He had no name, no memories. His mind was cold. Death had robbed him of all vital thoughts and feelings. He was detached, freed forever from sensation, from weariness, from pain and care. He haunted the place where he had once lived.

He was not part of it any more. He could only look at the world he had left, dispassionate. The things that had mattered so much when he had been alive were meaningless. Duty had ceased to be a concept. Hope was revealed to be a laughably perishable quantity. Victory was an empty promise someone once made.

The light of the heedless stars moved slowly. Across the deck, along the walls, across the ceiling, around and around like the morning, noon and night of a fast-running day. Perhaps this was how a ghost saw the world. Perhaps time and the day-night rhythm of life ran fast to the dead's eyes, to make eternity more endurable.

Except, no.

The stars weren't moving. The *Armaduke* was. Powerless, dead, inert and gravity-shot, it was tumbling end over end in real space.

The Ghost considered this with glacial slowness, forcing his frosted mind to think. The ship was moving. How had it come to this? What doom had overtaken them? Had death come upon them so swiftly and so traumatically that the memory of life's end had been ripped entirely from his recollection?

How had he died?

The Ghost heard drumming. It was getting louder: steadily, progressively louder.

He saw something in front of his eyes. It was a metal washer, a small one. It was hanging in the air before him, rotating very slowly, not falling at all. Light winked off its turning edges. Two more washers and an oil-black restraining bolt drifted across his field of vision from the left in perfectly maintained formation. They passed behind the first washer, creating a brief astrological conjunction before drifting on.

The drumming became louder.

The Ghost felt pain. Slight, distant, but pain nevertheless. He felt it in his phantom limbs, his spine, his neck. The aftertaste of the agonies he had suffered in death had come with him to the other side of the veil, to haunt his shade.

How fitting. How true to the universe's treacherous nature. Only in death does duty end, but pain does not end with it. That's the thing the priests and hierophants don't tell you. Death is not a final release from pain. Pain stays with you. It clings to you forever.

What other lies had he been taught in his brief existence? The revelation made him want to curse the names of the ones who had given him life, the ones who had pretended to love him, the ones who had demanded his loyalty. It made him want to curse the Throne itself for telling him that death was some kind of serene reward.

It made him want to curse everything.

The Ghost opened his mouth.

'Feth you *all*,' he said.

His breath smoked the air. His skin was cold.

Wait, *breath?*

The drumming became louder.

It was the blood pounding in his ears.

Suddenly, he could hear again. His world was abruptly full of noise: his own ragged breathing, the cries and moans of those nearby, the wail of alarms, the mangled shriek of the ship's hull and superstructure.

Gravity reasserted itself.

The washers and the restraining bolt dropped to the deck. The Ghost dropped too. He hit a surface that was slick with frost, and he hit it hard. All the airspaces and blood vessels in his body realigned to gravity. He half choked as his windpipe flexed. His lungs panicked. His gut sloshed like a half-filled skin of sacra. All around him, he heard other impacts, and realised it was the sound of every other loose and unsecured object aboard the old ship falling to the deck. Inside the *Armaduke,* it was raining things and people.

The Ghost got to his feet. He was not steady. A ghost was made for floating, not walking. Every part of him hurt.

He found his lasrifle on the deck nearby. He picked it up with hands that did not work as well as he would have liked. Could a ghost touch things? Apparently so.

Perhaps this was some penance. Perhaps he had been called back to mortality for one final duty. Another lie, then. Even in death, duty did not fething end.

The Ghost moved down the companionway. He heard whimpering. He saw a young Belladon trooper, one of the new intake, sitting on the deck with his back to the wall, his teeth clenched like a rat-trap, nursing a broken wrist. The boy looked up at the Ghost as he loomed over him.

'What happened?' the boy asked.

'Am I dead?' asked the Ghost.

'What?'

'Am I dead?'

'N-no. No, sir.'

'How do you know?' asked the Ghost.

He saw terror in the boy's eyes.

'I d-don't know,' the boy said.

'I think I am dead,' said the Ghost. 'But you are not. You can walk. Get to the infirmary. Consider us at secondary order.'

'Yes, sir.'

The youngster winced, and clambered to his feet.

'Go on, now,' the Ghost said.

'What are you going to do?'

The Ghost thought about that.

'I don't know. But I reckon the God-Emperor has some purpose reserved for me, and this gun suggests it will involve killing.'

'S-something you're good at, then,' said the boy, trying to seem braver than he actually was.

'Am I?'

'Famously, sir.'

'What's your name?'

'Thyst, sir.'

'Get to the infirmary, Thyst.'

The boy nodded, and stumbled away.

Nearby were two of the ship's crew personnel, deck ratings. One was bleeding profusely from a deep cut across the bridge of his nose. The other was trying to pick up all the labelled machine spares that gravity had inverted out of his push-cart.

'What happened?' the Ghost asked them.

The bleeding man looked up at him.

'I have no idea,' he said. 'It has never happened before.'

The left side of the Ghost's upper lip curled slightly in a frustrated sneer. He turned away. He knew pretty much nothing about voidships, but he was sure that this was what the commander had warned them about. The commander. The commander. What was his name? The Ghost was having such difficulty remembering anything about his life. It hadn't ended that long ago.

Gaunt. That was it. Gaunt.

What was it Gaunt had said? 'The *Armaduke* is experiencing drive issues. It might not bring us home. If we fall short or explosively de-translate, I want the fighting companies ready for protection duties.'

The Ghost tried a wall-vox, but nothing but static came out of it. They had light and they had gravity, but the ship was stricken. They were dead in the water. If something came upon them, they'd be helpless.

If something tried to board them, how would they even know?

The Ghost suddenly hesitated. He looked up at the ceiling. There was too much noise, far too much: the fething alarms and damage klaxons, the squealing of the hull de-contorting, the babble of voices.

It was probably his imagination, conjured by the trauma of his violent death, but the Ghost could swear he had just heard something else.

Something *wrong*.

Up. It was coming from above him, high above.

How did he know that? How could he discriminate one noise from the chaotic swirl of sounds coming from all around him?

Because he could. It was something else he was good at.

He clambered up a deck ladder. The soreness in his limbs was fading. Just bruises. Bruises and bone-ache. He felt a deep chill in his heart, in the very core of him, as if he were a slab of grox meat that had been dragged out of the vittaling freezers and left on a kitchen block to thaw. His fingers were working, though. The clumsiness was fading. Any minute now, he'd get back some useful faculty.

Like the ability to remember his own fething name.

He began to climb. He had purpose at least. Duty. A fething unasked for duty, whether he wanted it or not. That's why the Holy God-Emperor of Mankind, thrice cursed be His whim, had brought him back, dead from beyond death, to serve his regiment and his commander. It had to be him. That much was clear. It was a purpose, a duty fit only for him. Something he was good at. Otherwise, why would the Master of Terra have requisitioned his soul, and pulled him back through the veil for one last miserable tour in the life-world? But why did the God-Emperor need a dead man when there were evidently many living around him?

He clambered up. Ceiling hatch. Standard iris. He yanked the lever, and it dilated open. He knew how to do that. He didn't even have to think. He knew how the mechanism worked.

Loose objects fell past him. Broken machine parts, a couple of hand tools. A small wrench bounced off his shoulder on the way down. All things that had fallen onto the hatch when artificial gravity realigned.

The Ghost pulled himself through the hatch. He was in a service-way. The bulkhead lights flickered uneasily, like the sense-disturbing strobes of an interrogation chamber. Noises still, from above. Tapping. Scratching. He cradled his weapon and prowled forwards. He needed another vertical access.

He found a dead man. Another dead man. Unlike the Ghost, this one hadn't been reanimated and sent back to serve, so the God-Emperor clearly saw little value in his talents. He had been a fitter from the ship's Division of Artifice. He must have been floating upside down when gravity reset. The fall had driven his head into the decking like a battering ram, breaking his neck and crushing the top of his skull. The Ghost looked up and saw where the fitter must have fallen from. An engineering space above the service-way, a shaft that rose up through four decks of the ship at least. It was a tunnel of cabling and pipework.

The Ghost used the footholds inset in the service-way wall to reach the open bottom of the shaft, and then began to ascend the small-rung ladder.

He climbed at a pace, knowing that ghosts didn't tire. It occurred to him that immunity from fatigue was a benefit of death. He would miss food, though.

He reached the top of the shaft, and swung over the lip into a gloomy machine space. His breath fogged the air. Breath. Why was he respiring? Ghosts didn't breathe.

No time to wonder about the laws of the afterlife. He could smell something. Burned metal. The molten stink of a cutting lance. The Ghost moved forwards, soundless, like all ghosts.

He saw a glowing orange oval, a slice cut through the skin of the ship. The edges of the metal were bright like neon. The cut section, slightly dished, lay on the deck, surrounded by droplets of glowing melt-spatter. There were two figures in the gloom – men, but not men. The Ghost could smell the feral stench of them despite the hot stink of the burned metal.

One of them saw him.

It said something, and raised a weapon to fire.

The Ghost fired first.

But his rifle was dead.

Malfunction? Dead cell? No time to find out. Two las-bolts spat at him, deafening in the confined space. The Ghost lunged to the side, falling among oily bulky machinery. The shots banged off the wall behind him like hand slaps.

The Ghost had fallen awkwardly, hitting his head against a piston or bearing. The pain came as a surprise. He felt his head, and his hand came away bloody.

Ghosts bled. Odd. Unless...

The men-but-not-men came for him, shouting to each other in a foul language. The Ghost ditched his rifle, and drew his warknife. It fit his hand perfectly. The feel of it filled him with assurance, with confidence. He knew it. It knew him. They would help each other. Later, it could tell him who he was.

A man-but-not-man came out of the darkness to his left, leaning down to peer under the machinery. The Ghost reached out, grabbed the intruder by the throat and pulled him onto his blade. It sank deep into the man-but-not-man's chest. He shuddered violently, kicking the deck as though he were throwing a tantrum. Then he went limp.

The Ghost slid the blade out, let go of his prey and rolled clear. He crawled along the length of the machinery and came up against a work cart laden with tools. Pliers? No. Hammer? Perhaps. Cable hatchet? Better.

It was about the length of his forearm, with a slightly curved steel grip and a single-headed drop-blade. The blade was curved along its edge and had a long chin, perfect for hacking through burned-out cabling during emergency repairs. He took it in his left hand, straight silver in his right.

The second man-but-not-man appeared from nowhere. The Ghost silently commended his adversary for his stealth aptitude. He side-swung the axe, chopping the man-but-not-man's lascarbine aside. It fired uselessly, sparking a las-bolt along the machine space. The Ghost, legs braced wide, delivered a double blow, slashing from the outside in with both hands. The axe in his left hand and the warknife in his right passed each other expertly, so that the Ghost finished the move with his arms across his chest.

Both blades had cut through the man-but-not-man's neck. He toppled, blood jetting from the half-stump as his head hinged back like the lid of a storage hopper.

A third man-but-not-man appeared, running at him. The Ghost ducked, spinning as he did so, avoiding the spiked boarding mace that the man-but-not-man was swinging at him. He turned the spin into a gut-kick, and smashed his opponent back into the bulkhead. The man-but-not-man grunted as the air was smashed out of him. The Ghost hurled the axe, and skewered the man-but-not-man to the bulkhead by the shoulder.

Pinned, the man-but-not-man screamed. The sound was only approximately human.

The Ghost got up in his victim's face, straight silver to the intruder's throat. A little pressure from his left forearm tightened the angle of the firmly planted axe, and elicited more screams.

'Who are you?' the Ghost demanded.

He got a jumble of noises, half pain, half words. Neither made any sense. He leaned again.

'What is your strength? How many of you are there?'

More words-but-not-words.

He leaned again.

'Your last chance. Answer my questions or I will make it very slow indeed. Who are you?'

The man-but-not-man wailed. The Ghost wasn't getting anything. In frustration, he tried a different tack.

'Who am I?'

'Ver voi mortek!' the man-but-not-man shrieked.

Mortek. The Ghost knew that word. No, he was not death. That was wrong. The man-but-not-man was lying.

The Ghost knew that because his thawing brain had finally remembered his name.

He was Mkoll. Scout Sergeant Oan Mkoll, Tanith First.

He was Mkoll, and he was alive. He wasn't dead. He wasn't a ghost at all. Not that kind, anyway.

THREE

AND BACK

They had so very nearly got away with it. Got away with it and survived to tell the tale.

So very nearly.

Hell and back. That's how someone had described the Salvation's Reach mission. It sounded like the sort of thing Larkin or Varl would say.

Hell and back. They'd gone into hell and come out on the other side, and not for the first time. But after everything they had endured, it seemed as though they weren't going to make it home after all.

Four weeks out from the Rimworld Marginals, and the target rock known as Salvation's Reach, the doughty old warship *Highness Ser Armaduke* had begun to limp.

'How far are we from the intended destination?' Ibram Gaunt asked the *Armaduke's* shipmaster.

Spika, leaning back thoughtfully in his worn command seat, shrugged his shoulders.

'The estimate is another fifteen days,' he replied, 'but I don't like the look of the immaterium. Bad patterns ahead. I think we'll be riding out a proper storm before nightfall, shiptime.'

'And that could slow us down?' asked Gaunt.

'By a margin of weeks, if we're unlucky,' said Spika.

'Still, you're saying the storm isn't the real problem?' Gaunt pressed.

'No,' said Spika. He held up a finger for quiet. 'You hear that?'

Gaunt listened, and heard many sounds: the chatter and chime of the multiple cogitators ranked around the warship's bridge; the asthmatic wheeze of the air-circulation system and environmental pumps; the hum of the through-deck power hubs charging the strategium display; the deranged murmuring from the navigator's socket; the voxed back-chatter from the crew; footsteps on the deck plates; the deep, deep rumble of the warp drives behind everything else.

During the course of the Salvation's Reach mission, he had begun to learn the multifarious ambient running noises of the *Armaduke,* but not enough to become an expert.

'Not really,' he admitted.

'Not really?' asked Spika. 'No?' The shipmaster sounded disappointed. Though the life and the lifetime expectations of a Navy man were, quite literally, worlds away from those of a Guard officer, the two men had bonded during the mission tour, and had both gained insight into operational worlds quite alien from their own. They were not friends, but there was a measure of something that, nurtured, might one day resemble friendship. Clemensaw Spika seemed rather let down that Gaunt had grasped less shipboard nuance than he had expected.

'It's quite distinct,' Spika said, sadly. 'Number two drive. There's an arrhythmia in its generative pulse. The modulation is out of step. There. There. There. There.'

Like an orchestral conductor, he beat his finger to a pattern. It was a pattern that Ibram Gaunt did not have the experience of practice to discern.

It was Gaunt's turn to shrug.

Spika adjusted the brass levers on his armrests, and swept his command seat around. The entire chair, a metal-framed throne of worn leather with banks of control surfaces and levers set into each arm, sat upon a gilded carriage that connected it to a complex gimbal-jointed lifting arm. At a touch, Spika could hoist himself above the entire bridge, incline to share the point of view of any of the bridge stations below, or even raise himself up into the bridge dome to study hololithic star-map projections.

This more gentle adjustment merely turned the seat so he could dismount and lead Gaunt across the bridge to the bank of stations occupied by the Master of Artifice and his key functionaries.

'Output display, all engines,' Spika requested.

'Output display, all, aye,' the Master of Artifice answered. His hands – busy bionic spiders that dripped spots of oil and were attached to wrists made of rotator struts and looped cables jutting from the fine double-buttoned cuffs of his duty uniform – played across the main haptic panel of his console. Each finger-touch caused a separate and distinct electronic note, creating a little musical flurry like an atonal arpeggio. The Master of Artifice was not blind, for Gaunt could see the ochre-and-gold receptors in his enhanced pupils expanding and contracting his irises, but his attitude was that of a sightless pianist. He was not looking at what he was doing. His picture of the universe and the ship, which were, after all, the same thing, was being fed to him in a constantly updated flow through aural implants, and through data-trunks that ran up his neck like bulging arteries and entered the base of his skull through dermal sockets.

A hololithic display sprang up above the man's station. Side by side, in three dimensions, the rising and falling graph lines of the *Armaduke's* engines were arranged for comparison. Gaunt's limited expertise was not found wanting now.

'I see,' Gaunt said. 'Clearly a problem.'

'Clearly,' replied Spika. 'Number two drive is operating at least thirty-five per cent below standard efficiency.'

'The yield is declining by the hour, shipmaster,' the Master of Artifice said.

'Are you examining it?' asked Gaunt.

'It's hard to examine a warp drive when it's active,' replied Spika. 'But, yes. Nothing conclusive yet. I believe this down-rate is the result of damage we sustained during the fight at Tavis Sun on the outward journey. Even a micro-impact or spalling on the inner liner might, over time, develop into this, especially given the demands we've made on principal artifice.'

'So this could be an old wound only now showing up?' asked Gaunt.

Spika nodded.

'The Master of Artifice,' he said, 'prefers the theory that it is micro-particle damage taken during our approach to Salvation's Reach – ingested debris. This theory has some merit. The Reach was a particularly dense field.'

'What's the prognosis?' asked Gaunt.

'If we can effect repair, we're fine. If we can't, and the output continues to decline in this manner, we may be forced to exit the warp, and perhaps divert to a closer harbour.'

Gaunt frowned. They'd travelled non-stop since departing the Reach, except for one scheduled resupply halt at a secure depot, Aigor 991, a week earlier. It had not gone to plan. Resupply was urgently needed: the raid had expended a vast quantity of their munitions and perishable supplies, but they'd been obliged to abort and press on without restocking. Gaunt was reluctant to make another detour. He wanted to reach their destination as fast as possible.

'Worst case?' he asked.

'Worst case?' Spika replied. 'There are many kinds of worst case. The most obvious would be that the drive fails suddenly and we are thrown out of the warp. Thrown out of the warp... if we're lucky.'

'Is there anything,' Gaunt asked the shipmaster, 'which suggests to you that luck follows the occupants of this vessel around on any permanent or regular basis?'

'My dear colonel-commissar,' Spika replied, 'I've lived in this accursed galaxy long enough to believe that there's no such thing as luck at all.'

Gaunt didn't reply.

Spika walked back to his command seat and resumed his station.

'I will begin running assessment variables through astronavigation to see if there are any viable retranslation points,' he said. 'I intend to give this condition twelve hours grace. Twelve hours to correct itself or to be repaired. After that, I will be effecting the neatest possible real space translation in the hope of finding a safe haven or fleet support.'

Gaunt nodded.

'I take it this is all for my information?' he asked.

'Colonel-commissar,' said the shipmaster, 'if we are forced to terminate this voyage prematurely, or if the drive fails, it is more than likely we will find ourselves adrift in hostile space. There will, very probably, be no safe haven or fleet support. It is likely we will have to protect ourselves.'

He adjusted some armrest levers, and rotated his seat up into the navigation dome and the eternal glow of the star maps.

'I am telling you this,' he called down over his shoulder, 'so that you can ready your Ghosts.'

Gaunt walked aft from the warship's bridge, ignoring the salute of the Navy armsmen. He clattered down two companionway staircases and entered

Port Primary, one of the ship's main communication corridors. There was a general bustle to and fro; servitors and crew, and the occasional Tanith First trooper who threw him a salute.

The sounds and the smells of the ship were all around him. Warp stress was pulling at the *Armaduke*'s frame, and deck plates creaked. Wall panels groaned. Ice had formed in some places, glazing the walls, and unexpected hotspots trembled their haze in others. Blast shutters, which stood at twenty-metre intervals along Port Primary, ready to slam shut and compartmentalise the long thoroughfare in the event of a hull breach or decompression, rattled in their frames, temporarily malformed by the tensions of the warp.

If it's visibly doing that to the metal structure of the ship, thought Gaunt, *what's it doing to our bodies? Our cellular structures? Our minds? Our souls?*

He exited Port Primary and entered the tighter network of halls, companionways and tunnel ducts that linked the habitation levels and cargo spaces. Ceilings were lower, and the corridors were more densely lined with cabling and exterior-mounted switching boxes and circuitry. It was in these levels, less-well lit and claustrophobic, that the ancient ship felt more like a hive. An *underground* hive.

The light strings, glow-globes and wall lamps flickered at what seemed like a too infrequent rate, as if power was intermittent or struggling to reach the extremities of the ship. Bad odours gusted like halitosis from the air-circ vents: the rank stink of oil and grease, of sump water, of stagnant hydraulics, of refuse and badly draining sanitation systems, of stale cooking, of unwashed flesh, of grilles overheating because they were clogged with lint and soot and dust.

The *Armaduke* should have been scrapped long ago. It had been spared from the breaker's yards to perform the Salvation's Reach run, with little expectation it would be seen again.

Gaunt knew how it felt.

The mission had been a success – an astonishing success, in fact, given the odds. As had happened so often before, Gaunt took little satisfaction from that, because of the cost. The cost was too great, every time.

Gaunt passed the door of one of the mess halls, and saw Viktor Hark sitting alone at one of the long, shabby tables, nursing a cup of caffeine. A cold smell of boiled cabbage and root veg lingered in the hall. The room was too brightly lit. From the back, Gaunt could hear servitors prepping food for the next meal rotation.

'Viktor?'

Hark started to rise.

'Easy,' Gaunt told him. 'Briefing. In thirty minutes. Can you scare up the company officers and particulars for me?'

Hark nodded.

'Everyone?'

'Just those you can find. Don't pull people off duties. This is informal for now, but I want to get the word out.'

'The word?'

'Could be trouble ahead.'

Hark got to his feet and plonked his cup on the cart for empties and dirties.

'Ibram,' he said, 'there's always trouble ahead.'

They met in the wardroom. Hark had rounded up Ludd, Fazekiel, Mkoll, Larkin, Baskevyl, Kolea and most of the company commanders. The notable absences were Blenner, Rawne, Meryn, and Daur and Major Pasha, both of whom were still in the infirmary. Captain Nico Spetnin was standing in for Pasha, and Adjutant Mohr and Sergeant Venar for Daur.

'No Criid?' Gaunt asked Hark as he came in and the officers rose.

'Criid?' Hark replied. 'Tona's not company or particular level.'

Gaunt hesitated. His mind had been all over the place since–

He'd forgotten he hadn't mentioned it to anyone, not even Criid.

'All right, as you were,' he said, with a gesture to 'easy' themselves that they all recognised.

'Something awry, sir?' Baskevyl asked, pre-empting the standard comment of Gaunt's adjutant.

Beltayn, sitting up front, data-slate in hand ready to take notes, rolled his eyes at the trickle of laughter.

'Yeah, Bask,' Gaunt replied. They settled down quickly.

Gaunt took off his cap and unbuttoned his coat. The air got close in the wardroom when you packed it with bodies.

'It may be nothing,' he told them, 'but we need to come to secondary order as of right now.'

'Secondary order?' Kolosim repeated.

'Combat ready?' asked Kolea.

Gaunt nodded.

'I'm afraid so.'

'We're only four weeks out of that shitstorm...' Obel murmured.

Gaunt looked at him. The intensity of Gaunt's unblinking augmetic stare pinned Obel to his seat.

'Sir, I didn't mean–' he began.

Gaunt often forgot how hard his new eyes could be. He hadn't meant to discomfort an officer as loyal and dependable as Obel.

'I know, Lunny,' Gaunt said. 'We're all still licking our wounds. And I'm aware of our piss-poor supply levels. But the war works to its own schedule, not ours. I need the First to come to secondary order in the next twelve hours.'

There was a general groan.

'Any specifics you can give us, sir?' asked Bask.

'Shipmaster Spika informs me that the *Armaduke* is experiencing drive issues. It might not bring us home. If we fall short or explosively de-translate, I want the fighting companies ready for protection duties.'

'Shipboard? Counter-boarding?' asked Kolea, his voice a growl.

'Anything, Gol,' Gaunt replied. 'Just make sure your squads are ready to deal with any kind of contact. Anything they might reasonably be expected to counter.'

Kolea nodded.

'And make it generally known to all that in the event of action, munition conservation is essential.'

The officers took note.

'Ludd?' said Gaunt.

'Yes, sir?' Commissar Ludd answered.

'See to it that our friends are informed,' Gaunt told the company's youngest commissar.

'Yes, sir,' said Ludd.

'Hark?'

'Yes, sir?' Hark replied.

'I'll leave it to you to bring Rawne and B Company up to speed.'

Hark nodded.

'Well,' said Gaunt, 'that's all. Thanks for your attention. Get to it.'

On the way out, he caught Baskevyl's arm.

'If you see Criid, send her my way will you?'

'Of course,' Bask said.

Gaunt wandered back to his stateroom along Lower Spinal Sixty. He had a stop to make along the way.

He paused to look into one of the company decks, the hold spaces of the ship that served as accommodation for the retinue. This was home for the souls that had signed the accompany bond to travel with the regiment: the wives, the children, the families, and the tinkers and traders that made up the Tanith First's vital support network. Salvation's Reach had been a perilous venture, but every one of the regiment's extended family had signed the bond to come along. They had decided they would rather risk their lives and die with the Ghosts than stay behind on Menazoid Sigma and perhaps never catch up with them again.

Gaunt thought that showed more courage and faith than any soldier had. Guard life was made better by the constant strength of family, but it was a hard existence. He'd had to consider carefully before approving the issue of the bond.

He watched the children play, the women work, the lines of washing drifting overhead from the chamber's rafters. Their faith had seen them safely past the dangers of the Reach, but there were always new dangers. The implications of the drive problem troubled him, and the aborted resupply on Aigor 991 played on his mind. Major Kolea had encountered some form of the Ruinous Powers that seemed to be hunting for them. It had claimed to be the voice of Anarch Sek, and it had demanded the return of something called 'the eagle stones.' It had murdered several members of the landing party. Gol Kolea had done well to abort the resupply, but Gaunt had a lingering feeling that Gol hadn't told him everything about the encounter. Perhaps it had just been the terror of the experience that had made Gol seem unforthcoming.

No one had a solid idea what 'the eagle stones' might be, but if Sek's power had touched them at Aigor 991, then the Archenemy was closer on their heels than Gaunt liked to imagine. Against the odds, they had survived the Reach mission. Was an unforeseen and greater threat lying in wait for them all? Could he safeguard the families a *second* time? It was not the dispassionate concern of a commander. Gaunt had always been alone, but now *he* had family aboard too. His *son*...

He shook the thought off. One problem at a time.

Ayatani Zwiel was up on a bench, preaching the love of the God-Emperor to the family congregation. The old chaplain saw Gaunt in the doorway, and paused his sermon, climbing down from his perch with the aid of steadying hands.

'You look grim, Ibram,' he said as he hobbled up to face Gaunt.

'You noticed, ayatani.'

Zwiel shrugged.

'No, you always look grim. I was making a general observation. Why? Is there new trouble to keep us awake at night?'

Gaunt glanced aside to make sure no one could overhear.

'There's a drive fault,' he said. 'It may be nothing, but if we are forced to break shift to deal with it... Well, it could cause alarm and distress among the retinue. As a favour to me, stay here and keep watch. If the worst happens, try to calm fears. They'll listen to you. Tell them we'll be safe soon and that there's no reason to panic.'

Zwiel nodded. Since the loss at Salvation's Reach, his spirits had been lower. The old firecracker spark had grown dimmer.

'Of course, of course,' he said. 'I'll get them singing hymns. Hymns are good. And warm too, on a cold night.'

'Do you mean hymns?'

'Possibly not,' Zwiel replied, thinking about it.

Something cannoned into Gaunt's legs.

'Papa Gaunt! Papa Gaunt!'

Gaunt looked down. It was Yoncy, Tona Criid's little girl. She clutched his knees and grinned up at him.

'Hello, Yoncy,' Gaunt said. He scooped her up in his arms, and she gleefully took off his cap and put it on. She was so small and light.

'I'm Papa Gaunt!' she declared fiercely to Zwiel, glaring out from under the brim of the oversized cap. She threw a stern salute.

'Well, young lady,' said Zwiel, 'what you've just done is an abuse of uniform code, and Papa Gaunt will have you shot for it.'

'He will not!' Yoncy cried, defiantly.

'Not this time,' said Gaunt.

One of the women hurried over.

'There you are, child,' she exclaimed. 'I wondered where you'd run off to!' She took Yoncy out of Gaunt's arms.

'I'm ever so sorry she bothered you, sir,' she said. 'I was supposed to be watching her.'

'It's fine,' said Gaunt. 'She was no bother.'

'Papa Gaunt's going to shoot me, Juniper!' Yoncy laughed.

'Is he now?' the woman said.

'Papa Zwiel said so,' Yoncy told her.

'I'm really not,' Gaunt told the woman.

'Uniform infraction,' said Zwiel, mock stern, and scooped the cap off the child's head. 'A firing squad at the very least!'

'I think we can let this one go with a reprimand,' said Gaunt as Zwiel handed him his cap.

'You best consider yourself lucky this time, child,' Juniper said to the girl in her arms. She did a clumsy little bow and hurried off. Yoncy waved to them as she was carried away.

'She calls everyone "papa",' Zwiel said. 'It used to be "uncle", but now "papa" is the favourite.'

'A legacy of her curious upbringing, I suppose,' said Gaunt. 'She seems happy enough.'

'Does she...' Zwiel began. 'Does she seem small to you?'

'Small?'

'I was thinking it the other day,' said the chaplain. 'Just a child in pigtails, as she's always been. But Dalin is a grown man now, and there can't be too many years between them. She acts very young too.'

'Is that a defence, do you think?' Gaunt asked. 'Her life has never been safe. Maybe she plays on her childlike qualities to make sure we protect her.'

'You think it's an act?'

'Not a conscious one, no. But while she's an innocent child, everyone is her father or her uncle or her aunt. It's how she copes. How she feels safe.'

'Well, I imagine she'll sprout soon enough. Girls develop later. Overnight, she'll be a petulant teenager.'

'And we will protect her just the same,' said Gaunt. He reset his cap.

'Our children always need our protection,' said Zwiel, 'no matter how much they grow up. How is your offspring?'

'I'm still coming to terms with the fact,' said Gaunt. 'I have to go, father. I'll keep you advised.'

'And I'll stand ready,' said Zwiel.

Gaunt left the company deck and resumed his journey aft.

He suddenly heard music. It was jaunty music. It was cheerful. It rolled and echoed along the dismal connecting tunnel.

He approached the entrance to a side hold. The Belladon Colours band had assembled there, and were mid-practice. It was clearly an informal session. Most of them were not in full uniform code, and they were spread across the big, galvanised chamber of the holdspace, sitting or even sprawling on packing material, blasting out their music. Those not playing had got up and were dancing a sprightly formation polka in the mid-deck. Most of the dancers had discarded boots and jackets.

High above, the company's mascot, the ceremonial psyber eagle, flew from roof girder to roof girder, squawking from both beaks.

The music died away unevenly as the bandsmen noticed Gaunt in the hatchway.

'It's cheerful in here,' Gaunt remarked.

Captain Jakub Wilder wandered over.

'It's the Belladon way, sir,' he said. 'We celebrate the living and the dead. It's the best way to shake off a hard tour.'

Gaunt pursed his lips.

Commissar Vaynom Blenner had got himself up off a roll of packing material to join them.

'My idea, Ibram,' he said, hurriedly. 'Just a little loosening of the old collar, you know?'

Gaunt looked at his old friend. Blenner seemed remarkably relaxed.

'I'm sure we can all use some downtime,' he said.

'I was going to suggest a formal,' Blenner said. 'Get some decent food and wine out of stores. Everyone invited. The band can play. Dancing, eh? We can cast aside this mood. The First deserves it, Ibram.'

'It does,' Gaunt agreed.

'Good.'

'But now's not the time,' Gaunt said. 'We need to come to secondary order.'

'Since when?'

'Since now, Vaynom,' Gaunt said.

Blenner swallowed.

'Secondary order?' he asked.

'Yes. "Prepare to fight". Is that a problem?'

'No. No, no. Not at all.'

'My troopers are ready,' Wilder said.

'Good. Expect hazard within a twelve-hour threshold,' Gaunt said. 'If fighting starts, conserve your ammunition.' He turned and left the hold.

'Let's... let's finish up here,' Blenner said to Wilder. He needed a cup of water.

There was a pack of pills in his jacket pocket and he suddenly felt the urge to take one.

Gaunt paused outside the infirmary and hesitated before entering. He knew he had a good reason for the visit, and that it wasn't the real reason. The real reason Gaunt kept visiting the infirmary was that he was trying to get used to the place without Dorden.

He took off his cap and entered. Internal screen walls and shutter partitions had been rolled back to extend the space and accommodate the regimental wounded after the battle of Salvation's Reach. It was still pretty full. Several of the casualties, like the sniper Nessa Bourah, attempted to sit up and salute when they saw him.

He raised a hand.

'Stand easy, everyone, please,' he said.

He moved down the rows of steel-framed cots, pausing to speak to as many of the wounded as he could. He signed *How are you?* to Nessa, and she grinned back and replied with her voice.

'Ready to fight,' she said. Like many Vervunhivers, she'd lost her hearing during the Zoican War, and the sign language they had developed had proved vital to both their scratch company operations against the Zoicans and, later, to the stealth manoeuvres of the Tanith First. Chief Scout Mkoll had long ago adopted Vervunhive scratch-signing as the regiment's non-verbal code.

Recently, though, in personal circumstances, Nessa had been trying to use her voice more again. The words came out with that slightly nasal, rounded-out quality of a speaker who can only feel the breath of their words, but they touched Gaunt immensely.

'I know you are,' he replied, without signing.

She read his lips and answered with another smile.

Gaunt stopped at Major Pasha's bedside and talked for a while, assuring the senior officer of the regiment's new intake that her companies were in good order.

'Spetnin and Zhukova have things well in hand,' he said, 'and they are meshing well with the established commanders. Spetnin is a good fellow.'

'Not Zhukova, then?' Pasha asked.

Gaunt hesitated.

'She's an excellent officer.'

Pasha sat up and leant forwards, beckoning Gaunt close with a conspiratorial gesture made with hands that had choked more than one Zoican throat in their day.

'She is an excellent officer, sir,' Pasha agreed. 'But she is ambitious and she is beautiful. Not beautiful like her.'

Pasha nodded her chin towards Nessa, who had gone back to her reading.

'No?' asked Gaunt.

'The dear, deaf girl does not know she is beautiful. Ornella does. That is why your dear deaf girl is a marksman trooper, and Ornella Zhukova is a captain.'

'What are you saying?' Gaunt asked.

'I'm saying, Zhukova's a brilliant troop leader. Just treat her like any other cocksure ambitious male. Don't be fooled by her lips and breasts.'

Gaunt laughed. He liked Major Yve Petrushkevskaya immensely. She was a tall, strong, haggard veteran. He hadn't known her long, and it couldn't be said that they'd served together. Pasha had been miserably wounded in a hull-breaching accident before the Salvation's Reach fight had begun in earnest.

But Gaunt was sure she brought something to the Ghosts that was yet to be properly valued. A powerful, presiding, maternal force. A different wisdom.

'In truth, sir,' she said, settling back on her pillow, 'I feel... ashamed.'

'Ashamed?' he asked in surprise.

'Taken down before I could fire a shot in anger,' she replied, her mouth forming an almost comical inverted 'U' of a frown. 'Not a distinguished start to my service under your command.'

'You've got nothing to prove, major,' he said.

She tutted at him.

'Everyone always has everything to prove,' she replied. 'Otherwise, what is the purpose of life, sir?'

'I stand corrected. But enough of this "sir", please. You're one of the seniors and particulars. "Sir" in front of the troops, but "Ibram" to my face like this.'

'Dah,' she replied, holding up her hands in distaste. 'Formality is discipline.'

'Gaunt, then?' he said.

Her mouth made the doubtful, inverted U shape again.

'Maybe that.'

He could tell she wasn't comfortable. He'd tried to be open, but the sentimentality was not to her liking. He changed tack.

'Listen, major,' he said quietly. 'I need to be able to count on you.'

'Yes?' she whispered, craning forwards.

'We have a drive problem. A bad one. We may not get home. In fact, we could pop back into real space at any time.'

He kept his voice low.

'If we do, we could be at risk.'

'Attack?' she asked.

'Yes. If we're boarded, we may have to protect ourselves section by section. Will you run the infirmary for me? Rally all able-bodied to the defence?'

'Will you send a crate of rifles down here?'

'Supplies are limited, but yes.'

She nodded.

'Of course. Of course, I will,' she said. 'Count on me.'

'I already do,' he said.

She blinked in surprise and looked at him. He held out his hand and she shook it.

'Keep it to yourself, but get ready,' he said.

He got off the edge of her bed and turned to go.

'I will, Gaunt,' Pasha said.

A few cots down, Elodie was playing regicide with her husband. Ban Daur still looked very frail and weak from the injuries he'd taken. They had been married en route to the Reach.

'Captain. Ma'am Dutana-Daur.'

They looked around. Elodie started to get up.

'I'm just saying hello,' Gaunt said. 'Don't let me interrupt.'

'It's kind of you, sir,' Daur said.

'If I can't stop in on one of my best,' Gaunt said. 'How is it, Ban?'

'I'm doing all right. I'm still bleeding inside, so they say. Some mending to do.'

'You're strong, Ban.'

'I am, sir.'

'And she makes you stronger,' Gaunt said, looking at Elodie. 'I know love when I see it, because I don't see it very much.'

'You flatter me, sir,' said Elodie.

'Ma'am,' Gaunt began.

'Elodie,' she said firmly.

'Elodie,' he corrected. 'As you stand by and progress with this regiment, you will quickly come to know that I never flatter anyone.'

* * *

Towards the end of the first compartment, Gaunt encountered Doctor Kolding, who was conducting rounds. He was checking on Raglon and Cant, who were both recovering from serious injuries.

'I'm looking for Curth,' Gaunt said.

'I believe she's in the back rooms,' Kolding said. 'Can I help with anything?'

'No, she'll brief you,' Gaunt replied. He paused.

'Kolding?'

The albino turned to him.

'Sir?'

'Support her.'

'I am doing so.'

'The loss of Dorden is massive.'

'I barely knew him and I am aware of the magnitude,' Kolding replied. Gaunt nodded, turned and walked into the offices behind the ward.

In the first, he found Captain Meryn, stripped to the waist, sitting forwards over the rail of a half-chair as Curth's orderly Lesp went to work on his back with his ink and pins.

'Sorry, sir,' Lesp said, getting up.

Gaunt shook him a 'no matter'. Lesp was well known as the company inker, a man of skill and, as an orderly, hygiene to match. Gaunt had long since stopped trying to curtail the non-codex efforts of the Tanith to decorate their skin with tattoos.

'My apologies, sir,' said Meryn curtly, reaching for his shirt. 'It was downtime and I thought–'

'There was a company officer call, just informal,' Gaunt said.

'I wasn't aware,' Meryn said, and seemed genuinely contrite.

'It's fine. It was informal, as I said. But get Kolea to brief you. There may be trouble coming.'

'Of course,' said Meryn.

'What ink are you having?'

Meryn paused.

'Just... just names,' he said.

'Names?' Gaunt asked.

'The Book o' Death,' Lesp said, half smiling, then regretting it when he saw Gaunt's expression.

Gaunt signalled with a rotating finger, and Meryn turned to present his back. Meryn's torso was tough and corded with muscle. Down the left-hand side of the spine, Lesp had been noting a list of names in black ink. They were the names of the men in Meryn's E Company who had fallen at Salvation's Reach. Meryn had lost a lot, too many perhaps, to the Loxatl during the final evacuation.

Lesp had got halfway through the name 'Costin', a name that particularly troubled Gaunt. Before the raid, Trooper Costin, a chronically unreliable soldier, had been found guilty of death-benefit fraud through the Munitorum's viduity allowance. It had seemed an especially repellant crime to Gaunt. Someone had made large amounts of money by exploiting the regiment's dead and fallen. Costin had been killed before his associates in the fraud ring could be identified.

'I'm honouring my dead,' Meryn said quietly.

Gaunt nodded. The 'Book o' Death' was a common and popular tattoo among the Tanith officer class, so popular it had been adopted by several Verghastites too. Out of respect, a field officer had the names of men who had died under his command inked onto his skin.

Gaunt had considered it more than once. He wanted to show respect for Tanith tradition, and he felt that certain names – Corbec, Caffran and Bragg, for example – should never be far from him. He'd felt it even more for Dorden.

But it was not seemly for a commissar to break uniform code, he kept telling himself.

'It seemed only right, sir,' Meryn said.

It did. It really did. Except it *didn't* for a snake like Meryn, a man who had previously displayed absolutely zero company sentiment or sympathy for his troops. It didn't sit comfortably with Gaunt. Why now? Had Meryn really woken up to something after the knock his company had taken at the Reach? Or was this compensation? Was he trying to *look* like the grieving commander?

Was he trying to distance himself from a crime by having the name of the culprit inked on his back out of 'respect'? Costin *had* been killed before his associates in the fraud ring could be identified...

A common rule of law was that you didn't mess with or question the feelings of an officer grieving for his men. Gaunt wanted to say something, but genuine pity and sympathy checked him. If this *was* Meryn being odiously clever, then it was very, *very* clever.

And Meryn *was* very, very clever.

'Doctor Curth?' Gaunt asked Lesp. Lesp pointed to the second office.

Gaunt went in and closed the door behind him. Ana Curth was sitting at Dorden's desk, reviewing med files. She had grown a little thinner. There was a tension in her. Gaunt could smell alcohol that he hoped was medicinal.

'Can I help you, Ibram?' she asked.

'Can I help you?'

She shrugged. She seemed tired. Gaunt had heard from various private sources that she had taken the loss hard, and had been working too much and then drinking in order to sleep. The same sources said that Blenner had been looking after her.

Such selflessness hardly seemed likely from Vaynom Blenner.

Gaunt felt a sting of jealousy, but he could hardly complain. His own nights were filled with another woman, and Ana knew it. If there had ever been any sense of them waiting for each other, Gaunt himself had crushed it.

He'd always held back from Ana Curth, partly for reasons of regulation and decorum, and partly because he believed that he wasn't really the sort of man any decent woman would need or want.

'I keep coming in here,' Curth said, gesturing to the desk and the office. 'You know what? Each time, he's still dead.'

'Ana...'

She waved him off.

'Ignore me. I just can't get used to it.'

'Do you need–'

'I'm fine, Gaunt.'

'Ana–'

'Fine. *Fine.* All right?'

He knew that tone, that firmness, that 'don't push it' attitude. He'd known it from their first meeting at Vervunhive.

'What do you think of Meryn's ink?' he asked briskly.

'Meryn's a grown-up,' she said.

'I just wondered,' Gaunt began.

'Wondered what?'

'If he was compensating in some way?'

'For his dead men?' She had returned to her files, half listening.

'All right,' Gaunt said, 'compensating was the wrong word. Deflecting.'

She looked at him.

'Deflecting what? With what?'

'Guilt, with a notion of honour.'

'*What* now?'

'Costin, and the viduity scam. I think Meryn's complicit. Costin was not smart. He needed clever co-conspirators. Conveniently, Costin died before he could turn them over. And now Meryn's in mourning and untouchable.'

'So, what?' Curth asked. 'Meryn killed Costin before he could roll?'

'No, of course not–'

'You're a piece of fething work, you really are!' she spat out, tossing the file in her hand aside so forcefully it knocked a glass over.

'No,' he replied. 'I'm a commissar. I know what men are capable of.'

She got up and took off her smock. Then she turned away from him and pulled her crew-issue grey tee shirt up above her shoulders. Her back was slender, beautiful, the line of the spine–

There was a dressing just below her left shoulder blade. With the fingers of her right hand, she ripped it off.

Dorden.

One word, still raw and seeping blood from the needles.

'Silly of me,' she said. 'Sentimental. Against uniform code? I'm sure. Fething did it anyway.'

'Ana–'

She pulled her shirt down again, turned and sat back down.

'Forget it,' she said.

'The Book o' Death,' he said. 'You know how many times I've thought about following Tanith tradition and doing the same? Getting Lesp and his needles at my skin?'

She looked at him.

'What's stopping you? No, I can guess. Uniform code. Unseemly for a commissar to decorate his skin.'

'There's that. As a commissar, I take both uniform code and setting an example very seriously, funnily enough. But that's not the real reason.'

'What is?'

'The available area of my flesh.'

'What?'

'Dorden. Corbec. MkVenner. Bragg. Caffran. Colonel Wilder. Kamori. Adare. Soric. Baffels. Blane–'

'All right...'

'Muril. Rilke. Raess. Doyl. Baru. Lorgris. Mkendrick. Suth. Preed. Feygor–'

'Gaunt...'

'Gutes. Cole. Roskil. Vamberfeld. Loglas. Merrt–'

He stopped.

'I just don't have enough skin,' he said.

'You just don't have enough heart,' she replied.

'All right,' he said, but he wasn't all right at all.

'I came down to tell you that we might have trouble coming,' he said. 'A drive issue. Possible boarding. Be ready.'

'I'm always ready,' she said, blowing her nose loudly.

He nodded, and turned to leave.

Gaunt walked out through the first office area. Meryn was getting his back swabbed by Lesp. The smell of clean alcohol again.

'I'm just on my way now, sir,' Meryn said.

'Stay, Flyn,' Gaunt said as he walked past. 'Get the names done properly. All of them. All of the Ghosts. I miss them too.'

'Yes, sir,' said Meryn.

A long walk took Gaunt back to his stateroom. Maddalena Darebeloved was waiting for him.

Since joining the regiment, Maddalena had spent some portion of her time in Gaunt's cabin suite and the rest of it protecting Felyx Meritous Chass, the son Gaunt hadn't known he had. Felyx was integrating into the Tanith Regiment under the watch of Dalin Criid. Felyx's mother, Merity Chass of the Verghast House Chass, had insisted that he follow his father into war and learn the trade and value of combat from someone who excelled at it.

Excelled. Not the right word, Gaunt thought. Someone who was entirely devoured by it.

Maddalena was a lifeward, one of House Chass' most formidable bodyguards. Beautiful and supple, she carried her sidearm shrouded by a red cloth, as was the Vervunhive custom.

As he came in, she was cleaning her sidearm. Gaunt knew something was wrong. Their relationship had been generally and robustly physical. He understood his attraction to her. Her face had been augmetically modified to resemble that of Merity Chass, so as to reassure Felyx. Gaunt had responded to that on an instinctive level.

'What's happening?' he asked.

'You tell me,' she replied.

'You're strip-cleaning your sidearm,' he said.

She nodded, and rapidly slotted and slapped the weapon back into one piece. It was a .40 cal Tronsvass she'd taken from stores to replace her original weapon.

'There's trouble coming,' she said, checking the pistol for balance, and returning it to her holster.

'Why do you say that?' he asked.

'Are you mad, Ibram?' she replied, looking at him. 'The engines are making the wrong noise.'

He hesitated.

'That's very impressive,' he started to say.

But the words didn't come out right because, very suddenly and unpleasantly, the world was pulled inside out.

FOUR

DEAD IN THE WATER

'Get up,' said Brother Sar Af of the Adeptus Astartes White Scars.

'Yes, of course,' said Nahum Ludd. 'Of course. Sorry.'

It was, he knew, entirely inappropriate to lie on the deck when in the presence of three battle-brothers. Entirely inappropriate, especially for an officer of the Officio Prefectus. Officers of the Officio Prefectus did not lie down on the deck during audiences with Space Marines. Also, where was his hat?

He stood up.

'I... uhm,' Ludd began. He wasn't sure what he'd been in the middle of saying. He searched their faces for a clue.

The three Adeptus Astartes battle-brothers in the half-lit hold in front of him gave nothing away. Kater Holofurnace, the giant warrior of the Iron Snakes, very slowly buckled on his war-helm. Sar Af the White Scar seemed poised as though listening to something intently. Brother-Sergeant Eadwine of the Silver Guard seemed lost in deep thought.

'Have you seen my hat?' Ludd asked.

None of them replied.

'Uhm, Colonel-Commissar Gaunt sent me to respectfully inform you that we're experiencing drive issues,' said Ludd, suddenly remembering. 'So... so we're coming to secondary order in case we get bounced back into real space and experience... uhm... you know, an attack.'

Ludd realised he was blinking with his right eye.

'You told us this,' said Sar Af.

'Did I really?' said Ludd. 'When did I do that?'

'When you walked in here and told it to us,' said Sar Af.

'Oh,' said Ludd.

'About twenty seconds before the ship was... *bounced back into real space*,' said Eadwine, locking his helm in place.

The blinking was beginning to annoy Ludd. Something was getting in his eye. He reached up and found that his fingers were wet. He was bleeding from a scalp wound and the blood was running down his face.

'Ow,' he said. He began to remember the world lurching in a spasm, a feeling of... of something he didn't want to dwell on. He remembered flying through the air. He remembered the deck racing up to meet him.

'Gather your wits,' said Sar Af, putting on his own war-helm. 'This is just the beginning.'

'It is?' asked Ludd.

Holofurnace pointed at the roof of the hold with his lance.

'Listen,' he said.

Shipmaster Clemensaw Spika flopped back into his seat. He was breathing hard. His head hurt like a bastard. He knew that feeling. The lingering, sickening trauma of a bad translation from the warp. Everyone around him was disorientated and dazed, even the most hard-wired souls.

'Somebody mute those alarms!' he yelled. The stations and consoles of the bridge were a mass of flashing amber and red runes. The noise was overwhelming. One of Spika's aides made adjustments. The immediate row abated, though the ship sirens and warning horns continued to bay.

'Report, please,' said Spika, trying to catch his breath.

'No data, no feed, shipmaster,' the Master of Artifice replied.

'No data, no feed,' echoed the Master of Detection.

'Guidance is inert,' reported the chief steersman. 'The Navigator is unconscious.'

'Our location?' asked Spika.

'Not calculable at this time.'

'But real space?' asked Spika. 'We're in real space?'

He didn't have to ask. He could feel they were. The *Highness Ser Armaduke* had violently retranslated from the immaterium after a drive failure. It was a miracle they hadn't been annihilated, or torn apart, or void-blown by the extremity of it. An Imperial miracle, bless the divine God-Emperor. Maybe Gaunt had been wrong about their luck.

'I want a critical status report in five minutes,' Spika said, getting back on his feet. He was badly bruised from the gravity fall, and his cardiac flutter and irregular breathing were due to the physiological sympathies he felt with his ship's systems and drives.

'Five minutes,' he repeated. 'Casualties, damage, system status, repair schedules, local position, capacity, ready times, everything.'

'Shipmaster?'

Spika turned.

The junior vox-officer was holding out a headset to him. The man was pale and shaking. The trauma had left its mark on everyone.

'What?' asked Spika.

'Urgent vox-link from Eadwine of the Silver Guard,' he said.

'Routed through shipboard vox?'

'No, sir, that's down. This is direct from his suit system to my desk receivers.'

Spika took the headset.

'This is the shipmaster.'

'*This is Eadwine. Cancel all shipboard sirens.*'

'Noble sir, we have just suffered a traumatic return to–'

'*Cancel them.*'

'Why?' asked Spika.

'*So we can hear.*'

The shipmaster hesitated.

'Hear what, Brother-Sergeant Eadwine?'

'*Whatever it is that's trying to get in,*' the voice of the Adeptus Astartes warrior crackled back.

'The chances of us being boarded mere seconds after a translation are ridiculously low. It is an unfeasible coincidence. An Archenemy ship would have to be in precisely the right location, and ready for operation, and-'

'*Spika, you are confused. Reassess the situation. Prepare yourself. And cancel the damned sirens.*'

The link went dead.

Spika had to steady himself. He felt extremely unwell. What the hell had the battle-brother been talking about? How dare he talk to a shipmaster like that when...

He found himself staring at the main console, and specifically at the display of the ship's principal chronometer.

He swallowed, and felt a chill. It wasn't possible.

Sometime during the last few, terrible minutes of drive failure and brutal retranslation, they had lost ten years.

'Cancel the damned sirens!' he yelled. 'All of them! Right now!'

FIVE

V'HEDUAK

'The shipboard vox is down,' said Maddalena Darebeloved.

Ibram Gaunt nodded. He'd tried several wall outlets, and heard nothing but a death rattle of static. The quiet was unnerving. No transmitted throb of the engines, no purr of power conduits. There was just a slow, aching creak of metal moving and settling, as though the ancient tonnage of the *Armaduke* were begging for mercy.

Even the deck alarms had fallen silent.

Gaunt felt sick. His mind was numb and refusing to function clearly. He felt as though he'd been frozen and then defrosted. He was covered in bruises where gravity had smashed him back into the deck, but it was the slowness of his thoughts and the clumsiness of his hands that really bothered him.

From the look of her, Maddalena was suffering too. She was blinking fast, as if stunned, and her usual grace was absent. She was stumbling around as badly as he was.

Gaunt checked the load of his bolt pistol, holstered it and made off along the companionway. Maddalena followed him. There was a thin sheen of smoke in the processed air, and curious smells that mingled burning with the reek of spilled chemicals, and an odour that suggested that long stagnant sumps had been disturbed.

'I'm going to find Felyx,' Maddalena said.

Gaunt paused. He had expected as much. It was her primary duty, and he could hardly fault her for observing the orders of her House Chass masters to the letter.

He looked at her.

'I understand,' he said. 'But Felyx is in no more or less danger than any of us. The welfare of the ship as a whole is at stake. For Felyx's sake, it should be our priority to secure that first.'

She pursed her lips. It was an odd, attractive sign of uncertainty that Gaunt associated with Merity Chass. The duplicated face mirrored the expression perfectly.

'He is my charge. His life is mine to ward,' she said.

'He's my son,' Gaunt replied.

'You suggest?'

Gaunt gestured forwards.

'We need to assess several key things. How dead this ship actually is. What the level of injury is. How long it will take – if it's possible at all – to restore engineering function. On top of that, whether we're at external risk.'

'From boarding?'

Gaunt nodded.

'The longer we drift here helplessly...'

Maddalena smiled.

'Space is, forgive me for sounding simplistic, very large. To be prey for something, we'd have to be found by something.'

'You were the one prepping your gun,' Gaunt reminded her.

'I'll come with you to the bridge,' she said.

They moved as far as the next through-deck junction and stopped as they heard footsteps clattering towards them.

'First and Only!' Gaunt challenged. He didn't draw his weapon, but Maddalena had a tight grip on hers.

'Stand easy, sir!' a voice called back.

Gaunt recognised it.

'Criid?'

'Coming your way,' Tona Criid called back. She came into view, lasrifle ready. With her came the command squad from A Company, which included Larkin and the company adjutant, Beltayn. Their faces were pale and haggard, as if they had all just woken up from a bad night's sleep.

'We were just coming to find you, sir,' Criid said, 'when it all–'

She hesitated, and gave a shrug that encompassed the ship around them.

'–when all this happened.'

'What have you seen?' Gaunt asked.

'A few injured crew, not much else,' she replied. 'Everyone's been knocked around. I think grav was off for a moment.'

Gaunt nodded and looked at Beltayn. The adjutant was carrying his voxcaster set.

'Is that working, Bel?' Gaunt asked.

'Yes, sir,' Beltayn replied, nonplussed.

'All ship-side comms are dead,' Gaunt said. 'We're going to need our own field vox to coordinate. Set that up, see who you can reach. The regiment should have been at secondary order, so anyone still on his feet should be vox-ready.'

Beltayn unslung his voxcaster, set it on the deck, and lit it up. The power lights came on, and he began to adjust the frequency dials. Swirls of static and audio noise breathed out of the speakers.

'All companies, this is Gaunt. Report location and status, confirm secondary order. Send that by voice and voxtype, and tell me what you get back.'

Beltayn nodded, and began to set up to send the message. He tapped it into the caster's small keyboard, and then unhooked the speaker horn to deliver the spoken version. He was having trouble adjusting the frequency for clarity.

'What's the matter, lad?' asked Larkin.

'Beltayn?' asked Gaunt.

'Something's awry,' Beltayn replied, working with the dials.

'Such as?'

'I'm getting interference,' the adjutant replied. 'Listen.'

He turned the dial again very gently, and noise washed out of the speakers. It was a mix of pips, squeals, electromagnetic humming, dull metallic thuds and an odd, cackling signal that sounded like multiple voice recordings being played at high speed. The cocktail of sounds came and went in a haze of white hiss.

There was something chilling about it. Gaunt felt the back of his neck prickle.

'Holy bloody feth,' murmured Larkin.

'Swear by the Throne, sir,' said Beltayn, 'I have no idea what that is.'

Eszrah Ap Niht, called Ezra Night by his Ghost friends, slipped silently along the vast, helpless carcass of the ship, reynbow in hand. He was a grey shadow, flitting through the gloomy depths of the ancient vessel.

He felt as though he had been turned inside out. He was not clear-headed. But years of fighting the silent war in the Untill had taught him that danger did not wait until you were feeling fit enough to face it. When danger came, you made yourself ready, no matter how wretched you felt.

His wits, sharply attuned thanks to his upbringing as a Nihtganc of Gereon, had identified threat sounds. He had isolated them from all the thousands of other noises drifting through the stricken voidship.

The *Armaduke* had become a prison, a reinforced, rusting, iron prison, its sensory systems blind and deaf. Acute human or transhuman senses were the only tactically viable currency.

Principal artifice and engineering formed the aft sections of the vessel, and comprised an echoing series of cavernous assembly chambers, stoking vaults and drive halls. There was a stink of grease and soot, a stink of promethium and the dull, zincy dust kicked out by the overheated extractors.

Gravity was abundantly wrong in the rear portion of the ship. Ezra didn't really appreciate the concept of gravity. In his experience, drawn from the Untill of Gereon, the ground was that which a person stuck to, and to which all thrown or dropped objects returned. The same had proved to be true on the other worlds he had visited as part of the Tanith First retinue, and also true aboard the starships that carried them between battlefields.

Now that force, the authority of the ground, was gone. Ezra could feel the gentle, reeling tilt of the ship as it slowly spun end over end. It was like suddenly being able to feel the world turning on its axis. Starlight, filtering in through those dirty hull ports that remained unshuttered, slid like slicks of white oil across decks, up walls and across ceilings. Smoke glazed the air in uncomfortable swirls. For the most part, the deck underfoot drew him firmly as any ground should. But gravity wandered in places, where grav plates had failed, or mass-reactor rings had been misaligned by the violence of translation.

Ezra found himself walking down oddly sloping hallways and then, without warning, finding the vertical running briefly along the base of a wall. In one place, midway down a long loading hall, disrupted gravity fields took him off the deck, up one wall, over the ceiling until he was walking inverted, and then back down the other wall onto the deck again. All the while he had done nothing but stride in a straight line.

Ezra shook it off. It was disconcerting, but then, the galaxy was disconcerting. His life had, for all of his early years, been sheltered in the grey gloom of the Untill. Then he had joined with Gaunt and his men, and with them seen the marvels of the galaxy: space full of stars, cities and deserts, vistas he could not dream of and creatures he could never imagine.

Nothing surprised him. He had long ago accepted that anything was possible. Around any corner, anything might await. Including, he knew, death... from the least expected direction.

The disturbed gravity was disconcerting, but he refused to be disconcerted. Let the floor become the wall, or then the ceiling.

Danger was the only thing that needed to occupy him.

Sparks fluttered from wall panels that had shorted out. Overhead lighting rigs, suspended on chains, bellied out and swung in slow, wide, oval orbits, betraying the strange, sluggish rotation of the vessel.

He reached one of the main access gates into the engineering core. It was a huge structure, like a triumphal arch, decorated with brass seraphs and cherubs. Steel rail tracks ran through the archway, allowing for the process of wagons carrying stoking ore from the deep bunkers to the furnace mouth. The iron blast-gates filling the archway were ominously open.

Ezra took an iron quarrel out of his leather quiver, and dropped it nock-down into the muzzle of his upright reynbow. He heard it clink into place, then felt the slight hum and tension as the magnetic fields generated by the magpods at either end of the recurve bow assembly activated and locked the bolt in place.

He stalked forwards.

Beyond the towering archway lay a huge turbine hall. Part of the ceiling had come down, layering the deck with sheets of metal panelling and broken spars. Other torn shreds of panelling hung down on fibres and tangled wires, exposing dark cavities in the roof-space where flames swirled and guttered. Small fires burned amid the debris on the deck too.

The great chrome-and-brass turbines lining the room were silent. Oil ran out of several of them where seams and seals had burst. The dark liquid ran like blood, pooling on the deck in wide, gleaming lakes, like the black mirrors the elders of the Nihtgane used for glimpsing the future. Some were raining drops up from the floor towards the roof.

Ezra could see the future. Another hour or two and the spreading slicks would reach the fires... or the fires would burn to the slicks. An inferno would follow, and it would consume the turbine halls.

Where were the stokers? Where were the men of Artifice? Ezra moved forwards, bow ready, stepping silently and cautiously across the piles of debris and broken panelling. He realised that several of the dust-caked objects at his feet were the bodies of engineering crew, felled and crushed by falling wreckage.

Too few, though. Where was everybody else? He had observed this part of the ship on several occasions during the long voyage, marvelling at the scale and industry. Ordinarily, hundreds of workers toiled here, in rowdy, straining work gangs.

He followed the rails. The trackway ran down the centre line of the hall, between the turbine arrays. Passing between the first leaking turbine structures, Ezra came upon a row of forty bulk rail wagons that had been physically thrown off the tracks. They lay on their sides, ore loads spilling out like black landslides, like a giant, broken centipede. The mass of them had crushed and destroyed a great many of the brass condensers and sub-turbine assemblies on the starboard side of the chamber.

Ezra heard movement. He tucked himself in behind one of the overturned wagons. There was a rush towards him: raised voices, thundering footsteps. *Panic.*

Engineering personnel began to flood past, heading up the tracks. They were running, some hauling injured comrades. Ezra saw master artificers, junior engineers, huge ogryn stokers black with soot, servitors and robed adepts. Dozens went past, hundreds.

Then the shooting started.

It came from the rear of the chamber, in the direction Ezra had been heading. It was a ragged mix of las-fire and hard-round bursts. Ezra saw some of the fleeing engineers turn to look, then run faster. Others dropped, struck from behind by searing blasts. A bulky stoker was cut down just as he passed Ezra's hiding place. He staggered, turning awkwardly, and crashed against the side of the wagon, blood pouring from two hard-round exit wounds in his side.

The ogryn gazed at Ezra with uncomprehending, piggy eyes as he slowly slid down the wagon edge and thumped to the deck.

The firing became more fierce. A heavy stubber opened up. Looking from cover, Ezra saw dozens of the running engineers drop as the chewing impacts stitched across them. Men buckled and fell, or were knocked off their feet. Two, hit hard, were dismembered by the hefty rounds. Stray shots punched into the brass-work of turbine cylinders and copper venting kettles.

Ezra clambered up the end gate of the wagon, using the huge, oily coupling hook as a foothold, and bellied up onto the wagon side. He was about four metres off the ground. He crawled along to get a better vantage point.

The attackers were entering the turbine hall from the far end, where the hall opened into one of the ship's principal stoking chambers. They were clambering over mounds of debris and wreckage, firing as they came.

They were human... humanoid, at least. Men, but not men. They were dressed in ragged combat gear that mixed ballistic padding with plasteel breastplates and chainmail. Most had their faces covered with featureless metal masks that looked like dirty welding visors. The single, extended eye-slits glowed soft yellow with targeting arrays.

Their weapons were old, but clearly well maintained and effective. They were of the general kind that had been carried by the Astra Militarum for centuries.

But the emblems displayed on the breastplates and foreheads of the attackers were unmistakably the toxic sigils of the Archenemy.

Ezra sighted his reynbow. He took down his first target with a quarrel to the head.

The reynbow made only the slightest metallic whisper as the magpods charged and spat the dart. It was inaudible over the roar of gunfire.

The attackers only noticed they were being hit when the second and third of them went down, iron barbs staked into their chests and throats. Yellow visor arrays flickered in confusion.

Suddenly, sustained gunfire hosed along the wagon, hunting for Ezra.

He rolled fast and dropped to the deck, slipping to another point of concealment. He let the heavy framework of the wagon absorb the hard-rounds and las-bolts. Several large calibre shots punctured the belly of the wagon, punching holes through which beams of dusty light speared.

Ezra reached the inter-wagon coupling, knelt down and tracked one of the attackers with his bow. Stock to shoulder, he fired, clean-sighted. The quarrel penetrated the warrior's visor slit, and exploded the display reticule in a flurry of sparks. Gurgling and clawing at a visor that was now pinned to his face, the figure dropped to his knees.

Ezra reloaded. He tried a long shot at a bulky attacker with a heavy stubber, but missed. More gunfire spat his way, and he moved again, running back along the line of fuelling wagons, his feet crunching and slipping on the slopes of spilled ore.

One of the attackers suddenly appeared between wagons in front of him. Ezra's reynbow was loaded, and he fired instinctively from the hip. The quarrel went clean through the man's plasteel plating and his torso, spraying blood and specks of meat in the air. He fell.

A second attacker was right behind him.

There was no time to reload.

Ezra hurled himself into the warrior, using his reynbow as a club. He knocked the warrior's head sideways with the blow, but the man struggled with him. Ezra lost his grip on the bow. The warrior struck him, and Ezra fell on his arse. In a sitting position, he swung the reynbow again, this time more frantically, and managed to hook the warrior's legs out from under him. They slithered and struggled in the sloping spill of ore.

The warrior tried to rise. Ezra got up first. He stabbed the warrior repeatedly in the throat with a quarrel from his pouch, using the iron barb like a dagger.

The warrior gurgled and convulsed as he bled out.

Ezra reached for his reynbow, but it had not benefitted from being used as a cudgel. Part of the bow frame was twisted, and one of the magpods was misaligned. With a mixture of desperation and reluctance, Ezra grabbed his enemy's lasrifle. He had to tug it hard to free the sling from the dead man's clutches.

The Ghosts had taught him the basic use of an energy weapon, even though he did not care for the technology. He checked the rifle. The power-cell was charged, and the firing lock was off. He hefted it to his shoulder, searching for a comfortable grip and slipping his finger into the unfamiliar trigger guard.

Two attackers clambered through the space between the wagons. One fired at Ezra, and the searing las-bolt missed the Nihtgane by the width of a splayed hand.

Ezra shot back. He had not checked the discharge setting of his captured weapon. It juddered in his hands as it spat out a flurry on full-auto, mowing down both the attackers in front of him with a squall of shots.

Ezra ran to find new cover. As soon as he was sheltered from view, he adjusted the dial on the side of his new gun to 'single'.

The fight was escalating fast, but he knew it had only just begun.

Viktor Hark entered the brig area of the *Armaduke*. He was dazed and rattled. The vessel was clearly in a perilous state. Waking to find himself face down on the deck after the brutal retranslation, he had resolved to follow Gaunt's last instruction, and then proceed to restoring some order to the regiment.

Secondary order. Even before the accident, Gaunt had been anxious to make the Ghosts ready for a fight.

The ship was making odd, plaintive noises, and it was heeling badly. Hark clattered down a flight of metal steps and approached the heavy shutters of the brig. He realised almost immediately that he was in someone's crosshairs.

'It's me,' he said, feeling foolish.

Judd Cardass appeared, lowering his lasrifle.

'Just checking, sir,' Cardass said.

'As you should, trooper.'

'What's going on?' Cardass asked. He was surprisingly blunt for a Belladon. That was probably down to him being part of Rawne's mob for too long. Then again, the current situation was enough to breed tension and bluntness in anyone.

'I need to see the major,' Hark replied.

Cardass nodded, and led the commissar through the shutterway into the outer chambers of the brig, where security stations faced the inner hatches, and the walls were lined with cots for the guards.

B Company's first squad, the so-called 'Suicide Kings', had been charged with protecting the regiment's guest, an extremely dangerous military asset. They took their job seriously, and the outer chamber space had virtually become the company barracks. B Company had taken up residence in the brig after an attempt on the guest's life during the outward journey had proved the initial holding location insecure.

As Hark entered, he saw the Ghosts of B Company getting things straight. Some were picking up chairs and kitbags that had tumbled during the grav-failure. Others were checking the security instruments. Two or three were patching minor wounds and abrasions.

Major Rawne was on the far side of the monitor bay with Varl and Bonin. They were grouped around Oysten, who was setting up the squad's vox-set.

'Shipboard comms are down,' Rawne said to Hark without looking up.

'I see you're improvising.'

Rawne nodded. Only now did he glance at Hark.

'Drive accident?' he asked.

'I'm guessing.'

Rawne nodded.

'Is the asset safe?' Hark asked.

'He's secure.'

'I was coming down here to instruct you to come to secondary order,' Hark said.

'Done and done, sir,' replied Varl.

'Gaunt anticipated this. We're adrift and crippled, I believe. We may be assaulted.'

'Boarding action?' asked Bonin.

'He felt it likely,' replied Hark.

Rawne kept his gaze on Hark.

'Is the ship dead? Fethed? Are we going to die out here? Void-freeze? Like the damn space hulks they tell the old stories about?'

'I have no idea of our status, major,' Hark replied. 'I think we'd need to consult with the shipmaster to discern our viability.'

Rawne looked at Oysten.

'Anything?' he asked. 'Gaunt? The fething bridge?'

Oysten pursed her lips. A Belladon vox-specialist from the new intake, she had been transferred to Rawne's command after the death of Kabry, Rawne's previous adjutant. It was clear she was still an outsider in the ranks of the Suicide Kings.

'I don't seem to be able to set up any kind of vox-net, sir,' Oysten replied.

'Balls to that,' Varl snapped. 'This is the Tanith First. We're not arse-handed morons. Gods among men B Company may be, but we're not the only unit who'll have thought to go vox-live to coordinate.'

'Your point is well made,' said Oysten calmly. 'I'm just telling you how it is. The vox feels like it's being signal-blocked. Maybe it's the superstructure of the ship. We're pretty damn armoured down here.'

Rawne shrugged.

'Maybe it's you not knowing one end of a fething voxcaster from the other, Oysten,' he said.

'Maybe it's an after-effect of the real space shift?' Hark suggested quietly. 'Maybe we're flooded with energies that...'

His voice trailed off. He realised he was speculating in areas that even he, an educated and experienced senior officer of the Officio Prefectus, knew feth all about.

'Wait please,' said Oysten. 'I'm getting something. Voice, I think. Voice signal...'

She wound one of the dials hard, then flicked two toggle switches, moving the audio to speakers rather than the headset hanging around her neck like a torc.

They heard a blend of squeals, hums, e-mag burbles and bangs, out of which emerged a crackling signal that sounded like overlapped voice recordings. The whole mix was bathed in a white noise hiss.

'Can you tease that apart?' Rawne asked, craning to listen.

Oysten made a few adjustments in an attempt to isolate the individual signals.

'Just trying to clean it up,' she said.

She stopped suddenly. The thread of voices had become very clear. It was vox back-chatter between multiple operators, a scratchy to and fro of orders, acknowledgements and advisories. They could tell that from the tone and flow.

The content was impossible to discern. None of the words were being spoken in a tongue they recognised as human.

'Feth that,' said Varl.

'Archenemy transmissions,' Bonin said.

Oysten nodded.

'Shut it down,' said Rawne.

'Before we know what it means?' asked Hark.

Rawne shot him an ugly look.

'Seriously?' he asked.

'I think we're in deep shit, Rawne. I think we can use all the intel we can get right now.'

Rawne looked at Bonin and Varl.

'Bring him out,' he said.

The pair of them moved swiftly, gathering LaHurf and Brostin as they advanced to the door of the primary cell. Their weapons were ready.

'Open it!' Varl yelled to Nomis at the security station.

'Opening three!' Nomis called back as he threw the levers.

The outer hatch slid up, and the inner interlock doors opened.

Bonin entered first to sweep the cell. Then he re-emerged and waved in the other three.

It was about two minutes before they appeared. Hark knew that time had been spent adjusting shackles, removing deck-pins, and doing a tight search of hands, hems and mouth.

The four Suicide Kings appeared, advancing at a slow pace determined by the hobble-chain on the prisoner's ankles. They flanked him in a square formation.

It seemed to take forever for them to escort Mabbon Etogaur to the vox-station. Every man in the room watched the Archenemy prisoner as he shuffled along.

Mabbon's face lacked expression and personality. His shaved head was a mess of old ritual scars.

'What has happened, m–' he began to ask when he was brought to a halt.

'Don't ask questions,' Rawne replied bluntly. He gestured to the vox-set. 'Answer them. What is that, pheguth? What does it mean?'

Mabbon Etogaur cocked his scarred head and listened for a few moments. Then he sighed deeply.

'V'heduak,' he said. 'Four or perhaps five storm-teams are on board. To aft of the engine house, I think. They are making ground.'

'What was that word?' Hark asked.

'V'heduak,' replied Mabbon. 'You've been boarded by the V'heduak.'

'Meaning?'

'Literally? "Blood-fare", Mabbon replied. 'It is part of a longer phrase... *Ort'o shet ahgk v'heduak*... which means, "Those that will claim a price or fare in blood in return for conveyance".'

He glanced at Hark with his eerily expressionless face.

'What it actually means,' he said, 'is that we are, to use Sergeant Varl's vernacular, spectacularly fethed.'

SIX

PICK OUR BONES

Gaunt reached the bridge of the *Armaduke* about thirty seconds after Shipmaster Spika died.

Trailing the A Company command squad, with Criid on one side of him and Maddalena lurking on the other, he entered the bridge via the main arch and saw the crew gathering in a mob around a fallen figure.

Some of the bridge personnel – and there were an awful lot of them – had not left their stations or posts. Indeed, many could not because they were jacked and wired into their positions.

But even those who could not move were staring. Some were beginning to wail. Others had tears in their augmeticised eyes.

As soon as he saw that it was Spika, Gaunt pushed through the huddle, shoving robed bridge seniors and masters aside.

'What are you doing?' Gaunt asked them. As far as he could see they were all agitated and upset, but no one was offering any treatment.

'He fell!' one of the officers declared.

'He fell down! The shipmaster fell down!' moaned another.

'I think it is his heart,' said the officer of detection. 'I think our proud ship is mortally struck, and the sympathetic pain has–'

Gaunt ignored him. He looked at Maddalena.

'Get Curth!' he cried.

'But–'

'I said get her!' Gaunt yelled. Maddalena scowled, and then turned and ran from the bridge. Gaunt knew she was fast, faster than Criid, probably. Besides, he needed Criid and her authority.

Gaunt dropped to his knees and listened to Spika's heart. The shipmaster lay on his back, his skin as white as wax and his eyes empty.

'Feth,' Gaunt murmured. He knelt up and began compressions.

'Criid!' he yelled as he worked.

'Sir?'

'Secure the bridge! Get these people away from the shipmaster! Get them back to work, dammit!'

Criid looked dubious. The senior officers and high-function servitors of the *Armaduke* seemed fearful and outlandish creatures to her. They were staring at Gaunt and the other newcomers with puzzlement and distaste, as if they were invaders or zoological specimens.

'What if these good persons of the Imperial Navy do not recognise the authority of the Astra Militarum, sir?' she asked.

'Then see if they recognise the authority of a bayonet, Criid. Improvise.'

Gaunt kept working. Spika's body didn't betray the slightest hint of vitality.

Gaunt had saved lives before. His trade was taking lives, and he was miserably good at that, but he had saved a life or two in his time. Battlefield aid, trauma procedures. He had pumped lungs and hearts, bound up fast-bleeds with fieldwire tourniquets, and plugged gouting wounds with his fingers until the medicae arrived.

He was better at death than life, but the latter counted now. They needed Spika. More than that, Spika didn't deserve this end.

'Come on!' Gaunt snarled as he worked.

'We have been boarded,' a man said.

Maintaining the compressions, Gaunt looked up. A stout, sandy-haired battlefleet officer was looking down at him. Silver brocade decorated his dark blue tunic. He was command branch, not a master of anything or an officer of any specific department.

'We anticipated that,' Gaunt replied, his hands working steadily.

'You must clear the bridge,' the officer said.

'Can't you see what the feth I'm doing?' Gaunt asked.

'Our beloved shipmaster, may the Throne bless his soul, has departed this life,' said the officer. 'Stress. He had been fairly warned. His health was an issue. We will mourn him. Now he is gone, the life of the ship is all that matters. You will clear the bridge.'

'Like feth!' Gaunt answered.

'I am Subcommander Kelvedon,' the officer said. His voice was light and dry, like long grass at the end of a summer season. 'I stand second to the shipmaster in line of succession. At this hour of his death, I have command of the *Armaduke*. Its welfare is my business. You will clear the bridge.'

'He isn't even cold!' Gaunt snapped. He regretted his words. Spika's flesh, where Gaunt had torn open his frock coat and uniform shirt, seemed as cold as the void. Spika looked forlorn and forgotten, his chest a scrawny, shrivelled knot, like the belly of a fish. He had seemed a commanding man. Death had diminished him mercilessly.

'Clear my damned bridge, sir,' Kelvedon said. 'Have your meat-head troops gather in their appointed billets and stay out of our way. This is a fighting ship. We will secure all decks and drive out the enemy.'

'We fight better than you,' replied Gaunt. 'Imperial Guard. Astra Militarum. Best damned fighting bastards in the universe. Stop talking crap and collaborate with me, *Acting* Shipmaster Kelvedon. Spika knew our worth and how to profit from coordinated responses.'

'Spika made decisions that I would not have made,' replied Kelvedon. 'This entire run was not battlefleet business. It was some kind of undistinguished smoke and mirrors blackwork by your Commissariat masters and–'

Kelvedon suddenly made a curious sound, the sound that a cargo-8's tyre makes when it blows out. His eyes watered, his cheeks ballooned, and he sank to the deck, doubled up.

'Knee in testicles,' Criid announced to Gaunt as Kelvedon flopped onto his side in a foetal position. 'That the kind of thing you had in mind?'

'Superb work, Captain Criid.'

She half turned, then looked back.

'You what?' she asked.

'I've been meaning to tell you,' said Gaunt pumping at Spika's chest with the balls of his palms, 'there just hasn't been a moment. Promotion, Tona. Captain. Company command, A Company. I want you to run my company.'

'For kneeing some void-stain in the knackers?' she asked.

'I may have taken a few other factors into account. Your peerless combat record, for example. Now, Captain Criid, if you don't mind, would you kick Acting Shipmaster Kelvedon in the testes a second time?'

Criid frowned.

'Why?' she asked.

Gaunt stopped compressions and sat back on his heels.

'Because it would make me feel better. This isn't working.' He rubbed his hands together. The cold radiating from Spika's corpse had seemed to leech into him, numbing his hands, his wrists, his forearm.

'He's fething dead,' Gaunt sighed.

He rose slowly, stepped away from Spika's pathetic corpse and over Kelvedon's blubbering mass.

'Who's actually in charge here?' he asked the bridge around him. 'Not this blowhard runt,' he added, gesturing back at Kelvedon. 'Who is next in line? Come the feth on! This is an emergency!'

'I am,' said one of the robed figures waiting at the edge of the bridge platform. He stepped forwards. He was tall, as tall as Ezra Night, and just as rake-thin. His floor-length robes were blue, trimmed with an odd fabric that seemed opalescent. His eyes were gross augmetic implants, and one of his hands was a bionic spider. Input plugs and data cables threaded his neck, throat and chest.

'Darulin, Master of Ordnance,' he said to Gaunt, with a slight bow.

'Ordnance has precedence over artifice and helm?' Gaunt asked.

Darulin nodded.

'A ship is its weapons. Everything else is secondary.'

'Is it true that we've been boarded?' asked Gaunt.

'Available data says so. There is fighting in the engine houses.'

'Who's fighting?'

'I misspoke,' Darulin replied. 'There is *killing* in the engine houses.'

'Who has boarded us?'

'The Archenemy,' said Darulin.

'How did they find us?' asked Gaunt.

'Consult the chronometer,' Darulin invited, with a whirring spider-gesture. 'A moment passed for us, but we are missing ten years. We are adrift. The Archenemy had time to detect and triangulate.'

'What did you say?' asked Gaunt.

'The Archenemy had time to detect–'

'No, before that.'

'We are missing ten years. We have lost ten years because of the temporal distortion of the translation accident.'

Gaunt and Criid looked at each other.

'We were only unconscious for a moment,' murmured Criid. 'A moment.'

'Are you sure?' Gaunt asked the Master of Ordnance.

'Yes. Such time-loss is rare and troubling, but not unheard of. You are not void-experienced. You do not know such things.'

Gaunt regarded the deck for a moment, collected his thoughts, then looked back at Darulin.

'We must coordinate a counter-assault,' Gaunt said. 'My regiment. Your armsmen.'

Darulin was about to respond when Ana Curth entered the bridge. A couple of Tanith corpsmen followed her, and behind them came Maddalena Darebeloved. Larkin, Beltayn and the rest of A Company gathered in the doorway behind, looking on grimly.

'Who's hurt?' Curth asked.

'The shipmaster,' Gaunt told her. 'It's too late for him.'

Curth elbowed past Gaunt, heading for Spika.

'I'll be the judge of that,' she told him. She paused and glanced back at Gaunt.

'Don't send your bitch to fetch me, ever again,' she said.

He didn't blink.

'Behave like a professional,' he replied.

Curth knelt beside Spika, examined him, and checked his vitals.

'Compressions!' she ordered at one of the corpsmen, who rushed to oblige.

'I tried that,' said Gaunt.

'Let's see what happens when somebody knows what they're doing,' she shot back. She opened her case, lifted the folding layers, and selected a hydroneumat syringe. She loaded it from a phial, checked it, flicked it, then swabbed a place over the carotid on Spika's neck.

The needle slid in and she depressed the cartridge release.

Spika did not stir.

'Shit,' said Curth, and began mouth to mouth as the corpsman applied diligent heart massage.

Gaunt turned back to Darulin.

'My regiment. Your armsmen. You were saying?'

His route to the drive chambers had been blocked by a corridor that had suffered catastrophic gravity collapse. Scout Sergeant Mkoll had switched to service ducts and crawlspaces. He was edging his way down an almost vertical, unlit vent tube when the vox finally woke up.

A voice crackled, dry in the cold darkness.

'*Advisory, advisory,*' the voice said. '*The Archenemy is aboard this vessel. Arm and prepare. The Archenemy is in the drive chambers and advancing for'ard.*'

Mkoll braced himself on a welding seam, legs splayed. The vent duct was sheer. He let his rifle, now strip-checked and reloaded, hang off his shoulder and adjusted his microbead link. Cold air breezed up at him from far below, bearing mysterious sounds of clanks and bumps.

'That you, Rawne?' he asked quietly.

'*Identify?*'

'It's Mkoll.'

'*Where are you?*' Rawne asked over the link.

'Like I'm going to tell you that over an open channel. Report.'

'*We've been boarded.*'

'I know. I've met some. Not sure what they are.'

'*Intel says six storm-teams, which means about seven hundred hostiles. V'heduak.*'

'What's that when it's at home?' Mkoll asked.

'*No time to explain in detail. The Archenemy fleet, basically. Ever wondered how the Sanguinary Tribes get around? How the Blood Pact move from world to world? V'heduak, that's how. And when they're not acting as drivers for the bastard ground forces, they stalk the stars, looking for ships to pick off and plunder. We've been hit by cannibals.*'

'Tech cannibals?'

'*Yeah, and the rest.*'

Mkoll fell silent for a moment. He felt the sweat bead on his forehead despite the chill breeze gusting from below him.

'Where are you getting this intel from, Rawne?' he asked.

'*You don't want to know, Oan.*'

'But it's reliable?'

'*As feth.*'

'Where are you?' Mkoll asked.

'*In the brig, securing the asset.*'

'Rawne, is *anyone* moving aft to the drive chambers?'

There was a long pause.

'*Mkoll, it's all a bit uncoordinated. The vox is choppy. I think Bask's company is moving in. No word from Kolea. Nothing from Gaunt.*'

Mkoll sighed.

'Feth,' he whispered to himself.

'*Say again?*'

'Hold the fething line,' Mkoll said. 'I'm going to take a look.'

Toe-cap and fingernail, he resumed his descent.

Ezra Night threw himself headlong into cover. Enemy fire whipped at him, exploding the bulkheads and wall braces behind him. Sparks showered. Pieces of plastek and alumina whistled through the air.

Ezra rolled. He brought up his lasrifle and clipped off two solid bursts of fire. Varl would be proud of him. Varl and Criid. Those who had taught him.

The enemy dropped. The Archenemy.

Ezra had been fought back into the rear spaces of the drive chambers, vast as they were. He was just one man facing squads of hundreds.

He would fight and die. Fight and die. That was what Ibram always said. Better to fight and die. Do you want to live forever?

A little longer would be nice, Ezra thought.

He aimed again, and fired a burst. Two attackers flipped over on their backs, their torsos blown apart.

He was aware of a little amber rune winking on the rim of the clip-socket above his thumb. *Powercell low.* He needed a reload. Why hadn't he thought to take one off the corpse?

A series of heavy explosions detonated along the centre of the deck space, marching towards him. Debris showered into the air, whole deck plates and underdeck pipework.

The Archenemy had sent heavier units into the *Armaduke*.

Ezra spied the first of the stalk-tanks as it clattered along the drive hall towards him. Two more followed. He had seen such machines before. They were lightweight, with an almost spherical pod of a body just large enough to contain a single driver or hardwired servitor operator plus control packages and data sumps. Powerful quad-lasguns or plasma cannons were mounted on a gyro cradle beneath the body. The tanks walked on eight pairs of long, slender spider-legs.

These devices were heavier than normal. The body-shells were armoured against hard vacuum and heavy fire. The legs were more robust, and ended in flexible grab-claws. These things were designed to walk in the cold silence of the void, to scurry across the surface of starships, to find purchase as they sought to bite or cut a way inside. They were built to live like lice or ticks on the hull-skin of a shiftship.

The underslung gunpods were firing, the gyro-mounts turning each recoil slap into a fluid bounce. Deck plates erupted. Part of the chamber wall blew out in a dizzy gout of flame and sparks. One of the fueling wagons was blown to pieces.

An iron wheel squealed as it rolled across the deck.

Enemy foot soldiers, their visor slits glowing, advanced behind the stalk-tanks, firing as they came. Ezra felt a laugh building in his throat. He had survived the one-sided war by sticking to the hit-and-run resistance tactics of the Nihtgane. Stalk, kill, move, stay invisible. His situation was now beyond impossible.

Ezra knelt and took aim. He was partially shielded by the burning remains of a service crate. He aimed for the small, armoured window port on the nearest stalk-tank, and wondered if he could hit it. He was pretty confident he could. But could he penetrate it? Even if he poured on all the power left in the cell?

Yes. Yes, he could. He would kill it. It would be his last act as part of the Ghost regiment.

Ezra pulled the trigger. The gun did not fire. The rune was red. *Power out.* Ezra allowed himself to laugh.

'Is there any way of getting an external visual?' Gaunt asked.

'Are you commanding this ship now?' Kelvedon snapped back.

'Be silent, Kelvedon,' Darulin commanded.

They had descended to the main tactical strategium, a broad projector well in the forward section of the bridge. Kelvedon was back on his feet, though his face was flushed. Other bridge seniors had followed them. Gaunt was surrounded by towering robed men who were only marginally organic, and angry, blue-uniformed command echelon officers. He was entirely out of place. This was not his kind of war, nor his area of expertise. He was Guard. Battlefleet and Astra Militarum, they were ancient rivals in glory, with entirely different mindsets. They always had been, since mankind first left the cradle of Terra and set out across the stars. One branch of humanity conquered worlds, the other conquered the void. They were allies, brothers... closer than that, perhaps. But they had never been friends. Their philosophies were too different. For a start, each one presumed that the other depended upon them.

But Gaunt put himself in the middle of it all. There were two reasons for that. The first was that all their lives were at stake and he was hardly going to sit idly by and let the battlefleet officers determine his regiment's fate.

The second was that he had a sense of things. He had a sense of command. The thread of authority was the same in the Navy as it was in the Guard, and his years of service had left him with an instinct for it. The *Armaduke* was lost. It had lost its spirit. Spika was dead, and the confusion Gaunt had discovered on the bridge when he arrived was profound. These were high-functioning officers. They were brilliant and mentally agile. They should not have been frozen in shock and incapable of decision. They should not have been gazing down at the corpse of their commander wondering what to do next.

They should not have needed a scruffy Guard commander to push his way in and administer futile chest compressions.

They were lost. Gaunt didn't know why. He felt sure it was less to do with Spika's death, and much more to do with the shredding violence and incomprehensible time-loss of their retranslation. The *Armaduke* was crippled, and its crew – linked to it in too many subtle and empathic ways to count – was crippled too.

Someone had to take the lead. Someone had to ignite some confidence. And that someone wasn't Kelvedon, who saw only his own career path.

Gaunt remembered his time on the escort frigate *Navarre,* right at the start of his service with the Ghosts. There had been an executive officer, Kreff, who had been sympathetic. Most of what Gaunt understood about the battlefleet he had learned from Kreff.

The scions of the battlefleet, they were just men even if they didn't look like men. And men were the same the universe over.

'We need to get out of this,' Gaunt said. He started speaking generally, casually. That was the first thing you did; you brought everybody in and acknowledged them. He hated to be so clinical, but there was no choice.

'Can we light the strategium display?' he added. Casual, just a side comment. Confidence.

The hololithic well started to light up around them. Hardlight forms and numeric displays painted their faces and their clothes.

'I'm going to get my troopers ready,' he said, still casual. 'They're going to protect this ship. They're going to fight off anything that tries to get inside. I'll welcome the support of your armsmen too.'

Be inclusive. That was the next step. Breed a sense of common action and respect. Now it was time for truth.

'You're hurt, and you're dismayed. There's no shame in that. What has overtaken us is terrible and it has hurt you all. But the ship is you, and you are the ship. It will not live without you. Spika loved this old girl. He would have wanted her to see out her days in safe hands.'

Gaunt looked at Darulin.

'Externals?'

'Processing now, sir,' said the acting shipmaster.

'How badly hurt are we?' Gaunt asked. He aimed the question softly and generally.

The cowled Master of Artifice, flanked by his functionaries, sighed.

'No drive. No main serial power. No secondary power. No shields. No weapon commit. No navigation. No sensory auspex. No scope. No intervox. No real space stability. Massive and serial gravitic disruption.'

'I'm not Fleet,' Gaunt said. 'I take it that's not a good list?'

The Master of Artifice actually smiled.

'It is not, sir.'

'Then enumerate the positives for me.'

The Master of Artifice hesitated. He glanced at Darulin and his subordinates.

'Well... I suppose... we have environmental stability and general pressure integrity. Life support. Gravitics have resumed. We are running on tertiary batteries, which gives us six weeks real time, permitting use. We... we are alive.'

Now Gaunt smiled.

'That, sir,' he said, 'is the basis for most Imperial Guard fightbacks. We're alive. Thank the Throne. I never wanted to live forever, but a little while longer would be appreciated.'

'Ten years longer,' said Criid.

A grim ripple of laughter drifted around the strategium.

'External view?' Gaunt asked.

Darulin nodded and waved an actuation wand. The well filled with a massive data-projection map of the *Armaduke*. It presented nose-down like a drowning whale. Gaunt rubbed his mouth. He realised he'd honestly never known what the outside of the ship looked like. He was looking at something that had been the limits of his world for weeks.

He had known it was vast. He hadn't realised how vast. The *Armaduke* was a massive structure, and now it was a *helpless* massive structure.

'What are those?' Gaunt asked, pointing to three blob structures visualised at the aft of the ship's mass.

'Enemy craft,' replied Darulin. 'Light warp vessels of a much smaller tonnage than us. They have secured themselves to us to facilitate boarding.'

'Do they have a mother ship?' asked Gaunt.

Darulin dialled the strategium view back with his wand. The *Armaduke* shrank rapidly. The revised view showed another vessel sitting off them at a distance of seventeen thousand kilometres. It was large, a cruiser perhaps.

'Yes, there,' said Darulin. 'An Archenemy starship. No standard pattern discernible. A destroyer, I would imagine. Fast, agile, well armed.'

'And it's not firing on us because?' Gaunt asked.

'They want us as scrap. As prisoners, as raw materials,' said Criid. 'They want to pick our bones.'

Gaunt looked at her.

'I supposed so,' he said to her. 'I was hoping the acting shipmaster here might admit it.'

'Sorry, sir,' said Criid.

'Sorry,' said Darulin. 'That is... that is exactly what they're doing.'

SEVEN

THE LINE

Ezra was still laughing at his own doom when fury burst into the compartment. The slap of the shock wave threw him onto his side. The air filled with billowing smoke.

Huge figures emerged out of it.

Sar Af, the White Scar. Holofurnace, the Iron Snake. Eadwine, the Silver Guard. Full armour. Full weapons.

Three warriors alone against the mass of raiders flooding the vast compartment.

'Kill them all,' Eadwine said, a growl of sub-vox.

The Archenemy troopers, dazed and dismayed by the breaching blast, began firing. Las-bolts and hard-rounds pinged and slapped off the armoured Adeptus Astartes. In unison, they raised their bolt weapons and returned fire.

Bolter shots mowed down two rows of Archenemy foot troops. Explosive horror threw shredded meat and debris into the air. The enemy mass reeled back, recoiling as its leading edge was blown apart.

Ezra watched in disbelief as the three Space Marines charged the bulk of the foe. As they met the line, the impact threw bodies into the air. Eadwine's chainsword flashed, roaring. Archenemy troopers collapsed like harvested corn, their armoured bodies torn apart. Particles of flesh, blood, tissue and metal showered out of the carnage. A wet red fog began to cloud the burning air.

To Eadwine's left, Holofurnace hacked his way through the shrieking raiders. They were turning on each other, frantically fighting to get out of the giant's path. The Iron Snake reached a stalk-tank and split open its belly with his lance. Fluid, blood and toxic water spewed out of the sliced control bubble. Holofurnace stabbed the tip of his lance inside the wreck to impale the huddled body of the hard-wired pilot.

Another tank began firing, auto-tracking its target. Holofurnace was jarred back by the scorching impacts, but remained on his feet and hurled his lance like a javelin. Impaled through its core, the stalk-tank shivered, spasmed and collapsed, venting bio-fluid.

Holofurnace wrenched his lance out. Fluid spattered.

'For the Emperor!' he yelled.

At Eadwine's right hand, Sar Af pounced and landed on the back of another stalk-tank. It thrashed under his weight. He punched through the top of the main body to haul the driver out, and hurled the writhing body aside as he threw himself off the collapsing machine. Milling foot troops broke his fall. He killed them with his fists as they tried to scramble out from underneath him. More fled. Sar Af howled and followed them, cutting them down with his bolter.

Eadwine was murdering the foot troops too. Chainsword in one fist, storm bolter in the other, he was simply striding into the fumbling lines of the raiders like a man walking determinedly into a brisk gale, head down and unstoppable. Sparks flashed as hard munitions pinged and glanced off his armoured mass. He fired, selectively and methodically, toppling groups at a time, slashing into any bodies that came too close as though cutting back undergrowth.

Ezra left cover and cautiously followed in their wake. The Adeptus Astartes giants had cut a swathe down the engine house, littering the broad deck with burning wreckage and tangled corpses. The deck was awash with blood.

Ezra crouched, and pulled a lasgun from the dead grip of a fallen enemy. This time, he took spare clips too.

It was time to stop dying. It was time to win back the ship.

Ornella Zhukova led a portion of Pasha's company along the ventral tunnel that approached the engine compartments from the bow of the ship. She could hear the rattle and boom of fighting from the chambers ahead, and she could smell burn-smoke. Every few seconds, the deck shook.

Everything had a glassy feel, a slightly out-of-focus softness. She didn't know if that was the smoke getting in her eyes or her own mind. Something had happened. An accident. Something distressing that involved the physics and processes of shiftship travel, and it made her feel sick.

The company had been prepping for secondary orders. Then everything had gone to hell. Had they been hit, or was it something worse than that? She'd woken with a grinding headache, and many of her troopers had been sick, or complained of nausea or nosebleeds.

'Vox?' she hissed.

'Nothing!' the caster-man replied. Wall-mounted units wheezed nothing but static, and the squad's voxcasters coughed and crackled.

'Keep it tight!' she ordered. The men were in disarray. Confusion did that, confusion and fear. They didn't know the situation, and they didn't know what they were facing. Worse, they had so little ammo. There had been no time to send carts down to the munition stocks, and even if there had been, Zhukova knew the racks were almost bare.

The regiment was in no position to fight another war.

One of her scouts appeared from a transverse duct and hurried to her.

'Spetnin?' she asked.

'In lateral two, advancing, ma'am,' the scout replied. He looked out of breath. His face was filmy with soot and grease. Spetnin had taken half the company to shadow Zhukova's mob along the parallel hallway in the hope that, between them, they could block any forward movement along the aft thoroughfares. That's if they'd remembered the deck plans right. Zhukova's head hurt so much, she could barely remember her own birthday.

'What does he report?' she asked.

The scout shrugged.

'A shrug is not an answer,' she snapped.

'Same as here,' the scout replied, wary of her famous anger. 'Fighting ahead.'

The hallway had been damaged by frame stress. Wiring in the walls was shorting out and crackling with white sparks that floated like snowflakes onto the deck. Oil dripped from the ceiling and dribbled from ruptured pipes. Some of the deck's grav plates had worked loose or become misaligned, and they shifted uneasily underfoot, like boards floating on a lake. In one section, an entire twenty-metre portion of deck plate had broken away and slammed flat against the ceiling, held there by its own, unsecured antigravity systems. The exposed underdeck was a mass of wires and stanchions, and cables trailed from overhead like vines. Blood dripped down. Someone had been standing on the plate when it had snapped free, and had been sandwiched against the roof by six tons of rapidly elevating metal.

The blood was the first sign Zhukova had seen of any of the ship's crew.

Up ahead, Trooper Blexin raised a hand. He had stopped. She knew that tilt of the head. He'd heard something.

She was about to say his name. Blexin buckled and fell, sprays of blood gouting from his back as shots tore through him. Gunfire cut down the three men with him.

The company hit the walls, scrambling into cover behind bulkheads and hatch frames. Shots whined past. Zhukova hoisted her carbine, leaned out and snapped off return fire. Some of the men around her did the same. They had no idea what they were shooting at, but it felt good to retaliate.

The gunfire coming at them fell away.

'Hold! Hold it!' Zhukova shouted. 'No wastage!'

She risked a step forwards, keeping to the wall. The first squad followed her, shuffling down the hallway, hunched, their rifles to their shoulders, tracking.

She edged past the bodies of Blexin and his mates. The deck plates quivered restlessly. She took another step. There was a sharp pistol-shot bang, and one of the plate's restraining pins sheared. A corner of the plate lifted from the underfloor, flexing, straining, like a tent sheet caught by the wind, wanting to snap its guy wires and fly away.

Zhukova swallowed hard. Sliding her feet rather than stepping, she worked along the trembling plate. She guessed three or maybe four heavy duty pins were all that were keeping the damaged section down, all that stood between her and a grotesque fate squashed like a bug against the ceiling.

She stepped onto the next deck plate. It was firmer. Gorin, Velter and Urnos followed her. She could smell the garlic sausage stink of Urnos' fear-sweat.

A shape moved in the drifting smoke ahead of her. She saw the enemy. Some robed heathen monster with a slit for eyes.

'Hostile!' she yelled, and snapped off two shots. The enemy trooper caught them both in the chest and slammed backwards. Answering gunfire raked out of the smoke, hard-round shots that swirled the smoke into plumes and weird spirals. She hit the wall, willing it to swallow her up. A bullet ripped open the musette bag on her hip. Velter went down, head shot, and Gorin toppled backwards, hit in the shoulder and chest. Urnos dropped on his belly and started to fire and yell.

The angle of the enemy fusillade altered, raking the deck, trying to hit Gorin and the yelling Urnos. Zhukova saw plating buckle. She saw the edge of the damaged plate she'd slid across taking hits.

'Back! Back! Back!' she yelled at the rest of the company behind her.

A deck pin blew out. No longer able to anchor the restless plate, the other pins sheared explosively under the strain. Unstable gravitics slammed the loosed deck plate into the ceiling like a flying carpet. It fell up the way a boulder falls down. There was a terrible, crunching impact. Zhukova had no idea how many of her trailing first squad had been standing on it when it broke free. All she saw was Gorin, who had been sprawled on his back across the join. The plate swept him up like a hoist and crushed him against the roof, crushed his head, arms and upper body. His legs, dangling clear, remained intact and hung, impossibly, like a pair of breeches strung from a washing line.

Dust and flames billowed along the tunnel. The firing stopped for a moment. Zhukova grabbed Urnos and hauled him up to the wall. She couldn't see any part of her company in the tunnel behind her. All she could see was Gorin's heavy, slowly swinging legs.

'We're screwed, captain,' Urnos whined.

She slapped his face hard.

'Get on your feet, Verghast!' she said.

Gripping her carbine, she started to edge forwards. Urnos got up and followed her. She could hear the hoarse gulps of his rapid breathing.

'This is madness...'

'Just shut up, Urnos. Operate like a soldier.'

A few metres beyond, two bodies lay against the wall. Archenemy boarders. They were dirty and roughly armoured, patchwork soldiers that reminded Zhukova of the scratch companies that had hunted the Zoican Rubble. She had no idea who had cut them down. It could have been her or Urnos. She fumbled with their webbing, and found some hard-round clips, but nothing that would suit her carbine or Urnos' rifle.

She heard movement from ahead. She pushed Urnos against the wall, then clamped her hand around his mouth and nose to dampen the noise of his frantic breathing.

Trapped smoke made the tunnel air thick and glassy. She saw two of the enemy picking their way towards them out of the haze. Two more followed. They were shrouded in heavy, filthy coats and their body-plate was dull and worn. Their faces were covered by blast visors or mesh hoods. Red light glowed from the visor slits, suggesting enhanced optics or even dark-sight systems.

But she'd spotted them before they'd spotted her. Verghast eyes were strong, and beat corrupt tech enhancements. Because Vervun was strong, built to endure and survive, its youth born strong into freedom, healthy and vital, in the image of the God-Emperor...

Zhukova swallowed. It was all so much bull. She'd been listening to Major Pasha's patriotic speeches too long, listening to the crap spouted by the commissars as they conditioned the fighting schools.

The enemy hadn't seen her because she and Urnos were cowering behind a wall strut. Another few seconds, and their optics would pick up their body heat through the ambient fuzz of the smoke. Optic enhancers didn't necessarily mean heat-readers too, but Zhukova's experience told her that the universe took every opportunity it could to be as cruel as possible.

They had to move, or they'd be dead in seconds.

She slowly withdrew her hand from Urnos' mouth. She held up four fingers, then tapped herself and indicated left with two fingers. Then she tapped his chest and forked two fingers right.

Urnos nodded. He was scared out of his wits.

She made a fist he could see, and bounced it, one... two...

Three.

They came out of hiding together, firing. It was a simple, effective play, one the company had done in drill many times. She'd take the two on the left, he'd take the two on the right. Surprise was in their corner.

Their disadvantage was that Urnos, damn his garlic-reeking hide, didn't know his left from his right.

The two boarders on the left went straight down. Zhukova had tagged one with a headshot, and the other had been slammed over by las-bolts from both their weapons. Urnos was in her way, jostling her, trying to occupy the half of the tunnel he thought she'd told him to be in. Her next shot went wide, and he put two precious bolts into the floor.

She never got to ask him if he was just plain stupid, or if the fear and tension had scrambled his wits.

The two raiders on the right returned fire immediately, before their comrades had even hit the deck. Muzzle flashes leapt and flickered in the closed space. Hard-rounds spat at them. Urnos took a round in the forehead and another in the cheek, the impacts twisting his face into a gross cartoon of itself. He rotated away from her, blood jetting from his ruptured skull, hit the far wall and slid down, his legs kicking.

Zhukova turned, unflinching, and dropped the raiders with single shots, pinpoint. She ran into the smoke, ducked into the shadows, and shot at the next wave of raiders as they pushed forwards, hitting them in the ribs and the sides of their heads.

She risked a look. More raiders were advancing on her. She snapped off a shot or two, and a hail of gunfire came in reply.

There was no one with her, no one behind her, not even close.

She could stay down and wait to die, or move and strike. It would cost her her life, but it was a chance to put a stop to the enemy advance. Scratch company tactics. She remembered Pasha's lectures. Do the unexpected. Take the risk. Deal a wound to the enemy when you get the chance, even if you pay for it. Because it's not you, it's the fight entire. You do your part when you can. You don't step back so you can enjoy reviewing the battle when it's done, because the result you review will probably be a loss.

Zhukova swung out, firing. She had switched to full auto. Las-rounds kicked out of her carbine and ripped through the first rank of raiders. The next rank began to topple and collapse. Some got off shots, but they went past her, wild.

'Gak you all to hell and back!' she screamed.

Zhukova kept firing. Damn wastage. Damn aiming. Damn even seeing. Urnos' blood was in her eyes and all over her face.

The boarders came apart like bags of meat. They fell towards her. Shaking, Zhukova looked down at her weapon. The alert sigil lit up, telling her the cell was out. How long had it been out? Had she emptied it making the kills?

The boarders had fallen *towards* her...

She blinked, and wiped blood off her mouth with a shaking hand.

Mkoll appeared through the smoke behind the bodies of the enemy. He raised his hand, and beckoned to her with a double twitch of his fingers.

On the company deck, the women of the retinue had gathered the children and the elderly into the storage rooms and set up barriers at the main hatches using cot frames. Ayatani Zwiel hurried around, helping the injured, and making reassuring speeches to dispel fear. It was going to take more than a few kind words.

Yoncy wouldn't stop crying.

'It's all right, it's all right,' Juniper soothed her. 'We'll be safe.'

It wasn't all right. Juniper could smell smoke in the air, and every few minutes there was a thump or bang from aft, some of them fierce enough to shake the deck. Most of the children were crying or at least whimpering, but Yoncy's sobbing seemed particularly piercing.

It didn't sound like fear. It sounded like pain.

'Juniper?'

Juniper looked around and saw Elodie.

'What are you doing here?' Juniper asked.

'I was in the infirmary when it happened,' Elodie said.

'But what happened?' Juniper asked.

'I'm not really sure,' said Elodie. She could see that Juniper was scared. 'I thought I could help down here. Help with the kids.'

She took Yoncy out of Juniper's arms.

'Honne's taken a knock to the head,' she said, gesturing towards a woman sprawled in the walkway nearby. 'Get her on a cot and see if you can fix a dressing.'

Juniper nodded and hurried to Honne's side.

'It's all right, Yoncy,' Elodie said. Yoncy was crying loudly, and it was setting off the younger children all around them.

'Yoncy, calm yourself,' said Elodie. 'You're a big girl now. Stop your sobbing.'

'The bad shadow,' Yoncy wailed.

'What? What, honey?'

'I want Tona. I want my brother. I want Papa Gol!'

'They're busy, Yoncy,' Elodie said, stroking the girl's hair.

'Busy with the bad shadow because it came back,' she said.

'What's the bad shadow?' asked Elodie. She didn't really want to know. Sometimes, the imaginations of children conjured horrors far worse than anything real. In the cot rows some nights, she'd talked small children down from nightmares that had chilled her heart.

'I want my papa,' said Yoncy, wiping her eyes clumsily on her over-long sleeve. 'He knows what to do. He knows how things are meant to be.'

'Major Kolea is a brave soldier,' nodded Elodie. 'He'll be here soon, I'm sure of it, and he will chase the bad shadows away, Yoncy.'

The child looked at her as if she were stupid.

'*Shadow*,' she said, overemphasising the correction. 'Papa Gol can't chase the shadow away. He's not bright enough.'

'Oh, now! Gol's a clever man,' said Elodie.

'Not *bright* bright, silly,' frowned Yoncy. '*Bright* bright. When Papa comes, everything...'

She hesitated.

Elodie smiled.

'Gol will be here soon,' she said.

'You don't understand, do you?' asked Yoncy.

'I... No, not really.'

'No one does,' said Yoncy. 'No one can see in the dark.'

Yoncy tilted her head and looked up at the broad, ducted ceiling of the company deck.

'It's almost here,' she said. 'The bad shadow will fall across us.'

EIGHT

BAD SHADOW

The screaming was Vaynom Blenner's first clue that he wasn't dealing with just another hangover.

He got off his cot and stumbled into the hallway. The deck seemed to be at a slight angle. That wasn't right; shiftship decks didn't slope. They had systems, gravitic whatchamacallits, to make sure the horizontal true was maintained. Maybe his head was sloping.

That wasn't ideal either, but it was a local problem.

'What's the feth-name commotion?' he growled, grabbing Ree Perday as she hurried past.

'The ship's foundered, sir!' she replied. She was scared.

'Foundered? What does foundered mean?' he asked.

She shrugged.

'Swear to the Throne, Perday, I'm not in the mood–'

'I don't know what it means!' Perday snapped, her anxiety getting the better of her discipline in the face of a senior officer. 'It's a word. Someone said, just now. Someone said we'd foundered.'

Blenner looked around.

'The hell is that screaming?'

'Cargo shifted,' she said. 'People are hurt. And upset.'

He pushed past her and entered the practice chamber. The instruments of the Colours band, most of them packed in crates or cases, had broken free of their packing ties and stow-nets and created a pile like a rockslide across the floor. Corpsmen were treating bruises, cuts and the occasional twisted ankle of bandsmen caught in the spill.

'Throne of Terra!' Blenner snorted. 'I thought someone was actually hurt!'

'Get this mess stowed again!' he shouted.

'We were getting it stowed, commissar,' said the old bandmaster, Yerolemew. 'For secondary orders, as per instruction. You remember that?'

'I don't like your tone, old man,' Blenner snapped. Yerolemew took a step back, and lowered his gaze. Blenner swallowed. It had slipped his mind. He was foggy, but he remembered the warning. The ship was running poorly. It could fall out of warp. Then they'd be sitting ducks, so the regiment had to come to secondary.

At which point, apparently, he had decided to take a nap.

'I was just in my cabin, checking inventory,' he mumbled. 'How do we stand with secondary?'

Yerolemew gestured towards Jakub Wilder, who was dealing with a bandsman named Kores. Kores was almost hysterical. In fact, most of the screaming seemed to be coming from him.

'What's the problem?' Blenner asked.

Kores started to wail something.

'Not you,' Blenner snarled, 'you.'

'The shock tore the cargo loose,' said Wilder sullenly. 'Heggerlin has broken an arm, and Kores here, his hautserfone got smashed.'

'His instrument?'

'It's an heirloom,' said Wilder. 'It probably can't be repaired. The valves are busted.'

Blenner sighed. His contentment that he had been placed in charge of a bunch of fething idiot bandsmen, who were unlikely ever to see action and thus reward him with an easy, carnage-free life, came with a downside, to wit they were a bunch of fething idiots.

He was considering how much to shout at them when the fog cleared slightly. The slope of the deck, the toppling of the packed cases, Perday's use of the word 'foundered.'

'Oh, feth,' he murmured. The *Armaduke* had fallen out of warp. They were in trouble.

'Get Gaunt,' he said.

'Comms are down,' replied Wilder.

'Have you sent anyone to get Gaunt?' Blenner asked.

Wilder half shrugged.

'You're a bunch of fething idiots,' said Blenner.

'Commissar!'

Blenner turned. Gol Kolea had entered the chamber, flanked by troopers from C Company. They were all armed. They all looked like actual proper soldiers. Rerval, Kolea's adjutant and vox-man, had a dressing on his head that was soaked in blood, and he was *still* walking around performing duties. Fething idiot bandsmen.

'Everyone all right here, sir?' Kolea asked.

'Not really, major,' said Blenner, 'and in ways you couldn't possibly want to imagine.'

Kolea frowned.

'This... with respect, commissar, this doesn't look much like secondary order to me.'

'Or me,' Blenner nodded. 'I think I'll shoot the lot of them for being idiots.'

'I'd rather you got the Colours Company on their feet and held Transit Six,' said Kolea. 'What's the munition situation?'

Probably plentiful, thought Blenner, seeing as my mob hardly ever shoot at anything.

'I'll check,' he said.

He paused.

'Hold Transit Six?' he asked.

'The ship's been boarded,' said Kolea. 'We have hostiles advancing from the aft section, from the engine house.'

Blenner's guts turned to ice water.

'Boarded?'

'That's as much as I know.'

'Who's coordinating? Gaunt?'

'We've got no central coordination because the comms are out and vox is patchy. I'm trying to coordinate with Kolosim and Baskevyl. They're advancing into Lower Transitionary Eight. Elam and Arcuda have Nine covered. According to Elam, there's fighting in the engine house, and hostiles reported.'

'What kind of hostiles?' asked Blenner.

'The hostile kind,' said Kolea. 'That's all I know.'

Blenner nodded.

'Brace yourself, major,' he said. Kolea looked nonplussed, but nodded.

Blenner turned to the bandsmen. He was a genial man, but he possessed a powerful voice, especially in times of crisis, such as the bar being noisy when he wanted a round, or when a waiter was ignoring him.

'You're a disgrace to the fething Emperor, may He bless us all, Throne knows why!' he bellowed. 'We are under attack, Colours! Forget farting around with your fething musical instruments and get yourselves formed up! Wilder!'

'Yes, sir?'

'Munition count! Get everyone stocked and loaded! Anyone shows short, get people to tip out their musettes and even things up!'

'You're shouting and I'm right in front of you,' said Wilder.

'Damn right I'm shouting! I want Colours in secondary order in two minutes, or I will take a fething hautserfone and start clubbing people to death with it! Find that Fury of Belladon and find it fast!'

The bandsmen started to scramble. Blenner turned back to Kolea.

'We'll be secure in five, major,' he said. 'I'll have them advance and hold Transit Six.'

Kolea nodded.

'Move out!' Kolea told his company. 'May the Emperor protect you,' he said, looking back at Blenner.

Blenner went back to his cabin. At least, he thought, at least with Kolea, Kolosim, Elam and Baskevyl in the field, there would be a buffer between him and the hostiles.

He found the bottle of pills in his campaign chest. He took two, then a third just to be sure. He knocked them down with a swig of amasec.

He could do this. He was a fething fighting man of the Throne. Of course he could.

And if he couldn't, there were plenty of places to hide.

Dalin Criid was in charge, and he didn't like it much. There was no sign of Captain Meryn – the last word was that Meryn had gone to the infirmary – so although there were several men senior to him in the company, Dalin, as adjutant, had command.

E Company's barrack deck was in uproar. He had to yell repeatedly to get some kind of order. The last command received had been to go to secondary order, so that's what Dalin intended to do until he heard otherwise.

'Secure the barrack deck!' he shouted. 'I want watches and repulse details at every hatch! Let's scout the halls nearby too! I want to know what shape everyone else is in!'

E Company started to move with some purpose. Support and ancillary personnel looked scared. There were a lot of minor injuries, but Dalin could see that fear was the biggest problem.

'What do you want us to do, sir?' asked Jessi Banda. Dalin didn't rise to the sarcastic emphasis she put on 'sir'.

'Help anybody that needs help,' said Dalin. 'Try to calm fears. Leyr? Neskon? Take a party to the far hatches and sing out if anyone approaches from aft.'

The men nodded.

Dalin wanted to head to the retinue holds and find Yoncy. He desperately needed to know if his kid sister was all right. But he knew he couldn't show any kind of favouritism. The situation needed to be controlled, and essential personnel needed to be–

He turned.

'Get things settled here,' he told Banda and Wheln.

'Where are you going?' asked Banda.

'I'll be right back.'

The private and reserved cabins were at the for'ard end of the company deck. He pushed his way through the jostle of bodies and headed that way. Gaunt's son, Felyx, was billeted in one of those cabins. Dalin knew Gaunt would want the boy secured. The colonel commissar hated the fact that his offspring was here at all. He'd made a special point of asking Dalin to watch Felyx.

And Dalin wanted to check too. He liked Felyx. He felt they had become friends. He was a little afraid that the bond he had formed was part of a selfish urge to impress and please Gaunt. He liked to dismiss that idea, and tell himself that he had found a friend, and that Felyx needed a comrade he could count on, but the nagging doubt wouldn't go away.

In all honesty, Dalin Criid wished he could work out what it was that drew him to Felyx Meritous Chass so strongly, and hoped in his heart of hearts that it wasn't a psychological need to impress his beloved commander.

He found the cabin and banged on the door.

'Felyx? Felyx, it's Dalin.'

After a short delay, the hatch opened, and Dalin stepped in.

'Are you all right?' he began.

Felyx was sitting on the cot, his jacket pulled around his shoulders. He looked pale and ill. Nahum Ludd had opened the door for Dalin.

'Sir, what are you doing here?' Dalin asked.

'I came to check on Felyx,' said Ludd. 'The ship's under attack.'

'I know,' said Dalin.

'It's serious, trooper,' said Ludd. 'I knew the colonel-commissar would want to make sure Felyx was all right, and comms are fethed.'

Dalin nodded. He felt annoyed. He and Ludd were not far off in age, and like him, Ludd had gone out of his way to bond with Felyx. They had become almost like rivals feuding over a girl. It was stupid, but Dalin felt somehow jealous finding Ludd here. He was sure, damn sure, that Ludd was motivated by the same urge Dalin feared in himself. A desire to cover himself in acclaim and ingratiate himself to Gaunt. It had been remarked before that Ludd and Dalin represented the new generation of Ghosts, that one day Ludd might be senior commissar of the regiment, and Dalin a full company officer. One day, if the fates proved kind, and the regiment lasted that long. They were emblematic of the future, of the campaigns to come, Ghost commanders in the making. And as such, both wanted the approval and notice of Ibram Gaunt, who would make the decisions and recommendations that would shape their careers. Gaunt was a father figure to them both, and here they both were, sucking up by trying to be the man who 'looked after' Gaunt's son.

Ludd had the rank, of course. He was more like the father they were both trying to impress.

'Are you all right?' Dalin asked Felyx.

Felyx nodded, but it was clear he was hurt.

'He was knocked off his feet by the violence of the retranslation,' said Ludd. 'I found him unconscious. That locker had fallen on him.'

'I'm fine,' said Felyx. 'Just dazed.'

'He was out cold,' said Ludd.

'We should get him to the infirmary,' said Dalin, worried. 'Gaunt would–'

'The ship's overrun,' said Ludd. 'We have no idea which decks the enemy has seized. Movement without decent force strength would be a bad idea. I decided it was better to look after Felyx here until the emergency passed.'

'I have E Company on hand–' Dalin began.

'Good. Then secure the aft hatches and cover the rear hallways. That's the direction they're coming from.'

Dalin hesitated.

'Come on, trooper,' said Ludd.

'Was that an order?' asked Dalin.

'Yes,' said Ludd. 'Meryn not with you?'

Dalin shook his head.

'Then it's your day of glory, trooper – you're in charge. Get those hallways blocked. Barricades, if you can. The main spinal here runs straight down to the retinue holds, and there are women and children there who need protecting.'

Dalin nodded.

'If you're sure you're all right?' he said to Felyx.

'Yes. Go.'

Dalin nodded, and went out.

* * *

Ludd closed the door behind him and looked back at Felyx.

'You're not going to tell him, are you, Nahum?' asked Felyx.

'What?'

'What you saw when you found me–'

'I didn't see anything,' said Ludd.

'I'm serious, Nahum. No one can know. No one knows except Madd-alena. No one can know–'

'Calm down,' said Ludd. 'I didn't see anything.'

'We should check it,' said Baskevyl. 'Shouldn't we? We should check it.'

Shoggy Domor shrugged.

'I suppose so, Bask,' he replied.

Baskevyl and Domor had advanced their companies – D and K respectively – into the vast hold and cargo spaces of the *Armaduke*'s low decks. The ship's intervox was dead, but patchy back and forth using the company vox-sets had established that they'd been boarded, and that the boarders were coming in through the aft quarters, especially the engine house. A few unreliable sources said that a massive firefight was already under way in the engine house block, and from the smell of smoke on the dry air, Baskevyl tended to give that story some credence. Other sources had suggested the boarding forces were cannibals. Void monsters, hungry for flesh. Bask was happy to dismiss that as scaremongering, though he had been alive long enough to know that the horrors of the galaxy usually exceeded a man's worst imaginings.

His company had formed up with Domor's, more by accident than design. The plan, such as it was, was to move aft incrementally until they made contact with the enemy. As far as Bask knew, six companies were making their way aft from the billet decks. He and Domor had decided to take the belly route through the cargo spaces while Kolosim and Elam took theirs along the main transits of the upper decks. 'Thorough coverage,' Ferdy Kolosim had called it. It made sense. No point marching to the engine house only to find that the cannibal freaks had taken the bridge by moving through the holds. Elam had advised checking every compartment as they came to it. Boarders might be holding out in ambush squads. Worse still, they might have found other entry points and be swarming in unnoticed.

Bask and Domor, spreading their squads through the massive and labyrinthine hold area, had checked each chamber and compartment they passed.

They had reached hold ninety.

'We should check it,' Bask said, as if to convince himself. He and Domor looked at the security seals that Commissar Fazekiel and the shipmaster's officers had placed on the hold's locks. Hold ninety was where they had stored all the material and artefacts recovered from Salvation's Reach during the raid, inhuman artefacts taken from the sanctum of the Archenemy. Fazekiel had compiled the inventory, and standing instructions were that the material remained sealed and untouched during the return trip, ready for immediate transfer to the highest authorities.

That was before the ship had fallen out of the immaterium and rolled to a dead, hard, helpless stop.

'Maybe we should just leave it alone,' said Domor. 'I mean, that stuff… It's bad stuff, isn't it? Fething evil Archenemy stuff.'

'Yeah,' Bask nodded, 'but important enough for us to retrieve it all. Gaunt says it could be vital to the war effort. That's why we brought it all back with us. If they've cut through an inner wall…'

Domor shrugged.

'Cordon here!' he called out. 'Rifles ready!'

Chiria and Ewler brought a fire-team up close, aiming at the hatches.

Domor pulled out his straight silver, and sliced off the first of the seals. Then he took cutters to the locks. Bask took a pry-bar from Wes Maggs. As soon as Domor was done, Baskevyl levered the hatch's heavy locator bolts free.

They opened the hatch.

'No power,' said Domor, looking in.

'Yeah, but do you see anything?' Bask asked. Domor's eyes, a complex set of augmetic mechanicals, whirred and clicked as they searched the darkness.

'I think some of the boxes have spilled,' he said. 'Some of the crates.'

'Boss?'

Baskevyl turned. Wes Maggs, his company's lead scout, had found a junction box in a shuttered alcove nearby.

'We got emergency lights here,' he said.

'Throw them,' Bask nodded.

The interior lights came on with a dull thump. Blue emergency light shone out of the open hatch.

Baskevyl picked up his lasgun.

'Let's take a proper look,' he said, 'then we seal it up again.'

He and Domor entered hold ninety, followed by Fapes and Chiria. The materials had been packed into plyboard crates and lashed onto metal shelves. Each carton had a small label, an inventory number, and stamped warnings about tampering and removal. Fazekiel had been thorough.

Two shelves had collapsed during retranslation, and their cartons were spilled out on the deck. Bask saw clay tablets, some whole, some broken, among the packing beads, along with data-slates, small statues and beads, and old parchment scraps. Just some of the unholy treasures they had risked their lives liberating from the Reach's college of heritence.

'We should clean this up,' said Domor.

'I don't want to touch it,' Bask replied.

'Well, we can't just leave it like this if it's so valuable,' said Domor.

'I think we should. We don't know what goes where. There's no one in here, so I say we lock it up tight again. When this mess is over, Gaunt and Hark can come down here with the inventory and sort it out.'

Domor nodded. He looked relieved.

'Sir?'

Bask turned. His adjutant, Fapes, had moved into the next bay.

'Some more have come down in here,' Fapes called. 'I think you should see this.'

Baskevyl and Domor went to join him. In the second bay, three more cartons had shifted off the shelving and spilled on the deck. More scrolls and old books, and some noxious looking specimen jars. Baskevyl didn't want to consider what might be in them.

'What the feth?' Domor began.

Baskevyl took a step forwards. He could think of no ready explanation. Eight ancient stone tiles had tumbled from one of the cartons. They were arranged in almost perfect lines across the deck: a row of four over a row of three, with a single tile centred beneath.

'They fell like that,' said Chiria, as if trying to convince herself.

'In rows?' asked Fapes.

The tablets were perfectly aligned, as though someone had painstakingly and carefully laid them out that way. Not a single one was out of true.

'How does...' Domor murmured. 'How does that happen? How does that even happen?'

Baskevyl knelt beside the rows. He stared at them. He remembered the frantic recovery efforts in the foul colleges of the Reach. He remembered Gaunt telling him that Mabbon had reckoned these stone tiles to be of particular significance. Xenos artefacts, of impossibly ancient manufacture. Each one was about the size of a standard data-slate, and made from gleaming red stone. They were all damaged and worn by time, and one had a significant piece missing. They were covered in inscriptions that Baskevyl couldn't make sense of.

'No one's been in here,' he said. 'You saw the seals. No one's been in here. They must've just fallen like this–'

'That's a bunch of feth,' said Domor.

'You got a better answer?' Bask asked, looking up at him.

'Not one I want to say out loud,' mumbled Domor.

Baskevyl reached a hand towards the tablets.

'Don't touch them!' Chiria yelled. 'Are you mad?'

'I wasn't–' Baskevyl replied, snatching his hand away. But it was a lie. He had been about to touch them. He'd needed to touch them, even though touching was the last thing he wanted to do.

He got to his feet.

'They look like an aquila,' said Fapes.

'What?' asked Baskevyl.

Fapes pointed.

'The way they're laid out, sir. Like wings, see, then the body? Like an eagle with spread wings. Sir?'

Baskevyl wasn't listening to his adjutant any more. He stared at the tiles on the floor. They were laid out a little like an eagle symbol.

He swallowed hard. He had a sudden, sick memory. The supply drop... the aborted supply drop on Aigor 991. There'd been a daemon there. *Something*. Something *bad*. They'd heard a voice. Well, *he* hadn't, but Rerval had.

Rerval first, then Gol. Gol had made a full report about it. The voice had claimed to be the voice of Sek.

It had demanded they bring the *eagle stones* to it.

They'd fought the... the *whatever it was* off, and aborted the drop. Gol had aborted the drop, and he'd made a full report to Gaunt. No one had been able to offer an explanation, and besides, it was warp-crap anyway. You never paid attention to warp-crap and the ravings of the Archenemy, because that was a sure route to madness.

But this... Those stones on the deck. Stones they had been told by the pheguth were precious, laid out in the shape of an eagle.

'Throne preserve us,' he murmured.

'Sir?' Fapes asked.

'Seal it up,' Bask said. 'Seal it up. Get a torch on the door bolts to weld them in place. We come back and deal with this when the crisis is over.'

Domor looked at him, then turned and walked out, calling for a trooper with a metal-torch.

Baskevyl looked at Fapes.

'See if you can get the vox up,' he said to the adjutant. 'Raise Gaunt. Tell him what we found down here. Don't dress it up. Just tell him straight what we found and what it looks like. Then ask him what he wants us to do about it.'

'Gaunt?'

Gaunt stepped away from the strategium display and went over to Curth. She was still working on Spika's frail body, massaging his chest.

He crouched at her side.

'I've got a heartbeat,' she whispered.

'You have?' Gaunt replied.

She nodded. 'I didn't want to shout it out and give these men false hope. It's weak. Ridiculously weak. And it may go again in a moment. But I have a heartbeat.'

Gaunt nodded.

'I want to see if I can sustain it for another five or ten minutes,' she whispered. 'If I can, I'll risk moving him to the infirmary. He needs immediate surgery. A bypass. His brain may already be gone, though.'

'I'll ask Criid to get a stretcher party ready.'

'Good,' said Curth.

'If you've brought the shipmaster back,' Gaunt said, 'you've done amazing–'

'Don't patronise me,' she said, without looking up from her work. 'This is my calling. A life needed saving. I was here.'

Gaunt rose. There was a sudden commotion around the strategium display. 'What's the matter?' he asked.

'I'm assessing,' said Darulin. 'Something just...'

'Something what?'

'Roll it back,' Darulin said to a tech-adept. 'Thirty seconds.'

The main display image flickered as it switched from real-time feed to recorded data. Gaunt saw no difference.

'Look there,' said Darulin. 'The enemy flagship, lying seventeen thousand kilometres off us, approximate. A carrier vessel.'

He touched the display, making a small haptic mark beside the dark dot of the enemy cruiser.

'Advance by frame, one hundredth speed,' Darulin told the adept.

The data began to play. At the four-second mark, the dark dot was replaced by a point of white light. The light point expanded then vanished. There was no sign of the dot.

'What did I just see?' asked Gaunt. 'An explosion?'

'Sensor resolution is very poor,' said Darulin, 'but yes. The enemy base-ship just went up. Total disintegration.'

'But it was bigger than us,' said Criid.

'It was,' Darulin agreed.

'So, what... a drive accident?' asked Gaunt.

'What's that?' asked Kelvedon, reaching in to point.

Another dark dot, a larger one, had appeared on the scope. It was moving past the point where the other dot had vanished. It was accelerating towards the *Armaduke*.

'That's a ship,' said Darulin. 'A very large ship.'

'Time to us?' asked Gaunt.

'It's on us already,' said Darulin. He turned to the bridge crew. 'I want identifiers now! Now!' he shouted.

'We have visual,' Kelvedon called.

Something was coming in at them, something so massive it was eclipsing local starlight. It was casting a vast shadow across the crippled, helpless *Armaduke*. The light on the bridge changed as the shadow slid over them, throwing the external ports into blackness.

'We're in its shadow,' said Darulin quietly. The bridge grew very still and very quiet. There was no sound except the rasp of the air scrubbers, the chatter of automatic systems and the occasional ping of the display system.

Suddenly, the vox went live. A screaming noise shrieked from every speaker. Everyone flinched and covered their ears.

The deafening noise became words. A voice that was not human. A voice that echoed from the pit of space.

'tormageddon monstrum rex! tormageddon monstrum rex! tormagged-don monstrum rex!'

'The daemon ship from Tavis Sun,' Kelvedon stammered.

'The enemy battleship,' Darulin nodded. He looked pale, resigned.

Criid looked at Gaunt, aghast. 'Sir?'

'Do we have shields yet, or...' Gaunt's voice trailed off. The name was still booming from the speakers, over and over, like a chant. Gaunt could see the look on Acting Shipmaster Darulin's face.

'I'm sorry, colonel-commissar,' said Darulin. 'Whatever hope we might have had is now gone. We are caught, helpless, in the sights of an enemy warship that dwarfs us and outclasses us in every way measurable. We are dead.'

NINE

BLOOD PRICE

The only sounds were the crackle of flames and the sigh of the fire suppression system as it struggled to activate. The corridor section was in a low-power state. Torn cables hung like ropes of intestine from the buckled ceiling panels. Sparks drifted.

The Archenemy raiders picked their way along, the soft glow of their visor slits flashing and darting. They were advance guard, the reavers who cut deep into a victim ship to kill any resistance ahead of the main force. They were more heavily plated across the chest, shoulders, arms and groin, the armour segments patched and las-scarred. Their weapons were clearance tools: shot-cannons, rotator guns, broad-snout laslocks and concussion mauls.

They made remarkably little sound as they advanced. Their long, filthy robes muted the sway of their under-mail, and the metal mesh of their gloves had been over-wrapped with rags. They communicated by gesture, and sub-vox squirts, the tiniest whispers.

They were good. Formidable. Stealthy.

Mkoll was impressed. He hoped he would be equally impressed with Captain Zhukova's stealth skills as the raiders approached. They had wedged themselves into a maintenance alcove, a tight through-deck duct. There was barely room to breathe. There was just room to hide.

Both of them had a tight grip on their weapons, ready to move and fire. Mkoll had half an eye on Zhukova, ready to suppress any movement or sound she might make that would give their location away. She had controlled her breathing well, but her eyes were wide. She was scared. That was good. Scared was good. A soldier who claimed he wasn't scared wasn't much of soldier.

Watching the approach, Mkoll ran the numbers. He could see at least a dozen of the enemy prowling forwards, and they were spaced in a way that suggested they were the spearhead of an advance, not a discrete squad. That meant what? Thirty? Fifty? If they had any sense, they'd have heavier gunners and crew-supported weapons close behind. That's the way the Ghosts would do it, and these devils seemed to have plenty of sense and plenty of skill.

Mkoll was good, but trying to tackle thirty plus of the enemy was suicide. If he'd had a few grenades to shock them back and scatter them, that might improve things. But grenades in a tunnel-fight were a bad idea. He'd deafen himself, blind himself too, probably. Any advantage the blasts would give him would be lost at once.

He saw one of the raiders gesture. They were opening side hatches and compartments as they advanced. Mkoll thought they'd spotted him and the Verghast woman, but they were moving to the other side of the corridor, approaching a compartment hatch eight metres down on the left.

One stepped in, and slit the lock-bolt off with a thermal cutter. Another wrenched the hatch open. It swung wide with a metal squeal. Mkoll heard a scream, a pleading voice.

The raiders fired booming scatter-shot blasts into the hatchway, then moved inside. More shooting, dull and muffled.

They'd found crew. Stokers probably, or artifice adepts, cowering in the only bolthole they had been able to find. They were systematically murdering them.

One broke free. A midshipman in a tattered Navy coat, wounded in the arm. He ran, screaming, into the corridor. One of the raiders waiting outside took him down with a shot cannon. The flash-boom of the weapon covered the grisly thump of the midshipman's exploded carcass slamming off the corridor wall.

Zhukova glanced at Mkoll. Her eyes were wider. He knew the look. 'We should help–'

Mkoll shook his head.

We can't save them. At this rate, we can't save ourselves. They're going to find us any moment now...

Mkoll signed to Zhukova, *You. Stay here. Wait.*

She frowned.

He repeated it, and added the gesture for emphasis.

She nodded.

He could slip across the corridor to the bulkhead frame on the opposite side. If they were going to be found anyway, and they were, two shooting positions were better than one. They could lay down a crossfire, and cover each other's angles. A better field of fire. She knew that. She knew there was no running away, and no point pretending they could remain undiscovered.

Mkoll prepared to move. The raiders were still busy clearing the side compartment. Their attention was directed. The poor souls getting butchered would buy Mkoll and Zhukova a moment's grace to set up a better stand.

The raiders suddenly stopped their clearance work. Mkoll watched as they halted and, to a man, looked up. They seemed to be listening to something.

He tightened his finger on the rifle trigger. It was about to begin. They'd have to make the best of their poor positioning. If there was any grace in the galaxy, the Emperor would protect.

Protect them long enough to take down a decent tally at least. To make a good account, that's all he could wish for now.

Mkoll heard the tinny, muted whistling of sub-vox comms. The raiders stiffened, and then moved away, fast, back in the direction they had come.

He waited. Was it a trick?

He waited some more. He heard nothing but the crackle of flames.

He moved to step out of the alcove. Zhukova grabbed his arm tightly. He looked back at her, made an open-handed sign of reassurance.

Mkoll slid into the open. He moved forwards, rifle at his shoulder, maintaining aim. There was no one around except the smouldering corpse of the hapless midshipman. Where the hell had they gone?

He glanced around. Zhukova was beside him, her carbine up at her cheek, matching his careful approach.

'Are we clear?' she whispered.

'We'll find that out,' he replied.

He hadn't thought much of her to begin with. The Verghast were good soldiers. They generally lacked the finesse of the Tanith, but they easily matched them in heart and courage. Some of the best soldiers in the regiment were Verghast. But Zhukova had struck him as too young, too pretty, too soft, too haughty. A classic example of the ambitious, well connected, politically advanced Guard officer that Mkoll had encountered too many times in his service career. All words, all personality, all orders, expecting others to do the scut-work because they lacked the talent and fibre to do it themselves.

He had to revise that a little. She'd led from the front today, and not wavered. She'd kept her head together. And she was as resolved and silent as feth. Her looks belied the fact she was a first-class trooper. He thought it was a shame she'd ever got promoted. She'd have excelled in a field speciality.

'Where did they go?' Zhukova asked.

'I don't know,' said Mkoll.

'They backed up fast,' she said.

He nodded.

They reached the next transverse junction. Ahead of them, and to either side, the corridors were empty. Just debris, signs of damage, a few small fires.

'Something's going on,' said Mkoll quietly.

They edged down the tunnel directly ahead. At the far end, blast doors had been buckled open. Smoke was wafting through the jagged gap. Mkoll put his back against the corridor wall and slid along it slowly, so he could maintain the best aim and angle through the twisted gap. Zhukova covered him from the other side, a few paces back. Perfect hand-off position.

Metal screeched. The buckled blast hatch bulged and tore in at them as something came through it, ripping the thick plating like wet plyboard.

Mkoll took his finger off the trigger at the very last moment. He was about to shout to Zhukova, but she was right in the zone, and shot off a trio of las-bolts at the centre mass of the thing coming through.

Then she stopped shooting.

Eadwine of the Silver Guard looked down briefly at the scorched shot marks on his torso plate. The bulk of him filled the ruptured doorway.

'Unnecessary,' he remarked, his voice a soft whisper through the helmet speaker.

'M-my apologies,' Zhukova replied, lowering her carbine. 'Lord, I thought you were–'

'Obviously,' said Eadwine. He took two steps forwards. Each pace felt like someone had taken a door-ram to the deck. They heard the micro-whine of his armour's power system as it flexed.

'Nothing beyond?' he asked Mkoll, towering over the Tanith scout.

'There were plenty,' said Mkoll, 'but they retreated fast about five minutes ago. Heading this way.'

'I met some,' said Eadwine. 'They no longer live. Others were moving rapidly towards the aft sections.'

'What does it mean?' asked Zhukova, daring to step forwards and approach the giant Adeptus Astartes warrior.

'It means something is going on,' replied Eadwine. 'Something strange.' Mkoll glanced at Zhukova.

'Told you,' he said.

'Something's going on,' said Oysten, listening to the 'phones of her vox-set.

Hark and the Suicide Kings stood around her, watching.

'And how would you define that exactly?' asked Rawne.

'Awry?' suggested Varl.

'It went quiet,' said the vox-operator, 'I mean really quiet, for a minute or two and then the transmissions restarted. They've gone berserk. No chatter discipline.'

'We should get up there,' said Bonin. Cardass nodded in agreement.

'I believe you have particular duties here,' said Hark, 'and I believe Major Rawne shouldn't have to remind you of that.'

'I shouldn't,' Rawne agreed quietly. He was staring at Oysten. He was thinking, and that made him look more dangerous than usual.

'Mach's right though, inn'e?' growled Brostin. The flame-trooper was sitting in a far corner of the brig, nominally watching the access shutter. His bulk overspilled the seat of his canvas folding chair. His greasy flamer kit lay around his feet, ready to uncoil, like a pet serpent.

'Meaning?' asked Hark.

'If we're dead,' said Brostin, 'if the ship's dead, I mean... "spectacularly fethed"... then guarding wossname here is not so much a priority.'

He glanced at Mabbon.

'No offence, your unholiness,' he added. Mabbon didn't reply.

'If this is our last ditch, we should go down fighting like bastards,' Brostin went on. 'Give 'em fething hell as they choke us out, 'stead of skulking around in a fething prison block.'

'To be fair,' said Varl, 'that's what most of us have spent most of our lives doing.'

'Not funny, sergeant,' said Hark.

'Sort of funny,' said Mabbon quietly.

'If we're dead,' said Bonin, 'we should die with the rest. Alongside the rest. Fighting. Go to the Throne by giving a good account of ourselves.'

'When have we ever not done that?' asked Cardass.

'And if there's a chance we're going to live through this,' said Bonin, 'then another company up at the sharp end has got to increase that hope.'

''specially us,' said Varl.

'They may need us right now,' said Cardass. 'We could be the strength that makes the difference.'

Hark looked at Rawne.

Rawne sighed.

'We have a duty,' Rawne said. 'Clear orders to guard and protect. I'm not going to end my days defying an express fething order.'

He looked at Mabbon.

'But we can work out how best to implement that order,' he said. 'Could be that the best way to protect our charge is to get out there and kill stuff a lot.'

'You should make that your company motto, major,' said Mabbon.

'I want more intel,' said Rawne. 'I want to know how the situation has changed.'

Mabbon got to his feet off the metal stool they allowed him to sit on. Flanked by LaHurf and Varl, he shuffled back to the voxcaster, his shackles chinking.

Oysten nervously held out the headset. Mabbon shrugged and smiled back. His chained hands wouldn't permit him to raise the headset to his ear.

'Feth's sake,' grumbled Varl, and took the headset from Oysten. With a look of distaste, he pressed one cup of the headset to Mabbon's right ear and held it there.

Mabbon tilted his head forwards, stooping slightly, and listened.

'Busy... a lot of chatter...' he said. 'Oysten is correct. There is no discipline, and that is unusual. V'heduak sub-sonics and vox is usually ordered and economic. There is panic.'

'Panic?' said Hark.

'We've kicked their arses, haven't we?' smiled Varl.

'No,' said Mabbon, still listening. 'I can make out transmissions from unit leaders and command staff trying to quiet the panic. They are... they are repeatedly stating that the ship is taken, despite resistance, and that boarding forces should continue to their goals and complete objectives. They...'

'They what?' asked Rawne.

'They say some unflattering things about their Imperial enemies,' said Mabbon with an apologetic tone. 'About how you are close to being crushed. I won't translate. It's just invective to stabilise morale.'

He listened some more.

'But the seize units are in rout. They are breaking formation and falling back. They are abandoning their efforts to secure the ship. They... they don't care about the ship any more. They care about... living. They are afraid of something.'

'Us?' asked Rawne.

'No, major,' said Mabbon. He stepped back from the vox-set.

'They are afraid of the great destroyer,' he said. 'They are afraid of the *Tormaggeddon Monstrum Rex.*'

TEN

VISITING DEATH

Immense, the Archenemy battleship slid towards the helpless Imperial wreck. The real space engines of the *Tormageddon Monstrum Rex* pulsed lazily in the stellar twilight, growling circles of red light that flickered and wavered like dying suns. The battleship's vast form, flaring back to jagged bat-wings, was almost entirely unlit, and the blackness of it blotted out the stars, as if the void, reflecting and emitting nothing, had become a living thing.

Its battery cowlings retracted like eyelids. In the opened gun-ports, weapons lit and began to shine like lanterns along its edge as power charged the feeding cables and generator ducts of the guns. Red volcanic light throbbed as it illuminated the ship from within, a ruddy glow within the charred black skin and bone of the monster's hull.

It was still murmuring its name, like the distant ragged breathing of some oceanic behemoth.

'Enemy vessel weapon banks have armed!' sang out the adept manning data-acquisition.

'Do *we* have weapons?' Gaunt demanded.

Darulin shook his head.

'All fire control systems are defunct,' he replied. 'We cannot arm or aim–'

'Shields, then?' Gaunt asked.

'Stand by,' said Kelvedon. He had taken station at a nearby console with the Master of Warding and three tech-adepts. The techs were attempting some kind of bypass, their augmetic hands fluttering over the banks of controls. Noospheric exchanges hissed between them as they frantically exchanged data. Gaunt could hear the squeaks at the very edge of his hearing.

'Some port-side shielding may be viable,' said Kelvedon. 'Artifice has re-routed through secondary trunking.'

'That won't hold,' warned the Master of Artifice. 'The power ratios are too significant for secondary branches to conduct them.'

'But we're trying it anyway?' asked Gaunt.

The Master of Artifice looked at him, the delicate metal iris of his optics dilating wide with a tiny whir.

'Of course, Guard soldier,' he said, 'for there is nothing else left to try.'

'Power in three!' Kelvedon announced.

'Ignite the shields,' ordered Acting Shipmaster Darulin.

'Shields, aye!'

There was a deep, low groan, a cthonic bass note, deeper than any a templum organ could have produced. The bridge vibrated. The lights dimmed.

'Shields!' cried Kelvedon.

The screens around the central bridge area turned red, alive with amber warning runes.

'Shields failed,' Kelvedon sighed.

The Master of Artifice checked his board.

'Power fluctuation was too great,' he said. 'We could not sustain shield integrity. Shields are dead.'

Felyx rose to his feet. The lights were coming and going.

'What the hell's happening?' he asked.

'I don't know,' said Ludd, 'but it can't be good.'

Eszrah Ap Niht sat on the walkway platform overlooking the main engine house. He'd climbed up the metal ladders to escape the worst of it. Fires were blazing in the compartment below, and the decks were littered with dead. The battle had been ferocious. He'd lost sight of the Adeptus Astartes warriors. The fighting had driven through the main house and into the secondary compartments behind it. He could still hear small-arms fire and the sporadic boom of bolter weapons.

He had no clear sense of victory or loss. The ship seemed to be dying anyway. He could hear the mighty system wheezing and coughing.

Instinctively, he knew that whatever path they had been following, it was about to end.

The *Tormaggedon Monstrum Rex* spoke. Three of its charged batteries lit and spat, lancing white-hot energy at the crippled *Highness Ser Armaduke*. The strikes hit the aft section, bursting out in huge cones of light and debris.

Streaming vapour and burning gas, the *Armaduke* began to tumble again.

Gaunt got up off the bridge deck. The chamber was in uproar around him.

'Are we dead?' he yelled.

Most of the displays had gone blank, including the light show of the strategium. Servitors were hosing several consoles with plumes of extinguisher gas as officers dragged injured crewmen back.

'We're blind! No data!' called the Master of Artifice.

'Well, clearly, we're not dead,' said Criid. 'Not actually dead.'

She'd cut her chin when she'd been knocked to the deck. She wiped the blood away.

'We took three strikes,' said Darulin. 'At least three.'

'Aft strikes,' agreed Kelvedon.

'To cripple the drives?' asked one of the data officers.

'Are they toying with us?' Gaunt asked. 'Darulin, are they playing with us? Is this sport? Drawing out our demise?'

'I do not have any information, sir,' Darulin replied helplessly. He barked orders to the adepts around him, and they moved to the strategium to repair and restart.

Over the bridge speakers, the *Tormaggeddon Monstrum Rex* spoke again. It was no longer chanting its name.

'What does that mean?' asked Curth. 'Is it making demands?'

'It's hard to translate,' said Mabbon Etogaur.

'Really try,' suggested Varl, holding the headset out to him.

Mabbon glanced at the Ghosts surrounding him in the brig. It was impossible to gauge his expression.

'Roughly then, it said, "That which is born must live",' he said.

'What is that?' asked Rawne.

'It's unclear,' replied Mabbon. 'The word "born" can also be used in the sense of "made" or "manufactured", and the word-forms for "live" can also mean "survive" or "endure". So... it could equally be understood as, "That which was constructed must remain whole".'

'Was that it?' asked Hark.

'No,' said Mabbon, pressing his ear to the 'phones Varl was holding out. 'It's repeating it, like another chant. "That which was made must remain whole... the offspring of the Great Master...".'

'Offspring?' said Hark, stepping closer.

'Again, that's open to interpretation,' Mabbon told him with an apologetic shrug. 'The word "offspring" can mean a thing made, or a child, or something spawned. It is the female noun...'

'What, like a daughter?' asked Oysten.

'No, I think not,' said Mabbon. 'Things are female. Ships, for example, are referred to as "she". The connotation is any significant creation.'

He paused.

'What?' snapped Rawne. 'What else?'

'It just said,' said Mabbon, 'it said, "All this shall be the will of he whose voice drowns out all others".'

He looked at Varl and shook his head. Varl lowered the headset.

'It has stopped speaking,' he said.

'I'm scared!' sobbed Yoncy. 'I want Papa to come!'

Elodie held her tight. She didn't know what to say.

'Come on!' Gaunt yelled at the Navy adepts repairing the strategium. They glanced up at him, puzzled, their optics blank.

'Barking orders may serve well in the Astra Militarum, sir,' said the Master of Artifice, 'but in the Fleet we favour a more effective system of encouragement and support.'

Gaunt stared at him, and then stepped back and shrugged.

'The colonel-commissar has displayed the virtue of dynamism in this crisis so far,' Darulin said to the Master of Artifice. 'He has been by far the most controlled of any of us. And if this is my ship now...'

His voice trailed off, and he glanced over at Spika's body on the deck nearby, where Curth was still tending him.

'It is my ship now,' he repeated. 'In which case... get this damn strategium functioning!'

Startled at his rage, the adepts resumed work with increased vigour.

'The primary optic relay is blown, master,' one of the adepts reported.

'Replacement parts are located in hold fifty,' said another, reading off the manifest the noosphere was displaying in front of his eyes.

'There's no time for that,' said Darulin. 'Bridge it. Splice in! Now!'

The adepts hesitated.

The Master of Artifice pushed them aside. He extended his arms and held his augmetic hands over the open casing of the strategium table. Prehensile cables, as slender as twine and as fluid as snakes, curled out of recesses in his wrist-mounts and wormed their way into the complex mechanism, attaching and connecting.

'Splice established,' he said. 'Temporary operational relay in place. You have approximately four minutes.'

Gaunt glanced at Darulin.

'The Master of Artifice has bridged the relay,' Darulin said. 'His own biomech system has become a replacement component.'

'Activate,' the Master of Artifice ordered. Power was thrown. He trembled and shuddered, but remained standing. Gaunt could see a faint halo of heat-bleed surrounding him.

'That looks dangerous,' Gaunt said.

'It has its limits,' replied Darulin. He moved to the strategium, entered the access code, and the display relit.

They peered at it.

'Resolution is impaired,' said Darulin. 'Data retrieval is a fraction of what we had before.'

He studied the display. Blocks of machine text and code swam hololithically around the three-dimensional representation of the *Armaduke*. It was the bones of the ship, a skeletal diagram. Gaunt could see three bright wounds around the aft section of the ship, damage points that glowed so brightly data was negated. The area around them was fogged with fragments of loose data.

'Are those imaging defects?' asked Gaunt.

'No,' said Darulin. 'That's the best the strategium overview can do to render the debris field.'

'We're hit badly then?'

Darulin frowned.

'We're not hit at all, sir,' he said softly.

'What?'

'Those three impact sites... they are the remains of the three boarding vessels that had clamped to us. The enemy raiders have been burned off our hull.'

'Are you being serious?' asked Gaunt.

'By that?' asked Criid, pointing at the predatory shadow of the enemy killship that was looming over the *Armaduke*. It was so vast only a small portion of it appeared in the spherical display field.

'Yes,' said Darulin. 'The enemy killship has annihilated our enemies. It... it has spared us.'

'Saved us?'

'With pinpoint accuracy. It would seem so.'

'Why?' said Gaunt. 'Why?'

'It is an attested fact that the logic and mindset of the Archenemy is alien to us,' said Kelvedon.

'I know that better than most,' said Gaunt. He took a step back. He realised he was shaking. It was panic. He'd been running on adrenaline, the rush that had seen him through years of war and combat. But now he felt fear, genuine fear. Not a fear of risk or danger, or the desperation of warfare. It was horror. A terror of the unknown. A simple inability to comprehend and fathom the dark workings of the galaxy. He could fight a physical enemy, no matter the odds. A practical problem could be attacked and extinguished. But this was beyond him, and he despised the feeling. There was no sense. The harder he looked for it, the less sense there was.

'Perhaps–' Criid began. Everyone looked at her.

'Perhaps,' she said, 'it's a territorial thing. Like gang versus gang. We're the enemy to both, but they are no kind of friends. Perhaps the big brute wants us for itself.'

'The notion is not without value,' Darulin nodded.

'We should anticipate, then, a further boarding action from the killship?' said Criid. 'I mean, re-form and stand ready to repel again?'

Gaunt nodded.

'If that's its intention,' he said. 'Yes, that would be wise. Whatever defence we can now muster–'

'Sir!' said Kelvedon.

Darulin turned to look.

'The enemy killship has powered down its weapons,' said Kelvedon, studying the tactical display. 'It is retraining power to its drives.'

On the display, the giant shadow began to stir.

The Archenemy warship, black as night, began to move. Starlight glinted off the bare metal buttresses that lined its coal-black hull. Its prow rose like the beak of a breaching whale, then it banked silently and plunged back into the abyssal trenches of space.

The *Armaduke*'s bruised sensors retained a track on its heat-wake as it extended away from them by sixty, eighty, one hundred thousand kilometres.

Then the Master of Artifice had to be uncoupled from the strategium for his own safety. His flesh was starting to smoulder, and he could no longer form intelligible words. The strategium display shut down.

By then, the *Tormaggeddon Monstrum Rex* was a million miles away, vanishing into the starfield.

ELEVEN

FORGE WORLD URDESH

Thunder rolled across the Great Bay of Eltath. It was high summer, and the air was dull with a haze that made the low, wide sky a bright grey. Cloud banks running out across the wide bay and the sea beyond stood like inverted mountains, dark and ominous as phantoms. Lightning sizzled like trace veins in the dead flesh of the sky.

It was not a summer storm breaking, though changes in the weather were anticipated before nightfall. It was the electromagnetic shock wave of a large magnitude ship entering the atmospheric sheath.

Descending at speed, the *Highness Ser Armaduke* sliced through the cloud cover, emerging into the hard sunlight in a squall of rain. It left a long furrow in the cloud system behind it, like a stick drawn through old snow, a trail that would take several hours to fade.

It came in low over the sea. It was running fast, the vents of its real space plasma engines shining blue, but it was limping too. It was a patched survivor, sutured and soldered, its broken jaw wired shut from the fight. It had taken six weeks to reach Urdesh, and that voyage had been made thanks to frantic running repairs, constant coaxing, desperate compromises and sheer willpower.

In atmosphere, it made a terrible noise: a droning, vibrating, clattering howl of breathless engines, weary mechanicals and straining gravimetrics. The sound of it boomed out across the bay like ragged thunder, like a bass drum full of lead shot being kicked down a long staircase.

Its bulk was ugly, blackened and scorched. Three massive wounds scarred its heat-raked flanks and one of the four real space drives was unlit, a black socket leaking tons of liquid soot and water. It left a long, filthy plume of vapour and oily black smoke behind it, smoke that puffed and popped from exhaust cowlings like the fume waste of a steam locomotive. Slabs of dirty ice peeled from its hull as the air shaved at it, taking paint and hull coating with it. The chunks scattered away, dropping like depth charges into the ocean below, so that to shoreside observers, the *Armaduke* looked like it was performing a low-level saturation bombing run.

Vapour clung to its upper hull, swirling in the slipstream, and traceries of wild static sparked and popped around its masts.

It came in across the bay. To the west of it, grav-anchored at a height of one-and-a-half kilometres above the sea, the battleship *Naiad Antitor* sat like a floating continent, half shrouded in sea mist, an Imperial capital ship nine times the size of the relentless *Armaduke*.

The three Faustus-class interceptors that had guided the *Armaduke* in through the fleet, packing high orbit, purred down out of the cloud in formation, and resumed their station as an arrowhead, chasing ahead of the *Armaduke,* their running lights winking. The *Naiad Antitor* pulsed its main lanterns. Vox-links squealed with the ship-to-ship hail. Crossing the *Naiad Antitor*'s bow at a distance of ten kilometres, the *Armaduke* blazed its lamps, returning the formal salute. On both ships, the bridge crews stood and made the sign of the aquila, facing the direction of the other vessel as the *Armaduke* crossed beside its illustrious cousin.

A squadron of Thunderbolts, silver and red in the livery of the Second Helixid, scrambled from the *Naiad Antitor*'s flight decks and boiled out of its belly like wasps stirred from a nest. They raked low across the grey water, leaving hissing wakes of spray, and rose in coordinated formation on either side of the racing *Armaduke,* forming an honour guard escort of a hundred craft.

Ahead, the Great Bay began to narrow into the industrial approaches of the wet and dry harbours and the vast shipyards of Eltath. The mound of the great city, dominating the head of the peninsula, rose in the distance. Sunlight caught the flags, standards and masts that topped the Urdeshic Palace at its summit.

The clattering *Armaduke* came in lower, reducing its velocity. Its shipmaster reined in its headlong advance, easing back the power, sensing it was finding a last burst of acceleration like a weary hound or horse in sight of home and shelter.

It passed over the harbour, bleeding speed. Beneath, watercraft left white lines in a sea that glowed pink and russet with algal blooms. The south shore approach to the harbour was lined with derelict food mills and the rafts of rusting bulk harvester boats that had once processed the algae and weed for food. Scores of Astra Militarum troop ships, grey and shelled like beetles, were strung on mooring lines at low anchor over the harbour slick. Tender boats scooted around them on the water or flitted around their armoured hulls like humming birds.

Then they were over land, the foreshore of the city. The immense dry docks like roofless cathedrals, some containing smaller warships under refit. The endless barns and warestores of the Munitorum and the dynast craftsmen. The towers and manufactories of the Mechanicus, clustered like forest mushrooms around the base of the volcanic stack. The huge foundation docks and grav yards of the shipyard, like cross sections of sea giants, structural ribs exposed, each one an immense, fortified socket in the hillside, waiting to nest a shiftship. Watchtowers. The bunkered gun batteries at Low Keen and Eastern Hill and Signal Point. The tower emitters of the shield dome and their relay spires, thrusting from the craggy slopes like spines from an animal's backbone. The skeletal wastelands of the refinery, extending out over the sullen waters of the Eastern Reach, one hundred and sixty kilometres wide.

The *Armaduke* slowed again. Its real space drives began to cycle down, their glow dying back, and the clattering noise of the ship abated a little. Gravimetrics and thrust-manoeuvre systems took over, easing the impossibly huge object in slowly above the towers of Eltath. The sound of the ship, even diminished, echoed and slapped around the walls of the city. Windows rattled in their frames.

The Faustus escort peeled away, winking lamps of salute as they banked into space on higher burn. The Helixid Thunderbolts stayed with the slowing bulk of the *Armaduke* a little longer, dropping to almost viff-stall speed. Then they too disengaged, curling in lines like streamers as they broke and ran back to their parent ship.

Guide tugs, lumpen as tortoises, lumbered into view, securing mag-lines and heavy cables to harness the warship and manhandle it the last of the way. The *Armaduke* was crawling now, passing between the highest spires of the city, so close a man might step out of a hatch and onto a balcony.

Horns and hooters started to sound.

The southern end of plating dock eight, a gigantic portcullis, groaned as it opened wide, exposing the interior of the dock – a vast, ribbed cavity open to the sky. Rows of guide lights winked along the bottom of the dock. The air prickled as the dock's mighty gravity cradle cycled up and engaged. Air squealed and cracked as the grav field of the crawling ship rubbed against the gravimetric buffer of the dock. The *Armaduke* cut drives. The guide tugs, like burly stevedores, nudged and elbowed it the final few hundred metres.

Lines detached. The tugs rose out of the dock, and turned. The dock gates were closing, re-forming the end wall of the coffin-shaped basin that held the ship.

The *Armaduke* settled, slowly releasing its gravimetric field as the dock's systems accepted and embraced its weight. The hull and core frame groaned, and weight distribution shifted. Plates creaked and buckled. In places, rivets sheared under the pressure, and hull seams popped, venting gas and releasing liquid waste that poured down into the basin of the dock.

With a final, exhausted shudder, the *Armaduke* stopped moving and set down, supported on monolithic stanchion cradles and the gravimetric cup of the dock. Massive hydraulic beams extended from the dock walls to buffer and support the ship's flanks. Their reinforced ram-heads thumped against the hull with the bang of heavy magnetics, taking the strain.

Quiet came at last. The engine throb and drone of the ship were stilled. The only sounds were the dockside hooters, the clank of walk bridges being extended, the whir of cargo hoists rolling out on their platforms and derricks, and the spatter of liquids draining out of the hull into the waste-water drains of the unlit dock floor.

With a long gasp of exhaling breath, the *Armaduke* blew its hatches and airgates.

Then the storm broke. Thunder peeled across the bay, across Eltath and across the Urdeshic Palace. Above Plating Dock Eight, the sky curdled into an early darkness, and rain began to fall. It showed up as winnowing fans of white in the beams of the dock lamps illuminating the ship. It sizzled off the cooling hull, turning to steam as it struck the drive cowling. It buzzed like the bells of a thousand tiny tambourines as it hit the invisible cushion of the grav field, and turned into mist.

It streamed off the patched and rugged hull of the *Armaduke,* washing off soot and rust in such quantities that the water turned red before it fell away.

To some on the dockside and ramps of the bay, it seemed as though the rain were washing the old ship's battle wounds, bathing its tired bones, and anointing it on its long, long overdue return.

The heavy rain drummed off the canvas roofs of the metal gangways that had extended out to meet the ship's airgates. Gaunt stepped out onto one of the walkways, feeling its metal structure wobble and sway slightly. He saw the rain squalling through the beams of the dockside floodlights that illuminated the *Highness Ser Armaduke.* He tasted fresh air. It smelt dank and dirty, but it was fresh air, planetary air, not shipboard environmental – the first he had breathed in a year.

Ten years, he corrected himself... Eleven.

There was activity on the dock platforms at the foot of the gangway. He began to walk down the slender metal bridge, ignoring the dark gulf of the dock cavity that yawned below.

A greeting party was assembling. Gaunt saw Munitorum officials, flanked by guards with light poles. An honour guard of eighty Urdeshi storm troopers had drawn up on the dockside platform in perfectly dressed rows, holding immaculate attention.

Gaunt stepped off the gangway onto the dockside. The wet rockcrete crunched under his boots. Now he was beyond the gangway's canvas awning, the rain fell on him. He was wearing his dress uniform and his long storm coat.

Someone called an order, and the Urdeshi guard snapped in perfect drill, presenting their rifles upright in front of them in an unwavering salute. An officer walked forwards. He wore the black-and-white puzzle camo of Urdesh, and his pins marked him as a colonel.

'Sir, welcome to Urdesh,' he said, making the sign of the aquila.

Gaunt nodded and returned the sign formally.

'I'm Colonel Kazader,' the man said, 'Seventeenth Urdeshi. We honour your return. As per your signal, agents of the ordos and the Mechanicus await to discharge your cargo.'

'I will brief them directly,' said Gaunt. 'There are specifics that I did not include in my signal. Matters that should not be contained in any trans- mission, even encrypted.'

'I understand, sir,' said Kazader. 'The officers of the ordos also stand by to take your asset into secure custody. That is, if he still lives.'

'He does,' said Gaunt, 'but no prisoner transfer will take place until I have met with the officers and assured myself of their suitability.'

'Their...?'

'That they are not going to kill him, colonel,' said Gaunt. 'Many have tried, and they have included men wearing rosettes.'

Kazader raised his eyebrows slightly.

'As you wish, colonel-commissar,' he said. 'You are evidently a cautious man.'

'That probably explains why I have lived so long,' said Gaunt.

'Indeed, sir, we presumed you dead. Long dead.'

'Ten years dead.'

'Yes, sir,' said the Urdeshi.

'I never lost faith.'

Gaunt turned. The voice had come from the shadows nearby, under the lip of the dock overhang. A figure stepped out into the rain, flanked by aides and attendants. Guards with light poles fell in step, and their lanterns illuminated the figure's face.

Gaunt didn't recognise him at first. He was an old man, grey-bearded and frail, as if the dark blue body armour he wore were keeping him upright. His long cloak was hemmed in gold.

'Not once,' the man said. 'Not once in ten years.'

Gaunt saluted, back straight.

'Lord general,' he said.

Barthol Van Voytz stepped nose to nose with Gaunt. He was still a big man, but his face was lined with pain. Raindrops dripped from his heavy beard.

He looked Gaunt in the eyes for a moment, then embraced him. There was great intent in his hug, but very little strength. Gaunt didn't know how to react. He stood for a moment, awkward, until the general released him.

'I told them all you'd come back,' said Van Voytz.

'It is good to see you, sir.'

'I told them death was not a factor in the calculations of Ibram Gaunt.'

Gaunt nodded. He bit back the desire to snap out a retort. Jago was in the past, further in the past for Van Voytz than it was for Gaunt. The general had been a decent friend and ally in earlier days, but he had used Gaunt and the Ghosts poorly at Jago. The wounds and losses were still raw.

At least to Gaunt. To Gaunt, they were but five years young. To Van Voytz, an age had passed, and life had clearly embattled him with other troubles.

Van Voytz clearly did not see the reserve in Gaunt's face. But then Gaunt's eyes had famously become unreadable.

Eyes I only have because of you, Barthol.

Van Voytz looked him up and down, like a father welcoming a child home after a long term away at scholam, examining him to see how he has grown.

'You're a hero, Bram,' he said.

'The word is applied too loosely and too often, general,' said Gaunt.

'Nonsense. You return in honour and in triumph. What you have achieved...' His voice trailed off, and he shook his head.

'We'll have time to discuss it all,' he said. 'To discuss many things. Debriefing and so forth. Much to discuss.'

'I was given to understand that the Warmaster wished to receive my report.'

'He does,' nodded Van Voytz. 'We all do.'

'The office of the Warmaster will arrange an audience,' said the aide beside Van Voytz.

'You remember my man here, Bram?' said Van Voytz.

'Tactician Biota,' Gaunt nodded. 'Of course.'

'Chief Tactical Officer, Fifth Army Group now,' Biota nodded. 'It's good to see you again, colonel-commissar.'

'I wanted to be the one to greet you, Bram,' said Van Voytz, 'in person, as you stepped onto firm land. Because we go back.'

'We do.'

'Staff is in uproar, you know,' said Van Voytz. 'Quite the stir you've created. But I insisted it should be me.'

'I didn't expect my disembarkation to be witnessed by a lord general,' said Gaunt.

'By a friend, Ibram,' said Van Voytz.

Gaunt hesitated.

'If you say so, sir,' he replied.

Van Voytz studied him for a moment. Rain continued to drip from his beard. He nodded sadly, as if acknowledging Gaunt's right to resentment.

'Well, indeed,' he said quietly. 'I do say so. That's a conversation we should have over an amasec or two. Not here.'

He looked up into the rain.

'This is not the most hospitable location. I apologise that the site of your return is not a more glorious scene.'

'It is what it is,' said Gaunt.

'Not just the weather, Gaunt.' Van Voytz turned, and placed a hand on Gaunt's shoulder, as if to lead him into the interior chambers below the lip of the dock. 'Urdesh,' he said. 'This is a bloody pickle.'

Gaunt tensed slightly.

'When you use words like "pickle", Barthol,' he said, 'it is always an understatement. A euphemism. And I immediately expect it to be followed by some description of how the Ghosts can dig you out of it with their lives.'

There was silence, apart from the patter of rain on the dock and the awnings.

'I declare, sir,' said Kazader, 'a man should not speak in such a way to a lord general. You must apologise immediately and–'

Van Voytz raised his hand sharply.

'Thank you, Colonel Kazader,' he said, 'but I don't need you to defend my honour. Colonel-Commissar Gaunt has always spoken his mind, which is why I value him, and also why he is still a colonel-commissar. What he said was the truth, emboldened by hot temper no doubt, but still the truth.'

He looked at Gaunt.

'The Urdesh War will be resolved by good tactics and strong command, Gaunt,' he said. 'It requires nothing from you or your men. The real pickle is the crusade. Fashions have changed, Bram, and these days are perhaps better a time for truth and plain speaking. This is a moment, Bram, one of those moments that history will take note of.'

'My relationship with time and history is somewhat skewed, sir,' said Gaunt.

'You suffered a lapse, did you not?' asked Biota.

'A translation accident,' said Gaunt.

'You've lost time,' said Van Voytz, 'but this time could now be yours. It could belong to a man of influence.'

'I have influence?' asked Gaunt.

Van Voytz chuckled.

'More than you might imagine,' he replied, 'and there's more to be gained. Let's talk, somewhere out of this foul weather.'

TWELVE

A PLACE OF SAFETY

Below him, through the heavy rain, Gol Kolea watched the *Armaduke* discharge its contents.

He was standing on an observation platform high on the ship's superstructure. The platform had extended automatically when the ship's hatches opened. Down below, like ants, slow trains of people processed down the covered gangways onto the dockside, and the dock's heavy hoists swung down pallets laden with material and cargo.

He smelled cold air, faintly fogged with petrochemicals, and tasted rain. He felt the cold wind on his skin. It wasn't home, because he'd never see that again, but it was a home. It reminded him of the high walls of Vervunhive.

In his life there, he'd only been up onto the top walls of the hive a few times. A man like him, a mine worker from the skirtlands of the superhive, seldom had reason or permission to visit such a commanding vantage. But he remembered the view well. His wife had loved it. When they had first been together, he had sometimes saved up bonus pay to afford a pass to the Panorama Walk, as a treat for her. He'd even proposed to her up there. That was an age ago, before the kids had come along.

The thought of his children pained him. Gol hated that he registered fear and pain every time they crossed his mind. Though it didn't feel like it for a moment, it was ten years since he'd led the drop to Aigor 991 for the resupply. Ten years since he'd heard the voice. Ten whole years since the voice had told him he was a conduit for daemons, and that he had to fetch the eagle stones or his child would perish.

The terror of that day had lingered with him. He tried to put it out of his mind. When you fought in the front line against the Archenemy, the Ruinous Powers tried to trick you and pollute you all the time. He'd told himself that's all it was: a warp trick. He'd made a report to Gaunt too, about the voice and its demand, but not about everything. How could he report that? For the sake of his child, how could he admit he had been condemned.

Then there had been the incident in the hold during the boarding action. Baskevyl had told him all about it. It seemed likely they knew what 'eagle stones' were now. Bask's theory, and the related accounts, had all been classified to be part of Gaunt's formal report to high command. Now they were safe on Urdesh, the whole matter would be passed to the authorities, to people who knew what they were doing, not front-line grunts like him.

If the wretched things in the hold were the eagle stones, then they were apparently precious artefacts. It made sense that the accursed Anarch Sek would want them, and would try manipulation to get them. According to initial data, Sek was here on Urdesh, leading the enemy strengths. *Well, you bastard. I've brought the stones to you, like you asked. You can leave me be now. Leave me and my children be. We're not part of this any more.*

'Besides,' he growled out loud at the rainy sky, 'it's been *ten years*.'

Kolea sighed.

He was high enough on the ship to see beyond the walls of the dock and out towards the city and the bay. It was a grey shape in the rain, a skyline dotted with lights. He didn't know much about Urdesh, except that it was a forge world, and famous, and it produced good soldiers, some of whom he had fought alongside at Cirenholm. They hadn't been the friendliest souls, but Kolea respected their military craft. The Urdeshi had been stubborn and proud, fighting for the spirit of this world, a world that had changed hands so many times and so often been a battleground. He got that. He understood the pride a man attached to his birth-hive.

It was a good view. A strong place. A landscape a man could connect with. Livy would have loved it, standing here in the rain, looking out...

'Gol?'

He turned. Baskevyl was stepping out of the hatch to find him.

'Where are we?' asked Kolea.

'About two-thirds discharged,' replied Bask. 'The Administratum has issued us with staging about ten kilometres away. The regiment and the retinue.'

'Barrack housing?' asked Kolea.

Baskevyl checked his data-slate. 'No, residential habs.'

'How so?'

'Apparently the main Militarum camps are already full of troops waiting to ship out to the front line, but the city has been largely evacuated of civilians, so we've been assigned quarters in requisitioned hab blocks.'

'Where is the front line?' asked Kolea.

Baskevyl shrugged.

'All right, let's send some company leaders on ahead to check out the facilities. Criid, Kolosim, Pasha, Domor.'

'*Captain* Criid, you mean?' asked Bask.

'Damn right. About time. Tell them to look the place over and draw up a decent dispersal order, so no one starts bickering about their billet. And let's get Mkoll to sweep the venue and give us a security report.'

'This isn't the front line, I know that,' Baskevyl smiled.

'Never hurts,' Kolea grinned back. 'How many times have things changed overnight and bitten us on the arse?'

'Gentlemen?'

They looked up from the data-slate as Commissar Fazekiel joined them. She pulled up the collar of her coat against the rain.

'Medicae personnel have arrived to ship off our wounded. Those still not walking anyway.'

'That's not many is it?' asked Kolea.

'About a dozen. Raglon. Cant. Damn glad to have Daur back on his feet.'

'Major Pasha too,' said Kolea.

Fazekiel nodded. 'I gather Spetnin and Zhukova are crestfallen. They were just getting used to running Pasha's companies.'

'What about the shipmaster?' asked Baskevyl.

'They're moving him off to the Fleet infirmary at Eltath Watch,' she said. 'I'm frankly amazed the fether's still alive.'

'I'm amazed any of us are still alive,' said Baskevyl.

'There's that,' Fazekiel agreed. 'Can you two spare a moment? We've got visitors, and I'd appreciate the moral support of some senior staff.'

'Thoust leaving, soule?' asked Ezra.

Sar Af glanced at him briefly, then finished instructing the servitor teams handling the equipment crates of the Adeptus Astartes. There was no sign in the hold of Eadwine or Holofurnace.

'Good as gone,' said Sar Af, walking over to Ezra once his instructions were given. 'Duty is done, and I never stay put long.'

'Gaunt, he will–' Ezra began.

'Eadwine sent him notice of our departure,' said Sar Af. 'We've tarried far too long on this mission. It was supposed to last six weeks.'

Ezra nodded.

'Eadwine's already gone,' Sar Af added. 'Gone to see the Warmaster in person. The Snake's left too. Apparently his brothers are engaged in the war here, and he's gone to find them. He will be glad to see them again, and join with them in a new venture.'

'And thee, soule?' asked Ezra.

Sar Af grinned.

'The Archenemy presses close,' he said. 'I smell killing to be done.'

He gestured at the reynbow strapped to Ezra's shoulder.

'Found your weapon, then?'

'Broken, but I made mend of it,' said Ezra.

'Should get yourself a proper piece,' said the White Scar. 'Something that will stop a foe dead.'

'This stops the foe,' said Ezra.

Sar Af peered at him.

'I'm not good at faces. Are you sad, Nihtgane?'

Ezra shook his head.

'Uh, that's good. Men can be too sentimental. They place unnecessary emotion on leave-taking and such. Parting is not an ending. Life is just the path ahead, so sometimes you leave things behind you.'

'No sentiment,' said Ezra. 'It was a journey and we walked it.'

The White Scar nodded. With a twist, he uncoupled the lock of his right gauntlet and pulled the glove off to expose his bare hand.

'That's right, Nihtgane,' he said. He held his hand out and Ezra clasped it.

'Follow your path, Eszrah Ap Niht,' Sar Af said. 'Only you can walk it.'

He clamped his gauntlet back on, donned his war-helm with a hydraulic click, and followed the servitor team out of the hold without looking back.

'You can show me the paperwork all you like,' said Rawne, 'S Company isn't handing him over until I get word from my commanding officer.'

'Your tone is borderline insolent, major,' said Interrogator Sindre of the Ordo Hereticus. A heavy detail of Urdeshi storm troops filled the brig hatchway behind him.

'Not for him,' Varl told the interrogator. 'There was definitely a silent "fething" before the word "paperwork".'

Sindre had a very thin, pale face and very blue eyes. His black uniform was immaculate, unadorned except for the gold and ruby rosette on his back-turned lapel. He smiled. In the close, gloomy confines of the armoured brig, his soft voice sounded like a slow gas leak.

'I appreciate the seriousness with which you uphold your duties, major,' he said. 'Custody of the prisoner is an alpha-rated duty. You are commended. But crusade high staff and the office of the ordos have agreed to his immediate transfer to secure Inquisition holding. The order was ratified by two lords militant and the senior secretary of the Inquisition here on Urdesh six hours before you even touched down.'

'Gaunt didn't signal anyone that the prisoner was still with us,' said Rawne. He spoke slowly and sounded reasonable. His men knew that was always a warning sign. 'I know for a fact,' he said, 'that the information he broadcast on approach in-system was extremely limited and contained no confidential information.'

'A sensible move,' replied Sindre. 'The Archenemy is close, and it is listening. In fact, there is some consternation among upper staff that details of your extended mission have not yet been supplied. They are awaiting your superior's full report.'

'Which he will deliver in person for the same reasons of security,' said Rawne.

'We, however, made an assumption,' said Sindre. 'If Gaunt is alive after all, then the prisoner might be as well, etcetera, etcetera...' Sindre shrugged and smiled. He seemed to smile a lot. 'So,' he said, 'on the presumption he was, preparations for immediate handover and securement were made and authorised in advance. Just in case the animal had survived.'

'Move aside,' said Viktor Hark. He entered the brig chamber, pushing past Sindre's security detail. They glared at him at first, then stood out of his path.

'Gaunt has signed off, Rawne,' said Hark. 'He's had assurances.'

'Let me see,' said Rawne.

Hark handed him a data-slate. Rawne read it carefully.

'You know they're just going to kill him,' said Varl.

'Varl...' Hark growled.

'Oh, but they are,' said Varl. 'He's no use any more. He's done what he was supposed to do. They won't let him live, not a thing like him. They'll burn him.'

Sindre smiled again. The Suicide Kings began to feel his smile was quite as alarming as Rawne's reasonable tone.

'Is that sympathy I hear?' he asked. 'One of your men sympathising with the fate of an Archenemy devil? If security is such a concern to you, Major Rawne, I would look to my own quickly.'

'The prisoner is an asset,' said Rawne. 'That's all my man here is worried about.'

'Of course he is,' said Sindre. 'On that we agree. We're not going to execute him. Not yet, anyway. Eventually, of course. But the ordos believes there is a great deal more that may be extracted from him. He has been cooperative so far, after all. He will be interviewed and examined extensively, for however long that takes. Whatever other truths he contains, they will be learned.'

'Bring him out,' said Rawne.

Varl stood back with a shake of his head. Bonin, Brostin, Cardass and Oysten walked back to the cell, and threw the bolts. After a few minutes spent running the standard body search, they brought Mabbon Etogaur out in shackles. With the Suicide Kings around him, Mabbon shuffled his way over to Rawne's side.

Sindre looked at him with considerable distaste.

'Storm troop,' Sindre called out. 'Take possession of the prisoner and prepare to move. Double file guard. Watch his every move.'

The Urdeshi storm troopers moved forwards.

'S Company, Tanith First,' said Sindre, 'you are relieved of duty. Your vigilance and effort is appreciated.'

'We stand relieved,' replied Rawne.

The Urdeshi moved Mabbon towards the hatch. It was slow going because his stride was so abbreviated by the shackles.

'Hey!'

They paused, and Sindre looked back. Varl had gone into the etogaur's cell and reappeared holding a sheaf of cheap, tatty pamphlets and chapbooks.

'These belong to him,' he said, holding them out.

Interrogator Sindre took the pamphlets and flicked through them.

'Trancemissionary texts,' he mused, 'and a copy of *The Spheres of Longing*.'

'He reads them,' said Varl.

Sindre handed them back.

'No reading material is permitted,' he said.

'But they belong to him.'

'Nothing belongs to him, trooper,' said Sindre. 'No rights, no possessions. And besides, he will have no need for reading matter. He will be... busy talking.'

Varl glanced at Rawne, and Rawne quietly shook his head. At the hatch, surrounded by the impassive storm troopers, Mabbon looked back over his shoulder and nodded very slightly to Varl.

'You... you watch him,' said Varl. 'He's a sly one, that pheguth.'

'You take care of yourself, Sergeant Varl,' said Mabbon. 'We won't meet again.'

'You never know,' said Varl.

'I think I do,' said Mabbon.

'That's enough. No talking,' Sindre snapped at Mabbon. 'Move.'

The storm troopers led him away.

* * *

Luna Fazekiel led Baskevyl and Kolea to the hatch of hold ninety.

'Our visitors,' she remarked sidelong.

A man in the plain, dark uniform of the Astra Militarum intelligence service was waiting for them, accompanied by a cowled representative of the Adeptus Mechanicus and a tall woman in a long storm coat who could only be from the ordos. A gang of Mechanicus servitors and several other aides and assistants waited in the corridor behind them, as well as intelligence service soldiers with plasma weapons. Elam, and a squad from his company, blocked them from the hatch door.

'Ma'am,' said Elam as the trio approached.

'Are you in charge here?' the intelligence officer asked Fazekiel. He was well made and handsome, with thick, dark hair, cut close, and greying at the temples.

'We have been kept waiting,' said the female inquisitor. 'You have the authority to open this hold?'

As they had approached, Kolea had been struck by the woman's appearance. She was tall and slender, and her head, with its shaved scalp, had the most feline, high-cheekboned profile he had seen on a human. She possessed the sort of attenuated, sculptural beauty he imagined of the fabled aeldari.

But as she turned to regard them, he saw it was reconstruction work. The entire upper part of her head that had been facing away from them was gone, from the philtrum up, replaced by intricate silver and gold augmetics, fashioned like some master-crafted weapon. Her mouth was real, and her eyes, presumably also real, gleamed in the complex golden sockets of her face. She had been rebuilt, and the surgeons and augmeticists had only been able to save the lower part of her face. Even that, Kolea fancied, was just a careful copy of what had once existed. The augmetic portion had obviously been destroyed beyond hope of reconstruction. It shocked him, and fascinated him. He was alarmed to realise that he almost found the intricate golden workings of her visage more beautiful than the perfect skin of her jaw.

'My apologies,' said Fazekiel. 'Disembarkation after a long journey is a demanding process. We have authority to break the seals. I am Commissar Fazekiel. This is Major Kolea, and Major Baskevyl.'

'Colonel Grae,' said the intelligence officer. 'With me, Versenginseer Lohl Etruin of the Adeptus Mechanicus and Sheeva Laksheema of the Ordo Xenos.'

The cowled adept twitched an actuator wand, and a small, plump woman stepped forwards from the entourage. She wore a simple robe and tabard, and her hair was tight curls of silver. She presented Fazekiel with a thick sheaf of papers.

'Documentation for the receiver party,' she said, looking up at Fazekiel. 'It lists and accredits all personnel present, including the servitor crew and the savants.'

'You are?' asked Fazekiel.

'My lead savant, Onabel,' said Laksheema, 'and her identity is not pertinent to this discussion. Please explain, I am concerned that the hold seal has been tampered with.'

'We ran into trouble, ma'am,' said Kolea.

'The ship was boarded. We fought them off,' said Fazekiel. 'However, we were obliged to open and search all the ship compartments to ensure that no agents of the foe remained in hiding.'

'Who opened it?' asked Laksheema.

'I did,' said Baskevyl. 'It was opened on my command.'

The cowled adept made a small, clicking, buzzing sound. Laksheema nodded.

'I agree, Etriun,' she said. She looked at Baskevyl. 'Operational orders stated that the material recovered from Salvation's Reach should remain sealed for the return voyage. There is potential danger and hazard to the untrained and uninformed.'

'Operational orders that are now over ten years old,' said Kolea.

'As my colleague explained, ma'am,' said Baskevyl, 'circumstances changed. I thought it better to risk the potential hazard rather than risk even greater danger. A field decision.'

Laksheema stared at him. 'A field decision,' she said. 'How very Astra Militarum. You are Baskevyl?'

'Major Braden Baskevyl, Tanith First, ma'am.'

'But you are Belladon born.'

'My insignia gives me away,' he replied, lightly.

'No, your accent. When you opened the hold, Baskevyl, what did you find?'

'Disruption to the cargo. Some contents shifted and spilled. I checked the area for signs of intruders, found none, and so immediately resealed the hold.'

'Because?' Laksheema asked.

'Operational orders, ma'am,' said Baskevyl.

'No,' she said. 'Something else. I see it in your manner.'

Baskevyl glanced at Kolea.

'One of the crates had spilled in a way I could not explain. Our asset had suggested that this particular set of items constitute perhaps the most valuable artefacts recovered during the raid. I touched nothing. I left them where they were and resealed the hold.'

The adept buzzed and warbled quietly again.

'Indeed,' Laksheema nodded. 'Define "in a way I could not explain", please, major.'

'The crate contained stone tiles or tablets, ma'am,' said Baskevyl, uncomfortably. 'They had fallen, but arranged themselves in rows.'

'Rows?' echoed Grae.

Baskevyl gestured, to explain.

'Perfect rows, sir,' he said. 'Perfectly aligned. It seemed to me very unlikely that they could just land like that.'

'And you left them?' asked Laksheema.

'Yes.'

'How did it make you feel?' asked the stocky little savant.

'Feel?' replied Baskevyl. 'I... I don't know... My inclination was to pick them up, but I felt that was unwise.'

'Anything else of note occur during the voyage?' asked Grae.

'Plenty,' said Kolea. 'It was a busy trip.'

'That you'd like to relate, I mean,' said Grae.

Baskevyl glanced at Kolea. Neither wanted to be the one to open the can of worms about the eagle stones and the voice. Besides, it was above their grade now, and part of the official mission report document.

'There is a great deal you are not telling us, isn't there?' asked the inquisitor.

'The mission report is long, complex and classified,' said Baskevyl.

'The details can't circulate until the report has been presented to high command and the Warmaster, and validated by them,' said Kolea.

'And the ordos do not warrant inclusion in that list?' asked Laksheema.

'It's a matter of Militarum protocol–' Baskevyl began.

'Shall I tell you what I think of protocol?' asked the inquisitor.

'Our commanding officer is on his way right now to deliver the full report to staff,' said Fazekiel quickly. 'He's presenting it in person. The details were considered too sensitive to commit to signal or other form that could be intercepted.'

'This is... Gaunt?' asked Laksheema.

'Yes, ma'am.'

'His reputation precedes him,' remarked Grae.

'Does it, sir?' asked Kolea.

'It does, major,' said the intelligence officer. 'Amplified considerably by death, which of course now proves to be incorrect. He has made quite a name for himself, posthumously. It is rare a man turns up alive to appreciate that.'

'I'm sure the colonel-commissar will deliver the report in full to you too,' said Fazekiel.

'Of course he will,' said Laksheema. 'The Warmaster has drawn up our working group to examine and identify the materials gathered. Full accounts must be collated from all involved, and all who had contact, as well as a detailed consideration of any events surrounding the mission that may be relevant.'

She looked at Kolea.

'Even those which may not appear to the layman to be relevant,' she added.

'We will need full lists of everyone who had any contact with the items during recovery and storage,' said Grae. 'Anyone who was... exposed.'

Kolea nodded. 'That's quite a large number of personnel, sir.'

'They will all be interviewed,' said Grae.

The adept whirred.

'Etruin asks who collated and indexed the material for the manifest.'

'I did,' said Fazekiel.

Laksheema nodded.

'The manifest is very thorough. You have a keen preoccupation with detail, Commissar Fazekiel.'

'I imagine that's why Gaunt charged me with the duty, ma'am,' Fazek-iel replied.

'You are methodical,' Laksheema mused. 'Obsessive compulsive. Has the condition been diagnosed and peer-reviewed?'

'Has it... what?' asked Fazekiel.

'Shall we open the hatch?' suggested Baskevyl. 'You can take charge of it. We'll be glad to see the back of this stuff.'

I know I will, thought Kolea.

A long column of cargo-8 trucks left the staging gates of plating dock eight and followed the old streets down the hill into Eltath. The rain had stopped, and the skies were puzzle-grey. Rainwater had collected in the potholes and ruts pitting the rockcrete roads, and the big wheels of the passing trucks sprayed it up in sheets.

The buildings of the quarter were old, and looked derelict. They had once been the headquarters and storehouses of merchants and shipping guilds, but war had emptied them long before, and they stood silent and often boarded. Time and weather had robbed some of roof tiles, and in places, there were vacant lots where the neighbouring buildings were propped with girder braces to prevent them slumping sideways into the mounds of rubble. The rubble was overgrown with lichen and creeper weeds. These were the sites of buildings lost to shelling and air raids. The spaces they left in the street frontages were like gaps in a row of teeth.

The motor column was carrying the first of the Tanith to their assigned billets. Tona Criid rode in the cab of the lead vehicle. She peered at the dismal buildings as they rumbled past.

'When did the war here end?' she asked.

'The war hasn't ended,' replied the Urdeshi pool driver.

'No, I mean the last war?'

'Which last war?' he asked, unhelpfully. He glanced at her. 'Urdesh has been at war for decades. Conquest, occupation, liberation, reconquest. The whole system, contested since forever. One war followed by another, followed by another.'

'But you endure?' she asked.

'What choice have we got? This is our world.'

Criid thought about that.

'Forgive me for asking,' said the driver after a while, his eyes on the road, 'you've come here to fight, and you don't know what the war is?'

'That's fairly normal,' said Criid. 'We just go where we're sent, and we fight. Anyway, it's the same war. The same war, everywhere.'

'True, I suppose,' the man replied.

They drove further through the old quarter. The streets were as lifeless as before. Criid began to notice material strung across the streets from building to building, like processional bunting. But it was sheets, carpets, old faded curtains, and other large stretches of canvas that hung limply in the damp air. The sheets hung so low in places, they brushed the tops of the moving trucks.

'What's that about?' she asked, gesturing to the sheets.

'Snipers,' said the driver.

'Snipers?'

'We string the streets up with cloth like that to reduce any line of sight,' the driver said. 'It blocks the scoping opportunities for marksmen.'

'There are snipers here?' asked Criid.

'From time to time,' the man nodded. 'The Archenemy is everywhere. Not so much here these days. The main fighting is in the south and the east. Those are whole different kinds of kill-zones. But the enemy sneaks in sometimes. Insurgents, suicide packs, infiltration units, sometimes bastards who have laid low in the bomb-wastes or the sewers since the last occupation. They like to cause trouble.'

Criid nodded. 'Good to know,' she said.

He glanced at her again.

'Learn the habits now you're here,' he said. 'Stay away from windows. Don't loiter outdoors. And watch out for garbage or debris in roads or doorways. Derelict vehicles too. The bastards like to leave surprises around. Seldom a day goes past without a bomb.'

They reached a junction, and ground to a halt, waiting as heavy cargo transporters and armoured cars growled by, heading towards the docks.

Across the junction, Criid saw the end wall of an old manufactory. Someone, with some skill, had taken paint to it and daubed the words 'THE SAINT LIVES AND IS WITH US' in huge red letters. Beside it was a crude but expressive image of a woman with a sword.

'The Saint,' said Criid.

'Beati Sabbat, may she bless us and watch over us,' said the driver.

'Good to see that Urdesh is strong in faith at least,' she said.

'Not just a matter of faith,' said the driver, putting the cargo-8 in gear and leading the convoy away again onto a long slope towards the garment district. 'She's here. Here with us.'

'The Saint?'

'Yes, lady.'

'Saint Sabbat is here on Urdesh?' she asked.

'Yes,' said the driver. 'Didn't they tell you anything?'

THIRTEEN

GOOD FAITH

The Urdeshic Palace occupied the cone of the Great Hill. Eltath was the subcontinental capital of the Northern Dynastic Clave, and like all of Urdesh's forge cities, its situation and importance were determined by the geothermal power of the volcanic outcrop. The Adeptus Mechanicus had come to Urdesh thousands of years before, during the early settlement of the Sabbat Worlds, and capped and tamed the world's vulcan cones to heat and power their industries. Urdesh was not just strategically significant because of its location: it was a vital, living asset to mass manufacture.

Van Voytz's transport, under heavy escort, moved up through the hillside thoroughfares, passing the towers of the Mechanicus manufactories and vapour mills that plugged the slopes and drew power from the geothermal reserves. Swathes of steam and smoke clad the upper parts of the city, hanging like mountain weather, the by-product of industry. Soot and grime caked the work towers and construction halls, and blackened the great icons of the Machine-God that badged the manufactory walls.

'At one time,' Van Voytz remarked, 'they say the Mechanicus employed as many work crews to maintain the forge palaces as they did in the forges themselves. They'd clean and re-clean, never-ending toil, to keep those emblems blazing gold and polish the white stones of the walls. But this is wartime, Bram. Looks are less important, and the Mechanicus needs all its manpower at work inside. So the dirt builds up, and the glory fades.'

'I'm sure there is some parable there, sir,' ventured Biota, 'of Urdesh itself. The endless toil to keep it free from ruinous filth.'

Van Voytz smiled.

'I'm sure, my old friend. The unbowed pride of the Urdeshi Dynasts, labouring forever. I'm sure the adepts have composed code-songs about it.'

'She's really here?' asked Gaunt.

Van Voytz looked amused, seeing how distractedly Gaunt stared from the transport's window at the city moving past.

'She is, Bram,' he said.

'Sanian? From Hagia?'

'She hasn't used that name in a long time,' said Van Voytz. 'She is the Beati now, in all measure, a figurehead for our monumental struggle.'

Gaunt looked at the general.

'Can I see her?' he asked.

Van Voytz shook his head.

'No, Bram. Not for a while at least.'

'It is a matter of logistics,' put in Biota helpfully. 'She is placed with the Ghereppan campaign, in the southern hemisphere, many thousands of kilometres from here, where the fighting is most intense. Access is difficult. Perhaps a vox-link might be established for you.'

'How long has she been here?' Gaunt asked.

'Since the counter-strike began,' said Van Voytz. 'So... four years?'

'Three,' said Biota. 'Colonel-commissar, many aspects of the campaign have changed since you... since you were last privy to the situation. I should brief you on the details as early as possible.'

'Much has changed,' said Van Voytz, 'yet much has remained the same. Ten years on, and the requirements of our endeavour remain fixed.'

He leaned forwards in his leather seat, facing Gaunt, his elbows on his knees. There was an intent look in his eyes that Gaunt had not seen since the earliest days of their campaigning together.

'The issue is the same as it's always been,' he said, 'ever since Balhaut. Imperial focus. Our beloved Warmaster insists, despite staff advice, on driving us against the Archon *and* the Anarch. We wage *two* crusades in one.'

'Slaydo underestimated the individual power of the magisters,' said Gaunt.

'Oh, he did. He did indeed,' Van Voytz admitted. 'And of them, Anarch Sek is by far the most dangerous.'

'The Coreward Assault necessitated a division of our efforts,' said Gaunt. 'We would have been utterly lost if we had not countered–'

Van Voytz held up his hands.

'I'm not arguing, Bram. It was vital. Then. But we have broken Sek and driven him out of the Cabal Systems. Those stars are freed. This, all down to the policy of internecine division that you advocated.'

'It worked?' asked Gaunt.

'We used Sek's ambition and power against him,' said Biota. 'After the Salvation's Reach mission, there were others, all framed with the same intent – to ignite the rivalry between Sek and Gaur. They no longer move in unity. There is conflict. Considerable fighting between Sanguinary tribes. Intelligence suggests that, for a period of two years, an all-out war raged between the Blood Pact and the Sons of Sek in the Vanda Pi systems. Sek was broken down, pushed out of the Khan and Cabal Systems, and Archon Gaur was hounded back to the stalwart line of the Erinyes Group.'

'But Sek is back, here?' said Gaunt.

'Either the Anarch has been brought into line again by Gaur,' said Van Voytz, 'and is making an effort to display his renewed loyalty, or he is making a last-ditch effort to consolidate his own power and resources. He has launched this counter-strike against a clutch of systems, with particular focus on Urdesh, because of its productive assets. This poor world, contested so many times. I doubt another world in the Sabbat Zone has changed hands so often in the last hundred years.'

'So the effort is to break him here?' asked Gaunt.

'For the last time,' said Van Voytz. 'While Lord General Eirik leads the push against Gaur. And that's the thing – we are on two fronts again. We are spread thin. It's a policy Macaroth will not let go of.'

'Because he recognises the threat of Sek,' said Gaunt.

'Sek is desperate,' said Van Voytz. 'A fleet war would be enough to punish him and keep him at bay. Our Warmaster, with the Beati at his side, should be leading the way against the Archon, not detained here.'

'You'd give up Urdesh?' asked Gaunt.

'It's been done before,' said Van Voytz bluntly. 'Many times. So, Sek makes some ground. Once the Archon is destroyed, Sek will just be part of the pacification clean-up. But it has become an obsession with Macaroth to contend with them both at once, and take them both down.'

'You disapprove?'

'I've been disapproving for fifteen years, Bram,' said Van Voytz. 'My dissent got me the Fifth Army Group and a charge to cover the Coreward Line.'

'With respect,' said Gaunt, 'at the time that looked like the Warmaster was passing you over in favour of commanders like Urienz. You and Cybon both. It looked like a demotion. History has shown differently. If you, Cybon and Blackwood hadn't been demoted to the Coreward Line, Sek and Innokenti would have broken the crusade in '76. Was that petulance on the Warmaster's part, or a strategic insight beyond the capabilities of any of us?'

'Insight only lasts so long, Bram,' said Van Voytz.

Their vehicle had reached the summit of the Great Hill. The motorcade rumbled over the metal bridges that crossed the gulf of the geothermal vents, and then ran in past blockhouse fortifications and watchtowers that protected the access gorge bisecting the inner cone of the volcano. The outer faces of the gorge mouth were blistered with macro-gun emplacements, like barnacles on the hull of a marine tanker.

Past the watchtowers, the procession drove into the shadow of the plunging gorge. The cliff walls either side were sheer, solid and impassable. There were weapons posts every twenty metres, and heavy Basilisk batteries on the cliff heads, their long barrels cranked skywards like the long necks of a grazing herd.

The gloom of the deep access gorge was dispelled by frames of stablights that had been fixed overhead between its walls. The light cast had an eerie, artificial radiance that reminded Gaunt of the ochre lumen glow of a ship's low holds.

The motorcade slowed several times as it passed gate stations and barriers along the ravine, Hydra batteries and quad guns traversing with a whir to track them, but the lord general's authority meant that it didn't have to stop. Solemn ranks of armoured Guardsmen stood in honour as the ground vehicles sped past.

Beyond the access gorge, the sky was visible again. The summit of the Great Hill was a vast amphitheatre, fringed by the ragged lip of the volcanic cone, and in it lay the immense precinct of the Urdeshic Palace. Towering inner walls surrounded an Imperial bastion of humbling size, its main spires reaching high above the surrounding cone peak into the dismal sky.

They drove up through concentric wall formations, passed across inner yards where armoured divisions sat like Guardsmen on parade: Basilisk carriages, storm-tanks, siege tanks, super-massives asleep under tarps. They sped past a long row of Vanquishers, identical but for their hull numbers, and then followed a skirt road up to the High Yard of the main keep.

As Gaunt got out of the general's heavy transport, the Taurox escort vehicles swinging to a halt around him, a formation of Thunderbolts screamed low overhead, filling the High Yard with sound, heading west over the keep. Gaunt looked up to see them pass, and then the second wave that quickly followed them. He pulled on his coat, walked across the yard and ascended the access steps to the wall top.

'Gaunt?' Van Voytz called after him.

From the wall top, Gaunt had a clean view out across the rim of the cone, the vast city below and the distant landscape. He could see the dull sheen of the sea. The dark industrial landscape spread away to the east, a mosaic of refineries and manufactory megastructures, vast acres of pylons like metal forests, and filthy, belching galvanic plants, some clearly extending across the waters of the Eastern Reach on artificial islands. Far to the east, thunder broke, and Gaunt saw a tremble of distant flames light up the skyline.

The Urdeshi and Helixid sentries manning the quad-gun positions on the wall-line glanced at him, puzzled. Who was he to just walk up here?

Another wave of aircraft screamed overhead, following the same track as the earlier ones. Marauders this time, a shoal of fifty, their heavy engines roaring as they dragged through the air, slower and more ponderous than the strike fighters that had preceded them. Gaunt watched them until the amber coals of their afterburners disappeared into the dark jumble of the landscape. Another rippling boom of thunder came in on the wind, and another flicker of fire-flash lit the horizon.

'The enemy is assaulting the vapour mills at Zarakppan,' said Biota, stepping up alongside Gaunt, and looking out.

'We try to preserve the precious infrastructure as much as possible,' he said, 'which is why the Urdeshi war is primarily a land war and not an orbital purge. But the Archenemy seems more intent on destruction than reacquisition. However, Zarakppan is too close for comfort. Air power has been deployed in preference to ground repulse to deal with the assault more decisively.'

'At the cost of the vapour mills?' asked Gaunt.

'Regrettably, yes. Such sacrifices have become an increasing feature of this campaign.'

'An orbital purge would annihilate Sek in days,' said Gaunt. 'Perhaps end his threat forever. The battlefleet-'

'-stands ready,' said Biota. 'It is a strategy we have in our pocket. It has its champions. The loss of Urdesh as a functioning forge world would be a major sacrifice. This must be weighed against the benefit of eliminating the Anarch for good.'

'So the Warmaster favours the ground war?' asked Gaunt.

'Vehemently. To defeat Sek and preserve the might of Urdesh. A worthy goal, and one I can certainly see the merit of. But it seems to ignore the Archenemy's methodology.'

Gaunt looked at him.

'What do you mean, Biota?'

Biota was impassive.

'At the best of times, sir, the Ruinous Powers are unpredictable, their tactics impenetrable. But here they seem outright incomprehensible. They seem to have come to take back Urdesh, and yet they–'

'They what?'

'Even by their inhuman standards, they are behaving like maniacs.'

The tactician looked at Gaunt with an expression Gaunt found curious.

'There is a theory,' said Biota, 'that Anarch Sek has gone insane.'

'And we can tell that how?' asked Gaunt.

Biota chuckled.

'A fair point. But it has become impossible to discern any tactical logic to his campaign. Not in comparison to some of his actions, which have often displayed extraordinary cunning. Many in tacticae and intelligence have concluded that he has suffered a psychotic break. Perhaps he has been psychologically damaged by the need to show obeisance to the Archon. Gaur has humbled him and brought him into line, and that may have been too much for an ego like Sek's. Or perhaps he is ill, or damaged, or corrupted beyond any measure we can understand.'

Biota looked Gaunt directly in the eyes. His gaze was solemn.

'You did that to him, you know? You broke him.'

'I've driven him mad?' asked Gaunt. 'I've triggered this bloodbath?'

'That's not what I'm saying,' said Biota. 'Please, come. The general is waiting for us.'

Designated Billet K700 was a cluster of old worker habs in the Low Keen district. The towering bulk of the Great Hill could be seen above the rooftops, from the yard, a pale shadow in the haze.

When Ban Daur arrived, the yard was already full of trucks off-loading. There were people everywhere, troopers, retinue and Munitorum staffers, all of them milling around, unloading and lugging transportation trunks and stuffed haversacks into the mouldering habs. The yard wasn't large. Cargo-8s had backed up along the approach track, or rumbled into the vacant lots opposite, and people were dismounting and walking the rest of the way rather than wait.

Daur thanked his driver and got down. He felt a slight twinge in his thigh and belly. The wounds he'd taken at the Reach were healed enough for him to be back on his feet, and he'd been exercising regularly, but just getting down from the cab reminded him to take things at a gentle measure. Curth and Kolding had saved his life and repaired his damage, but it was up to him to make sure that work was not undone.

He paused to chat with Obel, and shot a wave across the crowd to his old friend Haller. The site the regiment had been given was clearly dismal, but there was a decent mood. Open air, a breeze, daylight. They'd missed those things.

Mohr, his adjutant, wandered over with Vivvo as soon as he saw him.

'Company present, captain,' Mohr said.

'What does it look like?' asked Daur.

'Basic as feth, sir. What did you expect?'

'No hero's welcome for us, eh?' asked Daur.

'I think this is a hero's welcome,' said Vivvo.

'Then I don't want to know what the Munitorum does if your service has been poor,' replied Mohr.

'We'll make the best of it,' said Daur. He noticed that Vivvo had his eyes on the distance. Vivvo was the chief scout of G Company, and one of the regiment's best, trained by Mkoll himself.

'Something on your mind?' Daur asked him.

Vivvo screwed up his face.

'I don't like the layout much, sir,' he said. 'Our driver mentioned insurgents, even this deep in the old city. A lot of derelict sites in the vicinity. A lot of line of sight.'

Daur nodded.

'Find the chief and express your concerns,' he said. 'Tell him I'm asking.'

'He's probably on it already,' said Mohr.

'No doubt, but we have families here, and civilian staffers. Let's make sure we're thinking in a straight line. Vivvo, it wouldn't hurt to get a detail on watch while you're finding Mkoll.'

Vivvo nodded, and hurried off.

Daur wandered through the crowd. He passed E Company unpacking from the backs of their transports. The bulk of the material being unloaded by all the companies that had arrived so far was in the form of long metal munition crates, but it wasn't ammunition. The Reach mission and the boarding repulse between them had run the regiment's munition supply down to almost zero. They were awaiting a full restock from the Munitorum now they were on-planet. But the long munition cases, sturdy and khaki, made robust carry-boxes for all kinds of kit, clothing and personal effects, and both the companies and the retinue had salvaged crates in bulk for reuse during the disembarkation phase.

Daur nodded to Banda and Leyr, but ignored the cocksure smile that Meryn sent his way. He saw Meryn turn away, laugh, and make some private remark to Didi Gendler.

At the door of the nearest unit, he found Criid, Domor and Mklure.

'Your mob's in unit six,' Criid told him. Daur took a glance at the layout on the screen of her data-slate.

'You've got everyone arranged?' he asked.

She nodded.

'No favours, no privileges,' she said. 'So no arguing about who's got the best billet. Orders from the top. Everyone takes what they get.'

'Not that there's a lot of choice,' said Captain Mklure. 'There aren't any plum facilities. It's all much of a muchness.'

'It'll do,' said Domor.

Daur nodded. He could smell mildew-laden air exhaling from the doorway.

'I've sandwiched retinue blocks in the middle floors of each unit,' said Criid. 'Seemed like the best way to secure them and the buildings. There's a cookhouse, but we can't find any fuel for the stoves.'

'Munitorum says that's on its way,' said Domor, 'along with the fething ammo restock. Supply trucks should be here by late afternoon.'

Criid made a note.

'Excuse me,' she said. She pushed a way through the lines of troopers lugging cargo into the unit, and crossed the yard. She'd just spotted Felyx Chass and his minder.

Felyx saluted her as she came up. Maddalena just eyed her sullenly.

'Before you ask,' said Criid, 'I've assigned your charge a room of his own. Two bunks. Unit four, with the rest of E Company. I hope that's sufficient.'

Maddalena nodded.

'This place is unfit,' she said.

'We get what we get,' said Criid.

'I didn't mean the venue,' said Maddalena. 'I meant the site itself. It's open. Wide open.'

'I agree. We're setting up a perimeter,' said Criid.

'What's that way?' asked Maddalena, pointing. East of the hab units, there was rubble waste around the ruins of an old cement works, with another row of shabby worker domiciles beyond. Through the rusty chain-link fences, they could see Guardsmen in grey fatigues playing campball and sacking out in the feeble sun.

Criid checked her slate.

'That's another billet section,' she said. 'Seven Hundred and Two. Helixid Thirtieth. Someone should wander over later and greet their CO, just to be neighbourly.'

She glanced aside and noticed Dalin loitering nearby, his pack on his back.

'Need something?' Criid asked.

Dalin shrugged.

'Then I'm sure you've got something to do,' said Criid.

'Yes, captain,' said Dalin. It was obedient, but Criid was amused by the wink of pride she saw as Dalin said it.

'Get on then,' said Criid.

'He's your son, isn't he?' asked Maddalena abruptly.

Criid looked at her.

'I raised him, yes. Him and his sister.'

Maddalena pursed her lips.

'He is attentive to Felyx,' said Maddalena. 'Very attentive. Always around.'

'I think that might be because Gaunt ordered him to be,' replied Criid. 'To keep an eye on him. They're about the same age.'

'I keep an eye on Felyx,' said the lifeward.

Criid forced a smile. She didn't like the woman. She'd known too many of her breed – aristo or aristo staff – in Vervunhive, back in the day. Snooty fethers. She could feel that Maddalena didn't like her high-born charge mixing with the son of a common habber. Worse, an ex-ganger still sporting the crew tatts. Tona Criid couldn't quite understand what Gaunt saw in her... Except she could. Thanks to juvenat work, Maddalena looked very much like the beautiful Merity Chass, whose high-hive image had been such a common sight in the Vervunhive data-streams. The most famous and celebrated woman in Vervunhive, heir to the city.

That was a life Tona had left a long time behind her, a life she had been glad to leave. Now she had to look at its most famous face every day.

'Dalin?' Criid called out. Dalin had been walking away, but he turned back.

'Maybe you could show Felyx and his lifeward to their billet?' Criid said. 'Help him with his bags. Get him settled in.'

Dalin nodded. Criid showed him the location on her slate.

'This way,' said Dalin. Felyx picked up his kitbag and followed. Maddalena walked after them, casting Criid a dirty look that Criid enjoyed very much.

Criid spotted a lone figure down by the chain-link fence overlooking the Helixid compound, and jogged over.

'What you doing here, Yoncy?' she asked.

The little girl was watching the soldiers playing campball.

'You should get indoors, sweet,' Criid said. 'Go find Juniper and Urlinta.'

'My head itches, Mumma,' said Yoncy, scratching her scalp. Criid took a look. Lice again. The close quarters of the *Armaduke* had never let them get free of them. There'd be carbolic and anti-bac showers for the whole company, and a few heads shaved, otherwise this new billet would be infested too.

Criid glanced at the billet, and reflected that it probably had lice of its own.

'They're going to die, Mumma,' Yoncy said.

'Who are, sweet?' Criid asked.

Yoncy pointed through the rusty links at the figures kicking the ball around.

'Them soldiers,' she said.

'What do you mean?' Criid asked.

'They're soldiers,' said Yoncy. 'Soldiers all die.'

'Not all soldiers,' Criid assured her, and gave her an encouraging hug.

Yoncy seemed to think about that. The hem of her little dress shivered in the breeze.

'No,' she said, 'but those ones will.'

'Let's get you inside,' Criid said. 'Juniper will wonder where you are.'

There was a sound like a twig snapping.

Criid looked around. It had been a high, distinctive sound above the murmur of the regiment behind her.

She looked back at the soldiers in the distance. They'd stopped their game. Some were looking around as if they'd lost the ball. Two had run over to a man who'd clearly been brought down by an overenthusiastic tackle.

'He fell down, Mumma,' said Yoncy.

There was another crack. This time, Criid saw the man go over. He'd been standing over the man on the ground, shouting something. She saw the puff of red as he twitched and fell.

Criid turned and yelled.

'Shooter! Shooter!'

FOURTEEN

LINE OF FIRE

Ban Daur turned. He'd heard someone shouting. There was a lot of noise around him, the chatter of off-duty ease, but this had been fiercer. Urgent.

He turned and looked. He saw Tona running towards him from the fence line. She was carrying Yoncy in her arms.

What the gak was she shouting?

He saw her mouth move. He read her lips.

'Shooter!' Daur yelled. 'Shooter! Shooter! Get to cover now!'

The off-loading personnel around him scattered. Several took up the cry. Daur saw people ducking behind trucks and cargo loads, or fleeing through the doorways of the hab units. Panic, mayhem, like a pot of ball bearings poured onto a hard floor spinning in all directions. Children started to cry as the retinue womenfolk snatched them up and ran with them.

Tona reached him. Daur's rifle was still in the truck, but he'd drawn his sidearm.

'Where is he?' Daur asked.

'Feth knows,' Criid snapped. 'He's looping kill-shots into the yard next door. Two of those Helixid boys are down, at least.'

'Medic!' Daur yelled.

'Don't be mad!' Criid snarled at him. 'No one's going to make it across to them alive. It's wide open!'

Daur heard a snap-crack. No mistaking that. Distant, though. Where the gak was it coming from?

Mkoll ran up, pushing through the last of the stragglers jostling to get through the hab doorway. There were people prone all around the yard and the approach track, down in the dirt or cowering behind cover. Some troopers were scrambling in the back of trucks for their weapons.

'Angle?' Mkoll asked directly, unshipping his rifle.

'Not clear,' said Criid. She was struggling with Yoncy. The child was sobbing and squirming. 'East side, towards the old ruin.'

She pointed towards the derelict cement works.

Mkoll tapped his microbead.

'East side,' he said. 'Past the access track.'

At the end of the yard, near the mouth of the track, someone opened up. A burst of auto.

'What the feth?' Mkoll snarled. He started to run in that direction, across

the open yard. Major Pasha, Mklure and Domor broke into a sprint after
him.

'Ban!' said Criid. 'Can you take Yoncy? Get her inside?'

Daur looked at her. She had her rifle looped over her left shoulder, and
that was going to be a lot more useful than his sidearm. He took the child
from her. She was surprisingly heavy. He felt the effort strain painfully at
his freshly healed wounds.

'Go with Uncle Ban,' Criid said, and ran off across the yard.

'Come on, Yonce,' Daur said, his arms around the kid. 'Come inside with me.'

She was crying and thrashing. What was that she was saying, over and
over?

Bad shadow?

'Make room!' Daur yelled. People packed the doorway. He had to force
his way in.

Mkoll reached the trucks parked along the end of the yard, and slid into
cover with men from E Company. Didi Gendler was on his feet at the end
of one truck. He let off another burst of full auto. Las-bolts swooped and
spat across the vacant lot.

'Cease that!' Mkoll yelled.

'I can see the bastard,' Gendler replied, taking aim again.

'Didi reckons he can see him,' Meryn said, sidelong to Mkoll.

'He's a fething idiot,' Mkoll said to Meryn. He looked past him at the E
Company sergeant.

'Gendler, stop fething shooting!' he yelled.

Gendler paused, and glanced back. His face was flushed pink and sweaty.

'He's in the cement works,' he hissed.

'We can't fething track him if we can't hear him,' Banda said. She was
crouching behind the rear wheels, stripping her long-las out of its weather-
case.

'We need to be able to hear,' Mkoll said very firmly.

Pasha, Mklure and Domor dropped in beside them.

Everyone listened. The only sound was the hiss of the breeze, the wailing
of startled children and the murmur of everyone in cover.

There was a muffled crack.

'Cement works. High up,' said Banda. Mkoll nodded.

'I damn well said so,' said Gendler.

'Get your mouth shut tight,' Domor told him.

Banda wriggled up for a look. She ran her long-las out over the rear fender
and snapped in a cell.

'Firing away from us,' said Pasha quietly. 'Firing down at the other habs,
not us. The wind's cupping it.'

Banda bit her lip and nodded. Major Pasha had been scratch company.
She was an old hand at reading the sound-prints of gunfire in an urban
environment.

Larkin and Criid ran up and dropped in beside Mkoll. Larkin had his
long-las.

Mkoll signalled the old marksman to go up and around the front of the truck. Larkin nodded, and made his way on his hands and knees. Banda was hunting through her scope, moving her mag-sight from one blown-out window of the cement works to the next.

'No movement,' she whispered.

'Fether's probably upped and gone now,' mumbled Larkin from the far end. 'Opportunist. His job's done for the day.'

Mkoll shook his head.

'We'd have seen him move. That's open ground all the way to the wire.'

'So we flush the fether out,' said Gendler. He got off his haunches and sprayed another burst of fire over the engine cowling of the cargo-8.

'I'm going to fething gut you,' said Domor, slamming Gendler against the truck's side panels.

'Get off him,' barked Meryn, grabbing Domor's arm. 'Get the feth off!'

'Shut the feth up!' said Mkoll.

The cab window beside him blew out in a flurry of lucite. Another shot spanked through the truck's canvas cover. Everyone huddled hard.

'You feth-bag shit,' Domor said, his hands clamping Gendler's throat to keep him pinned. 'You've got his attention. Now we're the target!'

Three more shots tore into the cargo-8 sheltering them, and the one beside it. Larkin swore and ducked. A pool driver nearby squealed as shards of glass punctured his cheek and eyelid. Criid and Meryn dragged the man into cover under a wheel-well. He was bleeding profusely.

'Can you get a shot?' Pasha hissed to Larkin and Banda.

Larkin reset his position, his head low.

'Stand by,' he said.

'You see any flash?' Banda called to him.

Another round tore through the truck's canvas cover.

'Top row. Second window from the left,' Larkin replied. 'My angle's not good.'

'Mine is,' said Banda. Her long-las banged. Everyone was down too tight to see where the shot impacted. Banda paused, and then fired again.

'Hit?' Pasha asked.

'Not sure, ma'am,' replied Banda.

'Conserve, don't waste,' said Mkoll. 'We've got feth-all ammo left.'

'Yeah, I'm running on nothing,' said Larkin.

Criid looked at Meryn. Between them, the pool driver was sobbing and wailing, and Meryn was trying to irrigate his eye wound with bright yellow counterseptic wash from his field kit.

'Have you got anything? In the truck?' she asked.

'No fething idea,' replied Meryn, struggling to keep the man still. 'Fething nothing, is my guess.'

'Find out!' Mkoll snapped.

'Didi,' Meryn hissed, looking over his shoulder, 'do as the chief says!'

Didi Gendler shot Meryn a 'feth you' look, then reluctantly squirmed around to the tailgate. Larkin and Banda both cracked off shots. Gendler bellied up into the truck's rear, muttering curses, and began to rummage.

A shot ripped through the cargo-8's side wall, and they heard him swear colourfully.

'You hit, Didi?' Meryn shouted.

'Gak you, no,' they heard Gendler retort. More rummaging sounds.

'I can't get a good angle on that fether,' Larkin complained.

'There's a thirty in here!' Gendler called out. 'A thirty and its stand.'

'Ammo?' called Mkoll.

'No ammo!'

'Get it out, get it down!' Mkoll said. A .30 calibre support weapon could take the lid off the entire target structure. Gendler began to slide the carry cases to the tailgate. Pasha and Domor crawled around to lug them down.

'I think there's ammo for the thirty in one of the tail-end trucks,' said Meryn.

'Which one?' asked Criid.

Meryn looked around.

'Mkteesh? You were on loading. Which one?'

The Tanith trooper cowering nearby nodded. 'Third one down, captain,' he said.

'Go fetch!' Meryn ordered.

'I'm with you,' Captain Mklure said. He and Mkteesh got up, waited for another crack from Banda's rifle, then began to run down the line of vehicles, heads low, scurrying.

Domor, Gendler and Major Pasha unboxed the .30 behind the rear wing of the truck. Criid heard another crack. She turned in time to see Mkteesh topple and fall. Desperately, Mklure started trying to drag him into cover, but Criid could see the man was already dead.

Mkteesh had fallen to his left, against the side of the cargo-8 two back from the one they were cowering behind.

To his left.

He'd been hit from the right.

'Feth,' Criid hissed.

'We've got another one!' she yelled. 'Behind us!'

A second sniper had begun firing from somewhere in the derelict fabricatory that overlooked the front of the K700 billets. He had the whole yard spread out in front of him, including the line of trucks that were providing cover from the first shooter. They were pinned.

Everyone on the yard and the approach road tried to move to better cover. They crawled under vehicles or attempted to dash to the old hab blocks. A Munitorum aide went down halfway across the yard. A Ghost was smacked off his feet a few metres from a pile of crates. Criid saw a woman from the retinue sprawl sideways, ungainly.

'Feth!' Larkin said as he struggled to improve his position. 'That's more than one shooter! Two, maybe three more!'

Shots rained into the yard, sparking off the bodywork of the trucks. Some kicked up grit from the yard, or chipped dust out of the hab walls. A window shattered. A man from J Company was hit as he fled towards the latrine block. A squad mate ran to him and tried to drag his body out of the open. A shot took off the top of his head, and dropped him across his friend's body.

As if encouraged by the increased fire rate from this second angle, the sniper in the cement works began firing again. The truck that was sheltering them started to shudder as shots tore into it from both directions.

'Screw this,' Mkoll murmured. Major Pasha, under the truck's rear fender with the half-assembled .30, called out in alarm, but Mkoll was already up and running across the yard towards the hab.

Criid got up and ran after him.

Sustained shots from the fabricatory punched into the front of hab unit four, blowing the glass out of ratty windows and drilling holes through the aged masonry. Two men were hit in the crowd that had packed into the stairwell for cover, and another was clipped in the hab doorway. A tinker from the retinue collapsed in a third storey block room. The round had gone through the exterior wall before hitting him, and it still felled him with enough force to break his femur. People were shrieking and yelling, and children were screaming. Troopers wedged in the crowds that choked the lower hallways began to kick out the hab's rear doors in the hope that people would be able to exit into the back lot and find better cover there.

On the third floor, shots whipped into the room assigned for Felyx Chass, shattering the window. Maddalena threw herself over Felyx, tackling him to the floor. Dalin ducked behind the bunk.

Maddalena looked fiercely at Dalin.

'Get him out! The back stairs!' she yelled.

'To where?' Dalin asked.

'Anywhere out of the line of fire, you idiot!' Maddalena snapped. 'You want to be his special friend? I'm trusting you!'

'But where are you–'

Maddalena flipped the cover off her powerful sidearm, and drew it so fast Dalin didn't even see a blur.

'I'm ending this stupidity,' she replied. She bundled Felyx up, and shoved him at Dalin. Dalin grabbed the young man and rushed him out into the hallway, his hand pressed to the back of Felyx's skull to keep him low. He glanced back, in time to see Maddalena take a run up and jump through the window.

Maddalena landed in the yard like a cat. Augmetic bone and muscle absorbed the impact. She rose, men fleeing for cover all around her, and fired a tight burst up at the fabricatory. The boom of her Tronsvass echoed around the yard, and caused more panic. She broke into a sprint and covered the yard. Her speed was inhuman.

Criid and Mkoll had reached the back wall of the fabricatory ruin. Zhukova, Nessa and Vivvo arrived too, from different parts of the yard, desperately slamming into cover, backs to the brickwork. Under the line of the mouldering wall, they were close to the shooters, but tight under their angle of fire.

Mkoll signed to Vivvo and Nessa – *right*.

They nodded, and began to edge that way. Nessa had her long-las, and Mkoll knew she had a decent personal reserve of ammo for it. She had been injured early on at the Reach, and had expended little.

Mkoll looked around at Zhukova and Criid. Zhukova was flushed and breathing hard. Her sprint from the south-west end of the billet yard had been frantic and bold.

Mkoll indicated an access point to their left. They nodded, and began to slide down the wall towards it. Shots echoed in the air above them.

Definitely three, Mkoll signed.

The access point was a filthy chute where a rainwater pipe had once run. The brickwork was rotten and slick with wet dirt, but there was a low roof three metres up, the sloped gutter line of an annex or storeroom. Zhukova jammed her back to the wall, and made a stirrup of her hands. Mkoll didn't hesitate. He put his left boot in her hands, his left hand on her shoulder, and let her boost him to the rooftop. Zhukova grunted. A moment to check he wasn't going to get his face shot off, and Mkoll hauled himself onto the sloping roof, belly-down.

Criid immediately took Zhukova's place, and hoisted the Verghast captain with her cupped hands. Mkoll grabbed Zhukova's outstretched arms, and dragged her onto the roof beside him.

Keeping low, they looked around. The sloped roof led up to the lower main roof, which was flat and littered with the rusty wreckage of toppled vox-masts. Beyond that, there was a row of glassless windows. Mkoll pointed, and Zhukova nodded. She turned to look back at Criid, hoping to reach down and pull her up, but Criid had already moved around the corner of the block, looking for another way up.

Mkoll and Zhukova crawled up the slope towards the windows.

At the right-hand end of the building, Vivvo and Nessa shouldered open a rotting door, and slipped into the fabricatory's interior. It was a vast, dark space, crammed with junk, lit only by the daylight that shafted in through holes in the roof. The floor was thick with birdlime, and old, galvanic generators, rusted solid, loomed like parked vehicles. Nessa got her long-las to her shoulder, and started to pan around the roof. Vivvo guided her forwards, his lasrifle ready at his chest.

They edged through a half-open sliding shutter into a larger space. More rubble, more burned-out machine units. The roof was partly glazed, and the glass was filthy and fogged. Their entry scared up a flock of roosting birds that broke in a rush, and began to circle and mob around the rafters. The movement made Nessa start, but she eased her finger off the trigger the moment she saw what it was. Vivvo could hear the dull thump of shots from above them. He knew Nessa couldn't, but he signed to her, and indicated direction. She nodded. They stalked forwards a little further.

Another shot. Vivvo swung his head around, scanning the ceiling. Another shot, then another. This time, he saw the brief flash reflection on the dirty glass high above him. He pointed. They could just make out a heavy chimney assembly on the midline of the roof, through the filth coating the cracked windows. Was that a vent or...?

No, a figure, huddled down in position against the chimney block.

Nessa grabbed Vivvo, steering him until he was facing the distant shape. She rested her long-las across his right shoulder, using him as a prop, and crouched a little to improve her angle. Vivvo turned his head away, and plugged his right ear with his finger.

Nessa fired. One shot. A panel of glass blew out far above them, raining chips of glass down. A second later, the entire roof section collapsed, panes of glass and frame struts alike, as a body crashed down through it.

The falling body hit the rockcrete floor of the fabricatory with a bone-snapping thump. The rifle, a hard-round, Urdeshi-made sniper weapon, struck beside it, splintering the wooden stock.

They scurried over. Neither doubted the shooter was dead. Nessa's shot had taken out his spine.

Vivvo rolled him over. He was wearing a filthy Munitorum uniform and a patched cloak. Around his throat, wet with blood, was a gold chain with an emblem. A face, made of gold, with a hand clamped across the mouth.

The Sons of Sek.

Criid stalked into a rubble-choked alley at the left-hand end of the fab. Her lasrifle was at her shoulder, ready to fire, and she swung slowly and carefully as she prowled forwards, hunting for movement and hiding spots.

The rate of fire coming from above her was still steady.

She heard movement behind her, and wheeled. Maddalena Darebeloved ran into view, gun in hand. Criid blinked. She didn't know anything human could run that fast, or achieve that length of stride.

'Go back!' Criid hissed.

Maddalena ignored her. A flash of red in her bright body glove, the Vervunhive lifeward ran past her, vaulted onto the top of a fuel drum and sprang onto the roof. She'd cleared about three metres in one running bound.

Criid wanted to yell after her not to be an idiot, but shouting was just asking for trouble.

Furiously, she ran after her, scrambling up onto the drum, and then straining hard to drag herself up onto the roof. The augmetic, transhuman bitch had done it in one leap, and made it look easy.

Criid made the roof, and rolled into cover as soon as she got there.

'Maddalena!' she hissed. '*Maddalena!*'

Hunched behind a ventilation cowling, she surveyed the roof. It was a multi-gabled expanse, caked in lichen. Chimney stacks rose like trees from the ridges and furrows of ragged tiles immediately around her. Beyond, the incline of the roof grew steeper, forming the higher central section of the fabricatory's structure. This section had been planked out with flakboard and metal sheeting, presumably at some point in the past when the old tiles had decayed. The building had been abandoned at some point after that, and even the planking was loose and sagging under its own weight. Criid saw exposed rafters where whole portions had collapsed.

Far ahead, she spotted another flash of red. Maddalena had made it as far as the main roof, and was darting like a high-wire performer along the parapet. She had to have vaulted several metres more just to get up there. She was fast, but holy gak, had she never heard of cover?

Criid shifted position, and then dropped down again fast. A las-bolt blew the pot off the chimney stack beside her. Dust and earthenware fragments showered her. She'd been spotted, which was ironic, as she wasn't the one leaping about in the open, wearing bright red.

Another shot whined over her head. She grappled to get her lasrifle around, but she was crumpled in tight cover and the effort was too awkward. She let go of her rifle, and unbuckled her sidearm from the holster strapped to her chest webbing. Hunched as low as possible, she snaked her arm around the side of the chimney stack, and spat off a series of shots in the vague direction of the source of fire.

Two more heavy rifle shots came her way. Then she heard a clattering burst of fire from a large handgun.

Silence.

She risked a look. There was no sign of anyone, and no more shooting. On hands and knees, she wriggled forwards as fast as she could, heading for the next clump of chimney stacks.

Mkoll and Zhukova kept low and ran up the long incline of the roof. They reached a deep rainwater channel choked with waste, and then scaled the low ledge of the overhang and slid into cover behind a buttress. Spools of loose wire were staked along the lip of the roof, perhaps to deter roosting birds or perhaps just a relic of some previous phase of conflict. Feathers had caught on the wire, and the stakes were caked in birdlime. Mkoll worked one of the stakes free and made a gap that both of them could slither through.

Up ahead, repeated shots were ringing from the stout belfry that had once summoned fabricatory workers to their daily shifts.

Mkoll signed to Zhukova to move right. He went left. It was a poor and improvised way of staging a pincer, but the shooter in the belfry was clearly not going to stop firing into the yard until he ran out of munitions.

Zhukova crawled past the rusted drums and gears of machine heads that poked clear of the roof line, ancient bulk hoists that had once conveyed product from one of the fab's interiors to the other. She could still see Mkoll, sliding low across a section of galvanised roof plate. She had an angle on the belfry, good enough to see the muzzle flashes lighting up the oval window on its north side, but she couldn't get a draw on the shooter. She willed him to move, to adjust to a new position. Just a moment of exposure, that was all she'd need.

Mkoll had reached the base of the belfry on the opposite side to the shooter's vantage point. He signed to Zhukova – *sustained*.

She nodded back, adjusted her grip on her weapon, and lined up. She waited as Mkoll started to haul himself up the outside of the belfry, clawing up the old brickwork with fingers and toes. He reached the window on the opposite side to the shooter.

Time for a distraction.

Zhukova started to fire. She peppered the stonework around the shooter's slot with shots, splintering the stone surround and the window's ornate frame, and raising a billowing cloud of dust. The shooter stopped firing, and ducked back to avoid glancing injury. He was probably surprised to come under fire from such a tight angle. Zhukova fired some more, then paused to check on Mkoll.

There was no sign of the chief scout. During her distraction fire, he must have crawled in through the other window. Zhukova tensed, and started shooting again. More distraction was needed, fast.

She peppered the window area again. Her ammo was low.

Mkoll slid down into the darkness of the belfry, silent. The air was close and dusty, and stank of gunsmoke. He could hear Zhukova's suppressing fire cracking against the far side of the small tower. He squinted to adjust his eyes to the darkness after the bright daylight outside. Movement, beyond the jumble of boxes. A man crouching to get ammo clips out of a canvas satchel.

Mkoll was about to shoot. The man was only two metres away, and hadn't seen him.

Mkoll hesitated. The man wasn't the shooter. Though he couldn't see directly, Mkoll was aware of a second man just out of sight around the corner in the alcove facing the other window. The man he could see had no rifle. He was the loader, fetching fresh clips to feed the shooter at the window. If he shot him, the other guy would react and that would lead to the sort of tight-confine firefight Mkoll considered distinctly disadvantageous.

Mkoll slung his rifle and drew his blade. Using the darkness and the low beams as cover, he edged around the belfry dome and grabbed the loader from behind. Hand over mouth, straight silver between the third and fourth ribs. A moment of silent spasm, and the man went limp. Mkoll set him down gently.

Zhukova's firing had stopped. She was probably out of ammo. Mkoll heard the shooter call out.

'Eshbal vuut!' *More ammo, fast!*

'Eshett!' he called back. *Coming!*

He picked up the heavy satchel, and moved towards the alcove. The shooter was crouching in the window slot, his back to him. He was clutching his heavy, long-build autorifle, reaching a hand back insistently for a reload.

He started to turn. Mkoll hurled the satchel at him. The weight of it knocked the man back against the window. One-handed, Mkoll put two rounds into him with his lasgun before he could get back up.

Mkoll picked up the shooter's autorifle, and threw it through the window.

'Clear!' he yelled.

Captain Mklure slithered into cover beside the cargo-8. He was clutching two drums of ammo for the .30. He was soaked with Mkteesh's blood.

Major Pasha grabbed one of the drums, and locked it into position on top of the assembled support weapon. Domor already had his hands on the spade grips, and was turning it to face the cement works.

'Locked!' Pasha yelled.

Domor opened fire. The weapon let out a chattering roar like a piece of industrial machinery. The upper floor of the cement works began to pock and stipple. Black holes like bruises or rust-spots on fruit started to appear, clouded by the haze of dust foaming off the impact area. Then the wall began to splinter and collapse. Chunks of rockcrete exploded and blew out, fracturing the upper level of the ruin.

Drum out, Domor eased off the firing stud.

'Load the other one,' he said.

'Did we get him?' asked Pasha.

'Are you joking?' Meryn snorted. 'Shoggy took the top off the building.'

'Wait,' Larkin called out.

They waited, watching. The dust was billowing off the structure in the damp afternoon air.

'You made him scram down a floor,' whispered Larkin, aiming.

'How do you know?' asked Domor.

'I just saw him in a first floor window,' said Larkin. His weapon fired one loud crack.

'And again,' he said, lowering his rifle.

Criid paused. She'd just heard sustained fire from a support weapon. The Ghosts in the yard behind her had finally got something heavy up to tackle the sniper in the cement works.

It was quiet on the roof. There'd been some firing from the west side of the building a couple of minutes before. She presumed that was Mkoll and the Verghastite. Things had gone still since then. She was high up, and the wind coming in across the city buffeted her ears. Maybe they'd dealt with them all, or driven them off.

She heard a sudden crack. A rifle shot. Then a quick burst from an automatic handgun. Another louder, single shot.

Silence.

A figure broke cover on the roof ridge ahead of her. A man in filthy combat fatigues, lugging a scoped long gun. He was trying to scramble down her side. Hastily, she whipped up her lasgun and fired, blowing out roof tiles on the ridge to his left.

He flinched and spotted her, swinging his rifle up to fire. He got off one round that missed her cheek by a finger's length. Criid put three rounds through his upper body. He jerked a hammer-blow shock with each one, then pitched sideways. His limp body, almost spread-eagled, slid down the incline of the roof towards her, and rolled into a heap at the foot.

Her rifle up to her shoulder and aiming, Criid hurried forwards. The shooter was dead. No need to even check. Were there any more?

She went around the edge of the slope via a parapet onto a stretch of flat roof beyond. The space was jumbled with abandoned extractor vents, all rusting and pitted, and stacks of broken window frames lined up against the low lip of the roof.

No one in sight. She decided to circle back and find Mkoll and Vivvo.

She heard a sound. A chip of glass tinkling as it dislodged and fell.

She looked back at the stacks of window frames. She saw the foot sticking out.

She ran to it.

Maddalena Darebeloved lay on her back in the pile of frames. She'd crushed and shattered them. There were fragments of glass everywhere. Her weapon was still in her hand, but it was locked out and empty. Her face was as red as her bodysuit, glazed with blood that also matted her hair. She'd been hit twice by long gun fire. The first wound was to her hip, and it was cripplingly nasty, but probably not lethal. The second, to her head, was a kill shot.

Her eyes were still wide open. Droplets of blood clung to her eyelashes.

'Oh, feth,' Criid murmured.

Maddalena blinked.

Criid scrambled down beside her, ignoring the pain as glass chips dug into her knees and shins.

'Hold still! Hold still!' she said. 'I'll get a medic!' How was the woman still alive with a wound like that?

Maddalena was staring at the sky. She let out a sigh or a moan that seemed to empty her lungs.

'I'll get a medic!' Criid told her, fumbling in her pack for a dressing or anything she could pack the wound with.

'Criid–' Maddalena said. Her voice was tiny, her lips barely moving. It was almost just a shallow breath.

'I'll get a medic,' Criid reassured her.

'Look after–'

'What?' Criid bent to hear, her ear to Maddalena's lips. Blood bubbled as the lifeward spoke.

'Look after...' Maddalena repeated. 'You have children. You know. You know how. You–'

'Stop talking.'

'Felyx. Please look–'

Her voice was almost gone.

'Stay with me!' Criid said, trying to get the dressing packed across the head wound.

'You have children. Don't let her–'

'Who? Do you mean Yoncy? What about Yoncy?'

'Promise me you'll look after Felyx. Protect Felyx.'

'What? Stay with me!'

'Promise me.'

'I promise.'

Maddalena blinked again.

'Good, then,' she said. And was gone.

FIFTEEN

STAFF

Gaunt followed Biota through the halls of the Urdeshic Palace. The tactician seemed little inclined to speak further.

There were guards posted at every corner and doorway: Urdeshi in full colours, Narmenians with chrome breastplates and power staves, Keyzon siege-men in heavy armour. The fortress was pale stone and draughty. Footsteps echoed, and the wind murmured in the empty halls. Walls had been stripped of paintings, and floors of carpets. Rush matting and thermal-path runners had been laid down to line thoroughfares. The old galvanic lighting had been removed and replaced with lumen globes.

Biota swept down a long, curved flight of stone steps, and threw open the doors of a long undercroft with a ribbed stone roof. The undercroft was full of men, standing in informal huddles, talking. They all looked around and glared as the doors opened.

Biota didn't break stride, walking the length of the chamber towards the double doors at the far end without giving the men a second glance.

Gaunt followed him. He was aware of the eyes on him. The men, in a wide variety of Astra Militarum uniforms that generally featured long dark storm coats or cloaks, watched him as he walked past. There were a hundred or more, and not a single one of them below the rank of general or field commander. By a considerable margin, Gaunt was the lowest ranking person in the room.

Biota reached the end doors. Made of weighty metal, of ornate design, they were decorated with etched steel and elaborate gilt fixtures. Gaunt reflected that they were probably one of the fortress' original features, ancient doors that had felt the knock of kings, and seen the passing of dynast chieftains and sector lords. It was better, he felt, to reflect on that notion than on the thought of the combined authority of the eyes watching him fiercely.

Biota knocked once, then opened the left-hand door. Gaunt smelt the smoke of lho-sticks and cigars. He entered as Biota beckoned him, and then realised that Biota had shut the door behind him without following.

The chamber was large, and draped in wall-hangings and battle standards, some fraying with age and wear. A draught was coming from somewhere, fluttering the naked flames of torches set in black metal tripods around the circumference of the room. In the dancing glow, Gaunt could see the inscriptions on the wall, proclaiming this chamber to be the war room of the Collegia Bellum Urdeshi.

The floors were a gloss black stone that contrasted with the paler stone of the rest of the old fortress. They were covered in lists, lists etched in close-packed lines and then infilled with hammered gold wire. Legends of battle, military campaigns, rolls of honour.

There was a vast semicircular table in the centre of the room, its straight edge facing him and the door. The table was wooden, and looked as if it was a half-section of a single tree trunk, lacquered and varnished to a deep gleaming brown. A cluster of lumen globes hovered over it. Above them, in a ring around the table space, twenty small cyberskulls floated in position, their eyes glowing green, their sculpted silver faces mumbling and chattering quietly.

Thirty people sat at the table around the curved side. They were all staring at him. A thirty-first seat stood, vacant, at the centre of them.

Gaunt recognised them all. Their ranks and power, at least. Some he knew by pict and file reports, some from commissioned paintings. Some he knew personally. To the left, Grizmund, his old ally from Verghast, now a full lord general by the braid on his collar and sleeves. Grizmund nodded a curt greeting to Gaunt.

'Step forward, Bram,' said Van Voytz, with a casual gesture. He had a cigar clenched in the fist that beckoned, and the smoke rose in a lazy yellow haze through the lumen glow, reminding Gaunt of the creep of toxin gas on battlefields. Van Voytz was sitting to the left of the vacant chair.

Gaunt stepped forwards, facing the straight edge of the table. He took off his cap, tucked it under his arm, and made the sign of the aquila.

'Colonel-Commissar Ibram Gaunt of the Tanith First, returned to us,' said Van Voytz.

A murmur ran around the table.

'The Emperor protects,' said Lord Militant Cybon. 'I am heartened to see your safe delivery, Gaunt.'

Gaunt glanced at the massive, augmeticised warlord. Cybon's haggard face, braced with bionic artifice, was deadpan. Torch light glinted off the jet carrion-bird emblems at his throat.

'Thank you, sir,' Gaunt said.

'It's been a while,' said Lord General Bulledin, broad and grey-bearded. 'A while indeed. Monthax, was it?'

'Just prior to Hagia, I believe, lord.'

'Ah, Hagia,' said Bulledin with a dark chuckle. The chuckle was echoed by others at the table.

'Things work out for the best, in the end,' said another lord general further around the semicircle. Bulledin glanced his way.

'You're living testament to that, my friend,' he said archly.

The man he was speaking to simpered some retort as if it were all barrack room banter. Gaunt glanced his way. He saw that the man was Lugo. He stiffened. Lugo looked older, much older, than he had the last time Gaunt had seen him, as if age had sandblasted him. He wore the rich brocade of a lord militant general, perhaps the most showy of the various uniforms in the room. A lord general again, Gaunt thought. Times have moved on.

'You have a report for us, Bram,' said Van Voytz.

'I have, sir,' said Gaunt. He took his encrypted data-slate from his pocket. 'If you're all ready to receive.'

'We are,' said Cybon. He lifted a wand to alter the setting of the cyberskulls. They began to whirr and murmur, erecting a crypto-field that insulated the chamber from all prying eyes, ears and sensors. Gaunt activated the slate, and forwarded his confidential report to the data machines in the room. The lord generals took out or picked up their various devices. Some began to read.

'A personal summary, I think, Bram,' said Van Voytz, ignoring his own data-slate, which lay beside his ashtray on the table.

'By order of high command,' said Gaunt, 'specifically the authority of Lord Militant General Cybon and Lord Commissar Mercure of the Officio Prefectus, my regiment departed Balhaut in 781 relative. Target destination was an Archenemy manufacturing base in the Rimworld Marginals.'

'Salvation's Reach,' said Bulledin.

'Indeed, sir,' said Gaunt. 'The objective was threefold. To neutralise the enemy's manufacturing capacity, to retrieve, where possible, data and materials for examination, and to create prejudicial disinformation that would destabilise the enemy host.'

'Of which,' said Cybon, 'the third was the most particular. The Reach mission was part of a greater programme of false flag operations.'

'This devised,' said Bulledin, 'by you, Cybon, and by Mercure?'

'And sanctioned by the Warmaster,' replied Cybon. 'But the germ of the notion came from Gaunt.'

'By way of an enemy combatant,' said Lugo. He glanced at Gaunt, his eyes glittering. 'That's right, isn't it? There was a high-value enemy asset involved?'

Gaunt cleared his throat. He had a feeling he knew which way this could turn.

'A high-value asset is only high value if that value is used, sir,' he replied. 'The enemy officer had surrendered to our forces. A change of heart. He had been one of us, originally. He offered information.'

'To you?' asked Lugo.

'He trusted me.'

Several of the lords militant muttered.

'I can make no sense of that remark that is comforting,' said Lugo. 'Or that reflects well on either side of this war.'

'The truth can often be uncomfortable, sir,' said Gaunt.

'Why did he trust you, Colonel-Commissar Gaunt?'

The question came from a cruel-faced woman that Gaunt recognised as Militant Marshal Tzara, het-chieftain of the Keyzon Host, and Mistress of the Seventh Army. Her hair was a fading red, cropped very close, and her crimson cloak was fringed with a ruff of thick animal fur. Metal-wire patterns decorated the armoured front of her high-throated leather jacket.

'Do I need to repeat the question?' she asked.

'He trusted me because he understands warfare, and respects an able commander, marshal,' he said. 'I bested him, on Gereon. I was tasked to eliminate the traitor General Noches Sturm. The asset failed to protect Sturm from my justice. I won his respect.'

'So he brought this plan to you?' asked Bulledin. 'The Archenemy brought this plan to you?'

'I was wary at first, sir,' said Gaunt. 'I still am. I supported the plan only when I had brought it to Lord Cybon and Lord Mercure for consideration.'

'It was mercilessly analysed before we committed,' Cybon rasped. 'Mercilessly.'

'But the theory was to create a division between Gaur and Sek?'

Gaunt looked towards the speaker, a younger man seated towards the right-hand end of the line. This was Lord General Urienz, one of the shining stars of the Sabbat Crusade, a brilliant commander who had risen to glory on the tide of Macaroth's ascendancy. They had never met, and Gaunt was surprised to see him present. He imagined Urienz would be off commanding a warfront of his own, gilding his considerable reputation even further. For twenty years, Vitus Urienz had been marked as the Warmaster in waiting.

He was Gaunt's age. His hair and goatee were black, and his broad face pugnacious, as if he had boxed as a junior officer – boxed without the speed to fend off the blows that had flattened his nose, brows and cheekbones, but with a constitution that had let him soak up punishment without a care. There was menace to him, weight. His uniform was dark blue, tailored and plain. No medals, no cloak, no brocade, no show. Nothing but the simple gold pins of his rank.

'Just so,' said Gaunt. 'Gaur was unassailably powerful among the magisters of the Sanguinary Tribes. He won his rank as Archon through his military ferocity, but also by appeasing his key rivals. Sek, Innokenti, Asphodel, Shebol Red-Hand. He made them trusted lieutenants. It is reasonable to say that Sek was a far more capable military leader. By the time the asset approached me, Sek was ascending, and building his own power base. We knew that rankled with Gaur, and that friction was growing. The proposal was to fully ignite that rivalry, and trigger an internecine war.'

'To make our enemies fight each other, and thus weaken them overall?' asked Lord General Kelso.

'Exactly that, sir,' said Gaunt.

Kelso, venerably old and distinguished in his grey formal uniform, nodded thoughtfully.

'A wild scheme,' said Van Voytz.

'An understatement, old friend,' chuckled Lugo.

'It was inspired madness,' said Cybon quietly, 'even desperation.'

He turned, and looked down the table at Lugo.

'But it damn well worked.'

'In… a manner of speaking,' Lugo admitted.

'In no "manner of speaking", my friend,' said Van Voytz. 'Though we face fury ten years on, it is a different fury. Sek's forces would have broken us eight years ago if they had not been riven. What we face now, to use my friend Cybon's word, is desperation. The frenzy of a corpse that refuses to acknowledge it is dead.'

'A weakness we do not capitalise on,' said Marshal Blackwood. It was the first thing Gaunt had heard the celebrated commander say. Blackwood, in his storm coat, was the only man present who had not removed his cap. He was slim and saturnine, and his tone was a blend of sadness and malice.

'Let's not get back to that,' said Kelso.

'Let's not indeed,' said Bulledin. Blackwood shrugged diffidently.

'It can wait, Artor,' he said.

'It can, Eremiah, and it will,' said Bulledin. 'A more fundamental duty requires our attention before we descend into another round of tactical arguments and bickering. Gaunt's mission, however desperate some of us might consider it, was a success. A success of staggering consequences. It was deemed so back in '84. That was the official report, stamped and sealed by our Warmaster. The Salvation's Reach venture was added to the honour roll of critical actions in this war.'

'It's there on the floor somewhere,' said Cybon with a casual gesture. 'You can read it for yourself, Gaunt.'

'You were presumed lost, colonel-commissar,' said Tzara.

'A warp accident befell us, marshal,' said Gaunt.

'And though you now appear again, as by some miracle, we are conscious of the immense risks–'

'Suicidal,' growled Cybon.

'– immense risks,' Tzara finished, 'that you embraced to achieve it.'

'And the considerable losses you incurred,' added Bulledin.

'You missed it all, Bram,' said Van Voytz. 'In the years you were missing, you were celebrated as an Imperial hero, lost in glory, your name and the name of your regiment to be venerated for all time. There were posthumous citations, feasts in your name, dedications. Glory was heaped upon you, Bram.'

'Only in death, sir,' said Gaunt.

'As is so often the case with our breed,' said Bulledin.

'It is rare for a man to return to see the laurels that were placed upon his tomb,' said Cybon.

'I... thank you, lord,' said Gaunt. He bowed curtly and made the sign of the aquila again. 'I am humbled by your words.'

The marshals and generals glanced at each other. A few chuckled.

'Come now, Bram,' said Van Voytz. 'Take your seat.'

'There is only one, sir,' said Gaunt. 'We are waiting for the Warmaster and–'

'The Warmaster is indisposed, Bram,' said Van Voytz. 'He's busy with his strategising. This seat is not waiting for him.'

Van Voytz rose to his feet.

'In death, Ibram Gaunt,' he said, 'you were commended at the highest level, and awarded with a posthumous rank to honour your deeds and selfless contribution. Now that you have come back to us, alive and whole, it would be the height of disdain to strip you of that rank and pretend it was not earned. Take your seat amongst us, Lord Militant Commander Gaunt.'

They all rose, every one of them shoving back their seats. They began to clap, thirty lords general, marshals, lords militant.

Gaunt blinked.

SIXTEEN

THE INNER CIRCLE

The Munitorum had set up light rigs around the yard of the K700 billet. They cast a foggy white glow that caught the streaking rain. Rawne dismounted from his cargo-4, and walked with Hark and Ludd towards the mobile medicae unit that a Munitorum transporter had hauled in just before dark. Gol Kolea, waiting under the awning, nodded to them.

'What happened?' asked Rawne.

Kolea shrugged.

'Insurgents,' he replied. 'Sons of Sek. Eight dead here, another four over in the neighbouring billet. The Helixid.'

'Feth,' said Rawne.

'Did we get them?' asked Hark.

Kolea nodded.

'We got 'em all,' he said. 'A mess, though. I wasn't on site when it went down, but Pasha says it was a shambles because our ammo was so low. They were scrambling around for munitions.'

'Do we have munitions now?' asked Rawne.

'We've got lights, a food drop and a medical trailer for Curth,' said Kolea. 'No ammo train yet.'

'I'll get onto it,' said Hark.

'We've made repeated calls, Viktor,' said Kolea.

'They haven't heard from me yet, Gol,' Hark said in a soft but dangerous tone. 'I'll get onto it.'

As Hark stalked away, Rawne looked around at the area. He could hear rain beating on the roof of the medicae unit and the plastek awning, and water gurgling down the broken chutes and water pipes of the ancient buildings.

'Did we–' he began.

'I've got perimeter guards and sweep patrols, yes,' said Kolea. 'They won't get at us again.'

'I thought this was a safe city,' said Ludd.

Kolea looked at him.

'Apparently, this is common here,' he said. 'The main front lines are porous. Insurgent cells are getting into the habitation and safe zones.'

Rawne nodded.

'Gaunt?' he asked.

'Still up at staff,' said Kolea. 'We're deciding who gets to talk to him when he gets back.'

Rawne narrowed his eyes quizzically.

Kolea jerked his head towards the medicae unit.

'Probably you, Eli,' he said.

'Why?'

'He hates you anyway,' said Kolea.

Rawne sniffed and walked up to the door of the medicae unit. Ludd shot a puzzled look at Kolea, then followed. He stopped short when he saw Felyx standing with Dalin beside the entrance.

'What are you doing here?' Ludd asked.

'They won't let me see her,' said Felyx.

'He's fine,' said Dalin. 'Let him be.'

'Don't tell me what to do, trooper,' said Ludd. He looked at Felyx again. 'They won't let you see who?' he asked.

Rawne stepped into the cramped medicae unit. Kolding was suturing the face wound of a Munitorum driver. Curth was slotting instruments into an autoclave. She looked up as Rawne entered, her face cold and drawn, then jerked her head towards the nearest of the gurneys racked up in the back-bay of the unit.

Rawne crossed to it, and lifted the end of the sheet.

'Feth,' he said.

'Gone before I got there,' said Curth.

'Who else?' asked Rawne.

'List's on the side there,' said Curth.

There was a thump in the doorway as Criid entered. She handed a set of medical clippers to Curth.

'Thanks,' she said.

'I don't imagine she took it well,' said Curth.

'Yoncy's hair will grow back, Ana,' said Criid.

'You used the salve?'

'Yep. You'll be using those clippers a lot in the next few days,' said Criid.

'I'll do a full inspect,' said Curth. 'I've ordered powders from the depot so we can treat all bedding. Lice should be easier to control here than on the ship.'

Criid noticed Rawne. He was lowering the sheet.

'She was brave,' said Criid. 'Went right for them, defending. Defending the boy, more than anything. Taking out a threat to him. And the regiment, but he was the point. She was fast. Trained for intense close protection. Of course, she knew feth-all about street fighting. And in that red suit...'

'I'll talk to Gaunt,' said Rawne.

'No, I'll do it,' said Criid. 'I was with her at the end.'

'I'll do it,' said Curth. 'It's the chief medicae's job.'

They both looked at her.

'I'll do it,' said Rawne, more firmly.

'Sir?'

Rawne glanced around. Ludd was in the doorway.

'Felyx... that is to say, Trooper Chass, he wants to see the body.'

'There'll be time for that later,' said Curth.

'She was like a mother to him,' said Criid quietly. 'I mean, probably more of a mother than his actual mother. Even if she was a psycho b–'

'Stow that, captain,' said Rawne. He looked at Curth. The medicae took a thoughtful breath, then nodded.

Rawne beckoned Ludd. Ludd brought Felyx up the steps into the trailer. Dalin hovered behind them in the doorway.

Felyx looked especially small and slender, more like a child than ever, Rawne thought. He went across to the gurney where Rawne was standing.

'You don't have to look,' said Curth.

'He does,' said Rawne.

'He probably does, Ana,' said Criid.

'You fething soldiers,' murmured Curth. 'You think horror inoculates against horror.'

'It's called closure, Ana,' said Criid.

'If you ask me, there's far too much of that in the world,' said Curth.

Rawne reached out to lift the edge of the sheet again, but Felyx got there first. Rawne withdrew his hand as Felyx raised the hem of the bloodstained cover.

He stared for a moment at the face staring back up from the cart.

He said something.

'What?' asked Rawne.

Felyx cleared his throat and repeated it.

'Did she suffer?'

'No,' said Criid.

'She was protecting you,' said Rawne. 'That was her job. Her training. Her life.'

'She died protecting me?' asked Felyx.

'Yes.'

'That doesn't make it any better,' said Felyx.

'It was going to happen eventually,' said Rawne.

'Oh, for feth's sake, Eli!' Curth snorted.

'He's right,' said Kolding, from the far side of the trailer. 'A lifeward's life belongs to the one he or she wards. They put themselves in the line of danger.'

'There are ways of doing that...' Criid began.

'What does that mean?' asked Felyx, glancing at her sharply.

'Nothing,' said Criid.

'Tell me what you meant,' said Felyx.

Criid shrugged.

'Your lifeward excelled at close protection. I mean, she was hard-wired trained for it. Sneak attacks, assassinations. In the environment of a court, or a palace, or an up-spire residence, she was built to excel. But she was no soldier. A warzone like this is a very different place. You don't run in, heedless and headlong. You don't rely on speed and reaction alone. You don't wear red and make yourself a target.'

Felyx's lip trembled slightly.

'I'm sorry,' said Criid. 'She was brave.'

'She'll need a funeral,' said Felyx.

'They'll all get funerals,' said Curth. She reached for a data-slate on her crowded workstation. 'The Munitorum has issued interment permits, and assigned spaces in... Eastern Hill Cemetery Two.'

'No,' said Felyx. 'A formal funeral. With a templum service and a proper ecclesiarch to say the litany, not that idiot chaplain of ours. I won't have her laid to rest in some mass war grave zone.'

'Is there something wrong with a military funeral?' asked Rawne.

'Or our fething ayatani?' muttered Criid.

'Felyx,' said Ludd, 'the Astra Militarum provides for all who fall in its service. The services are simple but very honourable. There is a dispensation allowance from the Munitorum–'

'A private service,' said Felyx. 'A private funeral. I have... I have access to funds. Through any counting house here on Urdesh, I can transfer sums from my family holdings. From House Chass. She will have a proper funeral.'

'She died with us,' said Rawne. 'She served with us. She'll be set in the ground with us, in our custom.'

'As has been pointed out, major,' said Felyx, his eyes bright, 'she was not a soldier. She will be buried as I deem fit.'

Rawne seemed to be about to reply, but stopped as Criid gently caught his arm and shook her head.

'Uhm,' Ludd began after a moment. 'I'd request that Trooper Chass be taken into the supervision of the Commissariat for the time being.'

'Your care, you mean?' asked Rawne.

Ludd's face became hard and unfriendly.

'I was charged with the trooper's welfare, given his particular circumstances. With his lifeward gone, there is the matter of his ongoing protection. I will stand as his guardian until–'

'He's part of E Company,' said Dalin from the doorway. 'What are you going to do? Transfer him? He can't have a commissar personally watching over him, day and night. Or do you want him moved away from barracks quarters?'

'I think I made it clear what I want, trooper,' said Ludd.

'No,' said Criid. 'He stays put. He stays in the ranks.'

'That's not your call, captain,' said Ludd.

'Chass came to us to learn to be a soldier,' said Criid. 'That's what his mother wanted. That's what his high-born house wanted. And that's what Gaunt wants too. He's not going to learn the ways of the Astra Militarum by being mollycoddled.'

'I'm not talking about special treatment–' Ludd began.

'But you are,' said Criid. 'He stays put. He has a decent bond with Dalin. Dalin will look after him and bunk with him. Keep an eye on him. A less obtrusive eye than a commissar.'

Ludd glared at her with what looked like suppressed anger.

'You're only saying that because Dalin is your son. You wish to earn him favour in Gaunt's eyes. It is entirely unsuitable.'

'And you're not trying to earn favour?' asked Rawne.

'I'm interested in... the boy's welfare, major,' Ludd snarled.

'Enough,' said Curth. 'This trailer is small, and there are too many people in here already. Settle this or take it outside.'

She looked at Felyx.

'Sorry,' she said. 'I don't mean to sound unfeeling. I'm very sorry for your loss.'

'I didn't say what I said because Dalin's my son,' said Criid quietly. 'I said it because that's what Maddalena wanted. When I got to her, she was still alive. Barely. I knew... I knew she wasn't going to make it. She made me promise. She made me swear, that I would do the best for you.'

'You?' asked Ludd.

'Not because Dalin's my son, but because I am a mother,' said Criid.

'She... she was alive?' whispered Felyx, staring at Criid.

'For a moment,' said Criid gently. 'Just a moment or two. It was too late. She made me promise. She... she trusted me. Feth knows why. She made me promise.'

'Well, that's all well and good,' said Ludd, 'but–'

'A soldier's promise is a serious thing,' said Rawne quietly. 'Simple, but serious. Like a soldier's funeral. Criid was asked, and she promised. We do it the way Criid says.'

'Major, I object!' cried Ludd.

'Object all the feth you want, Ludd,' said Rawne. 'I'm senior commanding in this room. Throne, except for Gaunt, I'm senior commanding in this fething regiment. I've just given an order. That's how things will go. Gaunt can overrule me if he likes, but you won't, Ludd. You should know by now I have feth-all truck with directives from the Officio Prefectus. Which will be the end of me, in due course. But right now, we do it Criid's way.'

'I'll take this to Hark,' said Ludd, his face grim.

'Knock yourself out,' said Rawne.

Ludd looked at Felyx. There was a softness in his voice that surprised all of them.

'Will you..?' he started. 'Are you all right with this? Will you be all right?'

Felyx looked back at him. It was quite clear he wasn't, but he nodded anyway.

'Dalin?' said Rawne. 'Take Trooper Chass, get him bunked in a room with you. Just the two of you. Shuffle sleeping arrangements if you have to. My authority.'

'Yes, sir,' said Dalin.

He stepped into the trailer to escort Felyx out. Rawne put a hand on his shoulder and stopped him in his tracks. He leaned forwards and whispered in Dalin's ear.

'Look after him, Dal. Eyes on him, you hear me? He's in shock. And don't let Meryn feth with him.'

'Yes, sir. No, sir,' Dalin said. He glanced at Criid, who nodded, and then led Felyx out into the rain.

* * *

After Rawne, Criid and Ludd had departed, Curth finished her clean up, and then turned to look at the death reports piled in her workspace.

Kolding had just sent the patched-up driver off with a bandage around his face.

'Shall I finish the reports, doctor?' he asked.

'I can do it, Auden.'

'You are tired, ma'am,' he said. 'Besides, death and paperwork are two of my specialties.'

She smiled, and nodded.

'Thank you. I could do with some air at least.'

She stepped out of the trailer into the artificial glare of the yard. The rain had eased to a drizzle, and beyond the limits of the lamp rigs, the world was black and cold.

'Finished for the day?'

She glanced around and saw Vaynom Blenner strolling up to join her.

'Yes,' she said.

'A trying day,' said Blenner. 'You know what I always find is an efficacious cure for a trying day?'

'In your medical opinion?'

'I am a physician of life, Ana,' he chuckled. 'And in my experience, the trials that life spits at us are best deflected by a glass or two of liquid fortification. The Munitorum driver who conveyed me here today was most helpful in releasing a bottle of amasec into my care. If you'd like to join me?'

She looked out into the darkness. There was a faint radiance in the distance, the glow of the city, she presumed. Perhaps the lamps and flares of the Urdeshic Palace that overlooked them all.

'No, thank you, Vaynom,' she said. 'I find, of late, I drink too much.'

'Surely not,' he smiled.

'You should know, Vaynom. I do it all in your company.'

'And we set the affairs of mankind to rights, two great philosophers together.'

'No, Vaynom. There's no philosophy in me either.'

He shrugged.

'There are, of course, many other ways to unwind, Ana.'

She looked at him. He was startled by the hardness in her eyes.

'You're very persistent, Blenner. Very persistent. I think I was clear.'

'Well, I certainly meant nothing by it, Doctor Curth.'

'Vaynom, you mean nothing by anything, and everything by everything. I have appreciated your friendship these last few months. Truly, I never expected to find any kinship with a man like you.'

'A man like–? You wound me, doctor.'

'I have come to know you, Vaynom, and you certainly know yourself. You have a raucously uplifting soul, but there is always an agenda with you.'

'Never!' he protested.

'Always,' Curth said firmly. 'You seek to serve yourself, in any way you can. To cushion your life against inconvenient hardship. When I spend time with you, I laugh, and I forget myself.'

'How is that a bad thing?'

'I forget that I serve others,' she said. 'I am medicae, Vaynom. It is my duty and my purpose. Always has been. I fear that if I dally with you too often, I will lose sight of that. I will begin to subscribe to your more self-interested way of living. I will end up serving myself, not others.'

'Is that how you see me?' he asked.

'You know what you're like,' she replied. 'It is not approbation. You are a man of distinguished qualities, if you'd only own them. In fact, I think the Imperium could be improved if there were more people like you. People who are able to find, against all odds, seams of joy and delight in this fething darkness.'

'You're saying I'm a bad influence?' he said, with a waspish smile. He leaned towards her.

'I'm completely fething serious, Blenner,' she said. 'I have lost myself of late. I have no wish to lose myself any more.'

She turned and began to walk away.

'This is because she died, isn't it?' he called after her. As he said the words, he flinched. He knew they had come out too bitterly.

Curth turned back.

'What?' she snapped.

'I heard she died,' he said. 'We all heard. Now she's out of the picture, you can stop wasting time with me and set your sights on–'

She strode right up to him and grabbed him by the lapels.

'A woman died. Eight people died. And you call it a "trying day"?'

'You didn't even like her!' he blurted, pulling against her grip.

'I did not, but I am a doctor and that doesn't come into it. I save lives, Blenner. I don't judge them.'

'You just judged mine.'

She let him go, and looked away at the puddles in the yard.

'I apologise,' she said. 'I am not perfect and I am sometimes inconsistent.'

He put a reassuring hand on her shoulder.

'You didn't like her, Ana. You told me so enough times.'

Curth shrugged off his hand.

'She was a human life, sir,' she said. 'She was brave. She was not a nice person, but she was a good person. She had a duty that she performed steadfastly to the end. An object lesson to both of us, perhaps.'

'I think you're upset,' he said softly, 'not because she is dead, but because you're happy she's dead.'

She wheeled to face him.

'How dare you?' she asked.

'You don't mean to be. You don't want to be. The fact that you are upsets that precious sense of self you just lectured me about. Gaunt's bitch is gone. The way is clear for you to finally–'

'Stop talking.'

'–and you cast me aside in the process as disposable–'

'Stop talking, Blenner,' she growled, 'or our friendship, which I value, will be over and done. I confided in you that I had feelings for Gaunt–'

'*Always* had feelings...'

'The duration is hardly the point, you idiot. I confided in you. A friend to a friend. I confided in you, when worse the wear for your procured drink, about *your* childhood comrade. Your best bosom pal from the bad old days. Ibram Gaunt, the man you like to tell anyone who is listening is your oldest, dearest friend of the ages! Why do you do that? Because it makes you look good to be able to say it?'

'He *is* my best friend,' said Blenner. He looked mortified.

'Then act like he is. His companion died today. As far as I'm aware, he doesn't even know it yet. I never cared for her. She was hard to like. But he liked her. He found some consolation in her–'

'Her face. She looked like–'

'It doesn't matter, Vaynom. If you truly know Gaunt, you know he is distant. Alone. He has been his whole life. It's the old affliction of command. As a colonel and as a commissar, he has to stand apart, to retain his authority, and that makes him remote. I know damn well he's impossible to reach, and I think his life has made it hard for him to reach out. For whatever ridiculous reason, that woman offered him something that was valuable to him. Now she's gone. Does that not, for a moment, worry you? How will it affect him? And how will it affect the regiment if he slips into a darker place because of it?'

Blenner sneered.

'I don't think you believe a word of that,' he said. 'I think... I think you're good at making generous, principled arguments of care and concern that entirely ignore your own feelings. It's just smoke. You're glad she's gone, and you despise yourself for being glad about it.'

'This conversation is over, Blenner,' she said.

'You know I'm right. Stop dressing it up. Stop pretending there's some moral principle here...'

He paused.

'What?' he asked. 'Are you going to strike me?'

'What?' she said. 'No!'

He nodded. She looked down and saw that her right fist was balled. She relaxed it.

'No,' she repeated.

'Well, then,' he sighed.

'You're wrong,' she said.

'We'll differ. And I will check on my old friend the moment he returns.'

'Good night, then,' she said. She paused.

'Vaynom?'

'Yes, Ana?'

'You... you are feeling better, these days?'

'Better?'

'The nerves? The anxiety?'

'Hah,' he said, a dismissive gesture. 'I am more settled. Good conversations with a friend have helped.'

'You haven't... you haven't asked me for pills. Not for a while.'

'The placebos, you mean?' he chuckled.

'I told you, sir, I was simply following the course of support Doctor Dorden prescribed.'

'Sugar pills to salve my troubles,' he said. 'You know, the placebo effect is very powerful. I am feeling myself again, these days.'

'Vaynom, if you are not... if, Throne save us, this business between us tonight has unsettled you–'

'My, but you think a lot of yourself, doctor,' he said.

She hesitated, stung.

'Do not backslide,' she said. 'Whatever the dispute between us, do not let it cloud you. If you struggle, you can come to me. I will help you. Don't go turning to the low lives who peddle–'

'I am enlightened by your low estimation of me, Doctor Curth,' he said. He tipped his cap.

'Good night to you,' he said, and walked away.

She watched him cross the yard, and then turned to find whatever dank billet they had assigned to her.

The banquet had been cleared from the grand salon adjoining the war room of the Collegia Bellum Urdeshi. The generals and lord commanders sat back as servitors brought in amasec and fortifiq. A fire burned in the great hearth.

The company had been convivial, despite Gaunt's state of shock. It was as if the staff seniors had been keeping straight faces before and could finally share the joke, and celebrate both Gaunt's elevation and his amusing disorientation.

He had found himself seated between Van Voytz and Bulledin, with Grizmund facing him. Van Voytz had been particularly garrulous, getting to his feet at regular intervals to raise a glass and toast the newest of the lords. Lugo, to Gaunt's surprise, had been the most entertaining, lifting his soft, hollow voice above the din of feasting to regale the company with genuinely amusing stories, many of them self-deprecating. One tale, concerning Marshal Hardiker and a consignment of silver punch bowls, had been so uproarious that Gaunt had witnessed Lord General Cybon laugh out loud for the first time. Marshal Tzara had smashed her fist on the table so hard it had shaken the flatware, more in mirth at Cybon's reaction than at the hilarity of the tale itself.

At one point, Urienz had leaned across the table and gestured to Gaunt with the half-gnawed leg of a game fowl he was devouring.

'You'll need a good tailor, Gaunt,' he said.

'A tailor?'

'You're a militant commander,' said Urienz. 'You need to look the part.'

'I... What's wrong with my uniform? I've worn it all my career.'

Urienz snorted.

'He's right, you need to look the part,' said Tzara.

'This admixture of commissar and woodsman guerrilla is very rank and file, young man,' chuckled Kelso.

'I have the mark of office,' Gaunt replied. He picked up the large, golden crest of militant command that Bulledin had handed him. It was lying beside his place setting. He had not yet pinned it on. Just raising it brought a chorus of cheers and a clink of glasses.

'It's not about modesty and decorum,' said Grizmund. 'You don't restyle yourself as a lord of men out of arrogance.'

'Well,' said Blackwood, 'some do.'

'I heard that, Blackwood, you dog!' Lugo called out.

'It's a matter of apparent status,' said Grizmund, laughing.

'My men have never had a problem discerning my authority,' Gaunt said.

'In a company of five thousand?' said Urienz. 'Perhaps not. But in a warhost of a hundred thousand? Five hundred thousand? You look like a commissar.'

'I am a commissar.'

'You're a militant commander, you stupid bastard!' roared Van Voytz. 'When you step upon the field, you need for there to be no doubt who wields power. You don't want men asking, "Who's in charge here?"... "That man there!"... "The commissar?"... "No, the man standing with the other commissars who isn't just a commissar"...'

'It's not pride, Gaunt,' said Grizmund. 'It's necessity. You need to look like what men of all regiments will expect.'

'You need to stand out,' growled Bulledin.

'A cloak, perhaps?' suggested Tzara. 'Not that ratty rag you wear.'

'Perhaps an enormous void shield parasol supported by battle-servitors!' cried Lugo.

'I will take the wise advice of my lords and turn myself at once into the most colossal target for the enemy,' said Gaunt.

The table shook with laughter.

'Take the address of my tailor, at least,' said Urienz. 'He's a good man, in the Signal Point quarter. A clean jacket, a sash, that's all I'm talking about.'

As the meal ended, the generals began to leave, one by one. Duties and armies awaited, and some had been from their HQs too long already. Every one of them shook Gaunt's hand or slapped him on the back before they left.

It came down to Van Voytz, Cybon, Bulledin, Blackwood, Lugo and Tzara.

'I feel I should return to my company,' said Gaunt, finishing the last of his amasec. 'They've barely disembarked.'

'There are still some matters to discuss, Bram,' said Van Voytz. He shot a nod to the house staff waiting on them, and they withdrew, closing the doors behind them.

'The state of the crusade, and the campaign here?' asked Gaunt.

'Oh, yes, that,' said Cybon. 'We'll get to that.'

'I was eager for full intelligence reports,' said Gaunt. He gestured to his crest on the table. 'Now, more so, for I believe it is my duty to review.'

'My man Biota will furnish you with everything you need,' said Van Voytz. 'A full dossier, then a briefing tomorrow or the day after to examine strategy.'

'And when do I get an audience with the Warmaster?' Gaunt asked.

Logs crackled and spat in the grate. Bulledin reached for the crystal decanter, and refilled his glass and Gaunt's.

'Our beloved Warmaster,' said Van Voytz, 'may he live eternally, is a very removed soul. Few of us see him these days.'

'He abides alone here, in the east wing,' said Tzara. 'He was ever a man of tactics and strategy–'

'Brilliant strategy,' put in Lugo.

'I do not dispute it, Lugo,' said Tzara. 'How one man can assemble and contain the data of this entire crusade in his mind and make coherent sense of it is a marvel.'

'It was always his chief talent,' said Gaunt. 'To see the Archenemy's intent five or ten moves ahead. To orchestrate the vast machineries of war.'

'An obsession, I think,' said Blackwood. 'Isn't there some obsessive quality to a mind that can negotiate such feats of processing?'

'It is an obsession that consumes him,' said Cybon. 'He withdraws more and more each day into a solitary world of contemplation, ordering scribes and rubricators to fetch him the latest scraps of data constantly. He scrutinises every last shred with fearful precision, looking for that clue, that opening, that nuance.'

'You speak as if he's ill,' said Gaunt.

'These last years, Bram,' said Van Voytz, 'the machinations of the foe have increasingly made less and less sense.'

'I have heard speculation that they are driven by a madman,' said Gaunt.

'You do not think that bastard Sek mad?' asked Lugo.

'Of course,' said Gaunt. 'But deviously so. There was a cold logic, a strategic brilliance that could not be denied. Sek is an unholy monster, but like Nadzybar before him, he is undoubtedly an able commander of war. As good, dare I say, as any we have.'

'I'll summon the ordos, shall I?' sniggered Bulledin.

'I mean to say, sir,' said Gaunt, 'at least, he was. His record was undeniable. Of course, my knowledge is ten years out of date.'

Light laughter ran around the table.

'If Sek is insane,' said Blackwood quietly, 'if he has fallen into a despairing insanity and lost that touch which, I grant you, he did possess... then what do you suppose happens to a man who studies Sek's plans in obsessive detail, day after night after day, searching for a pattern, for the sense of it?'

'Are you saying...?' Gaunt began.

Van Voytz sipped his amasec.

'If you look into madness, Bram, you see only madness, and you run mad yourself seeking a truth in it, for truth there is none.'

'Maybe I should summon the ordos,' said Gaunt stiffly.

'Macaroth's great weapon is his mind,' said Cybon, his voice almost a whisper like steel drawn from a scabbard. 'I deny it not. The man is a wonder. But his mind has been turned against him by too many years of gazing on insanity.'

There was a long silence.

'This is the matter you wished to discuss?' asked Gaunt.

'We are the inner circle, Bram,' said Van Voytz, his good humour gone. 'The six of us here. Seven, if you sit with us. Among us, some of the most senior commanders of the crusade. A Warmaster is only as good as the lords militant who surround him, lords who follow his orders, but who also check his decisions. We keep him true.'

'He shuts us out,' said Bulledin. 'Not just us, but all thirty who were present tonight, and other revered lords too. He takes no advice. He takes no counsel. He takes almost no audience.'

'We keep him true,' said Bulledin, 'but he will not let us.'

'The Sabbat Crusade is in crisis, Gaunt,' said Cybon. 'We do not speak out of disloyalty to Macaroth. We speak out of loyalty to the Throne, and to the hope of triumph in this long campaign.'

'You plot, then?' asked Gaunt.

'Your word,' said Blackwood. 'A dangerous word.'

'I don't like what I'm hearing,' said Gaunt. 'Are you contemplating a move against the Warmaster? To force his hand and oblige him to change his policy? Or are you planning to depose him?'

'Macaroth does not listen to us,' said Van Voytz. 'We have tried to advise, and he will not take our recommendations. His rule is absolute, far more than Slaydo's ever was. Bram, this happens. It's not unprecedented. Great men, the greatest, even, they burn out. They reach their limits. Macaroth has been Warmaster for twenty-six years. He's done.'

'Warmasters may be replaced,' said Cybon. 'Too often, they fall before it becomes necessary, but it is the very purpose of the lords militant to watch their master and check his thinking. If a Warmaster begins to falter, then his lords militant are failing in their solemn duty if they do not remedy that weakness.'

'We are the inner circle,' said Van Voytz. 'This is not a conclusion we have come to easily or quickly.'

'And not because he has overlooked or slighted so many of you during his mastery?' asked Gaunt.

Tzara looked at Van Voytz.

'You said he was bold,' she said.

'I said he speaks plainly,' Van Voytz replied. 'I've always admired that.' He looked at Gaunt.

'Has he slighted each one of us?' Van Voytz asked rhetorically. 'Yes. In some cases, many times. Have we seen past and borne those slights? Every time, for we have, ultimately, always come to see the greater sense of his intentions. This is not personal malice, Gaunt.'

'And you all think this way?' asked Gaunt. 'Not just the six of you? All thirty tonight?'

'Not all,' said Cybon. 'Some, like Grizmund, are new-made and still grateful to Macaroth. Some, like Urienz, had their careers forged by Macaroth and would never speak out against him. Some, like Kelso, are just too old and doctrinaire. But all feel it. All see it. And most would side with us if we made an intervention.'

'But you are the inner circle?' said Gaunt.

Tzara lifted her glass.

'We are the ones with no agenda except victory,' she said. 'The ones with nothing to forfeit from his favour. We are the ones with the balls to act rather than struggle on in silence.'

'And how will you act?' asked Gaunt. He took a sip of his drink to steady his temper.

'In coordination,' said Cybon, 'we can raise a declamation of confidence. This can be circulated through staff and countersigned. We all have allies. A majority will carry it. We are more than confident we have the numbers. Then we present it to him, and make our decision known to him.'

'A formal and confidential request has already been sent to the Sector Lord of Khulan, the Masters of the Fleet and the High lords of Terra for their support in the disposition of the Warmaster,' said Blackwood.

'This is no ward room coup, Gaunt,' said Bulledin. 'We have begun the process formally, and with due respect to the approved procedure. We are doing this by the book.'

Gaunt looked at the crest on the tablecloth in front of him.

'This makes more sense now,' he said grimly. 'Another vote to carry the numbers. A militant commander in your pocket. You know I owe personal loyalty to at least three of you. You count on me being your man. It makes this rather hollow.'

'It's deserved, Bram,' said Van Voytz. 'Fully deserved.'

Gaunt looked at him.

'Tell me, Barthol, before this was pressed into my unsuspecting hand tonight, did you have the numbers? Or am I the one vote that sways the difference?'

'We had the numbers, Gaunt,' snapped Cybon. 'We've had them for years. Your support would simply add to the strength of our voice, not force a majority.'

'That crest, militant commander, was given to you for your service,' said Lugo. 'As Barthol says, it is fully deserved. But the timing...'

'The timing, sir?' asked Gaunt.

'It was necessary to elevate you as soon as possible,' said Lugo.

'The process of deposition is under way,' said Bulledin. 'There was just one factor we did not have in place.'

'And what's that, sir?' asked Gaunt.

'Succession,' said Cybon.

'No man of rank less than militant commander could ever be elected directly to the post of Warmaster,' said Van Voytz.

'Are you...' Gaunt started to say. 'Are you insane?'

'We cannot simply depose Macaroth in time of war,' said Van Voytz. 'We cannot break the line of command. Deposition needs to go hand in hand with succession. To see this through successfully, we need to have the replacement standing ready. A candidate acceptable to all.'

'We all have baggage,' said Blackwood. 'It can't be any of us.'

'Besides, that would smack too much of personal ambition,' said Tzara.

'But you,' said Lugo, 'the People's Hero, the slayer of Asphodel, Saviour of the Beati, returned in glory, ten years missing, no litany of feuds and staff squabbles dogging your heels. And no history of ambition in the matter.

Your hands are spotlessly clean. Why, you were unaware of the entire initiative until tonight.'

'Slaydo almost did it after Balhaut,' said Cybon. 'You know that.'

'You are our candidate, Bram,' said Van Voytz. 'We do not need your support. We merely need you to be ready when we declare you Warmaster.'

SEVENTEEN

EAGLES

The regiment's psyber-eagle was roosting on a fence overlooking the billet yard, one head tucked asleep, the other wary and watching the dawn fiercely.

The sky was pink and the angles of the shadows long and hard. Zhukova wandered into the yard, greeting the sentries at the billet doors.

'Up early,' said Daur.

'So are you,' she replied with a smile.

'If I sleep for too long, the scar gets sore,' he replied, patting the side of his belly with a grimace. 'A little stroll stretches it out and eases the cramp.'

'Elodie not mind you leaving her bed now you're only just in it?' asked Zhukova.

'I'll be back directly,' said Daur with a grin. 'Anyway, she's been up half the night. Criid's little girl, Yoncy. Tona had to shave her head. Lice, you know. Poor kid's beside herself at the loss of her pigtails. They've been taking it in turns to sit with her and calm her down.'

'I thought I heard sobbing,' said Zhukova.

'Oh, that,' laughed Daur. 'That's just all the hearts you've broken. The men of T Company, crying in their sleep.'

Zhukova snorted.

'I was going for a run,' she said.

'Check with the scouts. They're watching the area. After yesterday.'

She nodded, and then paused.

'What's this now?' she asked.

An armoured transport, unmarked, was rolling down the track towards the yard.

'Is that Gaunt back at last?' she asked.

Daur shrugged.

'No idea,' he said.

Fazekiel, Baskevyl and Domor emerged from the billet units behind them. Each of them was in a clean number one uniform.

'What's going on?' asked Daur.

'Exciting day,' said Bask. 'We're summoned to the ordos.'

'What? Why?' asked Zhukova.

'Because *someone*,' said Domor, looking daggers at Baskevyl, 'was daft enough to feth around with the fething special cargo, that's why.'

'It's routine,' said Fazekiel. She finished pinning up her hair, and put her cap on, peak first. 'The ordos took charge of the trinkets we picked up, and they want to interview everyone who came in contact with them.'

'Trinkets, she says,' moaned Domor.

'Luna's right, it's just routine,' said Bask. He dead-panned straight at Zhukova and Daur. 'When we don't come back, dear friends, remember our names.'

Zhukova and Daur laughed.

The transport drew up in the centre of the yard, and a rear hatch opened. Inquisitor Laksheema's little aide stepped down.

'Fazekiel? Domor? Baskevyl?' she called out, reading off her data-slate.

'Keep it down, you'll wake the dead,' Baskevyl called back.

'Wouldn't be the first time,' said Onabel. She waited, sour-faced, as the trio walked over to her and climbed aboard. Baskevyl shot Daur and Zhukova a cheeky wave as the hatch closed.

'Well,' said Daur, 'fun for them.'

'They can keep that kind of fun,' said Zhukova.

'What is it?' asked Felyx. 'Is it my father?'

He was squirmed down in his bunk under a heap of blankets, just his face poking out. At the window, Dalin yawned as he looked out into the yard below.

'No, some transport,' he said. 'Baskevyl heading off with Shoggy and the commissar.'

'Ludd?'

'No, not Ludd,' said Dalin. He yawned again as the transport drove away. 'Fazekiel. We should get up.'

'Is it time to get up?'

'It will be soon. You don't have to wait for the hour bell. Officers are impressed by punctuality. People who are ready before they need to be.'

He went to yank the blankets off Felyx.

'Don't you fething dare,' snapped Felyx. Dalin backed off with a surrendering gesture.

'Just get up, Felyx,' he said. 'You need a shower. We probably both need to see Curth for a lice check too.'

'Lice?'

'Yes. Get up. I don't think you even got undressed last night.'

Dalin looked around the third floor room. It was the one Felyx had been assigned to share with Maddalena. Using Rawne's authority, Dalin had simply taken it over. As soon as he'd heard Rawne's name, Meryn hadn't even questioned it.

Dalin kicked the bunk.

'Come on, Chass. Get your lazy arse up. Get in the shower.'

'Go,' said Felyx. 'I'll be right behind you.'

Dalin grabbed his washbag.

'Make sure you fething are,' he said.

* * *

Zhukova jogged across the yard to the brazier where Mkoll and Bonin stood, sipping tin mugs of caffeine. She was shaking out her arms and flexing.

'Safe for a circuit?' she asked.

Bonin raised his eyebrows.

'Safe enough,' said Mkoll.

'Thanks, chief,' she said.

'Zhukova? Captain?'

She had been about to start running. She looked back.

'What is it, chief?'

'You got time for a word?'

She walked back to them.

'I'll check the perimeter again,' said Bonin.

'Stay lucky, Mach,' said Mkoll as the scout walked off.

'What's this about?' Zhukova asked.

'I've been thinking,' said Mkoll.

'Ooh, steady.'

Mkoll didn't smile.

'You know what your reputation was when you came to us?' he asked.

She scowled. 'Let me gakking guess,' she said.

'The pretty girl,' said Mkoll. 'Too pretty. Far too pretty to be a good soldier. Must've got her rank by being pretty. The trophy officer. Looks good on Vervunhive recruitment posters.'

'Feth you,' she said.

He shrugged.

'It's true, isn't it?' he asked.

'I fought, chief. Planetary defence force, scratch company, then militia, then Guard. I earned my bars. I earned my place.'

'Not saying you didn't. I'm saying that's what men always think.'

Zhukova sighed.

'It's followed me all my life. Men think what they think, and they tend to be dumb.' She pointed to her face. 'Didn't ask for this. In the Vervun War, sometimes I hoped for a shrapnel wound. Get caught in a blitz cloud from one of the gakking woe machines, you know? Mess this up a bit, so people would start taking me seriously.'

Mkoll nodded.

'Just this morning,' she said. 'Ban Daur's my friend. I've known him years. Even he made a crack. Didn't mean to be hurtful. Just the usual Zhukova jokes. "Oh, she's beautiful. Must've screwed her way through some officers to get that rank." I'm sick of it. It's not just the men. Elodie's all right with me now, but at first she thought I was some old flame come to scoop Ban away. And Pasha, Throne love her, is always warning men about me. That I use my looks to get what I want.'

'Do you?' he asked.

'What do you think?'

'I don't think you should be a captain,' said Mkoll.

She blinked. A flush rose in her cheeks.

'I expected...' she stammered. 'From you, at least. Feth you. Feth you to hell.'

'I don't think you should be a captain, because it's a waste,' he said.

She frowned.

'You're a good soldier, and you look the way you do,' said Mkoll simply. 'You're going to get promoted. Favoured. Chosen over others. Smart. Good-looking. Articulate.'

'You trying to get in my pants now, Mkoll?'

He snorted.

'I'm saying you took the obvious route. Career advancement. But I saw you work. On the *Armaduke*. And up on that roof yesterday. That wasn't just good soldiering. You can lead men, Zhukova, but you are very good at individual action.'

'Thanks,' she said, surprised.

'It made me review your service record. I gave it a lot of thought. See, I'm not just looking for good soldiers. I'm looking for specialists.'

'Really?' she asked.

'Pasha's back on her feet. Company command won't stay yours. So it'll come to you and Spetnin for T Company, and you'll get it, because you look like you. And that'll be a waste of Spetnin because, let's be fair, he's a fething good officer.'

Mkoll gazed idly up at the roosting eagle watching them.

'So that's a double shame. He'll get demoted, so we lose a good line commander. And you'll get the command, which is fine, but doesn't play to your true talents. You're wasted as a captain. Anyone can be an officer.'

'Well, not anyone,' she said.

'I don't know. Look at Meryn. Some people make decent officers. Some people make great officers. But almost no one makes a great scout.'

'A scout?' she asked.

'What do you think?'

'You're offering me a place in the scout cadre?'

'That's what I seem to be doing, yeah,' he said.

'I never asked to–'

'I pick the Tanith scouts, Zhukova. I don't take volunteers. You'd keep your rank, but you'd answer to me. You'd give up your company command.'

'What... what does Pasha say? Or Gaunt?'

'I don't know,' he said, with a careless shrug. 'I haven't asked anyone yet. I'm asking you first. Say no, and no one needs to be any wiser. Say yes... Well, Gaunt has very seldom *not* taken my recommendations.'

'I'm saying yes,' she said.

He nodded. He tried not to smile, but her smile was bright and infectious.

'Thank you,' she said.

'Oh, no, Zhukova. Don't thank me. No one ever thanks me for making this their life.'

'Well, I am. I'd kiss you, but that would not improve my terrible reputation.'

'It would not.' Mkoll shook out his mug and turned away.

'Enjoy your run,' he said.

* * *

Mkoll walked back to the billet habs.

'You ask her?' asked Bonin. He was watching Zhukova extend her stride as she made off along the entry track.

'Yup.'

'And?'

'She said yes.'

Bonin nodded and smiled.

'Good news,' he said.

'About time we had some,' Mkoll agreed.

The eagle took flight overhead.

'Look sharp,' Bonin said.

Vehicles were coming down the track towards the camp. Two Tauroxes, front and back of a Chimera.

'They're flying pennants. Staff vehicles,' said Bonin. 'We've got some fething lord fething general inbound.'

'Go get Rawne and Kolea, quick,' said Mkoll.

The vehicles pulled up in the yard, engines juddering to a stop. Rawne and Kolea had hurried out to join Mkoll, and Hark followed them. Startled troopers were hurrying out behind them, some yawning, some not fully dressed.

'Guard line, if you please!' Hark yelled. 'Come on, you fethers! Dress it up, dress it up! Vadim? Where's your weapon? Well, go and fething get it!'

'What's going on?' asked Pasha.

'Feth alone knows, ma'am,' said Obel.

'You want me to rouse the whole regiment?' Kolosim asked in Rawne's ear.

'No. If they're not up and tidy, keep 'em hidden and tell them to smarten up. We'll gussy up what we have here.'

He turned and called, 'Hark? Can we try to make this look reasonably professional?'

Women and children were looking out of the middle floor windows of the hab blocks.

'Back inside, please!' Rawne yelled, pointing at them.

The Chimera's hatch swung open. Two Tempestus Scions in gleaming grey carapace armour stomped out, followed by two more. They glanced around the yard, eyed the assembling Ghosts with mute contempt, then took up a line, four abreast, facing the company, hellguns across their chests.

'What are the fething glory boys here for?' Elam whispered.

'Something's awry,' murmured Beltayn.

Gaunt stepped down the Chimera's ramp. He winced into the sunlight, and pulled his storm coat close around him. Then he strode past the motionless Scions and stopped, face to face with Rawne and Kolea.

'Morning,' he said.

'Sir,' said Rawne. 'What's the big fuss?'

Gaunt glanced over his shoulder at the Scions.

'Them?' he said. He grunted. 'They've been assigned. To me.'

'What for?' asked Kolea.

'Close protection.'

'What did you do?' asked Rawne.

Gaunt smiled, and shook his head.

'I've been asking myself that,' he said.

'There's no one else in the transport?' asked Kolea. 'No lord general about to surprise us with an inspection?'

'No,' said Gaunt.

'No one important?' asked Rawne.

'No,' said Gaunt, more emphatically. 'Everyone can stand down. Just relax.'

He glanced at the ranks Hark had assembled, and the officers waiting with them.

'Stand down!' he called, pointing to them. 'Please, stand down and go back to your breakfasts.'

He started to turn back to Rawne and Kolea.

'This is going to get aggravating very quickly,' he began.

But Rawne grabbed at him. He grasped the front of Gaunt's storm coat and dragged it open. As Gaunt had pointed to the ranks, the coat had parted slightly, and Rawne had seen something.

'What the feth is *this?*' he said.

'Well,' said Gaunt. 'I'm going to tell you about that...'

'Is that *real?*' asked Kolea, wide-eyed, staring at the gold eagle crest pinned to Gaunt's chest that Rawne was unveiling.

The four Scions were suddenly all around them, aiming their weapons directly at Rawne. Rawne froze.

'Remove your hands,' said their leader, his grinding voice amplified by his threatening visor, 'from the person of the militant commander *now!*'

'You heard the instruction, scum!' barked another. Their optics glowed pinpoint red as auto-aiming systems kicked in.

'Whoa, whoa, whoa!' said Kolea.

'I'm letting him go! I'm letting him go!' Rawne exclaimed, releasing his grip.

Gaunt looked at the lead Scion.

'What's your name?' he asked.

'Sancto, lord.'

'Tempestor Sancto, this "scum" is my second in command. You will extend him every courtesy you extend to me.'

'Lord.'

'Now go and stand by the truck. No, go and face the fething wall. All of you!'

'Lord?'

'Did you not fething hear me, Scions? I'm a fething militant commander and you will do as I fething say, without question!'

'Yes, lord!'

The four turned, marched away, and stood in a perfect line facing the fabricatory, their backs to the yard.

Gaunt looked at Kolea and Rawne.

'Clearly,' he said, clearing his throat, 'clearly, I have to get a better handle on that. Not going to win friends that way.'

'You're a fething militant commander?' asked Rawne.

'I fething am, Eli,' said Gaunt.

'Are you... fething kidding?' asked Kolea.

Gaunt shook his head. He looked at them. It had gone extraordinarily quiet in the yard.

'Throne, your fething faces...' Gaunt smiled.

'I don't know whether to punch you or hug you,' said Rawne.

'Saluting would probably be the best option,' whispered Kolea. He turned. 'Commissar Hark?'

Hark swung to face the ranks, straight-backed.

'Tanith First, attention!' he bellowed. 'Tanith First, salute!'

The men snapped to attention and made the sign of the aquila.

'Tanith First, three cheers for our militant commander!'

Applause and cheering erupted across the yard. In the windows, the retinue and troopers too late to reach the parade whooped and waved. The chant 'First and only! First and only!' started up.

Gaunt shook Rawne's hand.

'You fething bastard,' said Rawne.

'Congratulations, sir,' said Gol, shaking Gaunt's hand as soon as Rawne had let it go.

Mkoll patted Gaunt on the shoulder.

'Tears in your eyes, chief?' Gaunt asked.

'Not a one, sir,' said Mkoll.

'Are you lying, Oan?'

'Allergies, sir.'

The men came over, clapping and chanting, mobbing around him.

'You cheeky fether!' Varl laughed, then added, 'sir.'

'I never thought I'd live to see the day, sir,' said Larkin. Gaunt gave the old marksman a hug.

'I see high command's finally made a decision I approve of,' cried Hark.

'I hope you don't come to regret that remark, Viktor,' replied Gaunt. They embraced, Hark bear-hugging Gaunt so tightly he lifted him off the ground for a moment.

From the doorway of the hab, Criid and Curth watched Gaunt moving through the mob of applauding, cheering troopers. Criid's grin was broad, Curth's smaller and sadder.

'Rawne's got to tell him,' she said.

'He will,' said Criid.

'He's got to do it now. It can't wait. He'll find out any moment.'

'He'll tell him, Ana,' said Criid.

'Let him have this moment,' said Blenner from behind them. They turned. Blenner looked very bleary and hungover, but there was a look of pride on his face, and he was welling up.

'Let him have this one moment, for feth's sake,' he said.

He pushed past them into the yard, walking towards the crowd, raising his hands and clapping enthusiastically.

'I've got a band somewhere, I seem to think!' he was yelling. 'Why aren't they gakking well playing? Come on! Ibram, you old dog! *You old dog!*'

Wet from the freezing shower, a towel kilted around his waist, Dalin raced down the hab hallway, his wet feet slipping and slamming him off the walls. The hab around him was rocking with chanting and cheering. Down in the yard outside, the band had started playing, not well but exuberantly.

'Felyx!' Dalin yelled. 'Felyx, get up! Get up! Get up *now!*'

He burst into the room. Felyx was out of bed and half dressed. As Dalin crashed in, Felyx let out a howl and grabbed a blanket, dragging it around himself.

'Oh my Throne!' Dalin gasped, stopping in his tracks.

'Don't you ever fething knock? *Don't* you?' Felyx yelled at him.

'Oh my fething *Throne...*' Dalin stammered. 'I'm sorry. I'm *sorry!*'

He turned to exit, floundering.

Wrapped in the blanket, Felyx pushed past him and slammed the door.

'I'm sorry,' said Dalin, staring at the inside of the door.

'You don't tell anyone,' said Felyx. 'Understand?'

'Y-yes!' said Dalin.

'Do you understand? You don't tell *anyone*,' she said.

EIGHTEEN

AND STONES

The stronghold of the ordos in Eltath lay in the Gaelen district. It had once been a gaol and courthouse, but its thick walls and private cells had long since been converted to Inquisitorial use. Fazekiel, Baskevyl and Domor were left waiting in the main atrium, a cold, marble vault. They sat together on high-backed chairs beside the main staircase.

'This is where they used to bring prisoners in,' said Fazekiel, 'you know, for trial.'

'Stop trying to cheer me up,' said Domor.

After an hour, Onabel came to fetch them, and led them to a long, wood-panelled bureau where Inquisitor Laksheema was waiting.

Three chairs had been set out in front of her heavy desk. Laksheema gestured to them, but did not look up from the data-slate she was reading. Several dozen more, along with paper books and info tiles, covered her desk. Colonel Grae of the intelligence service stood by the window, sipping a thimble cup of caffeine.

They took their seats.

Laksheema looked up and smiled. It was disconcerting, because only her flesh-mouth smiled. Her eyes, gold augmetic and fleshless, could not.

'Thank you for your attendance,' she said.

'I didn't think it was optional, ma'am,' said Domor.

Grae chuckled.

'We have been supplied, at last, with a copy of Gaunt's mission report,' said Laksheema. 'The Astra Militarum was kind enough to share.'

'Now the report has been delivered to the Urdeshic Palace, and lies in the hands of the beloved Warmaster, protocol permitted it,' said Grae.

'So we are now aware of all additional particulars,' said Laksheema. 'The matters you were reluctant to discuss yesterday, Major Baskevyl.'

Baskevyl felt his tension begin to mount.

'We have begun reviewing the materials you handed to us,' Laksheema said. 'Well, Versenginseer Etruin is conducting the actual review. It will take months–'

'Versenginseer?' said Baskevyl. 'You said that before. I thought I had mis-heard. You mean "enginseer"?'

'I spoke precisely, major,' she said. 'Etruin's specialty is reverse-engineering. The deconstruction, and thus comprehension, of enemy technologies and materials. As I was saying, it will take months, if not years. But we have focused our immediate attention on the stone tiles that you discovered so memorably.'

'We would have interviewed you in due course,' said Grae. 'You, and every member of the squad present at the discovery, and everyone else who came in contact with the materials. Just ongoing data-gathering in the months to come. But you collated the materials, Commissar Fazekiel, and you two – Major Baskevyl and Captain... Domor – you were in command when the disruption was discovered.'

'That's right, sir,' said Baskevyl.

'Even on cursory examination,' said Laksheema, 'Etruin assesses there to be great worth in the materials, collectively. Who knows what wars we may win and what victories we may achieve thanks to their secrets. Time will tell.'

She looked very pointedly at Baskevyl.

'The stone tiles seem to be key,' she said. 'And it would appear that the Archenemy thinks so too. Wouldn't you say, major?'

Fazekiel saw Baskevyl's unease.

'You're being remarkably forthcoming, ma'am,' she said.

Laksheema pursed her lips, an expression Baskevyl read as 'puzzled'.

'Well, commissar,' she said, 'circumstances have changed somewhat over-night, haven't they?'

'Have they?' asked Domor.

'I'll be honest,' said the inquisitor, 'given what I've read in the mission report, the interviews with all three of you should have been conducted individually, in less... comfortable surroundings, and with rather greater persuasion.'

'Charming,' said Domor.

'Do not test me, captain,' said Laksheema. 'That ship has not yet sailed altogether. But, due to circumstances, I find I am obliged to offer a greater level of cooperation, be less territorial. Colonel Grae is present to oversee that cooperation. And you three are now, of course, entitled to greater levels of confidence. You can be read in. So can any members of your regiment at company and particular grade or higher. That's correct, isn't it, colonel?'

'It is, ma'am inquisitor,' said Grae. 'As of midnight-thirty last night, the clearance rating of the Tanith First at company and particular level was raised by default to cobalt.'

'Cobalt,' said Laksheema. 'Which is a shame for me, because I felt I was likely to get a great deal more out of you all if I was permitted to function at a standard, basic level. Especially you, I think, captain.'

She smiled her non-smile at Domor.

'You think you'd acquire more and better information from us through enhanced interrogation than through... what?' said Fazekiel. 'Our honest cooperation?'

Laksheema shrugged. 'Probably not. Cooperation is always the most effec-tive. It's just a matter of trust, and I suppose I must trust you now you're cobalt cleared.'

'Wait,' said Baskevyl. 'I'm sorry. Could you start again?'

'From where, major?' asked Laksheema.

'The start?' suggested Domor.

'The point at which we could be suddenly read in at upper echelon level,' said Baskevyl.

'Oh dear,' said Laksheema. 'I don't understand what you don't understand.'

'Is this... is this part of the enhanced interrogation?' asked Domor, shifting uncomfortably in his chair.

'Shhhh, Shoggy,' said Fazekiel.

'I'm just all confused,' he said.

'Inquisitor,' said Grae. 'I believe they don't actually know.'

'Really?' said Laksheema, exasperated.

'Know what?' Fazekiel asked.

'Last night, Colonel-Commissar Ibram Gaunt received promotion to the rank of militant commander, and your regiment automatically becomes marked out for special status, with commensurate clearance.'

There was a long pause.

'He's a what now?' asked Domor.

'Are you going to say anything?' asked Rawne.

Gaunt took a deep breath and let it out. He stood facing the window of the small room in the hab block they'd cleared as his billet. Rawne stood by the door.

'It's done,' said Gaunt. 'I can't change it.'

'She, uhm... she was protecting the boy, of course. Her skills were not, I suppose, the right ones for urban war. She should have left it to us.'

'She was not one to be told,' said Gaunt.

'I suppose so.'

'Others died?'

'Seven others, sir. Some Helixid nearby too.'

'I'll see the list of names.'

'Yes, sir.'

Rawne paused.

'Criid, she wanted to explain it all herself. She was there when... She was there. And Curth, she wanted to break it to you. I decided it should come from me. I wanted to inform you straight away, but that was a moment down there in the yard and it felt wrong to ruin it. I'm sorry I had to kill your mood so soon after.'

Gaunt looked at him.

'It's fine. It's sad. It's fine. It's a life lost. Something to mourn. And I'll miss her. I will. But, in truth...'

'Sir?'

'That *was* a moment down there. To see the Ghosts uplifted like that. To see a celebration. We get so few.'

'There'll be more, sir,' said Rawne. 'I think Blenner wants a feast. I think he said a feast. Or a series of feasts.'

Gaunt laughed dryly.

'The truth, Eli,' he said, 'I'm glad for the Ghosts. I'm glad this cheers them. And vindicates them too, for all the years of courage and sacrifice. We are now a regiment of esteem, with special status, and that comes with benefits. But I am not as overjoyed by this day as I might have been. As I *expected* to be. It has come with other issues attached.'

'Issues, sir?'

'We'll discuss them, in time. Maddalena's death has not ruined a good day. The day, despite its apparent glory, was ominously marked already. Her loss simply seals that.'

Gaunt sat down, and gestured for Rawne to sit too.

'How has Felyx taken it?' he asked.

'Rough,' said Rawne. 'Like you'd expect. Criid's taken him under her wing. Apparently, that was your woman's dying wish, and I approved it. She's got Dalin to keep an eye on Felyx. Keep things as normal as possible. Guard routine.'

'That's good. I suppose I'll have to talk to him.'

'Well, he's kind of your son and everything. And he wants a funeral.'

'Of course.'

'No, he wants to pay for a private funeral. The works.'

'Not appropriate.'

'Oh, let him do it. Maddalena was a mother figure to him. It's the House Chass way, and he's rich as feth. Let him do it and save yourself some grief.'

Gaunt didn't reply.

'Save Felyx some grief,' Rawne added. 'Let him feel like he's done something.'

Gaunt nodded.

'I have to go back to the palace this afternoon. I'm needed at staff. There's a mass of tactical data to go through. This war's a mess.'

'It's a war. When weren't they a mess?'

'We're probably going to have to consider changes, Eli.'

'Changes?'

'In regimental structure. We're special status now. I have Tempestus goons trailing me around.'

'They're right outside the door and can probably hear you,' said Rawne.

'I don't particularly care. Anyway, this new rank elevates me too far above the regiment structure. The divide is too great. I'll need to promote from within.'

'Promote?'

'There needs to be a colonel in charge, especially if I'm not present, which I'm not going to be as much as I'd like.'

'Gol, Bask and I handle the regiment well enough when you're not around.'

'Not doubting that, but the Munitorum will insist for appearances and formal process. I'll have to raise one of you, or they'll bring someone in from outside.'

'Really?' asked Rawne, his face not relishing that prospect.

Gaunt smiled.

'It'll be one of you three. Well, I guess Daur, Elam and Pasha are in the frame too, but really it's one of you three. Ironic. One Tanith, one Verghast, one Belladon.'

Rawne nodded.

'It should be Gol,' he said.

Gaunt looked surprised.

'I'm asking you, Eli.'

'To be colonel? Colonel Rawne? I don't think so. Gol's the better man.'

'Gol's one of the best men I've ever served with. But it should be a Tanith because of this regiment's history and name, and it should be you because of your service.'

Rawne sat back and shrugged.

'Here's my thinking,' he said. 'You told me that staff promoted you for your service record, chief amongst the honours of which is Vervunhive. The People's Hero. If this is about appearances and show, then the hard-arse Verghast scratch company hero is the one for you. It's kind of poetic. The People's Hero and his doughty partisan second. Plus, and again for show, Gol was... like... blessed by the fething Beati and brought back from living death, so he's probably got feth-arse sainthood in his future somewhere.'

'She's here, you know?' said Gaunt. 'Here on Urdesh.'

'So I understand.'

Rawne put his hands flat on the tabletop.

'I don't want to be a fething colonel,' he said. 'Kolea's the man you want. We all have authority, true enough. Mine comes from... Well, people fear me. They love Bask. That's where his authority comes from. Gol... He commands through respect. Everybody respects him. Everybody. He's the one you want. Plus, he's never tried to kill you or sworn eternal vengeance against you or anything. I don't want to be a fething colonel. I'd never be able to look the woods of Tanith in the face again... oh, *wait*.'

He glared at Gaunt.

Gaunt laughed.

'And besides,' said Rawne, 'I could never ever take Corbec's place. Not ever.'

Gaunt nodded.

'We'll talk about this again,' he said.

'We fething won't,' said Rawne. 'It's a done fething deal, my lord militant commander.'

They sat together on a broken wall behind the billets, looking out across the rubble wastes.

'How long have you been–' Dalin said finally.

'A girl? Are you a simpleton? All my life.'

'Hiding this, I was going to say.'

Felyx shrugged.

'Since Verghast. Since birth.'

'Who knows?'

'Maddalena knew. Ludd knows.'

'Ludd?'

'Yes, "Ludd",' she mocked.

'Why does Ludd know?'

'Pretty much the same reason you do. He found out by accident. Maddalena went to great lengths to always secure me a private room. When the *Armaduke* fell out of the warp, I was alone, getting in kit for secondary order, and I was knocked unconscious. He found me.'

'And he saw–'

'Yes, he saw.'

'So that's why he–'

'Yes, that's why. That's why he wanted me to be placed in his care, to protect my secret. But he couldn't say so. And your damn mother–'

'Was doing what Maddalena asked. And trying to help you.'

Felyx shrugged.

'Doesn't it hurt?' Dalin asked.

'Doesn't what hurt?'

'The binding you put around your body, squashing up your–'

'My?'

'Your... bosom.'

'They're called breasts, Dalin. Grow up.'

'Sorry.'

'You get used to it,' she added.

'Why?' asked Dalin. He picked up a stone from the wall top and tossed it across the rubble. 'Why hide it? Why the secret? There are women in this regiment...'

'My mother,' she said, 'is heir to House Chass of Vervunhive-Verghast. You're Verghastite, Criid. You know this.'

'A bit. I was very young when I left. And I'm low-hive scum, right? So the politics of your world are lost on me.'

'My world is your world,' she said.

'Not really. My world is the regiment. For me, Verghast means the regiment.'

Felyx pondered this. She looked out across the rubble flats. The pink dawn was turning to a drab, overcast day, a scurfy, grey expanse of sky. An interceptor, probably a Lightning, soared across the distance, east to west, low over the city, leaving a long, rolling whoosh behind it.

'My mother is heir apparent to House Chass,' she said. 'House Chass is the most powerful of the Vervunhive controlling dynasties. She is the only heir. No sons. The first female ever to hold that rank. She must inherit the full title when my grandfather dies.'

Felyx paused.

'Time has passed. He is probably dead already.'

She shrugged.

'Anyway, the hive elders are against a female succession to House rule, and the other noble families... they see an opportunity to undermine House Chass and loosen its grip on the reins of power. Vervunhive-Verghast is a patriarchy, Criid. The Houses all have strong male heads or heirs. If my mother succeeds, she will be deemed weak – it will be a moment to topple House Chass from its long dominance. House Anko, House Sondar, House Jehnik... Throne, they will fight hard. It will be a dynastic war that could collapse Vervunhive more thoroughly than Heritor gakking Asphodel's Zoican War ever did.'

She glanced sideways at Dalin. He was listening, frowning.

'My mother is persistent and ambitious. Very ambitious. She cites continuity of bloodline, and her connection to the People's Hero who saved the hive from doom. She may carry the popular vote, despite her sex. Now, the city knows she has a child by Gaunt, the offspring of the hive saviour. So, in the absence of a direct male heir, the most elegant compromise to effect a popular succession would be to skip a generation. To make the child the new lord. For my mother to step aside, and become the Lady Dowager. For the son to succeed. That would be a big deal. It would strengthen House Chass' hold on power immensely. For Vervunhive to inherit a ruler who is both House Chass *and* the bloodline of the People's Hero.'

'But no one knows that child is a girl?'

'No one,' she said.

Away in the distance, in the direction of Zarakppan, the muffled thump of an artillery bombardment or a saturation bombing began to roll, like faraway thunder or the quiver of heavy metal sheets. A smudge of black smoke smeared the horizon.

'My mother is ambitious,' said Felyx. 'She wants power for herself. And she can't accede to the demands to step aside anyway, because that means admitting her child is another female. So she sent me away.'

'Just like that?'

'You really don't understand hive politics, do you? By sending me away, my mother makes herself the only candidate for succession. She avoids the issue of standing aside, and secures absolute primogeniture, which suits her ambition, no matter the political fight that might present to her. If I had stayed, the issue of my succession would have become a focus, and my gender would have been revealed. It would have weakened House Chass even more. There would have been no advantage to skipping, and there would have been, further, the prospect of an all-female succession. A woman followed by a woman. That would be too much for the traditionalists to bear. House Chass would have been done, then and there.'

'So she sent you away?'

'She sent me away.'

'So she could become queen?'

'It's not a *queen*. It's... head of the House.'

'She doesn't sound like a very nice woman,' said Dalin.

'She's not. She's a political animal. I respect her and loathe her for that in equal measure. I honestly wanted to find my father. I thought he'd be the better parent.'

'And he's not?'

'How do you think he's doing so far?'

Dalin swung his feet and shrugged.

'He's a great man.'

'He's a great soldier,' said Felyx. 'He's no father. Except, ironically, to the Ghosts.'

Dalin ran his tongue around his teeth and thought for a moment.

'We should tell him,' he said.

'No!'

'My mother, then?'

'Are you trying to be stupid?'

'Then Doctor Curth. Curth can be trusted. Doesn't *she* even know?'

'I have studiously avoided all medicae exams,' she said. She paused. 'The prospect of lice is a worry.'

'You're on the front line. What if you're injured? They'll find out. That's no way to find out!'

'You will keep my secret, Dalin Criid. You will swear this to me.'

She looked at him fiercely. She was not asking. It was the look of a person who had been raised to expect complete obedience.

'Look,' he said. 'Verghast high echelon may be a misogynistic mess... which, I have to say, comes as a surprise given how many female soldiers it has raised. Like my mother.'

'By necessity,' she scoffed, 'and because it is the only sphere of power in which a Verghastite woman may flourish. The war allowed women to show their strength. It is an empowering moment against the traditional patri-archy that my dear mother is using to the full extent to secure her position. It also factored into her decision regarding me. If I was sent out after my illustrious father, and served with him, and won rank and glory, then I could return and succeed her, and it wouldn't matter if I was a man *or* a woman. Because glory in war is a currency that all Verghastites understand. So she had the juvenaticists accelerate my growth and packed me off.'

In the distance, the thunder of the bombing had grown more intense.

'My point is,' said Dalin, 'you don't need to hide here. The Ghosts will accept you for who you are. There'll be no prejudice like there is in your home hive.'

'Word would get back to Verghast, and that would undermine her care-fully laid plans,' Felyx said.

'I think you should tell someone,' he said.

'I think you should tell no one,' she replied.

There was silence between them for a while.

'What do I call you?' he asked.

'Felyx,' she said. 'Or Chass, as you do.'

'What's your real name?'

'Meritous Felyx Chass. Merity Chass. After my mother. But my name is employed artfully to disguise the gender.'

Dalin heard someone behind him. He turned sharply.

'What are you doing out here, Dal?' asked Yoncy.

'Yoncy!' Dalin jumped down off the wall.

Yoncy scratched at her bald scalp. She looked thinner and older without the little girl pigtails. Her smock dress seemed more like the tunic of a pre-pubescent boy. She looked awkward, but oddly more beautiful than she had done as a pig-tailed child.

'Mumma cut my hair off, Dal,' she said.

'How long has she been there?' Felyx asked, jumping off the wall in alarm.

'She cut my hair off because of the lice,' said Yoncy. 'The itchy lice. She cut off all my tails.'

'How long has she been there?' Felyx repeated. 'What did she hear? Dalin?'

'What were you talking about?' Yoncy asked.

'Oh, just things,' said Dalin.

'Were you talking about Papa Gaunt?'

'Yes,' said Felyx, warily.

'He is milignant commander now,' she said. 'They said so.'

'That's right,' said Felyx. 'My great father, greater by the hour.'

Yoncy cocked her starkly shaved head, and looked at Felyx with big eyes.

'He's your papa too? Papa Gaunt is?'

'He's my father, yes.'

Yoncy frowned and thought.

'What else were you talking about?' she asked. 'Who's Merity?'

Laksheema led them through to the large workspaces adjoining her pan-elled office. Grae followed. The workspaces were several joined chambers, lined with examination benches over which hung glass projection screens. Ordo tech-savants bowed to Laksheema, before turning back to their diligent examinations.

Laksheema had brought a small silver cyberskull from her desk. She set it, and then released it into the air as if she were letting slip a dove. It rose and hovered over her shoulder. They all immediately felt a slight prickling sensation. The drone was generating a clandestine jamming field around them.

'The stones are the chief items of interest,' said Laksheema. She clicked an actuator wand, and images of the stones appeared on the hanging protection plates. Close up views, both back and front, in high resolution. Domor looked at them and shuddered.

'I understand the asset thought these especially significant?' she said.

'That's my understanding,' said Fazekiel.

'Did he say why?'

'Neither Fazekiel nor I were present at the time of recovery,' said Baskevyl.

'I was,' said Domor. 'I was part of Strike Beta that went in with Gaunt, and made the recovery. We went into that foul fething place. It was like animals lived there, but Mabbon, he called it a college.'

'Mabbon?' asked Grae.

'The "asset",' Domor replied, surly.

'What else did he say?' asked Laksheema.

Domor shrugged.

'I don't know. We were under constant fire, and I was too busy shovelling this shit into carry-boxes. We all were. I wasn't really listening.'

Fazekiel pulled out a data-slate and consulted it.

'The record states that the area was a "college of heritence", a weapons lab, run – according to the asset – by the Anarch's *magir hapteka,* or weapon-wrights. All the material was said to be inert. That is to say, not actively tainted.'

'You had the asset's word on that?' asked Laksheema, dubiously.

'There were compelling reasons to believe it so,' Fazekiel said. 'More volatile, warped material was held in other areas.'

'A college of heritence,' Grae said.

'For weapons development,' Fazekiel said, reading from her thorough notes. 'One of many facilities constructed by Heritor Asphodel to supply war machines to the Anarch.'

'Asphodel, the insane genius,' mused Laksheema. 'Very probably a corrupted adept of the Mechanicum, possibly immensely old, sharing Mechanicum perverted secrets with the enemy.'

'That supposition is probably not cobalt-rated, ma'am,' said Grae.

'The drone hasn't blocked it,' she replied, glancing at the cyberskull hovering nearby. 'However, if I had said, in addition, that Asphodel is reckoned to be-'

Her mouth continued moving, but they could no longer hear her speaking. A faint buzzing from the cyberskull was blocking her words, redacting the classified information. Grae was nodding. He could hear her.

'Yes,' he said with a shudder, 'that's definitely vermilion clearance.'

Baskevyl, Domor and Fazekiel glanced at one another.

'Asphodel, curse his soul, is dead,' said Domor. 'Long dead, on Verghast. Colonel-Commissar Gaunt killed him. I mean... Militant Commander Gaunt.'

'The asset suggested that Asphodel was just one of many "heritors" working for the enemy,' said Fazekiel. 'The greatest, perhaps, but one of many. A cult of demented weaponwrights, presumably "inheriting" secrets from the Mechanicum, to follow your line of thought.'

'I am already fully aware of those theories,' said Laksheema curtly. 'I want to know details of your regiment's experience at the point of collection. What did the asset say about the place and these stones?'

'According to Gaunt's verbatim report,' said Fazekiel, returning to her transcript, 'the asset called them the *Glyptothek*. A "library in stone". He remembered them being brought to the Reach years before, and being treated as valuable even then. They were said to be xenos items of significance, recovered from one of the Khan Worlds. He wanted them collected, and considered them very important. He didn't know why, he just appreciated their significance, the significance the weaponwrights considered them to have. He considered them "a discovery of singular value".'

'They now have another name, do they not, Major Baskevyl?' asked Laksheema.

Baskevyl sighed and nodded.

'There is reason to believe they may be called eagle stones, ma'am,' he said.

'Because of the Aigor Nine Nine One incident?' she asked.

'Yes.'

'Which you were present for?'

'Yes, I was.'

Laksheema looked at her data-slate.

'You, and Major Kolea, whom I met yesterday, and two troopers, Maggs and Rerval?'

'That's correct, ma'am,' said Baskevyl.

'You heard a voice?'

Bask shook his head.

'I did not, ma'am,' he said. 'The voice was only heard by Rerval and Gol. Uhm, Major Kolea.'

'But you saw something?'

'We *fought* something, ma'am. A daemonic shadow. It slew two of our party. We drove it off.'

'Horrible,' said Grae, wrinkling his face in disgust.

'Afterwards,' asked Laksheema, 'did Gol relate what the voice had said?'

Don't use his name like that, Baskevyl thought. Don't talk about him like you know him.

'He made a full report, to our commanding officer. To Militant Commander Gaunt,' said Baskevyl. 'He also told me what the voice had said.'

'In private?'

'Yes.'

'Why did Gol confide in you?'

'Because I'm his friend,' said Bask.

'And what did Gol say it said, major?'

'The voice... identified itself as the "voice of Sek". It said, "Bring me the eagle stones".'

'And at the time, this meant nothing?' asked Laksheema.

'It meant nothing to anybody,' said Fazekiel.

'But then after that, during the boarding action?' asked the inquisitor.

'We found the damn stones had spilled out on the deck,' said Domor. 'In a pattern. Fapes... that's Major Bask's adjutant... he said they looked like an eagle. Wings spread.'

Laksheema turned to the bank of screens. She adjusted her wand again. The eight hololithic images copied themselves onto one screen, and formed into a pattern.

'Like that?' she asked.

'Just like that,' Domor nodded.

'And from the shape, and prompted by your adjutant's remark, you made the connection?' Laksheema asked Baskevyl.

'It's just a guess,' he said. 'A gut feeling. A coincidence that made too much nasty sense.'

'Are they here?' asked Domor. 'The actual stones?'

'No,' said Grae. 'Versenginseer Etruin is examining the artefacts at the Mechanicus facility at–'

A soft buzzing blocked out the end of his sentence.

'That's vermilion, colonel,' said Laksheema.

'My apologies,' said Grae.

'There is another detail which lends weight to the proposition that these are the eagle stones prized and desired by the Archenemy,' said Laksheema. 'Your ship was spared.'

'That's in the report too,' said Fazekiel stiffly.

'You suffered a translation accident, and were helpless,' said Laksheema.

'You were overrun by enemy personnel. An enemy killship of significant displacement, the–'

She checked her slate.

'–*Tormageddon Monstrum Rex*, had you at its mercy, but elected instead to destroy the Archenemy units boarding you. It then left you alone.'

'The grace of the Emperor is strange and beyond our understanding,' said Baskevyl. 'He works in–'

'Spare me the platitudes,' said Laksheema. 'An enemy battleship, not the most stable, restrained or logical entity in this universe, saved you and spared you. Does that not suggest there was something on board your vessel that was too valuable to annihilate?'

'That's one way of reading it,' said Baskevyl.

'It looks very much like it was ordered not to vaporise you,' Laksheema continued. 'Indeed, that it was ordered to protect said treasure, even from its own kind.'

'It would take the command of a magister or the Archon himself to halt and control a killship of that aggressive magnitude,' said Grae.

'Then there is the matter of the broadcast,' said Laksheema. 'The broadcast made by the killship.'

'I don't know about any broadcast, ma'am,' said Baskevyl.

'The broadcast was intercepted by a Major... Rawne,' said Laksheema. 'By his vox-officer. It was translated by your asset, the Etogaur.'

'I wasn't aware of this,' said Baskevyl.

'Me neither,' said Domor.

'It's in the mission report,' said Fazekiel. 'It was considered need-to-know only.'

'It seems this Major Rawne has some appropriate notion of confidentiality,' said Laksheema.

'Domor and Baskevyl are cobalt-cleared now, inquisitor,' said Grae.

Laksheema smiled. She looked at her data-slate and began to read. 'Let's see how far I get,' she said. 'The transcript of Mabbon Etogaur's translation reads, "That which is born must live" or perhaps "That which was constructed must remain whole". In full, "That which was made must remain whole... the offspring of the Great Master... all this shall be the will of he whose voice drowns out all others".'

She glanced up at the cyberskull.

'Well,' she said. 'All cobalt after all. Presumably because it is vague.'

'What does it mean, "offspring"?' asked Baskevyl.

'According to your asset,' said Laksheema, 'that is open to interpretation. Allegedly, the word "offspring" can mean a thing made, or a child, or something spawned. It is the female noun, so it might refer to a female child, but apparently in the Archenemy tongue, things are female. Ships, as an example, are called "she". In all likelihood, the statement refers to some construction of immense significance. My interrogators are pursuing the matter with the asset.'

'Where is Mabbon?' asked Baskevyl.

Laksheema replied, but the drone's buzz obscured her words.

'Do you know what the eagle stones are, ma'am?' asked Fazekiel.

'Undoubtedly xenos. Etruin is confident they match artefacts and cultural relics of the Kinebrach, a species that is known to have existed in the Khan Group until about ten thousand years ago.'

'The age of the Great Crusade,' said Fazekiel.

'They persisted for a short while beyond that,' said Laksheema. 'Into the age of Heresy.'

'But they no longer exist?' asked Fazekiel.

'Xenoarchaeologists believe they became extinct during that period.'

'As a result of the Great Heresy?' asked Baskevyl.

'My dear major,' said Laksheema, 'you know full well how patchy our records of ancient history are. We have no idea what happened to them.'

'I've heard the name, though,' said Baskevyl. 'When we were on Jago. The Kinebrach. They were the ones said to have built the fortress worlds.'

'Oh, they didn't build them,' said Laksheema. 'But they almost certainly used them.'

'What are the stones for?' asked Baskevyl.

'We have no idea,' said Laksheema. 'Nor do we have any idea why the Archenemy considers them to be so valuable. But it is quite apparent they are held in high esteem. Your friend Gol is our most direct corroboration of that.'

She looked at the three of them.

'Is there anything else you'd like to add?' she asked. 'Anything else you'd care to share? I advise you, in full view of Colonel Grae, that now is the time, in this convivial atmosphere. If it later transpires that you have withheld any pertinent information, your cobalt clearance and association with a militant commander will not be sufficient to shield you. If we are obliged to speak again, our discourse will be far less agreeable. Are we understood?'

They nodded.

'Anything?'

Domor and Fazekiel shook their heads.

'No, ma'am,' said Baskevyl.

'A moment,' she said, and turned to Grae. The two exchanged a few remarks that were entirely screened by the drone's aggravating buzz.

Laksheema looked back at them.

'That will be all,' she said.

They walked out into the stronghold's courtyard. Savant Onabel had told them to wait, and that transport back to the billet would be arranged. Baskevyl was certain that meant they had several hours to wait. It was starting to rain. It wasn't clear if the distant grumbling was thunder or a bombardment.

Baskevyl let out a deep, long breath. Fazekiel stood and fiddled obsessively with the buttons of her coat. Domor sat on a stone block and lit a lho-stick.

'I'll be happy for that to never happen again,' he said.

Bask nodded.

'I will talk Gaunt through it,' said Fazekiel. 'Relate what happened. Was it just me, or did either of you sense territorial gamesmanship here? The ordos, with their agenda, grinding against the Astra Militarum? Squabbling over how they divide information?'

'I got that,' said Baskevyl. 'Grae was uncomfortable. This is clearly very big.'

'I thought we were all on the same side,' said Domor, exhaling a big puff of smoke. His hands were shaking.

'We're supposed to be,' said Fazekiel.

'But who pulls the most rank?' asked Domor. 'I mean, when it comes down to it? The Inquisition, or Astra Militarum high command?'

'I would say the Warmaster,' said Baskevyl. 'In the long run, no matter the clout of the ordos, the Warmaster must have final authority. He's the representative of the Emperor.'

Domor glowered.

'Anyway,' he said, 'we should warn Gol as soon as we get back.'

'Warn him?' asked Baskevyl.

'Well, we pretty much sold him down the river,' said Domor. 'Didn't matter what we said or how we answered, Gol stayed in the frame. He was the poor feth it spoke to. Feth, right at the end there, what they were saying about him.'

Baskevyl looked at him.

'What do you mean, "at the end"?' he asked. 'The drone was redacting them. We couldn't–'

'Feth me, Bask,' said Domor, rising to his feet and grinding the butt of the lho-stick under his heel. 'All these years serving with Verghast scratch company grunts, and you don't watch mouths automatically?'

He tapped his augmetics.

'Screw the fancy drone and its crypto-field,' he said. 'I was lip reading them the whole time. Second nature.'

'What the feth did they say, Shoggy?' asked Baskevyl.

'That fancy bitch wants Gol. She told Grae as much. Says she wants him brought in right away, no arguments,' replied Domor. 'And from the look on Grae's face, it wasn't going to be a pleasant chat like the one we just had.'

NINETEEN

WEEDS

The yard in front of the Tanith billet was bustling. The munition resupply had finally arrived, in the form of three cargo-10 trucks in Munitorum drab. Hark, who had discovered that being the senior commissar attached to a militant commander carried more clout than being the senior commissar attached to a colonel, stood in discussion with the Munitorum adepts, processing the dockets. Spetnin, Theiss and Arcuda were supervising the men transferring the munitions off the flatbeds. Theiss and Elam had sand-bagged and dug-in one of the hab's old washroom blocks as a dump, and ghosts were lugging the long boxes and crates down the path.

Gol Kolea sat on a hab doorstep, enjoying the pale sun that had emerged briefly between the day's showers. In the makeshift kitchens nearby, the folk of the retinue had gathered to begin preparations for the 'big feast' Blenner had announced to celebrate Gaunt's elevation. There was a lot of bustle and commotion, and a lot of laughter. Zwiel was lending a hand, and apparently seeing fit to bless every utensil and every ingredient. The children, bored by the work, had broken off to play, chasing through the ruined edges of the compound area, and playing skipping games in the yard. He could see Yoncy, skipping across ropes swung by two younger girls. He could hear them chanting, some weird sing-song thing that he'd been told was a play-yard song from Tanith. 'The King of the Knives'. It sounded ominous, but then all the old scholam playsongs and nursery chants had darkness beneath their innocent words.

He watched Yoncy. Her shaved head was brutal, and she suddenly seemed bigger next to the smaller kids, almost ungainly. Tona had warned him. She was growing up now. She wasn't really a child any more, no matter how she behaved. Maybe the haircut had been a good thing, though Gol knew she hated it. No more pigtails. No more pretending she was just a baby.

Nearby, the Colours band started to play, a practice session. The noise seemed to make Yoncy jump. She covered her ears with her hands, and scowled. The children playing with her laughed.

What kind of life was she going to have as she became a young woman? Gol wondered. She'd stay among the retinue, because it was her family. Then what? Gol didn't see her following Dalin into the regiment. Would she just become one of the women folk? Would she marry some fine young lasman? It seemed like only yesterday she had been running around his feet and drawing him funny, simple pictures to pin over his bunk.

Gol reached into his jacket pocket and took out the last drawing she'd given him. He unfolded it and looked at it. It still gave him a chill. Just before the Aigor run, he'd eaten supper with Criid, Dalin and Yoncy. She'd done it for him then. Every detail of the Aigor horror was there: him and Bask and Luffrey, the two moons, the silo, the bad shadow.

How had she known that? Just another gruesome coincidence? The voice of Sek had reached Gol Kolea, and had threatened his offspring. If it could do that, then it could toy with the mind of a little girl. The idea disturbed him very much, that she could have been touched by that darkness. He would protect her, of course, if it ever came to it, but there was something about her that troubled him. He'd been estranged from both his children, but he'd managed to become close again with Dalin. But Dalin was a grown-up, and a lasman, and they had a connection. He loved Yoncy, but she always felt like a stranger. Remote from him.

It didn't matter. She was his child. He would keep the bad shadow away from her.

'Feth, but that haircut's cruel.'

Gol looked up. Ban Daur had wandered up. He tucked the picture away.

'Lice,' he said. 'Tona said it was for the best.'

Daur nodded.

'They'll all be like it in a day or two,' said Gol. 'Dozens of little shaven-headed children running about the place.'

Daur chuckled.

'Poor thing,' he said. 'It makes her look like a little boy.'

Gol glanced at him.

'Oh, no offence, Gol,' he said.

'None taken,' said Gol.

'Ironic, though,' said Daur.

'What's ironic?'

Daur shrugged.

'You know,' he said. 'Because of the misunderstanding.'

'What misunderstanding, Ban?'

Daur sat down on the step next to him.

'Elodie was telling me, oh, this is months ago. Back on Balhaut.'

'Years, you mean?'

'Right!' Daur shook his head. 'Elodie was asking around about me among the Verghast women. She wanted some dirt. Thought Zhukova and I had a thing.'

Gol raised his eyebrows.

'We didn't,' said Daur, tutting at his look. 'The point is, she was talking to the women about you, and asking if I'd known you back at Vervun-hive, and it came out that several of them swore blind your kids were both boys.'

'This is the women?'

'Yes,' said Daur, amused. 'Galayda, I think. Honne, maybe. I don't know.

They were completely sure of it. Came as a shock when Elodie put them straight.'

'They thought I had sons?'

'Yeah. You know how stories get all mangled up. Most people didn't even know you had kids with the retinue for a long time. They were convinced you had lost two sons on Verghast. Gol?'

Daur looked at him.

'Gol? Are you all right? Gol?'

Gol didn't answer. A memory had just dug into his brain, like the sun coming out through rain, like something sprouting up out of the ground. Him and Livy, Throne love her. On the high wall of Vervunhive, the Panorama Walk where he'd proposed to her. One of their rare, precious visits. A special day. He'd saved up bonus pay to buy them passes. Up above the hive, taking in the view, mixing with the high-hivers out on their constitutionals. The looks they got from those snooty bastards...

Livy had put her hand on her belly. There was barely a bump to show.

'It's a boy,' she had said.

That's how she'd told him. He'd roared with joy. The snooty bastards had all turned to look. That's how she'd told him.

About Dalin. It had to be. That's how she'd told him that Dalin was on the way. That was the first time. Throne, his memory had been so buckled and ruined after Hagia. Gol could only remember some of his old life. Some small, bright details. The rest was a blur.

It's a boy. He could hear her saying it. That's how she'd told him.

Except there'd been the cart between them. The babycart with the baby in it. Dalin. He'd had to save extra, pay extra, almost a full half-fare, so they could bring the babycart too.

It's a boy. And Dalin had been there, right there, already.

It's a boy.

Gol felt as if he was going to fall over, even though he was already sitting down.

'Gol, stop fething around. Are you all right?'

His head swam. He looked up and saw Daur staring at him. Daur had his hands on Gol's shoulders, propping him up.

'Gol? Feth it, you're white as a sheet.'

'A headache,' he said. 'I'm fine... Just a sudden headache.'

'It looks like more than a fething headache,' said Daur. 'I thought you were going to keel over.'

'I get them from time to time,' Gol said. 'You know, since...'

Daur nodded. The injuries Gol had taken on Phantine had been so severe, his recovery had been genuinely miraculous. Daur helped Gol up.

'I'll go see Curth,' he said.

'I think you'd better. Let me come with you.'

Kolea shook his head. His vision was still swimming.

'No, it's all right.'

Concerned, Daur stood and watched as Gol shuffled away. He watched as Gol turned and took a long look at Yoncy, playing in the yard.

* * *

'What's this now?' asked Didi Gendler, flicking aside a lho-stick.

A large, gloss black transport was pulling into the yard, followed by two staff vehicles. They were gloss black too, gleaming in the watery sunlight. The vehicles edged around the bottleneck of the munition trucks and the men unloading them, and drew up beside the medicae trailer.

'They're burying her, Didi,' said Meryn.

'Gaunt's bitch?' asked Jakub Wilder.

Meryn nodded. The three of them were standing at the side of the yard, under one of the plastek awnings.

'She gets a fething funeral?' asked Gendler.

'Yeah,' said Meryn.

'A private funeral?' asked Wilder.

'Of course,' said Meryn. 'She was... what do you call it? High-hive.'

'She was a gakking lifeward,' snarled Gendler. 'Some low-born tart. No House blood in her.'

'No blood in her at all, now,' said Meryn.

'That's fething cold,' said Wilder.

'She worked for the aristo scumbags, though, didn't she?' said Meryn. 'Employed by House Chass. All that fancy kit and augmetics. So she gets the works.'

'She gets the works because she's Gaunt's bitch,' said Gendler.

'She gets the works because she was lifeward to Gaunt's brat, and Gaunt's brat is high-hive blood, so that's the way it goes,' said Meryn.

He could see that Gendler was seething. Didi Gendler had been high-hive once, but he'd lost it all in the Zoican War, and Guard service during the act of Consolation had been about his only option. Sometimes, he got so wound up at his loss of status, Meryn thought the man would split right out of his pale, fair-haired skin and his raw bones would go stomping off to strangle someone. Gendler's resentment for Felyx Chass was legendary. He hated the privilege that got Felyx his sinecure in the regiment, and his special treatment.

'If I died,' Gendler said, 'Gaunt wouldn't even drag his heel in the dirt to make a grave.'

Meryn nodded.

'I have a question,' said Wilder. 'Fancy private funerals like that? They cost a lot. A fething lot. So who's paying for it?'

'Histye, soule,' said Ezra.

Gaunt looked up from his work. The Nihtgane was staring out of the window into the yard below. Gaunt got up. His desk was covered in data-slates. True to his word, Biota had couriered full technical specs for the Urdesh theatre over to Gaunt. There was a lot to go through, and what he'd studied already had left him worried.

Besides, he was distracted. The shade of Maddalena stood over him. He felt a numb sense of loss. Part of him worried that the loss would grow sharper as he processed it. Another part was afraid that his life had simply made him unfeeling towards death, that his capacity for emotional connection had withered to nothing.

Whatever, he'd lost track of time. It was almost noon.

He went over to the window and saw what Ezra was looking at.

The cortege had arrived. The hired mourners, in their long black coats, had got out and were walking towards the medicae trailer.

'Can you go find Felyx and tell him we'll be setting off shortly?' he asked Ezra.

The Nihtgane nodded.

'Ezra?'

'Soule?'

'I've asked Dalin to keep an eye on Felyx, now Maddalena's gone. But as a favour to me, could you...'

Ezra cocked his head quizzically.

'Just watch over him,' said Gaunt. 'Nothing intrusive, just from the shadows. But watch him, and look after him, and if things get dangerous, step in and help Dalin.'

'You need not ask it,' said Ezra.

Ezra passed Blenner as he left the room.

'Got a moment, Ibram?' Blenner asked lightly.

Gaunt was putting on his black armband.

'No, Vaynom.'

'Oh, is it that time already?'

Blenner went to the window. He watched as the mourners brought the coffin out and slid it into the back of the transport. Curth, arms folded, supervised them.

'Well, it can wait,' said Blenner. 'Later on.'

'I'm at staff later on,' said Gaunt.

'This evening, then?'

'All day, Blenner. I've been called in for a round of more detailed debriefs, then there's all that to work through.'

Gaunt nodded towards the data-slates on his desk.

'I'm sure staff knows all about the war, Ibram,' said Blenner.

Gaunt looked at him.

'I'm not sure they do,' he said. 'I've been looking at that material. I think I've seen something they've missed.'

'You've seen something they've missed?' said Blenner with a smile. 'Something that all the lords militant and fancy-pants generals and chief tacticians and intelligence service officers have–'

'Yes,' said Gaunt. 'Because they're too close. I'm fresh eyes. And it's startlingly obvious to me.'

Blenner swallowed. He felt his stress rising, his palms beginning to sweat. He knew that look. When Ibram Gaunt got that look, you knew shit was coming. Blenner did not want shit to be coming.

He crossed to the side table and helped himself to a glass of amasec.

'I presume you're not going to share your special theory with me?' he asked. As he poured the drink, he used his body to shield the fact he was slipping a pill from his pocket. Feth! Almost the last one.

'I'm not sharing it with anybody except staff just yet,' said Gaunt.

Blenner palmed the pill and knocked it down with the amasec.

'Throne, but elevation has changed you,' he said, trying to sound light. Gaunt didn't rise to it.

'Have you spoken to Ana?' Blenner asked.

'No. Why?'

'Not at all?' asked Blenner.

'In the course of regular duties, yes, but not otherwise. Why?'

'I think you should,' said Blenner, regretting that he'd knocked the amasec back in one and wondering if he could get away with a top up.

'Why?' asked Gaunt, staring at him.

'Well, things have been so hectic, Ibram. So much has happened. And now that poor lady is dead, and you and Ana were such good friends–'

'Did she say something to you?'

'Ana? No! No, I just think... you know... You must be aware that Doctor Curth is very fond of you...'

Gaunt picked up his cap.

'I don't have time for this, Vaynom, and even if I did, it isn't appropriate.'

'A man talking to his best and oldest friend isn't appropriate?' asked Blenner, helping himself to another amasec anyway.

'Feth's sake, Blenner. What do you want?'

Blenner looked wounded.

'Well, if you're going to be like that, lord militant commander,' he said. 'I think you and Curth should talk. She's troubled.'

'I understood,' said Gaunt, 'that you were keeping good company with Doctor Curth. A fact you've clumsily dropped into conversation on several occasions.'

'I am. I have. We have an understanding.'

'What have you done, Vaynom?'

'Nothing.'

Gaunt took a step forwards.

'Have you messed with her?' he asked.

'What?'

'I know you, Blenner. Remember that. You're a rogue. A lush. A ladies' man. You get what you're after and then you leave without a goodbye. You don't care about people.'

'Now hang on–'

'If you've strung her along,' said Gaunt. 'If you've messed with her affections and then done your usual trick of bolting. If you've hurt her–'

'That's rich, coming from you!' snapped Blenner.

'Lose the tone! What did you do to her? What have you said?'

'It's not like that at all!' replied Blenner. His hands were shaking. 'We're not together or anything. We're friends. Feth you, Ibram! You're the one she has feelings for. You always have been. Take a long look at yourself. A long, hard look! Because if anyone is messing Ana Curth about, it's you! She cares! She's worried about you! She's worried that your grief might–'

'That's enough, commissar,' said Gaunt.

'Yes, well.'

'I've known you a long time, Blenner. I've put up with your antics and your flaws for a long time. You can talk to me with a familiarity that very few other people in this regiment can get away with. But when you're in uniform, you don't address me like that.'

'I'm sorry,' said Blenner. He put the glass down.

'That charm of yours only runs so far,' said Gaunt. 'Sort yourself out, and fast, or I'll have to review your posting with this regiment.'

'Yes, sir.'

There was a knock at the door. One of the Tempestus Scions looked in.

'I'm coming, Sancto,' said Gaunt.

'My lord,' said the Scion, 'word has just arrived. You are summoned to the palace.'

'No, I'm due this afternoon.'

'The summons was very clear, my lord. You are to report immediately.'

'But I've got a funeral to–'

Gaunt stopped. He took a deep breath.

'Bring the transport round, Sancto,' he said. 'I'll be right there.'

Blenner looked at Gaunt.

'That's bad timing,' said Blenner. 'I know you would want to go with your son. Do you want me to–'

'No, Vaynom. I don't want you to do anything.'

Gaunt buckled on his sword, straightened his coat, and left the room.

Alone, Blenner stared at the glass on the side. His hands were shaking badly and his heart was racing. He saw his future sliding away from him. Gaunt's intimation that bad trouble was coming was bleak enough. He didn't want that. But he had comforted himself that now he was posted to the command group of a militant commander, privilege would protect him. That kind of swing could get a man out of the front line.

But if Gaunt was tiring of him, if he'd pushed the friendship too far, then he'd get a posting. He'd get rotated out. He'd get a placement with some feth-knows regiment, and he'd probably end up smack on the line.

At the fething shitty end of the fething war.

Blenner killed the drink in one. He needed to be calm. He needed pills. He needed to call in a favour with Wilder.

Hark walked in.

'The cortege is here,' said Hark. 'Where's Gaunt?'

'I haven't seen him,' said Blenner.

'What's up with you, Vaynom?'

'Nothing,' said Blenner. He forced a smile. 'Nothing at all, Viktor.'

He walked out and left Hark staring, baffled.

'Don't get up,' said Gaunt. Criid did anyway.

'What's the matter, sir?' she asked. Gaunt stepped into her room and pulled the door closed.

'I've been called to staff. I have to go.'

'I'm sorry,' she said.

'I wondered if you could–'

'Of course,' Criid said. 'I was going anyway.'

Gaunt took off his armband and handed it to her.

'And, Tona, I hoped you might explain–'

'I will, sir,' she said.

'Express my apologies. Try to make Felyx understand.'

'I will, sir,' she said.

'Thank you, captain.'

A crowd had gathered in the yard. Some had just come to look at the cortege out of curiosity. Others had come to stand in respect.

Felyx walked into the yard and approached the gloss black vehicles. He was wearing his number one uniform. He looked very drawn and solemn.

'Where is... the militant commander?' he asked.

Curth shook her head.

'I'm sure he's coming, Felyx,' she said.

'He's late. I sent Dalin to find him,' said Felyx.

Zwiel came over to stand with them. The three of them stared at their reflections in the smoked glass of the transport's rear windows.

'Saint Kiodrus Emancid is a good templum,' said Zwiel. 'A fine place. Very tall. I hear the ecclesiarch is a splendid fellow too. Not stupid, which is a benefit at times like this.'

He held out a small posey of flowers to Felyx.

'Just a simple garland I made,' he said. 'For you to take. Islumbine.'

'Where did you find islumbine?' asked Curth, surprised.

'I found it growing by the Sabbatine altar in the chapel near here,' said Zwiel. 'Nowhere else. It seemed like a blessing to me.'

He looked at Felyx.

'They're the holy flower, sacred to Saint Sabbat.'

'I know what they are,' said Felyx. He took the flowers.

Criid joined them. She looked tall and very commanding in her formal uniform. The black band was around her arm.

'We're waiting for Gaunt,' Curth told her.

'Dalin's gone to fetch him,' said Felyx.

'Felyx,' said Criid. 'The militant commander has been called to the palace. A priority summons from staff. He sends his sincere apologies.'

'Oh, that's fething unbelievable,' whispered Curth.

'My father's not coming?' asked Felyx.

'He is very sorry,' said Criid. 'He's asked me to attend on his behalf, as captain of A Company, to represent the regiment.'

'He can't be bothered to come?' Felyx asked.

'It's not like that,' said Criid.

'He can't be bothered to come,' said Felyx. 'Fine. I don't care. He can go to hell.'

'Aw, look at that,' whispered Meryn at the back of the crowd.

'The little fether's tearing up,' said Gendler with far too much satisfaction in his voice. 'Boo hoo! Where's your high-and-mighty daddy now, you little brat?'

'Typical,' said Wilder. 'Gaunt doesn't care about anybody. Not even his own son.'

'It's tragic, is what it is,' agreed Meryn.

'I still want to know who's paying for all this crap,' muttered Wilder.

'That would be Felyx Chass,' said Blenner, appearing behind them. They straightened up fast.

'As you were,' said Blenner. 'I was actually looking for you, Captain Wilder. Just checking in while I remembered. I wondered if... if any of your recent inspections had turned up any more contraband? Any pills, you know?'

Wilder glanced at Meryn and Gendler. Both pretended to look away, but Meryn shot Wilder a wink.

'Pills, commissar?' replied Wilder. 'Yes, I think I might have stumbled on some somnia, just yesterday.'

'Deary me,' said Blenner. 'Well, I had better take that into my safekeeping as soon as possible.'

'I'll go and get it for you directly, sir,' said Wilder.

'We really should find out where that stuff's coming from,' said Meryn idly. 'Someone could end up with a nasty habit.'

'That would be unfortunate, captain,' Blenner agreed.

'So, the boy?' Gendler said to Blenner. 'Gaunt's son, he paid for this rigmarole?'

'Yes, Didi,' said Blenner. 'Deep pockets, that one, apparently. Rich as feth. Just sent a message to the counting house to access funds.'

'Did he now?' echoed Gendler. 'Well, well.'

Dalin hurried up the stairs to the hab floor where Gaunt's quarters lay. There was no sign of Gaunt anywhere, and the cortege was waiting.

There was someone in Gaunt's office, though. He heard voices through the half-open door, and went to knock.

He paused.

'Can you do it, Viktor?' Kolea was asking. 'Can you authorise it?'

'It's highly unorthodox, major,' Hark replied. 'I mean, highly. But I seem to have more robust clout with the Munitorum these days. I'll get on the vox and place the request.'

'Will Gaunt have to know?' asked Kolea.

A pause.

'No, we can keep this between us, for now. It's rather personal, after all. If anything comes of it, we can decide how we talk to him about it.'

'Thanks, Viktor.'

'Come on, Gol. Don't mention it. I can see how important this is. Do you know, does Vervunhive maintain its own census database, or is it a planet-wide list?'

'Vervunhive has its own census department. I remember them sending the forms out every five years. Births, deaths, marriages. The usual.'

'And you just want a confirmation of recorded gender?' asked Hark.

'Boy or girl, Viktor. That's all I want to know.'

Dalin froze, his hand reaching for the doorknob.

They knew. They had fething worked it out.

'What are you hovering there for, trooper?' said a voice behind him.

Dalin wheeled. It was Major Pasha. There were several men with her. Tall, stern-looking men in cold grey uniforms.

'S-sorry!' Dalin stammered.

'I'm looking for Major Kolea,' said Pasha. 'I was told he'd come up here.'

'He's inside, I think,' said Dalin, gesturing to the door.

Pasha knocked and entered.

'Can I help you, major?' Hark asked with a smile. His grin faded as he saw the men behind Pasha.

'These gentlemen, sir,' said Pasha. 'They're looking for Major Kolea. They say they've come to fetch him.'

Colonel Grae stepped into the room, flanked by the intelligence service security detail he had brought with him.

'Major Kolea,' he said.

'Colonel Grae,' Kolea replied.

'I'm sorry, Kolea,' said Grae. 'I need you to come with me.'

'What the feth is this about?' asked Hark.

'Please stand aside, commissar,' said Grae, showing more composure in the face of an angry Viktor Hark than many would have been able to summon. 'By order of Astra Militarum intelligence, Major Kolea is under arrest.'

TWENTY

OFFENSIVE

The main keep of the Urdeshic Palace loomed over Gaunt as he stepped out of the transport into the High Yard. The day was turning into what seemed to be a vague haze typical of Urdesh. The sky seemed flat and back-lit, as if bandaged with cloud, smog from the city's plants and refineries, and fyceline smoke from the bombardments in Zarakppan. It made the keep seem like a black monster, improbably tall, a void designed to swallow up his life.

He'd brought Daur, Bonin and Beltayn with him. Beltayn, because he was Gaunt's aide and adjutant, Bonin to represent the regiment's scouting speciality, and Daur as a member of the officer cadre. Those were the nominal reasons, anyway. It was more because Gaunt felt comfortable having good soldiers at his side. The four Tempestus Scions followed them up the steps. They were good soldiers too. The best, depending on how you measured such things, but Gaunt didn't know them, and they smacked too much of the zealous indoctrination of the Prefectus. They reminded him of his own early days, his training in the Commissariat Scholam. He might have become a Scion too, had he not shown brains.

Or perhaps if he had shown more ferocious, unquestioning fervour.

Bonin sniffed the air. There was a pungent, vegetable stink that was undoubtedly the sea, and a sharper reek of sulphur. He wrinkled his nose.

'The volcanic vents leak sulphur,' said Beltayn, noticing.

'Volcanic?' asked Daur.

'The Great Hill,' said Gaunt. 'This entire precinct is built in the plug of the volcanic cone.'

'Great,' said Bonin.

'Geothermal energy, Mach,' said Gaunt. 'That's what drives the industry of this great world. That smell is the reason Urdesh is such a critical holding.'

'Just adjusting to the idea we're standing on a volcano, sir,' said Bonin.

They entered the palatial atrium, Sancto and his Scions in match step behind them. The bare stone walls rose to soaring arches, lined with regimental flags that draped down their mast-like poles now they were sheltered from the wind. Four immense iron siege bombards sat on stone plinths, yawning at the doors. Officers stood in groups, talking in low voices. Messengers scurried to and fro. An aide informed Gaunt that Biota would attend him shortly, and that he should wait in the White Hall.

The White Hall was a banqueting room of considerable size, its walls whitewashed plaster. The room had been cleared of all furniture, except a long trestle table and a bench, and the emptiness made the place seem bigger.

The walls were covered in framed picts. Gaunt wandered over to examine some as he waited. They were regimental portraits: dour-faced men in stiff poses and stiffer formal uniforms, grouped in rows like sports teams. No one was smiling. Gaunt read the hand-scripted titles. Pragar, Urdesh Storm Troop, Jovani, Helixid, Narmenian, Keyzon, Vasko Shock, Ballantane, Volpone, Vitrian, Gelpoi... The history of the crusade in the form of the faces that had waged it.

Ban Daur joined him, and looked at the pictures thoughtfully.

'I wonder...' he began, 'I wonder how many of the men in these pictures are still alive.'

Gaunt nodded.

'Indeed, Ban,' he replied. He had been wondering how many had been long dead before their images were unpacked in this room and hung on hooks.

Along the base of the wall were stacks of old frames that had been taken down at some point to make room for the Imperial display. The whitewash of the wall was marked with smoke lines and faded oblongs where other pictures had once hung and their replacements had not matched in size. Daur bent down and tipped through the unhung frames.

'Look, sir,' he said. Gaunt crouched next to him.

These pictures were much older, dusty. Some were paintings. Images of proud warbands, and gatherings of stern industrialists. Gaunt lifted a few to read the captions. Zarak Dynast Clan, Ghentethi Akarred Clan, Hoolum Lay-Technist, Hoolum First Army, Clan Gaelen Dynast...

'I don't recognise the names,' said Daur, 'or the uniforms.'

'This is Urdesh's history, Ban,' said Gaunt. 'Its long and troubled history.'

'They aren't all military,' said Daur.

'Urdesh has always been a place of industry, from its first settlement onwards,' Gaunt replied. 'The Mechanicus has been here from the start, exploiting the planet's energy sources, building enclaves and forge manufactoria. But Urdesh... It's a geographical mosaic of archipelagoes and island chains.'

'A mosaic?' asked Daur, confused.

'A patchwork,' said Gaunt. 'Balkanised, without central government. I mean, for the longest time, there was no central authority. Urdesh was riven by low-level conflicts as warlords and feudal dynasties vied with each other.'

'Noble families held local power?' asked Daur.

'Right, they did, controlling city states, and squabbling for resources. Eventually, as Urdesh's importance grew, the Mechanicus exerted its influence, forcibly unifying the world under its control. The dynast families and city states were brought into line or eliminated.' Daur frowned.

'So the Mechanicus made Urdesh?' he asked.

'They made it the pivotal world it is now,' said Gaunt, 'and are regarded as the planet's owners and saviours.'

'What happened to the nobility?' asked Daur.

Gaunt shrugged.

'The most powerful families retained power in partnership with the Tech Priesthood,' he replied, 'providing ready work forces and standing armies. The dynasts that survived unification prospered, building their enclaves around the Mechanicus hubs, and even forming brotherhoods.'

'Brotherhoods? What does that mean?'

'Unions, allied labour groups... even some technomystical orders as the Mechanicus shared and farmed out its lesser mysteries in return for loyal service. Some of the most able weaponshops on Urdesh are not Mechanicus, Ban. They're dynastic lay-tech institutions, where the old warlord families of Urdesh machine weapons the Mechanicus has taught them to make.'

They rose from the pictures.

'You've studied your briefing material, I see,' smiled Daur.

'I read up as best I could,' said Gaunt. 'To be honest, I attempted to read the precis background of the world, but I cast it aside. The history and fractured politics are more complex than the damn crusade.'

Daur chuckled. He'd had briefing packets like that come across his desk.

'Besides, it's pointless,' said Gaunt.

'Pointless?' asked Daur.

'Whatever Urdesh has been, Ban, that era is dying. The crusade will either fully liberate the world and centralise its control in a new Imperial order, or the world will become extinct. These pictures, relegated to the floor, are a footnote to a complex and involved chronicle that has ceased to be relevant.'

They turned as the door opened. Urienz strode in, acknowledging the smart salute of Gaunt's Scions. He left his own entourage of aides and soldiers waiting in the hall. Gaunt stepped to meet him, Daur, Beltayn and Bonin hanging back.

'Heard you were here, Gaunt,' Urienz said.

They shook hands.

'Just passing by,' said Urienz. 'I'm called to Zarakppan. It's hotting up. The devils are pushing closer.'

'A futile effort, surely?' said Gaunt.

Urienz shrugged.

'Anyway,' he said, producing a slip of paper from his pocket. 'The address of my tailor, as promised.'

Gaunt took the note and nodded his thanks.

Urienz took him by the elbow and stepped him away from the three Ghosts and the Scions.

'A word,' he said, quietly.

'Of course.'

'We know,' he said.

'Know?' asked Gaunt.

'Of the scheme Van Voytz and Cybon are cooking up.'

'Who's we?' asked Gaunt.

Urienz shrugged.

'Other senior staff. It's an open secret. Some of us have been approached to lend our support.'

'You turned the opportunity down?'

Urienz smiled.

'There are many who do not share Cybon's view. Many who remain loyal to Macaroth.'

'I believe everyone is loyal to Macaroth,' said Gaunt.

'I'm advising you to think carefully, Gaunt,' Urienz said. 'I have no quarrel with you, and I can see why they've picked you as their man. Few would block you. That's not the point. We're on a knife edge. The last thing we need is a change of command. The disruption would be catastrophic.'

'So this is a friendly word?' asked Gaunt.

'There are some, perhaps, who would be more hostile,' Urienz admitted. 'Just think about what I'm saying. The crusade doesn't need a headshot like this. Not now.'

'The proposal can be blocked,' said Gaunt, 'very simply. It's not a conspiracy. It's a political effort. If you know, then the Warmaster must be aware too.'

'Who knows what he's thinking?' said Urienz. 'None of us are going to confront him with the matter. He's been known to shoot the messenger, even if that messenger is bringing valuable intelligence. Look, if it goes forward, he might step down quietly. But he could as easily go to war with Cybon and his cronies. None of us want to step into that crossfire. And that's where you'd be, Ibram. You'd be standing right in front of Cybon. The political bloodbath could put us back years. Throne, it could cripple us. Lose us the entire campaign.'

'You mean Urdesh?'

'I mean the damn crusade. Macaroth isn't perfect, but he's Warmaster, and he's the Warmaster we've got right now. This is not a cart of fruit that needs to get upturned.'

'If your concern is this great, sir,' said Gaunt, 'you should speak to the Warmaster. Inform him of what's afoot. Encourage discussion.'

'I don't need that flak, Gaunt. No one does. Turn Cybon down. Don't go along with him. They don't have another decent candidate to sponsor, none that the rest of staff would accept. You step aside, and they can't move ahead. The whole affair dies off. Let it blow over, bide your time. Once Urdesh is done and finished with, once the heat is turned down and we've got time to breathe, more of us might be willing to consider the process favourably.'

'Thank you for your candour,' said Gaunt.

Urienz smiled.

'We're all on the same side, eh? I like you. I mean you no ill will. You've walked straight into this, and you're barely up to speed. I thought a word to the wise was a good idea. And might save us all more grief than we can handle.'

Gaunt nodded. They shook hands again. Urienz turned to leave.

'Check out that tailor of mine,' he called over his shoulder as he strode out.

'What was that about?' asked Daur.

'Appropriate clothing,' said Gaunt.

'What?'

'About looking like the right person for the job,' said Gaunt.

The door opened again. Chief Tactical Officer Biota entered.

'Lord militant,' he said. 'Sorry for the delay. We must begin at once.'

Felyx looked up.

'Why have we stopped?' he asked.

Criid sat forwards in her seat and peered through the vehicle windows at the funeral transport ahead. Dalin said nothing. He'd been quiet since they'd set off, not just respectful, but as though he was brooding on something. Criid hadn't wanted to ask him what in front of Felyx.

'Traffic,' Criid said. 'At the next street junction. We'll be under way again soon.'

'On Verghast,' said Felyx, 'traffic parts for a cortege. Out of respect. The cortege does not stop.'

'Well, this is Urdesh,' said Criid.

'A place where respect seems to be in pitifully short supply,' murmured Felyx.

Criid looked at him. Gaunt's son was almost cowering sullenly in the seat corner, gazing out of the side window at nothing. She decided not to press it.

One of the hired mourners, a stiff figure in black, had climbed out of the funeral transport and was stalking back to their vehicle.

'Stay with Felyx,' she said to Dalin and got out.

'What's the problem?' she asked.

'The street is closed, ma'am,' said the mourner. 'There are Astra Militarum blockades here. Down as far as Kental Circle, I believe.'

'Why?' asked Criid. The man shook his head. She glanced at the street around her. It wasn't busy, but the traffic was stationary. Pedestrians, most of them civilians, seemed to be hustling away, as if they had somewhere urgent to go.

The mourner checked his pocket chron.

'The service is not for another seventeen minutes, ma'am,' the mourner said. 'We have plenty of time. We will find another route.'

'Do that,' said Criid.

'I'm waiting for the explanation,' said Viktor Hark.

Colonel Grae looked at him. The man was annoyed. The grey Chimera they were riding in was rumbling through the Hollerside district, and Hark had no idea of their destination.

'There was no reason for you to accompany us, commissar,' said Grae.

'I think there's every reason,' said Hark. 'You've taken a senior officer of my regiment into custody with no explanation. I'm not going to let you just march him off.'

He glanced back down the payload bay. Kolea was sitting on a fold-down seat near the rear hatch, flanked by security troops from the intelligence service. They hadn't cuffed him, but they had taken his sidearm, his micro-bead and his straight silver.

'The issue is sensitive,' Grae said.

'And I can probably help you with it, if you bring me up to speed,' said Hark. 'Colonel, this man is one of our finest officers. He's a war hero. I'm not talking small stuff. He's blessed by the Beati–'

'I'm aware of his record,' said Grae.

'He's in line for promotion to regimental command,' said Hark. 'Quite apart from Major Kolea's fate, I am, as you might expect, keenly concerned for the welfare and morale of my regiment.'

Grae looked him in the eye. Hark was disturbed by the trouble he read in the man's face.

'Major Kolea's significance and record are precisely why I've taken him in,' he said. 'Matters have arisen. The ordos have taken an unhealthy interest in him.'

'Unhealthy for whom?' asked Hark.

'For Major Kolea.'

'This is the Inquisitor Laksheema I've heard about?'

Grae nodded.

'The ordos wants Kolea. I tried to deflect, but intelligence is very much the junior partner in this,' said Grae. 'I have instructions to protect Kolea as an asset–'

'Instructions from where?' asked Hark.

'Staff level,' said Grae. 'High staff level. We need him shielded from the ordos. Laksheema could cause us some major and unnecessary set-backs if she gains custody.'

'I thought we were all playing nicely together,' said Hark.

'Come now, Commissar Hark,' said Grae, 'you are a man of experience. With the best will in the world, and despite aspiring to the same high ideals, the departments of the Imperium often grind against each other.'

'This is territorial?'

'Let's just say that the stringent application of Inquisitorial interest will slow down the ambitions of the Astra Militarum.'

Hark frowned.

'You've taken him into custody to prevent the ordos doing it?'

'I was obliged to agree with Laksheema that Kolea's detention was urgently required,' said Grae. 'I couldn't disagree. But I could get there first.'

'He's in detention, just as she wanted...'

'But not *her* detention.'

'This is protective.'

'It will take the ordos a while to work out where Kolea is, and longer to process the paperwork to have him transferred to their keeping. That buys us time. In the long run, they'll get him. The Inquisition always gets what it wants. But we can delay that inevitability.'

Hark exhaled heavily in wonder.

'Tell me about these issues,' he said.

* * *

Chief Tactical Officer Biota brought them to the war room. The first thing that struck Gaunt was the temperature. Several hundred cogitators, arranged over five storeys, generated considerable heat. Despite the size of the chamber, the air was swampy. Immense air ducts and extractor vents had been fitted into the chamber ceiling, and hung down like the pipes of a vast temple organ over the main floor. They chugged constantly, and the breeze they created flapped the corners of papers stacked on desks.

Entry was on the first floor, a broad gallery that extended around the chamber's sides and overlooked the busy main hall. Three more galleries were ranged above the first, and Gaunt could see they were all teaming with cogitator stations and personnel. At the centre of the main floor below lay a titanic strategium display, the size of a banqueting table, its surface flickering with holographic data and three-dimensional geographic relief. Nineteen vertical hololith plates were suspended around the main table, projecting specific Urdeshi theatres and the near-space blockade. Adepts with holo-poles leant across the strategium table to sweep data around, or used the poles like fishing rods to move captured data packets from one plate to another. There was a constant murmur of voices.

Biota led them up the ironwork stairs to the second gallery, which was packed with high-gain voxcaster units. The trunking spilled across the floor was as dense as jungle creepers, and the Munitorum had laid down flakboard walkways between the stations to prevent tripping and tangling. Message runners darted past, carrying urgent despatches from one command department to another.

'This way,' said Biota. They climbed to the third gallery. The war room had once been the great hall of the keep, Gaunt presumed. The towering windows were stained glass, and cast a ruddy gloom across the scene. Each desk, cogitator and work station was lit by its own lumen globe or angle lamp.

The third level gallery was divided into sections for the main division chiefs, each with its own smaller strategium system and cogitator staff. Each zone was privacy screened with a faint, shimmering force field. Gaunt passed one where three Urdeshi marshals were arguing across a table, then another where Bulledin was briefing Grizmund and a quartet of armour chieftains.

Van Voytz and Cybon were waiting in the third. Colonel Kazader and about twenty officers and tactical specialists were with them.

Biota wanded the privacy veil open to admit Gaunt.

'Your men can wait here,' he said.

'The Scions can,' said Gaunt. 'These Ghosts are my staff, so they'll be coming with me.'

'I really don't think–' Biota began.

'Bram! Get in here!' Van Voytz called jovially.

'Follow me, please,' Gaunt said to Daur and the others.

Van Voytz got up and clapped Gaunt on the arm paternally. Cybon, sullen, sat at the strategium.

'Good morning to you, my lord militant,' Van Voytz said. He was in 'good humour' mood, but Gaunt had known the lord general's moods long enough to catch the tension.

'We were scheduled for this afternoon, sir,' said Gaunt.

'Things have moved up,' said Cybon, just a steel hiss.

'I doubt very much you haven't absorbed the briefing data already, Bram,' said Van Voytz. 'You always were a quick study. Diligent.'

'I have, as it happens,' said Gaunt. 'I would have appreciated longer. It's considerable and complex.'

'Well, we'll have the room to begin with,' said Van Voytz, nodding to Kazader and looking significantly at Gaunt's men.

'I'm going to have to brief my men anyway,' said Gaunt. 'This is Captain Daur, G Company lead, one of my seniors. Beltayn is my adjutant. Bonin is scout company, so he represents the Tanith specialty. It'll save time if they hear it first hand. I believe time is of the essence.'

Bonin, Beltayn and Daur had all drawn to salute the lord generals. Van Voytz glanced at Cybon, got a curt nod, then accepted the salute.

'Stand easy,' he said. 'Good to meet you.'

'They're here to take notes, are they?' asked Cybon.

'They are, sir,' said Gaunt.

Cybon looked at Bonin. Daur and Beltayn had both brought out dataslates. Bonin was standing with his hands behind his back.

'That man doesn't have a pen,' said Cybon.

'He doesn't need one,' said Gaunt.

'Immediate update, as of this morning,' said Van Voytz. Biota flipped the table view to a projection of a southern hemispheric area.

'The hot spot is Ghereppan,' said Van Voytz. 'All eyes on that. Major conflict reported in the over-nights. We think Sek is concentrating a new effort there. He may be in that zone in person.'

'That's where the Saint is?' asked Gaunt.

'Leading the main southern efforts,' said Biota.

'Also of note, however–' Van Voytz started to say.

'She's a target,' Gaunt interrupted.

'What?'

'Is that deliberate or accidental?'

'She's leading the forces there,' said Van Voytz.

'Nominally,' Cybon added.

'But she's bait,' said Gaunt. 'Is that by design?'

'What are you saying, Bram?' asked Van Voytz.

'You put our highest value asset on the ground under Sek's nose,' said Gaunt. 'He's biting. Was that deliberate?'

Van Voytz glanced at Cybon.

'I'm asking,' said Gaunt, 'if this is part of a projected policy by the Warmaster. To bait the Archenemy.'

'She's a senior commander,' said Cybon.

Gaunt pointed to the table.

'Of course. But she is also a symbolic asset. If the Ghereppan action was commanded by you, sir, or Urienz, or me, do you suppose the enemy disposition would be the same? You kill one of us, you kill a senior officer. You kill the Saint, then you win an immense psychological victory.'

Van Voytz cleared his throat.

'There is fury here,' said Gaunt, running his finger along the lines of the three-dimensional modelling. 'An urgent, careless onrush. Look, they clearly haven't secured these highways, or either of these refinery areas. This vapour mill has been bypassed. Those are all strategic wins. The Archenemy is effectively ignoring them in its effort to reach Ghereppan and engage. Sek sees the Saint as a vital target, more vital than any of the forge assets on this world. Of course he does. So see how he reacts? His tactics are hasty, eager and over-stretching. They are not typical of his usual, careful methodology.'

'I have... I have already noted to you,' said Biota, 'that there is a madness in the Anarch's battlefield craft. No logic. This has been going on for a while.'

'You have, sir,' replied Gaunt, 'and no wonder. There *is* a logic, it's just not the logic we would apply. I'll ask again, is the Saint being used as bait to draw the Anarch into an unwise over-stretch?'

'We are aware that she is a tempting prospect,' said Van Voytz.

'Really?' asked Gaunt. 'A tempting prospect? I've heard neither of you confirm that her deployment is a deliberate tactic of provocation. I'd be reassured if you said so. It's clinical, and risky, but it's ruthlessly effective. What troubles me is that staff is unaware of the effect.'

'Once again, sir,' said Kazader indignantly, 'you speak with an insulting tone that–'

'Shut up,' Gaunt told him. He took the wand from Biota and adjusted the table view to a greater scale.

'The Archenemy of man is an unholy monster,' said Gaunt, 'but we'd be fools to underestimate his intelligence. And idiots to presume his motives are the same as our own. See? In the Ghereppan zone, Sek's entire approach has shifted. By placing the Saint there, we have altered the enemy's plans. He's not interested in Urdesh. He's interested in the Saint.'

'We did...' Cybon began. 'That is to say, the Warmaster did reckon on a shift of tactics. The Saint isn't bait. More... a goad. You have pointed out that Sek's mode of warfare has altered. We have begun to push him into rash structural positioning and unsupported advance.'

'Thank you, sir, for confirming my appraisal at last,' said Gaunt. 'Yes, it is working... but it must be capitalised on. Sek could be broken at Ghereppan. You've made him clumsy, and weakened his core. But if this ruse fails, he takes the Saint and we suffer a critical loss.'

'It will be capitalised on, sir,' snapped Cybon.

'It can be capitalised on by the commander on the ground,' said Gaunt. 'There are huge opportunities to throttle or even crush the enemy forces. Of course, the commander on the ground needs be *aware* of the situation in order to capitalise on it. Is she?'

There was silence.

'Does the Saint know she's your goad, Lord Cybon?' asked Gaunt. 'If she doesn't, for feth's sake... She won't appreciate the enemy's weakness and won't be able to exploit it.'

'She has senior officers,' said Van Voytz. 'Advisors...'

'Is staff here advising her too?' asked Gaunt. 'Or are we just assuming? Bait needs to know that it's bait if the trap is going to work.'

Cybon rose to his feet.

'That crest, Gaunt, has made you impudent,' he said. 'You lecture us about tactics?'

'I think these are Macaroth's tactics,' said Gaunt. 'I think he sees it very clearly. He has assigned staff to implement them, perhaps without fully explaining his thinking. Staff is executing a plan without fully appreciating *why* it's a plan. This, I think, is an example of the lack of interchange you complained to me about.'

'Now listen, Gaunt,' said Van Voytz, his face flushed.

'I want to win this war, general,' said Gaunt. 'I doubt I'm the only person in this room who thinks that's the foremost priority. Before we implement the Warmaster's orders, we need to comprehend his ideas.'

'Are you done?' asked Cybon.

'I've barely started,' said Gaunt. 'It's not just the Saint. You think she's the only bait here on Urdesh? Chief Tactical Officer Biota related to me the "madness" of Sek's operations on this world. Both sides should be striving to acquire, as intact as possible, the considerable resources of this forge world. After all, that's why the reconquest wasn't given to the hammer-fist of the fleet. Sek's schemes have, for months, seemed to be disjointed, as if the monster has lost his way, descended into feral nonsense. But what we're seeing today at Ghereppan can be enlarged planet-wide. From the outset, Sek has been less interested in Urdesh than in the value we place upon it. We are holding back so that Urdesh remains intact. He is counting on that. He is counting on the fact that we value this planet as a commodity to be preserved. I believe that he is so anxious to prove his worth... or so anxious to repudiate his reputation in the eyes of the Archon... that the possession of Urdesh is secondary to him. He has set the trap. He has laid the bait for us. That bait is Urdesh and Sek himself. We are so eager to take this world whole and end him. So eager, we have brought the Saint. The Saint, the Warmaster, and a significant section of high command staff.'

Gaunt looked at them.

'Sek doesn't want Urdesh,' he said. 'He wants to decapitate the crusade.'

The late morning had brought heavy rain in across the bay and Eltath. It was dismal. Baskevyl, Domor and Fazekiel had sheltered for two hours under the colonnades of the ordo stronghold, listening to the rain patter off the yard's paving slabs. The last time Baskevyl had tried the porter's office, a surly man had emerged after repeated knocks and told him that transport would be arranged, and that because of a scarcity of drivers, they would have to keep waiting.

'We've been waiting for a while,' Baskevyl had replied, biting back the urge to shout at the man.

The porter had shrugged as if to say, 'I know, what can you do, eh?'

This time, Fazekiel had gone to the door and hammered hard. There was no response. She tried the door, and found it was locked. So was the door to the main atrium.

'Have they just left us out here?' asked Domor, knuckling rain drops off his nose.

'This is ridiculous,' said Baskevyl.

'No, it's typical,' said Fazekiel. 'They made us wait when we got here, they're making us wait again.'

'Why?' asked Domor.

'It's a game,' said Fazekiel.

'What's the point of the game?' Domor asked.

'To show us who's in charge,' she said.

Baskevyl buttoned up his jacket.

'How far is it to the billet?' he asked.

Domor shrugged.

'Seven, eight miles?' he said.

'We could have walked home by now,' said Baskevyl. He started off towards the gate and the street beyond.

'Where are you going?' asked Fazekiel.

'Walking it,' said Baskevyl.

Apart from the rain, Gaelen quarter was quiet. Baskevyl hadn't paid much attention on the drive in, but now he was conscious of how empty and bleak the streets surrounding the ordos stronghold were. It wasn't derelict. The area was full of mercantile offices, commercial buildings and counting houses, and they were all well kept and in good repair. But they were all shut, closed, locked and barred. Shutters covered their windows, and cages were padlocked across their doors. There was no sign of life. Baskevyl wasn't sure if it was simply a non-business day, a holy day, perhaps, or if the premises were permanently closed. They all looked like they'd been locked up the night before, never to be opened again.

'We just walk,' said Baskevyl.

'You know the way?' asked Fazekiel. 'We don't know this city.'

Baskevyl grinned at her, and jerked a thumb towards the despondent Domor.

'Shoggy's Tanith, Luna,' he said. 'He's not going to get lost.'

Baskevyl looked at Domor.

'You're not, are you?'

Domor shook his head.

'This way,' he said, taking the lead. 'Top of the hill, then to the left. I don't remember the route they brought us, but I can find Low Keen from here.'

They trudged up the hill in the rain, soaked.

'There's a good omen,' remarked Fazekiel.

Someone had daubed the words THE SAINT STANDS WITH US on the side of a nearby townhouse.

'If she stands with us,' said Domor, 'she's soaked to her underwear too.'

The hill was steep. At the top, on a junction, they were able to look back and see the grey smudge of the bay beyond the sloping rooftops. The weather was coming in off the sea, a grey haze. They could see the shadows of heavy rain slanting from even heavier cloud.

Baskevyl heard a sound and looked up. An aircraft. Its engine noise was reflected off the low cloud, and he had to search to spot the actual object. It was a dot, cutting low and east across the city. After a moment, two more specks followed it, slicing fast across the clouds.

Domor frowned.

'That's not one of ours,' he said quietly.

Somewhere, far away to the north, an anti-air battery opened up, a distant rapid thumping. Several more joined in.

'Oh, feth,' said Domor.

A vehicle was approaching along the hillside street. A cargo truck. Baskevyl stepped off the pavement and tried to flag it down. It rushed past, oblivious, hissing up standing water in a spray.

The distant rattle of gunfire got louder, like firecrackers in a neighbouring street.

'We need to get back quickly,' said Baskevyl.

Another vehicle was approaching, a Munitorum transport rumbling through the rain with its headlamps on.

'Leave this to me,' said Fazekiel.

She stepped into the road and stood in its path, one hand raised.

The transport ground to a halt in front of her. The driver peered out, regarding the commissar with some trepidation.

'We need a ride,' Fazekiel told him. 'To the Low Keen quarter.'

'Ma'am, I'm ordered to go to Signal Point,' said the driver nervously.

'Let me rephrase that,' said Fazekiel. 'Officio Prefectus. I am commandeering this vehicle, now.'

As they scrambled into the cab of the transport, Baskevyl heard more aircraft. He turned and looked up.

Planes were approaching from the south west, emerging from the heavy cloud. Hundreds of aircraft, grumbling in wide, heavy formations.

They weren't Imperial.

'Drive!' Baskevyl ordered, slamming the cab door.

The rain had put a dent in the high spirits raised by Blenner's proposed feast. Smoke and steam continued to billow out of the cookhouses, but the work had slowed down. People had drifted off, and only a few of the women and the camp cooks had stayed to keep things warm and stop them burning. The band had packed up.

'They are coming here,' said Yoncy.

Elodie had been playing catch with her in one of the billet hallways. Rain had driven the children indoors, and they were getting fractious. Yoncy had at least stopped complaining about her hair. Elodie was glad of that. She was pretty sure she didn't have lice, but every time the child mentioned it, she wanted to scratch.

'Who are, Yonce?' she asked.

Yoncy frowned at her.

'They are full up with woe,' she said.

There was noise from the yard. Elodie went out to see, leading Yoncy by the hand.

The funeral transports had returned.

'They're back soon,' Elodie said to Rawne.

'That's what I was thinking,' said Rawne.

Criid got out of the transport and hurried across to Rawne. Elodie could see that Felyx was still in the back of the vehicle. Dalin was sitting with him. Then she noticed that the coffin was still in the back of the transport.

'What's going on?' Criid asked Rawne.

'About to ask you the same thing,' he said.

'The roads are shut,' said Criid. 'We got to the templum, and that was locked. The attendant said the service was postponed.'

Rawne made a face.

'Felyx is upset,' said Criid. 'We had to bring the coffin back with us.'

'Of course he is,' said Zwiel, appearing at her side. 'That won't do at all.'

'He's actually angry more than upset,' said Criid, glancing back at the transports. They could see Felyx yelling and gesturing at the sympathetic Dalin, though they couldn't hear what he was saying.

'Angry with everything and everyone,' said Criid. 'Angry at the whole fething galaxy.'

'The dead must rest,' said Zwiel, tutting, 'they really must.'

'Noted, father,' said Rawne.

Across the yard, a Ghost shouted and pointed up into the rain at the lowering sky. Formations of aircraft were passing over them. There were packs of them, hundreds. The shrill scream of their chugging engines was distinctive. The formations seemed to slide across the grey sky. They were heading for the Great Hill.

'Secondary order!' Rawne yelled. 'Get up, get up, get up! All companies! Secondary order now!'

Around him, the Ghosts scattered fast, heading for their bunk rooms and the arsenal.

'Retinue into shelter!' Rawne shouted. 'Elam! Meryn! Get the retinue settled as best you can.'

Ludd and Blenner ran up. Blenner looked flushed and out of breath.

'See to discipline in the camp, Blenner,' said Rawne.

'Yes, but–'

'See to discipline in the damn camp now!' Rawne snapped.

'Yes, major.'

Rawne looked at Ludd.

'Secondary order, and ready to move,' he said.

'Yes, sir.'

'That includes crew-served.'

'Yes, sir.'

'Do we have any transport?'

'A few of the cargo-eights,' said Ludd.

'Load them up. Munition support, plus heavier weapons. Everyone else can walk.'

'Yes, sir,' said Ludd. 'Walk to where, sir?'

'Well, it's not happening here, is it?' said Rawne. 'Unless you want to take pot-shots at those planes? Something's coming in, and we need to be ready to meet it.'

Ludd nodded.

'Not dig in here, major?' asked Zwiel.

'Do you want the fight to be here, ayatani?' asked Rawne. 'Here where the retinue is?'

'No, I do not.'

'If we're fighting here, it'll be a very bad sign,' said Rawne. 'It'll mean the enemy has taken everything south of here, and that's most of the city. So if we're fighting here, it means we're neck-deep in shit.'

Oysten, Rawne's adjutant, pushed through the milling crowds of troopers, and ran to him. She held out a slip of paper.

'This from staff, sir,' she said.

Rawne took it and read it.

NOTICE OF HIGH ALERT ++ ALL STATIONS IN CITY ZONE TO SECONDARY IMMEDIATE ++ AWAIT PRIMARY ORDERS

'No fething shit,' he said, crumpling the paper and tossing it aside. He glanced at the flocks of aircraft droning overhead.

'Like I needed brass to tell me that.'

Felyx got out of the transport and looked at the sky, mouth open.

'By the Throne, what is this?'

'Come on,' said Dalin. 'We have to move.'

Since accidentally overhearing Kolea and Hark, Dalin had been lost in worry about the prospect of Felyx's secret coming out. But circumstances had changed so badly, that hardly seemed an issue. Felyx Chass' stupid secret seemed insignificant now the city was under attack.

'Will you come on?' he urged.

'But Maddalena–'

'Move, now,' said Dalin, grabbing Felyx by the arm.

Elodie scooped Yoncy up in her arms and hurried with the rest of the retinue into the billet houses. Elam's company had opened up the basements and were sandbagging the windows of the lower storeys. They were urgently ushering the non-coms inside.

'Downstairs,' a trooper said to Elodie. 'Quick now.'

'I said they were coming, didn't I?' Yoncy whispered in Elodie's ear as they bumped down the cellar steps.

Elodie looked at her.

'The enemy? You meant the enemy?'

Yoncy nodded.

'They are always really close,' she said.

The wall batteries of the Urdeshic Palace began to fire, echoing the sustained barrage from batteries around the skirts of the high city. The storm clouds lit up with specks and flurries of light. The palace itself groaned and trembled. Deep-core generators kicked into life, and with a cough and pop of pressure drop, the fortress' massive void shield system engaged, encasing the entire summit of the Great Hill in a globe of phosphorescent green energy against the incoming raid. The air stank of ozone.

In the war room, contained pandemonium reigned.

'What are we looking at?' demanded Cybon.

'The situation in Zarakppan has deteriorated in the last hour,' said Biota, scanning the data that flooded the strategium. 'Faster than anticipated. Much faster.'

'Urienz is on the line there, isn't he?' asked Van Voytz.

'He's en route, sir,' said Biota. 'But the line has already broken in three places. The enemy is progressing into the refinery district.'

'Damn it!' Van Voytz snapped.

'But that's just a feint,' said Gaunt.

'It is,' agreed Biota. 'It's drawn our main power. Their main assault is coming from the south west, out of the margins of the Northern Dynastic Claves. A principal force, predominately infantry with fast armour support. Plus air cover, of course. Fast strike, slash and burn. They're using the suburbs here on the south shore of the bay.'

The stained-glass windows of the war room rattled in their frames, shaken by the over-pressure of the massive void shield outside. Gaunt thought he could hear the first crisp stings of munitions spattering off the outside of the shield. On the hololithic display, the fuzzy patch of imaging that indicated the enemy aircraft formations was merging with the upper contours of the Great Hill.

'We need to restructure,' said Van Voytz, studying the chart and sliding the code-bars of brigade indicators around as if he were laying out playing cards for solitaire. 'We need to pull garrison elements down from the north. Where's Blackwood?'

'Why do we need Blackwood?' asked Gaunt.

'Blackwood has principal command of the Eltath position,' said Cybon. 'This is his watch.'

'This needs to go to the Warmaster,' said Gaunt.

'The Warmaster is indisposed,' said Biota. 'Marshal Blackwood has command precedence here.'

Gaunt looked around. The chamber was bustling with staff, but there was no sign of Blackwood.

'For Throne's sake,' Gaunt said to Cybon. 'Interim orders at least. Start the fething restructure! Blackwood can take over when he arrives.'

Van Voytz looked at Cybon. Cybon sighed, and walked to the balcony rail. He amped up the volume of his throat-vox.

'Attention!' he boomed. 'I am assuming command until relieved by Marshal Blackwood! All data to my station! Await orders!'

He looked back at the table. Van Voytz and Biota were already pushing data blocks across the hololith map, suggesting deployment structures for the reserve garrisons stationed inside the city.

'Good,' Cybon nodded, considering their suggestions. 'Confirm these routings and send them to the main table. Get them despatched now! And make sure the damn Munitorum knows where and what it needs to support.'

'Yes, sir!' said Biota.

'Let's look at the rest of the list,' said Cybon. 'Anything we can reposition in the western corner there?'

Van Voytz pointed at the city map.

'That's your mob, Bram,' he said.

Gaunt nodded.

'Any requests?'

'I think they could make the south bayside in under an hour. Perhaps mount a support of the Tulkar Batteries?'

Van Voytz nodded.

'Yes, and we push this armour in at their left flank. Cybon?'

'Do it,' Cybon growled, busy with the deployment authorisations for another eighteen regiments.

'We have retinue with us, sir,' Gaunt said to Van Voytz. 'Permission to have them transported inside the palace precinct?'

'Granted,' said Van Voytz immediately, then paused. He gestured to the chamber's high windows, lit by the eerie green glow outside. 'But nothing's getting in or out with the shield up.'

'Once this raid is driven off,' said Cybon, looking up from the chart, 'we'll have to drop the voids. Power conservation.'

Van Voytz nodded, and looked back at Gaunt.

'Get them ready to move at our notice,' he said. 'They can come in once the raid has cleared.'

Gaunt nodded a thank you. He beckoned to his waiting adjutant.

'Beltayn?'

'Yes, sir?'

'Get me a link to the regiment. Call me when it's up,' said Gaunt.

'Yes, sir.'

Beltayn hurried off to the vox-centre. Gaunt took Van Voytz aside.

'The Warmaster must be on top of this,' he said quietly. 'Now.'

'We can manage.'

'This is his fight! On his doorstep!'

'He's busy with the big picture, Bram. This isn't the only warzone on Urdesh.'

'Someone should go and–'

'His area is off limits to all,' said Van Voytz. 'I'm sure he's been made aware of the situation. He will intervene if he thinks it's necessary. It's staff's job to keep on top of this.'

Gaunt looked at him, unconvinced.

'Dammit, Bram,' said Van Voytz, 'this is exactly what I've been talking about. Macaroth's detached from everything. Everything. It's all grand theory to him. He probably hasn't even noticed we're voids up.'

'I can't believe the Warmaster is so divorced from reality,' said Gaunt.

Van Voytz's voice dropped to a whisper.

'Throne's sake, Bram. We told you. We told you plain. He's not fit. Not any more. He's not the safe hands we need driving this. Not this fight, not the theatre, not the damn crusade. He's been holed up in his quarters for months, sending out strategic orders by runner. I don't think he's been out of the east wing in weeks.'

He put his hand on Gaunt's shoulder and turned him away from the officers around the busy strategium table.

'That's why we need to settle this,' he whispered. 'And we need to do it now. In the next few hours.'

Gaunt looked at him, hard-faced.

'You want to move against him now? Replace him? In the middle of this?'

'If not now, when, Bram? When? The inner circle is ready to act. The declamation of confidence is prepared. All the formalities are in place. With your cooperation, we were hoping to act this week anyway. This crisis is forcing our hand. The Archenemy has shifted tactics, a hard turn. Throne knows what's coming in the next few hours, here or on the Southern Front.'

'At least wait until we've pushed back this assault,' said Gaunt.

'The enemy is hitting Eltath, Bram. Two days ago, that was an unthinkable scenario. This offensive demonstrates the failure of command. It's primary evidence to support our demands.'

'Barthol, I refuse to accept that the best time to enforce change at the very upper level of command is during an enemy assault. Macaroth's hands need to be on the reins–'

'But they're not, Gaunt, they're not! He's not engaged with the matter at hand. He's letting it happen. The Warmaster's hands need to be on the reins, all right. But not Macaroth's.'

Van Voytz looked him in the eye.

'We need theatre command, and we need it now,' he said. 'Not tonight, not tomorrow. We need it now. If we leave it a day or two, Throne knows what we'll be facing across Urdesh. Throne knows how the game will have changed. I'm not going to wait to let a catastrophic defeat prove that we need new leadership.'

'Barthol, you know the rest of staff knows all about it?'

Van Voytz made a careless shrug.

'It's been plain to me,' said Gaunt. 'Staff knows what your inner circle is planning, and significant numbers of them oppose the idea. Even those sympathetic to the idea don't think this is the right time to consider it. Those against you would block it.'

'We have the numbers,' Van Voytz sneered. 'It will be a procedural formality. Look at what's going on, Gaunt. This is a shambles. After this, staff will thank us for it... If we get fresh blood to haul us out of this offensive with renewed vigour. Come on. Think about it. We should be thanking the Anarch for giving us the push we need. It trounces all counter-arguments.'

Gaunt took a deep breath. The windows were still quivering in their frames, and the sound of munition strikes and airbursts was now very distinct.

'The inner circle,' he said. 'It's not well liked...'

Van Voytz raised his eyebrows.

'What's the matter, Bram? Afraid you're going to be tarnished by association? Afraid you'll catch lice lying down with the bad boys?'

'I am concerned with the calibre of some of your co-conspirators,' said Gaunt.

'Oh! "Co-conspirators" now, is it?'

'You know what I mean,' Gaunt growled. 'Lugo is a paper general. He's never been better than barely competent–'

'Screw Lugo,' replied Van Voytz. 'He's a rat's arse. But we need him, because he's connected. He has strong links with the Ecclesiarchy in this sector and Khulan Sector. We need the approval of the Adeptus Ministorum and he brings that. A move like this slips down a damn sight easier with the church backing us. They'll bring over the sector lord and the Imperial court. We need him, so we tolerate him.'

Gaunt didn't reply.

'As soon as Blackwood gets here, we're calling the circle together,' said Van Voytz. 'And then we're pushing the button. An hour or two. Now, are you with us?'

'Give me two hours, sir,' said Gaunt.

'What? Why?'

'I need to issue direct instructions to the Ghosts. I owe them that much. I'm not leaving their feet in the fire like this.'

'All right, but after that?'

'I'll give you my answer in two hours.'

Van Voytz stared at him for a moment, as if trying to read his thoughts in his face. Gaunt's eyes, their impenetrable blue a result of Van Voytz's own command calls, made that impossible.

'Two hours, then,' Van Voytz said.

Gaunt snapped a salute. Van Voytz was already turning back to the strategium table where Cybon was yelling instruction to his juniors.

Gaunt looked over at Daur and Bonin.

'With me,' he said.

Beltayn was in the vox-centre on the gallery below. He'd taken command of one of the high-gain voxcaster units, ordering the vox-men aside so he could operate it himself.

'Linked to Tanith First, sir,' he reported, handing a headset to Gaunt.

Gaunt took off his cap and put the headset on.

'This is Gaunt.'

'*Reading you, sir,*' came the reply. He recognised the voice of Oysten, Rawne's new adjutant.

'I need Kolea or Hark,' said Gaunt.

'*I'm sorry, sir,*' Oysten's crackling reply came back. '*Neither one is here.*'

'How can they…? Never mind. Baskevyl, then. And quickly.'

'*Sir, Major Baskevyl is not on-site either.*'

'Feth me, Oysten! What's going on?'

'*One moment, sir.*'

There was a muffled thump from the other end of the connection, then a new voice came on.

'*Gaunt?*'

'Rawne? What the hell is happening?'

'*The explanation will take some time, and it will annoy you,*' said Rawne. '*Do you really want to hear it right now?*'

'No. Dammit, I was about to promote Kolea to brevet colonel to get the regiment together.'

'*Well, Gol's not present, and I don't think a brevet promotion is going to do him much good right now.*'

'All right. Rawne, looks like you got the job after all.'

Silence, a crackle.

'You still there?'

'*Yes.*'

'Are we going to have that argument again?'

'*I don't know. Shall we?*'

'Does this seem like a good time, Rawne?' Gaunt snapped. 'Are you the senior officer present or not?'

'*I am.*'

'Then you're in charge. I can't get there. The palace is locked down. What's the situation?'

'*We're at secondary order, and ready to move. I was anticipating marching orders.*'

'Yes? Well, here they come. You're moving south, to the Tulkar Batteries. The enemy is advancing from the south and south west. Garrison forces are moving in to cover the line. How fast can you get there?'

'*Hold on... Checking the charts... Fifty minutes if we leave now.*'

'Make it fast. Rapid transfer, and expect to hit the ground running when you arrive. The enemy may already be there. Orders are to hold the batteries and hold that line. I'll get any supplementary data I can find relayed via the war room. Munitions?'

'*Adequate, but we'll need more before long.*'

'Munitorum is aware. I think you may get some armour support in another ninety minutes, but you'll probably be on station first.'

'*What about the retinue?*'

'Permission's been granted to transfer all non-coms to the palace precinct. Transport will be despatched, but it will be a while. The retinue will have to remain at the billet site until the raid's over and the shield's down. Suggest you–'

'*Leave a couple of companies to protect them, got it,*' said Rawne.

'Good. Get on with it. Rapid deploy. Do you need a brevet rank?'

'*No, I fething don't.*'

'You've got it anyway, Colonel Rawne. You are primary order as of now. Get moving. The Emperor protects.'

'*Understood.*'

'Are my orders clear and comprehended, colonel?'

'*They are. They are... my lord militant.*'

'Straight silver, Rawne. I'll make contact again as soon as I can.'

'*Understood. Rawne out.*'

The connection dropped. Gaunt handed the headset back to Beltayn.

'Colonel Rawne?' asked Daur.

'Seems so,' said Gaunt.

'What happens now, sir?' asked Beltayn.

'We have to pay a visit,' said Gaunt.

'In the middle of this?' asked Daur.

'It's important,' said Gaunt. He looked at Bonin.

'Think you can lead me to the east wing of this place?' he asked.

TWENTY-ONE

LICE

Rawne walked out of the K700 billet buildings into the yard. Rain was still coming down hard.

'Listen up!' he yelled. He had to raise his voice to be heard over the constant drumming and rumbling of the raid. On the dismal skyline, the Great Hill was lit up, strobing with flashes and fizzles of light as the enemy air craft assaulted the shield and the lower slopes.

The officers, adjutants and seniors gathered in.

'Primary order,' said Rawne. 'We're moving in force towards the Tulkar Batteries. Expect enemy contact at that site. Be prepared to engage the enemy before we reach the batteries. We're moving in five. Rapid deploy.'

'Is this from the top?' asked Kolosim.

'No,' said Rawne sarcastically. 'I'm making it all up. Five minutes, are we clear?'

There was general assent.

'Sergeant Mkoll?'

'Yes, sir.'

'I want the approaches to the batteries scouted in advance, so your boys will tip the spear.'

Mkoll nodded.

'Do we have street plans?' he asked.

Rawne glanced at Oysten, who held out a waterproof bag of city maps and charts.

'Read and digest,' said Rawne. 'In fact, everybody get a look, please. Make sketches if you have to.'

'What about the retinue?' asked Blenner.

'E and V Companies will remain here and guard the non-coms,' said Rawne.

'Are you joking?' asked Wilder, unable to contain his annoyance. Once again, the Colours Company was being relegated from the front line.

'No, I'm not, captain,' said Rawne.

'V Company isn't just a marching band!' Wilder protested. 'This is simply another insult to our soldiering–'

'Enough, captain, enough,' said Blenner. He tried to sound stern, but secretly, he was pleased. His attachment to V Company meant that he wouldn't be advancing into the field.

'How long is this babysitting going to last?' asked Meryn.

Rawne glanced at him.

'An hour or two. Maybe slightly longer. Transport is being arranged to bring the retinue to safety inside the palace precinct. When it arrives, your job will be to escort the transit. Is E Company lodging a complaint too?'

Meryn shook his head. He was perfectly content to sit out the fight. And he knew full well why Rawne had made the call. If E Company stayed at the billet, then Felyx Chass would stay at the billet, and Rawne could sideline the boy from front-line deployment without making an obvious exception.

'Request permission to remain on station with E Company,' said Ludd. His concerns for Felyx's welfare were all too obvious again. Rawne saw Dalin glance at Ludd with a frown.

'Denied, commissar,' said Rawne.

'But–'

'I said denied. Hark and Fazekiel are basically missing in action. I need a competent commissar at the line with us.'

Blenner thought about objecting, but he kept his mouth shut. If he said anything, he might end up switching out with Ludd. Better to live with an insult to his abilities than to get himself a walk to the line.

'All right, that's it,' said Rawne. 'Get ready to move. This is going to get ugly. I won't dress it up. Chances are, whatever we're heading to won't be prepped. We'll have to hit the ground and improvise. Maintain contact at all times – we're going to need coordination. But vox discipline too, you hear me?'

He paused.

'One last point,' he said, reluctantly. 'I've been given the rank of colonel for the duration of this. I don't like it, but it may be useful authority if we're dealing with allied units.'

'You are our second in command anyway, sir,' said Pasha.

Rawne nodded.

'And now I have the rank to match,' he said. 'I probably should finish with some uplifting remark, but I'm fethed if I can think of anything. Get moving. Don't feth this up.'

Gaunt's Ghosts exited the billet camp rapidly, heading out along the access road and then turning south. Blenner stood and watched them fade into the rain, first the marching lines of troopers, then the half a dozen transports laden with munitions and heavier gear.

He heard Meryn shout, 'Get the site secure! Come on now!' The buffeting slap and thump rolling across the city from the Great Hill was growing more intense. Lightning laced the rain clouds, and it was hard to tell where the lightning stopped and the furious aerial bombardment began.

Blenner glanced around the yard. Wilder was talking to the hired mourners who staffed the funeral transports. The gloss black vehicles were still parked at the edge of the yard, glistening with raindrops. Death was clinging to Gaunt's men. Urdesh should have been a deliverance for them, a well-earned respite after the struggles of the Reach, but it was dismal.

He wandered over to the abandoned cook tents. Water pattered from the edges of the canopy. He could still smell smoke, but the stoves had been put out, and the food was cold. There would be no feast now, no celebration. Blenner doubted Gaunt would care. Gaunt had come home to glory, to the insulating sanctity of high rank. His friend Gaunt. His old, dear friend. How many of his friends would Gaunt remember now he was ascending the dizzy heights? How many would he take with him?

Few at best, Blenner reckoned. Gaunt had made that snake Rawne a colonel, but that wasn't anything. Just a field promotion so that the Ghosts had a leader. It was a way for Gaunt to wash his hands of the regiment. The Ghosts were just a historical footnote now, a minor citation in the history book entries on the career of Lord Militant Ibram Gaunt.

Blenner found the pills in his pocket, scooped up a ladle of water from an abandoned steamer, and washed down a handful. When he got to the safety of the palace, he'd work hard, make a few contacts, maybe inveigle his way into the good graces of a more agreeable commander. He'd secure himself a more comfortable future with some ceremonial company or honour guard, and he'd do it fast before Gaunt made good on his threat and transferred Blenner to some mud-bath line company.

He could do it. He was charming and persuasive. He'd always been able to work the arcane systems of the Astra Militarum to his own benefit.

'Do you know where the keys are?'

He looked around. Wilder had come over.

'What keys?' asked Blenner.

'The keys to the medicae trailer. The funeral staff want to be gone, and I don't blame them. They won't take the coffin with them. I said we'd store it in the trailer.'

Blenner nodded.

'I think Meryn has them,' he said. He called Meryn's name across the yard.

Wilder took out a hip flask, and took a swig while they waited for Meryn to join them. He offered it to Blenner, who knocked some back, too.

'I was talking to them,' said Wilder.

'Who?'

'The mourners,' said Wilder. 'The paid mourners.'

'They can't really leave the woman's body here. It has to be buried.'

Wilder shrugged.

'I hardly care,' he replied.

'Will they come back tomorrow?' Blenner asked. 'Will they reschedule the service?'

'Ask them yourself,' said Wilder. 'I said, I don't care.'

'Maybe we can take the coffin with us to the palace...' Blenner mused.

'I was talking to them, anyway,' said Wilder.

'And?'

'I asked how much this service and everything was costing.'

'The boy's paying for it all. Private funds. I told you that.'

Wilder nodded. He took another swig.

'You did. You have any idea what it costs?'

Blenner shook his head. Wilder mentioned a figure.

Blenner looked at him, his eyes wide. He took the flask from Wilder and drank again.

'Are you joking?'

Wilder shook his head.

'The boy's loaded,' he said. 'He just drew down that kind of money. It was triple rate because of the short notice.'

'Holy Throne,' murmured Blenner.

'Them and us, Blenner,' said Wilder. 'The great and eternal divide between the dog-soldiers like us who crawl through the mud and the high-born who can do anything they fething want.'

'You two talking social politics again?' asked Meryn, wandering into the cook tent with Gendler.

'Oh, you know, the usual,' said Blenner.

'I was just telling the commissar how deep that brat's pockets are,' said Wilder.

'You can spare them the details, Jakub,' said Blenner.

Wilder didn't. He repeated the figure to Meryn and Gendler. Meryn whistled. Gendler's face turned red with rage.

'Makes me want to slit that little bastard's throat,' he said.

'Now, now, Didi,' said Meryn.

'Come on, Flyn. He's a rancid little toerag. He's so gakking arrogant.'

'Didi, we all know the axe you have to grind against the Vervunhive elite,' said Meryn.

'And Gaunt,' said Wilder bluntly.

'Look at you,' Meryn laughed, nodding to Wilder and Gendler. 'Didi, robbed of his wealth and birthright by the war, and the captain here, seething with animus towards the man he blames for his brother's death... Or at least, his brother's lost reputation. You're both pathetic.'

'You despise Gaunt too,' Gendler snapped. 'He cost you your world.'

Meryn nodded.

'He did. And I'd love to see him suffer. But bitching and moaning behind his back is hardly productive. You should do what I do. Take that hate and make it work for you.'

'Yeah?' sneered Wilder. 'And how do you do that?'

'Well,' said Meryn with a shrug, 'for a start, I don't openly discuss vengeance against Gaunt, or his arse-wipe son, or the high spires of Verghast aristocracy, or any other iniquity, in front of a fething commissar.'

He looked at Blenner.

'Probably wise,' said Blenner. 'He *is* my friend.'

'Is he?' asked Gendler. 'Is he? He seems to treat you like crap on a regular basis.'

Blenner opened his mouth to reply, then decided to say nothing.

'You're all missing the point,' said Meryn quietly. 'You're all too worked up with your own grievances. You need to learn the long game.'

He walked over to one of the stoves, and sampled the contents of a cook-pot. He wrinkled his face and spat it out again.

'Gaunt's at the palace,' he said. 'Out of the way, and probably too good to mingle with the likes of us any more. The company's moving to the front line, and feth knows if they'll come back alive. We're here alone. We're in charge.'

He smiled at them. It was a dangerous expression.

'So, Didi, you could slice that runt's throat. Wilder, you could put the boot in too, if you felt like it. Get a little payback for your brother. And we could ditch the body in the rubble wastes, and claim Felyx Chass was lost during the retreat operation. What would that get you? Ten minutes of private satisfaction? A temporary outlet for your resentment?'

'So?' asked Gendler.

'That's if you got away with it,' said Blenner bleakly. 'There'd be an inquiry...'

'You're all so dense,' Meryn laughed. 'We don't need to off the boy. He's an asset. He's rich, you idiots.'

'What are you saying?' asked Wilder.

'I'm saying the profits we've enjoyed over the years have reduced significantly since Daur's bitch of a woman blew the viduity scam,' said Meryn. 'Booze and pharms make a little pocket change. We need a new revenue stream.'

'What, we milk him?' asked Gendler.

'Deep pockets, you said,' replied Meryn.

'Are you talking extortion with menaces?' asked Blenner. He felt very cold, suddenly.

'I'm suggesting we have a quiet word with Felyx,' said Meryn, 'and illustrate how life will be much better for him in this regiment if he has friends looking out for him. Friends like us, who can make his existence a great deal more bearable. In exchange for, say, regular withdrawals from his family holdings. We could split it comfortably, four ways – maybe even set aside enough so that one day, not too long from now, we could just ghost ourselves away, score passage on a merchant ship and get the feth out of this life.'

'Whoa, whoa,' said Wilder. 'I'm... I'm not comfortable with this conversation.'

'Really, Jakub?' smiled Meryn. 'Not even the thought of screwing over the man you hate by means of his own bratty son? That not doing it for you?'

'I think Captain Wilder is concerned that you're talking about extortion with menaces, and desertion,' said Blenner. 'This conversation alone counts as conspiracy to commit. And as you pointed out yourself, Captain Meryn, it's not a conversation you are wise having in my earshot. I thought you were smart, Meryn. I knew you were crooked as feth, but I thought you were meticulously careful. That you "played the long game".'

Meryn grinned more broadly. He took Wilder's flask and helped himself to a swig.

'I am, commissar,' he said. 'I plan ahead. I cover the angles. I don't open my mouth until I'm sure it's safe to do it. Who's going to tell?'

'This conversation ends now,' said Blenner. 'If you don't think I'll report you if you carry on with this–'

'How are those pills working out for you, Vaynom?' asked Meryn.

Blenner hesitated.

'What?'

'Contraband somnia. Oh, that's bad news. Possession, well... that would get a man flogged. And a *commissar*, what do we think? Execution? Or the worst possible punishment squad posting, at the least, I should think. A Delta Tau-rated posting. A death world, Vaynom. Want to end your days on a death world?'

'A-are you threatening me?' asked Blenner.

Meryn made a casual gesture.

'Me? No. You're one of us, Vaynom. One of our inner circle. We're all friends. We can talk freely. None of us is going to rat on the others, is he?'

Meryn wandered across the tent and stopped face-to-face with Blenner. Blenner couldn't meet his eyes.

'We need you on this, Vaynom,' he said. 'The sweet, cures-all-ills protection of the Officio Prefectus. And you'd benefit too. You like your life, Vaynom. You like it comfortable.'

'Damn you,' murmured Blenner.

'Oh, all right. Damn me.'

Meryn turned away.

'Your choice,' he said. 'But we've got you cold. You flip a coin on us, you're done. You really think I would have opened my mouth in front of you if I didn't already own you? Long game, Vaynom, long game.'

Blenner swallowed hard. He felt unsteady. He could feel all three of them staring at him. The self-preservation that had seen him safe his entire career kicked in faultlessly.

He lit his most charming smile.

'I was just testing you, Flyn,' he said. 'I wanted to make sure you were serious. It's about time we stopped picking up scraps and got ourselves a decent score.'

'Are you serious?' asked Wilder.

'Throne, Jakub,' said Blenner. 'My only hesitation was whether to do this myself or bring you in on it.'

Meryn nodded and smiled his crooked smile.

'We have to put this in motion now,' he said. 'The next hour or so. Better here than once we're inside the palace.'

'We need him alone,' said Gendler.

'Everyone needs to get scrubbed and showered before we ship to the palace,' said Blenner. 'Carbolic soap, anti-bac. We'll only be admitted if there's no lice infestation. The instructions are specific.'

'They are?' asked Wilder.

'They are if I say so,' said Blenner.

'What about that fether Dalin Criid?' asked Gendler. 'He's shadowing Felyx.'

'He's my adjutant,' said Meryn. 'He'll do exactly what I tell him to.'

'But what,' Wilder asked, haltingly, 'but what do we use as leverage? The boy's an arrogant little bastard. What'll stop *him* telling on us?'

'He'll be too scared to talk,' said Gendler.

* * *

They'd already had to double back four times. The road links across the city between Gaelen quarter and Low Keen were frantically congested. Instead of taking shelter from the raid, the population of Eltath seemed to have taken to the streets. Convoys of traffic, transports laden with people and belongings. It was like an exodus. People seemed to be trying to flee north.

Baskevyl had seen this before. It was like resignation. When a population had been beaten and deprived for too long, it finally snapped. In the face of another attack, the promise of another destructive cycle of death and dispossession, they turned their backs and fled, unable to face the danger any more.

Ironically, this meant they were fleeing into danger.

The main air raid was concentrated on the Great Hill. The cloudy skies above were backlit by flashes and blinks of light and fire as the Archenemy attacked the shield. Some sections of the enemy air mass had peeled off, choosing to strike at other targets in the city, strafing and unloading sticks of bombs. The constant drumming thump of anti-air batteries across the city was relentless. From the cab of the Munitorum truck they had commandeered, Baskevyl could see the glow of street fires in neighbouring blocks. The sky was stained amber.

They had come to a halt again. Traffic choked the street ahead. Transports were lined up, stationary, drivers arguing. On the pavements, tides of people hurried northwards, some pushing their lives in hand carts and barrows.

'Back up,' Fazekiel told the driver. 'Go around.'

'Where exactly?' the driver complained.

'Down there. That side street,' she told him.

'That'll just take us back towards the harbour,' the driver said.

'At least we'll be moving,' Fazekiel snapped.

There was a sucking rush as an enemy aircraft passed overhead. A moment later, the jarring crump of detonations shuddered from no more than three streets distant. Grit and scraps of papery debris drizzled down on the road, and people screamed and hurried for cover.

'Moving is good,' said Domor.

The driver put the truck in reverse, swung the nose around, and edged down the sharp incline of a narrow side street. Pedestrians had to get out of the way. They yelled at the truck, and beat on its side panels. Baskevyl wasn't sure if that was anger at the imposition of letting the truck pass through, or desperate pleas for help.

He glanced at Fazekiel. They'd been on the road for two hours, and seemed no closer to the billet. It felt like a year had passed since they had set out for the ordos stronghold that morning.

Baskevyl wondered if they should just stop. Stop and find cover. Stop and find somewhere with a voxcaster or some communication system. He wanted to warn Gol what was coming his way. He had a sick feeling it was already far too late.

At the bottom of the side street, the driver turned left, and they rumbled along the service road of a hab area. They passed people hurrying to nowhere, people who didn't turn to give them a passing look. Anti-sniper sheets and curtains, tapestries and carpets, flapped overhead like thread-bare parade banners.

Up ahead, a truck had broken down and was half blocking the service road. The engine cover was up, and people were working on it. The driver had to bump up on the pavement to try to ease around the obstruction. People shouted at them. Some clamoured for a ride.

'Hey,' said Domor. He slid down the cab's window and craned to listen. 'That's artillery.'

Baskevyl could hear the thumping, sporadic noise in the distance. Heavy shelling. That was a worse sign. If the artillery belonged to the enemy, then it meant they were facing a land assault too, one that was close enough to hear. If the artillery was Imperial, it meant that there were enemy targets close enough to warrant a bombardment.

'We need to find shelter,' said the driver. They could tell he was beginning to panic. The stink of his sweat in the cab was unbearable.

'Keep driving,' said Fazekiel.

There was a flash.

The street ahead, thirty metres away, vanished in a blinding cloud of light and flames. Then the sound came, the roar, then the slap of the shock wave. The transport shook on its suspension. Debris cracked and crazed the windscreen. Baskevyl shook his head, trying to clear his ears. Everything had become muffled, the world around him buzzing like a badly tuned vox.

'The feth was that?' he heard Domor say.

The street ahead had become a crater, deep and smoking. Outflung rubble was scattered everywhere. The buildings on one side of the street were ablaze, flames licking out of blown-out windows. On the other side, the front of a hab block had simply collapsed, exposing layers of floors like some museum cross section. As Baskevyl watched, an anti-sniper curtain, on fire, broke from its moorings over the street and fell, billowing sparks.

There were bodies everywhere. Bodies of pedestrians who had been rushing to nowhere, and were now not rushing at all. Debris had killed some, mangling them, but others had been felled by the blast concussion. They looked like they were sleeping. Pools of blood covered the road surface and gurgled in the gutters.

'Where's the driver?' Fazekiel asked, dazed.

The cab door was wide open. The driver had bolted.

'Can you drive?' Fazekiel asked Baskevyl.

He nodded. He was still hoping that the ringing in his ears would stop. He got into the driving seat, and fumbled to find the engine starter.

'We've got to turn around,' said Domor. 'The whole fething street is gone. We have to back up and turn.'

'I know,' said Baskevyl. He was pushing the starter, but the engine wasn't turning. He thought the driver had stalled the transport out, but maybe they'd taken damage.

He fiddled with the gears in case there was some kind of transmission lock-out that prevented engine-start if the box wasn't in neutral. He pushed the starter again.

He could hear a pop-pop-pop-pop.

Was that a starter misfire? An electrical fault?

'Get out!' Domor yelled to them.

Baskevyl could still hear the popping, but his finger was no longer on the starter button.

It was small-arms fire. He was hearing small-arms fire.

A moment later, they heard the slap-bang of the first rounds striking the bodywork.

Colonel Grae told Hark that the site was called Station Theta, apparently one of several anonymous safe house strongholds Guard intelligence controlled inside Eltath. Intelligence service troopers in body armour opened the gates and ushered the Chimera into a fortified yard behind the main building.

Hark got out. The raid had been under way for a while, and the skies were florid with fire-stain. Through the razor wire on the wall top, Hark could see enemy aircraft passing overhead, heading to the apex of the city.

'This is bad,' he said to Grae.

The colonel nodded.

'No warning this was coming,' he said. 'Nothing on the watch reports of this magnitude. We had no idea they had moved principal strengths so close to the city limits.'

Grae looked at his detail.

'Get Major Kolea inside, please,' he said.

'I should rejoin my regiment,' said Hark. 'With this shit coming down, they'll be mobilising.'

Grae frowned.

'True,' he said, 'but I don't like your chances. It's all going to hell out there. Maybe when the raid is over...'

Hark looked him in the eye.

'I said I should,' he said, 'not I would. I'm not leaving Kolea here. Not even with you, though you seem sympathetic. The Ghosts are big boys, and they have good command. They'll be all right for a while.'

'As you wish,' said Grae.

'You'll get me use of a vox, though,' said Hark. 'So I can get a message to them?'

'Of course.'

They walked into the blockhouse, following the guards as they escorted the silent, solemn Kolea. There was a holding area and a loading dock. Hark saw side offices filled with cogitators, planning systems and vox-units.

'Where is everyone?' Grae asked.

Hark knew what he meant. He had expected to see the place in a frenzy of activity. This was an intelligence service station in a city under assault.

'Where's the head of station?' Grae called out. 'Someone find me the head of station or the rubrication chief!'

A couple of troopers from the detail moved forwards to look. Grae led the main group through a station office and down a hallway to the situations room.

The console station in the situations room was active, chirping and buzzing, but it was unmanned. A tall figure stood waiting for them in the centre of the room.

She turned to face them.

'Inquisitor,' Grae said, startled.

'Colonel Grae,' said Laksheema. 'Did you honestly think that you could disguise your movements and deceive me?'

'I was... merely taking Major Kolea into custody, as we agreed,' said Grae.

'This is not what we agreed,' said Laksheema.

'This is her, is it?' Hark asked Grae.

'Yes,' said Grae.

For a moment, Hark had thought Grae had walked them into a trap, that he'd been playing them all along. But from the look of dismay on his face, it was evident that his part in delivering them to Inquisitor Laksheema had been unwitting.

'The intelligence service is extremely proficient,' said Laksheema, 'but it is an amateur operation compared to the omniscient surveillance of the Holy Ordos. You've made a fool of yourself, Grae. Inter-departmental rivalry is ridiculous and counter-productive. I will be speaking to your superiors.'

She looked at Hark.

'You are Viktor Hark?'

'I am,' said Hark.

'You are known to me from the files,' she said. She took a step towards Kolea, and waved the intelligence service guards surrounding him out of her way.

'And Gol Kolea. Face-to-face, again.'

Kolea said nothing.

Laksheema eyed him with curiosity. She tilted her head, and her gilded augmetics caught the light.

'With respect, ma'am,' Hark said.

She looked at him sharply.

'A phrase which always means "without any respect at all", commissar.'

'True enough,' said Hark. 'What do you want with Kolea? I am here to watch out for his welfare, and I intend to do everything in my power to do that.'

'You have no power at all,' she replied. 'However, unlike Colonel Grae, I see great benefit in inter-discipline cooperation. You will assist me in learning the manner of truths from Major Kolea.'

'Like what?' asked Hark.

'Major Kolea clearly has a connection of some sort to the so-called eagle stones,' she said. She looked at Kolea. 'Don't you, Gol? We will explore that connection.'

'Will we?' asked Hark.

'Yes,' said Laksheema. 'And let us first consider this. The city is under attack. It has been a safe stronghold for months. Now, suddenly and without warning, it is the focus of a major assault, one which we did not see coming. And, just days ago, the major here, and his regiment, and the secrets they guarded, including the eagle stones, arrived in Eltath. Do you not suppose the timing is significant? Do you not imagine that the Archenemy of mankind is descending upon us to get the stones back?'

Night was falling, and the rain was still beating down hard. A minimum number of lamps had been lit at the K700 billet because of the danger of air raid. The void shield of the Urdeshic Palace, a dome of green light just visible through the filthy air, was still lit. The waves of enemy aircraft had finally stopped coming about an hour before, but the shield was still up. Areas of the city on the slopes of the Great Hill glowed amber in the gloom: blocks and streets turned into firestorms by bombing overshoot.

Outside the wash house units behind the billet, people were still queuing for the mandatory anti-bac showers Commissar Blenner had ordered. V Company had already run through shower rotation, and were supervising the civilian queues. E Company was lining up to use the blocks of grotty wash houses on the east side. The rainy air smelt of counterseptic gel and carbolic.

'I don't want to do this,' Felyx whispered to Dalin. 'I don't have to. I don't have lice.'

'Everyone has to,' said Dalin. 'Blenner ordered it. Instructions from staff command, he said.'

'Dalin–'

'Don't worry. We'll use the block on the end. There are only four stalls. I'll cover the door while you're in there, make sure no one else comes in.'

'This is stupid,' said Felyx.

'What's stupid is us not telling anyone,' said Dalin. 'Then we wouldn't have to go through this pantomime.'

'Don't start on me.'

The group ahead of them was waved over to the left-hand shower block by Trooper Perday.

'Next group,' she called.

'We'll take the right-hand block,' said Dalin.

Perday frowned.

'It's the commander's son,' Dalin whispered to her with a meaningful look. 'A little privacy, all right?'

Perday nodded.

'Understood, Dal,' she said. 'On you go.'

Dalin and Felyx walked across the puddled cobbles to the end block. A couple of E Company troopers followed them.

'Use that one,' Dalin told them. 'Only two of the stalls are working in here.'

They reached the door of the end block. It was a grim, tiled chamber with four curtained brick stalls. The place reeked of mildew. A couple of troopers were exiting, towels around their necks.

'Go on,' hissed Dalin. 'Get in there and be quick. I'll watch the door.'

Felyx glared at him and stomped inside. Dalin heard the pipes thud and water start to spray. He pulled the wooden door to and waited.

'Trooper?'

Dalin turned. It was Meryn.

'You done yet, trooper?' Meryn asked.

'No, sir,' said Dalin. 'I'm just...'

'Is it full in there?'

'No, sir. Uhm, Trooper Chass is in there. I was just watching the door. Giving him some privacy.'

Meryn nodded.

'I want to know where the transports are,' said Meryn. 'They should be here by now. Seeing as how you're still dressed, run up to the gate and ask if they've seen anything inbound.'

'Oh. B-but-'

Meryn frowned at him.

'That's a fething order, Trooper Criid,' he said.

'Of course.'

'Come on,' said Meryn, smiling slightly. 'I know you take your duties seriously. This'll take you five minutes. Don't worry. I'll watch the door and keep precious Trooper Chass safe.'

Dalin hesitated.

'Get the feth to it!' Meryn barked.

With a sigh, Dalin turned and began to run down the breeze-way towards the yard and the gate.

Meryn leaned back against the shower block wall and folded his arms. Gendler and Wilder appeared out of the shadows.

'Get on with it,' said Meryn, 'and make it fast.'

He walked away.

'Keep watch,' said Gendler to Wilder. He pushed open the door and stepped inside.

The ragged curtain was drawn on the end stall. Gendler could hear water hissing.

He approached the curtain, and drew his straight silver.

'Hello, Felyx,' he said.

There was a long pause.

'Who's there? Who is that?'

'I just want a little chat, Felyx.'

'Is that you, Gendler? Is it? I know your voice.'

Gendler smiled.

'Yeah. It's time to have a little chat with your Uncle Didi.'

'Stay out! Stay the feth out!'

'Oh, that's not very friendly is it, Felyx,' said Gendler. He poked the tip of his knife through the curtain at the top, near the middle of the rail, and ripped it down, cutting the old curtain in half.

He expected to find the boy cowering inside. He didn't expect Felyx to come flying out at him like a fury.

Something sliced into Gendler's shoulder and he yowled in pain. Instinctively, he lashed out, swatting the boy aside with the back of his fist. Felyx lurched hard to the left, cracked his head against the side wall of the stall, and collapsed in a heap. His straight silver clattered from his hand onto the tiled floor. The water started to swirl Gendler's blood off the blade.

Gendler stood for a moment, breathing hard. The bastard had knifed him in the shoulder. Blood soaked the front of Gendler's uniform. *Little bastard! It hurt like a fether!*

Shaking, he looked down at the unconscious boy. He hadn't meant to hit him so hard. The boy had cracked his head on the bricks, and blood from the wound was spiralling into the stall's drain plate and soaking the grubby towel that the boy had half wrapped around himself–

'Holy gak,' Gendler breathed.

Not a boy. Not a boy at *all.*

'What have you done?'

Gendler looked around. Wilder had entered the shower block. He was staring in shock at the crumpled, half-naked body on the tiles.

'Oh, *shit,* Gendler! What have you *done?*'

'The little brat went for me,' said Gendler. 'Bloody stuck me. I'm bleeding!'

'Fething Throne, Gendler,' said Wilder. 'She's a girl. It's a *girl.*'

Wilder looked at Gendler.

'What the feth do we do?' he asked, panic rising. 'You have just dropped us in so much shit.'

'We... we say she slipped. Slipped in the shower,' said Gendler. 'Yeah, she slipped. We found her. We helped her.'

'You gak-tard! What will *she* say?' asked Wilder.

Gendler thought about that for a second. Then he knelt down, wincing from the pain of his stab wound, and put his hand around Felyx's throat.

'Nothing,' he said, calmly. 'She slipped and she fell and she died.'

'Throne, Gendler!' Wilder gasped.

Gendler's knuckles began to tighten.

There was a spitting hiss. Gendler tumbled back as if he'd been hit with a mallet. He landed sitting up, with his back to the brick wall. An iron quarrel was lodged in his chest.

Eszrah Ap Niht stood in the doorway, his reynbow aimed.

'Touch her not, soule,' he growled.

Gendler coughed blood.

'You feth-wipe,' he gurgled. He wrenched his sidearm from its holster, and aimed it at Ezra.

The reynbow spat again. The quarrel hit Gendler in the middle of the forehead, and smacked his skull against the bricks. He lolled, head back, staring at the ceiling with dead eyes.

Jakub Wilder wailed in dismay. He pulled his sidearm.

But Ezra had already reloaded. The quarrel punched through the meat of Wilder's right thigh in a puff of blood, and dropped him to his knees. Wilder squealed, and tried to aim his weapon. Ezra dropped another iron bolt into his bow, and fired again, quick and methodical. The quarrel hit Wilder in the shoulder of his gun-arm, spun him sideways off his feet and sent the pistol skittering away across the floor. Wilder lay on the ground, sobbing and moaning, blood leaking out onto the tiles.

'The feth is going on in here?' Meryn yelled as he and Blenner stormed in. They looked at the bodies on the ground in dismay.

'Feth...' Meryn said.

'They would to kill her,' said Ezra.

'It's a fething girl!' said Meryn.

Drawn by the commotion, people were crowding around the door outside. Meryn turned and yelled at them.

'Out! Get out! Get out now!' he bellowed, driving them back, and slamming the ratty wooden door shut.

He looked at Ezra again.

'Are you... are you saying Gendler and Wilder attacked this... attacked this girl?'

Ezra nodded.

Meryn glanced at Blenner. Blenner was shaking. He could see the frantic desperation in Meryn's eyes.

'That's... that's actionable, isn't it, commissar?' Meryn said. 'Gross assault? That's summary, right there!'

'I...' Blenner began.

'That's *right,* isn't it, commissar?' Meryn urged.

'Feth... Meryn, please...' Wilder moaned from the floor. 'For pity's sake, help me...'

'I'm right, *aren't I,* Commissar Blenner?' Meryn demanded. Blenner could read the message Meryn was sending him, the message blazing out of his eyes. *Shut this down. Shut this down before Wilder sells us out too. Shut this down and keep this contained.*

Vaynom Blenner's sense of justice crumbled beneath the weight of his fear. Somewhere, during that, his heart broke.

He drew his sidearm.

'Captain Jakub Wilder,' he began. His voice sounded very small. 'You have shamed the honour code of the Astra Militarum with actions base, vile and cowardly.'

'Oh, no,' Wilder cried, trying to rise. 'Are you bloody kidding me? Blenner, no! No!'

'By the authority of the Officio Prefectus,' said Blenner, 'punishment is immediate.'

Jakub Wilder started to scream. Blenner shot him through the head. Blood flecked the walls. His body fell hard on the tiles.

Meryn looked at Ezra.

'Good work,' he said. 'Very good work, Ezra. Thank the Holy Throne you were here.'

'Gaunt, he told me to watch his child,' said Ezra.

'Well, you've served him well,' said Meryn. He stooped to recover the laspistol Wilder had dropped. 'Very diligent. Really, thank Throne you were here. The Emperor protects.'

Meryn fired Wilder's sidearm three times, point-blank, into Ezra's upper back between the shoulder blades. Ezra fell without a sound.

Blenner stood and stared with his mouth wide open.

'What a mess, eh?' Meryn whispered to him, putting the gun down beside Wilder's lifeless right hand. 'Ezra saved the girl, but Wilder shot him, so you *had* to execute him.'

He looked at Blenner.

'Right?' he asked firmly.

'Meryn, I–'

'We're in this together, Blenner. You and me. It's a simple, sad tale, and our stories will match. *All right?*'

Blenner nodded.

'Good,' said Meryn. 'Now let's find a fething corpsman.'

TWENTY-TWO

THE TULKAR BATTERIES

The sea was close, less than half a mile away, but all Rawne could smell was the rank promethium smoke blowing in from the south. Vast banks of black smoke were making the night air opaque, as though a shroud lay over the city. Ten kilometres south of his position, a zone of mills and manu-factories along the edge of the Northern Dynastic Claves became an inferno. The horizon was a wall of leaping orange light that back-lit the buildings nearby. There was a steady thump of artillery and armour main-guns, and every now and then a brighter flash lit up the flame belt, casting sparks and lancing spears of fire high into the darkness.

The Ghosts were waiting, silent. Rawne had eighteen of the regiment's twenty companies with him, a complement of over five thousand Guards-men. The Tanith First had advanced south from K700, moving fast, and had entered the Millgate quarter of the city under cover of darkness and rain. There, they'd ditched their transports and hefted the heavy weapons and munitions by hand.

The area was deserted, and the Ghosts companies had fanned out across a half-mile front through empty streets, advancing fire-team by fire-team down adjacent blocks. Rawne knew they were tired from the fast deploy, but he kept the pace up and maintained strict noise discipline. The Ghosts had melted into the zone, pouring down the dark streets, one company flanking the next. The only sounds had been the quiet hurrying of feet.

At a vox-tap from Rawne, the regiment had halted in the neighbourhood of Corres Square, a few streets short of the batteries. Rawne knew the five thousand ready Guardsmen were in the vicinity, but they were so quiet and they'd hugged into the shadows so well, he could barely see any of them.

Marksmen from all companies had drawn in around the southern edge of the square. They'd fitted night scopes, so they had the best eyes. Rawne heard a tiny tap, barely louder than the rain pattering on the rockcrete. His microbead.

'Rawne,' he whispered.

'*Larkin*,' the response came. '*They're coming back.*'

Rawne waited for the scouts to reappear. Mkoll was suddenly at his elbow.

'Hit me,' Rawne whispered.

'The batteries are manned,' Mkoll replied quietly. 'But the main guns aren't firing.'

'Why?'

'Waiting for a clear target is my guess,' said Mkoll. 'They won't risk depletion. There's a brigade of Helixid dug in to the east of the batteries.'

Mkoll flipped out his lumen stick, cupped his hand around the blade of light, and showed Rawne the relative positions on the chart. 'The avenue here, to the west of the batteries, that looks wide open.'

'Between the batteries and the sea?'

'Yes.'

'What's this?'

'Maritime vessels, industrial units. They're moored together in a large block from the harbour side all the way down the coast. I think they're junked. Decommissioned. They effectively extend the land about half a mile from the shore.'

'Enemy units?'

'We spotted a few at a distance. And there are dead along the avenue, so the batteries have repulsed at least one assault. I think another rush is imminent.'

'Gut feeling?' asked Rawne.

Mkoll nodded. Mkoll's gut feeling was good enough for Rawne.

'We'll advance and stand ready to hold the avenue west of the batteries,' Mkoll said. He looked at Oysten.

'Get the word to the company leaders.'

'Yes, sir.'

Rawne glanced back at Mkoll.

'I don't want to risk open comms. Can you get runners to the batteries and the Helixid, and inform them we're coming in alongside them to plug the hole?'

Mkoll nodded.

There was another furious ripple of distant artillery, then it abruptly stopped.

'Move,' said Rawne. 'Here they come.'

The Tulkar Batteries were a cluster of heavy, stone gun emplacements raised on a steep rockcrete pier overlooking a broad esplanade. Their gun slots, like the slit visors of ancient war-helms, were angled to cover the bay, and Rawne presumed they had once been sea forts for coastal defence. But they had enough traverse room to cover the shorefront and the esplanade, and defend against any ground attack that came from the south west along the coastal route.

Though the Ghosts were on the edge of the Great Bay, the sea was invisible, merely a concept. The rolling banks of smoke had closed down any sense of space or distance, and choked out the view over the water. What Rawne could see, beyond the rockcrete line of the esplanade, was a rusty mass that seemed like a continuation of the shoreline. This was the junk Mkoll had described.

In better days, the city, like much of Urdesh, had employed fleets of mechanised harvester barges and agriboats to gather and process the weed growth of the shallow inshore seas as a food staple. War, Urdesh's long and miserable history of conflict, had brought that industry to a halt. The huge agriboats had been moored along the bayside and abandoned. The machines were big, crude mechanical processors, some painted red, some green, some yellow, all corroded and decaying, their paintwork scabbing and flaking. They had been moored wharf-side, and around the jetties of the food mills and processing plants that ran along the seawall on the bay side of the avenue. The long, rusting, rotting line of them extended as far as Rawne could see, right down to the coast, hundreds if not thousands of half-sunk barges, chained five or six deep in places. It was a graveyard of maritime industry. Rawne could smell the festering sumps of the old boats, the pungent reek of decomposed weed, the tarry, stagnant stench of the mud and in-water ooze the agriboats sat in. These were the first scents strong enough to overpower the stink of smoke.

The esplanade, wide and well maintained, was also well lit by the flame-light of the distant mills. The horizon, more clearly visible now, burned like a hellscape. Rawne could see the black outlines of mills as the fires gutted them.

In half-cover, he stared at the open road. The obvious route. Fast-paced armour could flood along it in a matter of minutes. There was little cover, but if the enemy had enough mass in its assault that would hardly matter. The sea road was a direct artery into the southern quarters of Eltath. If the Archenemy opened and held that, they'd have their bridge into the city.

Via Oysten, he issued quick orders to Kolosim, Vivvo, Elam and Chiria. They scurried their companies forwards, heads down, and set up a block across the road under the shoulder of the batteries. Old transports and cargo-carriers were parked on the loading ramps of the mills along the sea wall, and the Ghosts began to roll them out to form a barricade. Rawne heard glass smash as Guardsmen punched out windows to enter the cabs and disengage the brakes. Fire-teams worked together, straining, to push the vehicles out onto the road and lug prom drums and cargo pallets to the makeshift line. He moved his own company, along with A and C, into the narrow streets under the batteries on the south side of the avenue. This was another commercial zone, an extension of the Millgate quarter formed of narrow streets and packing plants. Curtains and rugs had been strung between buildings to deter snipers.

Rawne kept a steady eye on the dispersal. This was his game, and he wasn't about to feth it up. Oysten was almost glued to his side, passing quick reports from the company leaders. The tension in the air was as heavy as the smoke, and there was almost no sound except the thumps and quick exchanges from the teams forming the barricade. The Ghosts seemed to be as efficient as ever. That was a small miracle. They were down two commissars, three if you counted Blenner, which Rawne never did. With Kolea, Baskevyl and Domor missing, Daur off at the palace with Gaunt, and Raglon still away in the infirmary, five companies were operating under the commands of their seconds or adjutants: Caober, Fapes, Chiria, Vivvo and Mkdask respectively. It was Tona Criid's first time in combat at the head of A Company. That felt like a lot of new faces to Rawne, a lot of Ghosts who had proven themselves as good soldiers but had yet to go through the stress test of full field command.

That applied to him too, he reminded himself. He'd commanded the Ghosts, by order or necessity, many times, but this was different. He was named command now, Colonel fething Rawne. The reins had been handed to him, and he had a sick feeling he would never pass them back again.

'What are you thinking?' Ludd whispered to him.

'If I had armour, I'd drive up the road,' Rawne replied quietly. 'Do it with enough confidence, and you'd get momentum. Break through, and circle the batteries from behind.'

He glanced at Criid, Ludd and Caober.

'But if I was using the Ghosts,' he said, 'I'd come up through this district, off the main road. Push infantry up into Millgate. You could get a lot of men a long way in before you were seen.'

'And if you had both?' asked Criid.

Rawne smiled.

'They have both, captain,' he said.

'So... snipers and flamers?' asked Caober.

'Yes. Spread them out. Cover the corners here. All cross streets. If infantry's coming this way, I want to know about it, and I want it locked out. Oysten?'

'Sir?'

'Signal up J and L Companies. Tell them to move in behind us and add a little weight.'

'Yes, sir.'

Wes Maggs came running up.

'Word from Mkoll, sir,' he said. 'The battery garrison and the Helixid are aware of our deployment. The Urdeshi commander of the batteries sends his compliments and invites us to enjoy the show.'

'Meaning?'

Maggs shrugged.

'The batteries have the road locked tight. We are apparently to expect a demonstration of Urdeshi artillery at its finest.'

Rawne glanced at the massive batteries that loomed behind them. He could hear the distant whine of munition hoists and loading mechanisms. Artillery was a principal weapon of ground warfare, and could be decisive. But for all its might, it was cumbersome and unwieldy. If the tide of a fight moved against it, artillery could be found wanting. It lacked the agility to compensate fast and counter-respond. It was a superb instrument of destruction, but it was not adaptable.

And war, Rawne knew too well, flowed like quicksilver.

'I wish the Urdeshi commander success,' Rawne said. 'May the Emperor protect him. Because if He doesn't, we'll be doing it.'

As if hurt by the thinly veiled cynicism in Rawne's voice, the Tulkar Batteries spoke. There was a searing light-blink, and then a shock wave boom that hurt their ears and made them all wince. Two dozen Medusas and Basilisks had fired almost simultaneously. The ground shook, and windows rattled in the buildings around them.

'Ow,' said Varl.

The batteries fired again, hurling shells directly over them. This time, past a hand raised to shield against the glare, Rawne saw the huge cones of muzzle flash scorch out of the gun slots. He heard a more distant thunder, the staggered detonations of the shells falling a mile or so away.

'Positions!' he yelled, and ran for the nearest building, kicking in the access shutter. Oysten, Ludd and Maggs followed him through the old packing plant, up the stairs and out onto the low roof.

The batteries continued to fire overhead. They could hear the almost musical whizz of shells punching the air above them. Fyceline smoke descended like a mist across the streets, welling out of the batteries' venting ports. It had a hard, acrid stink, familiar from a hundred battlefields.

The concussion pulse from the bombardment made Rawne shake. He could feel each punch in his diaphragm. He kept his mouth open to stop his eardrums bursting, and took out his field glasses with fingers that tingled with the repeated shock.

In the distance, two kilometres away, the shells were dropping on the mill complexes and the western head of the sea road. Each flash was blurred and dimpled by the shock-force it was kicking out. Rawne saw buildings flattened, outer walls cascading away in avalanches of burning stone. Some buildings just evaporated in fireballs. Others seemed to lift whole, as though cut loose from their foundations and gusted up on boiling clouds of fire-mass before disintegrating. He saw vast steel girders spinning into the sky like twigs.

There were tanks on the sea road. Urdeshi-made AT70s, rolling hard, lifting fans of grit, thumping shells from their main guns as they ran. They were emerging from the firezone of the mills in the Clave district. SteG 4 light tanks scurried among them. A fast armoured push right down the artery. Just what Rawne had predicted.

That's what had woken the batteries up.

He kept watching. Artillery shelling continued to drop on the mill complexes. Some hit the sea road too. He saw an AT70 light off like a mine. He saw two more annihilated by direct hits. He saw a fourth get hit as it was running, the blast lifting the entire machine end over end and dropping it, turret down, on a speeding SteG 4. Munition loads inside the wrecked vehicles cooked and blew.

'It's not enough,' he said. No one could hear him over the thunder of the bombardment. He looked at Maggs, Oysten and Ludd, and signed instead, Verghast-style.

Not enough. They're moving too fast.

The enemy armour was taking brutal losses. They were driving through a hellish rain of heavy, high-explosive shells. But they had an open roadway, and they were pushing hard, as fast as their drives could manage. A dozen tank wrecks burned on the ruptured highway, but the majority of shells were falling behind the heels of the leading machines. The Urdeshi commander was traversing and adjusting range rapidly to stop the armour force moving in under his fire-field, but the distance was closing. How short could the long-range guns drop their shells? How far around to the north west could they traverse? It was a simple matter of angles. There would come a point at which the gun slots of the massive battery fortress would simply not be wide enough to allow a main gun to range the road and sea wall to its extreme right.

That moment was coming. By risking the open highway, and accepting brutal losses, the enemy armour had forgone safety in favour of speed.

Maggs grabbed Rawne's sleeve and pointed. Less than a kilometre away to the south west, SteG 4s and stalk-tanks were breaking out of Millgate quarter onto the sea road. Smaller and faster than the main battle tanks, these war machines had moved up under cover through the streets of the district. The big tanks of the main road assault had been a misdirection. The lighter machines were already onto the open highway, and were coming in under even the shortest drop of the batteries' cone of fire.

Pasha, Rawne signed to Oysten.

At the roadblock line, Major Petrushkevskaya had already spotted the sleight of hand. SteGs and stalk-tanks were rushing her position. She, Elam and Kolosim had got their tread fethers un-crated and in position, and crew-served weapons were set up along the roadside and among the line of trucks.

'Steady!' she ordered calmly over her link. The weapon mounts of the advancing enemy had greater range than her infantry support weapons. She wanted no wastage, even if that meant they had to take their licks first.

Shells from the .40 cal cannons of the SteG 4s began to bark their way. Some went over, others blew craters out of the road surface short of the line. The light tanks were rolling at maximum speed to reach their target, and that made them unstable, imprecise platforms. The stalk-tanks, scurrying like metal spiders, were spitting las-fire from their belly-mounts. Shots struck the line of trucks, puncturing metal and blowing out wheels. A round from a SteG 4 howled in, and blew the cab off a transport in a cloud of shredded metal.

Men went down, hurt by shrapnel. Pasha took her eyes off the road to shout for medics, but Curth and Kolding were already on the ground.

'Do you need help?' Pasha called to Curth.

'Free a few bodies from the line to help us carry these men clear, please!' Curth shouted back.

'Squad two!' Pasha yelled. 'Work as corpsmen! Take instruction from Doctor Curth!'

Her troopers slung their lasguns over their shoulders and hurried to help Curth. The medicae officers started pulling the injured clear with the help of troopers seconded as corpsmen. Pasha looked back at the approaching armour.

'Hold steady,' Pasha said.

'*Sixty metres,*' Kolosim voxed.

'Understood,' she nodded. Another few seconds...

She raised her hand. At her side, her adjutant Konjic was watching as if hypnotised, his thumb on the vox-tap switch.

Another shell tore at them, and flipped one of the trucks, scattering debris. Two more shells ripped in, punching clean through the bodywork of barricade transports, killing Ghosts sheltering in their lee.

Pasha dropped her hand. Konjic sent the tap command.

At the left-hand end of the barricade line, Captain Spetnin led two teams out of the roadside culvert. He had shouldered a tread fether himself. Trooper Balthus had the other. Kneeling, they lined up and fired. Each tube weapon gasped a suck-whoosh, and anti-tank rockets spat out across the road. Spetnin blew one of the leading stalk-tanks apart. Balthus stopped a SteG 4 dead in its tracks. It slewed aside, on fire, a gaping hole under its engine case. A SteG directly behind it tried to steer out and cannoned into the wreck, shunting it forwards and twisting its own chassis violently.

The men loading Spetnin and Balthus were already slotting in fresh rockets. From the midline of the vehicle barricade, Venar and Golightly fired their tread fethers. Venar's rocket burst a stalk-tank, flinging it around hard, toppling it into a burning pool of its own fuel. Golightly hit an oncoming SteG so square and low it flipped as if it had tripped over something. It tumbled and blew up.

On the right-hand flank of the barricade, Chiria's company fired its anti-tank weapons. More rockets streaked across the open highway. One made a clean kill of a running SteG, the other ripped the turret off a second. The crippled tank kept going, trailing fire in its wake, but either its crew was dead or its steering was ruined. It veered off, headlong, hit the rockcrete siding of the seawall and overturned, its six oversized wheels spinning helplessly.

A second and third wave of rockets spat from the roadblock line. More of the advancing tanks exploded or were brought to a standstill. The road was littered with wrecks. Big AT70s could have piled through, but the light SteGs and the delicate stalk-tanks had to slow down and steer around and through the burning hulls. The Ghosts' support weapons opened up, punishing the slower targets with .30 cal hose-fire. Armour shuddered and buckled under the sustained hits. Melyr swung the spade grips of his tripod-mounted .30 and poured a stream of fire into the body of a stalk-tank, ripping it open and shredding the pilot. The stalk-tank remained upright, but began to burn: spider legs frozen, supporting a fierce ball of flame, one leg lifted to take another step that would never come. Seena and Arilla focused their .30 on a SteG that was trying to turn past a blazing wreck, and shot out its engine. Fuel loads and hydraulics gushed out of the punctured hull like blood, and the vehicle shuddered to a halt. Its turret was still live, and it traversed, pumping two shots in the direction of the roadblock.

Arilla, small and scrawny, tried to retrain to finish the job, then cursed. Her weapon had suffered a feed-jam. Seena, twice her size and all muscle, reached in and cleared the jam with a fierce wrench of her fist, then fit a fresh box to the feed.

'Go!' she roared.

Arilla squeezed the paddles, and the weapon kicked into life. Her torrent of shots mangled the SteG's turret, and sheared off its gun mount. The impact sparks touched off the fuel gushing out of its ruptured tanks, and it went up like a feast day bonfire.

On the roadway, Archenemy crews were dismounting from damaged and burning vehicles, and trying to advance through the smoke and billowing flames. The Ghosts on the makeshift line now had human targets their rifles could take. Las-fire rattled from the jumbled row of trucks, chopping down men before they could move more than a few metres.

Smoke and haze from the killzone blocked any decent view.

'Advise!' Pasha yelled into her mic.

'*Another pack of SteGs about two minutes out,*' Kolosim voxed back. He had a better view from the right-hand edge of the sea road. '*We can hold them off with the launchers. Major, stand by.*'

Kolosim scurried along the line of the sea wall to get a clearer angle. He could feel the heat on his face from the burning tanks.

He touched his microbead.

'Pasha, I think at least two of the big treads have got past the bombardment. They're coming in, four minutes maximum.'

Pasha acknowledged. AT70s. They would swing things. The big tanks were robust and heavily armoured. They could shrug off the support fire and only the luckiest hit with a launcher would make a dent. Chances were the big treads would blow straight through the wreckage belt, and they'd have the meat and firepower to punch through the roadblock too.

Pasha had fought in the scratch companies during the Zoican War. Far too many times, she and under-equipped partisan fighters had been forced to hunt big enemy armour and woe machines that had massively outclassed them.

'Remember Hass South?' she asked Konjic.

'Is that a joke?' Konjic asked.

'No. Grenades. Fast. Not loose, boxes.'

'Gak!' said a young trooper in her first squad, 'Which unlucky bastard gets to do that?'

Pasha grinned. 'For that remark, Trooper Oksan Galashia, you do. But don't worry. I'll come teach you how we did it in the People's War.'

Galashia, a very short, thick-set young woman, turned pale.

Konjic returned with six men lugging metal crates of grenades.

'All right, lucky ones,' said Pasha, 'you're with me.'

She led them out, past the roadblock and onto the open road. Rockets whooshed over them, striking from the line at the next pack of SteGs.

Heads down, they began to run towards the burning enemy wrecks.

'Feth!' said Rawne. 'Is that Pasha? The feth is she doing?'

The batteries had fallen quiet. There was nothing left they could hit. From the roof of the packing plant, Rawne had a good view of the sea road and the resistance line of the roadblock. He could see figures – Ghosts – sprinting out from the cover of the roadblock into the open.

'Criid's calling, sir,' said Oysten.

Rawne cursed again, put away his field glasses, and hurried back into the street.

'You were right,' said Criid. 'Obel's scouts have spotted enemy infantry moving up through Millgate.'

'Let's go welcome them,' said Rawne.

They started to move through the narrow streets, fanning out in fire-teams.

'Marksmen in position?' Rawne voxed.

'*Affirmative,*' Larkin replied. '*Main force seems to be coming in along Turnabout Lane.*'

Still moving, Rawne found it on the map.

'Can we box them in, Larks?' he asked.

'*We can try, but the locals have proofed this area against snipers.*'

Rawne frowned. Overhead, carpets and drapes hung limp over the street in the smokey air.

'Varl!' he said.

Varl came up. Rawne showed him the map.

'This is Turnabout Lane. We want to clear back to about here. Here at least. Give each long-las as much range as possible.'

'We'll be giving them range too,' said Varl.

'Yeah, but they're moving and we're dug in. Get to it.'

Varl nodded.

'Brostin! Mkhet! Lubba! Shake your tails!'

Varl and the three flame troopers moved ahead, with Nomis and Cardass in support.

'Are we gonna burn something?' Brostin asked as they hurried along.

'Yup,' said Varl.

'People?' asked Brostin.

'No,' said Varl. 'Fething carpets.'

Over by the sea wall, at the right-hand end of the roadblock, Zhukova found Mkoll staring out at the graveyard of rusting agriboats.

'Signal from Cardass,' she said. 'Confirmation – enemy infantry extending up Millgate towards Rawne's position.'

Mkoll glanced across the broad road towards the dark maze of habs and mills south west of the batteries.

'Sir?'

'Rawne was on the money,' he said quietly. 'Armour push on the road, infantry in the cover of the streets. That would have been my call too. The armour's the distraction.'

'The tanks are still coming,' said Zhukova. 'They're going to be more than a distraction.'

'To an extent, but the infantry's the big problem, if there's enough of them, and there will be. In those streets, it'll be the worst kind of fighting. House-to-house, tight. With numbers, they could break, force an overrun. Maybe even take the batteries.'

'Rawne's on it, sir,' she replied.

He nodded. He kept looking at the flaking metal waste of the industrial barges.

'You seem distracted,' she said.

He looked at her, surprised by her frankness.

'Just thinking,' he said.

'What are you thinking?'

'I'm trying to think like an etogaur,' he said. 'Like a Son of Sek.'

Her expression clearly showed her alarm at the idea.

'They're not stupid, Zhukova. They are the worst breed of monsters, but they're not stupid. And that fact makes them even worse monsters. This isn't an opportunist assault. It's been planned and coordinated in advance. There is strategy here, we just can't see it.'

'So?'

'So if the Sons of Sek are working to a plan–'

'If the Sons of Sek are working to a plan, then we define their scheme and deny it.'

He nodded.

'An opportunist assault is hard to fight because it has no pattern,' he said. 'This has a pattern. So, you put yourself in their boots, Zhukova. If you were at the other end of this road, what would you be trying to do?'

'Uh... blindside the main obstacles. Get around them. The Ghosts, the Helixid, the batteries.'

'Right.'

'Isn't that what they're doing? Pushing troops up through the packing district, the hardest area to defend?'

'Yes,' said Mkoll. He didn't sound sure.

'What are you thinking now?' she asked.

'I think we should take a walk,' he said.

Pasha led her crew through the fires and wreckage of the SteGs and the stalk-tanks. On the wind, through the crackle of flames, she could hear the clattering rumble of the big treads moving towards them. Despite the cover of the smoke, she felt exposed. She felt nostalgia. She felt the edge-of-death rush she'd known as a young woman at Vervunhive.

'Move fast,' she ordered. 'Keep those crates away from the fires or they'll torch off.'

'They're about a minute away,' called Konjic.

'How many?'

'Two. AT-seventies. They're not slowing. They're going to pile through here.'

Pasha knelt down with one of the crates, opened the lid, and took out a grenade.

'Do what I do,' she told Galashia. Konjic was already working on the third crate. 'Slide the lid shut,' she said, working steadily and with practised hands. 'Wedge the grenade upright at the end. Slide the lid in tight to hold it in place. Now, fuse wire or det tape. You'll need about two metres. Loosen the pin of the wedge grenade. Not too loose! Tie the wire tight to the pin. Now play it out, back under the box. Leave a trailing end.'

Galashia watched what Pasha and Konjic were doing, and tried to copy it as best she could. Her hands were shaking.

The clatter of the advancing tanks was growing louder.

'All right!' said Pasha. 'One man to a box, grenade towards you. One man on each wire, keeping it under the box. Don't gakking pull. Lift them up, keep them steady. The real trick is placement.'

Pasha hefted her box up. Trooper Stavik held the end of her wire. Konjic lifted his box, with Kurnau on the end of the wire. Galashia got her wire wound in place, and lifted her box. Aust took up the end of her trailing thread.

'All right,' said Pasha. 'This is how this madness works...'

The two AT70s were approaching the burning wreckage clogging the highway. They were moving at full throttle, one ahead of the other. Neither slowed down. They were going to ram their armoured bulks through the wrecks, and charge the roadblock. No amount of small-arms or support fire would be able to slow them then.

The first AT70 smashed into the wreckage. It crushed the flaming ruin of a stalk-tank under its treads, then shoved a burned-out SteG out of its path in a shiver of sparks. Visibility in the smoke and flames was almost zero.

Pasha and Stavik ran out in front of it, Pasha struggling with the weight of the box. They had been waiting behind another wrecked SteG, concealed by the fires spewing out of it. This close to the front of the speeding battle tank, they were outside the driver's very limited line of sight. Both were sweating from the heat, and they were covered in soot.

Timing and placement were everything. Too hasty and you missed the line. Too slow, and the tank simply ran you down and churned you to paste.

Pasha slammed the box down in front of the advancing tank's left tread section. Stavik kept the wire straight so when the box came down, the wire was trapped under it and lying in a line running directly towards the whirring tracks. To do this, he had to keep his back to the tank about to run him down. The roar of it was deafening. The ground shook. It was as if it were falling on him.

Pasha and Stavik released, and threw themselves clear. The tank crew didn't even know two people had been in their path for a moment.

The left tread section rolled over the wire. The weight of the tank ground the wire between track and road, and pulled on it, drawing it back and dragging the box with it. Less than a second later, the track met the back of the placed box and began to push it forwards.

Less than a second after that, the track assembly would have crushed the box or, more likely, smashed it out of the way.

But by then, the draw on the wire and the pressure on the end of the box had combined to pull the pin from the wedged grenade.

The grenade exploded, detonating all the other grenades in the box. By placing the box in front of the treads, Pasha had made sure that the violent blast was channelled up under the tank's armoured skirts and into the wheel housing, instead of bursting uselessly under the armoured treads. The box went off like a free-standing mine.

The searing explosion rushed up under the skirt, shredding drive sprockets and axle hubs. The blast actually lifted the corner of the AT70 for a second. Torsion bars, segments of track and parts of the skirt armour went flying. With one tread section entirely disabled, the tank slewed around hard, driven by its one, still-working, track. It crashed headlong into a wrecked SteG and came to a halt, coughing clouds of dirty exhaust.

The second AT70 was on them. Glimpsing its partner lurching aside through the flames, the tank slowed slightly, opening up with a futile burst of its coaxial gun. The shots chewed up empty roadway. Konjic and Kurnau dropped their box in its path, and sprinted clear, but the tank was turning to evade. Its tracks chewed over the wire sideways, yanking out the pin, but the box was still clear of the track and the blast, an impressive rush of dirty flame, washed up its skirt armour without doing any damage.

Galashia and Aust ran through the flames and smoke. Galashia had never been so scared in her life. This was the behaviour of lunatics.

She was screaming as she got the box in place. The tank was starting to turn and accelerate again, but she'd made a good line.

Aust tripped. He went down on his face, and the tank's right treads went over him before he could even yell for help. His death, though swift, was the most horrible thing Galashia had ever seen. He was ground apart with industrial fury.

Facing it, she saw it all. She fell backwards. She could evade neither the blast nor the onrushing tracks.

The tank suddenly lurched into reverse. Fearing mines or sub-surface munitions, it backed out hard, smashing a burning SteG wreck out of its way. It left Aust and the box behind it. Nothing remained of Aust except a grume of blood and his spread-eagled arms and legs. The box was intact.

The tank halted and began to traverse its turret with a whine of servos. The .30 mount started coughing again.

Pasha reached Galashia, and hauled her to her feet.

'Grab it! Grab it, girl!' Pasha yelled.

They scooped up the box. Pasha had to peel the wire out of the jelly slick of Aust's remains, carefully, to stop it sticking and pulling the pin.

Together, they ran behind the tank. Pasha kept so close to the tank's hull she might as well have been leaning on it. It was counter-intuitive to be so close to such a terrifyingly indomitable enemy object, but staying tight kept them out of sight and out of the line of its coaxial fire.

'Here! Here!' Pasha yelled.

They placed the box behind the right-hand tread.

'It's stopped moving!' Galashia yelled.

Pasha bent down. Holding the wired grenade in place, she slid the lip open, and fished out one of the other hand-bombs.

'What the gak are you doing?' Galashia screeched.

Pasha ignored her, and slid the lid shut, bracing the wired grenade.

'Come on,' she said.

They started to run. Pasha pulled the pin on the grenade she'd lifted, and hurled it high over the tank. It landed on the road in front of the AT70, and went off with a gritty crump.

'What–' Galashia stammered.

Pasha threw her flat.

The AT70 driver assumed the grenade blast in front of him was evidence of a frontal attack or another mine. He threw the transmission into reverse. With a jolt and a roar of its engines, the tank backed over the box-mine.

The blast took out its back skirts and wheel-blocks. Galashia felt grit and debris rain down on her. Shrapnel from the blast penetrated the tank's engine house, and in seconds, the rear end of the massive vehicle was engulfed in fire.

Two members of the crew tried to escape, bailing from the hatches. Pasha was calmly waiting for them, pistol in hand. She cut them both down.

'Let's get clear,' she said, hurrying Galashia away from the burning tank. 'The fire will reach the magazine.'

The first AT70, crippled and immobile, was trying to train its main gun on the roadblock. Konjic, Stavik and Kurnau rushed it. Konjic fired his lasrifle repeatedly into the armoured glass of the gunner's sighting slot, blinding the machine. It fired the main gun anyway, but the shell fired wild, wide over the roadblock line.

There was no way to crack the hatches from the outside. Konjic hoped that the commander would pop the hatch to get a target sighting. If that happened, he'd be ready to hose the interior with full auto. But then tanks often had auspex. It didn't need to see in order to aim. They'd stopped it, but they hadn't killed it.

'What do we do?' asked Kurnau frantically.

'Get the feth clear,' said Chiria.

She had run from cover at the roadblock to join them, her tread fether over her broad shoulder.

'Shit!' said Konjic.

'Can't miss at this range,' said Chiria, and didn't.

Even AT70 hull plating couldn't stop a tread fether at less than six metres. The rocket punched a hole in its side, and there was a dull, brutal thump from within. The tank didn't explode. It simply died, smoke gusting from the rocket wound, its crew pulverised by the overpressure of the blast trapped inside the hull.

Chiria turned and grinned at the others.

She was about to say something when a colossal blast knocked them all off their feet. The second AT70's magazine had detonated.

Debris and burning scraps fluttered down on them. They got up, coughing and dazed. The centre of the road where the second AT70 had been was a large crater full of leaping flames. Pasha limped towards them, her arm around Galashia's shoulders.

She was smiling.

'Back into cover, lucky ones,' she said.

* * *

Varl's flamers were at work, at the head of Turnabout Lane. Loosing jets of fire, they were burning down the makeshift drapes and rugs strung up by the Urdeshi to block line of sight. Lubba and Mkhet burned out the ropes securing the top corners of the hanging sheets so that they dropped away, and fell, limp and smouldering, against the fronts of the buildings supporting them. Brostin seemed to prefer to hose the drapes, decorating the streets with flaming banners that slowly disintegrated.

'You only have to burn the ropes,' Varl said. 'Just bring them down.'

'Where's the fun in that?' Brostin asked.

Nomis and Cardass ran up.

'Enemy sighted,' Cardass told Varl. 'Two streets that way, advancing fast.'

'Infantry?'

'Yes.'

'A lot of infantry?'

'Far too many,' said Cardass.

Varl checked his microbead.

'Larks?'

'*I hear you.*'

'Can you see better now?'

'*Much better, thank you, ta.*'

Varl turned to his squad.

'Fall back. Come on, now.'

Lubba and Mkhet made their flamers safe. Brostin looked disappointed and reluctant.

'There'll be more to burn later,' Varl reassured him.

'Promise?' asked Brostin.

'Cross my heart.'

Larkin had taken up position in a third floor room in one of the plants on Turnabout Lane. He had a commanding view down the thoroughfare. Nessa and Banda were in position in adjacent buildings, and other Tanith marksmen were on nearby rooftops on the other side of the street.

He settled his long-las on the sill and clicked his microbead.

'Larkin,' he said.

A crackle.

'*Rawne, go.*'

'We've made ourselves a kill-box, Eli,' he said. 'They'll be on us in a matter of minutes. We'll take as many as we can, but–'

'*Don't worry, Larks. You've got full companies either side of you and capping the end of the street. Once it gets busy, you'll have serious support. Let's just walk them into a surprise first.*'

'Happy to oblige,' said Larkin. He shook out his old shoulders, and took aim. The street was clear and empty. The smouldering rags left by Varl's flamer squad had all but gone out.

He waited. He was good at waiting.

'*They're not coming,*' Banda said over the link.

'Shut up, girl.'

'*They've gone another way.*'

'Just wait. Keep your shorts on and wait.'

A minute passed. Two. Three.

Larkin saw movement at the far end of the lane. A figure or two at first, furtive. Then more. Assault packs, advancing by squad, weapons at their shoulders, drilled and disciplined. Big bastards too. Sons of Sek. There was no mistaking the colour scheme or the brutal insignia.

'*Feth,*' he heard Banda say. '*Look at the bastards.*'

'Keep waiting,' he answered, calmly.

'*There are hundreds of them, you mad old codger.*'

There were. There *were* hundreds of them, close to a thousand, Larkin figured, advancing urgently down the commercial lane. And many more behind that, he reckoned. This was their way in. This little, dark, undistinguished street was their route to victory.

'*Do we take shots?*' Banda asked.

'Wait.'

'*For feth's sake, they're almost on us.*'

'Wait.'

He paused, sighed.

It was time.

'Choose your targets and fire,' he said into his microbead.

He lined up. Who first? That one. That one there. A big fether. An officer. He was gesturing, barking orders.

Larkin lined up his sights. The man's head filled his scope.

'Welcome to Eltath, you son of a bitch,' he breathed, and pulled the trigger.

The agriboats were huge and old, but now they were on them, Zhukova could feel them shifting slightly underfoot in the low water.

Mkoll led the way, making so little noise it was inhuman. Zhukova felt like a clumsy fool as she followed him. They went from deck to deck, crossing from one rotting barge to the next, following old walkways and scabby chain bridges. The derelicts were just rusted hulks. In places, hold covers and cargo hatches were missing, and she saw down into the dark, dank hollow interiors of the barges, hold silos that contained nothing but echoes. The place stank of cropweed, a vile smell that had the quality of decaying seafood. The reek of bilge waste and shoreline mud made it worse.

Mkoll stopped at the side rail of the next barge and peered down between the vessel and its neighbour. Zhukova joined him and looked down. She saw shadows and, far below, the wink of firelight on the oil-slick water.

'What do you see?' she whispered.

He pointed. Ten metres below them, near the water line, there was some kind of mechanical bridge or docking gate connecting the barge they stood on with its neighbour.

'The agriboats are modular,' he said quietly. 'They could work independently, or lock together to operate as single, larger harvester rigs.'

'So?'

'I guess they could also dock to transfer processed food cargos,' he mused.

'So?'

He beckoned. They went to an iron ladder and descended through the rusting decks into the darkness. The barge interior stank even worse. Slime and mould coated the walls and mesh floor. It was as black as pitch.

Mkoll jumped the last two metres of the ladder, and landed on the deck. Zhukova followed.

He led her to a large open hatch, and she saw they had reached the rusting bridge linking the two vessels. She looked into the darkness of the neighbouring agriboat.

'They connect,' he whispered. 'They connect together. Docked like this, mothballed, the chances are all the agriboats in this graveyard are hitched to each other, all connected. Most of them, anyway.'

'That's several miles of junk,' she said.

He nodded.

'All connected.'

Mkoll knelt down and pressed his ear to the deck.

'Listen,' he said.

Zhukova wasn't sure she was going to do that. The deck was filthy.

'Listen!' Mkoll hissed.

She got down and pressed her ear to the metal flooring.

She could hear the creak of the ancient hulls as they rocked in the low water, the thump of rail bumpers as the tide stirred one boat against another.

And something else.

'You could walk all the way from the west point of the bay to the batteries without being seen and without using dry land,' he whispered.

'If you went through the hulks,' she replied, horrified.

'The armour push wasn't the only distraction,' said Mkoll. 'The infantry surge in Millgate is a feint too.'

Zhukova listened to the deck again. The other sound was clearer now. Quiet, stealthy, but distinct. Movement. A lot of people in heavy boots were stealing closer through the bowels of the graveyard ships.

'They're using the agriboats,' said Mkoll. 'This is the main assault. They're coming in this way.'

'We have to warn Colonel Rawne,' said Zhukova, her eyes wide.

'No fething kidding,' said Mkoll. He tried his microbead.

'It's dead,' he said. 'Try yours.'

Zhukova tried, and shook her head.

'They're jamming us,' he said. 'That buzz? That's vox-jamming.'

'What do we do?' asked Zhukova.

'Get Rawne,' Mkoll replied.

TWENTY-THREE

THE WARMASTER

The east wing of the Urdeshic Palace seemed empty, as if it hadn't been used in a long time. Bonin led the way. They passed rooms that were full of abandoned furniture covered in dust sheets, and others that were stacked to the ceilings with boxes and junk. The carpet in the halls was threadbare, and the ancient portraits hanging from the corridor walls were so dirty it was hard to make out what they were of.

The crack and boom of the raid continued outside. The air held an uncomfortable static charge from the palace's massive void shield, as though a mighty thunderstorm were about to break. When they passed exterior windows, they could see the light of the shield outside, encasing the dome of the Great Hill with its magnetospheric glow.

Time was ticking away. It was already almost two hours since Gaunt had given Van Voytz his deadline. Well, Van Voytz would have to wait for his answer. The east wing was like a warren.

'I thought there would be guards,' said Beltayn. 'I mean, he is the Warmaster. I thought there'd be high security, trooper checkpoints.'

'I think his authority keeps people out,' said Gaunt. 'His sheer authority, forbidding visitors.'

'Really?' asked Beltayn.

'He is the Warmaster.'

'If he doesn't like company...' Daur began.

'He'll have to make an exception,' said Gaunt.

'But if he forbids people...'

'I'll take my chances, Ban.'

It was certainly odd. The central parts of the massive keep, the war room, the command centres, were packed with people and activity, and every corner and doorway was guarded. But as they'd moved into the east wing they found an increasing sense of emptiness, as if they'd gone from a living fortress into some abandoned derelict, a place from which people had hastily evacuated and never returned.

'They're still with us,' muttered Bonin. Gaunt looked back down the hallway. Sancto and the Tempestus detail, their faces impassive, were following Gaunt at a respectful distance. Gaunt had tried ordering them to go back or to remain in the command centre, but Sancto had firmly refused. Protecting Lord Militant Gaunt was his duty. He would go wherever Gaunt went.

'At least they've hung back at my request,' said Gaunt. 'And they haven't tried to stop us.'

'That's because their orders are simple,' said Bonin. 'No one's told them to stop you. Not yet, anyway. I suppose we'll find out if a Warmaster's direct and angry order overrules a bodyguard command.'

He held up his hand suddenly, and they stopped. Bonin moved ahead to a half-open panelled door. He pushed it wide.

It was a bedchamber. Not a lord's room – they'd passed several of those, vaulted chambers with beds raised on platforms, the walls adorned with gilded decoration. This was the room of a mid-status court official, a servant of the house. The wood-panelled walls were smoke-dark with old varnish, and the drapes were closed. The only light came from a single glow-globe on the night stand beside the large four poster bed. The stand and the floor were stacked with old books and data-slates. A portable heater whirred in one corner, shedding meagre warmth into the chilly room. That was the sound Bonin had heard.

'No one here,' he said.

Gaunt looked around. It was a handsome enough room, but dank and dusty. Surely the bedroom of a servant or aide. This was not the accommodation of a man whose authority dominated a sector of space. The bed hadn't been slept in, though it had clearly been made up months or even years before and never used. The sheets and coverlet were grey with dust and there were patches of mildew on the pillows.

'Sir?' said Daur.

He'd walked around to the other side of the bed, the side with the nightstand. Gaunt went to look.

There was a nest on the floor beside the bed, half under it, a nest made of old sheets, pillows, the cushions from sofas and grubby bolsters. More books and slates were muddled into the lair, along with several dirty dishes and empty, dirty mugs. Whoever used this room didn't sleep in the bed. They hid beneath it, to the side away from the door, in the darkest part of the chamber, curled up in the kind of fort a child would make when he was scared at night.

Gaunt had seen that kind of paranoia before. He'd seen it in soldiers, even in officers, who had been through too many hells. Sleep eluded them, or if it came, they slept with one eye open. They always faced the door. They would sleep in a chair, or in a dressing room, so they could watch the bed that was in plain view of anyone entering the room, and remain unseen.

Sancto and his men had reached the bedroom door and were looking in at them.

Gaunt glanced at Sancto.

'Stay there,' he said.

'Sir–'

'I mean it, Scion.'

'Door, sir,' said Bonin. He pointed at the wall panels.

'What?' asked Gaunt.

Bonin held out an open hand towards the wall. 'I can feel a draught.'

He walked to the wall, ran his hands along the moldings of the panels, and pressed. A door clicked open.

Gaunt pushed the door wider. It was dark beyond. He could smell old glue, dust and binding wax.

'Everyone stay here,' he said.

Gaunt stepped into the darkness. It was a passageway, crude and narrow, just a slot cut in the stone fabric of the keep. He adjusted his augmetic eyes to the low light level and made his way along, skimming the stone wall with his left hand. A dusty curtain blocked the far end of the passage. He drew it back.

The room beyond was a library. Its high walls were lined with shelves stuffed with ancient books, rolled charts, parchments, file boxes and slates. Gaunt presumed he must be in the base of a tower, because the shelf-lined walls extended up into darkness, as high as he could see. Linked by delicate, ironwork stairs, narrow walkways encircled every level. Brass rails edged each walkway, allowing for the movement of small brass ladders that could be pushed along to reach high shelves. Several large reading tables and lecterns stood in the centre of the room, their surfaces almost lost under piles of books and papers. Some were weighed open with glass paperweights, and others were stuffed with bookmarks made of torn parchment. Gaunt saw old books discarded on the carpet, their pages torn out and cannibalised as a ready source of page markers. There was a litter of torn paper scraps everywhere. Reading lamps glowed on the tables, surrounded by pots of glue, rolls of binding tape, tubs of wax, book weights, pots of pens and chalk sticks, magnifying lenses and optical readers. Motes of dust whirled slowly in the lamp light, and in the ghost glow cast by the single lancet window over the tables. It was warm. More portable heating units chugged in the corners of the floor, making the air hot and dry, but there was a bitter draught from the open vault of darkness overhead.

For a moment, Gaunt was overcome by a memory. High Master Boniface's room in the schola progenium on Ignatius Cardinal, a lifetime before. He felt like a child again, a twelve-year-old boy, all alone and waiting for his future to be ordained.

He stepped forwards. His hand rested on the hilt of his power sword. He did not know what he was expecting to defend himself from, except that it might be his own resolve. Coming here, he felt, he was going to make enemies, one way or another.

'Hello?' he said.

Something stirred above him in the darkness. He heard brass runners squeak and rattle on rails as a ladder shifted.

'Is it supper time already?' asked a voice. It sounded thin, exhausted. 'Hello?'

Someone shuffled along a walkway two storeys above him and peered down. A small figure, his arms full of books.

'Is it supper time?'

Gaunt shrugged, craning to see. 'I don't know. I'm looking for the Warmaster. For Warmaster Macaroth. It is imperative I see him. Is he here?'

The figure above tutted, and hobbled to the end of the walkway. He began to climb down, precarious under the weight of the books he was trying to manage. He was old. Gaunt saw scrawny bare legs and heavy, oversized bed socks made of thick wool, patched and darned. He saw the tail of a huge, grubby nightshirt hanging down like a skirt.

The man reached the walkway below, somehow managing not to drop any of his books. He looked down at Gaunt quizzically, frowning. His face was round, with side-combed hair turning grey. He looked unhealthy, as if he hadn't been exposed to sunlight in a long time.

'Warmaster Macaroth is busy,' he said petulantly.

'I can imagine,' said Gaunt. 'Sir, can you help me? It's very important I speak with him. Do you know where he is?'

The man tutted again, and shambled along the walkway to the next ladder. A book slipped out of his bundle and fell. Gaunt stepped up neatly and caught it before it hit the floor.

'Fast reflexes,' the man remarked. 'Is it supper time? That's the real issue here.'

'I'm sorry–'

'Is it supper time?' the man asked, glaring down at Gaunt and trying to keep control of the books he was lugging. 'Not a complex question, given the great range of questions a man might ask. You're new. I don't know you. Has the usual fellow died or something? This won't do. The Warmaster is very particular. Supper at the same time. He is unsettled by change. Why don't you have a tray?'

'I'm not here with supper,' said Gaunt.

The man looked annoyed.

'Well, that's very disappointing. You came in as if you were bringing supper, and so I assumed it was supper time, and now you say you haven't brought any supper, and my belly is starting to grumble because I had been led to believe it was time for supper. What have you got to say to that?'

'Sorry?' Gaunt replied.

The man stared down at him. His brow furrowed.

'Sorry is a word that has very little place in the Imperium of Man. I am surprised to hear the word uttered in any context by a ruthless soldier like Ibram Gaunt.'

'You know who I am?' asked Gaunt.

'I just recognised you. Why? Am I wrong?'

'No.'

'Ibram Gaunt. Former colonel-commissar, commander of the Tanith First, formally of the Hyrkan Eighth. Hero of Balopolis, the Oligarchy Gate and so forth. A victory record that includes Menazoid Epsilon, Monthax, Vervunhive-Verghast, Bucephalon, Phantine, Hagia, Herodor, so on and so on. That's you, correct?'

'You know me?'

'I know you're good at catching. Help me with these.'

The man held out the stack of books in his arms and released them. Gaunt started forwards and managed to catch most of them. He set them down on one of the reading tables and went to pick up the few he'd dropped. The man clambered down the ladder. He looked Gaunt up and down. He was significantly shorter than Gaunt. His stocky body was shrouded in the old, crumpled nightshirt, and Gaunt could see the unhealthy pallor of his skin, the yellow shadows under his eyes.

'The Warmaster is not receiving visitors,' he said.

Gaunt eyed him cautiously.

'I feel it's my duty to inform the Warmaster that Eltath is under primary assault,' he said.

'The Warmaster has figured that one out, Lord Militant Gaunt,' the man snapped. 'The shields are lit, and there is a ferocious din that is making concentration rather difficult.'

'This is more than just a raid,' said Gaunt. 'The Warmaster needs to be aware of-'

The man started to rummage in the stack of books Gaunt had rescued from him.

'A primary assault, yes, yes. The argument over Zarakppan has finally broken wide open. Thrusts are coming from Zarakppan across the refinery zone, using the Gaelen Highway and the Turppan Arterials. Primary formations of enemy forces, moving rapidly. That's just interference, of course, because the main assault is coming from the south west, from the Northern Dynastic Claves, up along the southern extremity of the Great Bay, carving along a median line through the Millgate, Albarppan and Vapourial quarters. Messy and sudden, a rapid shift in tactics. I believe there are twenty... three, yes, three... twenty-three lord militant generals present in the Urdeshic Palace who ought to be capable of dealing with the issue competently. Any one of them. Pick a lord militant. That is why they are lords militant. They are born and raised and authorised to handle battlefield situations. Well, except Lugo, who's a bastard-fingered fool. But any of them. Do you know how many battles there are under way on Urdesh right now? At this very minute? I mean primary battles, class Beta-threat magnitude or higher?'

Gaunt began to answer.

'I'll tell you,' said the man. 'Sixteen. Sixteen. And Ghereppan's the one to watch. That's where the business will be done. The Warmaster brings an array of lords militant to Urdesh with him, the cream of the corps, ninety-two per cent of the crusade high staff. You'd think, wouldn't you, that they could get their heads out of their arses, collectively, and deal with sixteen battles. The question really is... where's my jacket?'

'Here,' said Gaunt. He took an old, black tail-jacket off the back of a chair. The brocade epaulettes were dusty, and the left-hand breast sagged under the weight of medals and crests.

'Thank you,' said the man as Gaunt held it for him so he could put it on over his nightshirt. 'The question really is not what is happening here in Eltath, but why.'

He fiddled awkwardly with the collar of his jacket, trying to get it to sit straight, and looked at Gaunt.

'Why? Isn't that the curious question, Lord Militant Gaunt? Why now?

Why like this? Why the tactical shift? What factors have influenced the timing? What has prompted such a drastic effort? Do you not suppose that it is those questions that should really occupy the consideration of the Warmaster?'

'I do, sir.'

'Is the correct answer. Tell me, Gaunt, was it you who started referring to me in the third person or me?'

'You, sir.'

'Honestly answered. Yes, well, I can't be too careful. There are bastards everywhere. Let's say it was you, because if we say it was me, then people would begin to doubt the clear function of my mental faculties, when I was merely occupied with thoughts of Melshun's victory at Harppan when you came in and distracted me with notions of supper and the tray you don't have. Why are you saluting?'

'Because I should have done it earlier, sir,' said Gaunt.

'Well, you can stop it. We're beyond that moment. You're here now, and bothering me. I don't like interruption. Not when I'm working. Interruptions break the flow. I can't abide them. I need to get on. There's so much to do. I had a man shot last week for knocking on the door.'

'Shot?'

'Well, he came in to polish my boots. Some Narmenian subaltern. I didn't actually have him shot, but I made it very clear to him that if he did it again, there'd be a wall in the parade ground and a blindfold with his name on it waiting for him. But I actually wrote out the order. Didn't send it. It was just boots, after all. I can always cross out his name and write in someone else's next time it happens.'

'I felt that I had to interrupt you, sir, I–'

The Warmaster swatted Gaunt's words away as though they were a fly buzzing around his face.

'You're all right. I had a mind to summon you at some point anyway. Interesting character. I've followed your service record. Low key, compared to some, but remarkable. Vervunhive. That was a superb piece of work. And after all, but for you, the Beati would not be standing with us. Have we met?'

'No, my lord.'

'No, I didn't think so. Balhaut was a big place. It would have been there, if at all. I've kept my eye on you, over the years. You and your curious little regiment. Specialists, I do like specialists. People talk about Urienz and Cybon and their extraordinary track records, and they *are* remarkable, but you, Gaunt. Over the years, you have achieved on the field of war things that have truly shaped this undertaking of ours. Perhaps more than any other commander in the crusade's ranks. Apart from me, obviously.'

He peered at Gaunt.

'On the whole, that's gone unrecognised, hasn't it? Your contributions have often been small, discreet and far away from the major warzones. But they've chalked up. Do you realise, you are responsible for the deaths of more magisters than any other commander? Kelso would wet himself in public to have that kind of record. I suppose you've been overlooked because you've never commanded a main force, not a militant division of any size, and there's that whole business of you being a commissar *and* a colonel. That made you a bit of a misfit. I suppose Slaydo was trying to be generous to you. He saw your worth. I see it too.'

He paused.

'I miss Slaydo,' he said quietly. 'The old dog. He knew what he was doing, even when what he was doing was killing himself. A tough act to follow. The burden is... it's immense, Ibram. Constant. Big boots to fill. More than a Narmenian subaltern can polish. Do you know Melshun?'

'No, sir,' said Gaunt.

'Urdeshi clave leader, two centuries back. Fought in the dynastic wars here. Where's the book gone?'

Macaroth began to leaf through the pile Gaunt had put on the desk. A few volumes fell onto the floor.

'This library,' he said as he rummaged, 'it's the dynastic record of Urdesh. Centuries of warfare. I believe in detail, Gaunt. The study of detail. The Imperium has fought so many wars they cannot be counted. So many battles. And it records them all, every last aspect and scrap of evidence. It's all there in our archives. Everything we need to win supremacy of the galaxy. Every tactic, every fault and clue. Every battle turns, in the end, on some tiny detail, some tiny flaw or mistake or accidental advantage. Look here.'

He opened the old book and smoothed the pages.

'Melshun's clave was fighting the Ghentethi Akarred Clan for control of the Harppan geothermal power hub. He was getting his arse handed to him, despite a beautifully devised three-point assault plan. Then an Akarred officer, very junior, called... What's that name there? I don't have my glasses.'

'Zhyler, sir. Clave Adjunct Zhyler.'

'Thank you. Yes, him. He failed to close the lock-gate access to the island's agriboat pen. A tiny thing. A detail. Nonsense really, in the grand scheme. But Melshun's scouts spotted it, and Melshun sent forty per cent of his main force in through the lock on jet-launches. Forty per cent, Gaunt. Think of it. Such a risk. Such a gamble. Such a potentially suicidal commitment.'

He smiled at Gaunt.

'Melshun brought down the Akarred. Took Harppan in a night. All thanks to one lock-gate. All thanks to one mistake. All thanks to Clave Adjunct Zhyler. I don't look at the big picture, Gaunt. Not any more. It doesn't interest me. The victory isn't in it. It's in the details. I look at the wealth of information that we as a race have retained. I analyse the details, the tiny errors, the tiny fragments of difference. And I learn, and I apply correctives.'

'Your approach is micro-management?' asked Gaunt.

'Boo! Ugly term. This war won't be won by a Warmaster, or a lord militant. It will be decided by a single Imperial Guardsman, a common trooper, on the ground, doing something small that is either very right or very wrong.'

Macaroth sat down and stared up at the books surrounding them.

'It's all about data, you see?' he said quietly. 'The Imperium is the greatest data-gathering institution in history. A bureaucracy with sharp teeth. It's a crime of great magnitude that we fail to use it. This chamber, for instance. Just a dusty library that gathers the records of one planet's conflicted past. But it is full of treasure. You know, there's not a... a mystical tome in this whole place? Not so much as one book of restricted lore or heretic power. Nothing the damned ordos would value and seek to suppress. Those wretched fools, locking data away, redacting it, prizing unholy relics. They wouldn't look at this place twice. They have their uses, I suppose.'

He leaned back and stretched.

'Your mission to Salvation's Reach. I understand it may have brought back the sort of Throne-forsaken artefacts that gets the Inquisition damp in the crotch.'

'Yes, sir.'

Macaroth nodded.

'And it will have value. I'm not an idiot. It will be reviewed and studied, and its use will be applied. Victory may well be hiding there. I am open to these possibilities. No, what really delights me about the Salvation's Reach mission is the tactical insight. The use of data. Your insight, I suppose. To disinform, and set the factions of the Archenemy against each other. That, Gaunt, is detail at work. Triggering a war between Sek and Gaur. To me, the artefacts that you have returned with are merely the icing on the cake.'

'Perhaps,' said Gaunt. 'I wonder–'

'Spit it out, Gaunt. I perceive value in you, but you are self-effacing. Too timid, which surprises me given your record. Speak your mind.'

'You mentioned the timing of this attack on Eltath, sir,' said Gaunt. 'The suddenly galvanised response. Just days after we returned with the spoils of Salvation's Reach–'

Macaroth nodded.

'They want them back,' he said quickly. 'They know they're here, and they want them back. This had crossed my mind. It is on my shortlist of explanations for their change in tactics. Analysis will confirm it. If it's true, then it's another detail. Another error. I estimate that the change of tactics and the assault on Eltath will cost them...'

He rummaged on his desk and found a notebook.

'Here. Nineteen per cent wastage. Sek accepts a crippling loss as the price of changing direction and attacking a near invincible Imperial bastion. So it must be worth it to him. Ergo, the artefacts are of immense value to whoever possesses them. Sek has shown us his cards.'

'You have prosecuted Sek since day one,' said Gaunt.

'Sek is potentially more dangerous than the Archon. If we ignore him and focus on Gaur, we will lose. If we don't take Sek down first, we will never get clear to deal the grace blow to the Archon.'

'And your scheme was to set bait for him here on Urdesh?'

Macaroth smiled and waggled a knowing finger at Gaunt.

'Sharp as a tack, you. Yes. To bait him.'

'With you, and the Saint, and the majority of the high staff?'

'How could he resist?'

'Is Sek a genius, sir?'

'Quite possibly. Superior in cunning to Gaur, at the very least.'

'Then have you considered that he might be playing the same game?'
Macaroth frowned.

'How so?'

'You come here, with the Saint and the staff, to bring him out and finish him. Might he have placed himself on Urdesh to do the same to you?'

Macaroth pursed his lips. He stared into the distance for a while.

'Of course,' he said. 'Like the end game of a regicide match. The last few pieces on the board. The most valuable pieces. Monarch against monarch.'

'What if he has pieces left that you don't know about?'

'We've analysed in detail—'

Gaunt drew out a chair and sat down, facing Macaroth across the stack of books. Macaroth seemed very frail and tired. Gaunt could see a small tick beat in the flesh beneath the Warmaster's left eye.

'My lord,' he said. 'I agree with you wholeheartedly that data is the key to victory. The Imperium does know so very much about itself. Too much, perhaps. That resource must be used. But my experience, as a common trooper on the ground, is that we know virtually nothing about our enemy. Virtually nothing. And what little we do know is sequestered and restricted, for the most part by the Inquisition, and deemed too dangerous to consider.'

Macaroth started to reply. No words came out. His hands trembled.

'I miss Slaydo,' he whispered.

He looked up at Gaunt. His eyes were fierce.

'I know detail. You, for instance. Your character and demeanour, as reflected by your service record. Your body language. You came here today, though orders reflect my desire to be left alone and the east wing is out of bounds. It was not arrogance that brought you. Not entitlement that you, the newly minted lord militant, should get his audience with me. That's not you. You feared I was neglecting my duties and oblivious to the assault at our door, that everything the staff said about me was true. That I was a fool, and a madman, a recluse, out of touch. That I am no longer worthy of my rank. You came to warn me.'

'I did, sir.'

'But not that the city was under assault. I can see it in you. Some greater weight you carry.'

Gaunt hesitated. He felt a weight indeed. He could feel enemies, waiting to be made, on either side of him.

'Lord,' he said, 'a significant proportion of the commanders at staff level have lost confidence in your leadership. As we speak, they have a process in motion to unseat you and remove you from command.'

Macaroth sighed.

'There's gratitude,' he said, his voice a hoarse whisper. 'I have watched for enemies with vigilance. I sleep with one eye open. But the enemies are inside these walls already. Cybon, is it? Van Voytz? Who else? Bulledin? Who do they intend to replace me with?'

'Me,' said Gaunt.

Macaroth blinked.

'Well, well… They're not idiots, then. I am reassured at least that they have a keen grip of politics. Of talent. In their position, you would be my choice too. But, Gaunt... You stand to succeed to the most powerful rank in the sector. An outsider, brought to the very forefront, just as I was at Balhaut. You stand to inherit. Yet you come here to tell me this? To warn me?'

'I do, sir.'

'Do you not want the job?'

'I haven't even considered my feelings about it,' said Gaunt. 'Probably not, on balance.'

'Which is why you're the right man, of course. Why, then?'

'Because you are the Warmaster,' said Gaunt. 'I have served you since Balhaut. Duty and history tell me that we are as good as lost the day men like me turn against their Warmaster.'

TWENTY-FOUR

I AM DEATH

'We can walk from here,' said Baskevyl.

'Oh, come on,' said Domor. 'It's not far now.'

'Let me rephrase,' said Baskevyl. He tapped the transport's fuel gauge. 'We're going to *have* to walk from here.'

He pulled the transport to a grumbling halt, and they got out. The street was deserted and lightless, but the night air was heavy with the smell of fyceline, and the sky above the rooftops was blooming with an amber glow. They could hear the distant sounds of warfare from several directions, rolling in across the city.

Fazekiel looked at the Munitorum transport ruefully. The bodywork was punctured in dozens of places, and the rear end was shot out.

'Close call,' she said. Bask nodded. If the engine hadn't started, they'd have been sitting targets. The ride out had been fierce and blind. Baskevyl had driven like a maniac, his only direction 'away from the gunfire'.

Domor glanced at the burning sky.

'Close call's not over yet,' he remarked. 'The whole city's up against the wall.'

They started to walk. They crossed streets that were shuttered and dark, and passed buildings that had been abandoned. Shrapnel and air combat debris littered the roadway, smouldering and twisted, some scraps still twinkling with heat. The stuff had been raining down indiscriminately for hours, and though the main air raid seemed to have ended, soot and sparks continued to flutter down. Up on the Great Hill, the glow of the palace's void shields was dying away. A calculated risk, Bask supposed, but the main fighting zones were clearly ground wars at the edges of the main city, and the void shields would urgently need time to recharge. Another aerial assault could come at any time.

Twenty minutes brought them through the derelict quarters of Low Keen to the head of the service road. They walked in silence, weary, out of words. The battle had escalated around them and left them out of the main action. It was time to catch up and hope there was still a chance to rejoin the regiment.

Whatever warning they thought they might bring was surely now too late.

From the service road, they could see the Tanith K700 billet in the gloom of the industrial scar-land. Lights moved around the buildings. They could see transports.

'Someone's still there, at least,' said Bask.

Halfway down the service road, they were challenged by sentries. Erish, the big standard bearer from V Company, and Thyst, another trooper from his squad. They seemed punchy and ill at ease.

'Major Baskevyl?' Erish said in surprise as they drew close enough for him to recognise them.

'What's going on, trooper?' Baskevyl asked.

'Just prepping to move out, sir,' said Erish. 'Up to the palace.'

'The whole regiment?'

'No, sir, just V and E Companies, moving the regimental retinue to shelter.'

'Where are the rest of the Ghosts?' asked Domor.

'Front line, sir,' said Erish.

Baskevyl and Domor glanced at each other. Their companies had gone to secondary without them. Possibly primary. They might already be fighting and dying.

'Who's in charge here?' asked Fazekiel.

'Captain Meryn, ma'am,' Erish replied. 'With Commissar Blenner.'

Fazekiel looked at him closely. She was a good study of body language, and Erish seemed unusually tense. No, not tense. Unsettled.

'Vox the gate, Erish,' said Baskevyl. 'Tell Meryn we're on our way in.'

'Yes, sir,' said the trooper.

'What's going on, Trooper Erish?' asked Fazekiel.

Erish looked nervously at his comrade.

'What do you mean, ma'am?' he asked.

'What aren't you telling us?'

'There's been an incident, ma'am,' said Erish.

'How the feth did this happen, captain?' asked Baskevyl.

Meryn shrugged. Around them, in the K700 yard, men from his company were loading cargo onto the Munitorum trucks, and the huddled members of the retinue were lining up to clamber aboard. There was an uncomfortable quiet, more than just a wartime quiet. A sense of shock.

'A shrug's not going to cut it, Meryn,' Baskevyl said.

'I don't know what the feth to tell you,' Meryn replied. 'It's a feth awful mess. What do you want from me? You want me to say that an arsehole from my company went psycho? Is that it?'

'You and Gendler were close.'

'So?' Meryn sneered. 'He was still an arsehole. I just didn't realise how big an arsehole. Attacking a girl like that.'

'Gaunt's... daughter?'

'Seems so.'

'Where is she?' asked Domor.

'In one of the trucks. She's conscious now, but she's woozy and in shock. Once we arrive at the palace, we'll get her to a medicae.'

'I want to talk to her,' said Baskevyl.

'I told you,' said Meryn, 'she's not in a fit state. Leave it. Leave it for now. Give her some time.'

'There'll be an inquiry,' said Bask.

'Don't doubt it,' said Meryn. 'There should be. Blenner and I are ready to provide full statements.'

'I can't believe Wilder would–' Domor began.

'Well, he did,' said Meryn bluntly. 'There was always some loose wiring there. You must have seen it. Too much booze, and a grudge the size of the Golden Throne. Didi must've... Gendler must have put him up to it. Feth-wipes, the both of them.'

'Wilder killed Ezra?' asked Baskevyl.

Meryn nodded. 'I can't believe it,' he said. 'I mean, Ezra... fething Ezra.'

'And Blenner sanctioned Wilder?'

'What else could he do?' asked Meryn.

Domor and Baskevyl looked at each other.

'Look,' said Meryn, 'we don't have time for this now. Priority is to get the retinue up and into the sanctuary of the palace, while the shields are down. That's a direct order from Gaunt. We can't hang about here, no matter what's gone down. We have to get this lot moving in the next few minutes.'

'All right,' said Baskevyl reluctantly. 'Double time, everyone. Let's move them to safety.'

Meryn threw a quick salute, and turning, began shouting orders at the loading parties. Baskevyl saw Elodie Dutana-Daur approaching, with one of the women from the retinue in tow.

'Major?'

'Yes, Elodie?'

'Juniper's lost Yoncy,' she said.

'She was with me, sir,' said the older woman. 'We were getting all packed away, then the commotion started, and I turned around and she was gone. I think she got upset. People were talking, saying that there'd been shooting. That people were dead. She thought it was them snipers again and got upset. I think she went to hide.'

'I can't find her,' said Elodie.

Bask swore under his breath.

'We'll hunt around,' he said. 'She can't be far.'

'Yeah, we'll find her,' Shoggy echoed. He knew that he and Baskevyl were thinking the same thing: there'd been enough bad turns for one day. They weren't about to lose Criid's little girl too. Criid's little girl... *Gol's* little girl. Meryn had told them that the Astra Militarum intelligence service had taken Gol away. Wherever he was now, Gol Kolea would need his friends to look after his family for him.

'Where's Dalin?' asked Baskevyl.

'On the truck, looking after Gaunt's child,' said Meryn.

'I'll go and ask him if he knows anywhere Yoncy might've hidden,' said Baskevyl.

'I'll start looking,' said Domor. He turned to Elodie and Juniper.

'Where'd you last see her?' he asked.

* * *

A voice spoke in the night. It spoke in the crump of the artillery bombardments, in the distant roar of firestorms, in the clunk of mortars.

It was the old voice, the shadow voice. It had no words; it just spoke of war in sounds made out of war.

But its meaning was clear. So clear, it seemed to drown out all the sounds and furies bearing down on Eltath.

In the blue darkness of the unlit waste-ground behind the billets, Yoncy cowered in the rubble heaps. It was time. Papa was telling her it was time. Time to come home. Time to be brave and grow up. Time to go to Papa.

'I don't want to!' she whispered, rubbing tears from her eyes with her grubby wrists. Then she wished she hadn't spoken. Someone would hear her.

Someone *had* heard her.

Someone was close. She could hear boots crunching over the rubble in the darkness around her. People moving.

People coming for her. Ready or not.

'What are you doing, exactly, Luna?'

Fazekiel stopped taking images, and lowered her small hand-held picter. Blenner was standing in the wash house doorway.

'Recording the scene,' she said. 'Or did you do that already?'

'Me? No,' said Blenner. 'Why? Why would I?'

'Three deaths in billet,' she said. 'We can't preserve the scene here, so we'll need as much evidence as we can get.'

'Evidence?' asked Blenner. 'Evidence for what?'

'Are you serious, Blenner?'

'It's cut and dried!' Blenner snapped. 'Feth's sake, Luna... Gendler went crazy. Wilder was in on it. They attacked Gaunt's girl, then Ezra–'

With each name, Blenner was pointing angrily at a different blood pattern on the walls and floor of the old wash house. Fazekiel started taking pictures of every dark stain.

'Stop it!' Blenner snapped.

'This incident is bad enough,' said Fazekiel. 'It would warrant a full hearing anyway, but the fact that the child of a lord militant is involved? You think Gaunt will just let this go on a field report?'

Blenner shrugged helplessly.

'He'll want to know everything. Ezra was his friend, and...' She trailed off and stopped. '*You're* supposed to be his friend, Blenner. His oldest, dearest friend. Why the hell aren't you doing this for him? Why aren't you doing your duty as a friend and a commissar, and wrapping this up in a bow for him? I mean, impeccably? No stone unturned? Why aren't you doing that for him?'

'I executed the bastard who–'

'Just get out of the way, Blenner. I'll deal with this.'

'It doesn't need to be dealt with,' said Blenner petulantly. 'I have a full report. Meryn was a witness to it. There's nothing to–'

'I'll deal with it, I said. My report, my case.'

'Just a fething minute, lady!' Blenner yelled. 'You weren't even here!'

'Exactly. Officio Prefectus procedural provision four hundred and fifty-six slash eleven. Independent review of any serious or capital crime. Don't you even know the fething rulebook? Why am I not surprised? This can't be your case because you were an active in the incident. Summary powers only cover so far. Get out, Blenner. My case, as of right now.'

She stopped suddenly, and looked around.

'What was that?' she asked.

'What was what?'

'That noise? Outside? It sounded like a bone-saw.'

The people had found her. Yoncy looked up.

Eight figures stood around her in the gloomy rubble. Men. Soldiers. Masks hid their faces.

'Go away!' she said. 'Go away!'

She hid her head in her hands so she couldn't see them.

The Sons of Sek raised their weapons and stepped closer.

'This way, maybe?' said Elodie hopefully.

'She did like to play out in the open ground,' said Juniper, hurrying along behind them. 'Out the back, in the waste-ground. She'd play hide and seek, sometimes.'

'We'll take a look,' said Domor. He adjusted his augmetics to the lower light. Behind the billet, away from the lamps of the yard, it was pitch dark, and the ground was loose and uneven.

They stopped and peered around.

'Check that way,' Domor said. 'Juniper, go along to the latrines. I'll look over here.'

They separated and stumbled into the darkness. Elodie moved along the rear of the billet buildings, groping her way. She called Yoncy's name a few times, but there was something about the darkness that made her reluctant to speak. It was cold, and thick like oil. A fathomless shadow.

A bad shadow.

Elodie heard something. Movement, or a faint voice, perhaps. She turned, and started to move in the direction it had come from.

'Yoncy?' There was someone up ahead.

'Yoncy, are you there?'

Something ran out of the darkness and flung itself into her. The impact almost knocked Elodie down.

'Yoncy?'

Yoncy was clinging to her legs, sobbing.

'It's all right,' said Elodie, trying to prise her free and get her on her feet. 'It's all right, Yoncy. We've found you now.'

'They've found me too,' wailed Yoncy.

Elodie froze. She looked up and saw the big, black shapes stepping out of the night around them.

'Oh, the Emperor protect me,' she gasped. 'By the g-grace of the Throne, and all l-light that shines from Terra...'

She could smell the dirt-stink of them, the unwashed filth, the dried blood. Their masks leered at her like remembered nightmares.

'*Ver voi mortoi,*' said the leader of the Sons. He had drawn a blade.

The darkness grew thicker. It swallowed Elodie up. She clung to the child, but the darkness ate her whole. A swooning red-rush, then blackout.

There was a shrill, screeching noise, like a power saw ripping through hard bone in a surgeon's theatre.

Blood flew everywhere.

Domor heard the noise. He started to run.

'Alarm! Alarm!' he yelled. It was a weapon of some sort. He'd heard a weapon. Insurgents. The fething enemy was among them.

He ran towards the spot where he'd last seen Elodie. Ghosts were moving out from the yard in response to his yells. Lamps were bobbing and flashing.

'Secure the perimeter!' Domor shouted to them. Fazekiel and Blenner shoved their way through the men to join him.

'Shoggy?'

'There's someone back here, Luna,' Domor yelled, running forwards. 'Get fire-teams to the rear fast! I think it's a raid!'

Fazekiel grabbed him. 'Wait! Wait, Shoggy! What's that?'

The lamps and torch packs were illuminating something in the rubble dead ahead of them. Two bodies, twisted together.

Everyone came to a halt.

'Holy Throne...' whispered Domor.

Elodie lay on the ground, her body and arms curled protectively around Yoncy. The two of them were soaked in blood.

Around them, every scrap and stone and brick and rock was dripping with gore. Steam rose from it in the night chill. Domor had seen shells detonate among squads of men. It had looked like this.

As if half a dozen or more men had been torn to shreds by some immense and violent force.

Blenner gagged and turned aside to retch. Domor and Fazekiel stumbled to the bodies. The Ghosts looked on, bewildered.

There were body parts everywhere, scraps of flesh and bone, chunks of shredded uniform, pieces of weaponry. Fazekiel crouched beside Elodie and Yoncy. As she touched them, her hands grew slick with blood.

'They're alive,' she called out, her voice hoarse with horror. 'They're unconscious but they're alive.'

'What the feth did this?' asked Domor.

The western end of Turnabout Lane was carpeted with bodies. Many had been felled by the Tanith marksmen during the first advance, the rest had been mown down in the two desperate pushes that had followed. Sons of Sek lay twisted and sprawled on the open roadway and the narrow pavements, piled up in places, smoke rising from clothes punctured by las-shots. Enough blood was running in the downslope gutters to make a clear gurgling sound. Smoke draped the air like gauze.

'*Movement at the head of the road,*' Larkin voxed.

'Copy, Larks,' Criid acknowledged. Her company and Obel's had the top end of Millgate covered. They were dug in, but that wasn't saying much. Street fighting was luck as much as craft, and the old mill area was a warren.

She glanced at Varl.

'You honestly think they're stupid enough to try again?' Varl asked. 'We cut them to ribbons. Three times.'

'I don't think stupidity has anything to do with it,' Criid replied. 'They want to come through, so they're going to keep trying.'

Obel ran across and slid into cover beside them.

'We've got a six-street section covered, backyards and breezeways too,' he said. 'Any wider, and we'll be spread too thin.'

Criid nodded.

'Rawne's pushing units up to the right of us. The Helixids are supposed to have the left.'

'I haven't seen any Helixids,' said Varl dubiously. 'We're supposed to be the invisible ones.'

'Check it out,' Criid told him. 'Get a vox-man on it. If the Helixids aren't in position, I want to know fast.'

Varl nodded, and dodged back to the street corner, head down.

Criid heard a *plunk*. A second later, a section of pavement high up Turn-about Lane blew up in a ball of flames. More, rapid *plunk*s. Explosions turned into the left side of the street, blowing out the facade of one of the mill houses. Masonry tumbled down.

'Mortar fire,' Criid cursed. The shells were dropping thick and fast, and creeping towards her line. Incendiary shells. Flames were already begin-ning to lick into the mill houses and habs of the street.

'Larkin!' she voxed. 'Fall back to me. All marksmen fall back!'

She heard a brief yelp of acknowledgement over the link.

'Feth this,' Criid said to Obel. 'Infantry didn't work, so they're trying to burn us out.'

'We'll have to fall back,' said Obel. 'I dunno, Vallet Yard, around there?'

That would mean giving up about seventy metres of territory. But the shells were falling fast. She could barely hear herself think.

'Contact!' a trooper yelled from nearby.

Criid poked her head up. Down the lane, through the billowing flames, she could see silhouettes scurrying forwards, low and quick.

'Hold them off!' she yelled.

The Ghosts around her, huddled into cover, began shooting down the lane into the fire. Almost at once, she heard sustained gunfire kicking off in the streets parallel to her.

'A Company to command!' she called into her microbead. 'Rawne, receiving?'

'*Go, Criid.*'

'They're coming again. Laying down fire-shells and advancing behind them. A whole lot of the bastards.'

'*Understood.*'

'I need that support. At least two companies, preferably four. I need holding strength to come in via Vallet Yard and secure Hockspur Lane and Darppan Street.'

'*Stand by.*'

'Do you copy, Rawne? I'm not fething around.'

'*Stand by.*'

Rawne pulled his microbead off and looked at Zhukova. She was so out of breath she was bent double, her hands planted on her thighs.

'Tell me again,' he said.

'They're coming through the scrapped boats,' she said. She straightened up. 'Significant strength.'

'You're sure?'

'Mkoll's sure.'

'Good enough,' said Rawne.

'Look,' said Zhukova, 'they're not *going* to come through, they're already *in* there.'

Rawne looked at Oysten.

'Tell Pasha to hold the highway, but be ready to spare me as many bodies as she can. Half her strength, if possible.'

Oysten nodded.

'What about Criid?' asked Ludd. 'What about here?'

'Take C Company, Ludd – back her up.'

'One company?'

'If Zhukova's right, one company is all I can spare.'

Ludd looked at him, pinched and fierce.

'The Emperor protects, Nahum. Go put the fear of the Throne in them.'

'Sir,' Ludd nodded, and beckoned Caober to follow him.

'The other companies with me,' said Rawne. 'We're going to cross the highway behind Pasha's position, and defend the east end of the scrap boats. Mkdask, get your men moving and lead the way.'

'Sir?'

Oysten was pointing to the microbead in Rawne's hand. It was emitting a piping squeak. He put it back in his ear.

'Rawne, go.'

'*Eli, it's Varl! The fething Helixid–*'

'Say again, Varl.'

'*They're falling back! The mortar fire's hit them hard, and they're falling back fast. The left flank's open all the way from Penthes Street north to Turnabout.*'

Rawne grimaced. Everyone was looking at him.

'Acknowledged, Varl. Stand by.'

He looked at the officers around him.

'Change of plan,' he said. 'B Company with me. We're going after Mkdask. Vivvo, lead the rest to the left and cover Criid's arse at the Penthes Street junction. Don't just stand there, move!'

Rawne strode into the narrow street, B Company assembling around him.

'Double time, straight silver,' he instructed. 'If you thought street fighting in an old mill quarter was tight fun, get ready to have your minds blown.'

He looked at Zhukova.

'Lead us back to Mkoll.'

She nodded.

'How many men did he have with him when you left him?' Rawne asked.

'Men?' she asked. 'Major, he was on his own.'

Here's where it starts to get interesting, Mkoll thought.

The first few to reach him were forward scouts. He picked them off with his knife, one by one, as they came through the dank guts of the rusted boats. But the main force was on their heels, and it had become necessary to ditch the subtle approach.

He crouched below a metal railing thick with lichen and wet weed, and used a row of heavy tool chests for cover. He started pushing shots at anything that stirred on the deck of the agriboat and its neighbours. He saw Sons of Sek attempting to haul themselves through rotted hatches, and blew them back inside. Head shots, throat shots. He heard shouting and cursing from the hulls below him. Las-fire started to kick back in his direction. It shattered the chipped windows of the drive house, dented the corroded metal of the engine house wall and spanked off the metal tool chests.

Mkoll crawled clear. He ran along a jingling companionway bridge, ducked into fresh cover, and leaned over to fire multiple shots down the throat of a through-deck hatch. He heard bodies fall as they were blown off rusty ladders.

He got up again, swung over the rail and jumped onto an inspection-way that ran the length of the agriboat. A figure in yellow combat gear was clambering up through one of the ladder-ways ahead. He fired from the hip, knocking the man sideways. The Son of Sek fell six metres into the bottom of an empty catch hold.

Mkoll swerved, and cut laterally across the boat. A man rose through a deck hatch in front of him, and Mkoll landed a hard kick in his masked face as he jumped over man and hatch together. The Son jerked backwards, his head bouncing off the back of the hatch ring, and he fell, senseless, knocking men off the ladder beneath him.

Las-fire ripped across the boat, a few shots, then a flurry. Sons of Sek had climbed on top of the engine housing, and were firing at him from cover.

He ducked, and crawled into the shelter of a hoist mounting. He changed clips fast. From his position, he could see the road line and the barricade. Ghosts were moving up from Pasha's position. He estimated they would be in the hulks in six or seven minutes. Were they just responding to the gunfire flashes or had Zhukova got through? Did the Ghosts even know what they were about to meet head on?

More shots poured at him. He got down, took aim, and dropped two Sons of Sek off the roof of the engine house. He checked his musette bag. Four grenades. He took them out and started to crawl.

He reached a hatch, listened and heard movement below. He tossed a grenade in, and then kicked the open hatch shut to maximise concussion. The dull blast thumped through the deck under him. He crossed, head low, almost on his hands and knees, and reached a vent chute that aired the lower decks. He set a long fuse to the next grenade and rolled it down the chute. He was at the next hatch when he heard the deadened bang of the blast. Thin smoke was issuing from the vent grilles in the deck behind him.

He slung a grenade into the next hatch and kicked the cover down, repeating the drill. The hatch flapped like a chattering mouth with the force of the blast from beneath.

How long now? Five minutes? Could he keep them busy for five more minutes? He remembered being a dead man, waking up dead, a ghost, on the *Armaduke* after the accident, with no memory and no sense of self, just an urge to protect and defend. A one man war. Time for that again. Time for that same single-minded fury and drive. Whatever it took, the Emperor protects.

What had that thing said to him? The man-but-not-man, in the machine space of the ship? 'Ver voi mortek!' *You are death.*

Mkoll had picked up the language on Gereon. It had been essential to survival.

Gunfire chopped at him. He felt a las-bolt crease his leg, a searing pain. Sons of Sek were rushing him from a service hatch.

He shot the first two, point-blank, then swung the butt of his gun up to greet the face of the third, poleaxing him so hard the Archenemy soldier's feet left the ground and he almost somersaulted. The fourth got a bayonet stab in the forehead. Mkoll hadn't fixed his war blade, but he lunged the rifle with a perfect bayonet-stab thrust and the muzzle cracked the enemy's skull.

More in the doorway. He leaned back and fired, full auto, sweeping. Las-rounds speckled the metalwork either side of the hatch, took the hatch off its hinges and ripped through the Sons of Sek in the doorway.

One man war. Last stand. Time was running out, running out too fast for him to stop it.

He saw more yellow-clad warriors coming at him, coming from all sides. They were pouring out of every hatch of the agriboat in their dozens, hundreds.

'Ger tar Mortek!' Mkoll yelled. 'Ger tar Mortek!'

I am death. *I am death.*

Some of them faltered, stunned by his words, the unexpected threat of their own barbarian tongue.

He cut them down.

Time was running out. His ammo was running out.

He was almost done, but they were still coming, more and more of them rushing him from all sides.

'I am death!' Mkoll screamed, and proved it until his shots ran dry, and his hands and warknife ran wet with blood.

TWENTY-FIVE

EXECUTOR

If anything, the level of activity in the war room was more furious than before. Marshal Blackwood had arrived, some thirty minutes earlier, relieved Cybon of command, and taken his place at the main strategium. The massive hololithic plates quivered with rapidly updating data streams. Van Voytz, Cybon and nine other lords militant were supporting Blackwood's command and supervising the mass of personnel.

Gaunt stood in the doorway for a moment, surveying the commotion. Hundreds of men and women filled the main floor below him, and the upper galleries too – hundreds of men and women processing information, making decisions and determining the lives of millions more across the surface of Urdesh and its nearspace holdings.

Even from a distance, Gaunt could read the general trend of the incident boards. Their glowing plates prioritised the main crisis zones. Ghereppan in the south was a massive focus. Zarakppan was in disarray. Eltath itself was clearly on the brink. Sub-graphics showed the seat of the fighting was in the south west, along the bay, and in the fringes of the Northern Dynastic Claves.

The Ghosts were in that mess somewhere. That's where he'd sent them.

He drew a breath, and walked down the steps to the main floor.

Van Voytz saw him through the crowd, handed a data-slate back to a waiting tactician and came storming over.

'The hell have you been, Gaunt?' he snapped.

'Achieving what you wanted, sir,' Gaunt replied.

'What does that mean? The hell you have! We should have moved two hours ago! This situation is beyond untenable and–'

'I believe you wanted a viable Warmaster,' said Gaunt.

'I wanted this done cleanly and quickly,' replied Van Voytz, 'and I'm having sincere doubts about your suitability. For Throne's sake, you don't play games with something this vital–'

'You don't,' replied Gaunt calmly. 'I agree. And I agree about my suitability too. But I've got you what you wanted. Just not in the form you expected, perhaps.'

Van Voytz began yelling at him again, loud enough to still the activity in the immediate area. Militarum personnel turned to look in concern. Cybon and Blackwood also turned, hearing the raised voice.

Gaunt ignored Van Voytz's tirade. He moved aside and looked back at the main staircase.

Warmaster Macaroth walked slowly down the stairs, chin up. He hadn't bothered to shave, but he had dressed in his formal uniform, the red sash across the chest of his dark blue jacket, the crest of his office fixed over his heart. Sancto and the other Scions flanked him as a makeshift honour guard, and Beltayn, Daur and Bonin followed in his wake.

The chamber fell silent. Voices dropped away. There was a suspended hush, and every eye was on Macaroth. The only sounds were the constant chirrup and clatter of the war room's systems.

'Attention,' said Gaunt.

The several hundred personnel present shot to attention. The twelve lords militant made the sign of the aquila and bowed their heads.

Macaroth strolled past Gaunt and Van Voytz, and walked up to the main strategium. Tactical officers scooted out of his path. He picked up a data-wand, and flipped through several strategic views, making the light show blink and re-form.

'This is a pretty mess,' he said, at last.

'Warmaster, we have containment measures–' Blackwood began.

'I wasn't referring to the war condition, Blackwood,' said Macaroth. 'Well, only in part. I can see your containment measures. They are fit for purpose. I will make some adjustments, but they are fit enough. I had no doubt, Blackwood, that you and your fellow lords were perfectly able to prosecute this war. That's how you were bred. That's why you were chosen. Continue as you are doing.'

Blackwood nodded.

'But it is clear you doubt *me,* don't you, my lords?' Macaroth asked. His gaze flitted from Cybon, to Blackwood, to Van Voytz, to Tzara. Each lord militant in turn felt the heat of his stare.

'You doubt my fitness. My ability. My resolution. My methods.'

'My lord,' said Van Voytz. 'I hardly think this is the time or place–'

'Then when exactly, Van Voytz? When would be a good time for *you?*'

'Warmaster,' said Cybon, stepping forwards, 'this is not a discussion to have in front of the general staff–'

'They're not children, Cybon,' said Macaroth. 'They're not innocents. They're senior officers. There's not a man here who hasn't been bloodied in war and witnessed first hand the miseries of this conflict. That's why they're in this room. They don't have sensitivities that need to be spared from the uglier difficulties of warfare. Such as questions of command.'

Macaroth looked at them.

'Which one of you has it? Whose pocket is it in?'

'My lord?' asked Cybon.

'The declamation of confidence. Countersigned, no doubt. The instrument to remove me from my post.'

A murmur ran through the crowd. Officers glanced at each other in dismay.

'Hush now,' said Macaroth. 'It is perfectly legal. We're not talking insurrection here. If a commander is unfit, he may be removed. The mechanism exists. My lords militant have been meticulous in their process. By the book. They have considered the matter carefully, as great men do, and they have made a resolution, and stand ready to enact it.'

He looked at the data-wand in his hand thoughtfully.

'My fault,' he said quietly. 'My oversight. I have been well aware of your disaffection for years. Some of that I put down to thwarted ambitions, or differences in strategic thinking. I knew there was dissent. I knew that many were unhappy with my focus and my style of command.'

He looked up again.

'I ignored it. I trusted in the loyalty of your stations. Whatever you thought, whatever our differences, you knew I was Warmaster. That, I thought, was all that mattered.'

Macaroth put the wand down on the glass tabletop.

'Not enough, clearly. Not nearly enough. And whatever awareness I had of your discontent, it needed one man to stand up and tell me so. To my damn face. To risk everything in terms of his career and future, his alliances and political capital, and simply *tell* me. That, I think, is loyalty. Not to me. To the office. To the Throne. To the *Imperial bloody Guard*.'

Cybon turned slowly to look at Gaunt.

'You bastard,' he rumbled. 'You told him, you treacherous bastard–'

'"Treacherous, General Cybon?' said Macaroth mildly. 'I don't think that's a word I'd throw around, if I were you. And certainly not a word I'd expect you to use of the man *you* personally chose to replace me.'

He walked over to Cybon and looked up at the towering warlord.

'Gaunt told me, because it was his duty to do so. You put him in a situation worse than any war he's ever faced. Conflict of interest at the highest degree. Yet he served, as every good Guardsman serves. Served with unflinching loyalty to the Astra Militarum, to the oath we all uphold. He came and he *told* me. He simply *told* me, Cybon. He told me the depth of your unhappiness. He supplied the one vital piece of intelligence missing from my overview of this crusade.'

Van Voytz snarled and swung at Gaunt. Gaunt caught his wrist before the blow could land, and pushed back hard. Van Voytz stumbled backwards, collided with Kelso and crashed into the side of the strategium table. He steadied himself.

'Is that where we're going now?' Gaunt asked. 'Is it, Barthol? Open insurrection? Legal process fails, so you resort to violence?'

'He just wants to break your face,' said Cybon. 'All of us do.'

'*All* of you?' asked Macaroth. 'Everyone in this chamber? Really? My lords, officers, soldiers, now is the moment. If you would see me gone, then stand together. Now. Go on. I will accept your declamation of confidence and all your instruments of removal. Come to that, I will accept your blades in my back and your bullets in my brain. If I am unfit and you want me gone, get it over with.'

Macaroth closed his eyes, tilted his head back and opened his arms serenely as if to welcome an embrace.

'For Throne's sake!' Van Voytz growled. 'We are obliged to act! The crusade is failing! We're losing this war! We must serve the declamation and rid ourselves of this infantile leadership! We must act for the good of the Imperium, in the name of the God-Emperor, and usher in a new era of clear and forthright command!'

Gaunt crossed to face him. He drew his power sword and lit it.

'Do it, Barthol,' he said. 'But you go through me.'

'You're a thrice-damned idiot, Gaunt!' Van Voytz raged, 'You've ruined us all! We had a chance here. A chance to find new focus! Cybon, for Throne's sake! We have to do this! *We have to do this!*'

'Not like this,' said Cybon quietly.

'By legal resort, yes,' said Blackwood. 'Not by bloody coup. Never that way.'

'Would you raise your hand against Macaroth?' asked Kelso in dismay.

'Step back, Van Voytz,' murmured Tzara.

'I have my grievances,' said Cybon. He looked at Macaroth. 'Throne knows, many. I am keen to discuss them. But I will not devolve to insurrection. Damn it, Van Voytz, he *is* the Warmaster.'

Macaroth opened his eyes, and slowly lowered his arms. He smiled.

'Put down your famous sword, Lord Militant Gaunt,' he said. 'I see only loyal men in this room.'

Gaunt glanced at Van Voytz, and then depowered and sheathed his sword. Blackwood took off his cap and his gloves and set them on the table.

'You have my resignation, lord,' he said. 'My resignation for my part in orchestrating your removal. I cannot speak for the others, but I trust my colleagues will have the dignity to do the same.'

'Oh, I don't want your resignation, Blackwood,' said Macaroth. 'I don't want your frightened obedience either. Resolving this isn't so simple. I have been at fault. I have been absent. I have lost my connection with staff command. I aim to remedy that. I intend to take direct control of this battle-sphere and win this cursed war.'

He tapped his index finger on the glass plate of the strategium.

'I am here *now,*' he said. 'Any man, *any* man present who finds no confidence in me can stay and have that lack of confidence disabused. Any who wish to go, go now. There will be no retribution. No purge by the Officio Prefectus. Just go, and you will be reposted to other zones and other sectors. But if you're going, get the hell out *now.*'

He looked at Blackwood, Cybon and Tzara.

'If you wish, stay. Serve me here. Don't cower or meep weak platitudes of loyalty. Serve me here at this station. Bring me the insight and ability that made you lords militant in the first place. Help me as we fight for Urdesh and drive the Archenemy to ruin.'

The room began to stir. Officers began to move back towards the table.

Macaroth clapped his hands.

'Come on!' he yelled. 'Move yourselves! This war won't win itself! I need data revisions on zones three, eight and nine immediately!'

Tacticians and data-serfs began to scurry.

'Get me oversight reports on Zarakppan!' Macaroth demanded. 'I want a

link to Urienz on the ground. And set up a vox-link with Ghereppan immediately! I need to advise the Saint of our strategic approach. Blackwood, put
your damn cap back on! Where's that zone three data?'

The noise and mass activity resumed. At the heart of the war room's reignited frenzy, Gaunt faced Van Voytz.

'You made a mistake, Gaunt,' said Van Voytz.

'I don't think so,' Gaunt replied. 'History will decide.'

'I trusted you.'

'As I have trusted you many times. The outcome is what matters, isn't
that what you always told me?' Gaunt looked at him. 'It may not come in
the form we expect, and it may cost us personally in painful ways, but the
outcome is what matters. For the Emperor. For the Imperium. Whatever
price we as individuals pay.'

'Damn you. Are you really throwing Jago back in my face? That was a necessary action! Sentiment doesn't enter into–'

'So is this. You heard the Warmaster. Do your job, or get out. I just heard
him calling for zone nine data.'

Van Voytz glowered at him. Gaunt turned away.

'My lord Warmaster,' he called through the hubbub. 'General Van Voytz
had oversight of zone nine. I believe he has tactical advice in that regard.'

'Tell him to get over here!' Macaroth shouted back.

Gaunt turned back to Van Voytz. Van Voytz glared for a moment more,
then pushed his way through the staff to the Warmaster's side.

'Sir?'

Gaunt looked around and found Beltayn standing beside him.

'What is it?'

'Um, signal from transfer section, sir. Our retinue has just entered the
safety of the palace precinct, with two companies in escort. Major Baskevyl
asks to report to you at the earliest possible opportunity.'

'Baskevyl? Tell him I'll see him as soon as I can. In fact, send Captain Daur
down to admit him and take his brief. Any word on the main Ghost force?'

'Nothing, sir,' said Beltayn. 'Vox-control suggests there may be signal jamming in their sector.'

Gaunt nodded, and pushed through the press towards Biota.

'Do we have an update on the Tanith First?' he asked the tactician.

Biota took him aside to one of the hololith plates, and wanded through
data.

'They log as still in position, as per orders,' he said. 'Tulkar Batteries
defence, at the east end of Millgate.'

'They're holding?'

'Yes, sir.'

'Contact?'

'Heavy jamming, sir,' Biota replied with a shake of his head.

Gaunt looked at the data display. 'Throne,' he murmured, 'that's a bloodbath. They're right at the heart of it. I sent them right into the heaviest
fighting in the zone.'

'My lord,' said Biota. He hesitated. 'My lord, we have an unconfirmed report that a significant enemy advance is pushing along the south shore into Millgate. Your Ghosts, sir... They are the principal unit standing in its way.'

The transports rumbled in through the gatehouses, and entered the compound of the Urdeshic Palace. It was almost dawn, but the sky was choked with smoke plumes running north off Zarakppan and the burning mills. Munitorum staffers with light poles guided the vehicles to parking places on the hard standing, and cargo crews moved in to help the retinue unload.

'How many are you?' a Munitorum official asked Meryn. Meryn handed him the manifest list.

'We have accommodation assigned in the west blockhouses,' the man said. 'The crews will show you the way.'

'I need a medicae,' said Meryn. 'We have a concussion injury.'

The official waved over a medicae. Meryn pointed him to Fazekiel and Dalin, who were helping Felyx out of one of the trucks. He had a bedroll and a combat cape wrapped around him like a shawl, and looked pale and unsteady.

She, Meryn reminded himself. *She.*

'Looks like you escaped the worst of it, captain,' the Munitorum official said lightheartedly. 'They say it's a living hell down in the zones.'

'Yeah,' said Meryn. 'We got away with it, all right.'

He looked across the crowd of off-loading personnel, the women and children of the retinue and the Ghosts escorting them. He saw Blenner, and tried to catch his eye.

But Blenner determinedly did not look back.

Elodie moved through the busy crowd in the half-light. She was still shaken. She wasn't sure what had happened at the billet, but fear and shock still clung to her like a camo-cloak.

'Yoncy? Yoncy?'

The girl was standing alone behind the trucks, away from the rest. Her shaved head seemed very pale and fragile in the gloom. They'd sponged the blood off her, but her shift dress was dark and caked with bloodstains. She hadn't said much since she'd recovered consciousness.

'Yoncy?' said Elodie. 'Come on, honey.'

Yoncy was staring at the fortress gatehouses, apparently fascinated by the sight of the massive gates as they slowly closed on their hydraulic buffers.

'Yoncy?' Elodie took her hand. 'Come on, it's cold out here.'

'We're home now,' said Yoncy softly. 'Home and safe. Just like Papa told me to be.'

'That's right,' said Elodie. For a second, she heard the bone-saw shriek, an echo in the night. She shuddered. Just a memory. Just a sharp, brief recall of the night's horror.

'Come on,' she said.

The gates slammed shut with a resounding boom. Yoncy sighed, and turned as Elodie led her away to join the others. The officials with light poles were leading processions of new arrivals across the compound.

As she was led along, Yoncy glanced over her shoulder at the thick darkness under the high walls of the yard. She frowned, as if she had seen something or heard something.

'Bad shadow,' she whispered. 'Naughty shadow. Not yet.'

The fire rate coming at them was breathtaking. The whole sky over the shore was on fire, and las-rounds rained in like a neon monsoon. Two Ghosts directly beside Rawne had just been cut down.

'Medic!' Rawne yelled over the deafening hail of fire. There was blood on his face that wasn't his.

'We have to get closer!' Pasha yelled to him, down in cover nearby.

Rawne knew they did. But they were outgunned at a ratio of about five to one. The agriboat fleet was swarming with Sek's warriors, and they were laying down so much fire, Rawne couldn't get any of his units past the sea wall. There was no way to call in air support, and the promised armour had never arrived. Runners from Ludd had brought him word that Criid's companies were facing a meat-grinder in the throttled streets around Turnabout Lane.

'If we could just get a foothold on those boats,' Rawne growled.

Beside him, head down, Oysten nodded. But she had absolutely no idea what to suggest.

'You'll have to pull back!' Curth snapped as she struggled to patch one of the fallen troopers. There was blood all over her too.

'Yeah, right,' Rawne replied. 'Do that, and we basically open the city to the fethers.'

'Have you seen our casualty rate?' Curth yelled back. 'Much more of this and you won't have any troops *left* to pull back!'

'What the hell?' said Spetnin suddenly.

Rawne looked up. The fire rate had just dropped dramatically. The withering storm of las-bolts had reduced to just a few sporadic shots.

Rawne waited. A last few cracks of gunfire, then something close to silence.

He started to rise.

'Be careful!' Pasha snapped.

He rose anyway, and took a look over the chipped and splintered lip of the sea wall. A haze of gunsmoke lay across the rusting agriboat fleet. Some of the vessels were burning, and they all showed signs of heavy battle damage.

There was no trace at all of the enemy force that had been hosing them with shots a few minutes before.

'The feth..?' Rawne muttered.

'It's a trick,' warned Pasha.

'What kind of trick?' Rawne replied. 'One squad, with me. Pasha, reposition our units. Get them in better order in case this starts up again.'

Rawne slithered over the sea wall, surprised to find that no one shot at him. The rockcrete was dimpled with shot holes and wafting smoke.

The settling fyceline was so thick it made him cough. Ghosts slipped over the wall with him. Weapons up, they scurried towards the dock and the condemned fleet.

His regiment's gunfire and rocket assault had damaged all the boats in the vicinity. Rawne could hear water gushing in and filling hulls holed by tread fethers. He saw the enemy dead on upper decks, or hanging over broken railings. More corpses choked the low-water gap between the dock wall and the hulls.

'Where the feth did they go?' asked Brostin, his flamer ready.

Rawne clambered onto the nearest hull, stepping over enemy dead. Where the feth *had* they gone?

'We have to listen,' said Zhukova.

'What?'

She moved past Rawne, and slipped down a through-deck ladder. He followed. Down inside the dark, stinking hull, she got on her knees and pressed her ear to the deck.

'Movement,' she reported. 'Like I heard before.'

She looked up at Rawne, and wiped grease off her cheek.

'But moving *away* from us,' she said.

'What?'

'They're retreating, back through the hulks. Back the way they came.'

'I don't get it,' said Brostin, on the ladder behind Rawne. 'Why'd they do that? They 'ad us dead.'

Rawne shook his head.

'The only reason you'd call a withdrawal is if you're losing,' he said. He paused. 'Or you've already won and got what you wanted.'

'Colonel! Colonel Rawne!'

Rawne, Brostin and Zhukova looked up. Above them, Major Pasha was peering down through the deck hatch.

'What is it, Pasha?' Rawne asked.

'You must come,' she said.

Rawne hauled himself back up the ladder onto the deck.

'What?' he asked.

'There's a great mass of corpses down in the hold space here, colonel,' Pasha said, pointing to the rim of a rusty catch-tank nearby. 'Caober and Vivvo have climbed down to search, but most are too burned and disfigured to–'

'Stop. Why did they go down?'

'Because I found this on the deck,' she said.

She held out a bloody object for him to see. It was a Tanith warknife, the blade broken.

Mkoll's.

'There is an old rank,' said Macaroth. 'From back in the days of the first crusade. Saint Sabbat's crusade...'

'My lord?' asked Bulledin.

Macaroth shook his head and raised his hands dismissively.

'Never mind,' he said. 'Take your seats. I was just musing to myself. I have spent a long time alone with history books. A long time musing over the details of the old wars, of Urdesh, of the Sabbat Worlds. I find myself thinking out loud.'

The lords militant took their places around the table in the Collegia Bellum Urdeshi. There were more than thirty of them present, and additional seats had been placed along the straight side of the vast wooden semicircle. Chairs scraped across the polished black floor with its golden inscriptions. Thousands of candles and lumen globes had been set to light the chamber, and the warding cyberskulls floated and murmured overhead.

'Yes,' said Macaroth, sorting through the reports and files placed in front of him, 'a long time alone with history books. Too long, I'm sure you will agree, Cybon?'

Cybon coughed awkwardly.

'Let's review,' Macaroth said. 'Together, as a group, as staff. Further evidence, I hope, that I am eager to refocus my manner of command.'

'My lord-' Lugo began.

'Don't fawn, Lugo,' said Macaroth testily. 'Now, would anyone care to explain what occurred in the last two hours?'

'The Archenemy has withdrawn into the Zarakppan basin,' said Kelso. 'And also has fallen back from the southern edge of Eltath. Mass withdrawal. Immediate and focused. They are outside the bounds of the city. They are present and more than ready to resume assault. But they gave up ground.'

'More than that,' said Urienz. His face was still speckled with petrochemical dirt from the journey back to Eltath. 'They gave up significant advantage. They had us by the throat, and they let go.'

'I said explain not describe,' said Macaroth. 'The enemy let us go. Sek let us go. Another few hours, and they would have been into the southern hem of the city, and the east. We would have fallen to them... or at least been caught in a fight so disadvantageous it would have cost us bitterly just to survive.'

'I believe we would have had to call in the fleet,' said Grizmund. 'I appreciate that's a sanction we wish to avoid, but it would have been necessary. We would have had to begin sacrificing the forge world's assets to purge the enemy.'

Macaroth nodded.

'We would, I fear,' he agreed. 'But something changed. Something turned the enemy back, despite his gains and advantage. With respect to the valiant Guardsmen fighting this action in all zones, it wasn't us. Not our doing. We didn't win. We survived because they allowed us to live. Chief tactical officer?'

Biota stepped up to the table. He was one of a number of senior tacticians waiting in the candlelit shadows beside them.

'My lord?'

'Does tactical have any wisdom?' asked Macaroth. 'Any data at all to explain the change of heart? Did we do something we're not aware of? Did we, for example, take down a significant senior commander and cause-'

'My lord, there is no evidence of anything,' said Biota. He cleared his throat. 'Except that... it is postulated by a number of parties that the enemy had... achieved his goal. Whatever Sek wanted, he got.'

'For now,' said Cybon. 'They're still out there.'

'If Sek got what he wanted,' said Macaroth, 'we have no idea what it was. I've read the reports concerning the trophies Gaunt recovered from Salvation's Reach. The so-called "eagle stones". Intelligence and the ordos believed those were his primary objectives, yet they remain in our custody. The enemy never even got close to the site where they are secured.'

Macaroth looked at his staff.

'I want answers, my lords. I appreciate our stay of execution, but it troubles me deeply. I want answers. I want to understand this, because if there's one thing I hate it's an absence of fact.'

A Tempestus Scion entered the chamber and handed a message slate to the Warmaster.

'Hmm,' said Macaroth, reading. 'A link has finally been established with our beloved Beati in Ghereppan. Perhaps she and her lords can furnish us with some information.'

He looked at the Scion. 'I'll be there directly,' he said. The Scion hurried out, and Macaroth rose to his feet. The lords militant began to rise too.

'No, as you were,' he said. 'I want you thinking. I want ideas. I want theories. We need something. The fight for this world isn't over.'

He started to walk out, then paused and turned back.

'There is an old rank,' he said, thoughtfully. 'Back in the day. The Warmaster or his equivalent was aided by a first lord. An executor who formed a link between the supreme commander and the command staff. Sabbat herself had one. Kiodrus, you know? Now Saint Kiodrus. History tells us this. *Books,* Cybon. I fancy I will reinstate this role. It will help mend and facilitate my connection with you great lords. I am not good with people. I don't like them. I feel I shall let someone do that job for me. Someone to keep you informed and keep you in line on my behalf. Keep me in line too, no doubt. He will be defacto leader, and my chosen successor should the fates take me. Warmaster elect.'

He looked at Cybon.

'When will you announce this post, my lord?' asked Cybon.

'Now,' Macaroth replied. 'And you know who it is, because you chose him yourselves. He's the ideal candidate, for no better reason than he doesn't want to do it. Ambition can be such an encumbrance.'

He looked at Gaunt.

'First Lord Executor Gaunt,' he said. 'Kindly proceed with this meeting while I am gone. I want answers, remember?'

He strode away. The thousands of candle flames shivered in his wake.

Gaunt sat back. He looked up and down the table at the faces staring at him. Bulledin, Urienz, Kelso, Tzara, Blackwood, Lugo, Grizmund, Cybon, Van Voytz...

He cleared his throat.

'Let's begin, shall we?' he said.

ANARCH

With thanks to Lord Militant Nick Kyme, versenginseer Matt Farrer, and, always, Nik Vincent-Abnett for noticing when something's awry.

This book is dedicated to the memory of Rob Leahy, and to everyone who has marched with the Tanith Ghosts since the very beginning.

To the high-most God, who is of the throne above, and to whom falls mastery of All Things, the mind, the blood and the tech ever after, we dedicate our service, and trust that, from him, and from the priests who serve at the Eight corners of his throne, we may inherit the knowledge of the Use of Fire, and the Forging of Devices, and the Making of All Things, so that, from the hands of our brotherhood, even to the last regeneration, we shall fashion the Secret Instruments and Weapons that will assure his eminence hereafter and provide for his Eternal Victory.

– Dedication scripture common to the lay-tech dynastic orders of Urdesh Forge World; also a recitation found, in variation, in a number of non-aligned, non-Imperial, and xenos cultures in the Sanguinary Worlds

'In the opening months of 792.M41, the thirty-seventh year of the Sabbat Worlds Crusade, Warmaster Macaroth's prosecution of the Anarch Sek, focusing on the contested forge world of Urdesh, reached a critical pass. The Imperial victory at Ghereppan, led by Saint Sabbat herself, had broken the Archenemy's main strength and exposed the callow ruthlessness of his intended strategy – to behead the Imperial high command even if it meant sacrificing the precious forge world. Sek's decapitation strike at Eltath had been repulsed, and many tacticians believed that a tide had turned. The Anarch was spent, and the crusade force, now focused under Macaroth's chosen Lord Executor, Ibram Gaunt, would deliver the Urdeshi theatre in a matter of months, if not weeks. After that, the Archenemy Archon Gaur would be alone. At last, a credible end-point to the crusade seemed within reach.

'But the war on Urdesh was not done, nor was the Anarch as disarmed as many supposed. Then began the bloodiest and most astonishing period of the campaign thus far, a sequence of events that many history texts have reported with the utmost credulity. Whatever the fine truth of it, it is no exaggeration to say that the fate of the entire sector hung in the balance, to be determined by just a handful of the Astra Militarum. Failure at Urdesh during those few, bleak weeks would end the crusade, wipe out thirty-seven years of Imperial gains in the Sabbat Worlds, and hand the victory to the enemy of mankind...'

– From *A History of the Later Imperial Crusades*

ONE

THE KING OF THE KNIVES

Under the watchful glare of mosaic saints, the floor was a lake of blood.

The saints were ancient and Imperial, and their names were mostly forgotten. Tesserae were missing in places, making their shapes ill-defined, their features indistinct, their frozen, pious gestures vague. But their eyes remained, weary eyes that had seen long histories pass, with all the blood and loss that histories claim as their price.

Still, they seemed appalled. The eyes of some were wide, in astonishment or horror; in others, they were half-closed in denial. Some looked away entirely, as if it was too much to bear, diverting their gaze to the distance, perhaps to some golden light of promise that might appear on a far horizon and spare them from witnessing more atrocity.

The blood was shin-deep. It had been dammed inside the great chamber's floor by the short flights of ouslite steps that rose to each entry. It was bright, like a glossy red mirror, rippled by the movement in the room, glinting in the torchlight. It had frothed and clotted into curds around the piled bodies. Half-submerged, soaked in blood, they seemed like tumbled island outcrops rising from a red sea, or moulded plastek forms lifting from run-off liquid composite on a manufacturing rack.

The hot stink of it was unbearable.

The screams were worse.

Damogaur Olort oversaw the work, hands behind his back, barking orders to his sonpack. Sons of Sek brought the captives in one by one. Some struggled and fought, shrieking and spitting obscenities. Others came placidly, stunned by the fate that was overwhelming them. Each of the Sons had made more than one visit to the chamber, and their ochre battle gear was dappled with gore. From the very sight of them, any prisoner brought up from the pens knew what awaited them.

Even when they fought and cursed, and had to be beaten and dragged, the sight and smell of the chamber silenced them. Some fell mute, as if dazed. Others wept. A few prayed.

The chamber was the inner precinct of the Basilica of Kiodrus on Sadimay Island. A holy place. That it had been transmuted into a hell was too much for most of the prisoners to bear.

Olort studied the next captive as he was brought in. The man stumbled, splashing through the blood, as though led to a baptismal pool against his will.

'Da khen tsa,' Olort said. *Hold him*.

The Sons, big brutes, their faces covered by glowing optic units and the human-hide leatherwork that stifled their mouths, obeyed, dragging the man upright. Olort approached, noting the insignia and unit marks of the captive, the torn and filthy state of his uniform. The man flinched as Olort lifted his dog tags to get his name. Kellermane. There was a paper tag pinned to the left breast of the man's tunic. It read 'Captured near the Tulkar Batteries,' in handwritten Sanguinary block-script.

Olort saw a tear running from the man's eye, and wiped it away with his fingertip. The almost tender gesture left a smudge of blood on the man's cheek.

Kellermane. Artillery officer. Captain. Helixid.

'Kell-er-mane,' Olort said, switching to the clumsy language of the foe, of which he had some small measure. 'An offer. Renounce your god. Assent now, pledge fellowship to He whose voice drowns out all others, and keep your life.'

The captive swallowed hard, but didn't reply. He stared as if he didn't understand.

Olort tried to look encouraging. He had unclasped his leather mouth guard so that the captives could see and appreciate the honesty of his smile.

'Cap-tain Kell-er-mane,' he said. 'Repudiate, and pledge. Thus, life is yours.'

Kellermane mumbled something. Olort leant in to hear.

'Join you?' Kellermane asked in a tiny voice.

'Yes.'

'A-and you won't kill me?'

Olort looked solemn, and nodded.

'Th-then I swear,' stammered the captive. 'Yes. Please. Yes. I w-will s-serve your Anarch...'

Olort smiled and stepped back, the blood pool swirling around his boots.

'Vahooth ter tsa,' said Olort. *Bless him*.

One of the Sons took out his ritual blade, the hooked skzerret of the Sanguinary Worlds, and opened the captive from throat to sternum with one downward slash. The man convulsed, useless noises of dismay and loss coming from his mouth, and collapsed. Arterial spray hit the temple wall and jetted across the faces of disgusted saints.

The Sons let the body fall.

How simply they fold, Olort thought, when faced with something so brief as death. Where is their trumpeted mettle? He whose voice drowns out all others has no use for cowards.

Olort resumed his place, hands behind his back.

'Kyeth,' he said. *Next*.

The Sons waded back across the chamber and left. Two more entered, a sirdar and a packson flanking another captive.

This one didn't look promising to Olort. His black hair was matted with blood and dirt, and he evidently carried several minor injuries. But at least he walked unaided. The Sons didn't have to drag him or frog-march him.

Olort approached, noting how the prisoner refused to make eye contact. There were no rank pins or regimental patches on the man's torn black fatigues, and the paper label was missing.

Olort glanced at the sirdar.

'Khin voi trafa?' *Where is his label?*

The sirdar shrugged apologetically.

'Let'he het?' Olort asked. *Circumstances*?

'Tyeh tor Tulkar, damogaur magir,' the sirdar replied, and continued to explain that the captive had been taken alive after fierce fighting in the boat-docks near the Batteries. He had fought, the sirdar said, like a cornered ursid.

Interesting after all, thought Olort. A man of courage. He reached for the captive's dog-tags. The captive did not flinch.

Mkoll. Recon. Sergeant. Tanith First.

'Mah-koll,' Olort said, in the foe's ugly tongue again. 'An offer. I make this now. Renounce your god. Pledge fellowship to He whose voice drowns out all others, and keep your life.'

The captive did not reply.

'Repudiate and pledge,' said Olort. 'Do you understand?'

The captive remained silent.

Olort considered things for a moment. The man was evidently strong. He had borne a great deal. He had not broken. This was the mettle that the Sons watched for. He whose voice drowns out all others had no place for cowards.

But some could be too brave. This man stank of a silent defiance that would not submit and could not be broken. That was the way of things. Most were too weak. Some were too strong.

Olort glanced at the sirdar, who already knew what was coming and was unfastening his skzerret.

'Vahooth ter tsa,' Olort instructed.

The blade flashed up. Olort abruptly stopped the sirdar's hand.

He had noticed something.

The captive had an insignia pin after all. A small dark badge fixed to his torn collar. It had been blackened to dull its gleam, which is why Olort hadn't spotted it at first.

He unfixed it. A skull, with a straight dagger placed vertically behind it.

'Mortekoi,' he said. *Ghost*.

'Magir?' the sirdar asked, blade poised.

'Ger shet khet artar, Sek enkaya sar vahakan,' said Olort. *This is one of the special ones, the ones He whose voice drowns out all others has told us will lead the way to the Victory.*

Olort looked at the pin again, then slipped it into his tunic pocket.

'Voi het tasporoi dar,' he ordered. *Make him ready for transport.*

The sirdar nodded and sheathed his blade.

Olort looked at the captive.

'Mah-koll,' he said, with a soft smile. 'Ver voi... you are a ghost, kha? A ghost? *Mortekoi*, kha?'

The captive looked directly at him.

'Nen mortekoi,' he said. 'Ger tar Mortek.'

Olort jerked backwards. The sirdar and the Son started in surprise, and looked at the damogaur, bewildered. The Imperial had just used their language fluently. *I am no ghost. I am death.*

Mkoll lashed out with his right hand. The brass hook-pin that had once fastened his missing label had been straightened and concealed in his palm. He punched it into the packson's neck just below the ear.

The Son reeled away, yelping and clawing at his neck. Mkoll was already turning on the sirdar. He grabbed the sirdar's right wrist, snapped his arm straight, and twisted, forcing the officer over in a helpless, painful stoop. Mkoll brought his knee up into the officer's bowed face.

The sirdar dropped to his knees, lifting a spray of blood. Mkoll maintained the arm lock, reached over the officer's hunched back, and yanked out his skzerret.

He pivoted, locking the arm in a tighter twist with his left hand, meeting the charging Son with his right. The packson still had the pin jutting out of his neck. The ritual blade sliced through the Son's throat. He staggered backwards, blood jetting between his clamping hands, and fell sideways, lifting waves that churned the surface of the blood pool.

Olort lunged at Mkoll. Mkoll kicked him in the gut and folded him up. Everything was slick and sticky with blood. The kneeling sirdar managed to wrench his wrist out of the armlock.

He tried to tackle Mkoll. Mkoll blocked him with a forearm, grabbed him just below the left elbow, and forced him to turn with another twist. The sirdar barked in pain. He was rotated. Mkoll forced the trapped left arm up like the lever of a pump, and punched the skzerret hilt-deep in the sirdar's armpit.

Mkoll wrenched the blade out, and the sirdar dropped on his face in a violent splash. Olort was trying to back up, trying to rise, trying to breathe. He floundered in the blood pool.

He pulled out his sidearm, but Mkoll kicked it away. Mkoll grabbed him by the front of his soaked tunic, dragged him to his feet and slammed him back against the mosaic wall. He put the skzerret to the damogaur's throat.

The saints watched, eyes wide.

No one was coming. The Sons in the anteroom outside were used to cries of pain and dismay echoing from the chamber.

'What did you mean... special ones?' Mkoll hissed.

'Voi shet–'

'My language!' Mkoll whispered. 'I know you have some. Why are we marked out by your Anarch?'

'Khet nen–' Olort gurgled.

Mkoll pinned him by the throat with his left forearm, and used the edge of the ritual knife to cut open the seam of the damogaur's tunic pocket. He fished out the Tanith pin and held it up for Olort to see.

'Why does this matter?' he growled.

'Y-you are the ones,' Olort gasped. 'He whose voice drowns out all others has identified this. You are enkil vahakan. You–'

'Those who hold the key of victory.'

'Kha! Kha! Yes!'

'So he fears us?'

Olort shook his head.

'Nen. He will take the key from you. For the woe is already within you.'

'Woe?'

'The Herit ver Tenebal Mor!'

'The bad shadow? The Heritor's bad shadow?'

'Yes. It was cast upon you a long age ago, mortekoi.'

Mkoll glared into the damogaur's eyes. He relaxed his grip.

'Next question,' he whispered. 'How do we get out of here?'

TWO

OTHER BUSINESS

'Enough,' said the First Lord Executor.

More than forty people were present in the chamber, and all of them had been talking. At his word, most of them stopped: all the regimental commanders, tacticians, adepts and advisors at least. Only the lords general and militant kept going, because they were used to being the senior figures in any room.

As quiet descended, even they trailed off. Someone coughed, uncomfortably.

'It seems there's been a misunderstanding,' said Lord Executor Ibram Gaunt quietly. He sat at the head of the table, the area in front of him stacked with data-slates, folders and strap-bound blocks of Munitorum forms. He was studying one of the data-slates. His long, lean face carried no expression. 'This isn't a discussion. Those are orders.'

Gaunt looked at them. Everyone at the table, even the most senior lords, winced. There was still no expression on Gaunt's face. But no one liked to be fixed by the fierce and cold gaze of his artificial eyes.

'Go and execute them,' he said.

Chairs scraped across the etched black stones of the floor. Staff members rose to their feet, and gathered their papers. There was some quick nodding, a few salutes. Murmuring, the personnel left the Collegia Bellum Urdeshi.

Only Adjutant Beltayn remained, perched on a chair by the wall. He clutched data-slates in his lap, and a portable field-vox sat in its canvas carrier at his feet.

'Me too, sir?' he asked.

'Stay,' said Gaunt.

The four Tempestus Scions assigned to him as body-men stayed too. They closed the hall doors after the departing officers, and took up their stations, silent and rigid, hellguns locked across their broad chests. There was no point dismissing them. They went wherever Gaunt went.

Gaunt had come to consider them as furniture, the dressing of any room he occupied. Sancto and his men were humourless, sullen and unyielding, but that was the product of indoctrinated loyalty, and such loyalty ensured confidence and discretion. Gaunt had been First Lord Executor for little more than three days, but in that time he had learned many things about what his life would be like from now on, and one of those things was that the Scions were simply bodyguard drones. However annoying their constant presence, he could speak freely around them.

Gaunt sat back and steepled his fingers. He could hear the distant crackle of the void shields surrounding the Urdeshic Palace and, more distant, the moan of raid sirens echoing across the city of Eltath. Occasionally, a burst of klaxon welled up from the palace beneath him. A recurring fault, he had been told.

The air in the Collegia smelled of stale cigar smoke and hot wax. The many candles flickered, shimmering the more constant light of the hovering lumen globes.

'What's done?' Gaunt asked.

Beltayn rose to his feet, and consulted one of his slates.

'Called in Militarum reinforcement to Eltath, Zarakppan, Orppus and Azzana. Despatched Lords Kelso and Bulledin to secure the Zarakppan front. Instructed Lord Grizmund to consolidate the south-west line of the Dynastic Claves. Sent Lord Humel to coordinate the liberation of Ghereppan. Brought the war-engine legions up to the ninth parallel. Asked Lord Van Voytz to prepare for the arrival of the Saint–'

Gaunt watched his adjutant read down the list. There was no sign of it ending in the near future.

He raised his hand.

'That was sort of rhetorical,' he said.

'Ah,' said Beltayn. He lowered the slate. 'Not clear from context, sir.'

'My apologies,' said Gaunt. 'I was looking for concision. Your answer could have simply been "everything on the day list", Bel.'

'Noted, sir,' said Beltayn. 'Except–'

'What?'

'Well, it's not everything on the day list. Generals Urienz and Tzara have both requested audience, the Munitorum has a list of queries regarding resupply quotas, an inquisitor called... umm...' He checked the slate. '... Laksheema, Inquisitor Laksheema, has asked for urgent attention–'

'Concerning?'

'Unstated. Above my pay grade, sir. There's also, of course, the other regimental business you asked me to note–'

'Ah, that,' said Gaunt.

'Yes, and also the matter of your staff personnel selection.'

Gaunt sighed.

'I just need good people,' he said. 'Tactical. Communication. Administration. Can't they be assigned?'

'I think the feeling is you should appoint them, sir,' replied Beltayn.

Which meant interviews, evaluations, isometrics. Gaunt sighed again.

'This is the Astra Militarum,' he said. 'People are supposed do what they're ordered to do. It's not a personality contest.'

'There's a certain... prestige involved, sir,' said Beltayn. 'Appointment to the private office of the Lord Executor. It carries... significance. You're the chosen instrument of the Warmaster...'

'I am,' said Gaunt. He rose to his feet. 'I set the rules now. Rule one. People follow orders. I don't care if it's front line grunts or lofty staff level Astra Militarum. Do as you're told. I need a good tacticae core.'

'Biota seemed willing, sir,' said Beltayn.

'Well, he's very capable. But he's been Van Voytz's man since forever.'

'I think Tactician Biota is eager to distance himself from the lord general since... since the lord general's disgrace.'

'Van Voytz is not disgraced.'

'Well, you know what I mean, sir.'

'Tell Biota he's got the job. Tell him to hand pick three... no, two advisors he deems capable.'

'Yes, sir.'

'Tell Urienz and Tzara I'll see them in an hour.'

'And this inquisitor?' asked Beltayn.

'The inquisitor can go through channels and make the nature of the matter clear. Then I'll assign time.'

'Yes, sir. Uhm, I expect you'll want a staff adjutant assigned too. I mean, I'm happy to fill in for now–'

Gaunt looked at him.

'You're my adjutant.'

Beltayn pursed his lips. 'I'm a company level vox-officer, sir,' he said. 'I'm not–' he gestured at the hall around him, as if the grandeur of it somehow made his point for him.

'You're my adjutant,' Gaunt repeated.

'Yes, but you'll be transferring me back to First Company soon,' said Beltayn. 'I'm a line trooper. Lord Grizmund did advise about–'

Gaunt looked at Beltayn sharply. He was well aware of the off-the-record conversation he'd had with Grizmund a few hours earlier.

'You're not Tanith any more, Ibram,' Grizmund had said with a sad smile. 'Your line days are over. Oh, the Tanith will remain in your purview, but the scale has changed.'

'You remain the commander of the Narmenians,' Gaunt had replied.

Grizmund had nodded. 'Yes, but that's fifteen armoured and eighteen infantry regiments. Brigade level. Backbone of my divisional assets numbering seventy thousand men. I don't ride a tank any more. Nor do you personally command a little recon scout force. Put someone else in the top spot, form up division assets – in your position, you can have a free choice – and put your Ghosts somewhere in the midst of them. They'll still be yours, but they're a small part of a much bigger picture. Regimental business is no longer your business, Ibram. Make the break. No sentiment. And make it fast. That's my honest advice. Take it from me, it's heartbreaking otherwise. All those years of toil together then you elevate above them. Make the break, and make it fast and clean.'

'Something awry, sir?' Beltayn asked.

Gaunt hesitated. He wanted to say it was too much, to confide in his adjutant that there was now so much to consider. The constant dataflow, the push-back from the command staff, the clashing personalities...

But that was an unfair burden to drop on Beltayn. 'Above his pay grade,' wasn't that how Beltayn had put it? Gaunt was another breed of creature now.

Rather than reply, he waved his hand at the piles of slates and documents. 'A lot to process,' he said.

'And they don't listen,' said Beltayn.

'Who?' asked Gaunt.

'The lords,' said Beltayn. He looked reluctant to say any more, but then plunged on anyway. 'It'll take them a while to get used to the fact you're above them now. Leap-frogged them all. In my opinion. Just take them a while to get used to taking orders from you.'

'How long did it take you, Bel?'

Beltayn smiled. 'I was a common-as-feth slog trooper, sir. I did as I was told right off the bat because otherwise you'd, you know, shoot me and everything.'

Beltayn looked over at the stacked documents.

'As for that,' he said. 'Triage.'

'Triage? Meaning?'

'Permission to speak candidly, my lord?'

'Always.'

'Most of that, it's just noise,' said Beltayn. 'I'm a field adj, a vox-officer. How do you think I kept my eye on the actual vitals in the thick of it? When it was all going off, and the artillery was coming in, and there was fething las shrieking hither and yon? How did I keep it neat and get you the stuff you needed, no extraneous crap?'

'Tell me.'

'Focus. Triage. Data triage. Most of that stuff is only wildfire las whipping around you. Screen it out. Filter it down. Or find someone who can do that for you. Always worked for me.'

'You ignored things?'

Beltayn shrugged. 'Only the stuff that didn't matter, sir.'

'I'm almost glad I didn't know this before now.'

'You're still alive, aren't you?'

Gaunt smiled. 'Judgement call, then?'

'Always. Works on the ground. Should work for you. I mean, your judgement is what got you that high and mighty rank, right?'

Gaunt nodded. His smile faded.

'I've got ten minutes. I'll handle that other business now.'

'The regimental business, sir?'

'The regimental business,' said Gaunt.

He was learning things, learning them fast as part of his new role. One was that he could walk and read at the same time.

The Scions flanked him at all times, two in front, two behind. If he stayed aware of the heels of the men in front of him, Gaunt could speed-read data-slates as he strode along, confident that Sancto and his men would steer him around corners, avoid obstacles, and open doors without him even having to look up.

He reviewed the slate again. Disposition reports on the Tanith First, laid out in simple unfussy terms. The main strength of the regiment, under Rawne, was still down at the Tulkar Batteries in the Millgate Quarter, following the brutal repulse of the enemy push three days before. Two companies – V and E – nominally under the command of Captain Daur were billeted in the palace itself, along with the retinue.

For nearly four days, he hadn't been able to find time to go and see either element in person, not even the section secure in the palace with him.

And just four days before, Ibram Gaunt would not have allowed such an oversight to happen. He'd been colonel-commissar then, and his men had been his only priority.

How things changed. How perspective shifted. Maybe Grizmund had been right. He'd had no reason to lie. Make the break and make it fast. No sentiment. Otherwise it's heartbreaking.

The trouble was, it *was* heartbreaking.

As a soldier rose through the ranks of the Imperium, he was obliged to leave many things behind. Gaunt knew that. He'd walked away from the Hyrkans after Balhaut. He wondered if he could ever do the same to the Ghosts.

But it wasn't the officer in him responding to these things, it was the human being. It was personal, it was sentiment. The feelings made him doubt his suitability for the rank he now held, and he had hidden them from other lords militant for fear of their scorn.

Just a few lines on a report, and they had cut him through. Line items that mattered to him as a man, not as a soldier.

At the Tulkar Batteries, there had been significant losses. He'd reviewed the casualty lists sadly, wearily. It had always been a painful task.

One thing had stood out. Sergeant Mkoll, MIA. Presumed dead. Mkoll, chief of scouts, had always been core to the Ghosts, one of the most able soldiers.

And a good friend.

Gaunt couldn't believe that Mkoll had finally gone.

Then there was the report, filed by Commissar Fazekiel, of an incident during the evacuation of V and E companies from the Low Keen billet. It made so little sense. Three Ghosts dead, one of them Eszrah ap Niht. Another miserable personal loss.

Gaunt wanted an explanation. The three had died during an incident involving his son.

Except Felyx Chass was, apparently, no longer his son.

And that was the hardest thing of all to understand.

Captain Daur was waiting for him in the anteroom of the private quarters assigned to him. He stood as Gaunt entered with his Scion honour guard, set aside the book he had been reading, and snapped smartly to attention.

Sancto and his men looked at him dubiously.

'Wait outside,' Gaunt said. The Scions withdrew. He could feel their reluctance.

'At ease, Daur,' Gaunt said.

'My first opportunity to congratulate you, my lord,' said Daur.

'Thank you,' Gaunt replied. 'My first opportunity to attend to any regimental matters. My apologies. You've been holding the fort, I trust?'

'Both companies and the retinue are housed in the undercroft, lord,' said Daur. 'There are the usual run of issues to deal with. I have them in hand, though Major Baskevyl is very keen to speak to you directly.'

'About?'

'Major Kolea, lord. Detained by the Intelligence Service in regards to the assets recovered at the Reach.'

'I'd heard something about that. I have a hunch that explains why the ordos are sniffing around too. Tell Baskevyl to come up and I'll get to him as quickly as I can.'

'Yes, lord.'

'I need to deal with this first,' Gaunt said. 'It's overdue.'

'Of course. She's in there,' Daur said, gesturing to the inner door.

'An account, please,' said Gaunt.

'I wasn't present,' said Daur. 'Blenner and Meryn were the officers of record at the time. Fazekiel is in charge of the investigation.'

'And I'm sure she'll be thorough. A summary, please.'

'Gendler attacked Felyx in the shower blocks at Low Keen,' said Daur. 'The piece of shit... Excuse me, sir. It seems he believed Felyx has access to private funds, and wanted a slice. Jakub Wilder was in on it too. Never liked him either. Too much in the shadow of his war-hero brother... which, by the by, will give you problems as far as the Belladon are concerned. That's two Wilders deceased under your–'

'I'm aware, Ban.'

Ban Daur studied his face, frowned slightly, then continued.

'Gendler attacked Felyx,' he said. 'Bungled it. Ezra discovered them, killed Gendler. Wilder killed Ezra. Meryn and Blenner found this total fething lunacy in progress. Witnessed it, for the most part. Blenner executed Wilder on the spot.'

'And Felyx?'

'Is your daughter. Merity Chass. She'd been disguising her gender.'

'Why?'

Daur shrugged. 'The son of the great hero of Vervunhive stands to advance faster than any daughter? I don't know, to be honest. Verghast was always damned patriarchal. There's an issue of honour here, primogeniture, succession. Shame.'

'Shame?'

'Take your pick,' said Daur.

'She's in there?' Gaunt asked.

Daur nodded. 'You haven't asked how she is,' Daur said.

'I'm going to find out, Ban,' replied Gaunt.

'Do it gently,' Daur suggested.

'I'm aware of the sensitivity,' said Gaunt. 'Her mother is de facto governor of Verghast. That means F– *Merity* could succeed in turn. If she acquires enough status here at the front line for the families of Verghast to take her seriously. To return with any disgrace or stain on her reputation would guarantee a lack of confidence from the rival houses, and that would in turn lead to a power struggle and instability on the planet that–'

'Not that,' said Daur. 'I know *that*. I meant because she's scared.'

He let himself into the room, closing the door behind him. His bedchamber was a simple space of white-washed stone. There was a folding cot and a wash stand, and his kit bag and effects had been brought up by an attendant and piled in the corner. A freshly laundered uniform had been laid out on the cot. Items had been ordered up from the Munitorum stores: black trousers with dark silk piping and a black pelisse jacket with black frogging. Gaunt had been very specific about a lack of ostentation. He wondered if the clothes would fit.

A side door led through to the small tower room that served as a study. Merity was sitting at the desk under the window. She looked small, dressed in the simple black fatigues of a Tanith trooper. When she turned to face him, he saw, despite her close-cropped hair, how much like her mother she truly looked.

She rose to her feet, and stood like a soldier on review. Her face was pinched-pale, and there was a clean field-dressing on her forehead.

'Are you all right?' he asked.

'Yes, sir,' she said.

'I'm sorry this has occurred.'

'Sir.'

'I'm sorry you... you felt compelled to conceal your real identity from me.'

'Females do not advance on Verghast,' she said. 'Coming here was a chance to achieve some credibility. Some capital that rendered my gender irrelevant.'

'I thought coming here was about finding your father?' said Gaunt.

'I found him,' Merity said. 'He was a soldier. Occupied with the war. He was not family-minded, nor do I blame him for that. I never expected a happy family reunion. I saw only political gain.'

'Really?'

Her face remained hard-set.

'Who knew?' he asked.

'Only Maddalena. Then Dalin and Ludd.'

'Both of them?'

'I swore them to secrecy. They both honoured that.'

'You could have told me,' said Gaunt.

She half-shrugged. 'Not really,' she said.

'We could talk about it.'

'I apologise for the problems I've caused. I expect to be returning to Verghast as soon as circumstances allow.'

'We could talk about it now, I mean.'

'You have time?'

'I have... ten minutes or so.'

'Ten minutes of the Lord Executor's time. I'm honoured.'

'I didn't–'

'I wasn't being sarcastic. I'm impressed you're even here. Honestly, I don't want to talk about it. About any of it. I'd rather–'

'What?'

'No one's really talked to me about anything for the last four days. Commissar Fazekiel has been very sensitive in her questions. But I'd rather talk about... well, absolutely anything else.'

Gaunt took a seat.

'Like what?'

'This war, maybe?'

'This war?' he echoed. He gestured to the desk chair and she sat back down.

'I have been shut in here for three days,' said Merity. 'I know nothing about anything. I'm hoping for distraction, I suppose. You have been named Lord Executor?'

'I have,' said Gaunt.

'Which makes you Warmaster elect. Second only to Lord Macaroth. His–'

'Fixer,' said Gaunt.

She looked surprised.

'You're not pleased at the promotion?'

'It's a huge honour, and unexpected,' said Gaunt. 'But I'm not a fool. Macaroth is a private man, and his detachment from staff business has become a chronic problem. I'm supposed to bridge that gap, become his mouth. I've no illusions. A fair amount of dirty work will come with the role. Most of it political.'

'You must learn the art of delegation,' she said.

'You're not the first person to tell me that today.' He smiled.

'The Munitorum, the Administratum, the Officio Tacticae and the Office of the Militarum exist to take ninety per cent of that burden off your desk. Leaving you only with the command effect decisions. A Warmaster elect can surely establish his own cabinet to filter and process information, just as a secretarial cabinet of the Administratum would–'

He raised an eyebrow.

'I had no idea you were so well-versed,' he said.

'Only in terms of civil administration,' she replied. 'I didn't mean to speak out of turn.'

'Please do,' said Gaunt. 'We're only having a conversation.'

'I was raised as the heir of House Chass,' she said. 'Civic Administration was considered a fundamental skill-set, so my primary at Vervun Didact was administrative proceeding. My mother believed any scion of House Chass needed a full grounding in housekeeping, and I say "house" in the fuller sense of the dynasty itself. I had begun to broker those qualifications into a placement with the Verghast-Vervun Munitorum as a way to acquire some military credentials. Then a more direct path appeared.'

'Coming here?' asked Gaunt.

'Coming here,' she agreed. 'Clearly, now, an idiotic plan. But the rivals of House Chass, House Anko, for instance, barely tolerate my mother's seniority. To accommodate, when the time came, a *second* female successor... well, that successor would need exemplary credentials. Significant military experience, of any sort. And even then–'

'You're ambitious?'

Merity stared at him.

'Of course,' she replied. 'Like my mother. Like my father.'

'I don't know how ambitious your father is,' he said.

'It doesn't really matter, does it?' she replied. 'Given the lofty position he now finds himself in.'

There was a long silence.

'Is Sek defeated?' she asked. 'The raids have subsided.'

'That is the question,' said Gaunt. 'The assaults on Eltath and Zarakppan have been repulsed for now, but there is considerable enemy activity in the surrounding zones. Fresh assault could begin at any time. Our forces under the Beati have dealt the Archenemy a considerable blow at Ghereppan. In fact, we don't know how badly the Saint has hurt Sek. He may even be dead. Certainly his death, or serious incapacity, could explain the sudden collapse of the assaults at Eltath. Then again, he could be regrouping. Intel operations are in progress. The next few days will show us. Either we're approaching the final battle with the Anarch's forces, or we're facing a long suppression and purge of surviving enemy elements. Whichever, Urdesh is far from won.'

'Why do you believe he could be regrouping?' she asked.

Gaunt paused, then allowed himself a small smile.

'That's the question I keep asking,' he said. 'Sek could be wounded and running, or even dead. But the nature of his breakaway in Eltath has... I just have a feeling about it. It didn't feel to me like a burn-out. Like an assault that had lost momentum. It felt like a deliberate cessation. As if some objective, unknown to us, had been achieved. The halt was deliberate, as though a phase was over. We don't know what the next phase is.'

'But you have suspicions?'

'Yes, I do.'

'Concerning?'

'That, I'm afraid, is entirely classified. I'm sorry.'

'Of course,' she said, dismissively. 'Though I wager it connects to the materials recovered during the Salvation's Reach operation.'

'I couldn't comment,' said Gaunt. 'But I am impressed by your appreciation of the circumstances.'

'I was there, at the Reach.'

'You were.'

'Do others share your appraisal? Other lords, I mean? Macaroth himself?'

'There is some dispute,' said Gaunt. 'At staff level, there is seldom consensus. I'm going to have to work hard to keep everyone who matters convinced of the critical danger we may be facing.'

'You don't have to convince anyone,' she said. 'You are Lord Executor. If you believe there's a present danger, you order them to fall in line. They are obliged. Isn't that the point of a Lord Executor?'

'You would think so,' he agreed. 'In practice...'

He shrugged.

'This is the Imperial Guard,' he said. 'Orders are supposed to be orders, not points of debate. I fear the problem is that there are too many chiefs here. Too much authority, concentrated in one place.'

'And you're an unknown factor. Untested. They're not used to your supreme authority.'

'There's that,' he agreed.

'Then you should exercise it. Demonstrate it. Make an example of someone.'

'I don't think–'

'Before everything else, you were a commissar. You need a little of that, perhaps.'

He nodded. 'Perhaps so.'

'What about Van Voytz?' she asked.

'What about him?'

'He is disgraced,' she said.

'Who told you that?'

She winced. 'Your adjutant mentioned–'

'Beltayn's wrong,' Gaunt said gently. 'Van Voytz took action he deemed was right for the crusade. It was misguided. He has been reprimanded.'

'But not disgraced. Have you sent him away to some fourth tier duty?'

'No. I thought it better to keep him at hand. Punishment sometimes sends the wrong message. I've taken the Fifth Army off him for my own division, and charged him with preparation for the Saint's arrival.'

'Is that...' she paused. 'With respect, is that wise? His insubordination was a slim legal definition away from treason. The two of you were close, in times past. Could this not be read as you going easy on an old ally?'

'Where making an example of him would demonstrate my authority shows no one favours?' he asked.

Merity nodded.

'I was a commissar, as you said,' said Gaunt, 'then a line officer too. My whole career, I have tried to temper the ruthlessness of the former role with the consideration of the other. A balance. To be unswervingly strict when necessary, but also not to make enemies needlessly. There are more than enough of those in this galaxy as it is.'

'Yet you are, in fact, neither of those things now,' she said. 'You are First Lord Executor. You don't need to make enemies or friends.'

He looked at her quizzically.

'Have I amused you, sir?' she asked.

'No,' he said.

'I was just talking,' she said. 'Chattering, I suppose. I have felt very isolated. I am...'

'What?'

'I am sorry they died. Ezra, and even those men.'

Gaunt was about to respond when someone knocked hard at the outer door. It opened.

'My lord?' Sancto called.

Gaunt rose, and motioned Merity to stay. He walked through the bed-chamber. The Scion Sancto stood in the doorway, Beltayn hovering behind him.

'I told him you were busy,' Beltayn said.

'Be quiet,' Sancto said to Beltayn, sidelong. He looked at Gaunt. 'Inquisitor Laksheema requests immediate audience, my lord,' he said.

'Inquisitor Laksheema was instructed to go through channels,' said Gaunt.

Sancto didn't reply, as if his part in the entire exchange was complete. Behind him, Beltayn grimaced.

'I think this is her idea of going through channels, sir,' he said.

Gaunt pushed past them. The inquisitor awaited him in the outer room, flanked by Colonel Grae of the Intelligence Service and members of Laksheema's retinue. Ban Daur was standing in the corner of the room, glaring at Laksheema.

Behind Laksheema, in the doorway, stood Viktor Hark and Gol Kolea.

'Lord Executor,' said Laksheema, nodding her head in a quick bow of deference.

'What's this about?' Gaunt growled.

THREE

THE EFFECTS OF THE DEAD

The alarms went off, screeching through the halls of the palace undercroft. Then they cut out again, just as sharply.

'Feth's sake,' Baskevyl muttered. That was the sixth time it had happened in the last two hours. The Tanith personnel and retinue billeted in the cold cellars of the Urdeshic Palace were getting seriously spooked. They were well below ground in arched basement chambers beneath the palace's Hexagonal Court, spaces once used to store wine and grain. There were no windows to look out of, no windows through which they could see if an actual attack was underway. Baskevyl was sick of asking the Munitorum work crews what the problem was, and sick of their vague answer of 'probably faulty wiring'.

He set aside his half-finished cup of cold caffeine and got up to take another stroll through the billet and calm some nerves.

Blenner was standing in the archway of his billet area.

'False alarm?' Blenner asked.

'Seems so,' replied Baskevyl.

'Again?'

Baskevyl pulled on his coat, and didn't reply.

'Are you, ah...' Blenner began.

'Am I what, commissar?' Baskevyl asked.

'You seem to be giving me the cold shoulder a little, Bask,' said Blenner, trying a friendly smile.

Baskevyl turned and looked at the commissar as he buttoned up his jacket. His look did not return the friendship.

'Not everything is about you, Vaynom,' he said.

'No. Obviously.'

'We're the personal company of the First Lord Executor,' said Baskevyl. 'Privileged and elevated. And this is what our privilege gets us. Stuck here in a wine cellar. There are matters to deal with that aren't being dealt with. I have feth-all idea what's going on, and I'm itching to re-join my company, which is out in Millgate somewhere, facing Throne knows what. So that might account for my demeanour.'

'Of course.'

'Unless there was something else you think might be weighing on me?'

'Just...' Blenner shrugged awkwardly. 'Just the matter of Jakub Wilder.'

'Because you executed him?'

'Yes, Bask. That.'

'He had just committed murder, had he not?'

'He had. Poor Ezra–'

'So I should think your field execution was entirely justified under the discipline code. You are a commissar.'

'Is that... is that what Fazekiel is writing up?' asked Blenner eagerly.

'Her investigation is ongoing,' said Baskevyl. 'I can't imagine how she could find in any other way. Unless there's something you and Meryn aren't telling us.'

'Well, no. Nothing like that.' Blenner cleared his throat. Baskevyl got the distinct impression that Blenner was glancing around in the hope of spotting a bottle he could pour a glass from.

'Look, Bask,' said Blenner. 'The thing of it is... the thing of it is, morale really. And confidence.'

'Go on,' said Baskevyl.

'Don't make me spell it out, Bask.'

Baskevyl sighed. 'Your specific assignment in V company,' Baskevyl said. 'A Belladon company. The colours band. Of which Wilder was c.o. You are concerned how they regard you now you've shot their senior. How any of us Belladon will regard you.'

'Well, I mean, given the history,' said Blenner. 'Jakub Wilder, Lucien Wilder. An illustrious Belladon fighting family–'

'Jakub Wilder was not a model soldier,' Bask snapped. 'He let the name down. He murdered, for feth's sake. And attacked the person of the First Lord Executor's daughter. You were doing your duty.'

'I was.'

'Then you and me, we don't have a problem. Jakub Wilder brought shame to the Belladon contingent. Unless, as I said, there's more to this.'

'There really isn't.'

'Good.'

'I'd still request,' said Blenner cautiously, 'reassignment.'

'Reassignment?'

'Attachment to another company. The boys of V Company keep looking at me like I'm a bad smell.'

There was a bad smell, all right. The background fug of sulphur from the volcanic vent the palace straddled was particularly noxious in the undercroft area. And the latrines had flooded again. Another technical issue the Munitorum work crews couldn't adequately explain.

'First of all, just bring them into line,' said Baskevyl unsympathetically. 'It's not a popularity contest. Second, that's not my call.'

'You're senior officer present.'

'By rank, yes. But Daur has operational oversight of the Tanith here. Take it up with him if you must. Except don't, because Ban's not an idiot, and he'll give you the same answer I just did.'

'Where is Captain Daur?' Blenner asked.

'Fethed if I know, Vaynom.'

'Is... is the girl all right?'

Baskevyl looked at him. 'Gaunt's daughter? Again, fethed if I know. Is that all?'

Blenner nodded. Baskevyl pushed past him to exit. He paused.

'Any word from Hark?' he asked Blenner.

'I've heard nothing.'

'Nothing through Prefectus channels?'

'No, Bask.'

'So we have no idea where Kolea is?'

'We don't,' Blenner agreed.

The alarms suddenly went off again. They shrieked for a second before shutting off. Blenner flinched.

'Feth that,' said Baskevyl, and strode away.

Alone, Blenner leant against the door jamb and breathed out slowly, trying to calm himself. His hands were shaking, so he stuffed them in the pockets of his storm coat.

'Nice chat?' Meryn whispered.

Blenner jerked with a start. The Tanith captain was standing right beside him in the shadow of the archway.

Meryn grinned his crooked grin.

'Don't do that,' Blenner hissed.

'I've got something for you, Vaynom,' Meryn said. He took a baggie of pills and stuffed them into Blenner's top pocket. 'Something to take the edge off.'

Then Meryn leaned in until he was eye-to-eye with Blenner, and the back of Blenner's head was pressed against the stonework behind him.

'I heard all of that,' Meryn said. 'That talk with Bask. You're a fething idiot. How guilty do you want to look exactly? Play it chill, for feth's sake. I'm not kidding, Blenner. If I go down, you go down. And if it comes to that, I think I can throw you to the damn wolves a lot more effectively than you can throw me. Are we clear?'

'Yes.'

'Good.' Meryn smiled. He raised both hands and smoothed the front of Blenner's coat as if he was a tailor finalising a perfect fit. 'Don't make me have this conversation with you again.'

Meryn walked away, humming to himself. Blenner took out the packet of pills. Somnia. He took two.

He knew it would hardly be enough.

Long rows of cots had been set up down the lengths of the arched undercroft chambers. Heaters were running, and lumen globes hovered under the arches. The close air smelled of sweat and volcanic fumes and the damned latrines.

And fear. The whole retinue was afraid. Apart from the dirty business with Wilder and Gendler, everyone had heard the story about Elodie and poor little Yoncy. Some kind of monster out in the wasteland behind Low

Keen had taken out an entire squad of enemy soldiers and almost killed them both too.

Baskevyl walked the length of the billet, pausing to chat with troopers and members of the retinue. He did what he could to reassure them. They did what they could to appear reassured.

Baskevyl spotted old Ayatani Zweil gingerly feeding scraps of dried meat to the regimental psyber-eagle mascot.

'Fattening him up, father?' Baskevyl asked.

'Oh no, no,' Zweil replied, offering another scrap and trying to guess which head would take it. 'Gaining the beast's confidence. Making friends, you see? I have named him Quil. He didn't have a name. It's short for–'

'I get it,' said Baskevyl.

'It puts us on good terms, see? Makes us friends. So I can get close enough to groom him.'

'Groom him?' Baskevyl asked.

'Groom him and maybe slip a garland of islumbine over each of his heads... ow! Bastard nearly took my finger off!'

'Because why?' Baskevyl asked.

'I presume because he was hungry,' said Zweil.

'No, father. Why do you want to groom him?'

'Well, because there'll be a parade. When she gets here. We want the bitey little bastard looking his resplendent best.'

'A parade?'

'For the Beati, man.'

Baskevyl frowned. 'Father, the arrival of the Saint is not open knowledge. How did you find out? Who told you?'

'No one,' Zweil replied, his eyes fixed on the raptor as he held out another chunk.

He glanced at Baskevyl.

'I'm ayatani imhava, major,' he said. 'One of her roaming chosen. I know these things. Just as I know the imhava are gathering in Eltath. Coming from all over. It's taken years for some of them to get here, following the long routes of the Saint's pilgrimage. I believe even some delegations of the templum ayatani are coming here too. Her priesthood, major, gathering at her side at the site of the victory.'

'This is a victory?' asked Baskevyl dubiously.

'It will be,' replied Zweil.

'It doesn't feel much like one.'

'I didn't say whose victory,' said Zweil. 'Oh, don't look at me like that, major. I wasn't being pessimistic. The paths of the esholi have not yet revealed the outcome of the future, even to those of her chosen, like me. All we know is, we should be at her side at this time and feth! Bastard! Shit! Bugger!'

'Did it bite your finger again, father?' asked Baskevyl.

'I find it has a tendency to do that,' said Zweil, sucking at his fingertip.

'Maybe don't put your fingers in its beaks, then?'

'I'll get a stick,' said Zweil.

'So you can offer the scraps at arm's length?' asked Baskevyl.

'Oh,' said Zweil, 'that's a better idea.'

Elodie was helping several troopers from E Company to mop the outer hallway of the undercroft where groundwater had sopped up through the washhouse drains.

'The Munitorum can handle that,' Baskevyl said to her as he walked up.

Elodie leant on her mop. 'In the meantime, the billets flood, major,' she replied.

'It's a mess,' he agreed.

'They say it's the heavy rain,' said Elodie. 'Backing up along the storm drains.'

'Does that happen a lot?'

'Apparently, it's never happened before,' she replied.

'Well, then we're blessed,' said Baskevyl. 'Are you all right?'

She shrugged and nodded. She didn't look all right. She was drawn, as though she hadn't slept much or well, and where her hands gripped the mop, Baskevyl could see that she'd bitten her nails off short.

'I don't know what happened, major,' she said. 'I still can't get the stink of blood out of my clothes. The Sons of Sek were right on us and then... they were dead and the world folded up.'

'Folded up?'

'I passed out. I don't know. There was a sound.'

'What sound?'

'Like a... a bone saw. I've seen some bad things, major, and been in some dangerous places, but that was the most terrifying thing that ever happened to me. Terrifying because I have no idea what it was.'

'But the child's all right?'

'I haven't seen her. She's with Dalin, I think. I suppose she is. Yoncy never says much, but-'

'But?'

Elodie looked at him.

'She's a very strange child.'

'She always has been, mam.'

'She says things sometimes,' said Elodie. 'Creepy things, really. I... I used to think that it was because she was just a child, but she's not, is she? I mean she's not a child anymore. She acts much younger than she is, like it's a defence mechanism. A way to get people to like her.'

Baskevyl nodded. 'To be fair,' he said, 'she's had a tangled upbringing. What she's seen in her life, I wouldn't wish that on any child. If she acts young to make people like her, then it's probably an effort to get some security.'

'Maybe,' Elodie replied with a shrug.

'What?' asked Baskevyl.

She shook her head. He felt he shouldn't press her. Ban Daur was due back soon. Maybe she'd confide in her husband.

'Do you know what a changeling is, major?' she asked suddenly.

'Like... in the faerie tales?' he asked.

'Yes. Sometimes, I honestly think she's that. Not human. Switched at birth.'

'Isn't that... a little unkind?' he ventured.

'Of course it is,' she agreed. 'But you know the story about her, don't you? Half the retinue was convinced that Kolea had two sons, not a son and a daughter. Naturally, that's nonsense. But why would so many people think it?'

'Hearsay?' Baskevyl suggested. 'Crossed wires? Stories getting mixed up?'

'There's no point asking Gol,' Elodie said. 'I think a lot of his memories are missing, you know, since Hagia. It's as though he doesn't even know his own children properly.'

'He hasn't been much of a father to them,' said Baskevyl. He grimaced. 'That came out wrong. What I mean is, he hasn't had much chance. He thought they were both dead for the longest time, and by the time he found out they were alive, Criid had taken them on. Saved them both. Anyway, we can't ask Gol.'

'Is he still missing?'

Baskevyl nodded.

'Look, don't say anything,' Elodie said. 'I mean, what I said about Yoncy. Everyone's on edge and I'm just jumping at shadows because of what happened at Low Keen. That shook me up, Bask, it really did. So this is just my nerves talking.'

'I won't,' said Baskevyl.

At the far end of the undercroft billet, a space had been set aside for supply crates and piles of kitbags. The Munitorum had shipped in the personal effects of the Tanith troops still deployed in the field at Millgate. Bonin, Domor and Sergeant Major Yerolemew were sorting through the kitbags, working from a list.

Baskevyl knew what they were doing. The list was the casualty list from the Millgate action. The men were setting aside the personal belongings of the troopers who wouldn't be coming back to claim them.

It was a miserable task, one they had to do all too often. The effects of the dead would be sorted through, dispersed, recycled where possible. Decorations would be returned to the regimental coffer. Personal trinkets might be given to close friends as mementos.

Baskevyl watched them work for a while, then admitted to himself that it was unkind not to help them.

They nodded to him as he came over. Along with Commissar Fazekiel, Baskevyl and Domor had endured a tough time together prior to the evacuation from Low Keen.

'Any word on Gol?' Domor asked immediately.

Baskevyl shook his head.

'And we can't even get a warning upstairs to the chief,' Domor sighed. 'Since when did Gaunt fail to respond to a request from the ranks?'

'He's First Lord Executor now, Shoggy,' said Baskevyl. 'He's got a plateful.'

'But it's urgent,' Domor stressed. 'The fething ordos sniffing after Kolea's blood.'

'Daur's on it,' said Baskevyl. 'He's promised to take the matter right to Gaunt, first chance he gets.'

'If the fething ordos are sniffing after Gol's blood,' said Bonin quietly, 'getting word to the chief isn't going to help. They'll have him. That's what they do.'

'Cheerful,' said Domor.

Bonin shrugged. There was nothing cheerful about him. With Mkoll gone, Bonin had been made chief of scouts. But that was only a title. Circumstances prevented Domor, Baskevyl and Bonin from re-joining the main regiment elements in Millgate. They all felt the frustration of being stuck, inactive, away from their companies. Out in the field, Caober or Vivvo would be running scout operations.

Bandmaster Yerolemew was looking grim too. The old, one-armed sergeant major was working methodically through the kitbags. Jakub Wilder had been his direct superior. Baskevyl could feel the shame hanging on the old man's shoulders, and the responsibility. Yerolemew was acting lead of V Company for the duration.

'Damn,' the old man whispered. He'd just unzipped a kitbag.

'What?' asked Domor.

'It's Mkoll's,' Yerolemew replied.

'I'll take that,' said Bonin. 'Don't sort it.'

Yerolemew zipped the bag back up and handed it to the scout.

'You know the procedure, Mach,' Baskevyl said gently.

Bonin nodded.

'I do,' he said. 'But Mkoll's MIA. He's not dead. Not until we find a body. Until then, I'll take care of this.'

'What are you doing?' asked Dalin.

He'd found his sister standing alone in the hallway outside the billet area. She was staring at the broad flight of steps that led up into the palace.

'Papa's coming,' she whispered, not taking her eyes off the steps.

Dalin breathed out heavily. Yoncy had a habit of calling everybody 'papa' or 'uncle'. He was getting sick of it. It had been cute when she was small, but she was a young woman now. With her hair shaved short after the recent lice problem, she looked like a teenage pilgrim. What did they call them? Esholi?

Dalin wanted to tell her to stop it with the infantile chatter. It was grating. She showed no sign of puberty yet, but she was getting taller. She was only a head shorter than he was.

But he refrained. Something bad had happened to her at Low Keen. He decided to cut her a little slack.

'Gol will be here soon enough. Tona too,' he said.

'Papa said to wait for him, Dal,' she said. 'He would send word. I have to wait and listen for him.'

'What happened at Low Keen, Yoncy?' he asked.

'Papa said it was time. I don't want it to be time. I don't want it, Dal. But he said it was. And he said I had to be brave about it. Then the men came, so the shadow fell.'

'The shadow?'

'The bad shadow, silly.'

Dalin gritted his teeth. 'Please stop it with the baby-talk, Yonce,' he said. He remembered a dinner on board the *Highness Ser Armaduke*, now genuinely years ago, and a drawing she'd made for Gol Kolea. She'd talked about a bad shadow, like it was her new bogeyman.

Of course, she had just been a child then.

Yoncy looked at him.

'It's not baby-talk, Dalin,' she said. 'You know. You know what Papa says too.'

'What's that on your neck?' he asked, reaching forward. She flinched back. 'Nothing,' she said.

He could see a sore patch of skin around the base of her throat.

'Is that the eczema again? Yoncy? Has it come back?'

Before the mission to Salvation's Reach, Dalin had given her a medallion, a souvenir of the Saint. She'd proudly worn it around her neck until it had been lost. The metal of what had undoubtedly been a cheap, mass produced medal had caused a reaction and given her eczema.

'It's all right,' she said. 'Doesn't hurt.'

'Come inside,' Dalin said. 'We'll find some food.'

'I have to wait here,' she replied firmly. 'Papa told me to wait here for him. It's time, and he wants to talk to me. You should wait too, Dalin. He'll want to talk to you as well.'

'Gol may be a while yet,' Dalin said.

'I don't mean Gol. Not Papa Gol. I mean Papa.'

'Who... who is Papa, Yoncy?'

She looked at him so fiercely it made him recoil slightly.

'You know,' she said. 'Weren't you listening to him too?'

Dalin raised his hands and backed away. She'd clearly been much more upset by the incident than he thought. He'd ask someone about it. Maybe Doctor Curth when she returned. It was some kind of trauma. He'd seen it in soldiers before.

'All right,' he said. 'All right. You stay here and wait for... for Papa. I'll go and get you some soup.'

She nodded.

'Thank you,' she said softly. 'I love you, Dalin.'

'I'm your brother. You're supposed to.'

She smiled.

'I do what I'm supposed to do,' she said, and then turned back to stare at the steps.

FOUR

VAPOURIAL QUARTER

The shots came again. Las-rounds, a short burst.

Down in cover, Wes Maggs glanced at Caober.

'Building down at the end of the street,' he said. 'Second or third floor.'

The chief scout nodded. 'Discouragement fire,' he said. 'They haven't got a target, but they've spotted us moving up.'

Hugging the wall, Gansky scuttled up to their position, and dropped down beside them.

'Word from Fapes,' he said. 'He's done a vox-check. There are none of ours in this area.'

'Not Helixid stragglers, then,' said Maggs.

'More Sek bastards,' said Caober. 'Cut off when they fell back. We have to flush them.'

He peered past the heaps of rubble that was suffering them limited protection. Visibility was poor. Heavy rain was still falling, and three days of constant downpour had raised a thick mist through the Millgate and Vapourial quarters. A lot of it was steam from the countless fires and burned-out buildings, the rest was smoke streaming in from the blazing mills and well-fires on the Northern Dynastic Claves.

'Take a squad,' Caober said to Maggs. 'Move off to the left there.'

Maggs nodded, and slid out of cover. Caober tapped his micro-bead link.

'Larks, this is Caober. You got eyes on this?'

'*Stand by,*' the vox crackled back.

On the far side of the mangled street, Larkin and Nessa moved, heads low, across the third floor space of a merchant house that had been gutted by tank shells. They picked their way through broken furniture and partly burned piles of inventory paperwork, and set up at one of the windows. There was no glass. Concussion had blown it out like an eardrum. Rain dripped steadily from holes in the ceiling as though a tap had been left on somewhere.

The marksmen lined up with their long-las rifles, and adjusted their scopes.

'Chief?' Larkin whispered into his micro-bead. 'Definitely third floor. Whup! Yeah, that was muzzle flash.'

'*Can you angle from there?*'

'Stand by,' Larkin replied. He moved to another window. Nessa had also repositioned herself further along the gutted office space.

'I can't get a clear shot,' she signed. 'I can't see in.'

'And the wall's too thick,' Larkin agreed, signing back.

'If we moved down,' Nessa suggested, 'to the next building along...'

Larkin shook his head. 'There is no "next building", Ness,' he said quietly, echoing the words with gestures. 'Just a heap of bricks that used to be a hab before said hab had a life-changing encounter with aerial munitions.'

'Ah,' said Nessa Bourah, remembering. She was tired. After three days, one hab shell looked like the next.

She settled back against the wall for a moment, and wiped the rain off her face, an action which did little more than rearrange the dirt on it.

'This sucks,' she said.

'Agreed,' said Larkin.

'When are they going to pull us back? We were at the sharp end of it. The fething Helixid have gone.'

'We're specialists, aren't we?' he grinned. 'They want this area cleaned out. Our expertise is in demand.'

Nessa explained in clear, anatomically precise terms what high command might do with their expertise. Larkin chuckled, and slid along to the next window gap.

'We'll get relief,' he said, 'sooner or later.' He set up again, training his weapon, peering with an unblinking eye through the powerful scope.

'Caober?' he voxed.

'*Go.*'

'We can't deliver from here.'

'*Understood. Maggs is moving left of the target.*'

Larkin adjusted his aim.

'I see him, chief,' he whispered. 'Tell him if he follows that alley, it'll bring him around to the back of the walled court behind the target site.'

'*Keep your eyes on him,*' Caober replied over the link.

The alley was high-walled and almost ankle-deep in water and debris. Maggs moved at the head of his team, lasrifle up to his cheek and aimed. He made a series of quick, clear hand signals to the Ghosts behind him.

Gate. Go around me. Either side.

They stole around him, weapons trained on the old wooden gate in the yard's high wall. The gate was the only access. Going over the wall would draw fire from the building.

Maggs pointed to Gansky, signalled 'kick it in' and then raised three fingers to count him down.

'*Maggs, hold position!*'

Maggs froze. He adjusted his micro-bead.

'Larkin?' he whispered.

'*Hold position,*' Larkin replied over the vox-link. '*I've got a view into that yard. Definite movement behind the wall.*'

'I read that,' said Maggs. He glanced at his squad, and pulled a grenade from his musette bag.

'I request, not for the first time,' said Rawne, 'permission to withdraw the Tanith First from this line.'

'I'm not unsympathetic, colonel,' said Major Maupin. 'But the lord general's orders are specific. The Tanith must hold here for a while longer.'

Rawne looked the Narmenian officer up and down. Maupin's clothes were clean, and he'd had a shave that morning. A few hours earlier, he'd been asleep in a bed somewhere. Probably the Urdeshic Palace.

'We held this line and took a bruising,' Rawne said. 'Now you're here to reinforce. It's time to rotate us out.'

Rawne looked at the signal the Narmenian had handed him again. A direct communique from Lord General Grizmund. Raindrops flicked and tapped the flimsy paper.

They were standing in a street in the Millgate Quarter, under the shadow of the now silent Tulkar Batteries. It had been the scene of the heaviest fighting against the Sons of Sek four days earlier. From the seawall and esplanade, the edge of the city was a mess of burned and bombed habs and manufactories, through the tight warren of Millgate Quarter south-east into the mercantile districts of Vapourial and Albarppan. Smog rolled in from the sea in the heavy rain, and behind the fume of petrochemical smoke that made the sky seem oppressively low, huge fires burned to the south of them in the Northern Claves, as though pit-gates down to the inferno had opened up.

Maupin's column had arrived ten minutes before. His line of Vanquishers and Conquerors stood waiting on the esplanade highway, tailing back into the upper streets of Millgate, engines idling.

'Grizmund has command of this theatre, does he?' Rawne asked.

'Lord Grizmund does, yes,' Major Maupin said, stressing the 'lord' gently to correct Rawne's lack of protocol. 'Staff has charged him with the securement of the south-western line in advance of further enemy assault.'

'So secure it, sir,' said Rawne. 'You've brought your big guns and everything.'

Maupin smiled.

'The lord general's approach is two-pronged. To secure these quarters of the city, house-to-house, using infantry, and to advance the armour into the Northern Claves and hammer a proper pushback against any remaining enemy forces holding there.'

'My Ghosts are tired,' said Rawne. 'They were in the thick of it four days ago. We drove the bastards back. They haven't slept since.'

'Resources are stretched,' replied Maupin. 'We are awaiting reinforcements. You are a vital infantry asset.'

'You withdrew the Helixid.'

'In part.' Maupin sighed. He looked at the tired and filthy Ghosts standing around them, watching, and drew Rawne aside.

'In all candour,' he said quietly, 'the Helixid forces are competent at best.'

'They broke here,' said Rawne.

'They did. It's been noted. Inquiries will follow. Your Ghosts, colonel, are a prestige unit. Famously specialised. Lord Grizmund knows you of old, I gather, and values your abilities. You might consider this a compliment.'

'Doesn't feel like one,' said Rawne.

'I'm sure it doesn't, right now. We have signals of assurance that brigades of Urdesh, Keyzon and Vitrians will move up to relieve you in the next thirty hours. The Urdeshi will be on station before that, in fact. Look, colonel, the First Lord Executor gave Lord Grizmund this command personally. The two of them have a history, you know that. And your Ghosts are the Lord Executor's personal regiment. Lord Grizmund wants people he can trust to keep this line tight. And he trusts Gaunt's Ghosts.'

'Major,' said Rawne, 'you keep making everything sound like it's doing us a favour and bestowing an honour on us. Gaunt would have pulled us out of here long since.'

'The Lord Executor has delegated zone command to Lord Grizmund, and Lord Grizmund has chosen the Lord Executor's elite troops to assist him in this endeavour.'

Rawne sighed and nodded.

'Then...' he said. 'Signal received. Happy hunting, major.'

'You too, colonel,' Maupin replied as he walked back to his waiting tank.

Colonel. That still sat uneasily with Rawne. He wandered back to the waiting Ghost squads.

'We've been delegated,' he said.

'What?' asked Ludd.

'Skip it,' said Rawne. 'We're holding this quarter for now. Another thirty hours.'

They tramped into the partial shelter of a damaged manufactory. Rain pattered down through sections of missing roof. Oysten, Rawne's adjutant, had spread area maps out on a printmaker's table.

'We're stretched thin,' remarked Elam.

'I know,' said Rawne.

'The armour could clear this zone out in a couple of hours,' said Obel.

'The tanks are moving south,' said Rawne.

'And this area is still inhabited,' said Ludd. 'We can't just flatten it.'

'Update on that?' Rawne asked.

'These quarters were not evacuated before the assault began, sir,' said Major Pasha. 'There are hundreds of citizens and workers cowering in these ruins, waiting to get out. They've been sheltering in basements and whatever. Now the shelling has stopped, they are emerging. Short of water, food, medical supplies.'

'Our sweeps are making contact with them all the time,' said Obel. 'They're risking exposure because they can't stay where they are any more. We're sending all we find into the city, to the nearest waypoints. There are camps in Gaelen that can take them.'

'Which makes our job harder,' said Varl. 'Any contact we encounter on the sweeps could be a friendly. Could be women, kids. We're holding ourselves in check, every building we clear, every door we kick–'

'I know,' said Rawne.

'Which means no flamers,' said Brostin, as if this was the biggest disappointment of his life.

'I feel your pain,' said Rawne. He stared at the map and scratched at a scab on his chin. It was a mess. Even before the recent assault, the city of Eltath had been porous. The Tanith had found that out to their cost at the Low Keen billet. There were insurgent forces inside the city, either Sek soldiers moving in unseen or sympathisers already embedded in bolt-holes. The recent fighting had left the Millgate and Vapourial Quarters even more penetrable. Add to that, enemy units that had been left behind or detached during the withdrawal.

And the withdrawal itself. Rawne's mind kept coming back to that. The Ghosts and other Imperial defence forces had held off the full-on assault. A victory to be proud of. Except, they shouldn't have won. The Archenemy had fielded significantly superior numbers, backed by armour momentum against thinly stretched and hastily prepared defence lines. Despite extraordinary individual actions by Ghosts like Pasha and her anti-tank teams, the marksmen, and – Throne rest him – Mkoll, the outcome should have been decisive in favour of the Anarch's forces. Millgate should have been broken. The batteries should have been overrun. Eltath should have been opened up.

But the Archenemy had, suddenly, fallen back. Not in defeat. By choice. A deliberate retreat.

As if, Rawne thought, they had achieved their objective.

The thought troubled him. He knew it troubled his officers too, and hoped it troubled staff, and the lords general, and even his newly crowned excellency the First Lord Executor. Sek was a wickedly cunning bastard. He'd done something, and they had no idea what it was. He'd had a knife to the Imperial throat, and he'd taken it away without finishing the slice.

'Because the knife was a distraction,' Rawne murmured to himself.

'What's that?' asked Varl.

'Nothing,' said Rawne. He wanted to know. To figure it out, he had to try to think like a Sek packson, and that was something he didn't relish. Archenemy tactics on Urdesh had been incomprehensible from the very start of the campaign. It was like trying to play a game when no one had bothered to teach you the rules.

Well, he was going to learn them. Lord Grizmund, one of the few senior commanders Rawne had any time for, had misjudged things. Operations in Millgate and Vapourial weren't a simple matter of hold and secure. Though the main fighting had ceased, there was still a coordinated enemy action going on, as far as Rawne was concerned.

He looked at the crumpled signal again. 'Secure and hold south-western line – Millgate, Vapourial – and deny enemy action in zone.'

When he'd dictated that order, Grizmund had clearly intended some hab-to-hab clearance, and the construction of more permanent defences, pickets and trenches. But it was open to interpretation. Rawne was good at interpretation. 'Deny enemy action in zone.' That was the choice phrase. The enemy was taking some kind of action, it just wasn't obvious.

Rawne had a gut feeling the Millgate assault had been a feint. Now he had specific orders to deny. He was going to follow them to the letter. There was intelligence to be gathered.

He looked at the officers around the table.

'We'll focus on sweeps, building by building,' he told them. 'Systematic, area by area. Advise all to err on the side of caution.'

'Because of the civilians–' Ludd began.

'No, commissar. I mean the opposite. If in doubt, shoot.'

'But–' Pasha began.

'No arguments,' said Rawne. 'I think the Archenemy is all over this area. Hiding like rats in the rubble. I'm not talking about stragglers and survivors. I'm talking active units. They're up to something. My orders are to deny.'

Pasha looked grim. 'We're going to kill friendlies that way, sir,' she said.

'There may be some collateral,' said Rawne. 'Be clear to your squads. If in doubt, shoot.'

'But–' said Pasha.

'How would the Ghosts take a city, major?' Rawne asked. 'Full on assault, or bleed in through the margins, probably while someone makes a very loud noise to draw attention from us?'

Pasha lowered her head.

'We thought we were fighting off the attack the other day,' said Rawne. 'I think the real attack is happening now. Shoot first. Make that explicit to all. I'm not letting them through this line just because we think the danger's passed and we can go easy.'

He walked down towards the esplanade. Elam and Obel followed him.

'No one likes this,' said Obel.

'I don't like it,' Rawne said.

'So, should we–' Elam began.

'I'm colonel now, so just follow my fething orders,' said Rawne.

Zhukova was standing by the sea wall, staring out at the rusting shells of the agri-harvester boats. Rawne knew why she was there, and why the sight preoccupied her.

She turned as she heard him approach.

'Help you, sir?' she asked.

Rawne stood for a moment, staring at the rotting hulks.

'He's not dead,' he said at last.

'I fear he is,' she replied.

Rawne shook his head.

'How can you be so sure?' Zhukova asked.

'Because there's nothing in this fething galaxy that can kill Oan Mkoll,' he replied.

He looked at her.

'He chose you for scout duties,' he said. A statement, not a question.

'Yes, sir.'

'Go find Caober and Vivvo. Spread the word in the scout units. I want one alive.'

'One...?'

'One of them. A Son of Sek. We need intel.'

'And you expect to get that out of a captured Archenemy trooper?' she asked.

'You have no idea how persuasive I can be,' he replied.

'What happened?' asked Tona Criid.

Caober glanced at her sourly. 'Non-combatants, sir,' he said simply. He sighed and shrugged. Smoke was lifting off a small, walled yard beside the derelict habs ahead, and Criid could hear shouting and the misery of the stricken and wounded.

'We were trying to clear that place,' said Caober, gesturing to the hab. 'Shooters in the higher floors. Larks got a bead on some movement in the yard, so Maggs tossed a grenade over the wall.'

Criid could guess the rest. It wasn't the first time it had happened. Civilians, hiding, trying to find shelter, caught in the crossfire. She watched the regiment corpsmen leading the injured out of the yard, men and women with burns and cuts from the shrapnel blast. They were sobbing, or wailing curses at the Ghosts. She saw children too. Nearby, she saw some Ghosts from Caober's team unpacking bedrolls so they could be used to cover the dead still laying in the yard.

It was only going to get worse. Rawne had just issued a 'shoot first' order.

'They must've known the civilians were there,' she said.

'Mmm?' asked Caober.

'The shooters,' she said.

'Oh yeah. They knew,' said Caober. 'Made a nice little buffer for the bastards. Shoot at us from up top, get us to storm in and kill our own. Bastards.'

He said the last word with a weary force that made Criid wince.

'Where did they go?' she asked. 'The shooters? You clear the building?'

'Of course, captain,' Caober replied. 'They're gone. Off on their heels into the back streets while we were dealing with the injured.'

Criid looked at the wounded children Lesp was trying to patch up. They were sitting in the rain, caked in dirt, glazed eyes looking into forever as the corpsman attempted to clean and close the gashes on their faces.

'They can't have gone far,' said Criid. She hoisted her lasrifle. 'You lot, with me.'

The Ghosts she'd summoned moved in close to her, eyes dark.

'You too, Maggs,' she called.

Maggs was leaning against the wall, smoking a lho-stick, staring at his boots.

'Leave him be,' Caober whispered to her. Criid ignored the scout. Going soft never worked. When a man was rattled, you got him back in the game as fast as you could.

She could see Wes Maggs was struggling. He'd lobbed the grenade. The blood was on him.

'Come on, Maggs,' she called, beckoning, then turning away to show that she expected him to follow without her having to check.

They filed down the alley and onto the adjacent street. Roof tiles covered the roadway like shed scales, and the rain drummed down. They hugged the left side of the street, checking the blown-out fronts of shops. Something had taken the top off the public fountain at the end of the street, and a broken pipe was jutting from the throat of a decapitated griffon, heaving a fat, irregular column of water into the air.

Sergeant Ifvan signalled, indicating something across the street. Criid led the way, keeping three men back to supply cover. She reached the side wall of a low building that had once been some kind of street kitchen or eating hall. Criid could smell rotting food waste and rancid spilled fat. Ifvan and Maggs slid past her, weapons up and aimed.

'Something in there,' Ifvan whispered. Criid nodded. She noticed that Maggs' index finger rested outside his trigger guard. He wasn't going to shoot unless he was sure of a target.

She edged into the dark interior, her weapon up to her cheek, grimacing at the smell of the place. The floor was covered in broken pots and beakers and dented tin plates. Trestle tables had been overturned. A chalkboard had been blown off one wall, and lay face up, revealing the prices and choices of the day's offerings, simple meals for the district mill workers.

She saw movement.

'Hold!' Maggs hissed.

He shone his flashlight. She saw huddled figures, a flash of blue.

'Come out!' she called. 'Right now!'

There were six of them, ayatani priests in blue robes. They were dirty and soaked through, and looked at the Militarum troops with suspicion.

'Praise be the Beati,' mumbled one.

'Praise be indeed,' said Criid. 'You sheltering here?'

'We tried to move on, but there was shooting,' said another.

'You're esholi?' she asked.

The ayatani looked at her in surprise. The term was quite obscure, and they hadn't expected to hear it from an outworld Guardsman.

'We are,' the first one said. 'Pilgrims come to the side of the Saint.'

'Pilgrims getting in the way,' muttered Maggs. 'This is a war zone.'

'We walk where she walks, and go where she goes,' said one of the esholi.

'This is no place for you–' Maggs began.

'That's enough, Maggs,' said Criid. 'How many more of you in here? More out the back? No? Then come on out.'

They led them back onto the street. The esholi blinked at the daylight and shivered.

'We cannot escort you,' said Criid, 'but head that way. Head west. When you reach the main thoroughfare, turn north. There's an aid station in Faylin Square. Move quickly. Don't look back.'

The esholi nodded. One tried to give Criid a sprig of islumbine. She refused it, and urged them on their way.

'Who walks into a war?' Maggs asked as he watched the ayatani move away.

'I heard the fleet was having trouble with pilgrim ships,' said Ifvan. 'They're trying to keep them off-world, and most ships haven't got the vittals to stay in orbit.'

'How do they even know she's here?' asked Mkvan.

'Same reason we're here doing this fething stupid job,' said Criid. 'Faith in something bigger than ourselves.'

Maggs had raised his weapon.

'More of them,' he said.

Across the street, another group of pilgrims had appeared from cover. There were more than twenty of them, wearing the blue robes, lugging bundles of possessions. Apparently encouraged by the sight of Criid's team allowing the other pilgrims to pass, they had come out of cover to refill their water-flasks from the broken fountain. They were all small and thin, stooped with age and fatigue. They reminded Criid of birds coming to drink.

'Fething idiots,' said Criid.

'I'll move 'em on, captain,' said Maggs. He crossed the street. Criid could see the confidence coming back into him. He'd taken a knock, but she'd made him push on. Now they'd saved a few lives, some tally in his head was beginning to even out. He was more like his old self, the smart-mouthed Wes Maggs who'd spit in the eye of anyone, including death.

More like his old self, she thought, but not whole. The kids with their empty stares and bloody faces would haunt him from now on. Another piece of a good man chipped away.

'You cannot stay here,' Maggs said to the esholi around the fountain. They looked at him silently.

'You have to move,' he said. 'Get walking, that way. That way.'

'Will you kill us, soldier?' asked the leader of the group. He straightened up slightly. He had some height when he wasn't hunched over, but it was hard to determine his age. He was rail-thin and haggard, and his skin lined and weathered, from long pilgrimages outdoors and meagre rations.

'No,' said Maggs. 'No, I won't. Just get moving. Get your things and move that way. Head west. What's your name?'

'Hadrel,' said the man. His eyes were as oddly flat and lightless as his tone.

'You're an ayatani?'

'I am Hadrel.'

'You need to get your group to move, father. You understand? Fast as you can. Off this street, head west.'

Hadrel glanced at his followers. They picked up their things and began to walk.

'That's it,' said Maggs. 'Off you go.'

Criid walked over to him.

'What's the matter?' she asked.

'With them?' Maggs asked, gesturing to the departing pilgrims. 'Shell-shock, I'll bet. They were just weird with me. Like they didn't care.'

'They've probably been through shit,' said Criid. 'And since when were ayatani not weird? You've met Zweil?'

Maggs smiled.

'They're alive, Maggs,' said Criid. 'When they get food inside them and their wits together, they'll offer thanks to the trooper who pointed them to safety.'

The House of Ghentethi sat halfway up the hill where Vapourial Quarter became Albarppan Quarter. It was a substantial manse made of worked ouslite, its street windows tall and blue. To the rear of its significant plot lay adjoining manufactory buildings and craft halls, high roofed and raised from local stone. Chrome chimneys vented from the furnace hall.

The house had survived the recent conflict in the district unscathed, but the Ghentethi had not so successfully weathered the past few generations. They had once been one of the most significant dynastic claves on Urdesh, lay-tech makers allied to the might of the Mechanicus. Their power had dwindled during the long years of the war as the Mechanicus relied less and less on the machine shops of the dynastic claves. Ghentethi holdings had reduced from three dozen properties of shop halls in the southern districts of Eltath to this one little fortress of industry, manufacturing bayonets, buckles and focus rings for the Urdeshi regiments.

In the main salon, the rain against the street windows washed the chamber in blue, moving patterns, like the bottom of a pool. Jan Jerik, ordinate of the clave, prodded the fire in the huge, ornate stove with a poker, and then closed the grille. He eyed his guests warily. They had done eating and now sat in silence.

Jan Jerik was a proud man, well-dressed in a dove-blue jacket and embroidered waistcoat. The silver keys and ciphers of his rank as ordinate hung around his neck on a long chain. His white shirt was high-collared, and the boss of his walking cane was the engine motif of his beloved clave.

Jan Jerik had nursed doubts about the endeavour since its first whispered suggestion. But Ghentethi came before everything, and it was his duty as ordinate to ensure its prosperity and survival. Since the earliest days of the dynasts, clave-wars had been fought in all manner of ways, and open violence was the rarest form. Trade wars, espionage, assassination... these were the arsenals of the Urdeshi claves. Clave-loyalty, survival, wealth and knowledge were the touchstones. Despite its risks, and its distasteful aspects, the endeavour promised unprecedented trophies of wealth and knowledge for Clave Ghentethi. He would have been remiss, as ordinate, in ignoring the opportunity.

He heard a knock from below, someone banging repeatedly against the street door. Jan Jerik nodded to a footman, and the footman hurried away to answer.

'The last few,' said the leader of his guests, rising to his feet. His accent was strong.

'They will be made welcome, sir,' said Jan Jerik, 'as you were made welcome.'

'I'm sure they will,' replied Corrod.

The footman returned, leading the visitors from below. They shuffled in, and stood, dripping wet, glancing around the high-ceilinged salon at the old murals.

'This place is... secure?' asked their leader.

'Yes,' said Corrod. 'You're the last to arrive.'

'They're sweeping the streets,' said the new arrival. 'Searching. Hunting.'

'How close?' asked Jan Jerik nervously.

'We'll be gone before they arrive to search your property, ordinate,' said Corrod. 'Provided everything is in place as you promised.'

'It is,' said Jan Jerik. 'Everything that was requested.'

'And the access?'

'Remains open, sir,' said Jan Jerik.

'Do we have data?' asked the leader of the new arrivals. 'Reliable intelligence?'

Jan Jerik took a packet of documents from inside his embroidered waistcoat. He unfolded them and spread them on a small side table. Corrod and the leader of the new arrivals looked over his shoulder.

'We believe the location is here,' said Jan Jerik, pointing to a section of the hand-drawn map.

'We?' asked Corrod.

'Information supplied by agents of my clave,' said Jan Jerik.

'There is certainty?' asked the leader of the new arrivals.

'Nothing direct,' replied Jan Jerik. 'The Mechanicus, and the other organs of the Imperial machine, keep such data secret. Their belligerent confidences are, of course, part of the problem–'

'Keep to the point,' said Corrod. 'We understand your grievance, ordinate. You help us, and we secure you a better future.'

Jan Jerik nodded. He hadn't known what to expect of his guests, but Corrod and his companions, and now the newcomers, seemed simply disappointing. Thin and shrivelled, unwashed and stinking from days in the open. They seemed frail and exhausted, and quite unsuited to the task ahead. He was disheartened.

'It is a matter of reading the hole in the available data,' he said. 'Movement and reassignment of specialist Mechanicus adepts from other facilities to this one. These transfers have been made since the arrival in the city of the warship *Armaduke*. Also, the classification of some data is specific to the ordos. So, by elimination, we can see... specialists moved to this location in the last few days. Higher classification to all data traffic relating to said location. They have masked what they are doing there, but we can see the mask. What you seek is there.'

'By your estimation,' said the leader of the new arrivals.

'The likelihood is high, sir,' said Jan Jerik. 'For the bargain we are striking, I aim to be diligent in my part of it. I would say a ninety-five per cent likelihood. There is one other location that might have potential. Here. But this, we think, is not research or analysis. The facility is too small. Prisoner holding, is my guess. The traitor, the pheguth.'

Corrod nodded. 'The equipment?' he asked.

'Laid out, in the sub-levels,' said Jan Jerik.

'Well then,' said Corrod. 'We can begin. I'll lead the effort here, at the primary target. You take the secondary one.'

The leader of the new arrivals nodded.

'We cover both possibilities,' said Corrod. 'If the second is the pheguth, then we win some justice.'

He looked at the new arrivals.

'Take off those damned robes. Burn them.'

The men stripped off their wet, blue silk garments, and pushed past Jan Jerik to stuff them in the mouth of the iron stove.

'Are you ready, sirdar?' Corrod asked.

'Yes, my damogaur,' replied Hadrel. 'His voice commands us, and we obey, for his voice drowns out all others.'

FIVE

LEAVING SADIMAY

The cloister air smelled of burning: burning history, burning faith, burning tradition. Packsons were in the record house and librarium of the old Basilica, sweeping books off the shelves and bundling them onto bonfires that had been lit in the low stone walk. Mkoll walked past them, his knife-hand pressed into the small of Olort's back, guiding him. His instructions had been plain, and he'd made them in Olort's language: draw attention to me and you're the first to die.

Some of the packsons even threw ritual salutes – the hand across the mouth – to the damogaur and his sirdar as they passed. The sirdar's uniform was a barely adequate fit. The man had been both taller and broader than Mkoll. But the chief scout made a few adjustments, hoping that dirt and drying blood would cover any discrepancies, and besides, the uniform discipline of the Sons of Sek never seemed that precise to him. They all looked like a mob of filthy, ragged barbarians to him, wasteland raiders who cared little if a button or epaulette was out of place, or a pair of boots unpolished.

But what did he know? He was Imperial bred. He understood and recognised the uniform codes of the Astra Militarum in all its variation. He could tell a Throne trooper from a non-Throne at a glance because of cultural familiarity. But the packs were not his heritage. This ruined island, this world, was no longer his culture. He was deep in the heart of the Archenemy, deeper than he had been on Gereon. What nuances was he supposed to notice, what details might he miss with his unfamiliar eyes? He found himself working obsessively about details. The mud on men's boots, the blood stains on their patched tunics. Was that just random, just dirt? Or was there some deliberate significance... marks daubed or smeared to signify something?

How was he giving himself away? The customs and habits of the Sanguinary Tribes, from whose far-rimward feral worlds Sek and that bastard Gaur drew their forces, were entirely alien to him.

Mkoll fancied that when, inevitably, he was finally discovered, it would be some ridiculously small detail that would give him way. Some tiny Sanguinary custom that he couldn't possibly have known.

As they walked along the cloisters, he decided it might be the helmet. He'd buckled it across his face, the foul-tasting leather mask across his nose and mouth. Tanned human hide, a boneless hand, a trophy turned into a

307

chin-strap that symbolised the Sons of Sek's gesture of humility to their Anarch. That was it. The touch of it against his mouth made him gag. He'd tear it off to be free of it, unmask himself, and be revealed.

They walked out onto a colonnade that overlooked the Basilica's harbour. The hillside below the Basilica plunged away almost sheer to the docks and stone-built ware barns below. Mkoll made Olort stop beside the low ouslite wall, and looked out.

The day was grey. There was rain in the air. Thirty kilometres ahead of him, across the unwelcoming waters of the strait, lay the mainland, the industrial shorelines and dingy habs of south-west Eltath.

That was where they'd brought him from.

He couldn't see the city itself. Its bulk, and the massive rise of the city mound and the palace mount were lost behind weather and wind-drawn banners of smoke. The fighting in those south-western wards had been intense. Whole areas were on fire, and the smoke plumes dragged back across the sky for kilometres, dense and dark.

It looked so close. The strait looked swimmable. But he knew the scale was deceiving him. A thirty kilometre crossing, in sub-zero water, with strong currents. If he made that, which he wouldn't, then it was another forty kilometres on foot through the industrial zones of the Dynastic Claves before he even reached the formal outskirts of Eltath. And that was all enemy ground, held by the Sons of Sek. Even the city fringes were disputed.

Mkoll changed his view. The great black crags and hilltop Basilica of Sadimay Island stood to his right, but over its rugged shoulder, he saw the hazed waters of the channel, and the mauve shapes of other islands. He searched his memory, trying to recall the overheads of charts he'd seen during briefings in the last few weeks. His focus had been on Eltath and its maze of streets and quarters. He'd paid little attention to what lay outside, the greater clave zones, the industrial heartlands, the neighbouring forge-towns. He knew the Strait ran from the bottom of the Great Bay of Eltath southwards, and was a major shipping channel. It separated the island chain from the mainland. Sadimay was one of the principal islands because of its religious centre. There had once been regular ferry links for pilgrims and forge devotees. But it was just one of many. The whole planet was blistered with islands in chains and groups and archipelagos, most of them volcanic. Sadimay was just one of hundreds in this particular chain, some closely spaced, divided by much narrower channels, no more than a couple of kilometres in places. Might he find sanctuary there, perhaps? Just for a while. Get himself to one of the small islands, something the Sons of Sek regarded as strategically unimportant, and just wait it out?

Was that even what he wanted to do?

Mkoll had an idea, a notion, and it made him fret to even think of it. Did it come from madness, or desperation, or some higher calling? He'd never believed in that last thing much, so he put it down to desperation.

He looked down at the small harbour. The island's little port was swarming. Watercraft were coming inshore in small fleets, some staying off-station while they waited for quaysides to clear. They were laden with Archenemy troops withdrawing from the mainland or bringing more Imperial captives to Sadimay for processing.

But the agriboats and barges were loading again as fast as they emptied. The enemy was in the process of abandoning Sadimay too. Packed tight and low in the water with the weight of men and vehicles, the barges were leaving the dockside and chugging out into the Strait, turning south on slow, steady curves of wake water.

Turning right. Heading towards the channel into the island chain.

Mkoll reached for Olort. The movement made the damogaur flinch.

'Be calm,' Mkoll hissed in the enemy tongue. He fished Olort's field glasses from his belt pouch.

He scanned the harbour, resolving greater detail through the small, grimy glasses. Miserable huddles of prisoners on the wharf, waiting to be loaded for transport. So they'd kept some alive, and were shipping them into the islands. The prisoners were all Guard. Were they men who had turned? Had they been offered the same choice Olort had offered him, and said yes?

If they were, then induction awaited them in the islands. Induction, and the pledging of their new loyalties. And you couldn't pledge without there being someone present to pledge to.

He loosened the vile chinstrap, and wiped his mouth. Who? An etogaur? A senior chieftain? Someone more significant than that?

He panned the glasses around again. At the north end of the docks, he saw a cluster of small craft tied up. Small cutters and jet-launches, and two or three skiff bikes.

Small and fast. Just sitting there. One of those could get him across the Strait in less than an hour. A sirdar on a one-man skiff, carrying confidential orders to officers on the mainland. Maybe he could pull that off. Maybe he could get down there, commandeer one of the jet-launches, and get clear.

Maybe he could even get as far as the harbour mouth before someone challenged him and the shore batteries began tracking to blow him out of the water.

It was a chance. It was as slim as a fething knife-blade, but that was the sort of chance he'd dealt with his whole life.

'Planning flight?'

Mkoll glanced at Olort. The damogaur was staring at him in vague amusement.

'Shut up,' he said.

'You wouldn't get far, Ghost,' Olort said. 'Someone would notice.'

'Not you,' said Mkoll.

Olort shrugged. 'Nen. Not me. I'd be dead. You'd cut my throat for my silence before you attempted such misadventure. But someone would.'

'Shut up,' said Mkoll.

'Give up now,' said Olort. 'Give up these dreams, Mah-koll. You won't be killed. This, I swear. You are special. You are enkil vahakan. We would transport you to where deliverance awaits. You would share words with he that speaks all truth. Life would be yours, if you repudiate and pledge. This, I can promise you.'

'You're not really in a position to make or keep any promises.'

'Oh, I am, despite the knife at my back,' said Olort.

'Don't pretend that you care whether I live or die,' said Mkoll.

'I do not,' said Olort with a surprisingly honest shake of his head. 'You are the archenemy. I would that I could bless you – vahooth ter tsa. Take your light from this world. But I think of myself. You are enkil vahakan. You have value, and such value may be transmitted to those who find you and deliver you. Our voice told us to be alert for you.'

'So you'd benefit?' asked Mkoll.

Olort shrugged again, diffidently, as if it was of no consequence.

'Bringing me,' said Mkoll. 'That would be a good mark for you? Raise your status? Win you favour? What would you get? A promotion? Etogaur Olort?'

Olort winced in distaste at the sound of the word on an enemy's lips.

'Kha,' he admitted, grudgingly. 'I would be elevated. Perhaps receive a bounty.'

'Money? Blood money?'

Olort frowned.

'The things your kind place value on, Ghost,' he muttered. 'Money. The elevation of rank. We do not chase these foolish nothings. I mean a gift would be bestowed. A passport – is that the word? A passport to the elite. A command posting. Responsibility. Authority. Presence. Or even perhaps a gift of reworking.'

'What's that?'

'The great blessing of the Eight Ways. A reshaping of form, an influx of holy gifts. To be wrought and reworked by our magir's ingeniants. To be chosen and changed, perhaps even as a Seneschal of Ways, or as a Qimurah.'

'A what? I don't know that word.'

'The chosen of chosen. The blessed reworked.'

Mkoll chewed his lip and studied the damogaur's smiling face.

'You're an ambitious little feth, aren't you?'

'I go where the voice calls me to go, Ghost, and I ascend through my devotion.'

Mkoll glanced back at the grey waters below. He had a choice. Either way, there was no coming back. A desperate, perhaps suicidal flight to find safety, or something even more insane.

'You found an enkil vahakan today, damogaur,' he said. 'If you'd kept control of him, if he hadn't got a knife at your back, what would you have done? Where would you have taken this special prisoner?'

'To the Fastness,' said Olort.

'Where's that?'

Olort gestured to their right. The island chain.

'So you'd have taken me to the voice?' Mkoll asked.

'Yes,' said Olort.

The rusting barge was an old agriboat that had long passed the end of its useful life. The sirdars running the quays had pressed all available water-craft into service. Its deck and flanks were a corroded mess, and it stank of rot and mildew. Almost seventy packsons were crammed aboard, along with a dozen manacled and terrified Imperial prisoners.

The barge chattered out of Sadimay harbour, engines groaning and rumbling, leaving the drab rock of the sea cliffs to aft. High above, the Basilica had been put to the torch. A crown of flames clung to the clifftops, lifting a thick pall of black smoke into the sea air. Soot and cinders fluttered down, as gently as snow.

The agriboat was one of eight in a small, puttering flotilla, barges and tub-hulks. One was even being towed by another on a long, caulked hawser. They nudged out into the Strait, wallowing in the chop, sluggish and heavy as a funeral procession. The men aboard held on to the side rails or to wire stanchions to stay upright in the churning swell.

They cleared Sadimay and its burning crown, and chugged south into the Strait. A couple of kilometres ahead, they could see other small flotillas like their own, turning south into the paler waters of the channel. Beyond that, islands, some crags and atolls, some larger bars of purple in the wet haze.

The voyage lasted three hours, passing islands and rock slopes on either side, until a great section of the sky ahead, what had appeared for some time to be the lowering black form of an approaching westerly storm, resolved and solidified.

Another island. High cliffs as black as the rich loam of the lost Tanith forests. It was huge, many times larger than Sadimay, its towering sides like the ramparts of some keep raised by the titans of old myth. There were rainbow slicks of promethium on the approach waters, and the air stank of bulk machines and heavy industry.

The chugging flotilla came in over the shadow of the cliff wall. There was a huge inlet, an arch like a sea cave a couple of kilometres wide. The barges followed the channel in, until they began to pass under the arch of rock, the island consuming them.

It grew dark. The noise of the flotilla's weary engines echoed louder in the wide confines of the rock-roofed passage.

Mkoll stood at the barge's stern, beside the rail. His hand at Olort's back. The darkness slid across him, blotting out the sky.

There was no going back.

SIX

PROTECTION

'You're conducting a Hereticus investigation of my regiment?' asked Gaunt.

'Your specificity is wrong, Lord Executor,' replied Inquisitor Laksheema. 'It is a more–'

'You're running an investigation?' Gaunt asked more firmly. The sharpness of his question stilled the room. They sat across a table in an empty ward room a short distance along the hall from Gaunt's chambers. Daur had claimed the ward room for what clearly had to be a private meeting.

Daur sat at Gaunt's side, his face impassive. Colonel Grae sat beside the inquisitor. Hark occupied a chair at the table's end, as if he was somehow moderating the discussion. He had chosen the seat himself. His eyes were narrow. He could see how Laksheema was testing Gaunt's patience, just as she had tested his.

Gol Kolea sat alone on a low-backed chair in the corner, staring at the floor.

'Yes, my lord,' said Laksheema. The burnished golden sections of her partly augmetic head glowed in the lamplight. She was impossible to read. Was she smirking? Annoyed? Amused? Viktor Hark knew there was no way of telling. Her face was a mask. That made her very good at her job. It was probably why she'd had herself rebuilt that way, after whatever grievous damage she'd suffered.

No doubt deserved, Hark thought.

There was no misreading Gaunt's annoyance.

'An investigation of my regiment? And of the Astra Militarum dispositions on Urdesh?'

'Yes, my lord.'

'Without approval? Without notifying anyone in high command?' asked Gaunt.

'The matter is sensitive–'

'So high command itself is under suspicion?'

'I didn't say–'

'You're not saying much, inquisitor,' said Gaunt. 'But you would have informed senior staff militant unless you thought senior staff were also potentially complicit.'

'I am informing you now, lord,' said Laksheema. 'I have come to you directly.'

'Not directly,' said Gaunt. 'First, you detained one of my officers.' He looked at Kolea, whose attention remained resolutely fixed on the floor. 'Then you come to me with questions, and not through official channels. That's not informing me. My man, my regiment. I fall within the compass of your investigation too, don't I?'

'Lord, this is a formality to expedite the–' Colonel Grae began.

'I don't think it is, colonel,' said Gaunt. Grae closed his mouth. Gaunt turned his unnerving stare back to the inquisitor.

'Ask. Speak. Inform,' he said. 'If you wish to expedite, get on with it and I'll cooperate.'

'You are correct, my lord,' said Laksheema calmly. 'We have issues of concern that involve the Tanith First and so, by extension, you. Those concerns stretch into other departments of the Astra Militarum and other regiments, and simply due to your status, to high command.'

'Lay these concerns out for me,' said Gaunt.

'There are issues of strict confidence that–'

'No,' said Gaunt. 'You're cleared, Grae is cleared, and I am cleared, all at the highest level. Because of my status, which you so delicately point out, the officers of my regiment present are also, by extension, authorised.'

Laksheema shrugged slightly.

'Certain ratification would be necessary,' she said. 'For Commissar Hark, Captain Daur and Major Kolea... paperwork and disclosure approval–'

Gaunt shook his head. 'Again, dissembling. If your investigation encompasses the entire Astra Militarum on Urdesh, who stands outside that purview to warrant and approve such authorisation? You're hiding behind the rules you're seeking to subvert, asking us to chase our tails through the Administratum, knowing we'd never get an answer. Let's be clear. I am ratifying them. Right now. With these words.'

'Yes, my lord,' said Laksheema.

'And you are clearing them with yours, on behalf of the ordos,' Gaunt added.

'Yes, my lord,' said Laksheema. 'We will consider them cleared to both our satisfactions.'

'Good,' said Gaunt. 'Begin.'

'There has been a crisis on Urdesh for some time,' said Laksheema, 'one that existed before your return. The obvious challenge of overcoming the Anarch's military threat, matched by a lack of understanding of his tactics. This is now, for the most part, resolved. It is clear that the Anarch's strategy on Urdesh was a mirror of our own, to whit, the enticement, containment and elimination of the opposing leaders. The obliteration of the Warmaster and his high command. The neutering of this crusade.'

'I think we can agree that the Lord Executor played no small part in the revelation of that stratagem,' Grae said to Laksheema. 'He saw Sek's trap, and prevented it from springing shut, and–'

'Please, don't,' said Laksheema.

'Don't what?' asked Grae.

'Attempt to flatter and support these men,' said Laksheema. 'They are of your institutions, Grae, not mine. I serve the Throne, directly. My intentions are not filtered through the strata of a vast and hidebound organisation like the Astra Militarum.'

'I advise you not to push that point,' said Hark quietly. 'Say your fething piece or get your fething arse out of the door.'

Laksheema looked at Gaunt. 'Will you not reprimand your man for such–'

'I find,' said Gaunt, 'as I grow older, the Astra Militarum indeed to be a vast and hidebound organisation, inquisitor. Starched with needless formality and protocol, and strangled by the chains of command. So, in this room, Viktor can speak his mind with my entire support. Say your fething piece.'

Laksheema sat back, her eyes fixed on Gaunt.

'Whatever your accomplishments in revealing the truth of the Anarch's stratagem,' she said, 'I do not believe it is ended or even halfway done.'

'Then we agree on something,' said Gaunt.

'And your very return is an issue,' Laksheema said. 'For it changed the nature of things. Of the crisis. Whatever long game Sek is trying to win on Urdesh, it altered overnight to accommodate you.'

'Me?'

'The material you brought with you from Salvation's Reach,' said Laksheema. 'Its import is unknown to us, but it is clearly of great significance to the enemy. Such significance, in fact, that he is willing to abandon – or at least, delay and modify – a scheme of war that he has been preparing and executing over a period of years.'

'The eagle stones,' said Gaunt.

'Yes, those artefacts,' said Laksheema.

'Apparently, a Glyptothek–' Grae began.

'Whatever,' said Gaunt. He looked at Laksheema. 'Again, agreed. I believe the late assault on Eltath was as much about recovering said items as it was about annihilating high command.'

'The attack was repulsed,' said Daur.

'Was it, captain?' asked Laksheema.

'Yes, Ban, was it?' Gaunt said, glancing at Daur. 'The main assault was repulsed. Perhaps. It certainly fell back without warning. Secured objectives were not capitalised on. It may have been a feint. A cover for some clandestine objective now invisibly secured.'

'But the Beati struck a blow at Sek at Ghereppan,' said Daur. 'That surely was the decisive factor? The timing was no coincidence.'

'It seems likely,' said Gaunt. 'He may have been disadvantaged by the Beati's work. Feth knows, he may even be dead. But his strategy isn't. My gut says so. Sek wasn't defeated four nights ago. He didn't walk away from Eltath and Ghereppan empty-handed with his arse whipped. Whatever it cost him, he achieved something.'

'And we don't know what it is?' said Daur.

'And we don't know what it is,' said Gaunt. 'But like an enemy under cover of darkness, we don't need to know where he is. We just need to prepare.'

'This is the thinking of high command?' asked Laksheema.

'This is my thinking,' said Gaunt. 'That's enough.'

Laksheema was about to speak when there was a knock at the door.

'Ignore it,' said Gaunt.

The knock came again. Both Daur and Hark were in the process of rising, but Gaunt shoved back his chair and strode to the doorway.

Sancto and the other bodymen stood in the hallway outside. Nearby stood Beltayn and Merity and the members of Laksheema's entourage, waiting where they had been told to wait, along with the tactician Biota and several Officio Tacticae officials Gaunt didn't know. Behind them stood two officers from the command echelon, their braid denoting them as members of Van Voytz's staff.

'My lord–' Sancto began.

'Not now,' snapped Gaunt, and slammed the door in his face.

He walked back to his seat slowly.

'What are the eagle stones?' he asked.

'We don't know,' said Laksheema. 'They are currently subject to detailed analysis.'

'Where are the eagle stones?' asked Gaunt, sitting down and straightening his chair.

'Secure,' said Laksheema.

'Where?'

'That's classified.'

'But they are of strategic significance?'

'My lord,' said Laksheema, 'they could be lumps of broken brick, but if the enemy considers them significant, we must too. Even if they are sacred objects of no intrinsic value or power, they may still provoke the Archenemy into action and response, to our disadvantage.'

She paused.

'We believe, however,' she said, 'that they are malign.'

'Malign?'

'My inquiry into their nature and purpose revealed a connection to your Major Kolea, which is why I had him detained for interview. Major Kolea has revealed, reluctantly, that he knows more about the stones and adjacent matters than he has admitted to you, or to anyone.'

Gaunt looked over at Kolea. Kolea was still staring at the floor. Gaunt saw the muscles of his jaw clench.

'A malign influence,' said Laksheema, 'one that has been exerting its power over your man there, and by extension your entire regiment, since you first obtained the objects. By the reckoning of world-time, Lord Executor, that's ten years. Some of the precarious events of your odyssey home may be connected to it. Your warp-translation accident... the curious sparing of your vessel by the Archenemy battlecruiser, which surely failed to annihilate a clearly identified enemy because it knew something valuable was aboard... even the replenishment drop to Aigor 991, a mission Major Kolea was personally involved with.'

'So,' said Gaunt, 'you wish to arraign the Lord Executor for heretical contamination?'

'My lord,' said Laksheema, 'you and your regiment have a worrying record of straying outside the safety of approved behaviour. I might cite your mission to Gereon in 774, and the suspicions that followed your return from that mission, that you had spent too long in the tainted environment of a Chaos-held world.'

'Cite all you like,' said Gaunt. 'Those matters are closed. We have been determined as loyal and true. I was reinstated, and my regiment returned to me, despite the naysayers.'

'Dirt and rumours cling to a man,' she replied, 'even one of your rank.'

'Perhaps you should discuss this with Warmaster Macaroth,' said Gaunt. 'He appointed me to this station. He has faith in me.'

'Your unorthodox reputation goes back a long way, lord,' said Laksheema. Her haunting non-smile ignited. 'Your unusual career path of colonel *and* commissar. Reports from 765 and thereabouts – I have Inquisitor Abfequarn's files at my disposal – suspicions that, for a considerable period, you sheltered in your regiment, and close to you, a suspected psyker. An unregistered boy. Also, the business of a Major Soric–'

'A boy? You mean Brin Milo,' said Gaunt. 'I haven't seen him in years. He left my company on Herodor, and joined the personal retinue of the Beati. I think that's a fairly glowing reference for his good standing. Or do you intend to interview the Saint when you're done with the Warmaster?'

'I do not,' said Laksheema.

Gaunt sat back. He watched her. She betrayed nothing.

He got up.

'Right,' he said. 'Stay here please, all of you. I want to talk with Major Kolea. In private.'

'We... wait here?' asked Laksheema.

'I'm sure we can entertain ourselves, ma'am,' said Hark.

Gaunt led Kolea out of the room. Biota and the other officials were still waiting expectantly outside the ward room. More had joined them, carrying data-slates and reports.

Gaunt could see questions and requests about to explode at him from all sides.

'Not now,' he growled.

'My lord,' said Sancto. The Scion stiffened as Gaunt turned to look at him. 'Sancto?'

'I appreciate this is not the time,' Sancto said quietly, 'but there are matters that demand your attention. *Many* matters. I hesitate to detain you, but–'

Gaunt raised a hand and Sancto shut up.

'Quickly,' Gaunt said to the rest of them.

Beltayn shrugged. 'Oh, just stuff. It can wait, sir,' he said.

'You requested my presence, lord,' said Biota. 'To form a tactical cabinet and–'

'I did,' said Gaunt. 'I wanted you specifically, Biota.'

'I'm honoured, sir,' said Biota. 'It will be a pleasure to serve. May I introduce–'

He had started to turn to the Tacticae officials with him.

'No,' said Gaunt. 'Not now. Just get to work. Choose effective people you can trust. Triage the data for me. Deal with the stuff that doesn't need my personal attention. My adjutant Beltayn has been doing your job single-handedly for the last four days, so use him. He can bring you up to speed.'

'My lord,' said one of the officers from Van Voytz's echelon. 'The lord general wishes you to know that the Beati is inbound to the palace and will be arriving shortly. He thought—'

Gaunt's hand came up again. He looked at Biota.

'Things like that, Biota. I'm delegating. Get everything in order. I will, of course, greet the Beati as soon as she's here.'

'Of course, sir,' replied Biota. 'And, uhm, if there are matters that *do* require your personal attention...?'

Gaunt sighed, and looked at the faces around him. He pointed to a figure at the back of the group.

'Along with Beltayn, add her to your cabinet,' he said. 'Merity Chass, of House Chass. Well-versed in administrative duties, and entirely familiar with the immediate business of my regiment.'

'Her?' said one of the officials, bewildered.

'Sir,' said Biota, looking pained, 'this is entirely unconventional. The personal cabinet of a Lord Executor can't be thrown together as a makeshift—'

'We're improvising today, Antonid,' said Gaunt. 'This is just expediency to keep things from leaving the rails. We can refine it all later. For now, get on with it.'

He looked at Merity.

'Are you all right with this?' he asked.

'I will be delighted to have something practical to do, sir,' she said.

'But why her?' asked one of the officials.

Gaunt glared at him. 'Because she's the only one of you that could knock on my door and not make me want to shoot them in the face. So use that advantage.'

'This is highly unorthodox, my lord,' said Biota.

'Apparently, that's my reputation,' said Gaunt. 'Run with it and let's see where it gets us.'

He turned to Kolea.

'With me,' he said.

Jan Jerik tapped his fingers on the head of his cane as he waited for the freight elevator to ascend. They could hear it grumbling and clanking its way up from far below.

Corrod stood with him in the dank chamber of the lift-head, a chamber seated deep in the basement crypts of House Ghentethi. They were the last to descend. His men, and those who had arrived with his second, Hadrel, had already gone down, escorted by house footmen and the subordinates of the clave. All told, Corrod's company numbered sixty-four, all scrawny, emaciated and filthy individuals who had seemed barely able to lift and load the crates of equipment Jan Jerik had provided for them. A singularly unimpressive mob, Jan Jerik concluded. The gear and uniform his people had procured, most of it standard-size trooper fit removed from an abandoned Munitorum depot in Albarppan, wouldn't fit them. They'd look like children dressing up in adult clothes. Jan Jerik's disappointment and unease had risen considerably. They were vagabond heathens clad in rags, stooped and bone-thin like the victims of famine, weak and frail. Beggars. They all reminded him of beggars. He hadn't expected beggars, and he hadn't asked for them. These wretches wouldn't be physically able to conclude the endeavour, and he doubted they'd make good on any promises. The deal was sour, and he should never have made it.

Still, the clave's thermal junction, far below, was quiet and out of the way. A good place to divest himself of this mistake. Five minutes before, he'd spoken quietly with one of his subordinates, out of earshot of his guests. His staff were set and ready. They'd make short work of the business, and dispose of the corpses in the geotherm vents.

Jan Jerik had pulled on a work-suit and protective boots for the descent. He carried a glowglobe set in a lantern holder. When he'd buttoned up the work-suit, he hung his keys and ciphers on the outside.

'Why do we go last?' Corrod asked.

Jan Jerik shrugged. 'Just a custom of the house, sir,' he said. 'The ordinate always comes to the workface last, once his crews have prepared the area. A protocol.'

'Damogaur,' said Corrod.

'I'm sorry?' said Jan Jerik, looking up.

'You called me "sir",' said Corrod. 'I hold the office of damogaur. That is the correct form of address.'

'Of course.'

'A protocol,' said Corrod.

Jan Jerik smiled thinly. Corrod was watching him. His eyes were dull and lifeless. The weather-beaten skin of his face had shrunk back to every promontory of cheekbone and jaw. His neck was like a reed, and his throat the slack, wrinkled wattle of a nonagenarian.

'A military rank?' said Jan Jerik. The elevator finally arrived, rattling into place. He stepped forward and dragged open the folding metal shutter of the cage.

'Yes,' said Corrod.

Jan Jerik ushered him into the freight car, and Corrod shuffled past him. The ordinate closed the cage, secured the lock latch, and pulled the lever down to the indicator for the lowest level. With a lurch and a whir of cable gears, the car started its descent.

'I hadn't realised,' said Jan Jerik.

'What?'

'That things had gone so badly for... for your forces. I now see why you would be so desperate to engineer a deal with men of, uh, Imperial leanings.'

'Your leanings seem quite fluid,' remarked Corrod.

Jan Jerik shrugged. 'Our loyalty is always to Ghentethi,' he said. 'Ghentethi before all. Our house has stood, like many of the dynastic claves, since the early times of settlement. We consider ourselves independent, and ally with those who will benefit us most. My dear s– damogaur. You know well that the mastery of Urdesh has changed many times over the centuries. The Throne, the rimward tribes, and back, and forth. We have worked with and for the Sanguinary Brood as often as we have distant Terra. Indeed, in some golden eras, past gaurs have favoured us more than the Throne or the forge-priests of Mars have ever done.'

The elevator continued to rumble down into the darkness.

'What did you mean?' asked Corrod.

'Mean?'

'Your comment... that you see now why we are desperate?'

Jan Jerik smiled. 'Oh, I meant no offence, damogaur,' he said. 'Merely an observation. I was expecting warriors. Soldiers. Strong and able men. But your forces are clearly so depleted that they send us old men. Veterans, I presume. I doubt not your courage, but you are a flimsy bunch. Presumably all that could be spared. I am sad to see the might of the tribes so wasted and reduced.'

'My lord Anarch has sent his best to accomplish this deed,' said Corrod, without emotion.

Jan Jerik chuckled. 'Rather my point, damogaur. If you are his best, then woe betide the Anarch's host. I had heard that the Guard had the measure of you, that the war had swung hard to the Throne on this world, and others. I had no idea that it was quite so parlous. Just dregs remaining. I am surprised the Administratum hasn't broadcast this jubilantly to raise the public mood. That the Archenemy in these parts is reduced to a tattered relic, and that the fire is gone from them.' Corrod looked at him almost blankly for a second, then shuffled across the car and threw the lever into neutral. The elevator halted abruptly, between levels. It rocked and creaked gently on its cables.

'What are you doing, sir?' Jan Jerik snapped. 'Have you taken umbrage at my words? Have I offended you? Well, then, forgive my spirit and my honesty. Let us resume.'

Corrod turned to face him.

'We came to you in guise, ordinate,' he said. He grimaced slightly, his lips curled back from his dirty teeth for a second, as if suffering some quiet anguish. 'We entered this city masked, so that we might pass unheeded. You have made a misapprehension.'

The ordinate chuckled, nervously.

'I crave your pardon, then,' he said lightly. 'Let us continue on. The lever, sir–'

'I wish to reassure you, ordinate,' said Corrod. He grimaced again.

'No need, no need! Let us–'

Jan Jerik stopped speaking. His eyes and mouth opened wide, and he took two or three involuntary steps backwards.

Corrod's eyes had lit. They shone with an ugly yellow light. There was acute intelligence in them now, and a predatory precision. He began to twitch, his thin arms pressed into his ribs, elbows bent, hands spavined into shaking claws. His lips drew back from his teeth in a snarl, and his mouth slowly opened under tension, as if he was screaming silently.

Neon tears began to well and drip from his eyes, the same luminous yellow that glowed inside his sockets. His skin began to ripple. Jan Jerik could see muscle, fibre and bone shift and undulate beneath the surface, bending and poking, twitching and pulsing. He heard a series of ugly cracks, the snap of bones and the click of joints, that made him flinch.

Corrod was growing taller. The weak, slack musculature was filling out and growing taut. Ribs stretched, and vertebrae rattled like beads. The dirty rags he wore tore in places across his shoulders as he grew within them. He tilted his head back in a rictus, mouth wide, spittle flecking from his brown and broken teeth. Neon tears ran from his hollow cheeks. His jaw clicked forwards.

'The Emperor protects!' Jan Jerik whispered. His voice shrunk to nothing.

'No,' said Corrod. 'He does not.'

The alchemy was done. Corrod towered over the ordinate, staring down at him. He was more than two metres tall. His limbs were longer. He was still cadaverously lean, a tall, thin spectre, but the muscles were hard under his fat-less flesh. His nose had all but receded into a cavity, and his mouth had extended like a snout, with a long, narrow chin. The teeth, top and bottom, were a tangled mess of canine points, some as long as the ordinate's little fingers.

Corrod's neon eyes glowed, yellow heat behind a milky surface.

'Now you may see us,' he said.

'What are you?' Jan Jerik stammered.

'We are the Anarch's chosen of chosen, the blessed reworked, the blessed of his voice, which drowns out all others.'

'I don't...' Jan Jerik gasped.

'We are his favourite sons. And we are few,' said Corrod, 'granted our rare and precious gifts by the holy Changer of Ways through the Ministry of the Great Anarch. We are the Qimurah, and within the Sabbat Worlds, a mere sixty-four of us exist as the Anarch's elite.'

Corrod paused, wiping a neon tear off his cheek with the back of his thumb.

'And all of us,' he said, 'all sixty-four, in unprecedented unison, have come to perform this task.'

'I'm sorry!' said Jan Jerik. 'I'm sorry!' He had backed to the far wall of the car in terror, and was pressed against the cage.

'Apology accepted,' said Corrod. He reached for the lever. 'Shall we continue?'

Gaunt led Kolea into his quarters, took one warning look at Sancto and the Scions as they took up position outside, and shut the door.

'Sit,' he said.

Kolea breathed heavily, and sat down on one of the chairs.

'Talk,' said Gaunt. He crossed to a cabinet and poured two cap glasses of amasec.

Kolea looked like he was in pain. He couldn't make eye contact.

'I don't know where to start, sir,' he said.

'Try,' said Gaunt. He handed one of the glasses to Kolea, who took it carefully, but didn't sip. Gaunt dragged over another chair and sat down, facing Kolea.

'Gol?'

Kolea sighed.

'What has she got on you?' asked Gaunt.

'I don't know. Falsehoods, lies.'

'She's making it up?'

'No. I mean... there are things that I don't... I don't even know if they're true. Things that have haunted me.'

He looked up into Gaunt's eyes for the first time.

'Things I should have told you long ago,' he said.

'About Aigor? The supply drop?'

'Mostly. Yes.'

'Now's the time, major,' said Gaunt.

Kolea looked down at his drink. He paused, then he sank it in one gulp.

'There was something there,' he said.

'You told me that. It was in your report.'

'A voice, that demanded the eagle stones.'

Gaunt nodded.

'Demanded they be brought to Urdesh.'

'All this I know, Gol.'

'It said it was the voice of... of him. Sek. It said it had power over me.'

'To deliver the stones?'

Kolea hunched his shoulders. 'We brought them anyway,' he said. 'To Urdesh, I mean. It's what we were doing. It's not like I had to steal them, or break orders, or do its bidding...'

'And this was all in your report, Gol. So what has Laksheema got hold of? What didn't you tell me?'

'It said I was marked,' said Kolea, his voice thin. 'It knew my name, and said I was... susceptible. That the harm done to me on... the injuries that were healed on Herodor, that they had made me vulnerable.'

'To Sek?'

'To the warp. Throne help me. The voice told me I was... I was a conduit for daemons.'

He looked up at Gaunt.

'How can a man say that? It damns him. It walks him to the scaffold or the stake.'

'Probably better to say it than to hide it, Gol. This is late to learn it.'

'I know!' Kolea snapped. He subsided. 'I know. But I told myself... I told myself it was all lies. Sir, we both know how the Ruinous Powers game us. Play with our minds. Whispering and polluting. I thought it was that. The warp trying to... to play me.'

'So your report was incomplete because you were protecting yourself?' asked Gaunt.

'No,' said Kolea, in the tiniest whisper.

'What, then?'

'The voice told me that if I didn't comply, it would kill my children.'

'Your children?'

'Dalin and Yoncy. It told me they'd perish, if...'

Gaunt nodded. 'They're safe, you know?' he said. 'Both of them. They got here safely. It was lying to you.'

'It's what I thought.'

'But what? Gol?'

Kolea sighed again.

'It's like I don't know what to trust any more. I thought it was my head, the old damage... so many things that don't make sense. I just locked it all up. Kept it to myself.'

Kolea rose to his feet abruptly. He fiddled with his empty glass, as if wondering where to put it down.

'I thought if I told you, you'd execute me,' he said. 'That, or the Black Ships. And the kids too, by extension. Named by the darkness. Feth, what? The Black Ships for them *too*?'

'So you told yourself it was all lies?' asked Gaunt.

'Yes,' Kolea replied. 'But I made a promise to myself. An oath, that I'd keep the children safe. Protect them. That if this darkness, this bad shadow, was real, I'd deny it and kill it. That's what we do. We're soldiers of the Throne.'

He looked at Gaunt.

'Aren't we?' he asked.

'We are,' said Gaunt.

'But it was getting too... too hard,' Kolea said. 'Spinning out of control. Just so much. Once Laksheema got her claws in me, I knew it was just a matter of time. That it would all come out.'

Gaunt got up, took the glass from Kolea's hand, and went to refill it.

'We didn't know what the eagle stones were, Gol,' he said. 'Not back then. Not at Aigor. It was much later we made that connection. Bask saw them after the accident. Spread out like wings.'

'Yeah,' said Kolea. 'That's when it all really started to unravel. Sir, I should have told you right at the start, damn the consequences. I was a coward.'

Gaunt held out the refilled glass. 'You're one of the strongest men I've ever served with, Gol,' he said. 'Whatever you are, you're no coward.'

'What happens now, sir?' Kolea asked. 'I'll resign my pins. You'll want me in the stockade at least.'

Gaunt wiggled the glass he was holding out slightly, reminding Kolea to take it.

'What happens now, Gol,' he said, 'is you tell me the rest.'

'The rest?'

'What started to unravel?'

Kolea took the glass. 'Have you heard...' He began, then winced as if he couldn't believe he was saying it out loud. 'Have you heard the rumours? About Yoncy?'

'Rumours?' asked Gaunt.

'I thought Dalin and Yoncy were dead and gone with Livy on Verghast,' Kolea said. 'Lost and gone. But then, like a miracle, it turns out Criid had saved them. Brought them into the fold. Raised them.'

He sighed.

'I guess a man can only have one miracle in his life, and mine was the

Beati saving me. The kids were alive after all. I blessed the Throne for that. I let them be. I stayed back. They were too young to remember me, and they'd been through too much. But, you know, Dalin's grown into a fine man. A good lasman.'

'There's distinction in him,' Gaunt agreed.

Kolea nodded. 'And Yoncy. Everyone's favourite. More of a damn mascot than that fething bird. All the women dote on her. And Criid, well, she coaxed me back into their lives. Said it was dumb for me to be apart from them. So I made that connection again and... well, I was glad of it. For all the obvious reasons. I don't need to tell you how it is to make a bond with a child you didn't know existed.'

Gaunt pursed his lips. 'No.'

'But it got me close to them, you see?' Kolea went on. 'And I thought, "here's how you look after them, Gol. If there's any fething truth in that voice's threat, I can be here. Right with them. Protect them, like I promised." Because I thought... thinking like a solider, you understand, that the threat would be violence. An attack.'

'But?' asked Gaunt.

'I think the threat was more venomous than that,' said Kolea. 'More... what's the word? Insidious.'

'How?'

'This rumour,' said Gol. He took a sip of amasec and glanced at his seat. Gaunt nodded, and Kolea sat back down. 'This rumour. Don't know where it started, but some women in the entourage, Verghast women, they thought my kids had both been boys. Two boys. Well, this got back to me, and I laughed. No, a boy and girl...'

He looked at Gaunt again, solemn. 'Now I'm not so sure. I can't trust my memory. I can't trust anything in my mind, not since the harm done to me, or since the voice was in my head. I get headaches and... well, anyway, I think it's right. There *was* no girl child. Two boys. I asked Hark to check, but there's been no word back from the Administratum.'

'It was just a mistake,' said Gaunt. 'You'd know. The women got it wrong. You know what camp rumour is like.'

'I don't reckon so,' said Kolea.

'Why would you think like that?' Gaunt asked, sitting down again and leaning forward.

'Yoncy, she's an odd child. Always has been. A little girl, reluctant to grow up.'

'She's had a tough life.'

'Not just that.'

'Exactly that. Lost her mother. Lost you. Been through hell. Her life now as part of a nomad regiment.'

Kolea shook his head. 'I don't know,' he said.

'I do,' said Gaunt. 'I've seen her. She acts young because it's safe. Subconscious, I'm sure, but she acts like a little girl, because people always look after the little girl. It's just a defence mechanism.'

'No, sir,' said Kolea. 'I've had... I've had memories. I'm increasingly sure she isn't my Yoncy. Before you say it, I know. Maybe *that's* the punishment. Maybe that idea, that uncertainty, is the cruel trick the voice threatened, playing with me. In which case, I'm tainted and damned. But maybe...'

'Maybe what?'

'Maybe I'm right,' said Kolea. 'Maybe the true punishment is this. This is what the voice promised on Aigor. My girl, my Yoncy. Not mine at all. Maybe this is the way the warp shreds me.'

'What do you think she is, then?' asked Gaunt.

Kolea exhaled hard, his eyes wide and wondering.

'Who the feth knows?' he said. 'Something placed among us? Some changeling thing. Something malevolent.'

Gaunt smiled. 'Yoncy?' he asked. 'You think the Ruinous Powers planted her among us years ago? *Years*, Gol. As what? Some elaborate plan to destroy us from within? That it's just been *waiting*?'

'Well...'

'Come on! If Yoncy's a daemon, Gol, or whatever... she's had plenty of chances. We'd know by now. The warp plays games, but not long-term games like that. And for what? To cripple or destroy a regiment that, until recently, was just another Guard unit? We're not that important.'

'We are now,' said Kolea. '*You* are now.'

'So it could see the future too?' Gaunt laughed. 'Predict? Project? Put an agent in place waiting for the day, the remote chance, *years* to come...?'

'The eagle stones–'

'Feth's sake, Gol!'

'I know how it sounds. But I know what my heart says.'

'We're sheltering a creature of the warp?'

'All right, when you put it like that...'

'Gol, you're all mixed up,' said Gaunt. 'I get why. I understand. We've been through many hells, all of us. We've all faced the darkness and felt it mess with us. It's what it wants. It's what the Archenemy does to us. It wants to ruin our bonds, our trusts... it wants us to suspect each other and collapse in fear and hatred. And we're not going to let it. That's our job, after all. Our calling. Of all the citizens in the Imperium, we're the ones that hold fast. The Imperial fething Guard. We're the ones that are supposed to fight. You're just messed up.'

'But–' Kolea began.

'Whatever state your mind's in,' said Gaunt, 'whatever confusion, maybe you don't know. But Dalin does.'

Kolea blinked.

'He'd know, wouldn't he?' asked Gaunt. 'Forget your doubts. A brother would know his sister.'

Kolea wiped his mouth. He took a few deep breaths.

'I suppose there's that,' he admitted.

'Fething right there's that,' said Gaunt.

'So what do we do?'

'We fix this. We deal with the actual problem. Coordinate with Laksheema and divine Sek's true intention. I need all the good men I can get, so I'm not losing you. And I have a way to get the inquisitor off your back and clear your mind about this.'

'You do?'

'Yes. Drink up, then come with me. I'm going to talk to Laksheema again. Later on, you can go down to the billets and see your kids. See them and hug them and know that everything's all right.'

Gaunt raised his glass.

'You know why?' he asked.

'Because you're Lord Executor and you said so?'

'No. Because the Emperor protects.'

The glasses clinked together.

They all rose to their feet as Gaunt walked back into the ward room with Kolea.

Kolea stood by the door. Gaunt resumed his seat, and gestured for them all to sit.

'So here we have it, inquisitor,' he said. 'I believe, absolutely, that we share the same desire. To serve the Throne. To deny and destroy the Archenemy of Mankind. To end the pernicious blight of Anarch Sek, and to achieve victory in this crusade for Terra. Sek, or at least his schemes, live on. Only a fool would believe the eagle stones play no part in them. So let's combine our efforts. Identify the nature and value of the stones, their use and implication. Defend them. And ascertain through that effort the Archenemy's intent, so that we may not only block it but also accomplish a total victory.'

Laksheema nodded. 'The Holy Ordos would find the cooperation and assistance of the Lord Executor invaluable.'

'Good. Where are the stones?'

'As I said previously, sir, the location is necessarily classified–'

'Laksheema,' said Gaunt. 'No more games. The ordos do not have combat forces of sufficient scale present on Urdesh to defend a location against mass attack. The Astra Militarum does. Please don't presume that keeping their location a secret is an adequate defence against a monster who deals in secrecy.'

'My lord,' Laksheema began to protest.

'You said it yourself,' said Gaunt. 'The Archenemy battleship withheld fire from my vessel – indeed, perhaps fought to save it – because something valuable was on board that it could not bring itself to destroy. We can safely assume it was the eagle stones. It knew they were aboard without even seeing them.'

'I will supply data on the location,' said Laksheema. 'But it must remain classified, even within the Guard and the high command. We are certain the enemy has spies throughout Eltath. It has been enemy ground for too long.'

'And the city leaks like a sieve,' agreed Gaunt. 'I have a regiment at my disposal that is cleared at my level. Have Grae give the data to Captain Daur.'

'What about the pheguth?' asked Hark quietly.

'The traitor general?' asked Laksheema. 'I think his uses are exhausted.'

'He's scheduled for termination,' said Grae.

'Mabbon led us to them,' replied Hark. 'He was the key that allowed the Salvation's Reach mission to happen. The strategy of division between Blood Pact and Sek came from him. I'm not saying he's lying, or withholding, but... he's still an asset. He may know things that can help us, even if he doesn't realise it.'

'Do you want him brought here?' asked Grae.

'Again, I want his location,' said Gaunt. 'I'll have him delivered to the palace by an escort who knows how to handle him.'

He turned to look at Daur.

'Go fetch Beltayn,' he said. 'I want a secure link to Rawne in five minutes.'

Jan Jerik wrenched the cage door open, and stepped out of the freight car. Corrod followed him, stooping slightly to move under the door frame.

The air stank of sulphur, and it was unpleasantly hot. Jan Jerik was already sweating. He led Corrod across the rockcrete loading bay outside the elevator and into a broad chamber where the others were assembled and waiting.

Corrod's men, under the supervision of Hadrel, were busy equipping themselves from the crates House Ghentethi had provided. They were pulling on drab Guard fatigues and regulation boots, and unshipping lasrifles and hellguns from the munition crates. Each packson was checking his chosen weapon with assured ease and familiarity.

Like Corrod, they had all changed. Each one was a towering spectre of tall bones and hard muscle, and taut; too tall, too thin. The uniforms, which Jan Jerik had feared would be too big for them, were, if anything, too small. Some had rolled up sleeves where cuffs fell far short of their bony wrists. Their eyes shone, like those of wild animals caught by lamp light in the dark. On the deck plates, Jan Jerik saw spattered drops of neon tears.

The ordinate's men, a dozen or more footmen and subordinates, were standing watch. Jan Jerik could see the pallor of their faces, and smell the fear. They were all armed with carbines as per his earlier private instruction, but they carried the guns as if ashamed of them.

'My ordinate,' said one of the footmen, coming forward quickly in concern.

Jan Jerik waved him off. They were committed now. He didn't dare think what might befall him and his men if he reneged, or tried to purge his guests.

'You... you have everything?' he asked.

Corrod was pulling on a faded Guard jacket and checking its fit.

'It would appear so,' he said. 'Sirdar?'

'Most of what we requested, my damogaur,' said Hadrel. 'Though the quality of the weapons and clothing is merely serviceable. Just standard lasrifles. And no support weapons or grenades as stipulated.'

'We got what we could,' said Jan Jerik. 'Sources are few at a time of war. And to ransack Munitorum property without detection–'

Corrod raised a lasrifle, checked its aim and feel quickly, shortened the carry-strap, then opened the receiver to load a powercell.

'It will suffice,' he said. 'Sirdar, share the ammunition equally between all. Hacklaw? Make sure everyone has a blade.'

His officers moved to their tasks.

'This... this is the lower level,' said Jan Jerik. 'From down here, we draw power from the geothermal vents to run our lathes and processors.'

'And the vent system links all Mechanicus and forge facilities in the city?' said Corrod, strapping on an ammunition belt.

'All of them, and beyond the city too,' said Jan Jerik. 'It was a network constructed by the earliest settlers, to harness the power of the mountain and–'

'Yes,' said Corrod, cutting him short. 'Let's begin. Give me the chart.'

Jan Jerik handed it over, then lit his lantern and walked through the preparing group towards a large hatch at the end of the chamber. He selected a silver cipher key from his chain, and unlocked the hatch. Stinking gases and heat billowed out.

Corrod gestured, and his men assembled.

Jan Jerik unhooked a rebreather mask from a rack on the wall. His subordinates did the same.

'You'll need these,' he said to the damogaur.

'No,' said Corrod.

'Damogaur, the heat alone can be treacherous,' said Jan Jerik. He adjusted a toggle on his worksuit to activate its cooling system. 'And the accumulated gases are noxious. They can blind and choke. Moreover, if there is unscheduled system venting or an upwelling from the–'

'No,' said Corrod again. He began to blink rapidly, and the neon glow of his eyes increased in intensity. His jaw clenched tightly, as if he was suffering discomfort. There was a sudden, wet, sticky noise of bubbling fluids.

Milky secondary eyelids formed over his eyes, a tough organic membrane oozing with mucus that resembled the bulbous, glassy stare of a deep sea fish. The lids dulled the light of his eyes a little. Another film of mucus oozed out to cover his raw stub of nostrils and his mouth, hardening like resin. It formed a bony sheathe across his nose and mouth, like a muzzle on a dog woven from intestine and coral.

Hadrel and the other men had all done the same.

'We will manage,' he said to Jan Jerik, his voice muffled to a low murmur.

Jan Jerik winced with distaste.

He raised his lantern.

'Then follow me,' he said.

SEVEN

ARRIVALS

They ran under the shadow of the rock and entered the Fastness. The deep water of the channel lapped against the huge rock overhang, stirred by the current and chopped by the wake of the watercraft. It was brisk and cold under the shadow, and the growl of the hard-running engines echoed off the rock.

Mkoll didn't know the Urdeshi name for the island, and there were no maps to hand. As they cleared the shadow, the nature of the Fastness became evident. It was a vast volcanic peak, long extinct. At some point in its long history, the sea had invaded the dead cone through fissures like the one they had entered by. The immense internal flue had become a sea-lake ten kilometres in diameter. Around it, the inner walls of the cone rose like cliffs, a kilometre and a half high. Above, the cone was open to the heavens, a ragged circle of grey sky fringed with vapour.

Urdesh's clave dynasts and agri-fleets had used the Fastness as a natural harbour. The wide internal water, deep enough to handle the draft of any vessel, was protected from all sides by the rock bastion of the cone, defending it from foul weather and oceanic gales. From the waterline up, the internal cliffs were clad in buildings: docks and wharfs, landing platforms, boat pens and salting houses. Above these rose habitats, administrative halls, workshops, warehouses and machine rooms, all built out over the water on rusted metal pilings, and stacked up like blocks, clinging to the cliff walls and linked by open staircases and suspended walkways. A small city, accumulated over the years around the inner circumference of the dead flue. In some places, the piled structures reached almost a quarter of the way up the cliffs. Everything was caked in a thick coating of algae.

The cold air stank of seawater, promethium slicks and venting exhaust fumes. Mkoll saw fleets of watercraft – landing barges and battered agri-boats – packing in at the landing stages, unloading war machines, cargo and hundreds of Sekkite troopers. This was the Archenemy's safe haven, the point of flight for the vast forces retreating from the mainland brawl. Cranes and industrial hoists swung the heavier items onto the docks from the agriboats, ponderously manoeuvring tracked armour and troop carriers to the ramps of the foreshore yards. Horns blew, their bass notes echoing across the hidden lake, and standards flapped along the walls of the waterline, company standards, battle flags and banners of the infernal powers proudly displayed for incoming vessels to see. There was a screech and chatter of machine tools from the work-barns on the waterside.

The most arresting sight, dominating all others, was the ship. It was an Archenemy cruiser, gnarled and scarred, a medium-displacement shiftship over a mile long. Like the tiny agriboats beneath it, it had taken shelter in the cone of the Fastness. It hung in place on its grav-anchors and suspensor arrays thirty metres above the water, and the bulk of it seemed to fill the open hollow of the cone's interior. Supply pipes looped from its flanks and belly to the dockside plants and manufactories. Bracing cables of woven wire as thick as a man's thigh strained tight between anchor points on the hull and the surrounding cliffs, as taut as the strings on a lyre. Vapour and steam vented in thick, slow, dirty clouds from the ship's aft drives. Bilge water and liquid grease poured in steady cascades from its underside. It had clearly not been at the Fastness long. The surface of the lake beneath the ship, black in the ship's immense shadow, rippled with moire patterns triggered by the invisible action of the suspensor fields.

The cruiser's down-lights were lit, illuminating the immediate wharfs with searchlight beams of an ugly radiance. Banks of lights had been set up on the docks too, angled to light the ship's paint-scabbed and warp-scorched plates. Mkoll could see the minuscule figures of men moving like lice on the ship's upper hull, work-crews engaged on field repairs and plate refits. There was the occasional blue-white twinkle of welding torches and fusion cutters.

Structures resembling siege towers had extended out from the docks, bridging the gap and linking ship to shore. As the agriboat passed beneath one, Mkoll could see the internal hoists lifting freight up to the access levels, and crews of stevedores and servitors hauling the loads across the bridge-spans overhead into the ship's open airgates. Small lift ships and lighters droned like flies, shuttling between the cruiser's gaping belly holds and the shoreline landing platforms. One flew overhead, running lights flashing, wings angled for low-flight mode, and the agriboat rocked in the wake of its thrusters.

The agriboat's engines started to mutter a new note, and the vessel began to slide sideways towards the waiting docks. Other boats in the small fleet slowed and moved in with it. There were dock crews, servitors and soldiers waiting on the quay.

Mkoll heard chattering. It was in his head, a constant hissing, like a thousand soft whispers.

Olort looked at him, noticing his reaction.

'He speaks to us all,' he said, 'to all and to every.'

Mkoll grimaced slightly. The psionic background drone would take some getting used to. It felt like fingernails scratching at his eardrums and the lining of his sinuses.

He was here. Close by.

They were moving in to dock. At the prow of the boat, men were standing ready to catch and throw the mooring lines.

'I don't know how you expect to–' Olort began.

'You have urgent business to attend to, damogaur,' Mkoll replied.

'Business?' asked Olort.

'Reports. Statements of deployment. You'll be inventive. We'll move directly through the crowd and get in.'

Olort sighed. He looked at Mkoll with an almost kindly smile.

'This is the end. You realise that? Whatever plans you were nursing, they end here. You have delivered yourself. Your own choice. You are here and this is it. There is no escape, and no opportunity for any course of action except surrender.'

Mkoll didn't reply.

'Come,' said Olort. 'Submit now. I'll take you in directly, and deliver you. It'll be a feather in my cap, but it will make things easier for you. I'll see to that. We have an understanding, don't we? You've spared me. I'll spare you.'

'Spare me?'

'Spare you the worst. You're a trophy. You have value, and for that reason, you will be treated with care.'

'And accept induction?'

'If you choose so. I appreciate you may not be able to bring yourself to that. But you are enkil vahakan, Ghost. Special status will be afforded you.'

Mkoll looked at him.

'Give me the blade,' said Olort.

'No.'

'You're a prisoner already,' said Olort. He shrugged. 'Look around. You have entered the heart of us. You have placed yourself in our bastion and in our midst. Your identity will not remain hidden for long. There is no escape. Give me the knife, and I will make things go as well for you as they can.'

The agriboat rocked against the quayside, grinding against the sacking bumpers. Men shouted instructions, hauled on cables, and jumped the gap to tie up. The boat's engines coughed into reverse.

'You have urgent business to attend to,' Mkoll said.

Olort's face fell. 'A knife at my back? You think that will get you in here? That will keep you alive?'

'It's worked so far.'

'I am but one life–'

'But you don't want to lose it. I'm sure you would die in the name of your lord. Cry out, and bring them all down on my throat. But you want to live, damogaur. You'd rather live. I see that in you. You see purpose and personal glory in this, and all the while that chance exists, you'll keep your mouth shut. So... you and your sirdar have urgent business to attend to.'

The agriboat had scraped to a halt, and sat rocking. The troops aboard began to clamber out, passing up packs and folded support weapons, and reaching out for proffered hands. Packsons barked orders and got the shackled prisoners on their feet.

Mkoll let Olort feel the solidity of the blade at the base of his spine.

'Let's go,' he whispered.

Olort moved forwards.

'Make way here!' he called. 'I have urgent business to attend to!'

They made their way along the pier, and Mkoll stayed close to the damogaur.

The whole structure had a cake of algae on it, hard-set from years of growth. It was pink, purple and ochre. The crowds were tight. At every side, packsons stood in loose groups, some resting, some swapping stories. A few had knelt down in what little space was available to offer prayers and observations. Sekkite officers and grotesque excubitors moved through the masses, marshalling the arrivals, and despatching them in ragged columns up the wharf to holding areas. Gangs of prisoners were being led away. Mkoll counted more than sixty captured men unloaded from the boats. How many more had already been brought to their doom?

The great horns roared above them. A cargo-lifter skimmed by, its shadow flickering in the searchlight beams.

'Keep moving,' Mkoll whispered.

A sirdar with a data-slate approached them. He threw a cursory salute to Olort with a quick hand to his mouth, a reflex gesture that to Mkoll had begun to read as blowing a kiss. The Tanith found the cultural mis-connect of the gesture unsettling. The sirdar and Olort exchanged a few words. The enemy tongue was fast and hard to follow, but Mkoll heard the phrase 'urgent business' more than once. The sirdar nodded, and pointed in the direction of the stilted buildings overhanging the wharf.

The scratching whispers in Mkoll's skull continued.

From the rail of the dock, he saw a rockcrete foreshore where Sons of Sek with flamer packs were torching piles of what looked like undergrowth. Thick clouds of black smoke billowed from the burning heaps. The smell was pungent and sweet.

'What are they doing?' Mkoll asked.

Olort answered, using a word Mkoll didn't know. There was no time to question further. They crossed a busy yard and entered the nearest building.

The place was old. Lumen-globe lamps hung from chains anchored to the ceiling. It was part modular build and partly carved from the rock wall. Industrial meltas had been used to fuse the rock and modular plate together. The hallway space was big, and echoed with voices and the tramp of feet.

The walls of the hallway were lined with engravings, tall and narrow. The place, Mkoll guessed, had been a centre of clave administration. The engravings displayed the Urdeshi loyalty to Terra in the form of images of the God-Emperor, but they reflected the interests of Urdesh. Here was the Emperor in the aspect of a sea god, coiling with scaled tentacles, and here he rose from the Urdeshi deeps in a vast bloom of algae. On another panel, he was festooned with weapon-pods, triumphing the product of the forge's war-foundries. On another, he was so augmeticised with cyber implants he resembled a Titan war engine with a single, human eye. Slogans had been daubed in yellow paint under each image, utterances of the Archenemy. But the images themselves had not been defaced.

'Why have these not been torn down?' Mkoll asked Olort.

Olort seemed surprised. 'They show him as he is,' he replied. 'Why would we break those?'

'I don't understand.'

'The Urdeshi know the deeper truths,' said Olort. 'They are kin to us. They understand the fluidity. You cannot stand upon a border line for generations and not see both sides.'

Olort glanced up at one of the images. 'See him there, not as a false emperor surrounded by saints. He is shown as the machine, as the mutation, a force of war. He has always been a creature of the deep warp, warped like us. You know him only as you want to see him.'

Olort made a gesture of respect to the engravings.

'You worship him?' Mkoll asked.

'Nen, we respect,' replied Olort. 'He is no god, nor is he an emperor. But a prophet? Kha. *Yes*. He has seen the enlightenments of the Eight Powers and witnessed the truth of the warp. Ghost, your kind... they follow blindly. They see what they want to see. The Holy Lord, blessed of all, defying the darkness. But he stands in the darkness, beyond the curtain of death, fed by the warp and changed by it. He is a brother to us, a brother we must sadly fight to subdue until he renounces his insurrection.'

Olort looked at him.

'You know nothing of this?' he asked.

'It makes no sense.'

'This is because of your breeding. The indoctrination of your heretical culture. Do you... not know why we fight?'

'You fight to annihilate.'

Olort shook his head sadly.

'You are a man of war, Ghost,' he said. 'You have spent your whole life, I'd wager, serving your Throne in the field of battle. And you have never stopped to wonder what those you fight believe in? What our cause is?'

Mkoll didn't reply.

'We fight to bring you back,' said Olort. 'We fight to break your mindset and your blind beliefs. To make you see the truth and embrace it. Your prophet-lord has seen it, but he can no longer speak it, so your kind, they fight on according to ancient decrees and fossilised laws, things you believe are what he would have wanted. He is of us, and will be welcomed back to our bosom on such day as his followers finally lay down their swords and accept the warp-truth. Your faith in a man that was never a god has blinded you for ten millennia.'

'No,' said Mkoll simply.

'This is the way of it,' replied Olort. 'You think we are the darkness. But you are the darkness. Your ignorance is a shadow on your eyes and a fog in your mind. We fight to deliver you from that. We fight, Ghost, to save you.'

They moved on past administrative chambers where rubricators worked at cogitation systems, then out across a suspended walkway towards another stacked complex of cliff-side buildings.

'You know this place?' Mkoll asked.

Olort nodded.

'You've been here before?'

'Twice, not for long.'

'I want to find... information,' said Mkoll. 'Data on layout. Personnel locations. Those chambers back there–'

Olort shook his head.

'Just the old processing centres of the Urdesh dynasts,' he replied.

'There were people at work. Using the cogitators–'

'They have finished stripping out the memory cores of the dynastic claves. A gathering of intelligence. Now those machines are simply being used to compose and circulate our litanies.'

'Then, assuming your life depended on it–' said Mkoll.

'Which I know it does,' Olort replied with some sarcasm.

'Where would you go?'

Olort pointed to the structures that lay ahead of them. 'The record rooms,' he said. 'There we collate deployment details and pack data by hand. Machines cannot be trusted on this world.'

'Lead me.'

'What do you seek, Ghost? Do you cherish some plan, some great scheme, whereby a lone man with a knife can bring down this host? How long will you persist in such fantasies?'

'Lead me. I know what I'm looking for. And to answer your question, until my life is over. The Emperor protects.'

'Not here he doesn't,' said Olort. He shrugged. 'Come, then.'

They began to cross the walkway. Below, the water of a dock inlet gleamed like a rainbow where the floodlights caught the scum of spilled promethium lapping the surface.

Packsons were coming the other way, hefting metal barrows laden with dead vegetation. More fodder for the bonfires on the rockcrete strand. As they passed, Mkoll saw what the vegetation was.

Islumbine. It had been torn up in great quantities, leaf, flower, stem and root.

'They're taking it to burn it?' Mkoll asked as the soldiers with the barrows moved past.

'I told you this.'

'Why?'

'It is vergoht,' Olort replied, using the unknown word again. 'The flower of your Saint. It never grew here, not on Urdesh. It was not...'

He hesitated, trying to find the correct word.

'Native?' asked Mkoll.

Olort nodded. 'Yet now it grows everywhere,' he said. 'Like weed. We cut it and it grows again. So we cut it and burn it.'

'Why bother?'

'Because it is her flower,' Olort said. 'It is a holy aspect of her heresy. We must purge it, for while it grows and flourishes, it means she is here.'

'Sir?' Oysten called. She held out the headphones of her vox-set.

Rawne sniffed and trudged back to her, tugging his collar up against the incessant rain. He was soaked to the balls and his mood was foul. From down the wet, rubble-strewn street came sounds of sporadic gunfire. He hoped there'd be some killing left to do when he got there. He needed to take his mood out on something.

He took the headset and pulled it on.

'Rawne,' he said. He looked at Oysten, who nodded. 'Link is secure,' he continued. 'Speak.'

The signal chattered and whined. A burst of static. Then a voice broke through.

'–do you copy? Repeat, Colonel Rawne–'

'Daur? That you?'

'Affirmative, sir. This link is bad.'

'Agreed. The weather. Tell me you've raised me to give a withdraw notice.'

'Negative, sir. Sorry. I have new orders for you.'

'I've just had new orders, Daur, from some arsewipe in Grizmund's brigade. I don't know what the feth is going on, but we're locked in grunt work, street cleaning, and–'

'These orders are direct from the Lord Executor, and they supersede all others.'

Rawne wiped his mouth.

'Why isn't he talking to me himself?' he asked.

'Don't be an arse. Because he's the Lord Executor and he's got shit on his plate. This is vital work, Rawne. I'm going to brief you, so get ready.'

'Stand by,' replied Rawne, waving a hand distractedly at Oysten. She jumped up and passed him a data-slate and stylus.

'All right,' said Rawne. 'Go.'

'First point. The Tanith First is now cleared at vermilion level. Copy that?'

'I heard.'

'Gaunt orders you to withdraw from the Old Town district, effective immediately. Pull everybody. Commandeer transports if you have to. Leave any wounded at field stations, or have them shipped to the palace.'

'Understood.'

'You have two targets, both inside Eltath limits. Orders are to secure both locations. Both are classified. Location one...'

Rawne wrote the details down on the slate in company code, then read them back to make sure there were no mistakes.

'Secure both sites,' Daur said over the link. *'The stones are at site one. Send the main force there. The pheguth is at site two. Smaller, mobile force there. Gaunt thought you'd want to handle that one yourself.'*

'Indeed.'

'You've got that clear?'

'I have. What's this shit about?'

'I don't know the half of it myself,' Daur replied. *'But this is direct from the top, coded special task deployment. I'm advising you to keep this to yourselves. You have waiver authority to pass where you need to pass, but don't discuss the details with any other units.'*

'Are we compromised, Daur?'

'We don't know anything, Rawne. Situation is fluid. But this is special task

deployment. Gaunt needs men he can trust to perform this, and you're the only ones in reach.'

There was a long pause. The rain pattered down.

'The only ones period,' Daur added. *'This is on us. The Ghosts are now a discretionary unit operating at the Lord Executor's personal instruction.'*

'So... outside the Guard command structure?'

'For the duration. Those two locations carry the highest confidence ratings. Update on this channel as you can. And don't feth it up.'

Rawne cleared his throat.

'How deep are we in this, Ban?' he asked.

'Assume it's the end of the world and your arse is on fire, then act accordingly,' said Daur. *'The Emperor protects–'*

'Feth he does. Rawne out.'

Rawne stood for a moment reading back over the notes he'd made. Then he took off the headset and tossed it back to Oysten, who caught it neatly.

'You weren't planning on living forever were you?' Rawne asked her.

'Sir?' his adjutant replied, puzzled.

'Skip it. Call the Ghosts in. All of them. Disengage and fall back to my marker. Now.'

Daur handed his headset back to Beltayn. Rain was lashing against the tall windows of the palace and the overhead lamps were flickering slightly, as if damp had got into the wiring.

'They're despatched,' he said.

'I'll inform the Lord Executor,' Beltayn replied.

'That'll have to wait,' said Hark.

They turned to look at him.

'He's got a greeting to make,' said Hark.

Gaunt led his small honour guard into the reception chamber. It was one of the finest rooms of the palace, its floor tiled, its pillars and cornices gilded. Mythical beasts of the ancient Cyberzoic Era ran rampant across the immense ceiling fresco, surrounding a luminous image of the God-Emperor, who they seemed to regard with a mix of appetite and dread. The God-Emperor looked down, sword raised, one mailed foot resting on the head of a vanquished and pliant cockatrice.

Rows of company and brigade banners had been brought into the hall and set up along its length specifically for this moment. Many were still damp and dripping. At the far end, a large hydraulic hatch had been opened, allowing for a view out onto the exterior landing platform. Gaunt could feel the wind blowing down the length of the hall, and see the veil of heavy rain outside.

He advanced. In step behind him were Kolea, Grae, Inquisitor Laksheema and the Tempestus squad.

At the far end, just inside the hatch, Lord General Barthol Van Voytz was waiting. There was a wet semi-circle on the floor at the hatch sill where the wind was blowing the rain in. Van Voytz had put on his finest uniform, the breast ribboned with medals. Accompanying him were a dozen other senior officers and adepts and a phalanx of heavy Urdeshi storm troops. Gaunt recognised their leader, Kazader of the 17th.

The storm troops were set either side of the hatch, rigidly at attention with weapons presented. They were as immobile as granite. Kazader matched their pose, but Gaunt could tell Kazader was watching him approach out of the corners of his eyes. Kazader was one of Van Voytz's inner circle. There was bad feeling there.

Van Voytz turned as Gaunt came up, and the party of officers turned with him. All snapped a salute in unison. Van Voytz's salute was a nanosecond slower than the rest. It wasn't because Barthol was an older man, Gaunt thought. He wasn't slow. That tiny delay was micro-aggression. A way of showing his resentment without being directly insubordinate.

Gaunt returned the salute.

'At ease,' he said. 'The Emperor protects.'

Van Voytz stepped closer, making a respectful head-bow with a smile on his face. All for show.

'My lord,' he said, like an old friend.

He held out his hand, and Gaunt shook it. Like we're all pals together, he thought. No grudge, no bitterness. He wants to stay relevant inside high command, and if that means making a show of friendship to a man who blocked his plans, a man whom he once regularly sent to do death's work...

Gaunt smiled. The informality of the handshake wasn't for his benefit. It wasn't a gesture of reconciliation. It was for the officers looking on. *Look at me. I am Van Voytz, the old wardog. I am so tight with the Lord Executor, I get to bypass protocol and shake his hand.*

'Has the transport arrived?' Gaunt asked.

'It touched down some minutes ago,' said Van Voytz, 'but no one has yet emerged.' Gaunt noted how Van Voytz avoided the honorific of 'sir' or 'my lord', yet could not bring himself to risk an 'Ibram'.

'Awaiting security clearance from the war room,' said Gaunt.

Van Voytz nodded. 'I'm sure,' he said.

'Then we have a moment, Barthol,' said Gaunt, drawing him to one side. Van Voytz went with him eagerly, but his expression was tight.

'There's bad blood between us, Barthol,' Gaunt said quietly.

'Not at all, not at all...'

'We need to work together, Barthol,' said Gaunt firmly. 'This is a precarious time. High command needs to be of one mind and one purpose. So don't deny it. There's bad blood here.'

'Well...'

'And there always has been.'

Van Voytz looked both shocked and pained. 'Now, sir–'

'Since Jago, and there's a lesson there. I learned it the hard way. Duty and service over friendship. My duty was to your command then, and it was what it was. I see a bigger picture that you always urged me to appreciate. Now your duty is to me. Our roles are reversed. It's uncomfortable for you, but at least I'm not sending you into a killing ground.'

Van Voytz cleared his throat, and sagged slightly.

'I appreciate that,' he replied.

'You were on the path to disgrace, Barthol. Macaroth wanted your head on a stick.'

'I was merely putting the safety of the crusade first–'

'I know. I know that. Which is why I talked the Old Man down, and found you a staff position that allowed you to retain your rank and privileges. No direct command, I know, but that may come in time.'

'If I behave myself,' rumbled Van Voytz.

'Feth's sake, it could have been an outworld command for you. The arse-end of everywhere. Or a penal regiment. I covered your back because I know you're a fine officer. Don't piss on that respect. What took place in the command chamber–'

'You don't have to explain yourself, Ibram,' Van Voytz said with a long sigh.

'I don't. And I won't,' said Gaunt. 'I drew you aside to tell you that I don't have to explain myself. Do we have an understanding?'

Van Voytz nodded. He saw the look in Gaunt's eyes, steel-cold eyes that Van Voytz's orders had cursed Gaunt with a long time before.

He straightened up and saluted.

'We do, my lord,' he said.

Gaunt looked back at the hatch. The rain was still falling.

'Someone check on the transport,' he said. Sancto made to move, but Kazader sternly broke line, held up a hand to halt the Scion, and strode out into the rain.

'And keep him in check too, Barthol,' Gaunt murmured sidelong to Van Voytz. 'He's got a bigger streak of resentment in him than you have.'

'Kazader's good Guard,' Van Voytz replied. 'He's got the makings of a high career. A generalship in a few years. In fact, I dare say, he reminds me of you.'

'Exactly my point,' said Gaunt.

Gaunt returned to his escort.

'This is peculiar,' said Laksheema.

'You'll find that a lot as far as she's concerned,' Gaunt replied. He glanced at Kolea. Gol looked tense and fidgety.

'Gol?'

Kolea shrugged. 'She's not out there, sir,' he said. He nodded towards an anteroom adjoining the hall.

'Really?' asked Gaunt.

Kolea shrugged again.

'Come with me,' Gaunt said. 'Stay here,' he added firmly to the others.

The pair crossed to the side door. Gaunt saw a single raindrop glinting on the gold handle.

He opened the door. The shifting air shivered the hundred candle flames burning in the anteroom. It was dark, like twilight, but Gaunt's eyes automatically reset.

She was standing in the centre of the room. She turned to face him, and lowered the hood of her simple woollen cloak. Her combat boots and fatigues were equally worn and filthy, and the silver breastplate she wore – part of an articulated, Urdeshi-made combat carapace that also covered her arms and upper thighs – was chipped and tarnished. The only things that shone were the pommel of the sword sheathed on her left hip, the gold grip of the autopistol holstered on her right, and – somehow – her face.

Gaunt dropped to one knee, and bowed his head.

She stepped forward, took his hand, and raised him back up.

'Ibram,' she said. 'Lord Executor.'

'Beati,' he replied. 'We were attending upon you without.'

'I require no formality,' she said.

'The Warmaster sends his apologies that he could not greet you in person–'

'Again, no formality.'

'There will be feasting and ceremonies in due course,' said Gaunt. 'Once the crisis is behind us–'

'And I will endure them. For now, there's work to be done.'

She was small. She looked up into his eyes. It seemed she had not changed. Perhaps a fleck of grey in her short black hair. She looked like the Esholi girl he had first met on Herodor. Sanian. The green eyes had not altered.

Her presence had. The room felt charged, as if some powerful electric or magnetic force had been loosed upon it. There was a faint scent of islumbine.

'It has been a long while for us,' she said. 'Our paths have diverged, now they come together again.'

'I hope there is a purpose to that reunion,' said Gaunt.

'Yes. To bear witness to victory. The Anarch is broken.'

'He fights on.'

'And so he is at his most dangerous. Together we will prevail, for the Throne. I faced him. He set a trap for me, but I confounded it and I hurt him.'

'You did?'

'After Ghereppan. We broke his malicious efforts there. Shattered them and shattered his control of the field. Immediately, I pushed on into Oureppan, believing it to be his stronghold. It was headstrong, I suppose. But there was such a chance. Not just to vanquish him on the field of war and drive his forces to rout, but to finish him.'

Gaunt realised she looked very tired. She had come to Eltath directly from the heat of combat. She had not taken time to rest or clear her mind. He wondered how inexhaustible her divine strength really was.

'I led an assault on the Pinnacle Spire at Oureppan early yesterday. It was a trap laid for me. A warp snare. But it failed. He fled. His ship was as damaged as he was. He has hidden to heal his wounds.'

'But he's close?'

'Too close. Our focus shifts here now. The last part of this business.'

'Your forces?'

'Are moving up country. I have left good people in charge. Ghereppan is secured. Oureppan will be by tomorrow. The brigades that stood with me there are now driving the Archenemy out of Lartane and the Northern Claves. They will be with us in, perhaps, ten days. I wanted to lead them in person, but the Warmaster summoned me.'

'And you came.'

'Of course.'

Gaunt became aware that there were others in the room. Two Guard soldiers, standing outside the ring of candles. They had assault weapons braced and ready across their chests. One was a small woman with an angular face and glossy dark hair. She wore the black-and-mulberry long coat of the Jovani Vanguard, and Gaunt noticed the insignia of the Collegia Tactica on her collar. The other was a man, his simple battle dress dark and ragged.

For a moment, Gaunt thought–

The Beati turned, and gestured to them to stand down. 'My seconds,' she said to Gaunt. 'Captain Auerben and Major Sariadzi. All the rest of my chosen people are with the main force moving north.'

The pair put up their weapons, and saluted, the simple salute of troops who were weary from the field and who had seen everything. They had marched with the Saint. A Lord Executor was nothing impressive.

'My lord,' they both said.

Gaunt took their salute.

'You remember my officer, Major Kolea–' he began.

The Beati had already turned to Kolea with a bright smile.

'Gol,' she said.

He tried to bow again, but she took his wrists and kept him on his feet.

'It is good to see you,' she said.

'Is it?' asked Gaunt.

She glanced at him sideways with a quizzical smile.

'I crave your indulgence for a moment, Beati,' Gaunt said. He pulled open the anteroom door and called out into the reception hall.

'Inquisitor?'

Laksheema strode in, followed by Grae. Gaunt closed the door in the faces of Van Voytz and anyone else following.

Grae and Laksheema stared at the Beati for a moment, as if surprised at the sight of her. It took a second for them to register the magnitude of her presence and see she was much more than a scruffy girl dressed like a gutter-trench auxiliary.

Grae dropped to his knee. Laksheema bowed respectfully. Gaunt saw an involuntary tear welling in her eye.

'Introductions can wait,' Gaunt said. 'Beati, I want you to vouch for this man, for Gol, in front of these people. Let them witness it.'

'And if you can't vouch for me,' said Kolea, 'then speak that truth too. Right here. Let it be over with.'

The Beati frowned. She looked at Kolea with deep intent, as if she was seeing through him. He averted his eyes, flinching like a man waiting in a foxhole for a shell to fall.

She stepped closer to him, uncoupling the cuff-lock of her carapace unit and removing the glove. With a bare hand, she reached up, and turned his face to look at her. She ran her fingers down his cheek, then traced lines up across his scalp, reading the map of his old scars beneath his hairline.

'Know that I know this man,' she said softly. 'From Herodor. He has remarkable courage, but then so do many of the infamous Ghosts, not least their commander. But in Gol Kolea of Vervunhive, there is a singular strength. A fortitude I've seen in only one in every hundred thousand. In you, Sariadzi, that day on Caliber Beach.'

Behind her, the solemn major blushed slightly.

'And perhaps you, Auerben,' she added. 'We have not known each other long, but I sense your potential.'

The woman laughed. The olive skin of her face was marked from collar to cheekbone by an old pyrochemical burn.

'I'll see what I can do, my lady,' said Auerben in a dry rasp.

'This strength is something I yearn for,' said the Beati. 'It is... I can't describe it. But those I choose to be close to me, those I make my seconds and my instruments, they all have it. And Gol Kolea was, I think, the first instrument I made.'

The Beati looked at Laksheema.

'You have doubts, lady,' she said. 'I see them in you. You are wary.'

'Major Kolea's reputation is formidable,' said Laksheema, 'but there are concerns that the Ruinous Powers have touched him. Made him a conduit...'

The Beati shook her head.

'No,' she said flatly. 'Well, the darkness has touched him. Burned him. Tormented him. But he is not of its part. The fortitude remains intact. You have no reason to mistrust him.'

She withdrew her hand. Tears were streaming down Gol's face.

'I think that will be satisfactory,' Gaunt said to Laksheema.

The inquisitor paused.

'I cannot question that verdict, my lord,' she replied. She wiped the corner of her eye with her knuckle.

'No apology offered?' asked Gaunt.

'She should not apologise for doing her duty,' said the Beati. She glanced at Laksheema. 'But Major Kolea should now be taken into your circle of trust.'

Laksheema nodded.

'Wait outside,' Gaunt told Laksheema and Grae. As they withdrew, he turned to Kolea.

'Your mind at rest now?' he asked.

Kolea nodded.

'Then go down. See to the company here. See your children.'

Kolea nodded again. 'Thank you–' he began to say.

Gaunt shook his head.

'Get on with you,' he said.

Kolea smiled, rubbed his reddened eyes vigorously, and walked out.

'There are things going on here,' said the Beati. 'For such great suspicions to exist, for such–'

'There are,' said Gaunt. 'We need to talk. At length.'

He hesitated.

'I wondered,' he said. 'When you came here, I wondered who would be with you. I wondered if Brin–'

She placed a hand on his arm.

'Brin Milo has gone,' she said gently. 'I'm sorry, Ibram. He stood with me during the assault on Oureppan. Brave to the last. He, and many others, including a warrior you know. Holofurnace of the Iron Snakes. It was a hellish fight. We won the day and hurt the Anarch Magister, but they were lost in that struggle. Caught in the warp snare and never recovered.'

The Beati gestured to Sariadzi, who stepped forward with a small bundle wrapped in a khaki ground sheet. She took it and handed it to Gaunt.

'Just... yesterday?' Gaunt asked. 'Milo died yesterday? After all these years, and–'

The Beati nodded. 'I have not had time to rationalise the loss,' she said quietly. 'Brin stood at my side longer than any other. I will grieve when this war permits me space to do so.'

She pressed Gaunt's hands around the bundle.

'I felt I should bring these for you,' she said.

Gaunt looked down, and slowly unwrapped the bundle. It was a set of Tanith pipes, old and worn, the same set Brin Milo had been playing the day Gaunt first met him.

EIGHT

DEPLOYMENT

'Well, Throne be blessed,' said Blenner. 'Major Kolea? Back from the dead?'

'Back from somewhere,' replied Kolea.

'Well, welcome anyway,' said Blenner. He offered up a little shrug, suggesting he was about to give Kolea a brotherly embrace, but Kolea looked distant. Blenner turned the shrug into a smoothing of his tunic, as if that's all he had intended to do in the first place. 'Welcome to our new home.'

Kolea glanced around. Blenner was the first person he had encountered since descending to the undercroft.

'Temporary home,' he said. 'Our homes are always temporary.'

'Well, that's indeed the truth of it,' Blenner replied cheerfully. 'Ever marching on, no bed to call our own. But this is better than some. I recall a billet on Sorclore where the lice, I tell you–'

'What's the smell?' asked Kolea.

'Yes, there is a smell,' said Blenner. 'An aroma. Latrines, I gather. Backing up. It's the fething weather.'

Kolea glanced around at the whitewashed stonework. The overhead lamps ticked and flickered.

'And the lights?'

'Another maintenance issue, I gather.'

'What are our numbers here?' Kolea asked. 'I was told two companies...'

'Uhm, E Company and V Company, along with the retinue, of course.'

'And they're all accommodated? Needs met?'

'Well, Major Baskevyl has that in hand. That and the maintenance issues. I gather–'

'You gather?' asked Kolea. 'You seem to gather a lot, commissar, but nothing seems gathered to me. You must be one of the ranking officers here. Why aren't you supporting Bask and getting things fixed?'

Blenner looked stung. 'I do what I can, major,' he said, then added, 'What they'll let me do.'

'What does that mean?'

Blenner dropped his gaze and his voice. He seemed miserable. Four women from the retinue went past, carrying baskets of laundry. When Blenner spoke, it had an air of confidentiality.

'Did you hear about Low Keen?' he asked.

'Yes, briefly. Gendler and Wilder. And Ezra.'

'Well, it's put a stink on things,' said Blenner. 'On me. Just now, I am not regarded with the same warmth as I once enjoyed.'

'You did your job, didn't you?'

'It's not a popular job. The Belladon–'

'It's a dirty job, is what you mean?'

Blenner nodded. Kolea eyed him. He'd never thought Vaynom Blenner much of a soldier, and his lack of discipline made him a poor discipline officer. Kolea suspected he'd only ever become part of the company because he and Gaunt went back. Now Gaunt was elevated above the Tanith, Blenner had no ally to hand, no shadow to lurk in. His chief value had always been his endless cheer and informal conduct, which Kolea had to admit had been an asset to morale at times. Even that seemed dimmed.

'A dirty job indeed,' Blenner said.

Kolea felt a pang of pity for the man. Blenner was good for little, but Kolea knew all too sharply what it felt like to lose status and relevance, or at least to stand on the brink of that.

'Bask doesn't trust you?' he asked.

'No, and I don't blame him,' said Blenner. 'No one seems to. I'm sort of out of the loop a little. Shunned, you might say. Throne knows, I'm–'

He shrugged, as if unwilling to finish any searching self-reflection.

'Good old Vaynom, you know,' he said with a half-smile. 'Good for a laugh. Fond of a drink. Fun to have around until the laughing stops.'

'Do you know what I think?' Kolea asked.

'Please tell, sir,' said Blenner.

'I think it's shock.'

'Mine?' asked Blenner.

'Theirs,' Kolea replied. 'You have a reputation for... good humour. People forget you're a commissar. You just reminded them. You executed a killer. You upheld the dictats and discipline of the Astra Militarum. You showed your true self to them. Give them a few days to reconcile that with the Blenner they know.'

'Well, I suppose. That's kind of you to say.'

'And there are always duties,' said Kolea. 'Gendler was Meryn's man, so I'd be looking at Meryn pretty hard right now if I was a commissar.'

'Ah, well, ah... Fazekiel is in charge of the investigation,' said Blenner nervously. 'I can't be involved in that, seeing as I was the one that pulled the trigger and all...'

'I suppose,' said Kolea. 'But there's always other work. You don't have to be asked. Do the asking yourself. For a start, it smells like there are drains to be unblocked.'

'I'm not unblocking drains, major,' said Blenner with a waspish smile.

'No, but you can order someone to,' said Kolea. 'Get on with things and make this situation better. Show them you don't care what they think of you.'

'Sage counsel, sir, thank you.'

'Blenner?'

Blenner looked at him.

'You did your job, and you saved her, didn't you?'

'I did, yes.'

'Gaunt's daughter, Blenner.'

'Ah, Throne knows what that maniac Gendler might have done...'

'Take pride in that, then. Gaunt knows what you did. Throne above, I know what it's like to be a father. Despite everything.'

'Despite...?' Blenner asked.

'What I mean is, that's a bond that ties a man's soul. Children. The future, and all that. If Gendler had threatened Yoncy, or Dal, I'd like to think a good man like you would have stood up to defend them. And I'd be blessed thankful for that. You did your job.'

Blenner looked almost embarrassed. Or ashamed. It was hard to read the expression on his face. For a moment, Kolea thought the commissar was going to blurt something out, as if he carried some awful burden he needed to set down.

'Major,' he said. His voice was hesitant. 'Gol, I–'

Raised voices suddenly echoed down the hallway, and they both looked around.

'Someone's annoyed,' said Blenner with forced lightness.

'Indeed.' Kolea looked back at Blenner. 'You were going to say something.'

'No, nothing,' Blenner laughed. 'Nothing, nothing. Just an idle... Really nothing.'

'All right,' said Kolea. 'Let's see what this is.'

Their spur of the undercroft hallway met another coming in from the vaults to the left. Baskevyl was arguing with a Munitorum overseer, with Bonin and Yerolemew looking on. The overseer's three man work crew, lugging their equipment panniers and bulky in their yellow overalls, stood sheepishly behind their boss. A small crowd of women and support staff from the retinue was gathering to watch.

'There's nothing to unblock, sir!' the overseer snapped.

'There fething well must be!' Baskevyl snarled back.

'I'm telling you, I know my trade,' the overseer retorted.

'Fifteen centimetres of soil-water in the second and third billet halls would seem to suggest otherwise,' said Bonin.

'Do I tell you how to fight?' asked the overseer.

'Would you like to?' asked Bonin, stepping forward.

'Whoa,' said Yerolemew, arresting Bonin's arm with a tight grip.

'Yeah, listen to the old chap,' the overseer said. 'We haven't come down here to do no brawling.'

'You misunderstand,' the old bandmaster told him. 'I just wanted it fair. Start with me, and see how you get on against a one-armed man. Then you can have a crack at the big time.'

The crowd laughed at this. The overseer blinked rapidly.

'We've checked the drains through to the north outfall,' he said. 'There's nothing blocked. I don't know where the water's coming from.'

'What about the lights?' asked Baskevyl.

'Circuit systems is on a different docket,' said the overseer. 'My docket says waste overflow.'

'Your docket is about to say "ow, my face hurts", said Yerolemew.

'Gentlemen,' said Kolea, stepping in.

They looked at him. A broad smile crossed Baskevyl's face.

'Gol,' he said, and gave Kolea a hug. Blenner looked on from the edge of the group. That was how good comrades greeted each other. He sighed.

'Back on duty?' Baskevyl asked.

'Back on the slog,' said Kolea. 'And not before time, looks like.' He glanced at the overseer. 'What's your name?' he asked.

'Taskane,' the man replied. 'Technician, first class.'

'I'm Kolea. Major Kolea. My company, we were pretty pleased to be staying in a palace for the duration. But it's hardly palatial.'

'Well, I grant you–'

'Taskane, I know you've got orders. Dockets, in fact. So have I. The Lord Executor wants his personal regiment well taken care of.'

'The Lord Executor?' asked Taskane.

'You've heard of him?'

'Well, of course.'

'He's an absolute bastard,' said Kolea. 'Kill you as soon as look at you. We don't want that. We don't want complaint reports filed with names on them, do we? What's that form again?'

'K 50715 F,' said Blenner quickly, trying not to grin.

'That's the very one, commissar,' said Kolea. 'Thank you. Oh, and commissar? Please keep your weapon holstered. This isn't a discipline matter.' He looked at Taskane and pulled a face. 'He's a right bastard too,' he whispered. 'We don't want to get him riled up.'

'We do not, sir,' said Taskane.

'So we've got water, backflooding.'

'I explained this, sir.'

'Soil water too, so from the latrines not the drinking supply. So that's a hygiene matter, which will bring in the Medicae.'

'I've explained,' said Taskane. 'It's the weather. Unseasonal quantities of rain, backing up the waste flows. We've checked the pipework.'

'You could check it again, though?' asked Kolea. 'I mean, a thorough double-check. Thorough never hurt, did it? Then maybe pole it out with extenders. Run a rod right through?'

'I could do that...' Taskane began.

'Then flush the whole system with a chem-sluice. It's old, stone built, so there's no danger of corroding metal pipe. And if that fails, you could set up a pump or two, and evacuate the flood water using suction tubes.'

Taskane hesitated. 'How come you know so much?' he asked.

'I was a miner before I took to soldiering,' said Kolea. 'I know how to dry-down a flooded section. Lives depended on it.'

'Well, I can imagine...'

'But I'm no expert,' said Kolea. 'Not municipal, like this. That's your area. I'll bet with your skills, you can get this handled by nightfall.'

'We'll get to it, sir,' said Taskane. He glanced at his men and directed them back the way they'd come. 'And we'll take a look at the circuit system too,' said Taskane. 'The problems could be related.'

'I appreciate it, overseer,' said Kolea. 'The Emperor rewards diligent service.'

The overseer and his team trudged back down the hall towards the flooded section.

'Direct orders from the Lord Executor?' Bonin asked.

'I may have re-worked the actual truth a little there,' Kolea said with a smile. 'Then again, I think there was a little invention at work with the complaint forms too.'

Blenner winked. 'Made the whole fething thing up,' he said.

'It's good to have you back,' Baskevyl said to Kolea.

'It is.'

Kolea glanced around. Dalin had appeared, gently pushing his way through the amused crowd of onlookers.

'Hello, son,' said Gol.

The morning showed no signs of ending. From the darkness outside the chamber windows, it looked like it was night already, and they had sat through the entire day, but Merity knew that was just the storm hanging over Eltath, a turbulent, rain-belting blackness that had despatched any sign of daylight.

Senior Tactician Biota had seized the room 'by order of the Lord Executor,' a phrase he seemed to enjoy using. The chamber was a prayer chapel adjoining the hub of the main war room, a vast place teeming with people that Merity had only glimpsed as they had gone past it.

The chapel was small, but a cogitation station and a strategium display had been brought in, along with an old, solid table that could accommodate ten. As part of the war room area, the chapel was screened and proofed against scanning and detection. The trunking on all the device cables was thick and reinforced, there was a small back-up power unit, and the walls had been crudely over-boarded with panels of bare flakboard that sandwiched suppression materials against the original stonework. Even the windows had been treated with anti-invasive dyes, which further darkened them, adding to the gloom, though Merity could still see the shifting speckle of raindrops striking them.

The back-up power unit was also an asset. Main palace power kept fluctuating, and twice during the morning had blink-failed entirely, causing displays to go dark. Biota had taken to kicking the power unit automatically every time the lights dimmed, to make it whirr into action. It had become a reflex gesture: he did it even when he was talking, without even looking at it.

She quite liked Biota. She believed his name was Antonid. He was a veteran, but no soldier. The small, bespectacled man had spent his career in the Departmento Tacticae, and he seemed fiercely clever, though his people skills were clumsy. She suspected he was the cleverest man she had ever met. Throughout the morning, he had led the way through a slew of documents, discussing everything from 'geographical suitability' to 'Munitorum

Asset efficiency', and displayed a knowledge of everything. He didn't even need to consult lists to be able to name, with accuracy, specific divisions, companies, unit commanders, or the numbers of men active in any bracket. Now he was leading the way through a review of orbital images, pointing out details she wasn't able to detect.

It was fascinating, yet still boring. Merity had a decent general grasp of the situation at Eltath, and on Urdesh at large, but the minutiae were lost on her. She could barely follow the logistic data, the deployment specifics, or the tactical nuance. Biota's team had spent ten minutes debating the weight tolerance of a single bridge in Zarakppan.

But she had always been fascinated by the sight of people, expert people, doing what they did best. There was a wonder to it. And these individuals, hand-picked by Biota to form her father's tactical cabinet, were the best. Among the best in the entire Imperium, and certainly within the crusade host.

It reminded her of the long afternoons when she had been forced to attend the congress meetings of House Chass, where matters of hive politics and house business affairs were discussed in forensic detail. Now, as then, she was but a witness. Beltayn had assured her she would come to grasp the finer points soon enough. She certainly had nothing to offer, except her attention and the promise of direct access to the Lord Executor, should the need arise.

She did not have an actual seat at the table. Biota had vaguely pointed her to a row of chairs in the corner. She started off taking notes, but Beltayn had seen her doing this and had shaken his head.

'Why?' she'd whispered.

'It'll end up in the burn box as soon as you leave the room. I'll get you an encrypted slate for tomorrow.'

Merity had put the noteblock aside, and tried to rely on her memory.

Aside from Beltayn and Biota, there were three others present. Two wore the same tacticae uniforms as Biota: a younger man named Willam Reece, who had the darkest skin she'd ever seen, and a rather tall, haughty woman called Geneve Holt. Neither seemed to smile, ever, and they matched Biota's pace and knowledge detail for detail.

The other person was a fierce, body-armoured Tempestus Scion called Relf. Relf had been assigned to guard Merity, and the Scion had taken it upon herself to remain standing throughout, at duty beside the door. Biota had broken his flow several times to offer the Scion a seat.

'Thank you, no,' Relf had replied each time.

Eventually, around mid-morning, Biota had insisted she sit down.

'You're in my eye-line every time I look at the display,' he said.

'I would prefer to stand,' Relf had replied. 'Standing, I can react more swiftly to danger presenting at the doorway.'

'If danger presents at the doorway, then the palace has fallen,' remarked Holt, 'and then we're all screwed, and you being here will make little odds.'

Reece had actually laughed at this.

'Take a seat, Scion,' Biota had said. 'I insist. By order of the Lord Executor.'

Relf had, reluctantly, sat, though she had taken Merity's chair and forced Merity to shift one seat down so that Relf could be between her and the doorway.

Merity hadn't argued. She was used to this kind of protection work. It wasn't the first time she'd had a lifeward.

Biota was finishing up the orbital scans when there was a knock at the door. Relf answered immediately, and after some wary discussion with the porters, admitted a very fierce woman in the uniform of a lord militant.

'Ah, Marshal Tzara,' said Biota. 'We're ready for your presentation. Please, take a seat.'

Tzara, het-chieftain of the Keyzon host and Mistress of the Seventh Army, eyed the chapel room and its occupants stiffly.

'The Lord Executor asked me to report to you and deliver yesterday's data from the suppression in the Northern Claves. I'm not sure why I couldn't send an adjutant to do this, nor why I am asked to report to a broom cupboard.'

'The Lord Executor wants the chain of command kept as short as possible, Marshal,' Biota replied. 'Senior officer briefings only, to reduce data dispersal and the risk of breaks in the confidence chain. Reporting to me, you may consider yourself reporting to the Lord Executor himself.'

'This is undignified,' said Tzara. 'This is his... tactical cabinet?'

'Yes, well...' Biota faltered slightly.

'Triage,' Beltayn hissed at him.

'You have requested his audience several times, and it was granted this morning,' said Biota.

'Indeed–' Tzara began.

'One does not need to be an expert on human behaviour to see that you want to ingratiate yourself with the new First Lord.'

'Is that so?' Tzara said. The tone of her voice dropped the temperature in the room.

'Well, yes,' said Biota. 'No one likes to fall from grace.'

'I have not fallen from grace,' Tzara snarled.

'No,' said Biota, 'but the precipice is close and sheer. You backed others in the move to disempower Macaroth. You've held on to your position, like Lord Blackwood and Lord Cybon, but there is a cloud over you. You need an ally, and the Lord Executor is the best ally to have. So please, take a seat. Consider my polite request an order of the Lord Executor.'

Tzara sat down.

'He really likes saying that,' Merity whispered to the Scion beside her. Relf trembled slightly. Merity realised the Scion was trying to suppress a snigger.

'Please walk us through yesterday's efforts in the Clave theatre,' said Biota. 'Be as specific as possible. We have received a summary document, but you will have detailed lists of enemy strengths and so on.'

Marshal Tzara produced a data-slate from her belt pouch. She took a last, sneering look around the room.

'The Astra Militarum has protocols,' she remarked. 'I fear they are being forgotten. There is a common line trooper here.'

She glanced at Beltayn, who suddenly found his notes fascinating.

'And as for her,' Tzara added, nodding in Merity's direction. 'I did not realise that the Guard had become a family business.'

'I was asked to attend,' Merity replied before Biota could answer.

'By your father,' said Tzara. 'The Guard operates through excellence. Training, experience, and hard-won seniority. Not nepotism.'

Merity felt her cheeks flush hot.

'I'm sure it does, ma'am,' she replied. 'I'm sure that's why the third, ninth and fourteenth companies of the Keyzon host are commanded by your sons.'

Tzara blinked. Her mouth formed a sharp, pursed, horizontal line.

'Ballsy,' she remarked, and turned back to Biota.

Biota had removed his spectacles and was looking at Merity with a frown.

'We reviewed the disposition of the Keyzon about four hours ago,' he said. 'You remembered that detail?'

'I'm trying to remember everything I can, sir,' said Merity. 'So there's some point in me being here.'

Biota raised his eyebrows, put his spectacles back on and turned back to the table.

'Right, let's continue,' he said. 'Marshal, kindly run us through–'

There was another knock at the chamber door.

'If that's Lugo, he's an hour early,' snapped Biota.

Relf answered the door. 'It's a commissar,' she reported stiffly. 'Requesting my lady Chass.'

'I'll step out so you can carry on,' said Merity, getting up. She went to the door as Tzara began her report.

It was Fazekiel.

Merity stepped into the hallway. Relf followed.

'No need,' Merity said.

'I'll say what's needed,' Relf replied. She closed the door behind them, then stood with her back to it, gazing at the wall opposite.

'I'm sorry to interrupt,' said Fazekiel. 'I see you're busy.'

'How can I help?'

'I'm still conducting the investigation. I want to re-interview everybody involved. Blenner, Meryn, you. Just go over it again.'

'There's nothing much I can add that you don't already have,' Merity replied. 'I was unconscious during the... the murders.'

'Well,' said Fazekiel, 'your memory might throw up something, even if it doesn't seem pertinent to you.'

'Her memory's very good, it seems,' said Relf from behind them.

'I don't know, commissar,' said Merity.

'Well, think about it,' said Fazekiel. 'I'm based in the undercroft with the regiment billet. If you think of anything, come and find me. Anything at all, all right?'

Merity nodded.

'And maybe tomorrow, when you're not tied up, we can run another interview just for the record.'

'Of course,' said Merity.

Fazekiel nodded.

'Thank you, ma'am,' she said. 'I won't keep you.'

An air battle was underway to the south. Most of it was hidden by the low cloud cover of the rainstorm, but they could hear the blow-torch growl of thrusters and odd pops and crackles. Occasionally, a white dart would become visible, rolling and swooping against the black clouds, a canopy briefly catching the sun. Varl had told her they were Lightnings, probably out of Zarak East, running an interdiction patrol to maintain Eltath airspace. Curth didn't know anything about that, but she knew that a skirmish was underway. She sat in the cab of the cargo-10, reviewing her medical reports, but the sporadic noise of the battle kept drawing her attention.

Something flashed. A silver dot, about five kilometres west. She saw it screw-roll down out of a great dark, buttress of low cloud, blurred by the rain. A flurry of tiny lights suddenly surrounded it, a cloud like fireflies or sparks cast up by a bonfire. They swirled for a second, then streaked away, lost in the cloud. A moment later, the entire cloud bank was back-lit by a fierce series of yellow flashes, flames blooming behind the dark vapour. The staggered pops of the multiple detonations reached her after a second. By then, the silver dot had gone. She saw something drop out of the cloud-bank. A streak of fire that fell straight down, the sunlight flashing off wing panels as they folded around the fireball and fluttered away. The streak of fire vanished behind the rooftops.

Someone rapped at the window of the cab door.

Curth got out and climbed down. The rain was worse than before.

'They're all loaded and secure,' Kolding told her.

'Thank you,' she said.

'I can go with them,' Kolding offered.

'Colonel Rawne's ordered me to do it, so...' she shrugged.

Curth's inclination was to move with the main force, but they were carrying forty casualties from the action at the Tulkar Batteries, and nine were critical. Her oath as a doctor made those souls her responsibility, and her position as the regiment's chief medicae landed the duty firmly in her lap. Rawne knew that. The casualties needed more than a field station. They needed the surgical and intensive facilities of the Urdeshic Palace.

Across the shattered street, beyond the line of waiting transports, Rawne was briefing the officers. The Ghost companies were drawn up along the length of the street, standing at loose order, resting, and using the blown-out shop fronts as partial cover from the downpour.

'Major Pasha has command of the primary group,' Rawne said.

'We can move at once, sir,' Yve Petrushkevskaya replied confidently. 'Three hours to the location, barring mishaps.'

Rawne nodded. 'Asa Elam and Ferdy Kolosim are your line officers. Chain of command flows through them. Pasha gets final operational say. All clear?'

The company commanders all nodded.

'First section, B Company, goes with me to the secondary,' Rawne continued.

'Just one section?' asked Obel.

'Don't question me,' Rawne replied.

'But it's a fair question,' said Criid.

'We're stretched as it is,' Rawne replied. 'The primary objective needs everything we can throw at it, which is fething little as it stands. The Suicide Kings have handled him before, so we can handle him now. In and out.'

First section, B Company had become known as the Suicide Kings when the regiment first took custody of the enemy asset known as the pheguth. No one doubted they had the best level of experience.

'But if there's trouble...' Kolosim began.

'Trouble can kiss my Tanith arse,' Rawne replied. 'Get your companies up and ready to move. That's it.'

'No cheery words of inspiration, sir?' asked Theiss.

Rawne paused. 'Am I known for that sort of thing?' he asked.

'No,' Theiss admitted with a grin.

'Then imagine me sending you thoughts and prayers,' Rawne said.

The officers laughed.

'I tell you what,' said Rawne. 'These orders come directly from Gaunt. That should be enough for all of you. Feth, imagine it's him standing here briefing you in this fething rain. I'd prefer that. I'd be much happier sitting in the palace with my boots up on a desk. Get on with it.'

The group broke up. The company officers – Criid, Kolosim, Theiss, Arcuda, Elam, Obel, Spetnin and the rest – strode back to their waiting men, shouting brisk orders. The drenched Ghosts began getting to their feet and shouldering their packs. Ludd moved among them, yelling strong words of encouragement.

Rawne turned and saw Curth waiting.

'Ready to go?' he asked.

'Honestly,' she said, 'I'd be happier going with Pasha's formation. It's bound to get ugly.'

'Pasha will have Kolding and the corpsmen,' said Rawne. 'Besides, this isn't about your preference. I gave you an order.'

'You did.'

'No disrespect to Kolding, but I think you're the only one who can get them to the palace alive.'

'You're probably right.'

'Now, about an escort,' he said.

Curth shook her head. 'You need everyone you can get. Don't waste anyone on a guard duty. We can get there.'

He looked at her.

'I'm serious,' she said. 'We're making a run to the palace through what should be friendly territory. We're not heading into danger. You are.'

'All right,' he said.

Curth turned away, then looked back at him, wiping rain off her face.

'I don't know what this is about,' she said. 'I don't know what you're getting into...'

'Join the club,' Rawne replied.

She rested her hand on his arm gently.

'Just don't die,' she said.

'I'll see how that goes,' he replied.

She turned and walked back to the waiting transports.

'Start them up!' he heard her shout.

The heat was fierce. Jan Jerik could feel the sweat pooling in his boots. He paused, wiping the visor of his mask, to check the duct number stencilled on the wall.

'This way,' he said, his voice muffled.

There was a junction ahead. The main shaft of the vent continued northwest. To the left was a grating mouth that had rusted open. The geotherm network had been built a long time ago, and the secondary ducts were not well-maintained. Only the grates of the principal ducts still operated, opening and closing huge iris valves in response to over- and under-pressure demands.

Jan Jerik sloshed to a halt in the soup of mineral swill that flowed along the base of the duct. He raised his lantern, and the light illuminated the old grating through the rolling steam.

'Here is your division,' he said.

Corrod and Hadrel stepped forward. The sirdar consulted his chart. Jan Jerik could hear the wet, rasping respiration of their mucus-thick snouts.

'This runs to the secondary?' Corrod asked him.

'All the way,' Jan Jerik nodded.

Corrod and Hadrel faced each other.

'Select your team,' Corrod said.

Hadrel nodded, and began pointing at packsons in the line behind him. Seven of the Archenemy warriors split from the main group and came to stand with Hadrel.

'He dies,' said Corrod.

'He dies,' Hadrel agreed.

They both raised a palm to their mouths in a brief salute.

Corrod turned to Jan Jerik.

'The main duct takes us to the primary?' he asked.

'Yes,' said Jan Jerik. 'I'll show you–'

'No,' said Corrod. 'You, and your men, you are no longer needed. We will find the way from here.'

'But we've not yet–' Jan Jerik began.

'Go back. You've done your part. Forget us. Say nothing. If the warp approves our endeavour, then we will return, and the voice of our lord will reward those who have served him in this. The courage of House Ghentethi will not be forgotten.'

'Well,' the ordinate wavered. 'His voice... his voice drowns out all others.'

'Go back now,' said Corrod.

Jan Jerik nodded. He signalled his men and they began sloshing their way back down the line, returning the way they had come. He looked over his shoulder, and saw Hadrel leading his team into the rusted grating.

He kept walking. At every step, he expected Corrod's daemon-men to fall on him from behind, to butcher him and his subordinates to ensure their silence.

No strikes came, but he would never shake the feeling of death at his heels, not for the rest of his life.

He looked back again. Through the darkness and steam, neon eyes watched his departure.

'You're all right then?' Kolea asked.

'Yes,' Dalin nodded. 'You?'

'It's been eventful,' said Kolea. 'Yoncy?'

'She's around here somewhere,' said Dalin. 'She's a little shaken.'

'I'd like to see her,' said Kolea. 'She'll be scared, especially as Tona's not here. Look...'

'What?'

Kolea looked uncomfortable. 'Dal, I've... I've never been much of a father to you, to either of you–'

Dalin laughed and held up a hand. 'Seriously?' he said. 'Where's all this sentimental crap coming from? This isn't the time or the place, and it probably never will be. We're Ghosts. This is our life–'

'I just wanted to say–' Kolea insisted, quietly urgent.

'You don't need to,' said Dalin. 'What's brought this on? It's not the end of the world... well, no more than it ever is.'

Kolea smiled. 'Things just don't get said, you know?' he replied. 'Not the things that matter. It's always too late. A day goes by and suddenly, someone's not there to speak to any more. So many times over the years, I've realised it's too late to talk to somebody.'

'Are you expecting to die?' Dalin asked.

'No.'

'Are you expecting me to die?'

'No,' said Kolea. He shrugged. 'My mind's been a jumble for a few weeks now. Gaunt helped me get it straight. Yoncy's really all right?'

'Seems to be.'

'Dal, have you ever thought there's something different about her?'

'She's my sister. She drives me mad.'

'I'd better find her,' said Kolea. 'She'll probably hear me out with more patience than you.'

'Look, I appreciate what you were trying–'

'Dal, feth take the sentiment of it, I want you to know... you and your sister... I'd walk into hell for you both. I mean it. While there's breath in me, I'll stand between you and anything–'

'I know,' said Dalin.

'Good then.'

'Can we go back to being normal now? This is awkward.'

Kolea laughed.

'Gol!' Baskevyl's voice echoed down the hallway. Kolea turned and, past two Munitorum workmen rolling out flexible piping for a pump unit, he saw Baskevyl wave to him and brandish a bottle.

'Come and join us!' Baskevyl called out.

Kolea shrugged a 'maybe'.

'Go on,' said Dalin. 'Do you good. I'll go and find Yoncy and bring her round to you.'

'All right. I really want to see her.'

Fazekiel appeared, striding down the hallway, stepping neatly over the unrolling pipes.

'The smell hasn't got any better, then?' she said.

'They're working on it,' said Kolea.

'Nice to have you back, major,' she said. 'Trooper Dalin?'

'Yes, ma'am?'

'I'd like some time with you. In half an hour or so?'

'Yes, ma'am. Concerning?'

'The incident at the billet. You were the last one with... Felyx before the attack.'

'Is she all right?' Dalin asked. 'Merity, I mean?'

'She seems fine.'

'I've got an errand to run. Half an hour, then?'

Fazekiel nodded. The three of them went their separate ways.

In a side room nearby, Meryn leaned against the cold stone wall beside the open door.

'She's relentless,' he said quietly.

Blenner didn't reply. He sat on the dirty cot, and knocked back a pill with a swig of Meryn's amasec.

'That's right,' said Meryn. 'You swallow it. Keep calm.'

Blenner looked at him with poorly disguised contempt.

'We're good, Vaynom,' said Meryn. 'For now. But she'll come back to both of us too. More questions. So keep the story straight and keep it simple.'

Blenner rose to his feet. 'Sometimes,' he said, 'you have to ask yourself if it's worth it. Throne knows, I don't want to lose what I have. And forget a shit-duty posting or a demotion. This? It'd be a headshot for me.'

He looked at Meryn.

'But Luna's good. She's got a ferocious eye for detail,' he said. 'I don't think she can catch anything, but if she does–'

'We stick to the story.'

'And live with the guilt? I've lived with shame most of my career, Flyn, one way or another. But guilt? Guilt this heavy?'

'Take another pill, Blenner,' said Meryn.

'Don't you just ever want to let it go?' Blenner asked. 'No matter the consequences, just let it all out? Get that weight off you?'

'No,' said Meryn. 'Because I'm not a fething idiot.'

Blenner smiled sadly. 'No, I don't suppose you are.'

'Are you going to crack on me?' asked Meryn. 'You sound like a coward who's close to giving up. But then, you always have. You suddenly going to grow a fething spine and face the music?'

Blenner shook his head. 'No,' he said. 'Actually, I'm not worried about me. It's you that bothers me.'

'Me?'

'You shift stories like you change clothes, and you've got the wit to sell them too,' said Blenner. 'I think if it gets close, you'd throw me under the wheels to save yourself. Feth, you did it to that idiot Wilder. Whatever it takes to cover your arse. Throne, I can imagine it.'

Blenner put on an earnest but wheedling voice.

'"It was all Blenner's plan. We had to go along with it because he's a commissar. He threatened us with the brute force of the Prefectus. Summary execution if we didn't go along with him. And he's hooked on pills too. I was too afraid to speak up, sir, but I need to clear my conscience now..."'

Blenner smiled at Meryn.

'I can hear you doing it. Blinking those wide, handsome eyes. I mean, no one likes you, Meryn, but they all just think you're a snake. A self-serving creep. They have no idea how truly toxic you are.'

'And they won't,' said Meryn. 'Will they?'

'No,' said Blenner. He put his cap back on. 'I'll keep to the story. But you keep leaning on me, I might decide the guilt and all that shit just isn't worth it.'

He patted Meryn on the shoulder.

'Feth,' he grinned, 'maybe I am growing a spine after all. How about that?'

Luna Fazekiel had a small room at the north end of the undercroft. Just enough space for a cot and a folding desk. She had the picts laid out there, all the images she'd captured on site at Low Keen. It was a damned shame they hadn't been able to preserve the scene, and an exam of the bodies brought back from Low Keen – Gendler, Wilder and Ezra – had revealed nothing useful.

Low Keen. The very thought of that place made her tense. Aside from the Gendler case, there had been the incident with Daur's wife and the girl, Yoncy. Fazekiel had been one of the first on the scene. Something had torn bodies apart. Some monster.

She'd heard it too. She'd heard the shrieking sound it made. Fazekiel was a strong soldier, but that sound had shaken her to an extent that troubled her. It had been more than a hazard – they faced those all the time. It had stirred some primal response in her.

She hadn't slept. The memory of the shrieking sound was playing on her nerves, and she was afraid it might unlock some of the old anxieties she had spent so many years learning to contain and control.

The unknown made her worry. Data comforted her. Solid facts gave her a way to understand the world and retain agency. The Gendler case was reassuring. It helped take her mind off the mysteries she couldn't address.

She sat down, and brushed invisible dust off the lip of the desk. The picts were telling her nothing. There was no inconsistency of evidence, no clash of accounts. She'd run each interview again – Merity, Blenner, Meryn, Dalin – perhaps twice more, to see if anything shook loose. But she was already sure how her report would run. The data upheld the story Meryn and Blenner had given.

The overhead lamps flickered.

Fazekiel sighed. She wished she'd brought some food with her from the canteen. That was the second time in two days she'd forgotten to eat.

The lights flickered again.

She stood up to fiddle with the lumen element and halted. She suddenly had a really uncomfortable feeling, as though something was scratching at her eardrums and her sinuses.

She coughed and tried to clear her nose. Probably just the damp down in the undercroft getting to her–

The lights went out.

Blackness. The lights didn't flicker back on. She groped her way to the door, and peered out. The hallway was pitch black too. She could hear voices from other chambers raised in complaint.

The damn circuit fault had finally become terminal.

She fumbled her way back to her desk, reached down, and fished her stablight from her kit pack. It wouldn't switch on. She slapped it against her gloved palm and the beam speared into life, lighting a frost-blue disc on the far wall. She panned the beam around quickly. Her ear drums itched again.

The beam passed over the open doorway. For a second, it starkly lit a face staring in at her.

Fazekiel jumped in surprise.

She played the beam back.

Yoncy stood in the doorway, hands at her sides, her face expressionless. She was staring right at Fazekiel.

'Yoncy, you scared the shit out of me,' Fazekiel said.

The girl didn't answer. She stared at Fazekiel for another few seconds, then just turned and walked away.

Fazekiel got up quickly, stumbling slightly against her chair.

'Yoncy?'

She reached the doorway, and stepped out into the hallway. More voices of protest and complaint were echoing through the undercroft. The scratchy sensation in her ears was worse. She played the beam to the left, then to the right. There was no one there.

'Yoncy?'

She started to move to her left. The overhead lights suddenly buzzed and came back on. Alarms whooped for a second, then cut off. Fazekiel blinked at the glare.

Meryn stood a few metres away, wincing in the light.

'Captain,' she said.

'Oh, ma'am. I... I was just looking to see what had happened to the lights.'

'With your silver out?'

Meryn looked down, He was holding his warknife.

'Well, to be honest, I thought I heard something,' he said.

'Did you see Yoncy?'

'What? No,' said Meryn. He rubbed at his left ear.

'You feel that?' asked Fazekiel.

'What?'

'In your ears. An itch.'

He nodded.

'It reminds me of–'

She stopped short. She could feel the anxiety rising inside her and quickly focused on the mental coping strategies she'd been taught to help her deal with her obsessive nature. She shut the anxiety down.

'Of what?' said Meryn, looking at her warily.

'Go and get Baskevyl or Kolea.'

'Why?' Meryn asked.

'Something's not right,' said Fazekiel.

'What are you going to–'

'I'm going to find Yoncy. She was right here and she's probably scared. Go and get Baskevyl. Now, please.'

Meryn sheathed his warknife and hurried away.

'Advise him amber status!' she called after him.

In the wardroom, the lights fizzled back on in a brief squeal of alarms. Baskevyl was standing with a bottle in his hand.

'As I was saying...' he said.

'They haven't gone off for that long before,' said Domor.

Kolea shrugged. 'Maybe the Munitorum took them off line to reconnect or test?' he said.

'You want me to go and check?' asked Bonin.

'Well, I was about to open this precious bottle of sacra to celebrate Gol's return,' said Baskevyl. He put it down. 'But we probably should.'

The others got up from their seats around his camp table.

Yerolemew and Blenner came in from the hall outside.

'A lot of fuss in the billet halls,' said Blenner. 'That black-out was the whole undercroft.'

'Go calm them down,' Baskevyl said. 'It was just a circuit fault.'

Blenner eyed the bottle on the table. 'Private party?' he asked.

'Go calm them down, Blenner,' said Baskevyl, 'and you might get an invitation to join us.'

Blenner nodded, and hurried out.

'What's the matter with you?' Bonin asked the bandmaster.

'Can't you hear that?' Yerolemew asked.

'Hear what?' asked Domor.

Yerolemew frowned. 'Like a... whistle. A note. High pitched.'

They shook their heads.

'You've spent too many years standing beside the full brass section,' said Domor.

'You really can't hear that?' Yerolemew asked.

Bonin glanced around. He looked at the shot glasses standing on the table beside the bottle.

'What, Mach?' asked Kolea.

Bonin reached out and placed his splayed hand down on the tops of the glasses.

'They were vibrating,' he said.

'Well, it must've been that,' said Yerolemew. 'The sound's gone now.'

Bonin lifted his hand.

'Now it's back,' said Yerolemew.

'What the feth?' said Domor. The sound made him uncomfortable. It reminded him of something he'd heard recently.

'My, uh, ears itch,' said Baskevyl. 'What the gak is going on?'

Meryn hurried in. 'Commissar Fazekiel wants you,' he said to Baskevyl. 'Why?'

'Something's going on. She said amber status. She's spooked about something.'

'What?' said Domor in surprise.

'Amber?' asked Kolea. 'On what grounds?'

Meryn shrugged mutely.

'Let's get some control back into this situation, please,' said Baskevyl. 'Come on! Act like you know what you're doing. Get the retinue calmed down and secure, get the companies stood to. Shoggy, find that Munitorum work crew and ask them if they know what the problem is. Yerolemew, send a runner upstairs and find out if this is just us or the whole palace. And get them to advise Daur we seem to have a situation down here. Gol, Mach, with me–'

The lights went out again.

This time, they did not come back on.

She'd been thinking about it all the while Biota had quizzed Marshal Tzara about the integrity of the bridges and causeways serving the Zarakppan and Clantine canals.

Dalin had been waiting for her outside the showerblock. Standing guard at the door to protect her modesty. As she'd stepped into the shower pen, she'd heard his voice through the door. Dalin speaking to someone.

It was so vague. Just a partial memory she didn't feel she could trust.

But the other person had sounded like Captain Meryn.

'I'm sure this can wait,' said Relf.

'I'm not sure of anything,' said Merity. 'But Commissar Fazekiel said to report anything to her. Anything at all.'

'But now?' asked Relf, following Merity down the steep stone staircase into the undercroft.

Merity turned to her.

'Can I ask?' she said. 'Do I take orders from you, or do you simply follow me where ever I go?'

'Uhm, the latter,' replied the large Tempestus Scion.

'That's what I thought,' said Merity, and continued on her way.

They reached the bottom of the steps and followed the white-washed corridor into the chambers of the palace undercroft. Merity glimpsed the billets of the retinue, through side arches. There seemed to be some general agitation.

'It smells down here,' said Relf.

'Never mind that,' Merity said. 'Let's ask someone where Fazekiel is billetted.'

They turned a corner and Merity recoiled. The hallway floor ahead was awash with drain water. It wasn't just standing water. The frothy waste was spilling towards her rapidly, as if it was being fed gallons at a time by some serious leak or overflow.

'Come on,' said Relf.

The lights went out.

Merity froze. She heard voices crying out from the billet halls in alarm.

'There is one circumstance in which you take orders from me,' Relf said in the darkness behind her.

'Yes?'

'Get behind me and do what I say.'

'You have, honoured one, no active knowledge of the Anarch's where-abouts?' asked Van Voytz.

'No,' replied the Beati.

'Or any views as to his plan of attack?' Van Voytz added.

'No,' said the Beati.

'But he lives still?'

'He lives, Lord General,' she said.

Van Voytz stood back and glanced at Gaunt. The three of them were standing at a strategium desk in a privacy-screened gallery room overlooking the war room. Kazader and the Beati's deputies were with them. Sancto and his Scions stood guard outside.

Gaunt wasn't sure what was wrong. The Beati could be unpredictable, but in the last ten minutes, her manner had become distracted and remote. He knew she was tired. He could see it. She'd come straight from the Oureppan fight. He wished they could give her time to recuperate, but synchronising intel was a priority.

Gaunt turned to Captain Auerben. 'You've brought reports from Oureppan?'

'Yes, Lord Executor,' Auerben replied. 'Full field accounts from the victory and subsequent miracle at Ghereppan, and supplementary command reports and pict records from the raid on Pinnacle Spire.'

'Then let's upload and review those at least,' said Van Voytz. 'And maybe we should bring in Blackwood and Urienz?'

'Let's run through it first,' Gaunt said. 'Then we'll brief high command as a group. Blackwood and Urienz have got plenty to be getting on with.'

Gaunt looked at the Beati.

'Is something wrong?' he asked.

She looked up at him. He was surprised by the distance in her eyes.

'I think I hear a voice,' she said very quietly. 'Nagging at my head. His voice. Scratching...'

'What?'

'Ibram,' she said. 'A shadow is falling. Something bad is about to happen.'

'An attack?' asked Gaunt.

'No,' said the Saint. 'It's already in here with us.'

* * *

Olort led the way into the record chambers. It looked like an old library space that had been requisitioned for the Sons of Sek. Packson scribes worked at the old wooden desks, scraping bare the pages of old shipping ledgers so that they could be reused as palimpsests.

There was no electronic activity or apparatus. The dark, high-ceilinged rooms were lit only by candles and wick-lamps.

'I want information about prisoners,' Mkoll whispered to Olort.

'Prisoners?'

'You've brought plenty here. There will be lists.'

Olort looked dubious.

'When we've found that, maps and charts. Plans of the whole Fastness.'

'You sound like an etogaur planning a campaign,' said Olort.

'Maybe I am.'

'You also sound like a hopeless fool.'

'Humour this fool, and the fool won't kill you.'

Olort spoke to two of the sirdars, and was directed to a side room. It was a small space, lined with shelves, with high windows facing the hollow mountain's interior lagoon. There was a maritime desk, with an empty crystal decanter on a silver tray. Mkoll fancied this had once been the office of the port master or a shipping baron.

Mkoll pushed the heavy door shut.

'Here?' he asked.

Olort turned to the half-empty shelves. The books were all old, leatherbound ledgers. Fresh labels marked with the spiked symbols of the archenemy had been glued to their spines. Mkoll unbuckled his helmet and took it off.

Olort pulled a volume from the shelf, set it on the desk, and opened it.

'This one,' he said.

Mkoll moved closer to look. He placed the helmet on the desk beside the ledger, nodding at Olort to stand back.

The pages of the ledger had been treated and scraped to remove the old ink. Faint ghosts of the original writing remained. Over the top, fresh script had been added, the jagged characters of the Archonate's tribal tongues. Symbols adorned the margins of the palimpsest, and in some places great effort had gone into the decoration of the words and letters that began chapters or sections. Illuminated images, rendered in different coloured inks, sometimes with a hint of gold leaf or egg tempera. Beasts with horns and wings and cloven hooves peered out from the shadows behind the large capital characters.

'It will be meaningless to you, kha?' Olort asked, amused.

It was dense, and the script hard to read. But a year on Gereon had taught Oan Mkoll more than the rudiments of the spoken language. He began to turn the old pages, running his finger along. He found lists. Pages of lists, with details beside what seemed to be names.

'That word means "captives", doesn't it?' he asked.

Olort nodded.

'This gives names. These are Imperial names. Here, location of capture. The names of the Imperial units the men belonged to, where given.'

'We are thorough,' said Olort.

'There must be a thousand names here,' Mkoll said. 'And this word, this indicates induction? Or a willingness to be inducted?'

Olort stepped closer and looked at the pages.

'Kha,' he said. 'Those willing are held here...'

He slid his finger across the page.

'...the holding spaces beneath the chapter house. These others, they are resistant but promising. Otherwise, we would not have brought them here. They are held in the livestock compound.'

'A thousand or more...' murmured Mkoll, reading on.

'Do you suppose you have an army, Ghost?' Olort asked, smiling broadly. 'Is that your hopeless plan? To release them? Then what? Mobilise them to fight? Stage a revolt within the Fastness?'

'A thousand men is a thousand men,' said Mkoll.

'A thousand starving men, unarmed. Beaten. Defeated. A thousand traitor sons of the Emperor. They would not follow you. And even if they did, they would accomplish very little. Unarmed men? Broken men? If this is your plan, you are no etogaur. I say again, give up, Mah-koll. Let me deliver you. You are alone at the heart of my Anarch's bastion. The sons of the pack surround you. Give me the skzerret and discard these hopeless dreams.'

Mkoll ignored him. He skimmed on through the pages.

'Nen, I see it now,' Olort said. 'Not an army. A distraction. Kha, kha... a distraction. That's what you plan. Prisoners released, chaos and confusion. Mayhem. You care not for the lives of these captives. You would use them. Use their lives as cover for your own activities. But not escape. You would have tried that long before now. Not escape, but...'

He looked at Mkoll sharply.

'You have come to kill,' said Olort, his eyes wide. '*Nen mortekoi, ger tar Mortek*. These words you said to me. You see your fate as an opportunity.'

Mkoll continued to ignore him. He was reading on, and had come upon a small separate section divided from the other lists.

'Enkil vahakan. That's what you called me. *Those who hold the key of victory*. There are three names here.'

'So?' asked Olort with a sneer.

'Held aboard the ship,' Mkoll said. He peered closer to read the three names. He blinked in genuine surprise. 'Feth,' he murmured.

Olort lunged. The old crystal decanter smashed across the side of Mkoll's head and hurled Mkoll across the desk face-first. He rolled, blood streaming down his neck, shards of broken crystal falling off him, and dropped to the floor. Helmet and ledger fell off the desk with him.

Olort ripped the skzerret out of his hand.

'Help me here!' Olort roared in the enemy tongue. 'Help me here! Intruder! Intruder!'

NINE

BAD SHADOW

Olort stabbed down with the ritual blade. Mkoll was blinded by his own blood, which was pouring out of the scalp wound the decanter had left. His head was spinning.

Somehow, he managed to block the stab with his forearm. The edge of the skzerret sliced his sleeve and broke the skin beneath.

Still shouting for help, Olort stabbed again, and again Mkoll blocked, grabbing his knife-wrist. Olort had Mkoll pinned under him. Mkoll grabbed frantically with his free hand, seized something, and swung it.

The sirdar helmet smacked into the side of Olort's face. He lurched sideways. Mkoll hit him again, fending him off with his left arm and swinging the helmet by the chinstraps with his right.

The second blow clipped Olort off balance and made him yelp. Mkoll kicked out and sent him staggering back across the room.

Olort came back at him, hatred in his eyes. Blood was running down his cheek from a cut above the left cheekbone. He thrust in with the dagger. Mkoll, barely on his feet, blocked the thrust with the dome of the helmet, using it like a buckler. Olort jabbed again.

'In here! In here!' he was yelling in the Archenemy dialect.

The skzerret punched through the top of the helmet and dug deep. Mkoll twisted his grip and wrenched the dagger out of the damogaur's grasp. The helmet, with the dagger transfixing it, bounced away across the floor.

Wide-eyed, Olort dived for it. Mkoll went for the damogaur, landing a glancing kick that knocked the diving man down short of his target. Olort landed on the floor and scrambled for the helmet.

Mkoll dived for it too.

He got his hands on the dagger's hilt. Olort merely managed to grasp the helmet. He clawed at it. Mkoll wrenched the blade out. Olort's hands got to it too late. All he managed to grab was the blade as it slid free of the helmet. The serrated edge sliced off all the fingers of his right hand.

Olort screamed.

Mkoll smashed the dagger back down again. It punched through the side of Olort's neck. Mkoll turned his grip with a sharp jerk and tore out Olort's throat. The scream turned into a gurgle.

Mkoll rose, dagger in hand. He was dizzy and disorientated. He was drenched in his own blood, and Olort's was still pumping out across the floor in a pool of astonishing size. Mkoll heard hurried footsteps outside.

He kicked the damogaur out of the way. Olort rolled, still making ghastly sucking sounds. Mkoll opened the door. Two packson scribes were right outside. One had drawn a laspistol.

'Voi tar karog!' Mkoll yelled at them, stepping aside to let them in. They rushed in, not knowing what to expect, just that a sirdar had ordered them to assist him.

They halted. One almost slipped in the widening pool of blood. They saw a damogaur bleeding out on the floor, his throat cut through.

Mkoll punched the skzerret into the ribcage of the scribe with the gun. With his left hand, he grabbed the laspistol as the man dropped to his knees. There was no time to turn the pistol. Mkoll swung it instead, hitting the other scribe in the face with the butt of the gun. The packson reeled away, blood and spit flying from his lip, and bounced off the door.

More footsteps. Mkoll stuck the blade in his belt and stepped out into the long hallway. Two more packsons were running towards him from one direction, three more from the other. They were shouting. They had weapons. Mkoll raised the pistol and fired, cutting the approaching pair off their feet with four neat snap-shots. Then he turned smartly, and fired on the trio. He dropped one and clipped the second. The third hurled himself into the cover of a doorway. The second tried to rise, and Mkoll plugged him in the side of the head with a single bolt. The man flopped back down.

From the adjoining chambers, Mkoll could hear raised voices and the frantic ringing of handbells. The whole building was scrambling to respond.

He stepped back into the room. The scribe he'd dropped with the pistol butt was stirring and moaning. Mkoll put a shot through his head. He shoved the bodies of the packson scribes out of the way, and closed the door. There was no lock, and merely the overpainted marks where a bolt had once been screwed in place.

He looked around and made a rapid assessment. Then he dragged the bodies of the two dead scribes and piled them against the foot of the door in an awkward heap. They would hardly keep the door shut, but they'd slow down any attempts to shove it open. There was no time to check the bodies for anything useful like spare clips or keys.

He crossed to the desk, bent down, and opened the ledger, brushing splinters of decanter glass off the pages. He found the page that had surprised him, the page of enkil vahakan, and tore it out. He folded it and stuffed it in his pocket. His hands were leaving bloody finger marks on everything.

He swayed slightly, and steadied himself against the desk. There was a dull, throbbing ache behind his right eye. The scalp wound was still bleeding freely. Shaking his head, he gritted his teeth and shoved the heavy desk against the end shelves.

Olort was still twitching, staring at him with wide eyes, his bloody mouth opening and closing dumbly.

'Vahooth voi sehn,' Mkoll said. *I bless you.*

He shot Olort between the eyes.

There were more footsteps outside, raised voices, thumps at the door, an attempt to shoulder-barge the door open. The door opened a crack, but the weight of the bodies slammed it shut again. The thumping resumed. Another fierce shoulder-barge.

Mkoll clambered up on the desk, and climbed the shelves to the high windows. There was no clasp or opening, but the sea air had rotted the ancient windows in their frames long since. He pushed out a pane of glass and heard it fall and shatter somewhere far below.

Then he hauled himself up and out through the gap. Cold air met him, and a strong sea breeze. He clung to the sill. The wall dropped away sheer directly below him, but there was an adjoining tiled roof three metres down to his left.

He jumped.

Behind him, the first las-rounds tore through the door.

Baskevyl was handing out stablights from a packing crate.

'One each. Check the charge, grab a weapon, and start searching.'

'What are we looking for, sir?' asked Leyr, taking the stablight offered and testing it.

'Commissar Fazekiel, for a start,' replied Baskevyl. 'She was the one who called this amber status. Right, Meryn?'

'Yes, sir.'

'Aside from her... I don't know,' said Baskevyl.

'Is this an attack?' asked Neskon. 'I mean, has the undercroft been penetrated, or–'

'We don't know anything,' said Kolea. 'This is probably just faults in the circuit. Spread out like Bask says and take the undercroft by sections. There will be stragglers, so round them up and send them along to the exit staircase.'

The darkness felt close, as if there was no room to move or breathe. The stink of the cellar level was getting worse, but Baskevyl thought this was probably just his imagination. That, or the air-circ pumps and vents had shut down too. And the scratching in their ears was persistent. That, more than anything, made Bask feel like this was more than a technical problem.

The chamber itself possessed the eerie qualities of a bad dream. It was so lightless, it was hard to tell who you were standing next to, even though it was packed tight. As stablights flashed on, the moving beams came at haphazard angles, like bars of pale blue glare that showed frosty details but nothing of the whole. The alarms kept stuttering and squeaking in short, fitful bursts, little shrill gasps of sound that came and went, truncated. Neskon had strapped on his flamer unit, and had used the ignition burner to light tapers. He was now passing these, one by one, to Banda and Leclan so they could light the wicks of little tin box-lamps. The box-lamps issued only a dull glow, but it was more diffuse than the hard beams of the stablights.

'Pass them out,' said Leclan. 'Maybe take a bundle of them up to the stairs. The retinue haven't got many lamps.'

'Do that, Luhan,' ordered Baskevyl.

'On it, sir,' replied Trooper Luhan.

'I could take them along,' suggested Blenner.

'Luhan's doing it,' replied Baskevyl, passing a stablight to Blenner.

'Well, maybe I should at least check on the progress,' said Blenner. 'There's a lot of women and children, in the dark, trying to find their way out–'

'Yerolemew and Bonin are running the evac,' replied Baskevyl. 'They've got it covered. Help with the section search.'

'All right,' sighed Blenner. 'Of course.'

'Has anyone seen Dalin?' Kolea called out. 'Or Yoncy?'

His voice was sudden and loud. Everybody, even Baskevyl as he called the shots, had been talking low, as though louder voices might somehow offend the choking darkness that had engulfed them.

'We'll find them, Gol,' said Baskevyl. 'Come on, shift your arses and get to it!'

Shoggy Domor hadn't waited for a stablight. He'd simply flipped his bulky augmetic optics to night vision and set off.

Now he was beginning to regret responding to Baskevyl's instruction so eagerly. He could hear an agitated murmur of voices several chambers behind him as the retinue hurried to evacuate and find their way to the undercroft steps. The alarm system kept piping in sudden, unnerving squelches of sharp sound.

His heart was racing. It was unnerving. Domor could feel an unpleasant rasping in his ears, as if someone was wiggling a pin against his eardrum. He wished he'd waited for some company. He wished he'd picked up a weapon. All he had was his straight silver.

He wondered why he felt he *needed* a weapon. Was it just the non-specific amber status that had been issued? Out on the line, that usually meant bad shit was coming, but this wasn't the line. Domor didn't scare easily, and this was surely just a power-out. But the darkness was oppressive. It didn't feel like the simple absence of light. It felt like a thing in its own right, as if darkness had poured into the undercroft and filled it like black water.

'Taskane?' he called. 'Overseer Taskane?'

The blackness seemed to eat his voice.

'Commissar Fazekiel?'

Domor moved forward, seeing the world as a cold, green relief map. He moved with one hand on the wall, feeling his way even though his augmetics gave him the best sight of anyone down on the undercroft level.

'Taskane? Overseer?'

Domor jumped as the alarms sounded again. This time it was a dying shriek that ended in a long, warbling throb of defective speakers. It tailed off into nothing, but while it lasted, for five or six seconds, it sounded less like a broken, misfiring alarm system and more like a baby crying.

'Feth,' he whispered to himself.

He edged on, following the hallway that led to the latrine area. The stone wall was hard and rough under his groping hand. Just to the right, he thought, the tunnel turns and–

There was a blank stone wall ahead of him. A dead end.

Domor stood for a second, and adjusted his optics. How was that possible?

He cursed himself. You got turned around, Shoggy, he thought. You took a wrong turn. Mach Bonin will have your guts when he finds out a Tanith man got himself lost in his own fething billet.

He turned and moved back the way he had come. Stupid. Just stupid. Just nerves. They'd been in the undercroft for four days. He knew the fething way around.

Domor came back under a low lintel into one of the main billet halls. His optics showed him the rows of empty cots, the rumpled sheets a brighter, almost incandescent lime green compared to the deep emerald of the bedrolls. Kitbags had been knocked over and left.

'Taskane! For feth's sake!'

He thought he heard something, but it was just the damn scratching in his ears. He turned back and took the correct exit this time, fumbling along another wall.

He went down a couple of steps and found himself shin-deep in water. It was cold as hell, rushing into his boots.

'Feth's sake!' he cursed.

He splashed on for a few metres.

'Taskane!' His optics winked out.

Domor stood stock-still for a moment. He tapped at the sides of his augmetics. Vision returned in a jumble of green noise.

Then it failed again. The temperature seemed to drop sharply.

In utter darkness, he sloshed his way backwards and found the reassuring solidity of the wall. Get your breathing under control, you idiot. You're not afraid of the dark. There's nothing down here to be scared of–

A noise shuddered through the darkness. It wasn't the burble of the faulty alarms. It was a rasping, keening whine.

He'd heard it before. A noise like a surgical drill. A bone saw.

He'd heard it down at Low Keen, while searching behind the billets for Elodie and Gol's kid.

Heard it right before the... the *whatever it was* slaughtered an insurgent pack of Sekkite troops.

Shoggy Domor drew his warknife, and felt the comfort of it in his hand. He tried to adjust his optics and get them working again.

Something grabbed him from behind.

'Good to see you,' said Daur.

'You too,' replied Curth.

He'd come down to a reception hall just off the palace east gatehouse as soon as he'd received word that the regimental casualties had arrived.

'I've got them all to the palace infirmary,' she said, handing Daur the casualty list. 'All stable. No losses en route.'

Daur nodded, reading the list. 'Some of these look grim,' he said.

'It was fething brutal at the batteries,' she said. 'Some of them should have been shipped back from the front line days ago. It's a miracle three or four of them made it.'

'I imagine that miracle was you,' said Hark as he joined them.

'No,' she said. 'Just luck and maybe the blessing of the Emperor. They're all with the palace medicae now. Best surgical teams in the crusade.'

She looked at Daur.

'I'd like to get back out there,' she said. 'Re-join Pasha's group, or Rawne's. Are you sending V or E out in support?'

'This is Gaunt's op,' said Daur. 'He's told us to sit here for now.'

'Well, can you authorise *my* return, Ban?' Curth asked.

Hark looked at her. She was filthy with dirt and blood stains, and had a dazed look in her eyes, a look he'd seen many times before. She clearly hadn't slept in days.

'I think a little turn-around rest here first, eh, Ban?' said Hark gently. He glanced at Daur.

'I think so,' he replied.

'Feth's sake,' she snapped. 'They're deploying into... well, who the feth knows what. No one's clear about it. The whole regiment's been on the line for nearly a hundred and fifty straight. They're burned through–'

'I know,' said Daur. 'And so are you. Take an hour or two at least, get cleaned up, and we'll talk about it again.'

'I'll take this to Gaunt, then,' she said, her chin jutting pugnaciously.

'Good luck,' said Hark. 'No fether's getting in to see him. He's with the Saint. He's the Lord high fething *Executor*, Ana. We're just getting scraps from his table, and the scraps say do this and get it done.'

Curth breathed out hard and her shoulder slumped.

'Is it true?' she asked.

'About what?' asked Daur.

'Ezra being dead? Felyx being...' her voice trailed off. 'Gaunt's daughter or some shit?'

'All true,' said Hark.

'Feth!' she said.

'It's been quite a time, all told,' said Hark. 'Ana, let's go find you a billet.'

'And a drink, maybe?' she asked.

'Oh, definitely that,' said Hark.

The three turned and began to walk back down the reception hall. It was filling up with Helixid and Keyzon troopers, just arriving off transports that had set down in the Hexagonal Court. The trio had to skirt between gaggles of men and stacks of fieldpacks and bagged support weapons. Munitorum staffers were shouting orders and herding the arrivals into formations. A squad of Urdeshi troopers hurried through the hall, and spat disparaging taunts at the Helixid as they pushed through.

There were some angry answers. Some of the Helixid squared up, blocking the big Urdesh men.

'You! Yes, you!' Hark yelled. 'That's enough. Back off and get about your business or I'll turn the lot of you arseholes-out!'

'That's an actual surgical procedure, right?' Daur murmured sidelong to Curth.

'Takes a steady hand, but it's highly effective,' she replied with a weak grin.

'Idiots,' muttered Hark as he turned back to join Curth and Daur. 'Is it me, or is there something in the air tonight?'

'The storm?' asked Daur. Hark didn't look convinced.

'No, Viktor's right,' said Curth. 'A really ugly mood. I thought it was just me, but you could sharpen steel on some of the looks in here.'

Hark nodded. 'Yeah,' he said. 'I know I've got a bastard of a headache. Right between the ears. Gnawing away.'

'Probably brain worms,' said Curth.

'That would explain an awful lot,' said Daur.

'The two of you are simply hilarious,' said Hark.

'Sir! Captain Daur!'

They turned at the sound of a woman calling out anxiously. Trooper Ree Perday, the helicon player from V Company, was pushing her way through the hall towards them, waving to be seen over the tall, solid mob of assembling Guard.

'Perday?'

She ran up, slightly out of breath, and threw a salute.

'Message from Major Baskevyl,' she said. 'There's a situation in the undercroft, sir.'

'Where?' asked Curth.

'Our spectacular billet,' replied Hark, 'also known as the old palace wine vaults that no one else wanted.'

'What sort of situation, trooper?' asked Daur.

'Well, the lights have failed. Total blackout,' she said.

'Then get a fething tech crew on it,' said Daur. 'Bask doesn't need my permission to call in a–'

'Begging your pardon, sir,' said Perday, 'he's already done that. It's f – *bad word* dark as arseholes down there – *sorry*, sir. It's totally dark. And Commissar Fazekiel, she's called an amber status.'

Daur and Hark looked at each other sharply.

'What?' asked Daur. *'Why?'*

'No one really knows, sir, but that's what happened. Sergeant Major Yerolemew sent me up right away to appraise you, sir.'

'Amber status is a hazard advisory...' said Daur, mystified.

'"Threat suspected",' Hark agreed. 'But that's a combat zone condition. This *isn't* a combat zone.'

'I think Rawne might disagree with that,' said Curth.

Hark scowled. '*Urdesh* is,' he said. 'The fething *palace* isn't.'

'Luna's not one to jump at nothing,' said Curth.

'No, she's not,' said Hark. 'Nor one to get a technical definition wrong.'

'Granted,' said Daur, 'but even so...'

'Major Bask, he's ordered the retinue out, sir,' said Perday. 'Personnel evac. They're making their way up now.'

'Luna and Bask don't piss around, Ban,' said Hark.

Daur nodded. 'I'll alert the palace watchroom. See if they've got anything. Then I'll take this to Gaunt immediately. In person. Viktor, you go down and take a look. Report back to me.'

'Of course,' said Hark.

'You think this is something?' asked Curth.

'I think someone's got their shorts in a knot,' said Daur.

'But you're taking it to Gaunt...' Curth said.

'Yes,' said Daur, 'because he'll put a rocket up the Munitorum and get specialist crews down there to sort it out.'

'*If* it's just a circuit problem...' Hark said.

'We're inside the void-shielded Urdeshic palace, Viktor,' said Daur, 'as you just pointed out. What else could it be?'

Curth and Hark exchanged uneasy glances.

'Well, that's why you're going to check it out, isn't it, commissar?' said Daur. Hark nodded.

'I'll be down as soon as I've spoken to Gaunt,' said Daur, and hurried away.

'There's an officer's mess on the third floor,' Hark said to Curth. 'Decent log fire, decent amasec–'

'Feth that,' she replied, 'I'm coming with you.'

The beams of their stablights criss-crossed the walls as they moved into the darkness.

'Gol, take the left there,' Baskevyl instructed.

Kolea nodded, and moved through an archway with a team of troopers from V Company.

Baskevyl shone his torch around to the right. 'Meryn?'

'Yes, sir?'

'Move through the billets in that direction.'

'Right,' Meryn replied. He sounded reluctant. Baskevyl couldn't blame him. The internal scratching was getting more intense, like a dry hum, a crackle. His own hands were shaking.

Meryn played his light around, picking out the faces of Leyr, Banda, Neskon and the E Company corpsman, Leclan.

'Let's go,' he said.

Baskevyl could feel Blenner's nervous presence at his elbow, even though he couldn't see him.

'We'll follow the main tunnel down to the latrine area,' he said.

'Close up behind,' Blenner said to the E Company men at their heels. 'Where's Shoggy?' he asked. 'Didn't he go this way?'

'I don't know where the feth he is,' said Baskevyl. He tried the micro-bead links several times, but there was some kind of interference pattern.

'Domor? Domor, this is Blenner,' he heard Blenner say behind him. 'Report your location, Shoggy. Have you found the work crew?'

'I've tried that,' Bask snapped.

'Just getting noise,' Blenner muttered. Their voices in the small, dark space sounded dead and muffled. 'Is that jamming?'

'In here?' Baskevyl replied. 'I don't know how that would be possible.' The palace was the most secure Imperial site on the Urdesh surface, and its void shields were up. Furthermore, they were in a sub-surface level. The undercroft might not be the most salubrious area of the palace complex, but it was buried in bedrock and sheathed in foundation stonework metres thick. None of the Archenemy dispositions on Urdesh could get within kilometres of the Great Hill, let alone undertake the engineering efforts necessary to undermine the foundations without being detected.

But Baskevyl's mind kept returning to two things: the weird acoustics that they were all experiencing, and the simple fact that Luna Fazekiel was trustworthy and meticulous.

Baskevyl called her name into the darkness. There wasn't even an echo, just a dull silence. Then he called other names... Domor, Dalin... Yoncy...

Nothing.

'Keep up,' he said to the others.

'Sir?'

Baskevyl looked back, shining his beam. It was trooper Osket.

'What?'

'Something's up with the commissar,' Osket said.

Baskevyl played his beam around. Blenner was leaning against the passage wall, breathing hard.

'Vaynom?'

He got a light on Blenner's face. Blenner flinched. He was sweating and almost panting.

'Vaynom?' Baskevyl said calmly. 'Vaynom? You're having a panic attack. Vaynom, just breathe with me–'

'There's no air,' Blenner gasped. 'There's no fething air...'

'Vaynom, breathe with me. Slow. Count of three in... Hold it, count of three exhale...'

'This is death,' Blenner gasped, his breathing painfully quick and shallow. 'This is death. It's fething death. It's fething *punishment*–'

'Vaynom, breathe. Slow. Slower than that. Now hold it. Fill your lungs.'

'What did I ever do, Bask? I mean really,' Blenner stammered. 'I didn't want it. Not any of it. Just wanted to mind my own business and–'

'Concentrate on your breathing,' Baskevyl said firmly. He gripped Blenner by the shoulder. 'Come on. That's better.'

'I'm sorry,' Blenner mumbled, 'I'm so sorry.'

'Nothing to be sorry for,' said Baskevyl. 'It happens to all of us. Just gets up in your head–'

He paused. Where he was gripping Blenner's shoulder, it felt wet to the touch. He took his hand away and shone his stablight at his palm.

'What is it?' Blenner asked.

'Oil, I think,' Baskevyl replied. 'There must be some on the wall. You've leant on it–' He sniffed his hand.

It wasn't oil.

Baskevyl pushed Blenner out of the way and shone his light on the wall. The wet spatters read only as black in the harsh glare. Baskevyl didn't have to see red to know it was blood.

'Are you hurt, Vaynom?' he asked. 'Are you cut or–'

'N-no,' Blenner replied.

Baskevyl ran his beam along the ground. More black spatters there, gleaming in the light.

'Someone's hurt,' he said. Then he pulled his lasrifle off his shoulder, clipped the stablight to the under-barrel lugs, and brought the weapon up in a ready position.

'Secondary order,' he said.

'I thought...' Erish began.

'What?' Kolea asked.

The big V Company bandsman hesitated.

'Just thinking out loud, sir, sorry. I just thought there was another room beyond this one.'

Kolea's team was in one of the smaller billet chambers. Forty cots in neat rows, head-ends to the cellar walls. Kolea turned his stablight on the end wall.

'There, you mean?'

'Yes,' said Erish.

'You'd know better than I would,' Kolea said. This was his first visit to the undercroft. Erish and the others had been down here for two days.

'The layout's really simple,' said Kores. 'Just a grid with...'

He paused.

'What?' asked Kolea.

'I don't like to say, sir,' replied Kores awkwardly. 'But Erish is right. I'd have sworn there was a door there. An archway.'

Kolea slapped the stone wall with his hand.

'Well, there isn't,' he said. 'Let's back it up and go on to the left.'

The squad started to turn.

'What was that?' asked Arradin, a little woodwind player.

'What?' asked Erish.

'Didn't you hear that?' asked Arradin. 'Sounded like crying. Sobbing.'

Kolea couldn't hear anything.

'Just the alarms again?' Erish suggested.

Kolea led the way back to the left-hand archway. 'Close up,' he said.

He aimed his light beam through. Nothing–

He played it back. He'd seen a damned figure. Someone standing there in the darkness. Gone now, gone before his beam could return to it.

'Yoncy?' he called. It had been her, he was sure of it. Just the flash of a pale face in the dark. 'Close up,' he said.

There was no one behind him.

'Erish? Kores? Where the feth have you gone? Erish?'

He heard Erish call back. It sounded distant. The acoustics in the basement were off-putting.

'Where the feth have you gone?' Kolea yelled.

'Where are you, sir?' Erish called back.

'I went to the left. You were right behind me!'

'Where are you, sir?' Erish called.

'Feth's sake!' Kolea growled. It sounded like Erish was on the other side of the wall. He went back a few steps to the archway.

'Erish!'

The archway was there. The chamber beyond was small, and stacked with munition boxes and kitbags.

Where the feth were the cots? Kolea snorted in annoyance. How the feth had he done that? He'd gone into a side room by mistake, not the billet they'd just searched.

'Erish! Follow the sound of my voice!'

'Where are you, sir?' Erish called from a distance. It didn't sound like a voice. It sounded like the echo of a voice, the echo returning slowly from Erish's previous yell.

Kolea heard a skitter of movement behind him and turned fast. His stablight was quick enough to catch a pale figure darting out of sight.

'Yoncy!'

He ran after her.

'Yoncy! It's me! Yoncy, don't be scared! It's just a power-down!'

The hallway ahead of him dead-ended in a solid section of curtain wall.

'Yoncy?' he called.

He heard muffled sobbing. He couldn't tell for the life of him where it was coming from.

Trooper Luhan moved up through the tail-end of the retinue, handing out the little box-lamps.

'Pass 'em out,' he said.

They were crowded into the wide stone hallway that led to the stairwell.

'Why's everyone stopped?' Luhan asked.

'I don't know,' said one of the women.

'They're jammed up on the steps,' said an elderly tailor, clutching his workbag to his chest so he could take a lamp from Luhan.

Luhan gave them the rest of the lamps to pass around, and began to push his way up the tightly packed hall.

'What's the hold up?' he asked several times, getting nothing but anxious shrugs in reply. The retinue was a fair size: women, children and support artisans. But they should have been filing out by now, up the long steps to the undercroft's single exit.

'We just stopped moving a couple of minutes ago,' Elodie said to him as he squeezed past.

'Maybe someone's had a fall on the steps, ma'am,' he replied. 'I mean, in this dark.'

Luhan saw her expression by the glow of the box-lamp he was holding. Captain Daur's wife was a strong woman. He didn't like the fear he saw.

'Let us through,' said Elodie, pushing forwards. Luhan followed. Elodie had become the spokesperson and leader of the retinue, partly because she was married to Daur, but mainly because she was well-liked and cool-headed. She didn't crumble easily. Luhan stuck close behind her. The retinue was letting her through with more civility than they might have shown him.

They reached the bottom of the stone staircase. The stairs too were packed with people. The air was very close. Luhan could smell sweat, anxiety and the fouled diapers of some of the babes-in-arms.

'What's the hold up?' Elodie called up.

'I think the door's locked,' Juniper called back.

'The door? The door to the undercroft?'

'I dunno,' the woman replied.

Pushing and apologising, Elodie shoved her way up the steps, Luhan close behind, squirming through the press of bodies.

'Mach!' she called up. 'Mach, what's the issue?'

High above, in the shadows, she saw the wink of moving stablights.

'Elodie?' Bonin's voice boomed down to her.

'What's the problem?' she shouted. 'We can't leave everybody here like this! We're crushed in! Get it moving!'

'Keep everybody calm,' Bonin called back.

Bonin looked at Yerolemew. They were painfully aware of the tight press of bodies on the deep stairs behind them.

'What do we do?' the sergeant major asked quietly.

'I don't know,' said Bonin.

'With respect, Mach, you're the fething scout.'

'These are the stairs,' Bonin growled. 'The only fething stairs. Unless there's another flight of stairs I didn't know anything about.'

'Just the one flight,' Yerolemew replied. There was a twitch in his voice, the faintest hint of anxiety breaking through. 'You know that.'

'Right,' replied Bonin in a low whisper. He shone his light at the wall. 'So where's the fething door?'

The hallway ahead was flooding. Baskevyl tipped his light-beam down and saw the dirty liquid spilling along the flagstones. It stank. The latrine area had backed up entirely. He wondered if it was still raining. How much more water was going to pour into the palace's ancient drains and force its way up into the lower levels?

'Form on me,' he instructed. All the Ghosts with him had weapons ready, as per his order to secondary. Blenner was hanging back, but he'd drawn his weapon.

'We're not going on, are we?' Blenner asked.

'Of course we are,' Baskevyl said. 'This is the area the crew was working.'

'Well, they're not working now,' said Blenner, stepping back as the water began to reach his boots.

That much was obvious. There was no sound of pumps, no sign of pump tubing. Baskevyl had a scenario in his mind: Taskane's crew had been working to drain the water, and there had been a short. It had blown the circuit and caused the blackout, and shocked Taskane and his men, who'd been standing in flood water. A maintenance accident, that's all this was.

They had to get in and help. The Munitorum crew could be seriously hurt. Maybe Fazekiel too, if she'd been with them when it happened.

The blood... there had to be some other explanation for that.

He stepped forward. In just a few steps, he had water gushing around his ankles as it back-fed along the hall.

'Stay sharp!' he said.

They splashed into the stream. It was getting deeper. Did the tunnel slant down at this point?

'Sir!' Osket called out.

The lamp's beam moved and Baskevyl saw an object floating along in the tide. A work boot. Old and worn, laces broken.

'That's Munitorum issue,' said Osket.

'Fish it out,' said Baskevyl.

'Why?'

'Don't bother then,' Baskevyl snapped, and took a step forward.

He fell, unable to catch himself. He crashed into water at least a foot deep, and thrashed around to get up again. He'd tripped over something.

'Bask?' Blenner called.

'Feth it!' Baskevyl replied. He groped around, swirling the water, trying to keep his light and his weapon raised out of the way.

He located the object he'd tripped on. He shone his light down.

A face stared up at him out of the filthy water. Overseer Taskane. Baskevyl jerked back.

'Throne,' he gasped.

'Bask?'

'I've found Taskane. He's dead.'

'Dead?'

Baskevyl swung the light around. There were other shapes in the water. Other bodies. Munitorum overalls.

'Bask?' Blenner called. 'How can he be dead?'

'They're all dead. I can see all of them. The whole crew.'

'How can they be dead? Did they drown?'

'No,' said Baskevyl. He rose slowly, weapon braced in his dripping hands. 'They were killed.'

'How do you know that?'

'Because not a single one of them is intact,' Baskevyl replied. 'They've been torn apart.'

TEN

WOE

'Down here?' asked Curth, dubiously.

'That's right,' said Hark. He led her off the well-lit palace hallway and down a broad flight of steps, Trooper Perday at their heels.

'They gave us the palace cellars,' said Hark, walking briskly. 'The undercroft.'

'It's quite cosy, really,' remarked Perday. 'Except, you know, in the dark. It really is black when the lights go.'

'Only the best for the Tanith First,' said Curth.

'As usual,' Hark replied with a nod.

They reached a large and heavy set of doors. The area was bare and white-washed, with simple rush matting on the floor. Overhead, old lumen globes burned in iron holders.

'You close the doors when you came up, Perday?' asked Hark.

'No, sir.'

'I thought they were bringing the retinue out?' said Curth. 'Where are they?'

'Maybe they have the problem sorted,' said Hark.

'Well, the lights are on,' said Curth.

'Up here,' said Perday quietly.

Hark gripped the door handle and turned it. Then he rattled it hard.

'Come on, Viktor,' said Curth wearily.

'It won't open,' said Hark.

'Stop messing around.'

'I'm not,' said Hark, and rattled the door again.

Curth looked at him. She could see the bewilderment on his face.

'Is it locked?'

'No. There's no lock. Bolts on the inside.'

'Who would draw those and lock us out?' Curth asked.

Hark shook the doors again. They wouldn't budge. He hammered his fist against the heavy wooden panels.

'Hello? Hello in there!' he yelled.

There was no reply. Hark hammered again.

'Open the damn door!' he yelled. 'This is Hark! Open it up!'

He waited.

'Can you hear that?' asked Curth.

'Hear what?'

'Viktor, I can hear someone crying. A child...'

Curth stepped to the door and pressed her ear against the wood.

'It's really faint. Far away. There's a child crying down there.'

She tried the handle herself, then yelled. 'Hello? Hello? Who's in there? Can you hear me?'

She looked at Hark.

'We need to break this down,' she said.

Gaunt and Van Voytz stood watching the Beati. She was standing at the railing, looking down at the seething activity of the palace war room. Then she tilted her head back and gazed up at the high ceiling of the huge chamber.

'What's she doing, Ibram?' Van Voytz asked.

'I don't know,' replied Gaunt. 'Waiting. Listening...'

'Listening?'

'I trust her instincts,' Gaunt replied. 'If she thinks there's something wrong... senses it... then...'

'Should we go to an alert?' Van Voytz asked. 'Inform the Warmaster and the others? If an attack is imminent—'

'She said it was here. Right here.'

'Then all the more reason,' Van Voytz began.

They heard voices behind them, and turned. Sancto's team was letting Beltayn and Gaunt's tactical cabinet into the gallery room. It was getting crowded in there. Kazader was still present, along with the Beati's deputies. Inquisitor Laksheema and Colonel Grae had also arrived a few minutes earlier.

'I'll go and talk to them,' said Gaunt. 'Barthol, I don't want to cause an uproar. The Beati is mercurial to say the least, and her insight isn't always true. But let's play it safe. Alert the Palace Watch. Then round up any high command in the building. Tzara's here, I think, also Lugo and Urienz.' 'I think everyone else is already in the field,' said Van Voytz. 'Grizmund, Blackwood, Cybon, Kelso—'

'I think you're right. Just get the seniors assembled and aware. Tell them to get all the strengths they have in the Great Hill zone brought to secondary order. Tell Urienz to take charge of the war room... no. No, scratch that. *You* take charge of the war room. Lock us down, bring us to order and watch for anything. Anything, Barthol.'

'Right.'

'Send Urienz to inform the Warmaster we may have a situation on site. He'll receive Urienz more readily than you.'

Van Voytz nodded.

'Tell Urienz that comes direct from me,' said Gaunt.

'I will.'

'Good. This could be a chance to demonstrate your mettle again,' Gaunt said.

'That had occurred to me, Ibram,' Van Voytz replied, 'but I rather hope that it won't be, for all our sakes.'

He made the sign of the aquila, and strode away.

Gaunt stepped off the gallery walk into the screened glass box of the briefing room.

'What's happening?' Laksheema asked immediately.

'The Saint has a presentiment of danger,' Gaunt began.

'Are our assets compromised?' the inquisitor asked.

'No,' said Gaunt. 'I have strengths moving in to secure them both as we agreed. The Saint's feeling is that the danger is here.'

'What sort of danger?' asked Kazader.

'She can't be specific yet,' said Gaunt.

'Can't be specific?' Kazader asked scornfully.

'I've raised the ready status of the palace, and the garrison is coming to secondary–' Gaunt began.

'But she can't be specific?' Kazader cut in.

'Her visions are not always particular,' said Sariadzi. 'We must give her time to focus–'

Kazader looked at her, his eyes narrowed.

'I think this is ridiculous,' he said. 'If there's a threat, we deal with it. If not, this is dangerous foment. Scaremongering. Are we really just going to wait for some peasant girl to–'

Auerben had to hold Sariadzi back.

'That's enough!' Gaunt snapped. 'Not in here. Not anywhere. Kazader, step out. Go get your men ready. There will be a reprimand on your record for that.'

Kazader glared at Gaunt, then saluted and walked out.

Gaunt looked at the rest. 'I've brought you here to consult and assist. Colonel Grae and the inquisitor are party to the most delicate confidences attached to the Urdesh situation. Biota, you and your staff need to be aware so you can support me.'

Biota nodded. The two tacticians with him were solemn and silent.

'Where's Merity?' Gaunt asked, an afterthought. 'I thought she was with you?'

'Mr Biota excused her, sir,' said Beltayn. 'She's gone down to the undercroft. Commissar Fazekiel wanted to ask her a few more questions about the Low Keen incident.'

'She's down there now?'

'Went down a little while ago, sir.'

'Alone?'

'She has an appointed Scion with her, my lord,' said Biota.

Gaunt nodded. 'Right. Let's run over what we know. Starting with the Beati's sense that there's a–'

Gaunt broke off. Through the room's glass door he saw Ban Daur arrive, and exchange words with Sancto. Sancto gestured to the room. Daur said something else. Sancto turned and looked through the glass at Gaunt.

Gaunt was about to shake his head. Regimental business could wait, and Daur knew it. But there was something in Daur's body language.

He nodded.

Sancto hesitated for a moment, as if surprised, and then opened the door for Daur.

'My apologies, Lord Executor,' Daur said as he stepped in.

'What do you need, captain?' Gaunt asked.

'I...' Daur hesitated. Everyone was looking at him. 'I need to report that there seems to be a situation in the Tanith billet. In the undercroft, sir.'

'An issue?'

'A power-out, my lord. It–'

Gaunt sighed. His gut had been wrong. Daur was fussing, and he should have known better.

'That's a technical issue, Captain Daur. Take it to the palace custodians.'

Daur wavered. 'I don't fully understand the circumstances, my lord, but an amber status has been issued. By Commissar Fazekiel.'

'Why?' asked Gaunt.

'I don't know, my lord. I came straight to you. Commissar Hark has gone to investigate directly.'

He looked at the others in the room.

'I apologise for interrupting this meeting,' he said.

Gaunt had risen to his feet.

'Amber status?' he asked. His voice was oddly fierce.

'Yes, my lord,' Daur replied.

'Is it in darkness?'

Everyone looked around. Daur blinked in surprise. The Beati had entered through the walkway door and was staring at him.

'Captain Ban Daur,' she said. 'I asked you, is the undercroft in darkness?'

'It is, my lady. Entirely. So I understand.'

'Are there children there? Children who might be afraid? Who might be sobbing?'

'Yes, my lady. There are children. The entire retinue.'

The Beati turned to look directly at Gaunt.

'Anarch,' she said.

'Sound the alarms!' Gaunt snarled.

Hark took another run at the doors, and bounced off again.

'You'll break your fething shoulder,' said Curth.

He didn't reply. He pulled out his plasma pistol and adjusted the setting.

'Stand the feth back, both of you,' he said. Curth and Perday stepped away. Perday's eyes were wide.

Hark aimed the weapon at the doors, and fired.

The whoop of discharged plasma echoed in the empty hallway, and Curth winced. Smoke drifted up and clouded the air around the hissing lumen globes overhead.

The doors were unmarked.

'How the hell–' Hark stammered.

'Is there something wrong with your gun, Hark?' Curth asked.

'What? No. That was a full discharge.'

He examined the door, running his fingers over the wood. Not so much as a blemish.

'I don't understand,' he said.

'I hear alarms,' Perday said, looking up. 'That's the threat alert.'

Klaxons were sounding in the corridors and hallways above them. The bells in the palace campaniles were being rung too.

'Try it again,' Curth urged Hark.

Footsteps clattered down the stairs from the hall above. They turned, and saw Gaunt striding towards them, with Daur at his side. Behind them came Gaunt's Scion guard, Beltayn, some tacticae officers, a woman with an augmetic golden mask, and several individuals who looked like scratch company partisans. Curth didn't know them at first. Then she saw the face of one of them.

'Oh feth, Viktor,' she whispered. 'It's the Beati.'

'Hark?' Gaunt said as he arrived.

'The door won't budge, my lord,' said Hark. 'I even took a shot at it.'

Laksheema pushed forward and stared at the door. 'A las-round will hardly tear down–'

'Plasma gun, inquisitor,' Hark said. 'Full load, point blank.'

'My lord?' said Sancto. 'Shall we?'

'No disrespect, Sancto, but I don't think you and your men are going to make a better dent than Hark,' replied Gaunt.

'It's bound shut,' said Laksheema. She had been stooping to examine the door. 'The warp is holding it.'

'You sense that?' asked the Beati.

'Don't you?' asked Laksheema. 'My lord, even if we could force it, we have no idea what's on the other side.'

'My regiment–' Gaunt replied.

'And what else besides?' asked Laksheema. She adjusted her micro-bead link. 'I will summon my staff. We need specialist assistance.'

She frowned.

'My link is dead,' she said.

'No response from any vox source below,' Beltayn called out. He'd set his vox-unit against the wall and was adjusting the settings. 'Dead air. No microlink. No vox-unit. Just–'

Beltayn jumped in surprise, and pulled the headset away from his ears.

'What the feth–?' he gasped.

'Bel?' asked Curth, crossing to him.

'I heard a voice,' Beltayn said. 'A child, weeping.'

'Speaker!' Gaunt ordered.

Beltayn switched the set to speaker output. There was a hiss of static, then they could all hear the tinny yet distinct sound of sobbing. A young voice, far away, in anguish.

'Grae?' said Laksheema over the eerie sound. 'Go get my team, please.' Grae nodded.

'And tell Van Voytz we have a red status location,' Gaunt added. 'Biota, you and your team go too. Start briefing on everything we know.'

'Which is precious little,' replied Biota.

'Do it anyway.'

Grae was already running back along the hall. Biota and his aides turned to follow him.

'Biota?' Gaunt called.

'My lord?' Biota responded, pausing to look back.

'You said my daughter went down there?'

'Yes, my lord.'

Gaunt cleared his throat. 'Carry on,' he said. Biota and his aides hurried after Grae.

Curth looked at Gaunt. She gripped his arm.

'We'll get in,' she said.

'I know,' Gaunt replied.

The offspring of the Great Master,' Laksheema muttered.

'What?' said Hark.

'Do you not recall, commissar?' Laksheema said, glancing at him. 'The signal from the Archenemy warship that spared the *Armaduke* so mysteriously. The translation provided by the pheguth spoke of "the offspring of the Great Master". A child, a daughter. The noun was female.'

'You remember all that?' Hark asked.

'I have reviewed the reports many times,' Laksheema said. 'Merity Chass was aboard the *Armaduke.* She is here now. She is the offspring of a Great Master... a Lord Executor perhaps? Major Kolea's misfortunes may have been a wilful distraction. *A creation of significance.* That's how it translated. *All this shall be the will of he whose voice drowns out all others.*'

'The feth are you suggesting?' Hark asked, stepping forward. Gaunt held up a hand to him in warning.

'We have been confounded by the Archenemy's actions,' said Laksheema. 'We have many elements that do not fit together. All we agree on is that Sek achieved something after the Eltath raid, and now enters a new phase of attack. It would seem that is here, now, beneath us. Elements begin to connect.'

'The hell they do,' said Hark.

The sobbing continued to crackle from Beltayn's vox-unit.

'Turn it off,' said Curth.

'Should I, my lord?' asked Beltayn.

Gaunt nodded. Beltayn reached for the speaker switch. Just before he could throw it, the noise of weeping shut off and was replaced by a hellish shrieking roar. The volume was so great, it blew out the vox-caster's speakers. Smoke wafted from the ruined set.

'What the Throne was that?' asked Auerben.

'It sounded like... a surgical saw,' Curth said.

'A bone saw,' said Daur. 'That's what Elodie said. Whatever attacked at Low Keen, it sounded like a bone saw.'

Gaunt took a step towards the undercroft doors and drew his power sword. The blade powered up with a fierce hum.

'No, my lord!' Laksheema cried.

'My daughter's down there,' Gaunt said. 'My daughter and my regiment.'

'And my fething wife!' Daur snarled at the inquisitor. 'Step the hell back!'

'Please, my lord,' Laksheema protested.

'Do it,' said the Beati quietly. 'There is death down there. The child is weeping. All the children. *Every* soul.'

'Positions!' Sancto growled. The Scions raised their hellguns and fanned out to flank Gaunt. Auerben and Sariadzi hoisted their assault weapons. Daur had drawn his sidearm.

Gaunt swung the power sword of Heironymo Sondar at the doors with both hands. Wood splintered and billowed out, burning. A bloom of flickering, sickly energy surrounded the blade as it slashed across the panels, as if the blade was biting not just through ancient wood, but through the skin of some subspace membrane. There was a flash, and Gaunt staggered back a few steps.

This time, damage had been done. The centre panels of the ancient, heavy doors were blackened and crumbling. Arcane energy fizzled and spat frothing residue from the collapsing wood.

Sancto and Daur moved in, tearing at the ruined wood, dragging sections of the damaged doors away.

'Be careful!' Laksheema warned.

'Are you all right?' Curth asked Gaunt. He flexed his grip on the power sword.

'It nearly overloaded,' he replied. 'I've never known it fight and buck in my hands like that.'

Stendhal, one of the other Scions, moved in to assist Sancto and Daur. The other two raised their weapons to their cheeks, and sighted the centre section of the door.

Daur, Stendhal and Sancto hauled the doors apart. Both doors fell away in their hands, disintegrating into hot dust and embers that the men threw aside.

'Something's awry–' Beltayn began to say.

'Oh, Emperor protect us!' Curth exclaimed, clasping her hands to her mouth.

Behind the burned and shattered doors, there was no doorway. Just the solid, white-washed stone of the wall, perfectly intact, as though no door had ever existed.

By the time the trucks rolled onto the rockcrete apron of Eltath Mechanicore 14, visibility had dropped to thirty metres.

Major Pasha peered out of the cab, then looked down to check the rumpled chart in its plastek sleeve.

'Grim place,' murmured Konjic at the wheel.

Pasha nodded and held out her hand. The adjutant passed her the vox handset without hesitation. Pasha held it to her mouth and thumbed it on.

'R Company lead,' she said, 'let's see who's home, and make our purpose clear. Elam? Please to do honours.'

She took her thumb off the button.

'Loud and clear, lead,' said Elam over the link.

She held the button down again.

'Convey my respect,' she said. 'Everybody else, stand by. This runs according to pattern agreed. Kolosim? Hold the rearguard on the approach road. No one get twitchy until I say they get twitchy.'

Konjic's vox set, on the seat between them, pipped out a little flutter of vox signal-bursts as each company leader in the convoy behind her acknowledged.

Pasha had the full muscle of the Tanith First with her, packed up in canvas-backed cargo-10s behind her. Only the first three trucks had pulled onto the apron: hers, Elam's, and a second strength from R Company. They'd come to a halt side by side, their headlamps on. Rain danced like digital static in the beams.

The rest of the convoy was on the long slope of the approach road, lamps hooded and set to dark-running. They were arranged in a double column, filling both lanes of the road. At the back of the formation, Kolosim deployed four sections to hold the road and form a rear guard. They set up crew-served weapons in the gutters. Bannard, Kolosim's adjutant, walked down the road a little way and scattered pencil-flares that fizzled in the rain. The flickering green glow of the flares illuminated little except the empty road behind them, and the dead ruins on either side.

The approach road was flanked by sheet-wire fencing. Mkflass eyed the fencing dubiously. Beyond it was just scrub wasteland. It was impenetrably dark. He could smell wet vegetation and rain-swilled earth.

He glanced at Kolosim.

'Get some cutters,' Kolosim told him. 'Get two sections through, one each side.'

Mkflass nodded. The men in his section started to cut the fence and drag it wide enough to let men pass.

Bannard returned.

'Ugly spot, sir,' he said. 'Feels wide open.'

Kolosim knew what he meant. They were boxed in on the road by the fence, the rain and the darkness. It was hard to see anything. But it felt unpleasantly exposed.

'With luck, we won't be sitting here long,' Kolosim replied. He keyed his micro-bead.

'Rearguard,' he said. 'Sit tight but get combat-light. Stow your packs. Exit on my word, not before. And let's kill the engines, please. If we can't see, let's hear at least.'

One by one, the idling engines of the big transports shut down. The low grumble was replaced by the sound of rain, hissing off the strip of road and pattering on the canvas truck-tops. It wasn't a great improvement. The sound of the rain seemed to magnify the emptiness to an unnatural level that suggested it wasn't empty at all.

Up on the apron, Pasha saw three figures dismount from Elam's transport: Captain Elam, Captain Criid and Commissar Ludd. Elam walked through the cold puddles of headlamp light and came up to her side door.

She pulled the window down and handed him the waiver certificate that Daur had sent through. It was a heat-printed flimsy produced by Konjic's vox-caster. Pasha had slipped it in a clear-plastek chart cover to keep the rain from turning it to mush.

'Don't take any shit, Asa,' she told him.

'I never do,' he replied with a smile.

Elam turned and walked across the apron, his rifle strapped across his chest. Criid and Ludd fell in step with him. The row of headlamps bleached the backs of them bone-white and stretched their shadows, long and thin ahead of them.

'Let's be confident about this,' Elam said to his companions. No one liked dealing with the Mechanicus, even when they had the authority of the Lord Executor to back them.

Criid glanced ahead at the ominous bulk of Eltath Mechanicore 14. Air raid regulations had placed it in blackout, like the rest of the city. The only lights came from the fortified gatehouse, a rockcrete bunker at the top of the apron that was protected by huge hornwork demi-bastions. The night was so black and the rain so sheer, she couldn't make out the main site beyond, but she had the impression of something invisible and vast. It had to be a big place. The scale of the demi-bastions told her that much. She'd seen smaller outworks on Militarum fortresses. Eltath Mechanicore 14 – EM 14 – was one of the many Mechanicus strongholds in the city, occupying a stretch of lowland hillside in Klaythen Quarter on the eastern flank of the Great Hill, surrounded by extensive worker habitats and just below the vast spread of the shipyards. It wasn't one of the principal forges, the huge structures dominating entire districts she'd seen on her first day on Urdesh. Indeed, even they were minor forge sites, she'd been told. Eltath was the subcontinental capital, an administrative centre. The giant forge complexes within its territory were nothing compared to the mass forge installations elsewhere on the planet. Pasha's briefing had described EM 14 as a research facility, one of the old tech-dynast manufactories that had been absorbed by the Mechanicus occupation and repurposed with a specific role.

Guard mindset regarded Urdesh as simply a contested world, a battleground to be cleared and secured. Criid reminded herself that it was contested because of what it was: a forge world. A place of industry and manufacture, the largest and most important of its kind in forty systems. To her, it was a place to be fought for. To the Priests of Mars, it was holy ground, a precious outpost of their far-flung technomechanical empire.

That's why it had survived. Other worlds so bitterly disputed would have been obliterated long before by the ultimate sanction of fleet action. Whoever held Urdesh held the most vital munition source in the rimward Sabbat Worlds. She knew that it had been held, lost and retaken by both sides many times in its past. She wondered if any world anywhere had suffered under so many temporary masters. Reign after reign, Archenemy and Imperial, changing hands with each occupation, claimed and reclaimed. No wonder it bred such ferocious warriors. She had often felt that the Urdeshi troops she'd met had been fighting for Urdesh above and before any other cause.

There was a furnace smell in the wet air that reminded her of Verghast, but she knew that Verghast, for all its mighty hives, was a minor industrial world compared to this.

They heard a sudden, throaty rush of air that sounded like the mother of all flamer units. The three of them halted in their tracks, bathed in an infernal glow. Above them, the sky burned for a few seconds, a massive, boiling rush of churning flame-clouds.

Not an attack. EM 14 had just vented a gas plume burn-off from its vapour mill. The burning clouds died back into blackness, but before they did, they briefly revealed EM 14 in red half-light. Criid glimpsed the outlines of vast rockcrete ramparts and cyclopean galvanic halls, heavy casemate defences, and outer thickets of razor-wire. Criid sucked in her breath. She wondered what the hell Gaunt thought was coming that a place like this would not be a sufficient defence.

The massive gatehouse straddled two defensive ditches lined with wire. Inside that was another ring of dead earth sandwiched between a heavy chain fence and the outer wall.

'What's that?' Ludd asked.

'What?'

'It sounds like an animal,' Ludd said.

Criid and Elam listened. They could hear the constant sizzle of the rain, which was dancing silver splashes on the rockcrete around their feet. Beyond that, they heard a bark, a growl somewhere in the night. It was a deep, ugly sound, full of pain and rage.

'Feth knows,' said Elam, lowering his hand to the grip of his strung weapon.

The growl died away, then others answered it, yaps and snarls that faded into scraps of noise. They were weird sounds, a blend of deep-throated reverberation and higher pitched whining.

Lights snapped on, blinding the three of them. They had tripped the gatehouse auto-sensors. Automated weapon mounts in the gatehouse's deep-set embrasures rotated to target them, whirring softly. Criid could see the targeting lasers moving across their soaked battledress like fireflies.

'Astra Militarum! Tanith First!' Elam called out. He held up the waiver in its plastek wrap. 'We require access!'

The laser dots continued to drift. The guns stared, occasionally micro-shifting with the pulsed hums of platform gears. There was a thump, and the gatehouse projected a fierce blue scanning beam. The horizontal blue bar tracked up and down them from head to foot and back. It shut off.

An outer hatch clanked open in the side of the bunker. Two men appeared, large, armed and armoured. They stepped out into the rain and approached. They were Urdeshi Heavy Troops from the infamous Third Brigade, the Steel-side Division. They wore full ballistic plate and grilled helmets, all finished in puzzle camo. Each one wielded a .30 'short-snout' hip-mounted on a gyro-stable bodyframe. Fat, armoured feed belts ran from their weapons to auto-delivery hoppers inside the gatehouse. Both of them had stylised Mechanicus emblems fused to their breastplates, denoting their proud secondment to the protective service of the forge.

'Explain your business,' said one, his voice amplified by his vox-mask.

Elam held up the waiver again.

'My business is the business of the Lord Executor,' he said. 'Here's my waiver authority. I have an infantry regiment under transport on the road behind me. My commander seeks access and immediate conference with the facility senior.'

'Not tonight,' the Urdeshi said.

'Oh yes, tonight,' said Ludd.

'The seniors of the forge will take no audience with the city on lock-down.'

'Then I'll take names,' said Ludd. He stepped right up to them, eye-to-eye with the massive troopers, and fished out his black pocket book. 'You wear the sigil of Mars and you do loyal work,' he said, 'but you're Astra Militarum, and I will have your names.'

With a gloved fingertip, Ludd casually wiped raindrops off the name tag bolted to the chest-plate of the man he was facing. He did it with such matter-of-fact calm it made Criid smile.

'Erreton. Captain,' Ludd said, and wrote the name down. 'And you?'

The other Steelsider didn't reply, so Ludd studied his name tag too.

'Gorsondar,' he said. 'I suppose you boys know who the Lord Executor is?'

'We do,' replied Erreton. 'We–'

'Find yourselves hurtling at near light speed towards a pile of shit for this, captain,' said Ludd. 'I'll give you a moment to reconsider and verify the waiver. Out of courtesy. The Mechanicus is a mighty institution, but it won't protect either of you from the Prefectus.'

'In,' said Erreton, jerking his head at the bunker.

They followed the men inside. The gatehouse command was lit with amber panel lights. A third Urdeshi Heavy manned a control station of multi-level display screens. Each screen showed a different low-light image of the apron outside. The slack of the sentries' ammo-feed belts retracted into the big autohoppers as the men entered.

Criid stood with Ludd, water dripping off them onto the deck grille. She saw the inside of the automated gun-points, the subhuman forms packed foetally inside tiny turret cages, wired by spine, hand and eye-socket into the weapon systems. Each of the embrasure weapons that had tracked them outside had been guided by a vestigial flicker of human consciousness. Mechanicus gun-slaves, the lowest and most pitiful order of the infamous skitarii.

Erreton took the waiver from Elam and passed it to the Steelsider at the station desk.

'Check it,' he said.

The desk officer took the waiver flimsy out of its wrapping, and slid it under the optical scanner. A digital version, instantly verified by the Urdeshic Palace war room, appeared on one of the monitors surrounded by a vermilion frame.

'My apologies,' Erreton said to Elam.

'None taken,' smiled Elam as though he was responding politely. 'Get your transport gates open so we can bring the regiment inside. And have a senior of this facility summoned to meet with my commanding officer.'

'Do that at once,' Erreton said to the desk officer, who began speaking rapidly into his vox-mic.

'Follow me,' Erreton told them.

He walked to the rear hatch of the gatehouse and opened it. The ammo-feed of his rig-weapon buzzed as it played out behind him. When it reached the limit of its tension, the whole hopper, an armaplas container the size of a fuel drum, detached itself from the wall and scuttled after him on short, thick insectiform legs.

They followed Erreton and his obedient, mobile ammo hopper out of the rear door and onto a caged walkway that ran across the ditches to a blast hatch in the main wall. Flood lights had come on, catching the spark of rain falling through the wire. Beyond the second ditch, the walkway bisected the ring of caged, dead earth outside the wall.

Criid peered through the chain link at it as they walked by, presuming it was a firefield, a boundary margin left deliberately open so that nothing could cross it without becoming a target for the main wall guns. Were the high chain fences and wire roofing just there to slow down an invader's progress?

A shape slammed into the chain link, making it shiver. Criid recoiled. Something feral was glaring at her, clawing at the chain link separating them.

'Keep back from the wire,' Erreton said. 'We keep shock-dogs in the inner run.'

It wasn't a dog. It wasn't even an animal, though it was making the animal growl the three of them had heard outside. It was a form of attack servitor, a grim fusion of cybernetic quadruped and human flesh. It barked and snarled at them, dragging its steel foreclaws across the mesh. Its steel jaws looked like they could bite a man's arm off. Criid couldn't see its face. Its scalp and nape were covered with a thick mane of cyber cables that draped across its deep-set eyes like dreadlocks.

Other shock-dogs appeared out of the darkness behind it, drawn by the lights and the smell of unmodified humans. They padded forwards, growling, hackles raised. Some sported spikes, or body-blade vanes, or saw-edge jaw augmetics. They were feral kill-servitors, permanently goaded to madness and hyperaggression by neuro-psychotic implants, most of their humanity long since surgically excised and replaced with biomimetic augmentation. Criid had heard of such inhuman monsters, but she had hoped never to see one.

Erreton waited while the inner blast door opened, then led them through the portal into the inner gatehouse. His hopper scuttled after him diligently. A full squad of Urdeshi Heavies and two towering adept wardens of the Cult Mechanicus Urdeshi were waiting for them. The wardens were robed in embroidered rust-red silk and stood almost two and a half metres tall. They carried ornate stave weapons, and their cowled faces seemed like nightmarish cartoons of Guard-issue gas-hoods: big, round ocular units staring out above pipework rebreather masks. Their duty was the protection and security of the forge facility. They turned to look at the visitors in perfect neurosync unison.

'This is unorthodox,' said one. His voice was a modulated arrangement of digital sounds emulating human words.

'You've seen the authority,' said Erreton.

'It has been relayed by the manifold,' said the other warden. 'Noospheric verification is complete. However–'

'–this is unorthodox,' the first finished. One voice, speaking through two bodies. 'We serve the Omnissiah.'

'Right now, you serve the Lord Executor,' said Ludd, 'who is protecting your interests on this world. My regiment is a Special Task Deployment sent by the Lord Executor himself. You will cooperate fully.'

The adept wardens looked at each other, a perfect mirror of movement, and exchanged a burst of machine code.

'Signal your commanding human officer–' said one.

'–the gates will open now,' the other finished.

There was a deep rumble of heavy machinery.

'Move in,' Elam's voice crackled over the vox.

'Understood,' replied Pasha. A bloom of light appeared through the rain, as the main gate hatches unlocked and yawned open, dragged by immense hydraulics. Outer defence barriers beside the gatehouse retracted into the ground, and a long metal ramp extended across the ditches like a tongue.

'Pasha to Kolosim,' she said. 'Please to hold back one quarter strength and take up a broad defensive position around the access road and surrounding waste-ground, as per pattern. Please also to cut damn fence down and get all transports off the road. I want a clear, unimpeded run when we come out. I'll want to be moving fast. Do it by book, Ferdy, and keep me advised of anything.'

'Understood.'

'I mean anything.' Pasha looked at Konjic. 'Start her up,' she said.

Konjic nodded and woke the big engine of the cargo-10.

'Engines live,' Pasha said into the vox handset. 'Recovery detail, orderly fashion, single file, follow me in, please.'

A voice in the darkness, a whisper barely loud enough to hear, told him, 'Stay still and don't make a sound.'

Domor obeyed, dumb. The firm hands that had grabbed him pulled him back against the cellar wall. He could feel the rough brick of it.

'Who is that?' he managed to hiss.

'Shhhhh!' the whisper replied.

The bone saw sound died away. Near silence settled like a stifling weight in the impenetrable blackness. All Domor could hear was the blood pounding in his ears and the water lapping around his knees. The quiet pressed in on him, robbing him of the ability to fill his lungs.

It wasn't the quiet doing it, it was fear. He tried to focus. He knew his cortisol levels had ramped right up. He wondered what his heart rate was. Higher than 140, and his motor skills would be eroded. Higher than 160 or thereabouts, he'd have tunnel vision and begin to slide into the decayed, non-rational world of fear.

He couldn't tell. He couldn't see to tell if his vision was tunnelling down. But he knew for a fact he'd never been so scared. Ever. And that was saying something, because he'd been through some wicked feth in his time. Domor knew fear. They all did. The story of their lives was punctuated by regular spikes of terror: the threat of death, the insanity of combat, the gnawing in-between times of waiting that whittled away the soul.

Domor had known men, strong men, freeze or panic, or lose the ability to speak, or perform simple motor skills. There was no hierarchy to fear. It bit everyone who came near it. The best of the Ghosts had learned, with only brutal experience as a tutor, to tame it. They had honed intuitive mechanisms to channel the adrenaline and the hindbrain threat responses, to overcome the drastic shifts in blood pressure and biological process, and remain operational. Gaunt was a master at it. Some, like Mkoll and – Domor fancied – Rawne – had been born with the knack. Others, like Baskevyl and Varl, had acquired the skills over time and hard use.

Domor had evolved that way. Most of the veteran Ghosts were only veterans because they could look fear in the eye and remain functional. The crucible of battle did that to a man or woman quickly, and they coped or they died. The initial startle response was still there, but you barged through it and used your heightened state to push on rather than be crippled by it.

Some called it the *rush*. Hark called it *fight time*. A good Guardsman turned his own poleaxing biological responses into a weapon.

But this... this wasn't a battlefield. There was no whip-crack of passing las to trigger the startle, no visible threat to engage the mind with. Domor had no idea why this was the most terrifying experience of his life.

That puzzled him, and it felt like a weight lifting. His bafflement acted like a sponge, blotting up the fear. His mind became occupied with the question of *why* he was so uniquely scared rather than the fact of being scared.

He wrested control of his breathing.

'Are you still there?' he whispered.

A hand squeezed his arm in affirmation.

Domor sheathed his blade, and fumbled with his optics. There was a fizzle of green light as the augmetics came back on. He glimpsed the chamber, awash with water; his own dripping hands, ghost-white and radiant. Then it went out again.

The reassuring hands gripped his shoulder and guided him backwards. His boots kicked blindly at step risers, and he felt his way up them. A dry floor. His right hand found the wall beside him.

His optics flashed back on.

He saw Zweil ahead of him. The old ayatani was trailing a hand behind him, trying to lead Domor as he groped blindly along the wall.

Domor reached out and tucked Zweil's arm under his.

'I can see, father,' he whispered. 'Move with me.'

'There's something down here,' Zweil said very quietly, cocking his head and trying to sense Domor in the darkness.

'It's just the lights,' whispered Domor. 'The lights have failed.' He knew he was lying. He knew the sound he'd heard.

'No, son,' said Zweil. 'It's just the darkness.'

* * *

The Scion Relf had a stablight slotted on the under-barrel rail of her weapon. When she turned it on, the light made Merity jump.

'Nice and calm now,' Relf said. There was a glass-squeak edge to her voice that undermined her reassurance. She brought her weapon up to her cheek, and aimed ahead. The weapon was a short-form lascarbine that had been strapped to her back from the moment Merity met her. It wasn't a battlefield weapon, but its compact length made it ideal for close-quarter protection duties in interior spaces.

'Feth nice and calm,' Merity said. 'It's just a power-out.'

Now there was light, the hard stripe beaming from Relf's weapon, Merity's anxiety dropped. What had it been about the darkness? The suddenness of it? No. The thickness, the density of it. The lights hadn't just cut. An airless darkness had swallowed them.

Relf's beam picked up the waste water extending towards them. In the wobbling oval of light, it looked like blood. Merity could hear it gurgling. It was a sound she'd heard before in the infirmary, and in the aftermath of hot contacts on Salvation's Reach. Blood leaking from wounds, the steady, hideous trickle of life leaking away. She looked at the black water slopping towards them and swallowed hard. It looked like blood. It looked as though the ancient bowels of the palace were bleeding out.

'Come on,' said Relf. She turned, tweaking the stablight in different directions.

Merity heard her curse. It seemed like an odd sign of weakness.

'Scion?'

'Where are the stairs?' Relf asked.

'What?'

'The stairs, missy. We just came down the stairs...'

She panned the light right and left. The smooth, whitewashed walls looked like snow-covered ground.

'And the billets...' Relf said.

'I don't understand,' said Merity.

Relf swung the light behind them and then forward again fast. Merity glimpsed the encroaching water.

'We came down the stairs,' Relf said, as if rationalising it to herself. 'Came down, turned, walked along. The flood was ahead of us.'

She twitched the stablight back and forth again.

'Flood there, stairs there. And archways... through to the billets, there.'

The disc of light hovered on glacial whitewash.

'I understand what you're saying,' said Merity. 'I just don't understand what you mean.'

Relf snapped around, tilting the light so it underlit their faces. She looked hurt, as if she'd been slapped for no reason.

'The stairs have gone. The access to the billets has gone. Where have they gone?'

'You're mistaken,' said Merity. 'We must be confused. The steps were behind us.'

She moved into the darkness, hands raised, expecting to catch her toe on the bottom step. Relf reached to stop her, but there was no need. Merity had come to a halt, her hands pressed flat against stone wall.

'That's just fething impossible,' she said.

Relf grabbed her arm. 'With me,' she said, pulling Merity after her. She was heading for the water, the light-beam bobbing.

'What? Where to? The water's that way–'

'I know, I know,' said Relf. Merity could smell the woman's sour fear-breath. 'But somehow we're in a... in a dead end. The water's rising fast, so we can't stay put.'

They were already sloshing into the spilling tide of water. It rose around their boots like a stream that had burst its banks after a rainstorm.

'Relf? Scion?'

'Just walk,' Relf said, pulling her arm. 'You're right. We're just confused. The dark confused us. There will be an exit. Just nearby.'

The water was shin-deep and flowing hard. Merity thought – no, she *knew* as an awful certainty – that Relf was wrong. Something had happened. Something had changed in the darkness. Things had shifted like the walls and faces in the stress nightmares that had haunted her as a child.

All of which was impossible. She wondered if it was still pitch dark and this was all some imagined nonsense. Maybe her concussion was worse than the medicaes had said. Maybe she was hallucinating. Her head ached. She had a rasping itch in her ears. But the water around her knees, her thighs, was not impossible. It was soberingly cold. In fact, everything had suddenly become much colder.

'Scion, stop.'

Relf wouldn't. She pulled at Merity, then she froze. They had both heard it.

A quick, purring buzz. A whine, as though someone nearby was squeeze-testing a drill or a powered saw. It came again, twice, like an insect droning past their ears.

'What was that?' Relf asked.

'Hello?' Merity called out. They'd heard voices from the billet spaces when they'd first come down. There had to be people close by. Why was it so quiet?

'Shut up!' Relf snapped. 'Shut up, shut up.'

There was a tremor in the light beam. The Scion's hands were shaking. Merity could hear Relf's rapid, shallow breathing.

The lights came back on, stark and over-bright. It made them wince. Then they died back down to a filament glow and went out again. While the light lasted, Merity saw the cellar hallway, thigh deep in gleaming black water, and an archway ahead to the left.

'That way!' she hissed. 'That way!'

The lights came back on, along with a brief chirrup of faulty alarms. They lasted two seconds, long enough for Merity to see that there was no archway ahead to the left.

Not any more.

Merity didn't have time to mentally process that. The cellar lights began to flash on and off like an intermittent strobe. The lights came on for half a second then off for two or three seconds, then back on. The rapid, erratic blinking made Merity feel nauseous. She reached out to hold onto Relf.

But Relf wasn't there.

In darkness, she gasped the Scion's name.

The light fluttered on and off again. In the third flash, she saw Relf on the far side of the tunnel, clawing at the wall. In the fourth flash, Relf had vanished.

In the fifth flash, Merity saw a figure standing directly ahead of her, its back to her. A figure standing nearly waist deep in the blood-black water. A figure waiting, still and upright, her hands at her sides. A simple smock dress. Head shaved.

Blackness.

'Yoncy?' Merity called out.

A saw buzzed somewhere in the darkness.

In the sixth flash, nothing.

Blackness.

In the seventh, a heartbeat later, the figure was there again, its back to her still. But it was closer. Three metres closer.

Blackness.

In the eighth flash, Yoncy was still there, and she was starting to turn. Starting to turn slowly to face Merity.

Blackness.

An angry warble of damaged alarms.

Abrupt las-fire ripped across the hallway in the dark. Merity flinched. She saw the searing bolts of energy, heard the close-by shriek of the carbine. One shot passed her head so close it crisped the downy hairs on her neck. She could smell the hot ozone as it went by, cooking the chill air. Scalding steam erupted where the las bolts hit the water.

Merity staggered backwards, eyes wide and hungry for light. She saw Relf's stab-beam moving wildly, reflecting in the water, tracking across the walls. More howling las-shots overlapped it.

'Go back!' she heard Relf yelling. 'Go back!'

Something that sounded like a surgical saw screamed in the tight confines. Merity covered her ears. Water splashed across her chest and face.

Silence. Blackness. The reek of superheated air and brick-dust. The lap and gurgle of the water. Merity moved, blind, hands out, splashing through the flood.

She saw a point of light ahead, a pale blue glow. It bobbed, then drifted down and away from her, foggy and distorted.

It was Relf's stablight, still attached to the weapon, sinking slowly in the black flood, the beam spearing up through the rippling water.

Merity plunged and grabbed at it before it sank out of sight. She pulled the short-form carbine out of the water, and turned it, holding the thing like a massively oversized flashlight rather than a gun.

'Relf? Relf?'

Debris floated on the choppy, dark water. Scraps of fabric, flecks of foam insulate from a body jacket liner, a few broken rings of armour scale. Small slicks of jelly.

Two human teeth. Some shreds of hair.

Merity gathered the dripping carbine up, and gripped it properly. It felt heavy as feth. Steam smoked from the muzzle as the heat of its recent discharge evaporated the water. She panned around, gripping it tightly with trembling hands.

The lights came back on, first a flutter, then straining half power. In the amber haze, she saw someone up ahead, someone wading through the flood towards her.

'Relf?'

Luna Fazekiel aimed her sidearm at Merity, then slowly lowered it.

'Merity?' she mumbled.

'Commissar?'

Fazekiel blinked. She looked unsteady and distressed. Her eyes were red and sore, and the expression in them was dull. Merity was shocked. Fazekiel was ordinarily the most immaculate figure in the regiment. Even the tiniest blemish on her uniform would famously irritate her deeply. Now, her clothes were torn and stained, and buttons were missing. Merity saw blood dribbling from Fazekiel's ears and one nostril.

'You're hurt,' Merity said, wading forward.

Fazekiel shook her head. 'Heard shots,' she said. 'You?'

'No, Relf. The Scion with me.'

'Where is she?'

'I don't know. She–'

'Did you see anything else?' Fazekiel asked.

'I saw Yoncy. I think.'

Fazekiel nodded. 'We're in hell,' she said.

'What?'

Fazekiel shook her head, gulping for breath. She had the zoned-out look of a soldier who'd been in contact for too long. She was soaked through, and pawed at the blood seeping from her left ear.

'We're in...' she began, then shook her head as if what she wanted to say was too hard to articulate.

'You're bleeding,' said Merity.

'Where?' asked Fazekiel, as though it didn't matter. 'So are you. Are you hit?'

'I'm not–' Merity said.

'There's blood on you. Your face and neck.'

Merity looked down and realised that the front of her tunic was soaked, and it wasn't just water.

'It's not my blood,' she said.

Luna Fazekiel wiped her hand across her mouth.

'When?' she asked. 'When did you come down here?'

'Just minutes ago,' replied Merity. 'Just before the lights went out.'

Fazekiel looked at her sharply. The dead exhaustion in her eyes scared Merity. 'That's not right,' said Fazekiel. 'The lights have been off for days.'

* * *

The undercroft lights had come back on at low power. It was a sickly, wavering light, an ochre glow no brighter than the trickling fizz of a slow fuse.

Gol Kolea sloshed through the shin-deep water of a flooded connecting passage. The cast of the wall lamps caught the moving surface of the water, and lapping reflections trembled along the whitewashed ceiling, creating an illusion that the ceiling was awash too.

The sobbing had stopped. Kolea hadn't heard anything in a while. At one point, he thought he'd heard Erish somewhere, and just after that, he was sure he'd heard Bask shouting, much further away.

He turned off his stablight to conserve power, but kept his rifle ready. The world was closing down, as though the malice of the under-universe had seized control. This was no longer a matter of technical problems.

It was here. He knew it was. It had followed him all the way from Aigor 991, across a decade and billions of kilometres. Gaunt's stoical reassurances seemed so flimsy now, Kolea was shocked at how readily he'd believed them. The Ruinous Powers had marked him, and they had come for him.

And they had lied. Everything the voice had said to him in that gloomy supply dump had been a lie. Even the promise that if they delivered the eagle stones it would cease to threaten him and his children.

Kolea hadn't done its bidding, but he hadn't denied it either. The Ghosts had brought the eagle stones to Urdesh. But that hadn't been enough. It had come for them anyway.

'What did you want?' he asked the shadows around him. The damp silence made no reply. 'What did you want us to do? Did we fail? The stones are here. Is here not where you wanted them?'

Nothing answered. That was a relief, in a way, but part of him wanted the voice to speak, so he could challenge it and deny it.

It had broken its promise. That's what the warp did, so it came as little surprise. The things that dwelt in the shadows that life cast were made of untruths and demented logic. They were lies incarnate and could never be trusted. Their promises meant nothing.

But his did. He didn't break them. Not his allegiance to the Astra Militarum, not his trench pledges to the brothers in his scratch company at Vervunhive, nor his fealty to Number Seventeen Deep Working that had been his living before that, and certainly not his vows to Livy Kolea. Livy Tarin, as was, bright in his mind as the day he'd met her.

He'd made an oath to protect his children, and all of his comrades, from the bad shadow stalking them. He'd face it down, and he'd kill it. And his promises couldn't be stronger if they'd been wrought from the metal ore he'd once dug out of the Verghast pits.

'When are you going to show yourself?' he asked. 'When are we going to have this out, you and me? Or are shadows your only trick?'

He knew they weren't, but he was angry, and taunting the darkness felt good. Maybe he could annoy it, and provoke it into revealing itself.

Give himself a target.

It had played with him all along. It had toyed with him, and its lies had even made him doubt his own kids.

Gol hesitated. His priority was to find Dalin and Yoncy, and anyone else stuck in this hellhole. He had to find them before the shadow did, and stand in its way. It had made an enemy of Gol Kolea, and any bastard could tell you that was a bad idea.

He moved forwards, swilling the flood around his knees.

'How dare you,' he murmured. 'How dare you make me think my kids were part of this. That was just torment, wasn't it? A way to plague me and make me weak.'

His mind went to the cruel fantasies that had been rattling around his head for months. Stupid, stupid thoughts. What had Gaunt said to him?

A brother would know his sister.

Fething right. It was so ridiculously easy to demolish the warp's falsehoods. If only he'd had the clarity to do that months ago. Some things just don't get thought when a man's head is all of a jumble. Some things just don't get said. They get left unspoken. Simple things that lasted and held more power than anything the warp had ever conjured. *I love you. I care. I'll walk into hell for you.*

Well, this was hell, and he was walking into it. But his mind was clear now, sharp as straight silver. The Ruinous Powers had threatened the wrong man.

At the end of the flooded hall was a flight of brick steps that led to the door of a billet hall. The lights in the stairwell were fluttering out. He thought he could hear voices.

He edged up the steps, shoulder to the wall, lasrifle aimed from the jawline. He peered out.

The billet hall was dry. Forty cots stood in two rows under a low arched roof of whitewashed stone, lit by low-power lamps. There were signs of disarray, of possessions disturbed, of people leaving in a hurry.

He hoped they'd all got out.

From the cover of the archway, he saw two figures sitting side by side on a cot at the far right end of the chamber.

It was Dalin and Yoncy.

Dalin was just staring at the next cot along, his arms in his lap, his rifle on the sheet beside him. Yoncy was snuggled up against his side, whispering quietly in his ear.

He heard Dalin murmur, 'No, Yoncy.' Like a denial. A weary refusal to accept.

Kolea took another step.

Yoncy looked up sharply, frowned at him, and then darted away.

'Yoncy! Come back, girl!' Kolea yelled, and ran down the chamber between the cot rows. She'd already vanished through an archway at the back.

'Where's she going?' Kolea asked.

Dalin didn't look up.

'Dal! What's she playing at? This isn't a game.' He turned back to look at Dalin. 'Get up, Dal,' he said. 'Right now. Help me fetch your sister.'

Dalin looked up at him, his face deadpan.

'She doesn't make any sense,' he said quietly.

Kolea frowned, and sat down beside him. 'You all right? Dal?'

'Yeah, yeah. This is all just a bit strange.'

'You got that right,' said Kolea. 'There's some ugly feth going on down here, Dal. So let's jump to it. Find your fething sister, and drag her out of here by the skirts.'

'She's only playing,' said Dalin.

'Well, this isn't time for games.'

'She said she was hungry.'

'Well, we'll cart her upstairs and get her a meal.'

Dalin nodded.

'Dal, have you seen anyone else? Bask or–'

'No.'

'Not anyone? They got everyone else up out of here? The whole retinue?'

'I think so. I was just looking for Yonce. She was playing hide-and-seek when the lights went out. Got scared, I think.'

'No doubt. Come on, move your arse before she gets too far ahead of us. Dalin?'

Dalin looked at him. It looked like he was trying to process something. Kolea didn't like the way Dalin seemed so lethargic.

'She said things,' said Dalin.

'What things?'

'She said... she said word had come. That it was time. She said there was a woe machine here.'

'A woe machine? What, like–'

'Yeah,' said Dalin. 'It's one of her games. "There's a woe machine coming" she'd say, and then she'd hide and you'd have to find her. She's been doing it for years. But when she said it just now, I thought...'

'What?'

Dalin shrugged. 'How does she know about woe machines? I've never thought about it before. I mean, I barely remember Vervunhive. I was just a child, and she's younger than me. How does she remember that?'

Gol scratched his cheek. He remembered woe machines all too well. It was the term Vervunhivers had used to describe the ingeniously grotesque death engines that Heritor Asphodel had launched against the hive. They had come in an inventively murderous range of designs. None of the Verghastites in the regiment, Guard and retinue alike, had ever forgotten their malevolence.

'She's just heard talk over the years,' said Kolea. 'Gossip in the camp, bad memories.'

'I suppose so.'

'And made a bogeyman out of it. You know how she is with games.'

'What, like her bad shadow?' Dalin asked.

Kolea said nothing.

'She said I should talk to you about it,' said Dalin.

'Me?'

'She said papa would explain it to me.'

'She calls everyone papa,' Kolea replied sadly.

He put his hand to Dalin's shoulder.

'What's the matter with you, Dal?' he asked. 'I don't like this. Are you sick?'

'I just...' Dalin stopped and sighed. 'She said such weird things. She's always been strange, but–'

'She's always been your sister,' said Kolea.

Dalin looked at him sharply. 'What does that mean?'

'Nothing. Dal, get your fething head in gear. We have to find her, wherever she's hiding, and get her out of here. There's bad shit going on and she shouldn't be down here. *We* shouldn't be down here.'

Dalin nodded and got to his feet. He picked up his lasgun.

'Yeah, of course,' he said. He seemed a little more together. 'I'd just spent so long looking for her in the dark, and then I found her, and I tried to calm her down, but she just wanted to play. And then the things she said just got to me.'

He looked at Kolea.

'You know about that thing that attacked her and Mam Daur down at Low Keen?'

'I heard,' said Kolea.

'What if that was a woe machine? I mean, it took apart a whole pack of enemy troops.'

'But spared the pair of them? Where's the logic in that?'

'Did woe machines ever have any logic?' Dalin asked. 'You'd know.'

'Not much,' Kolea admitted.

'And they were made by the Heritor.'

'Asphodel.'

'Right.'

'He's dead.'

'I know,' said Dalin. 'But there are other heritors. We know that. I mean, Salvation's Reach was a workshop for their breed. What if this is something made by one of the others? What if it followed us here from the Reach? What if... what if it's here? In the city. What if it was out there at the old billet, and now it's got in here?'

Kolea shook his head. 'A death engine like a woe machine couldn't get in here. The palace? Dal, it couldn't get past the guards. The walls. The–'

'Something has,' said Dalin quietly.

'Yes. Something has.'

They looked at each other for a moment.

'Let's find her, Dalin,' said Kolea.

'Oh, for feth's sake!' Baskevyl snapped and lowered his rifle.

Up ahead, in the low light of the bunk hall, Meryn and Banda lowered their weapons too.

'I nearly fething shot you, you fething idiots,' Baskevyl said.

'Likewise,' snorted Banda. 'How are you lot fething *in front* of us?'

'I'm telling you,' said Blenner, coming up behind Bask, his voice agitated. 'I'm telling you, there's something not right going on down here. How are Meryn's mob up there when they should be behind us? And where's everybody else? Hmm? Where is everybody?'

'There's definitely something shitty-weird going on,' growled Meryn. 'We can't find anyone and we can't find the way out.'

'What?' snapped Baskevyl. He looked past Meryn at Leyr, one of the regiment's finest scouts. Leyr looked deeply uncomfortable.

'I can't find the main stairs, sir,' Leyr said.

'Is everyone a fething idiot today?' asked Baskevyl. 'What do you mean you can't find the stairs?'

'I just can't,' said Leyr. 'They're not where they were. It should be back two rooms, and then to the right. But it's not. It's freaking me out.'

'*You're* freaking me out,' said Baskevyl.

'I'm not joking,' said Leyr angrily. 'It's like everything is shifting around. Doors, walls–'

'This palace,' said Baskevyl very calmly, 'has been standing for centuries. It's about as solid as anything gets. It's not fething-well shifting around in the dark. Have you been at the sacra, Leyr?'

'Feth you. I'm telling you what I know. The plan of the whole undercroft is not stable. Every time it goes dark, things move.'

'Bullshit,' said Baskevyl. 'Find me Bonin. Find me a scout who knows what he's fething doing.'

'Mach was leading the retinue out,' said Neskon. He was standing just behind Leyr. His eyes were hard. 'There's no sign of him, or the sergeant major. Or the retinue. It was a lot of people, sir. A lot. Women, kids. With the dark and all, and just the one staircase, they should still be filing out. An evac would take half an hour at least. We should still be able to hear them.'

'And we can't even find the stairs,' said Banda.

'Are you going to tell them what we found?' Blenner asked.

Baskevyl glared at him.

'We found the Munitorum work crew,' said Blenner, looking at Meryn's squad. 'What was left of them.'

'What?' said Meryn.

'They were very dead,' said Blenner. He palmed something from his coat pocket and swallowed it dry.

'So this is an attack?' Banda asked.

'I don't know what it is,' said Baskevyl quietly. 'We can't find Shoggy, or Luna, or Dalin, or the girl. We can't find anybody.'

'Not just me, then,' muttered Leyr.

Baskevyl glanced at him. 'Well, as long as your professional reputation is intact, we're all good,' he growled.

'Have you seen anybody at all?' Osket asked Meryn.

'Not a soul until you came along,' said Meryn.

'From the wrong direction...' Blenner whispered.

'Gol?' asked Baskevyl.

Meryn shook his head.

'All right,' said Baskevyl. 'We'll try to finish the section search. At the very least, Gol's team is down here somewhere. Then we'll pull back. Meryn, take your squad, circle back and find the fething stairs. Got any pencil flares? Any chalk?'

'I'll find a way to mark the route,' said Leyr.

'Good. Do it.'

Baskevyl turned and led his team back the way they had come. Meryn
glanced at Banda, Leyr, Neskon and Leclan.

'You heard him,' he said.

They turned around and moved back down the hallway. The lights were
flickering again. Every three metres or so, Neskon paused and scorched a
burn-mark on the wall with a quick burst of his flamer.

'That'll do the trick,' said Leyr.

The air began to fill with the stink of burned paint and scorched brick
dust. It mixed with the damp reek of burst drains, and caught in their
throats. They reached a T-junction that none of them could remember
being there before.

'Right or left?' asked Neskon.

Leyr paused.

'Left,' Meryn decided.

Banda held up her hand.

'What was that?' she asked.

'What?'

'It sounded like sobbing,' she said.

'I can't hear anything,' said Leyr.

Meryn gestured at Neskon, who damped the ignition flame of his unit.
The constant, chugging rasp of the flamer died away.

They listened.

'That's sobbing,' said Banda. 'Or giggling.'

'A kid...' said Leclan.

'Gol's brat,' said Meryn. 'Gotta be.'

'Well, we should find her,' said Neskon. 'Everyone was looking for her.'

'That way,' said Leyr, indicating the left-hand tunnel.

They advanced. Neskon and Leyr took the lead, but Neskon kept his
burner dead so they could hear. He roped the nozzle-gun over his shoulder,
and drew his sidearm. Banda and Leclan followed them, and Meryn lurked
in the rear. He kept glancing behind him.

'Oh feth,' Leyr murmured.

Up ahead, every few metres, there were burn patches on the whitewashed
wall.

'Somebody else had the same idea,' said Neskon.

Leyr shook his head. He touched one of the marks. 'Still warm,' he said.
'You did this.'

'Feth I did,' Neskon objected.

'We're following our own footsteps,' said Leyr.

'Shut the feth up,' Meryn told him.

The lights dimmed suddenly and went off. The darkness lasted about
three seconds, then the lamps began to glow again. They barely rose from
nothing. There was no more light than an overcast dusk, sallow and yellow.

The Ghosts flipped on their stablights.

'Door,' said Leclan, and nodded ahead. There was an archway to their left. A small storage room.

Leclan and Leyr advanced, and came in either side of the door. Leclan had his sidearm out, Leyr had the butt of his lasrifle tight in his shoulder.

They swung in.

The room was a small stone vault. On one side, the wall was lined with old wooden racks that had once held wine casks. Several broken packing crates stood nearby. The stone floor was wet, with a couple of centimetres of rank standing water. Several steady drips were spilling from the bowed ceiling.

Yoncy sat on a crate in the far corner with her back to them. Her head was bowed and her shoulders were shaking.

'Hey, Yoncy,' said Leclan. He holstered his sidearm and hurried in, pulling his medicae satchel in front of him. Leyr followed.

Leclan knelt down by the young girl.

'You all right? Yoncy? It's me, Leclan. Are you hurt?'

Yoncy glanced at him, her head still down. She had been crying.

'Papa Leclan,' she whispered, and sniffed.

'That's right. Are you hurt? I'm just going to check you over, and then we'll get you out of here.'

'I was hiding,' she said softly. 'Because the woe machine is here.'

'What did she say?' asked Leyr, moving closer.

'Something about a woe machine,' replied Leclan. He was trying to turn Yoncy's head towards him so he could check her pupil response with his penlight. 'I think she's in shock.'

'Woe machine?' said Neskon. He and Banda had followed the scout and the corpsman into the room. 'Tell her there's no fething woe machine here.'

Meryn stood in the doorway behind them.

'It's just a game she plays,' he said. 'Hide-and-seek. Stupid little freak.'

Banda glared at him. 'Feth you, Flyn,' she warned in a hard whisper. 'She's scared.'

Meryn shrugged. 'We're all fething scared, sweetie,' he replied.

'There's no woe machine,' Leclan told the girl gently. He opened her mouth and shone the penlight inside. 'Have you seen anybody? Yonce? Did you see anybody when you were playing your game? When it went dark?'

Yoncy closed her mouth.

'I saw Dal. And Papa Gol,' she said.

'Where were they?' Meryn called across from the door.

'They took a wrong turn,' Yoncy whispered to Leclan conspiratorially. 'I'm really hungry.'

'What's that mark on your neck here?' Leclan asked, tilting her head gently to look.

Banda looked back at Meryn.

'If Gol's close,' she said, 'or Dalin... maybe try your link again?'

Meryn sighed, and adjusted his earpiece. The deep itching in his eardrums was back. It suddenly seemed to have got very cold.

'Kolea? Dalin?' he called. 'Anyone read? Kolea?'

There was a sharp screech, a howl like grinding metal. Meryn started, and yanked the earpiece out, thinking it was the wail of feedback. But the noise continued even with the earpiece gone.

He looked back into the room. Something was happening to Leclan. He was standing with his back to them. His body and out-flung arms were vibrating violently. Meryn stared in utter incomprehension. What the feth was Leclan doing? He couldn't see Yoncy. Just Leclan, shaking and juddering like some fething ecstatic worshipper.

Leclan began to rise into the air, his arms still wide. Water dripped off his suspended boots. Meryn screwed up his face in disbelief. The screech turned into the excruciating, full-on howl of a bone saw.

Leclan disintegrated. Tissue, shredded clothing and shattered bone fragments blasted out in all directions, splattering the room. A small bone shard caught Meryn under the right eye with the force of a slingshot, even though he was metres away.

There was blood everywhere. A drenching mist of it.

Leyr stumbled backwards. A piece of Leclan's left clavicle had embedded in his throat. He tried to raise his weapon, arterial blood squirting from his neck.

Darkness, wailing like a cycling saw blade, boiled out of the back of the room. It came on like a wall of shadow, a flash-flood of darkness. Leyr loosed two wild shots. Neskon screamed and reignited his flamer. It took two or three frantic pumps to gun it into life.

By then, the rushing tide of shadow had reached him. The saw howled. Neskon shredded. He came apart where he was standing. It looked as though he had been sliced vertically by four or five separate blades. As the pieces of him toppled in a blizzard of blood, the trigger spoon still clutched in his right hand gouted, engulfing Leyr in a sheet of roaring flame.

Leyr, burning from head to foot, dropped to his knees and toppled forwards.

The entire horror had taken just a second or two. Meryn shrieked, and scrambled backwards out of the doorway. The darkness swept towards him, like black water filling the vault.

He ducked aside, about to run, but something clawed at him, holding his arm and shoulder tightly.

He snarled and fought back.

Banda was clinging to him with both hands. He could only see her head, shoulders and arms. She was folded around the door jamb by the armpits, the rest of her inside the room.

Her eyes were so big.

'Flyn! Flyn!' she screamed.

He fought to break her grip. It was like a vice on his arm.

'Flyn!' Banda shrieked. 'It's got me! It's fething got me! Pull me out!'

'Let go!'

'Pull me out, you fething bastard! Pull me out!'

Meryn thrashed wildly. He refused to look into her staring eyes. His churning elbow mashed her left wrist and her grip broke.

Meryn tumbled backwards into the hallway.

'You fething bastard!' she screamed as the room pulled her back in.

'You toxic fething-' Her fingers raked along the whitewash, leaving bloody scratches. Then she was gone, snapped back like a whip around the edge of the door.

He heard her final scream, mangled by the screech of the bone saw.

Blood squirted out of the doorway and spattered three slashing lines across the floor and up the opposite wall.

Meryn got up, almost crippled by terror. He was tangled in the sling of his rifle. Shadows began to ooze out of the vault like black silk swirling in a breeze. He could smell blood, promethium and burned flesh.

He opened up, firing from the hip at full auto as he backed away. Brick and whitewashed plaster exploded from the walls and ceiling around the doorway. The air clouded with white dust, and the shadow poured through it like a stain.

Meryn hurled the gun away and started to run. He screamed, sprinting for his life.

The hallway was suddenly very long and very straight. There was no end to it. Every three metres there was a burner scorch on the whitewash.

He kept running. Behind him, one by one, the low-burning lamps went out. He heard the pop and fizzle of each globe chasing him like gunshots.

He tried to run faster. He tried to stay ahead of the darkness. His bladder had gone, and he realised the piercing squeals he could hear were his own.

He fell, skinning his palms. He couldn't breathe. Terror had closed his windpipe.

He looked up. His vision had tunnelled down to a grey haze.

There were two people standing over him. Merity Chass was looking down at him in utter bewilderment. Luna Fazekiel was staring past him, her eyes narrowed.

'Stay the feth down, captain,' Fazakiel said.

Fazekiel and Merity opened fire. Meryn screwed into a foetal position, arms clasped around his ears, as Fazekiel's autopistol and Merity's carbine blazed over his head. Hot brass bounced off his cheek and neck.

And then it stopped.

'Check him,' he heard Fazekiel say. He felt Merity's hand on him, trying to turn him, trying to uncoil him. He wrenched away from her with a whimper.

He raised his head. Merity was staring at him.

'What the Throne happened to you?' she asked.

He didn't answer. He looked back at the hallway. He didn't want to, but he knew he had to.

Fazekiel had stepped past him and was staring down the hall, checking the clip of her weapon. The long hallway was empty. The three ceiling lamps closest to them were still lit, fizzling weakly. Beyond them, it was just shadow.

'I don't know what we saw,' said Fazekiel, 'but it's gone.' She turned and looked down at him.

'What was it, captain?' she asked. 'I don't understand what we glimpsed. We drove it off, but I don't know if we could do it again. I don't think I can

protect you again. I can't fight what I don't understand. Captain? Do you
hear me? What *was* it?'

Meryn shook his head. His mouth wouldn't work.

Fazekiel crouched down.

'What did you see, Meryn?' she asked without a scrap of compassion.

'I saw everybody die,' he said.

ELEVEN

CONTACT

Handbells were still ringing along the shore line. Squads of packsons hurried through the steep streets of the stacked little cliff-town, going building to building and stopping to question everyone they passed.

Mkoll watched from the top of a bale stack in one of the quayside barns. The roof of the open-fronted barn extended over him, preventing anyone spotting him from above, and he had taken a sheet of tarp from the loading dock and pulled it over him.

Every inch of him ached. His scalp wound had finally stopped bleeding, but the whole area behind his ear was too painful to touch. Dried blood crusted his scalp, the side of his neck and his shoulder. He didn't have a mirror, but he knew the side of his face was probably purple with trauma.

He was drawn tight with fatigue. He'd rested under the tarp for an hour, but hadn't dared sleep. Fatigue was just something he'd push through. He'd done it before. It was a matter of will. Body-tired didn't matter. Mind-tired was the killer. His mind was sharp. The pain had done that.

He watched the scene below him, wishing he still had Olort's field glasses. The whole of the Fastness was on security vigil – the equivalent, he fancied, of an amber alert in an Imperial garrison. The search teams didn't interest him much. They were sticking to the higher levels of the city, around the records building. They would have little idea who they were looking for. Their quarry had made a reckless escape across the rooftops of the high town. He was either hiding up there, or had fallen to his death in one of the ditch gullies between the stacked dwellings. They were probably dragging for a body already.

What interested him was the area directly below, a stretch of wharf around the base of one of the loading gantries. Internal freight hoists steadily ferried loads up to the level of the bridge spans where teams of servitors rolled them across to the cruiser's hold gates. Sixty or more men were working on the rockcrete pan below him, mainly servitors and stevedores, plus a few gangs of Imperial slaves. They were being supervised by several Sekkite officers. They rolled metal carts out from the barns beneath him, carts laden with bales and crates, and shunted them into the hoist cages. A few men rode up with them. The rest waited as empty carts came back down, then clattered them back to the barns to be restocked.

A lighter bumbled past at low level, heading for the ship. Mkoll kept

his head covered under the lip of the tarp. The small craft was chased by
a shadow that flickered across the working dock and then out across the
shivering water. Daylight had gone. Above the mouth of the cone, the sky
was a starless grey. The shadow had been cast by the banks of floodlights
framed on the edge of the wharf. Mkoll had thought about a lighter or a
small lifter, but he wasn't sure where they were working from. A landing area
would be guarded, and it was hard to be anonymous among a small crew.

He watched the lighter turn and settle, lights winking, into a hold cavity
further down the flank of the immense ship.

More agriboats were coming in, chugging sideways into the next dock
bay along with smoke spilling at water level from their straining motors.
They were loaded with more mainland personnel, a few shivering prisoners, and some small artillery pieces with sacks on their muzzles and their
split trail carriages closed.

The thousand whispers in his head welled up again like the dead channel
of a vox. The voice was speaking, a droning hiss he could feel in his sinuses
and jawbone.

I have some words for you too, he thought. I'll say them in person.

Down below, another train of carts rattled across the rockcrete, the gangs
steering them shouting and exchanging comments. Servitors dragged empty
ones back to the barn from the hoist. One of the officers, a sirdar, spoke to
a group of stevedores, then wandered towards the barn, marking items on
a slate.

The sirdar entered the lamplit barn and instructed the servitors which
load to move from the freight stacks next.

One of his men called to him. He finished what he was saying, and walked
around the bale stack to find out what the man wanted.

There was no one there.

Mkoll dropped down behind him, and snapped his neck with a practised
twist. The sirdar's feet jittered, and then he went limp. Mkoll dragged him
behind a heap of trench-wire spools, and stripped off his jacket, watching all
the while to make sure no one was coming. A decent jacket, and better boots
than the ones Mkoll was wearing, but the boots were a size too small. He
took the jacket, the Sekkite helmet and the weapons belt, which had a single
shoulder strap. The belt's pouches were full of hard-round clips because the
sirdar carried a long-nosed autogun. There were no las cells to fit the sidearm
he already had. But there was a small vox handset, a short-range unit, and
three small grenades. They were little silver cylinders. Two were marked with
red dots, which he guessed meant smoke. The other, its casing slightly ridged,
was marked with a black dot. Fragmentation. Anti-personnel.

Mkoll tucked the laspistol into the back of his waistband, then put on the
sirdar's undershirt and jacket, and buckled the weapons belt over the top.

He stepped back behind the wire spools. Two packsons from the labour
crews walked past the freight aisle. Once they had gone, he put on the sirdar's gloves and full-face helmet, gagging slightly at the touch of the tanned
leather and the acid smell of the sirdar's spittle. Then he picked up the
slate and stylus.

The sirdar walked back out onto the dock. A work gang was waiting beside a laden row of carts. A hoist car was returning to dock level, jangling with empty carts.

'Ktah heth dvore voi?' a stevedore asked him as he walked past.

'Nen, nen,' the sirdar replied, busy looking at his slate. 'Khen vah.'

A bare-chested packson lifted the hoist's cage door, and the servitors clattered the empty carts out.

'Kyeth! Da tsa herz! Kyeth! Kyeth!' the sirdar said, sweeping with his hand to urge the gang to load.

The men started to wrangle the heavy carts into the hoist. One of the packsons looked at the sirdar.

'Khin bachat Sird Eloth?' he asked. *Where is Sirdar Eloth?*

'Tsa vorhun ter gan,' the sirdar replied. *Gone to his rest.*

'Tyah k'her het!' the packson scoffed. *This early?*

'Khen tor Sird Eloth fagrah,' the sirdar replied. *Sirdar Eloth is a lazy bastard.*

The workers laughed. They pushed the cumbersome carts up the fold-down ramp, cursing each other as they handled them into the cage. Another lighter warbled overhead, heading towards the cruiser. Its shadow chased across the dock.

Three servitors and two packsons got into the cage with the new load. One went to pull down the cage door.

'Nen, coraht!' the sirdar barked, raising his hand.

He stepped forward and jerked his thumb, ordering one of the packsons out.

'Shet, magir?' the man asked.

'Hsa gor tre shet,' the sirdar replied, stepping into the hoist in his place. 'Voi shet tsa khen verkahn.' *I've got to go up. Go ready the next load.*

The sirdar pulled the cage shut. The hoist began to rise, slow and ponderous, the steel hawsers squealing through poorly greased drums.

The packson with him in the cage said nothing. The three servitors cycled their systems in neutral, and flexed their manipulator arms ready to resume effort.

The hoist reached the loading bridge level, and stopped with a jolt and a thump of block-brakes. The packson slunked open the cage door at the far end.

The sirdar waited while the servitors rolled out the first of the carts. More servitor crews and a few sweating labourers took hold of them, steered them clear, and began to roll them across the bridge.

The sirdar stepped out of the cage. He checked off items on his slate. Two Sekkite officers stood nearby with an excubitor, discussing loading options. None of them acknowledged him.

The sirdar fell in step behind the rumbling train of carts and followed them across the bridge span.

No one challenged him.

The hold gates of the Archenemy cruiser stood wide open to receive him.

* * *

'How do we open a door that isn't there?' Curth asked.

'Maybe we don't,' said Laksheema.

'Say that again,' said Curth.

Laksheema raised her voice to compete with the steady whoop of the red condition klaxons.

'I said maybe we *shouldn't*, doctor,' she said.

Curth shot her a foul expression.

Gaunt ran his hand along the old stonework.

'Maybe we need a drill,' someone suggested.

Gaunt looked around. Trooper Perday flushed.

'I mean, like in the Reach, sir,' she added, nervously. 'You know, a proper breaching drill. Just thinking out loud...' Her voice trailed off.

'Is there a breaching unit in the palace compound?' asked Gaunt. 'A Hades?'

'Must be,' said Beltayn.

'Think, think,' Hark interrupted. 'How do we get a fething Hades down here? Some of the halls between here and the transit grounds are too narrow, and there's stairs–'

'Go in from outside?' Curth suggested.

'Not viable,' said Auerben. 'Even if we could round one up.'

'Agreed,' said Sancto. 'The thickness of the root wall. It would take days.'

'And where do we drill?' Auerben asked.

'Someone find a fething plan of the undercroft level,' Gaunt said to no one in particular.

'Det charges,' said Sariadzi bluntly.

'Now, *that's* better thinking,' said Hark, nodding.

'Stop,' said Laksheema.

Everyone looked at her.

'With respect, your debate assumes we *want* to open the undercroft,' she said.

'Feth you,' said Curth.

'Feth me all you like,' Laksheema replied. 'This is a security matter. A warp incursion. There's something in there. I believe we would be derelict in our duty to the Throne to open that wall and let it into a palace containing the bulk of crusade high command and the person of the Warmaster.'

Daur looked away. Hark squeezed his shoulder.

The Scions snapped around, weapons raised. Grae was returning, bringing the inquisitor's savant Onabel and two robed interrogators.

'Let them through,' said Laksheema. She put her hand on the plump little woman's elbow and cradled it. 'Did Grae brief you?' Laksheema asked.

'He did, mam,' Onabel replied. She combed her fingers through her curly silver hair. 'All our meters are spiking. This is an incursion of serious grade.'

'Serious enough to evacuate the palace?' asked Gaunt.

Onabel hunched her shoulders. 'Not my place to say, high lord,' she replied. 'But I wouldn't stay here. I'm only here because I'm called to work. I'd venture that, at least, the removal to safe distance of senior echelon might be wise. That would include yourself, sir.'

'I'm staying,' said Gaunt. 'Beltayn, go to the war room and...' he hesitated. 'No, it's got to come from someone with authority. Van Voytz won't act on the word of a vox-man. Inquisitor?'

Laksheema beckoned the two interrogators. She handed them her ordo rosette. 'Convey to Lord General Van Voyz whatever the Lord Executor instructs you.'

They nodded.

'Tell him immediate evacuation, including senior level,' Gaunt said. 'Tell him to carry Macaroth out of the palace on his shoulders if he has to. Tell him... Ibram told you this. It's an unconditional order from the Lord Executor.'

'Yes, lord,' they replied, and hurried back the way they'd come, the tails of their robes lifting behind them.

Onabel had set her hands on the wall.

'Here?' she asked.

'Yes,' said Laksheema.

The little savant closed her eyes. She took one hand off the wall and pressed it against her bosom. The other she left in place, her index finger tapping on the stone.

They could smell the ugly aura of psionics immediately. Perday covered her mouth. The Scions took a step back, uneasy.

Clear liquid began to seep out of the stonework, welling up and running down the wall around her hand like heavy beads of condensation. It felt as though someone had opened the door of a walk-in freezer.

'Water?' said Daur. 'Is the flood up this high?' He reached towards the droplets.

'Don't,' said Laksheema.

'It's tears,' said Onabel. She kept tapping her finger, her eyes squeezed shut.

'Tears?' asked Curth.

'There is a great deal of pain on the other side of this wall,' said Onabel. 'Woe.' Her voice was soft, but a tiny break betrayed her increasing discomfort. 'I have voices,' she said. 'People are... there are dead people. Others crying out.'

'May we hear?' asked Laksheema. 'If you can bear it?'

Onabel nodded. When her mouth opened next, it wasn't her voice that came out of it.

'–can't find the door! There's no door!'

There was no mistaking the voice. It was Mach Bonin. They'd never heard him so agitated, but it was undeniably him. The savant wasn't impersonating. Bonin's voice, the product of an entirely different set of vocal chords, was issuing from her mouth.

'Mach?' Gaunt said, stepping forward. 'It's Gaunt. Tell him it's Gaunt.'

'Is he the other side of the wall?' asked Sancto.

Laksheema shook her head.

'There's no fething door, Yerolemew!' Bonin said through Onabel's mouth. 'How's that fething possible?'

'I don't know, Mach. Mach? Mach? There's something on the stairs.'

Onabel's speech had switched seamlessly to the gruff, rich cadences of the Belladon bandmaster. They'd never heard him panicking either. 'Mach, it's on the stairs. It's all shadows. The women are screaming.'

'Sergeant major!' Gaunt shouted at the wall and the savant. 'Sergeant Major Yerolemew! This is Gaunt! Can you hear me?'

'Sir? Sir?' Onabel's lips kept moving, but Yerolemew's voice had faded, as though he had moved away. The volume rose and fell like a 'caster looped on and off a signal. 'Mach, did you hear that? Bonin! I heard someone. I heard Gaunt!'

The noises from the savant became inaudible. Muffled sounds. Echoes of words.

'Bonin!' Daur called out, moving in beside Gaunt. 'Bonin? It's Ban! Let me know you can hear us.'

The voice coming out of Onabel suddenly giggled. A different voice in another register. A child.

'Feth,' murmured Hark.

Curth nodded. 'Yoncy.'

The giggle stopped. Onabel's mouth continued to move silently. Then suddenly, sharply–

'Ban?'

Daur shuddered. He fought to control the contortions of his face. His eyes filled with tears.

'Ban?' The voice was loud and very clear.

'Elodie?' Daur answered.

'Ban, get us out. Ban? The shadow's in here. We can't find the door. Everything... everything's moving around.'

'Elodie... we're trying to–'

'Everyone's scattering. Women and children. There was no door. The door just wasn't there. The shadow came up. The bad shadow. Filling up everything. People – Ban? Are you still there?'

'Yes,' he whispered.

'Ban, love,' said Elodie's voice, as though she was just on the other side of a curtain. 'Ban, it's killing people.' She started to sob. Tears ran from Onabel's eyes and more droplets scurried down the wall. 'I'm so afraid. There's blood everywhere. It's cutting through the retinue and– Ban? I think it's hungry. I think it's eating to... to get stronger. To grow. It's filling everything up. Blood levels are rising–'

'She means flood levels,' whispered Sancto.

'No, she doesn't,' said Laksheema.

'Elodie?' Daur grimaced through his tears. His fists clenched. 'Elodie, stay put. Hide. We'll get in there.'

'Blood levels are rising. The shadow's in us. It makes the sound I heard. The sound at Low Keen. The butcher sound. Juniper says it smells like a woe machine. I'm so scared. Get me out. Get me fething out. Please. I'm so sorry, Ban. So sorry. I was right. I was right about her, and I should have said before. I should have said. I knew what she was. I should have made someone listen–'

Elodie's voice dropped to a distant whisper.

'Oh Throne,' she breathed. 'She's right here.'

'Elodie?'

'Ban? I love you. I always will.'

'I love you, Elodie. I–'

Onabel fell silent. Her lips stopped moving.

'Elodie?' Daur murmured, staring at the savant.

Onabel let her hand slip off the wall. It flopped down at her side. She turned very slowly and opened her eyes. She stared right at Daur.

And opened her mouth. And somehow produced a sound it should have been impossible for a human voice to copy.

The howling shriek of a bone saw.

The light globes overhead shattered like autogun rounds.

Onabel coughed, and bloody phlegm sprayed from her lips. She fell down, twitching.

Daur sank to his knees.

'Holy fething throne,' murmured Beltayn.

Laksheema knelt beside her stricken savant. Curth ran to Daur, and tried to get him up. He wouldn't move, so she crouched beside him instead and wrapped her arm around him.

'Get charges,' said Gaunt. 'Viktor? Get charges now. A demolition team. We're taking this wall down.'

'My lord, we cannot let it out,' said Laksheema. 'Under no circumstances. It's your regiment, I know. I understand your despair. But we cannot permit this thing to exit the undercroft area.'

Gaunt looked down at her.

'I think if it wants to come out, it will,' he replied. 'I think it can come through that wall, or any wall, as easily as it can seal a door. I think killing the feth out of it is our only option. So kindly, inquisitor, shut the feth up.'

'I'll get charges,' said Hark.

Auerben put a hand on Gaunt's arm. He looked at her. She nodded her head to the back of the group behind them.

The Beati had been sitting on the floor beside Beltayn's ruined vox-set the whole time. She hadn't spoken a word. She hadn't uttered a sound. She had just sat as if chronic fatigue had finally overcome her entirely.

She rose to her feet.

'If we leave it in there, it will keep feeding and get stronger,' she said in a hollow voice. 'I've been trying to focus. Trying to... trying to know.'

'Know?' asked Gaunt.

'Know what I should do.'

'You should leave,' said Grae. 'You and the Warmaster. All the vital personnel. It's here to kill, to obliterate the command structure–'

'It is,' the Beati nodded. 'It's a Heritor weapon. An old one. A rare one. Asphodel made it. His finest and most nightmarish work. A woe machine like no other. It's been growing this whole time, learning, maturing.'

'How the feth do you know any of that?' Curth snapped.

'He told me,' said the Beati. 'Because I asked and I waited and he answered.'

'Who?' asked Curth.

The Beati looked at her with a sad smile as though the answer was unambiguous.

'Move your poor savant,' she said to Laksheema. 'Captain Daur? I need you to move too. Stand back. Weapons up.'

Laksheema and Grae carried Onabel clear. Daur got up, and allowed Curth to walk him aside. The others raised their weapons in a clatter of charging bolts, released safeties and slotting clips.

The Beati approached the wall.

'Wait,' said Gaunt. 'You're too valuable.'

'No one's too valuable, Ibram,' she replied, 'and no life is disposable.'

She put out her hand and touched the spot where Onabel had been tapping. There was no ceremony, no fanfare, no warning. The stone work crumbled. It collapsed around her fingertips. Blocks fell out and bounced across the floor. Some disintegrated into dust. The rupture widened, radiating out from her touch. A section of whitewashed stone three metres wide flexed, folded and fell back into the darkness with a rumble like an avalanche.

Dust billowed around them, glittering the red target beams of the Scions' aimed weapons.

There was a ragged hole, like the mouth of a cave. Beyond it, the air was a soft blackness tinged with red. They could smell smoke, the stench of waste water. Blood.

The Beati drew her sword. She looked weak and drained, as though collapsing the wall had sapped her fading strength even more, but her voice was strong.

'We kill it,' she said. 'We kill it before it eats its fill and becomes strong enough to kill *us*.'

Ordinate Jan Jerik checked his timepiece again. Just over an hour until middle night. According to schedule, Corrod's forces would be at the execution points by now. By sunrise, Urdesh could be a different world, a place of new prospects and possibilities. Indeed, the complexion of the Sabbat Worlds as a whole should have begun to change.

He snapped shut the engraved silver cover of the timepiece and slipped it back into his waistcoat pocket. An hour until middle night. It was quiet. The halls of House Ghentethi were almost silent, with only night staff at their stations. Outside, the rain had eased, and an easterly was spoiling in across the Great Bay, piling steep banks of dark cloud inland across the south-western limits of the city, black against the slate-black sky. *Full dark.* That, he gathered, is what soldiers called it.

It all seemed too still and silent for such a significant moment. The world, he thought, should be shaking apart as such fundamental changes were made.

There would be difficult and confusing times ahead, of course. He understood that. Existential transitions were painful. But Urdesh had weathered many such transitions in its history. It had grown resilient. His efforts would focus on keeping the house secure, and on ensuring that the Archon and his magisters appreciated and remembered the role of his clave appropriately. It would be an era of renewal, an end to the long conflict that had kept them cowering like starving dogs, an end to the decades of war that had convulsed the Sabbat Worlds. The chokehold of the Cult Mechanicus tyrants would be broken, and the claves would be free to prosper again in the ways they had done generations before. They would be the demiurge masters of the world-forge, and Urdesh would be the precious, beating heart of a new epoch. A new Archonate.

This had been explained and promised to him repeatedly by the intermediaries who had visited frequently over the last two months. Some had been insurgent chieftains, others rogue tech-shapers from the wasteland zones. Once or twice, Sekkite officers in hooded rain cloaks had appeared on the house loading docks in the dead of night. Some had conversed in Jan Jerik's tongue, while others had brought servitors as translators. One had channelled a voice which had spoken out of him like the wheeze of ruptured bellows.

The promises had been consistent. In return for assistance and specialist intelligence, Ghentethi would be spared and favoured. In the aftermath, it would have priority access to food supplies and resources, and after that, a pact-bond granting it first pick of contract-projects and commissions of manufacture. Jan Jerik had already made a comprehensive list of the forge assets and industrial facilities he would demand as Ghentethi's due recompense, as well as acquisition orders for the labour force he would require.

The war was about to end. It would not end all at once, and there would be lean years as the broken forces of the vanquished were prised out of the Sabbat Worlds and driven to flight. But it would be a victory, the victory long imagined, and it would begin in earnest tonight. Ruined and shamed, the crusaders would not attempt to return for generations to come. It would take lifetimes for them to recover from the loss, and gather strength enough to contemplate the prospect of a fresh campaign.

Lifetimes, if ever.

Jan Jerik took out his timepiece again, checked it, and put it away. Corrod would be in position. Hadrel would be in position. The future hinged on those uncanny creatures. There was no way to know how they had fared. One unscheduled venting of the thermal network could have ended them already, and no one would know. Dawn would come and the future would be unaltered. The hope of victory would have passed away invisibly.

But things needed to proceed on the assumption that they had prevailed. A data wafer lay beside his glass of amasec on the lacquered side table. On it was a code-burst written in Sekkite cipher, designed to be broadcast via wide-band vox on the lower frequency channel used by the Archonate's communications network. Corrod had helped him to compose the specifics. A call to arms. An order of uprising to all the insurgent forces in the tattered skirts of the city and beyond. Eltath had been pregnable for months. There were cells embedded everywhere, even in the inner quarters, along with Sekkite combat packs that had gone to ground in the city rather than flowing out with the general retreat a few days earlier. The code-burst commended their mettle and loyalty, promised them spiritual reward and deliverance, and specified critical targets.

They would be no more than noise, a violent disruption intended to fog the situation and draw Imperial attention from the key objectives.

Of course, if Corrod was already dead, the uprising would be a meaningless snarl, swiftly put down by the Militarum divisions for no result. And the code-burst transmission would be tracked, and Ghentethi erased by crusade prosecution.

Jan Jerik thought of Corrod, of the abomination that had revealed itself in the freight elevator. The image made him shudder. He had allied his House with abhuman creatures. It had been a gruelling choice. His doubts over the last few weeks had been many, not least at the sight of Corrod's apparently worthless wretches when they first arrived at the house door. It was a choice between the continued yoke of slavery to the Omnissiah of the Golden Throne, and the prospect of an age without the privations of chronic war. He still didn't know if he could trust the warp-words of Sek's changeling angels. He feared their terrible beauty. But he did know what a lifetime under the scourge of the Mars priesthood felt like.

He knew true monsters when he saw them. He knew where freedom lay. Life was a series of choices, and every choice contained an unknowable risk.

He reached for his timepiece again and stopped himself with a smile. He didn't need to know the time, for it no longer mattered. He had made his choice an hour earlier when he sent the code-burst.

He sat back and waited for the dawn to bring whatever it would bring.

Van Voytz looked at the ordo rosette again, and then handed it back to the waiting interrogators.

'This is from the Lord Executor?' he said.

'I have repeated his words precisely, lord,' one of them replied. 'He insisted on that.'

Van Voytz nodded, and they stepped back. He stood for a moment and surveyed the war room. He'd come down to the main floor, his favourite place, among the strategium tables and the bustle of tactical staff. They'd been on red condition for the best part of an hour. Chevrons still flashed on the alert boards, though he'd had the interminable klaxons muted to allow them space to think.

He went to his station, and quickly wrote down a general command on a signal pad. He tore the sheet off and handed it to a runner.

'Take this to the watch room,' he said. He looked at his console, and began to type his authority code in.

'You have accessed Central Classified Command Notation,' an adept at the desk beside him said immediately.

'I know,' said Van Voytz. He continued to type.

'This order burst will instruct on the General Band to all stations,' the adept said.

'I should hope so,' Van Voytz replied. 'I'm not so old I got the damn coding wrong.'

'You have entered a Priority One Red Condition mandate. This will be an Unconditional and General Order to all personnel in the palace zone.'

'Yes, it will,' said Van Voytz.

'What's going on, Barthol?'

Van Voytz looked up from the keypad. Urienz had crossed the war room floor to join him.

'I'm ordering full evacuation.'

'You're joking, surely?' The brows of Urienz's pugnacious face narrowed.

'No. Direct instruction from the Lord Executor.'

'This is an attack, then?' Urienz asked.

'There's something going off in the sub levels,' said Van Voytz.

'Well, they haven't got in there,' said Urienz.

'Gaunt says something has. An incursion. Clearly one he considers a credible threat.'

He resumed typing.

Urienz took hold of his wrist, gently but firmly. 'Macaroth won't wear this, Barthol,' he said.

'Well, he's not in a position to argue.'

'I did what Gaunt asked,' Urienz said. 'I went to Macaroth. As usual, he was furious about the interruption. I had to weather another of his tirades. I got a little sense out of him when his anger blew out. He's aware that there's a situation in the undercroft levels. He believes it's–'

'What?' asked Van Voytz.

'A misidentification. Perhaps the product of technical problems, perhaps some remote influence by the Archenemy. A distraction, Barthol. Macaroth insists that any significant Archenemy counter assault is a week away at least. There's nothing of substance within a hundred and twenty kilometres of Eltath. Look, in the last two hours we've stepped up from amber status to red condition, plus the secondary order. Macaroth's livid. The enemy's poking at us somehow, trying to get us to dance a jig and lose our grip on the game. And we're dancing, Barthol. Dancing like idiots.'

Van Voytz scowled at him. 'The Beati supported Gaunt's concern,' he said.

'And praise be to her,' said Urienz. 'But she's a figurehead, a field commander. It's not her place to direct strategy. An evacuation, Barthol? That would be a disaster. If this is anything solid, it's a psychological attack intended to spook us into disarray before next week's assault. An evacuation is exactly the sort of mayhem it's designed to cause. The Sek packs will roll in across Grizmund's line in the south west and find high command camping in the streets and shitting in doorways.'

'I have an order, Vitus,' said Van Voytz.

'Well, the Warmaster will have your balls in a monogrammed box if you follow it.'

Van Voytz shook his head. 'I know Gaunt,' he said. 'He's many things. But he's no fool. If he says there's cause, there's cause. Throne's sake, Urienz, he's seen more of this shit first-hand than you or me. And that doesn't matter anyway. He's the Lord Executor. This is his order.'

Urienz shrugged. His broad, powerful frame stretched at his tailored blue jacket.

'Your funeral,' he said.

'Better mine than everybody's,' replied Van Voytz.

He smiled at his fellow lord.

'Yours too, actually,' he added. 'Gather an escort company and convey the Warmaster from the palace.'

'You bastard,' Urienz replied, with a sorry shake of his head. 'Can't you charge Lugo with that?'

An adept at a nearby station called out and held up a signal form. Marshal Tzara strode across and took it. She brought it through the hustle of the floor to Van Voytz and Urienz.

'An alert from vox-net oversight,' she said, frowning. 'Unauthorised broadcast detected about an hour ago. Code-burst, wide-band, low numbers.'

'Origin?' asked Van Voytz.

'Vapourial or Millgate. They're working to lock the source.'

'Could be one of ours, strayed from the line,' said Van Voytz.

'Damn Helixid no doubt,' added Urienz.

'No,' said Tzara. 'It was encrypted. Cipher division is searching for a key. It's not a Throne pattern. Ciphers grade a seventy-eight per cent likelihood that it's a Sanguinary code, probably Sekkite.'

'What are they doing, transmitting from down there?' Van Voytz asked. 'That's under the line.'

'And they're painting a target on their backs,' said Urienz. 'Twenty minutes, and we'll have Valks executing gun runs on the position.'

'Call it in,' said Van Voytz. 'As soon as we have a lock.'

'The issue is not who is sending and how swiftly we can wipe them,' said Tzara. Her tone was gruff and no-nonsense. 'The issue is who was listening. Wide-band, a transmitter of that power... it could only be received inside the city bounds.'

Van Voytz glanced up. A section chief at strategium station four had just raised his hand, clutching a signal form. Within seconds, another hand had risen at station six, then two at station eight. Three at tac relay. Two at forward obs. One at vox coordination. Five, all at once, at acoustic track. Still more hands rose, brandishing forms.

'Shit,' said Urienz.

'Call them in!' Van Voytz ordered.

'Reporting small arms discharge in Albarppan,' the section chief called back.

'Sustained weapons fire, possible rocket grenades, East Vapourial into Millgate,' shouted the woman at six.

'Tracking mortars, two possible three, region of Antiun Square,' called out an adept at eight. 'Rapid, sustain, ongoing.'

'Gunfire, harbour-side. Gunfire, Lachtel Rise. Gunfire, Shelter Slope.'

'Vox activity, tight band, tight chatter, region of Kaline Quarter. Chatter reads as Sekkite.'

'Detonations in Plade Parish and adjoining arterial. Habs ablaze.'

'Movement reported, Millgate and surrounds. No confirmation of hostiles, but no ID tagging and no call response.'

'Coordinate response primary!' Van Voytz bellowed. 'Marshal, tracking now. I want target solutions for the city batteries.'

'At once!' Tzara replied.

'Air cover, up!' Van Voytz shouted, turning to station two. 'Call it in, call it in! Suppression and containment! Support divisions mobilise in five minutes or I'll have heads on sticks!'

He looked at Urienz.

'Get Macaroth out,' he said.

'You're going with the evac?'

'This isn't a damn coincidence, Vitus. Get a bird ready to take him out of the city.'

Urienz nodded and made off across the floor. Van Voytz turned back to his station. 'I want direct vox with Grizmund, Kelso and Bulledin in three! Advisory signals to Cybon and Blackwood. Tell them to stand by for instruction. And find me Lugo!'

He reached for the keypad. His screen flickered and went dark.

'What the hell? Technical here!'

He looked up. There was a thump and a dying moan of power as the strategium nearest to him shut down. The holomaps it was displaying shivered and vanished. One by one, the strategiums around the war room floor blinked, sighed and shut down. As the tables failed, the main screens went dark in rapid succession.

Then the overhead lights strobed and went out.

'Power down! Power down!' an adept yelled.

'No shit!' barked Van Voytz above the tumult of voices. 'Auxiliary power now!'

'Switching,' the adept replied. 'No automatic. Re-trying... Auxiliary, failure! Back-up generators, failure!'

'They can't fail,' Van Voytz snarled. 'Re-initialise and re-start! Fire them up!'

'Technical reports... the reserve batteries have drained,' the adept said. 'Support generation systems are experiencing a critical loss of capacity. No power to palace systems. No power to core-vox. No power to war room reserve and safety. Auspex is down. Detection grid is down. Fire control is down.'

She looked at Van Voytz in the half-light.

'Void shields are down,' she said.

'Holy shitting Throne,' whispered Van Voytz.

Ferdy Kolosim put the unlit lho-stick to his mouth and clasped it between his teeth, grimacing. A night this dark, he couldn't light it in the open.

The sky was a huge swathe of reddish black cloud, low and menacing. It spread out across the unlit city like a shroud. Kolosim could barely make out the outline of Eltath. Blackout conditions were still in force. He located a few spots of light; the twinkle of a pylon beacon, small building lights like distant stars, a floodlight washing something to the southwest, the brief vent flare of a gas plume at Millgate.

The rain had stopped. There was a smell of wet soil in the darkness. A slight breeze had lifted, stirring litter in the waste ground to his left. The breeze felt like the prelude to something stronger, maybe a big storm that would roll in from the bay by dawn.

Heat lightning growled in the low cloud. There wasn't much spark to it, but the mumbling sheet-flashes let him see the city for a fraction of a second every few minutes, the climbing skyline rising to the east, a key-tooth silhouette of spires and habs.

Sergeant Bray approached, effortlessly making no sound on the rough scree.

'Are we set?' Kolosim asked.

'Oh yeah. All four companies, left and right of the approach road. Wire's cut back. We've got support teams set up, decent, broad field with a focus on the road. Fire positions in a string off that way for about a kilometre.'

'Transports?'

'All off the road. Got them side-on, in case we need fall back cover. Scouts out on both flanks. It's mostly bomb-site ruins on both sides for five kilometres.'

Kolosim turned and looked back up the approach road towards EM 14. It was the only vaguely lit thing around. He could see the glow of the gatehouse lights. The road was dark. The steel fenceposts stood out starkly where they hadn't been pulled down. The oblong shadows of some of the transports were just about visible, rolled back on the rough slip.

'Quiet order?' Kolosim asked.

'Everyone's behaving,' replied Bray. 'Pretty decent alert level, actually.'

'An active purpose refines the mind,' said Kolosim.

Bray nodded at the Mechanicore complex.

'Taking a while,' he said.

'Red tape. Reluctance,' said Kolosim. 'The priests don't like to cooperate. Pasha's probably reading them the riot act.'

His micro-bead pipped.

'Kolosim, go.'

'Caober. You pick that up?'

'Be more specific.'

'Uh, mortars. Mortar fire. South-west.'

Kolosim glanced at Bray.

'Nothing here,' he said into the link. 'Crossing to you.'

They moved down the shallow slope and jogged across the road into the waste scree on the other side. Kolosim could see Ghosts hunched around him, the folds of their capes making them blend with the stone heaps and slabs of broken rockcrete they were using as cover. He and Bray moved along behind the outer line of them. Caober emerged from the darkness.

'Mortars?' asked Kolosim.

'Sounded like,' Caober told the big red-head.

They listened for a moment, and heard nothing except the breeze stirring litter. There was a faint flash of heat lightning.

A second later, a slow, soft peal of thunder.

'Not mortars,' said Bray.

Caober shook his head. 'It wasn't thunder just now. More punctuated. A little trickle of thumps. I'd put money on mortars.'

'Well, that could be coming up from the line,' said Kolosim. 'It's active beyond Tulkar.'

'We wouldn't hear it,' said Caober. 'Not at this distance, in these conditions. It was closer.'

Bray frowned. 'Listen,' he said.

'What?' asked Kolosim.

Bray raised a finger, his head tilted to hear.

Pop-pop-pop.

'That's not mortars either,' said Kolosim.

Pop-pop-pop.

'That's fething small arms,' said Bray. 'Autogun.'

Kolosim reached for his bead.

'Stand ready,' he said.

The distant popping stopped. About a minute passed, and they started to hear much louder cracks, like branches snapping.

'Las,' said Bray.

'Definitely,' said Caober.

'What do you think?' asked Vadim from his position nearby. 'Insurgents?'

'Must be,' said Kolosim. 'Can't be Sek packs this deep in.' He hoped he was right. The city edge was far from secure, but they were well inside the inner ring. If it was a company strength of the Sons, someone somewhere had made a big tactical error. Insurgents were bad enough. The small raid-cells were still pocketed throughout Eltath, lying quiet. They'd found that out to their cost at the Low Keen billet.

They couldn't see the first few shots. Then a ripple of bright bolts flashed in high, looping into the scrub behind them. Two or three at first, then a sudden riot of them, incoming from a dozen sources. They flashed and zipped across the highway bank, hitting rocks, raising tufts of dust from the edge of the slip, and spraying pebbles off the front portion of the scree. A volley stitched across the mouth of the approach road, and Kolosim heard a sharp twang as a fence pole was cut in half.

'Hold,' he said into the micro-bead. He flicked channels. 'R Company lead, R Company lead, this is rearguard. Be advised, we have contact at the gate at this time.'

'Copy, rearguard.'

Kolosim switched channels.

'All positions, hold fire. Let's see how busy this gets.'

A second flurry came in, stinging the night air with bright darts. The las-fire began to chop at the forward positions, cracking and splitting rock cover.

'They're correcting,' said Bray. 'Cutting in closer now.'

Somewhere out in the dark, a support weapon started to chatter. A hard round .30, crew served. The shots licked along a line from the outer fence post to the nearest transport. They heard the slap as the heavy rounds punched through bodywork, then a smash as a windscreen blew out. The firing stopped, then they heard it begin again, the distinctive clattering cough of a belt feeder. It was spitting blue tracers this time, every tenth round. The illuminated rounds seemed to float and drift as they came in, feeling the range.

'Seena,' said Kolosim into the link.

'Sir.'

'They're giving us tracers. Are you sourcing that?'

'Angle's wrong from here, sir.'

'Melyr?' Kolosim said.

'Sir. If he keeps chucking that at us, I can narrow it down to about a ten metre zone.'

'Don't be greedy, Melyr. Just make a mess of the whole area.'

'Pleasure, sir.'

'Pour it on, please,' said Kolosim.

Forty metres from him, one of the support positions opened up. The .30 howled for about ten seconds.

When it ceased, the tracers stopped skimming in.

'Thank you, Melyr. Do it again if he starts back up.'

Kolosim didn't hear Melyr's reply. The night opened up with an intense barrage of small arms fire. A rain of las and hard rounds swept across their position. The combined roar felt extreme after the long quiet. If these were insurgents, there were a lot of them, and they had coordinated with alarming effect. Kolosim guessed at eighty or ninety shooters. How did cells link up to deliver this?

For thirty seconds, the barrage was so intense it kept them down. The noise seemed deafening. A sheet of smoke and lifted dust rolled off the scree.

Kolosim rolled onto his back, and adjusted his bead.

'All right,' he said. 'They're determined to have this out.'

He lay on his back for a moment, watching las-bolts flit over him, dazzling against the black sky.

'Full contact, full contact,' he ordered. 'All positions. Light them the feth up.'

The moment he spoke, four prepped and ready companies of Ghosts opened fire. The light-shock lit the entire gate area.

Now the noise was truly deafening.

Major Pasha strode down the burnished arcade of the Mechanicus station behind the two adept wardens. Elam and Ludd led a squad of Ghosts in her wake. Behind them, Criid, Theiss, Spetnin and the other company officers were deploying squads to cover the front half of the complex.

The place was vast and the layout complicated. There were floors of polished brass and ornate walls dry with rust. Deep turbine halls throbbed with energy, and were criss-crossed by suspended walkways that would easily hinder standard practices of cover. Machine shops thrummed with power tools, dancing with sparks. Side vaults gave access to cryonic bays, and were bathed in cold blue light.

Everywhere they went, servitors and cowled adepts stared at them in curiosity and suspicion. They could hear the muted tick and chatter of machine cant as the adepts gossiped to each other. *Newcomers, outsiders...*

Halfway along the arcade of the inner court, Pasha was met by a senior tech-priest and a slender young man in black. The two adept wardens stepped back and stood to attention, their dendritic fingers holding their stave weapons upright.

'Pasha, commanding Tanith First,' Pasha said, snapping the sign of the aquila.

'Sindre, interrogator, Ordo Hereticus,' the pale young man replied. 'I present Versenginseer Etriun, the study lead.'

The cowled priest nodded. Mandelbrot-pattern electrodes in the flesh of his throat rippled with light. He emitted a soft buzz of code.

'You are aware of our business here?' asked Pasha.

'The gatehouse relayed the details,' said Sindre. 'The Mechanicus formally objects to this invasion by the Astra Militarum.'

'Invasion?' asked Pasha, amused.

'All these Guardsmen. So many. How many companies did you need to bring into the sanctity of the Mechanicore?'

'Sufficient,' said Pasha. 'I note that the priesthood objects to the intrusion of the Militarum, but not to the presence of the Inquisition.'

'You're not terribly good at politics, are you?' said Sindre.

'Don't have much call for it,' said Pasha.

'Well, for one thing, I haven't trooped a regiment in here,' said Sindre. 'For another, I am attached to the study. The ordo has a fundamental interest in the items. And for another, the versenginseer requires my assistance as an intermediary. Unless you speak mechmata hyper-bineric?'

'I do not,' said Pasha.

'That's a shame, captain.'

'*Major,*' said Pasha. She tapped her collar studs. 'Just dots. Not hard to remember. If you can't tell dots from dots, I wonder how you can tell heresy from a hole in the ground.'

The tech-priest made an urgent, buzzing sound. Sindre nodded.

'We find your tone aggressive, Major Pasha,' said Sindre.

Pasha shrugged. 'Aggressive? I am soldier. Aggressive is my mother. She would bite your throat right out. Grrrr! *Bite* it.'

Pasha clutched her own throat for emphasis.

'Now, eagle stones please, thank you,' she said.

'This is untoward,' said Sindre. 'The stones are xenos artefacts, under safe-keeping. Neither the Mechanicus nor the Ordo Hereticus has yet determined their potential or use. It was clearly understood that they should remain in our hands for the duration. This was a given, signed off by the Militarum, the office of the Warmaster, the Intelligence Division, your company commander Gaunt, and my associate Sheeva Laksheema.'

Pasha nodded, as if chewing this over.

'I tell you what is untoward,' she said. 'I am here, asking you for thing. It is not a matter of negotiation. My rearguard is already in hot contact with the Archenemy on your doorstep. My company commander, "Gaunt", as you speak him with shocking lack of respect, is Lord Executor. Lord Executor? You know this thing? My orders are his will, and his will, it cannot be challenged by Ordo Hereticus, Mechanicus of Mars, Intelligence Division, my fething mother, whatever. Also, I have asked you very nicely, please. Now get me the eagle stones, ready for transport, or I will stick my boot up your arsehole and go get them myself.'

'I'd do it if I were you,' said Ludd. He was standing at Pasha's side, his arms folded. 'I'd run and do it. She doesn't feth around.'

Sindre glared at them.

'I will take this up with the ordo senior,' he hissed.

'And he will take it up with the Lord Executor,' said Pasha. 'Then everyone will be happy, as long as they are the Lord Executor.'

The tech-priest's actuators buzzed.

'This way,' said Sindre, gesturing behind him.

Pasha grinned.

'You are lovely man,' she said. 'No matter what the other boys in the ordo say about you.'

They followed Sindre and Etriun along the arcade. As he walked, Sindre gestured to one side and then the other. The two adept wardens stayed where they were, but six skitarii emerged from the shadows and fell in beside the Ghost party, three on each side. They moved in perfectly synchronised step.

'Expecting trouble?' asked Ludd.

'Security is elevated,' replied Sindre, 'the Urdeshic Palace issued an amber status advisory for Eltath this afternoon. The skitarii are a precaution. We're lucky to have them. Few remain on Urdesh these days.'

The skitarii were the martial division of the Cult. They were as tall as the adept wardens, but seemed bigger because of their armoured mass and their breadth of shoulder. They were skitarii of the Cult Mechanicus Urdeshi, and wore the traditional double robes: short black coats over longer red mantles. Little of their original organics remained. Their augmetic hands were bare metal claws, clutching weapons across their chests. Their faces were silver masked, polished to a mirror sheen. Green pinpricks glowed in the deep recesses of the eyeslits. Four carried archeotech firearms across their chests: antique galvanic sleetguns. The other two – members of an officer caste, denoted by the intricate etching that covered their steel craniums – brandished black metal staves that were a metre and a half long, plainer versions of the ceremonial staves the adept wardens carried.

Without breaking stride, Etriun waved his actuator, and opened a massive golden blast hatch, then a second, and then a titanium iris valve six metres in diameter. Cold, sterile air blew out at them. They descended a metal ramp into a grand laboratory hall. Polished chrome workbenches gleamed in pools of stark, directional light. Each bench was equipped with manipulator robotics: long, delicately articulated alloy limbs that curled over each work surface ready to activate and begin work. They looked like huge metal whip-spiders clinging to the end of each workstation. They were dormant, shut down, limbs raised and splayed like hands raised in greeting.

'Access crypt K of the Gnosis Repository,' Sindre said to a trio of waiting adepts logis.

'Crypt K is released and waiting,' one replied in a synthesised voice.

Sindre led them across the lab. A compression hatch parted with a pneumatic hiss. What lay beyond resembled a detention bay. The deck was underlit and the general light levels were low. Thick pipework ran along one wall, connecting to a complex junction of ducts and vertical pipes at the far end of the bay. Massive hatches lined the other side. Light beading around each hatch glowed red, except for one hatch towards the far end, where the beading shone green.

Etriun entered the bay, followed by one of the skitarii officers and one of the warrior-caste. Sindre followed with Pasha's team. The other skitarii remained on the lab side of the hatch.

'Wait,' said Sindre. 'This is the Gnosis Repository. The crypt-safes contain their most precious relics. The versenginseer will perform the retrieval.'

The Ghosts halted. Etriun shuffled and approached the green-lit hatch. He hauled on the rail, and the crypt door swung open on galvanic hinges. Etriun paused for a moment, staring into the crypt, bathed in the soft white light that streamed out of it.

His actuator buzzed.

'What do you mean?' asked Sindre, stepping forward.

Las-bolts tore out of the open crypt, hitting Etriun in the thigh, groin, chest and head. He wobbled backwards, and fell against the wall behind him.

'Throne alive!' Sindre yelled. 'Close the crypt! Lock crypt-safe K!'

More bolts whickered down the length of the bay. A second shooter, out of sight in the ductwork at the far end. Sindre was hit in the upper chest and hip. He squealed and fell onto the lighted deck. The skitarii warrior beside Elam took four hits and spun around hard, sparks and fluid spraying from its body. It recovered and swung back immediately to re-aim. Gerin, the Ghost to Pasha's left, took a bolt in the face and collapsed on his back. He did not recover.

'Suppressing fire!' Pasha roared. Her side arm, a heavy Tronsvasse service pistol, was already blasting. The Ghosts opened up, raking the length of the Repository with assault fire. The two skitarii began unloading their weapons, advancing steadily. The damaged warrior fired its ancient galvanic. The sleetgun spat hails of micro 'chettes down the length of the bay. The officer's stave juddered and pumped out invisible bursts of force that rippled the air. Ducting at the far end crunched and buckled.

There was no cover. Multiple hostiles were concealed at the opposite end of the long chamber. The entire length of the bay lit up with a furious cross pattern of exchanged fire.

Ludd ran to Sindre, clamped his hand around the man's gouting chest wound, and started to drag him backwards. Wall panels shattered. A las-round went through Ludd's sleeve. Sindre was staring up at him, eyes wide, his mouth gaping. The shot had gone into the top of his chest, almost at the base of the throat. He was soaked in blood.

'Where the feth are they?' Pasha yelled, jerking as a las-round clipped her shoulder plate.

Elam was hollering into his link.

'All sections! We are compromised and taking fire! Intruders inside EM Fourteen! Repeat intruders inside EM Fourteen!'

Two figures emerged from the open crypt hatch. They were hard to see. The bright light shining out of the crypt seemed to attenuate them, making them seem eerily tall and unnaturally slender. One was using the open hatch as a shield and shooting a lasrifle at Pasha's group. The other dashed across the walkway, grabbed Etriun's body and dragged it back into the crypt. The skitarii officer drummed a pulse from its stave that dented the crypt hatch. Somehow, the slender man behind it braced it open. He returned fire. The las-bolt hit the skitarius directly in the left eye. There was a minor implosion inside its gleaming chrome skull. It wavered, and dropped to its knees so hard that it cracked the clearplex panels of the underlit floor. Three more shots found it, and blew out its neck with such force, its almost-detached head swung around at a wild angle and hung sideways off a stump of fractured ceramite vertibrae. The stave clattered from its hands. It did not move again.

The fire rate from the far end of the Repository increased. Within moments, two more Ghosts had been killed by las-bolts.

'Back! back!' Pasha bellowed. 'We are dead in the open!'

They backed towards the laboratory hatch, making their own cover with streaming las-fire. Ludd was dragging Sindre. Trooper Setz ran to help him.

The remaining skitarius did not retreat. It advanced steadily and remorselessly into the storm of shots. Its sleetgun whined as the voltaics cycled to power, then cracked as the galvanic charge launched a cloud of micro dart rounds. It got off four shots and almost drew level with the open crypt before sustained las-fire finished tearing it apart. It fell, its robes ablaze.

Pasha's survivors backed into the gleaming lab space. Shots shrieked after them. Elam and Kadle stood in the hatch frame and hosed with full auto while Pasha found the activator for the compression hatch and slammed it shut. The four skitarii who had remained in the lab were advancing, match-step, towards the hatch.

'Wait! You, wait!' she yelled at them. 'They just cut down two of your kin! And four of mine! That's a kill zone in there!'

The skitarii halted. Binaric code bursts snapped between them.

Ludd and Trooper Setz dragged Sindre to one of the chrome benches and laid him on it. They left a long trail of blood all the way back to the hatch. Setz tried to maintain compression, while Ludd opened his field kit with bloody fingers.

'Keep him still!' Ludd cried.

'How the living feth are they in there?' Pasha demanded, storming towards the nearest adept. The adepts logis in the lab seemed to have frozen in disbelief. A logic problem had made them cycle.

'We do not understand,' one said. 'The Repository space is secure. There cannot be danger within a secure space–'

'There must be another access point!' Pasha snapped. Her upper arm was bleeding. She ignored it.

'No,' said another adept. 'The Gnosis Repository is a sealed section. One access.'

'One access my backside!' cried Pasha.

'The thermal vents,' said the third, arriving at a viable hypothesis. 'If hostiles entered via the thermal vents–'

'Impossible,' replied the first. 'They would never have made it through the geotherm system alive.'

'Well, they fething did!' snarled Pasha.

The adept wardens strode into the lab through the iris valve, followed by Criid's first section and a squad from Theiss' company.

'What the feth is happening?' Theiss asked.

'Compromised!' said Pasha. 'Their fething security is compromised to shit! The enemy is in the vault! They have the fething stones!'

'They cannot exit,' said the remaining skitarii officer in a grinding voice that echoed from its chest plating. It and its three kin aimed their weapons at the compression hatch in neosynchronous unison. 'We will cancel their lives as soon as they try.'

'Do this,' ordered the adept wardens in unison.

'They can get out the same way they fething got in!' Pasha roared.

'Not possible,' said the adept wardens.

'Stop telling me that,' said Pasha. 'This vent system. This *ge-o-thermal* vent. Is there a way into it?'

'There is access at several points within the complex,' said an adept logis. 'The geothermal substrate is a network that supplies power to all aspects of this facility, and to all other forge sites on Urdesh. It underpins the city, connecting a subterranean duct network that draws heat and pressure energy from the natural volcanic–'

'Don't give me lecture!' Pasha cried. 'Show me way in! Show me fething access point!'

'Turbine Hall One is the closest,' said an adept logis.

The adept wardens looked at each other and then back at Pasha.

'We will show you the location,' said one.

'We will mobilise the remainder of our skitarii complement from cryonics,' said the other, 'and activate all automata gun slaves.'

'Tona!' Pasha called out. 'Go with this pair of... of... wardens. Ready a strike group. Prep to go in fast, cut the devils off!'

'Get flamers up front, Criid!' Elam added.

Pasha looked at him.

'Flamers? Not fething flamers!' she exploded. 'These devils came up through fething ge-o-thermal system! They are fething *fire-retardant*!'

'There's something about them, that's for sure,' said Kadle. 'I'm certain I clipped one in the firefight. One of the two who came out of the crypt. It didn't even jolt him.'

'Tona? Tona, go!' Pasha yelled. 'Shoot them, kill them with sticks, fething kick them to death! Whatever! Get in and cut them off!'

Criid was already yelling orders into her link as she followed the adept wardens out of the lab.

Under the hard light inside crypt K, Corrod looked down at Etriun. The versenginseer was lying on his back, fluids leaking from his multiple wounds. There was a spark of life in him, machine life at least. His electoos had gone a cold blue colour.

Ulraw entered the crypt. He had been clipped on the arm during the exchange, but the bolt had barely broken the skin.

'One casualty on our side, damogaur,' he said. 'Ekheer. Struck by flechettes. He's healing. The enemy has withdrawn to the lab level and closed the hatch.'

Corrod nodded. 'Bring the others up,' he said.

The Qimurah had entered the Gnosis Repository through a spur in the thermal vents that rose through the sub-levels of EM 14. As they drew close, Corrod had been able to smell the eagle stones, and feel their pull. He had been preparing a device to unlock the crypt hatch when the light surrounding it had gone green. Like a gift. The shapers of the dark had granted him a boon.

He had known what it really meant. Someone was approaching. He had sent the bulk of his force back to the vent access at the end of the bay to take up firing positions, and then entered the crypt with Ulraw.

The stones were lined up on either side of the crypt. Eight stone tablets, each encased in a sterile plastek cover and set in an illuminated alcove. The *Glyptothek* removed during enemy action from the College of Heritance on Salvation's Reach more than ten years earlier. An heirloom of past eras, prized beyond any other thing by He whose voice drowns out all others. They were *Enkil Vehk*, the key of victory. Not just victory over the scum of the Throne, but victory over the bloated Archon, Urlock Gaur. Anarch Magir Sek would crush both of them. He would drive the crusade of blighted Terra back into the stars, and he would claim his rightful place as Archon of the Sanguinary Tribes.

Ulraw returned with several of the others. They gazed at the tablets.

'Remove them carefully,' Corrod told Ulraw. 'We'll be moving out quickly.'

'The enemy will counter-attack within minutes,' said Hellek. 'They are not fools, sad to say. They will have realised we used the vents. They will block them or attempt to flush them.'

'Which is why we will move with haste, Hellek,' Corrod said. 'And why I will create a suitable distraction.'

Ulraw began to remove the stones from their alcoves. Corrod knelt down beside the dying adept.

Ordinate Jan Jerik had provided him with all the technical support he had demanded: access to the vents, schematics, pass keys, system codes. He had also supplied, at Corrod's request, a data plug of Mechanicus pattern loaded with a tailored code he had called *Berserker*. It was, Jan Jerik had explained with pride, sanctioned codeware dating back to the Dark Age of Technology, a machine plague that would poison and corrupt any system it infected. This, he had promised, would scramble and deactivate even the most secure Mechanicus holding crypt.

Corrod hadn't had to use it. The crypt-safe had been unlocked for him. But it seemed such a waste.

'Friend,' he said to Etriun, speaking in the Imperial tongue.

Etriun's eyes fluttered. Soupy fluids gurgled out of his mouth.

'I have something for you,' Corrod said. 'A gift from me, and from the Anarch whom I serve. You will share it with all of your kind, so they may delight in its wild ecstasies.'

Corrod yanked several cables out of the plug ports behind Etriun's left ear. The versengineseer shuddered and emitted several shrill, buzzing calls of despair. Corrod fumbled with the ports until he found one that matched the data plug. He pushed, and the plug connected with a snap.

Berserker initiated. The tech plague streamed from the data plug into Etriun's amygdala and cyber-cerebral implants. It flooded his micro-cogitators. It burned what was left of his flesh. It was feral code, magnificent in its ferocity and aggression.

Etriun spasmed. He was dying, but his neosync connections to the EM 14 noosphere were still open.

Kolding entered the laboratory space.

'There!' said Captain Elam, pointing to the workbench where Setz and Ludd were fighting to keep Sindre alive.

Kolding opened his kit and assessed the man's wounds. 'Keep pressure there,' he told Setz. 'I'll try to seal and then pack the wound.'

'I think he's bleeding out,' said Ludd.

'He is bleeding out,' replied Kolding simply. 'That's what I'm trying to prevent.'

Pasha glanced at Theiss. 'Are they there yet?'

Captain Theiss was listening intently to his bead. He nodded.

'Yes, mam,' he said. 'Criid and Obel have reached the vent access. They have squads with them. Preparing to enter.'

'Word from outside?'

'Major firefight at the gate,' Theiss replied.

Pasha paced. Waiting was always the worst. She'd give the vent parties ten minutes, then she'd re-open the compression door and storm the Repository bay. Cut the devils off at both ends.

She eyed the room. The four skitarii still stood motionless, weapons aimed at the hatch. Two of the adepts logis had left to activate the facility's automata weapon servitors. The one who had remained seemed most concerned that Sindre was leaking pints of blood onto the polished, sterile surfaces of the laboratory zone. Elam and the other Ghosts were just waiting, checking weapons and slotting fresh powercells. The firefight had keyed them up. They didn't want to crash. They wanted to manage the stress so it was ready the moment the fighting resumed.

She knew how they felt. She'd lost four men. Four fething men. And the Archenemy devils had reached the stones before her. She would not allow them to leave the site with such a precious cargo.

She would not allow them to leave the site alive.

Several of the laboratory's wall screens suddenly fluttered and started to crawl with odd, rapid lines of code script.

'What is that?' she asked. 'Is that data? Do we have new data?'

The adept logis stared at the screens.

'I do not recognise the code,' he said. 'I do not recognise it. Non-standard. Source unknown. Type unknown. Codeware has entered neosync. Codeware has penetrated internal cogitation. Codeware has penetrated the machine-spirit core. Codeware has–'

'What?' asked Pasha. 'Codeware has what?'

The adept logis didn't reply. He turned to look at her. There was something very wrong with his eyes. Watery blood was trickling from his sockets and the augmetic optic implants had hazed with roiling fields of static. A substance like treacle was oozing out of his breather mask.

'Berserker,' he said in a flat tone. 'Berserker. Berserker. Berserk. Berserk. Zerk. Zerk. Zerk. Zerk–'

He headbutted her with savage force. It took her by surprise, and she fell, clutching her face. The adept logis knelt on her and began to throttle her. He started screaming a high pitched stream of obscenities.

Asa Elam rushed forward and tried to pull the adept logis off her. It was like trying to shift a boulder. The adept logis had locked solid like a piece of machinery. His grip on Pasha's throat tightened. Her eyes bulged. Her tongue, protruding from her spittle-flecked mouth, went blue.

Elam smashed the butt of his rifle into the adept's head. The adept went limp and let go. Elam wrenched him off her. Pasha lay on her back, gasping, trying to breathe again. There were red hand marks around her neck.

The sagging adept logis suddenly came to life again and broke Elam's sturdy grip. Screaming further obscenities, he lunged at Elam and clawed at his face.

'What the feth is wrong with you?' Elam snarled, trying to fight him off. He threw a fast punch, the snap-jab special that had seen Asa Elam triumph in many garrison sparring bouts. Elam cursed as he broke a finger on the adept's brass faceplate.

'Throne's sake! Help me here!' he yelled.

The other Ghosts, aside from those fighting to save Sindre, were already hurrying to his side.

'Shit!' said Kadle.

The robot arms on all the benches had suddenly started to twitch and writhe. Blade limbs and cutter dendrites gouged blindly at the steel work surfaces, making metal-on-metal squeals that hurt their ears.

The four skitarii at the hatch turned. Facing into the lab, they started shooting.

The first sleetgun blast exploded Kadle's head and upper body in a cloud of meat and bone. The second, another tight cloud of micro flechettes, blew a hole through Mkjaff's torso, almost removing his entire right side. Gore painted the wall screens behind him. He gazed down in disbelief at the missing part of his torso, then his spine splintered and he folded and fell.

The others ducked for cover. There was little of it. A galvanic shot-cloud grazed Captain Theiss, and stippled the wall beside him with a thousand tiny punctures. He blinked and saw he was bleeding from dozens of small wounds across his right thigh, hip, and right arm. The pain was excruciating. The micro 'chettes were still boring into him. He began to scrape frantically at his skin.

The skitarii officer thumped a pulse from his stave. The bubble of hyperdense gravity bent light and air as it crossed the room. It hit Theiss while he still scrabbled at his own flesh, and pulped his head like an invisible jackhammer.

Ludd wheeled from Sindre's body. His bolt pistol boomed and the explosive shell struck a skitarius at very short range. The warrior's torso blew out. Ludd fired again, and knocked the Cult Mech officer sideways in a bloom of flame. On the far side of the lab, Konjic, Mkget and Dickerson unloaded on auto, side by side, hosing skitarii and the area around the hatch with a storm of las. Another skitarius fell, shorting out at every joint. The remaining two – a warrior-caste and the officer Ludd had damaged – kept advancing, firing, las-fire clipping and puncturing their armour. Caught in the middle, Kolding ducked his head and continued working on Sindre as las shrieked past him in one direction and galvanic bursts burned past in the other.

Pasha rose and spat blood. She started blazing at the skitarii with her sidearm. Elam, snarling in frustration, punched the frenzied adept logis in the gut and then the neck. As the adept staggered backwards, Elam swung up his lasrifle and shot him twice. Elam's right cheek was raked with claw marks. A graviton pulse shivered the air right in front of him, and then punched a dent the size of a medicine ball in the lab's metal wall. Elam threw himself flat. He fast-crawled, reached the nearest workbench, and got to his knees, using it as cover. He started to hose at the skitarii too.

The multiple flailing cyberlimbs serving the bench grabbed him, like a spider seizing its prey. Elam yelped. The limbs had his wrist, forearm and shoulder, and the digital claws were drawing blood. Mechadendrites slashed and whipped, trying to loop his neck. An additional servo-arm reached in, servos purring, extending a gleaming titanium scalpel towards his face.

Elam tore free, leaving most of his sleeve and part of his cape behind him. He landed clumsily on the polished floor. The manipulator limbs began to mercilessly dissect the scraps of fabric they had captured.

A galvanic shot-burst went through Dickerson and exited in a giant mist of blood and disintegrated meat. The spray drenched Mkget and blinded him for a moment.

Ludd heard Setz shriek. The manipulator arms on all the work benches were thrashing and clawing wildly. Drill-limbs and flashing surgical blades were ripping into Sindre's helpless form. They skinned and butchered him in a matter of seconds, dividing him into bizarre, geometric pieces.

Setz had still been trying to compress Sindre's wound. The limbs had seized him too.

Kolding tried to grab him. The hyper-mobile limbs slammed Setz face down into Sindre's steaming remains. Mechadendrite cables lashed around him, and constricted him, binding him to the bench. The cutting beams, shuttling side-to-side along rapid and precise lines, did the rest, slicing Setz from crown to shoulders into dozens of wafer thin cross-sections.

Kolding backed away, utterly dazed by the horror of it. Ludd body-slammed him, bringing him down out of the crossfire.

Elam and Konjic concentrated fire on the remaining skitarii warrior. The barrage of las-bolts ripped off its arm and destroyed its face. It fell, fluid jetting from the impact cracks crazing its bodyplate.

The last skitarius, the officer with the engraved skull, came to a halt. Cerebral fluid and hydrodynamic synthetics gushed from a large hole in the middle of its forehead. It died standing up, augmetic limbs locked.

Pasha lowered her sidearm. The air in the lab was thick with discharge smoke, and almost every surface was splashed and dripping with blood. A broken monitor was sparking and burning.

'Throne alive,' whispered Mkget.

'Alert!' Pasha yelled. 'Alert, all sections–'

She realised that her ear-bead had been yanked out when the adept assaulted her. She fumbled for it, found the trailing wire, and stuffed it back in her ear.

Before she could speak, she heard the frantic traffic from the Ghost units inside EM 14.

'–attacking! They're fething attacking! I say again, the Mechanicus have turned on us! The Mechanicus have turned on us!'

Outside the lab, rapid gunfire was rolling through the hallways and arcades.

TWELVE

QIMURAH

The man who was going to kill him at dawn came to save his life in the middle of the night.

Keys scraped at the locks of the old cell door. It took three keys to release the thick slab of battered metal. Usually, the unlocking routine was methodical and precise, but this sounded hasty and rushed.

Mabbon waited patiently. He could do little else. The iron manacles on his wrists attached him to the floor by a heavy chain. He could stand and walk in a small circle in the tight confines of the filthy cell, or he could sit on the rockcrete block that served as a stool. They always ordered him to sit when they were coming in, and he preferred it that way.

The heavy door opened, groaning on its metal hinges. Zamak looked in at him. Zamak was one of the six guards who watched Mabbon around the clock. He was Urdeshi, a thick-set man from the 17th Heavy Storm Troop cadre that provided all six members of the guard team.

Zamak looked flustered, his face red, sweat on his forehead. His puzzle-pattern jacket was open as if he hadn't had time to button it properly. He wasn't wearing his body armour.

He stepped into the cell, producing the set of keys that fit the manacles. No body search first. No thorough pat-down. None of the usual, painstaking protocols.

'I don't usually see you at this hour,' said Mabbon.

'I've got to move you,' said Zamak. He was trying to find the correct key. His hands were shaking.

'Is it dawn already?' Mabbon asked.

'Shut up,' said Zamak. He breathed hard. 'They're through the yard already. They're killing everybody.'

Mabbon had been aware of the gunfire for the past ten minutes. Las-fire, sporadic, its whip-crack sound muffled by the cellblock's thick stone walls.

'Who?' asked Mabbon.

'Your kind!' Zamak spat. 'Your filth!'

Mabbon nodded, understanding. It had been inevitable. He had been waiting for it.

'Sons?' he asked. 'Sons of Sek?'

'I don't know what they are!'

Mabbon shrugged, as much as the chains would allow.

'A kill team, I should think,' he said placidly. '*Mortuak Nkah*. An "extinction force". I imagine that's what they'd send.'

Zamak fumbled and released the heavy cuff around Mabbon's right wrist. 'I've got to move you,' he said. 'Get you clear. Get you to a safe location.'

'Why?' asked Mabbon.

Zamak stared at him. 'They're coming to kill you,' he said.

Mabbon nodded. 'I know they are,' he replied. 'Zamak, you're scheduled to shoot me at dawn.'

'Yeah,' Zamak said, struggling to fit the key to the other cuff. Garic, the S-troop squad leader, had explained the timetable to Mabbon two days earlier. At dawn, the six man team guarding him would take him from the cell, escort him down to the yard, put him against the wall, and shoot him. Mabbon didn't know which of them would actually end his life. It might be any of them. All six would fire their lasrifles at once. He would, he had been told, be offered a blindfold.

'Well, I don't understand,' Mabbon said. 'You want me dead. They want me dead. Stand aside and let them have me.'

'I can't do that!' Zamak exclaimed. He looked horrified at the suggestion. 'I've got to get you clear–'

'Why?' asked Mabbon. He was genuinely bemused. 'The packsons are killing people to get to me. Killing anyone in their way, or so it sounds. If you try to protect me, you will become a target.'

'So?'

'Zamak, the logic isn't hard. Let them have me. Save yourself.'

'I can't do that. I've got to move you. That's orders.'

'If you get me clear, are you still going to execute me at sunrise?' asked Mabbon.

'Of course.'

'Then what–' Mabbon began.

'Shut up!' Zamak snapped. He couldn't get the key to fit the left cuff.

'I'm serious,' said Mabbon. 'You're risking your life over a... what? A bureaucratic issue? By dawn, I'll be dead. Does it matter who does it?'

'It doesn't work like that!' Zamak said.

'Well, I think it should. There's a strong chance you'll die protecting me. If you don't, you'll only shoot me yourself. Go. Get out of here. By dawn, I'll be dead. You don't have to be dead too.'

'Shut the hell up!'

'I really don't understand the Imperium sometimes,' Mabbon said. 'It's so constrained by administrative nonsense and paradoxical–'

Zamak had become so flustered he dropped the keys. They landed on the floor between Mabbon's feet.

'Shit!' said Zamak. He bent down to pick them up. Outside, close by, a lasgun ripped out three shots. They heard a man cry out in pain. The cry cut short.

Zamak turned in fear. He drew his sidearm and stepped back to the cell door warily. He peered out.

'Shit,' he said again. He stepped out of the cell and disappeared from view.

Mabbon looked at the open door. He waited. He looked down at the keys on the floor at his feet. He cleared his throat and sat up straight, his hands resting in his lap.

He stared at the doorway.

He heard a man shouting nearby, then a burst of pistol fire. An auto side-arm, emptying its clip. The double-crack of two las-shots, then a third. Silence.

Zamak reappeared. He leant against the frame of the cell door. His breathing was laboured, and he was struggling to change the clip on his autopistol. He was making a mess of the task because his hands were both slippery with blood. There was a hole in his torso just below the rib line, and his jacket and undershirt were soaked, dark and heavy.

He'd just slammed the fresh clip home when a las-bolt struck him in the centre of his body mass. The impact bounced him off the door frame, and he half-fell, half-slid to the ground outside the cell with his body turned to the right and his legs splayed.

His killer appeared, framed in the doorway. He looked down at Zamak, then fired another shot into him for good measure.

The killer turned, and stared at Mabbon through the open door.

'Pheguth,' he said.

'Qimurah,' Mabbon said. 'I'm honoured. I did not expect him to send one of your kind.'

'More than one,' said the Qimurah. 'The vengeance of He whose voice drowns out all others will not be denied this time.'

Mabbon nodded.

'I am not trying to deny it,' he said. 'Not any more.'

The Qimurah stepped into the cell. He was fully worked and revealed, towering and skeletally taut. His neon eyes shone. The Anarch did make such beautiful things.

The Qimurah wore dirty, Guard-issue fatigues that didn't fit well. The old combat boots had bulged and split a little where they failed to contain his elongated, clawed feet. He carried a worn, humble lasrifle. His tangled rows of yellowed teeth, like little tusks, shaped into what was probably a smile.

'Shadhek,' said Mabbon.

'You recognise me.'

'It's been a long time. Fefnag Pass. Scouring the archenemy into the sea.'

'You are the archenemy now,' said Shadhek.

'No, not to anyone,' said Mabbon. 'And yet, to everyone. My end is sought by everyone under the stars.'

'Do you want me to pity you?'

'No, not at all.'

'I will not understand you, Mabbon,' said Shadhek. 'Not in a thousand thousand years. You were etogaur. A great warrior. No soul more loyal, no commander more shrewd. It was an honour to serve at your side. There were the makings of a magister in you. All who knew you said so.'

'That's consolation, I suppose,' said Mabbon.

'And then,' Shadhek murmured. He shrugged. 'Pheguth. Lowest of all. Lower than filth. A traitor. A betrayer of all trust. You turned.'

'I have turned more than once in my life. Neither path ever took.'

'Why, Mabbon?'

'Because no one ever offered me an answer, Shadhek,' Mabbon replied.

'An answer? What answer?'

'To the most simple of all questions. Why.'

'Why?'

'Why all of this? Why any of it? Why do we kill with such consuming intent? Why does this galaxy burn? Imperium and Archonate, eternally locked in rage. No one ever asking why. Who is right? Who is wrong? What secret domain of truth lies between those two extremes?'

Shadhek sneered.

'You have lost your mind,' he said.

Mabbon smiled.

'I think I am the only sane soul alive,' said Mabbon, 'but that amounts to the same thing.'

'Well,' said Shadhek, 'now you won't even be that.'

He raised the lasgun until the muzzle was just a hand's length from Mabbon's face. Mabbon did not cower. He did not try to shy away from it. He sat in place, back straight, staring into the notched barrel.

'Vahooth voi sehn,' Shadhek said.

The sound of the shot boomed in the close confines of the cell.

Mabbon's head snapped sideways. The las-bolt had scorched his right cheek and torn through the fleshy lump of his right ear before stroking the back wall of the cell. Blood poured down the side of his head.

He blinked.

Shadhek had been wrenched backwards at the last second, enough to swing his aim aside. The tip of a silver warknife protruded from the middle of his chest, neon blood oozing out around it. A man was clinging to him from behind, one arm locked around his throat, bending him back, the other driving the warblade into his back.

'Feth me, what *are* you?' snarled Varl.

The Qimurah still had his weapon. It fired twice as Varl wrench him backwards. One las-bolt missed Mabbon's shoulder by a centimetre. The other hit the stone block he was sitting on. Mabbon didn't flinch. He didn't even move.

'Ah,' he murmured wearily.

Cursing and raging, Varl hauled the Qimurah backwards, trying to turn him away from Mabbon before he fired again.

'Fething feth-bag shit-stain won't fething die!' Varl yelled through gritted teeth.

Shadhek snarled and shoved himself back, mashing Varl between himself and the door frame. Varl barked as all the air was crushed out of him. Shadhek tried to shake him off and turn. Gasping, Varl managed to jerk his straight silver out of the Qimurah's back before he lost his grip on it completely. As the reworked turned, Varl raked the blade in a frantic slash that opened a diagonal slit across Shadhek's chest and cut through the strap of his lasgun.

Varl kicked, planting the entire sole of his left boot in the Qimurah's belly. Shadhek lurched backwards and slammed into the cell wall. The impact forced neon blood from his chest wound. His rifle tumbled out of his grip and clattered across the floor.

Jaws wide, he lunged at Varl.

'Feth–' said Varl a second before he was driven into the corner of the cell. He'd been reaching for the lasrifle looped over his shoulder, but Shadhek didn't give him time to act.

Shadhek's paws locked around Varl's throat, squeezing to snap his neck. Thrashing, Varl rammed his warknife into Shadhek's sternum and shoved with both hands until the blade was buried to the hilt.

An agonised, mangled sound came out of Varl's mouth as the Qimurah throttled him.

Mabbon looked down at the keys again. He looked at the cuff on his left wrist.

He looked at Varl, as the Ghost sergeant reached the final moments of his life.

With one last burst of near inhuman effort, Varl shoved. Shadhek staggered back, his hands still locked around Varl's throat. Varl's hands, soaked with neon blood, were clenched around the grip of the warknife buried in Shadhek's solar plexus.

Mabbon stood up. He looped the heavy floor chain of his remaining cuff around Shadhek's neck, took up the slack, and wrenched the Qimurah away from the Ghost.

Shadhek stumbled, the loop of chain biting into his neck. Mabbon kicked the back of his knees and brought him down, then stood on his chest and pulled the chain as tight as he could.

'Gun,' he said.

Varl was coughing and retching. He snatched his dangling rifle and aimed it down at the Qimurah.

'Hurry,' said Mabbon patiently. 'I can't hold him for long.'

Varl roared, and put three rounds into the Qimurah's grimacing face. Incandescent blood sprayed out across the flagstones and spattered them both. Half of the Qimurah's face was a smoking ruin of neon gore.

Mabbon kept the chain tight.

'More,' he said.

'I've fething–' Varl gasped.

'More,' said Mabbon.

Varl fired again. Four shots, five, six. When he stopped, very little of the reworked's head remained. Broken tusk fangs stuck at angles in the shapeless, bloody mess.

Mabbon let the chain go slack, and took his foot off the body.

'They're hard to kill,' he said.

'No shit.'

'Qimurah. Their tolerances are beyond human.'

'Uh huh,' said Varl. He coughed, then turned and threw up on the floor. He stood bent over for a second, heaving and gasping.

'You had a rifle, sergeant,' said Mabbon. 'Why didn't you use that? Why did you lead with the blade?'

Varl spat on the floor. He straightened up.

'You were right in the line of fire,' he replied, his voice hoarse. 'I might have hit you too.'

'That seems to bother a surprising number of men today,' said Mabbon.

Varl saw the keys lying on the floor. He picked them up and reached for Mabbon's cuff.

'Come on,' he said. 'These fethers are all over the place. It's fething murder outside. Shift your arse.'

'I am not sure why you're saving me,' said Mabbon.

'Me neither,' said Varl. 'Gaunt's orders.'

'Ah.'

'Come on,' Varl said, stripping off the remaining cuff.

'I am resigned to die, Sergeant Varl,' Mabbon said, not moving. 'I have been waiting for it. Longing for it, probably. All of this is entirely unnecessary. You've risked your life and wasted your time–'

'Come. The feth. Along,' said Varl.

Mabbon looked at him.

'Please, I... I've had enough,' said Mabbon.

'Yeah? Really?' asked Varl. 'Then why did you step in? You sat there like a dozy fether while all of that went down, then at the last moment, bang, in you come. Why do anything if you want to fething die?'

Mabbon hesitated.

'I don't care about my life any more,' he said. He looked at Varl. 'But you were always decent to me, Sergeant Varl. Fair. One of the very few who were. My submission would have meant your death too.'

'Oh, gee,' said Varl. 'I'm touched. I'm getting a nice warm feeling in my... no, that's vomit. Move your fething arse now, Mabbon. We are leaving and it's not going to be pretty.'

They left the cell and headed down the dank blockway, Varl in the lead with his weapon ready. Tatters of gunfire continued to echo.

'I don't even know where we are,' said Mabbon.

'Camp Xenos,' said Varl. 'Used to be a civilian jail, but it got turned Prefectus pen during the occupation.'

'Where is that?' asked Mabbon.

Varl glanced back at him with a frown.

'Plade Parish,' he said. 'East Central Eltath.'

Mabbon nodded. 'They brought me in blindfold,' he said. 'I don't know what Eltath looks like. Is it a pleasant city?'

'Not right now,' said Varl.

Mabbon looked down at his hands. He flexed his fingers. 'I have only known the inside of cells for a long time. I have not been without manacles or leg irons for years–'

'Just keep it down and keep it tight,' Varl hissed. They passed through a rolling cage divider into another gloomy bay. Two corpses lay on the stone floor surrounded by puddles of blood that looked as shiny and black as tar in the low light. Their poses were clumsy, as though they had been frozen in the middle of restless sleep. One of them was Garic, the leader of the execution watch.

'Grab a weapon,' said Varl. Mabbon didn't.

The prison was old, just a series of rockcrete blockhouses. Most of the paint-scabbed cell doors were open, and Mabbon saw weeds growing between the floor slabs.

'Are there other prisoners?' Mabbon asked.

'No,' said Varl. 'They cleared the place to make it all special for you.'

'Me and six guards?'

'No, a garrison of thirty plus a six-man prisoner detail.'

They approached an open yard twenty metres wide. The area was roofed in with chain mesh. Above the high wall, Mabbon could dimly see the stacks of a vapour mill blowing slow, silent columns of pale steam up into the night air.

Varl made Mabbon wait before stepping out into the yard. Rawne appeared at a doorway on the far side.

He gestured, Tanith hand-code.

'Got him, colonel,' Varl said, signing back.

'Colonel?' asked Mabbon.

'Yeah, there's a lot of shit been going on,' said Varl.

On the far side of the yard, Rawne edged a little way out of the doorway, lasrifle ready, peering up at the rooftops that overlooked the chain mesh layer. Trooper Nomis got in beside him, forming a V cover. They drew no immediate fire.

Apparently satisfied, Rawne signalled to Varl.

'With me, double time, now,' Varl told Mabbon.

They started out across the yard. Within seconds, las-bolts slammed down around them, steep plunging fire from above and behind. The shots dug scorch-holes in the yard's rough ground, and left glowing, broken holes in the mesh above.

Rawne and Nomis both opened up, squirting shots up at the roof, and pinging more molten holes through the mesh. Varl got his arm around Mabbon and bundled him towards the door they had just left by.

Something landed hard on the mesh, making it jingle and undulate like a trampoline. The Qimurah had jumped from above. He turned, balanced in a low, splayed crouch on the wobbling mesh, and fired rapid, angled shots at the retreating Varl and Mabbon.

Rawne and Nomis hailed fire at the exposed figure. Hit multiple times, the Qimurah tumbled forwards, rolling and bouncing on the metal net. It was tearing in places where his weight combined with the heat-tear damage of gunfire. He wasn't dead. He was trying to regain his balance to shoot again.

Rawne and Nomis stepped out into the open, training their fire at him. Spurts of neon fluid spattered down through the mesh.

Brostin stomped out of the doorway behind Rawne. He was hefting up his flamer's nozzle.

'Feth him up!' Rawne yelled. 'We'll be all day killing the fether at this rate!'

Brostin's flamer belched, and hosed a broad, yellow cone of flame up at the netting. The Qimurah was engulfed. They saw him thrash and twist, fire encasing him.

The damaged security mesh tore with a series of sharp metal whip-cracks. Part of it flopped down, spilling the burning Qimurah down onto the yard.

'All right,' said Varl, dragging Mabbon back out of the doorway where they had almost fallen. 'Brostin's cooked his–'

'No!' Mabbon warned.

The Qimurah got up again, flames still licking and swirling off his body. His clothes had burned off entirely. His flesh, from head to toe, was a bubbling mass of yellow ooze, blistering and dripping.

He raised his lasrifle. His hands and the rifle were swathed in fire. He got off three shots. One hit Brostin, fusing and snapping the buckle of his tank pack and knocking him backwards. The other two hit Nomis in the face and throat and killed him outright. Then the intense heat made the Qimurah's rifle jam.

The Qimurah tossed it aside like a burning stick and began to limp towards Varl and Mabbon.

'Shitty shit shit!' Varl gasped, and started firing. Brostin was trying to wrestle with his now un-anchored tanks so he could let rip again.

'Trooper Brostin! Tight squirt! Tight squirt!' yelled Mabbon over Varl's head. 'Pull your flames tight!'

Brostin frowned, but obediently screwed the nozzle choke as tight as it would go. Varl had no idea how Brostin wasn't burning his hands on the metal of the flamer spout. Rawne had run forwards to help brace the heavy tanks swinging off Brostin's shoulder.

Brostin hosed again. His flamer made a much wilder, higher shriek. He shot a narrow, focused spear of nearly white-hot flame that struck the advancing Qimurah in the back.

The Qimurah staggered, seared from behind by the intense surge. He re-combusted in a rush of furious light, the flesh on his back rippling away in blackened flakes like paint stripping under the tongue of a blow torch. He became a column of fire in which they could see his ribcage and long bones in silhouette as meat and muscle transmuted into billowing clouds of ash and droplets of burning fat.

He collapsed, his remains making a heap like a pile of burning sticks. His skull, black as anthracite and steaming, rolled clear.

Varl pulled Mabbon out of the doorway. Brostin put the tanks down, panting. Rawne crossed to Nomis to check for a pulse, but one look at the man's wounds told him it was futile.

'Nice trick,' said Brostin to Mabbon.

'Qimurah secrete mucus through their skin,' said Mabbon. 'It makes them highly resistant to energy fire and to strong levels of heat. Blanketing them in flame is ineffective, but even they can't withstand a sustained, focused blast at the very highest temperature.'

'Good to know,' said Brostin, trying to cobble a make-do repair on his tank-straps. 'Because they're awful fethers.'

'What did you call them?' asked Rawne.

'Qimurah,' said Mabbon. 'The Anarch's chosen ones. Elite and very rare. Hello, colonel. I gather it's colonel, now. On your way to making etogaur at this rate.'

Rawne looked at him.

'Not really the time or place for a catch up,' he said. 'Varl, get him under cover. There could be more of the fethers up there.'

Varl led Mabbon by the arm towards the door Rawne had emerged from.

'How many are they, colonel?' Mabbon asked over his shoulder.

'We've seen six,' said Rawne.

'And killed two,' said Varl.

'I am flattered they sent more than one,' said Mabbon. 'Colonel, there will be eight of them. They either come alone, or in squads of eight.'

'Eight? You sure?'

'Please, colonel,' said Mabbon. 'It's the holy number. Only sixty-four Qimurah ever exist at one time. Eight times eight, you see? There will be eight. How many men are with you?'

'One section,' said Rawne.

'One?'

'Just the Suicide Kings. B Company, first section.'

'Then, with respect, you are dead,' said Mabbon. 'Six remain. It is unprecedented for the Anarch to deploy eight Qimurah together in this day and age.'

'You're clearly high on his to-do list,' said Rawne.

'But the pheguth's not the primary target, is he?' said Varl.

'What?' asked Rawne.

Varl shrugged. 'Their primary target is gonna be the same as ours,' he said. 'Collecting Mabbon's just a courtesy. We sent the bulk of our lot after the eagle stones. And if they sent eight here—'

'What's that?' asked Brostin. 'Sixty-four minus... that's fifty-six. Fifty-fething-six of these bastards?'

'To field all the Qimurah on one world at one time,' said Mabbon. He was clearly stunned. 'That's unheard of. That's never happened. It—'

'It means Pasha and the Ghosts are totally fethed,' said Rawne. 'Oysten! Get me the vox. Now!'

From the blockhouse ahead, gunfire renewed in serious, frantic blurts.

'Oysten!' Rawne yelled. He looked at Brostin and Varl. 'Close on him,' he said, pointing at Mabbon. 'We're going to take him straight through and out. Staying here is not an option.'

Lunny Obel opened his mouth to speak, then closed it again. He shook his head.

Finally, he said, 'Fethed if I understand any of this.'

He put another las-round into the already dead adept warden, just to be certain.

He looked around.

'How many?' he called out. 'How many did we lose?'

'Eight,' said Maggs quietly.

'Nine,' said Larkin. 'Nine. Etzen's over here behind the... the thing.' He waved his hand wearily at one of the turbine hall's control desks.

Tona Criid rose from the body of the other adept warden. She had picked up the ornate stave he had, without warning, used to kill three of the Ghosts. She turned it over in her hand. Then she looked around the hall. Fyceline smoke was still hanging in the air. Zhukova had just managed to manually close the outer hatch, locking out a Mechanicus automata that was now standing outside, emptying its munition hoppers against the hatch plate. The impacts were making a noise like a machine-hammer, and flecks of green paint were scabbing and flying off the inside of the door. Behind that immediate thundering, Criid could hear other gunfire. The automata, a squat gun servitor, had been one of several that had started shooting in the arcade outside the Turbine Hall just seconds before the adept wardens had gone berserk. By the sound of it, there was now a full-scale rolling battle tearing through EM 14, as the companies of Tanith Ghosts who had entered the facility with Major Pasha tried to fend off the Cult Mechanicus personnel who had turned on them for no reason.

Criid took a quick head count: Obel, Larkin, Zhukova, Mkhet, Boaz, Falkerin, Galashia, Cleb, Ifvan, Maggs, Lubba... all told thirty-one Ghosts from the two teams that she and Obel had assembled were left.

'What do we do?' Lubba asked.

'We go in,' said Obel. 'We go in now, as per Pasha's orders.'

Criid nodded.

'I think the situation has changed wildly since she issued that order,' said Larkin. 'The fething Mechanicus freaks are trying to end us.'

'I don't think they know what they're trying to do,' said Maggs. He gestured at the data screens that covered one wall of the imposing hall. They were rolling with broken codeware and half-formed runes. The hall's lights were flickering, and the huge turbine didn't sound as though it was running well. Even a tech-novice could tell that something catastrophic had swept through the Mechanicus facility.

'They didn't turn on us,' Zhukova agreed. 'They just all turned insane, like a switch being thrown.'

'How could you tell?' asked Larkin. 'They're freaks at the best of times.'

'You could tell,' said Zhukova. 'They went feral. Central system corruption. Maybe part of the Archenemy attack. I don't know. But if they'd simply decided to kill us, for whatever reason of logic, we'd be dead.'

She looked at the corpses of the two adept wardens. It had taken the combined, desperate efforts of all of them to drop the wardens, and only then because the wardens had attacked without any regard for their own safety.

'They went mad?' Larkin asked. 'How could you tell?'

'Because they behaved like humans,' said Criid. 'Emotion. Frenzy. That's not Mechanicus.'

'Well,' Larkin pouted. 'Whatever, are we still going in?'

'Orders still stand,' said Criid. 'Orders from Pasha, given to her by Gaunt. The objective is still essential, even if the game on the ground just turned bad.'

'All right,' said Ifvan. 'But how do we get in? And how do we know where to go? Those murdering shit-heads were supposed to show us.'

Zhukova pointed to an embossed metal sign bolted to the marble wall. It looked like a circuit map.

'That seems to be a schematic of the vent systems,' she said.

'Make some sense of it,' Criid ordered. 'Everybody get kit-light. We'll be moving fast because we've already lost time. Weapons, torches and ammo. And water. Check your reloads. Strip extras from the dead.'

Several of the Ghosts looked at her.

'They'd want us to have them,' she said flatly. 'They'd want us to use them. Lunny, see if you can raise Pasha. Or anyone.'

Obel nodded, and started trying his micro-bead. Criid crossed to where Zhukova and Maggs were studying the metal sign.

'Is that a plan?' she asked.

'Yeah,' said Zhukova. 'This is us here. Turbine Hall One.' She pointed. 'So access is that duct over there. It's a bit of a maze, but if I'm reading this right, we can follow the ducts down to the main geotherm shaft here. If the bastards got in this way, then that's the way they're coming out. It's the main spur to the city power system. So if we can get down here as quick as we can, we can block their route. Their only way out will be through us. That is, if I'm understanding this correctly.'

'You're our best hope,' said Criid. 'And our best chance for finding the way.'

Zhukova nodded grimly. The scouts in both Criid and Obel's team sections were amongst the dead, their flesh and bone demolished by the wardens' grav pulses. Ornella Zhukova was the closest thing they had to a fully fledged scout.

'Finding the way's not going to be our problem,' said Maggs. 'Stopping the bastards is. Pasha and Kadle reckoned they were like *bullet proof* or some shit.'

'We'll just have to pack as much punch as we can,' said Criid. 'Flamers–'

'And *fire-retardant*,' said Maggs.

'We've got Larkin and Okain, so we've got hotshots,' said Criid. 'We can bring the .20.'

'Snipers and a crew-served? In a tunnel?' Maggs said, mocking.

'We've got grenades and tube charges,' Criid went on firmly. She looked at the stave in her hand. 'And we can improvise.'

Maggs sighed. He looked at the sign. 'If I had some paper, I could make a rubbing of this. Or a data-slate, we could copy it.'

'All the data-slates have crashed too,' said Criid. 'Central link. The noospheric thing. And I don't think the Mechanicus uses paper.'

'It's all right,' said Zhukova, staring at the sign and moving her right index finger around her left palm as though she was sketching. 'I can memorise it.'

Criid, Lubba and Ifvan opened the duct cover. Automation was off, so they had to force the heavy bolts manually. They were sweating by the time they'd finished. It was work a power-assisted servitor would normally have performed. Lubba heaved the circular hatch open, and a wall of heat and gas fumes rolled out.

It made them all step back.

'Shit,' said Ifvan. 'That's gonna kill us.'

'We'll be fine,' said Criid.

'Do we need masks?' asked Lubba. 'You know, rebreathers and stuff?'

Criid looked around. There were plenty of equipment racks in the hall's workspace, but no masks or rebreather hoods. The adepts of the Cult had no need of such things.

'We'll be fine,' she repeated. She peered into the duct, and shone her stablight. It was a circular metal tube three metres in diameter, the interior black with soot and mineral deposits. Every three metres, it was banded with a big iron reinforcement ring. The duct stretched as far as her beam could reach.

'Let's go!' she called out.

Obel was gathering his kit, still trying his bead.

'Obel to Pasha. Do you copy? Obel to Pasha.'

In the laboratory space, Konjic passed the vox-mic to Pasha.

Pasha took it.

'Lunny? Is Pasha. Sorry, vox is being scrambled by whatever crazy has happened to our Mechanicus hosts. Konjic had to run re-routes, clever boy.'

'We're going in, major,' Obel replied on speaker. *'Not ideal circumstances–'*

'You do your best, Lunny Obel. Make Belladon proud.'

'I'm from Tanith, ma'am.'

'And where is that, these days, eh? Belladon will give you land and honour when you come home a hero. An adopted son. Do what you can. In five minutes, I start sending teams down from this end.'

'We've locked ourselves in here, major,' said Obel, his voice crackling with static. *'What's the situation?'*

'Is bad, sad to tell,' she replied. She looked over at the door that led from the lab into the arcade. Spetnin had a squad there and two more outside, fending off anything that came close. She could hear the constant chatter of lasfire. 'The Mechanicus makes deadly toys. Gun-servitors. Kill machines. Very bad. Also, the priests have gone insane. We are killing many, and so are they.'

'We'll be as quick as we can,' replied Obel. *'Can you contact the palace for reinforcement?'*

Pasha grimaced. 'I will try, Lunny. Now off you go. The Emperor protects.'

'Obel out.'

Pasha handed the mic back to her adjutant.

'Didn't have the heart to tell him,' she said. Konjic had been trying the Urdeshic Palace and high command channels for several minutes. They were all dead. It wasn't just scrambling or interference. The caster display read all those sites as non-functional. She dreaded to think what might have happened.

She took a deep breath. All she could do was focus on the job at hand, the job the Lord Executor had given her.

Spetnin hurried over. He was bleeding from a scalp wound.

'Well?' she asked.

'Almost an over-run,' he replied. 'All our companies inside the complex have been driven into pockets by the frenzy. The Mechanicus has run amok. But they're making easy targets. It just takes a lot to kill them. Our casualty rate stands at about thirty per cent.'

'Throne,' she rumbled. 'That was hundreds of men.

'Our big problem is going to be ammunition,' Spetnin said. 'We're burning through it, and we can't get out to resupply. Are we getting reinforcement?'

She shook her head.

'Not from the palace,' she said. 'But we have four companies outside.'

'Who are in a fight themselves,' Spetnin reminded her.

'They may be better off than us,' she said. 'They were ready for theirs. Konjic, please to see if you can raise Kolosim.'

On the scree around the approach road, the Ghosts were lighting up the night. Their position was holding, and they were answering everything the insurgents handed them with interest. Already, the fire rate from the Arch-enemy, invisible in the waste-ground on the far side of the highway bank, had begun to drop off. Kolosim reckoned that in another ten minutes the hostiles would run out of munitions, or the will to continue, or the Ghosts would have simply killed enough of them to break them.

He cracked off some shots himself, using a rockcrete post as cover, his cape drawn in around him to mask him in the night. Ripples of bolts were criss-crossing the highway, and the Ghost's extended line was dancing with discharge flashes and the big fire blurts of the heavy support weapons.

His link crackled.

'Kolosim, go,' he said.

'Pasha. It is shit-show in here. We're going to need some help.'

'Happy to oblige as soon as this breaks, major,' he replied.

'Make it fast, captain. We are running dry of ammunition. If you can get in here, bring plenty. And consider anything and anyone you meet who isn't a Ghost a hostile. The Mechanicus has turned.'

'They've turned?'

'Bah. Long story. Just get in. But bring ammo, and bring things that kill hard. Tread fethers. Grenades. Crew-served units. All targets have a high stopping factor.'

'Stay alive,' he responded. 'I'll advise you as soon as we're moving. Kolosim out.'

Kolosim ducked down and crawled through the rubble to Bray's position.

'Here's a twist,' he said. 'We're going in.'

'Into the Mechanicore?' Bray asked.

Kolosim nodded and quickly related what Pasha had said. 'I want you to get at least a company strength ready to fall back as soon as this dies down enough.'

Bray nodded. He looked back up the approach road at the dark, grim bulk of the Mechanicus fortress, a grey monolith in the night.

'Ironic,' he said. 'We thought our job was going to be defending that place. Not invading it.'

'You know what ironic gets you?' Kolosim asked.

'No, sir.'

'Fething nothing. Not a thing. This situation is ongoing and developing. I don't much fancy assaulting a fortified location like that head on, but I'm not leaving Pasha and the rest to die in there. That's over two thirds of the Ghosts.'

'If we can get the main gate open, we might be able to use the transports to move munitions inside in bulk. Faster than carry-teams.'

'All right,' said Kolosim. 'Clock's ticking.'

The fire rate coming in at them suddenly dropped away to almost nothing. Just a few lone shooters continued to pink away.

'The feth?' said Bray.

Kolosim pulled his bead close. 'Ghost formations, cease fire. Cease fire.'

Firing from the Tanith lines died back. An almost eerie silence settled over the nightscape, broken only by a few cracks and pops from persistent shooters and the distant grumble of heat lightning. A haze of smoke drifted.

'I don't like that,' said Bray.

Kolosim didn't either. He'd expected the attack to die away eventually, because the insurgents moved in small, mobile, ill-supported units and their ammunition was limited. But they hadn't all run out all at once. This fire-halt was coordinated.

They waited. After an anxious minute or two, they heard the engine.

A cargo-6 was coming down the highway from the east, lights hooded. It was moving at a fair pace. Kolosim couldn't see it clearly, but it looked like its cab windows had been plated with flakboard.

'Crap!' he said. 'Oh crap!'

He knew what it was. The Sekkite insurgence had driven bombs into several targets during the long months of the Urdesh campaign. They were rolling something in now. The foot attack had been to keep the Ghosts in position. Now the kill thrust was coming.

A cargo-6 could carry about ten tonnes. If it was fully laden, and that load was thermite or D60, both of which the insurgents used, then it would level a couple of square kilometres around the approach road.

Several Ghosts had taken aim at the approaching truck.

'No!' Bray ordered. A stray shot would set off an unstable load. A tread fether like the one Chiria was lugging would certainly stop the truck, but the result would be the same. It was already too close. A blast would take half of the Ghosts with it.

'Fall back?' asked Bray.

Kolosim shook his head. There was no time. No one would get clear. Not even at a run.

He dashed down the line to Nessa.

'Driver!' he said, signing. 'Driver or engine block! Nothing else!'

She nodded, and set her long-las, resting it on its folding bipod across the top of the boulder she was crouched behind.

The cargo-6 thundered closer, kicking up dust. It was running fast, and wavering across the centre-line of the highway.

'Nessa?' Kolosim urged.

'I have to wait,' she said.

'What?'

'It has to be side-on, or the round will go clean through to the back compartment.'

'Shit!' Kolosim hissed.

The truck came up the final stretch. Ghosts in the line nearby had ducked flat. It took the corner hard, tyres squealing, tilting hard on its suspension. Throne, it was loaded heavy.

Past the corner it began to accelerate up the approach road. It was almost level with them.

Nessa looked serene. She seemed to have stopped breathing.

Her long-las boomed.

The hotshot round went through the boarded side window of the cab. It must have delivered a straight kill to the driver, because the truck veered hard. Nessa ejected the cell, slammed home another, and fired again. Her reload cycle had taken less than a second. She didn't even appear to aim the second time. She fired, and the second hotshot punched through the truck's engine cover. Something blew out under the hood and the truck decelerated hard. Its motor was clattering and stricken. The truck came to a slow halt as its sudden lack of motive power worked with the incline of the approach road. It started to coast, then swung sideways and rammed a fencepost.

Kolosim had closed his eyes. He opened them. The truck had not detonated. Its front end was caved around the post. It started rolling backwards slowly, carried by its own weight on the slope.

'Feth!' Kolosim said.

The truck rolled silently, motor dead, and bounced off the approach road on the other side, rear axle down in the gulley.

Again, it did not go off.

Kolosim was up and running. So were Caober and Chiria, heedless of the fact that they were exposed with insurgents in range on the far side of the highway.

Chiria reached the truck first, and clambered into the back.

'Chiria?' Kolosim yelled.

'More D60 than I ever want to see in one place again,' she called back.

'Shit.'

'What?'

'It's on a timer.'

'How long?'

'You don't want to know. Run.'

Caober had opened the cab door. The driver, a Sek packson, was dead behind the wheel. Nessa's shot had entirely vaporised his head.

Kolosim got up into the back. His jaw dropped. He'd never seen so many boxes of D60. Maybe a tonne and half, plus some open crates of thermite mines. Chiria was hunched over them.

'It's pretty rudimentary,' she said. 'Impact trigger running the timed fuse. Very rough. Surprised they didn't die rigging it.'

'How long?'

'You still don't want to know.'

'Stop saying that!' he exclaimed.

'Just cup your balls and pray,' she said. She was good with explosives. If anyone could do it, it was Chiria.

'Uh oh,' she said.

'What!'

She turned to look at him. A big grin split her famously scarred face. 'We're still alive,' she said.

She tossed him the detached timer and firing pack. He caught it badly.

'Feth you,' he said. 'I nearly shat.' He kissed her on the side of the head.

'Get off,' she said.

They heard pops and cracks. The insurgents had started up again. It wasn't as heavy as before. They had little left to deliver.

But they were aiming for the truck. They wanted to finish the delivery of their gift.

Kolosim jumped down out of the cargo-6. Las-bolts and hard rounds were clipping the road and gulley around him. He heard one slice through the cargo-6's canvas cover.

'Light 'em up! Make 'em stop!' he yelled into his bead.

The Ghosts began firing, trying to drive the remaining insurgents down and keep them so pinned they couldn't fire.

But shots were still coming in.

'Over here!' Kolosim yelled. With Chiria and Caober, he was already straining to push the truck out of the gulley. The nearest fire teams ran over to join them. One was hit in the back of the leg as he ran forwards. Someone stopped to drag him back to cover, yelling for a corpsman. The others came to Kolosim's side, tossing down their weapons and planting their hands against the truck's bodywork. Kolosim had fifteen Ghosts heaving on the truck with him. They got it bumped out of the gulley and back onto the road. Caober leaned into the cab to correct the steering while he pushed. Backs breaking, they began to roll it up the long slope towards the Mechanicore. Shots pinged and cracked down around them.

All they had to do was get it out of range. Push it up the slope. Just a hundred metres would be enough.

A hundred metres. Under sustained fire. Pushing a five tonne truck carrying a tonne and a half of high explosive.

The air in the ship was stale and humid. It had clearly taken damage in the past week, and major environmental subsystems had been taken off-line for repair. The sirdar passed through areas where the main lighting was out and red-lensed lanterns had been hung from the spars to provide temporary illumination. Oil, grease and waste water dripped through the decks and pooled under the walkway grilles. Some sections were closed off entirely. The sirdar heard the whine of power tools and the sputtering pop of welding gear. Several other sections were stacked with structural debris and baskets of broken plasteks and ceramite. Gangs of servitors and haggard human slaves were working to clear the detritus from the companionways and compromised compartments. Packsons and gold-robed crewmen roamed past.

The hissing whisper was everywhere. It scratched at his ears, and tugged at his brain. It was far, far louder inside the ship.

At most junctions and compartment hatches, the sirdar passed easily, unchallenged by the packsons posted at each way point. At one, an over-zealous guard called out after him as he passed. The sirdar kept walking with confidence, as though he hadn't noticed the cry, and the guard didn't follow it up.

At another junction, he was stopped by two etogaurs who berated him for over a minute about the noxious heat aboard ship and the lack of circulating air. The sirdar nodded, checked his slate, and promised he would look into it directly.

Access was alarmingly easy. All that was required was confidence, the ability to look like you belonged there, and a few words of the language to get you past. Enough purpose in your stride, and no one gave you a second look.

And the Archenemy had no reason to be alert. They were in the heart of the Fastness, a secure location unknown to Imperial intelligence. The only Imperial humans in a radius of ninety kilometres were in chains.

The brig lay on the eighth service deck aft. Most prisoners were held ashore, especially those who had signalled they were ready to convert and accept impressment. Only the most significant and sensitive were chambered aboard the ship.

Like *enkil vahakan*.

The sirdar loitered in the shadows of a through-deck ladder well for a few minutes, and observed the operation of the brig access. There was an outer and inner cage, large and heavy sliding metal frames, and between them was a security post manned by two large packson watchmen. There was a small operations console built into the wall, a vox-link and security board, and a belt-fed Urdeshi-made .20 on a tripod, mounted to cover the inner bay of the brig block through the second cage.

While the sirdar watched, a damogaur and two packsons arrived, and gained access to the outer cage using a pass key. They talked briefly to the duty watchmen, who then used their own key to let them through the inner cage. A few minutes later, a different damogaur exited alone, locking the outer cage securely with his own key.

The sirdar followed him along the service deck to a traverse, waited while a detail of packsons hurried past, then called out a question to catch the damogaur's attention. The sirdar left his body stuffed in a service locker.

The sirdar returned to the brig with the damogaur's key.

Without hesitation, he let himself in.

The security watchmen looked up at him.

'Desh arad voi toltoom,' the sirdar said. *More interviews.*

'Who?' asked one of the watchmen.

'Enkil vahakan,' the sirdar replied.

The security watchmen hesitated. One said they hadn't been notified. Nothing was scheduled.

'He has set new questions,' the sirdar replied with a shrug. 'He wants them asked tonight. Are you going to be the ones who delay him getting the answers? It's on you, brothers. I'll just say you were doing your job.'

The watchmen glanced at each other. One got up, unlocked the inner cage, then slid it open.

'The grace of his voice guide you and drown out all untruths,' the sirdar said as he stepped through the cage. 'I will not be long.'

The brig block was a stinking, infernal realm. It was lit by age-stained lumen globes set in iron cages, and the deck and walls had never been cleaned. They were caked with the residue of pain and suffering. Some of the cells in the block were unoccupied. Through the open hatch of one, the sirdar saw a man being tortured by the damogaur he'd seen entering the brig ten minutes before. His packsons, stripped to the waist, were doing the work while the officer stood on and watched, asking the same question over and over.

The man was an Urdeshi colonel, a high value prisoner. He was so far gone, he was no longer making a sound or even flinching as the packsons worked at his flesh with flat-wire knives.

The man's eyes just stared out past his tormentors into the hallway, gazing at a freedom he would never know. He caught the sirdar watching him. Their eyes locked.

The man's staring eyes twitched. His mouth moved, leaking slightly. He *knew*. He saw what every Sekkite aboard had missed. Despite the uniform and the hand-strap mouth, he saw the sirdar's eyes. The expression there. The horror and the pity.

The sirdar hesitated. He wanted to go in, to lay vengeance on the officer and the two packsons. He wanted to put the Urdeshi out of his suffering.

He could not afford that kind of diversion.

Very slowly, he shook his head. *Don't.*

Then he made the sign of the aquila.

The Urdeshi did not respond. He simply closed his eyes.

The sirdar hurried on. Beyond the block of regular cells, there was an area reserved for more specialised containment. The notification mark on the page he'd torn out of Olort's book matched a sigil scratched above the archway. Highest level securement.

He checked there was no one close by, then deactivated the screening field and stepped through the arch. The dank and rusted chamber beyond was octagonal. Each wall section was formed by a heavy hatch with a vox-speaker set into a large window of reinforced glass.

The hatch windows were dirty, but it was clear that each looked into a flooded cell. The sirdar peered into the nearest one. The fluid beyond the glass was murky green, drifting with fibrous scraps, like the dredged sediment of some polluted canal. There was a shadow in it. A human cadaver, rotting back to bone, floating like a revenant apparition. It looked like the corpse of a drowned mariner who had been in the water for a long time.

There was a similarly ragged corpse in the silted water of the next cell. The sirdar squinted in at it. The corpse within suddenly jerked its head and glared at him with rheumy, lidless eyes, its fleshless mouth snapping and chewing.

The sirdar recoiled from the glass. He could hear a scratchy, gurgling voice. It was coming from the cell's vox speaker. He saw that cables were attached to the corpse's temples.

These were stasis tanks, filled with nutrient fluid. The prisoners were held in suspension, their minds wired via augmetic links to vox-grilles that articulated their thoughts.

He moved to the third tank. The fluid suspension here was a little cleaner, as though it had only been filled a few days before. A drowned man drifted inside. His hair was black, his clothes the tattered fabric of Imperial Guard fatigues. Cables were fixed to his temples too. His flesh was bloodlessly white and shrivelled by long immersion.

'Feth,' the sirdar murmured. He knew the face. Time had passed, and it was older, but it was unmistakable.

He put his hand against the dirty glass.

'Hello,' he whispered. 'Can you hear me? It's me. It's Oan.'

The figure inside stirred, as though it was twitching in a bad dream. A few oily bubbles broke from its lips.

The sirdar looked around. There was a control panel beside the hatch frame. He didn't know much about stasis suspension. He didn't know if abrupt removal would shock or damage the subject.

There was no time to debate it. He threw the switch that would open the sluices and drain the tank.

The fluid level inside the tank began to drop. The sirdar could hear it gurgling and flushing through the underdeck drains. The body inside was slowly revealed, losing its buoyancy and slumping into the corner of the metal vat.

As the fluid level dropped, the sirdar saw his own reflection in the glass, and took off his helmet. If the captive survived release, he wanted him to be able to see his face.

As soon as the fluid had dropped far enough, the sirdar opened the hatch. Excess water, stagnant and foul, sloshed out over his boots. The tank reeked of organic waste and bacterial processes.

The man inside was limp. Dead or unconscious. The sirdar grabbed him and dragged him out. His flesh was cold and extraordinarily colourless. The sirdar tore the cables out of his temples, leaving little bloodless punctures, and pumped at his chest. Brackish soup glugged out of his slack mouth and nostrils.

'Come on,' the sirdar whispered. 'Don't let this be hello again and goodbye.'

The man convulsed, and started to cough and choke. His eyes opened. He retched and spat out ropes of mucus and spittle while the sirdar supported him.

He looked up at the sirdar, blinking in the stale light. Some colour was returning, and his flesh began to show livid bruises from beatings and many minor combat injuries.

'Oan?' he asked, his voice made of nothing.

'Hello, Brin,' said Mkoll. 'It's been a long time.'

Mkoll locked his arms around Brin Milo, like a man greeting a son he'd thought he'd lost forever.

THIRTEEN

UP INTO THE LIGHT

Luna Fazekiel had an excessively ordered and compulsive mind. It had been remarked upon, not always in a complimentary manner, and accounted for her career path into the Prefectus rather than a regular Militarum command.

When the Ghost companies and the retinue had arrived at the undercroft, an event that seemed like months ago to her, she had walked every centimetre of the cellars to learn the layout.

The information was useless to her now, and that troubled her deeply. She liked to have solid, verifiable facts to give her power over her circumstances. That was gone, and she felt her long-conquered anxieties rising.

The hallway she was following was long. She knew that no single hallway in the entire undercroft was this long or this straight. The environment had turned against them, buckled by the warp-aura of whatever stalked them.

Whatever it was that made the noise she had first heard at Low Keen, a noise that had lodged in her ever since and thrown her into a downward spiral of anxieties.

She led the way, controlling her breathing to avoid the onset of panic. Merity and Meryn followed her. Merity seemed alert, but Meryn was either traumatised, or unwilling to hide his usual, sullen nature. He had said very little about what had happened to him, despite her questions. People had died. His squad. Something had torn them apart.

Information – specific detail – was a tool that allowed for greater control. Meryn's reluctance to help her with much compounded her sense that she was losing her grip.

'You're sure,' she asked, 'that we have only been down here an hour?'

'Thereabouts,' said Merity.

It was difficult to allow for that. It lacked sense, and wasn't backed up by the evidence of Fazekiel's own experience.

'I'm not sure any more,' Merity added. 'I'm not sure of anything.'

'Why did you come down?' she asked Merity. 'You came down to the undercroft. Why?'

'I...' Merity said. She eased her grip on the carbine. 'Does it matter?'

Fazekiel looked at her.

'You were working with the Lord Executor's cabinet up in the palace, but you chose to come down.'

'I came to find you,' said Merity.

'Regarding the Low Keen incident?' asked Fazekiel. She was fidgeting with the front of her coat in a futile effort to wipe the stains off it.

'Yes,' said Merity. She was painfully aware of the way Meryn was staring at her, his eyes hooded. 'Look, it's hardly important right now, is it, commissar?'

Fazekiel turned to Merity and presented her with what she hoped was a reassuring smile. She was finding it hard to know what expression her face was actually wearing, or how much of her mounting terror she was betraying.

'We don't know what's important,' she said. 'Things happened at Low Keen. The thing that attacked Yoncy and Elodie Daur. Mam Daur described a very distinctive noise associated with the attack, a noise I believe we have now heard. Yoncy was present at both places–'

'So?' asked Meryn.

'I'm just assembling facts,' said Fazekiel. 'You said she was also present when your squad died. And we both saw her before the lights went out.'

Meryn said nothing. He looked at the wall. His breathing was too fast, too shallow.

'I'm sorry,' Fazekiel said to Merity quietly. 'I... I am meticulous to the point of compulsion. I always have been. I like detail. I like to know the far side of everything. I suppose it is a weakness. An obsession. Detail gives me a sense of control.'

'I'm sure it makes you a very good investigator,' Merity answered. Merity was edgy and scared, and she could see how strung-out Fazekiel was. She didn't feel reassured by either of the people she was with, though she was glad she wasn't alone.

'Detail freak,' muttered Meryn. 'That's what everyone says about you. Taking great pains and giving them to everybody else.'

'There's no need for that,' Merity said to him.

Meryn glared at her. 'We're lost, little girl,' he said, 'and something out of a nightmare is hunting us. But yeah, let's swap a few personal secrets and braid each other's fething hair.'

'In the face of an unknown threat, assembling reliable data seems sensible,' said Fazekiel. 'Do you have a better idea, captain?'

'Give me a gun,' he replied.

'We only have two firearms,' said Fazekiel.

'And she's a fething civilian!' Meryn growled, indicating Merity with contempt. 'I'm a fething serving officer in the Tanith First.'

He looked at Merity.

'Give me the carbine,' he said.

'No,' she replied.

'Commissar?' he said, looking for support.

'What happened to your weapon, captain?' Fazekiel asked.

'Feth you. Both of you,' he murmured and looked away. Merity could see how badly his hands were shaking.

'Why did you come down here?' Fazekiel asked Merity.

'I just... I just did.'

'To find me. You had something to tell me regarding the Low Keen incident?'

'It doesn't matter now. It's not important.'

'You were in a meeting with Gaunt's tactical cabinet, ma'am,' said Fazekiel. 'It must have been important to tear you away from that.'

'I remembered something, that's all,' said Merity. She kept flicking her eyes in Meryn's direction, trying to show she didn't want to speak in front of him, but the commissar was too weary and anxious to notice the hint. Merity had always disliked Meryn intensely. She wasn't about to throw suspicion his way. Not in front of him. So, she thought she'd heard his voice outside the shower block? So what? How did that matter even slightly now?

Meryn had turned to stare at her, listening intently.

'What did you remember?' he asked. There was an edge to his tone. His eyes were bright and unblinking, like a snake's.

'I don't want to talk about it,' she said.

'It might be important,' said Fazekiel. 'It might relate to this.'

'It doesn't,' Merity insisted.

Fazekiel sighed, and turned to start walking again.

Meryn stood for a moment, staring at Merity. When she went to walk past him, he whispered, 'Careless talk, that's always a bad thing. Rumour, gossip. Don't want people getting the wrong idea, do we?'

Merity blanked him and kept walking.

They'd only gone another few metres when they heard the sound again. The saw-blade, screeching somewhere close by. It was like the shriek of an animal. The lights flickered.

'Feth this,' Meryn whispered. 'Give me the gun.'

'No,' Merity replied. It was the only thing making her feel remotely safe.

'What I think,' said Ayatani Zweil, 'is that darkness follows the light.'

'Is that so?' Domor replied. They sloshed, knee-deep, along the flooded hallway. Domor had his straight silver in his hand, for all the good it would do.

'Yes, oh yes, Shoggy,' Zweil replied earnestly. 'Like a shadow, you know? Imagine a candle.'

'All right.'

'The candle's lit, you see? So there's light.'

I'm familiar with the fething principles of candles, Domor wanted to scream. He didn't. The old priest was scared. He'd been talking non-stop for the last twenty minutes. Domor wanted him to shut up. He liked the old man dearly, but he longed for silence. He wanted to be able to hear things coming.

He sighed to himself. *And then what?* he wondered. He looked around at the half-lit gloom, the reflections of the low-power lamps flickering on the rippled surface of a waste water flood that was still rising.

This was going to be a grim old end. Not at all what he'd ever imagined. Domor had always known for sure he would die in the regiment. He was resigned to that. He'd come close often enough, including the occasion that had robbed him of his eyes and left him with the buggy optical augmetics that had earned him his nickname.

But he'd always pictured the end as a glorious one. On the field of battle, a valiant stand at Gaunt's side. A noble death. Maybe there'd be wreaths afterwards, and a bugle call or a gun salute.

But those days were gone. Life was changing. Gaunt was high and mighty now. He'd never stand in the line with his boys again. The glory days and noble ends of the First and fething Only were memories. Reality and the future was a colder place. He had to reimagine his own destiny.

And he couldn't ever have imagined this. Not this. A stinking, unwitnessed end in a sealed fething dungeon that shifted around him like a living thing, like a sorcerous labyrinth in the old-time myths. And a nightmare monster, straight out of those same childhood stories, coming for him, sniffing at his heels and tasting his tracks.

'So, the candle's lit, and there's light,' Zweil was saying. 'But the candle casts a shadow too, doesn't it? Doesn't it?'

'Yes, father.'

'The shadow's only there *because* of the light,' said Zweil.

Domor glanced at the old man. 'Is it?' he asked. 'Or is the shadow still there when the light goes out, and we just can't see it because it's dark?'

Zweil frowned. 'Shit me sideways, boy,' he exclaimed. 'That's some deep philosophy there.'

'Sorry.'

'No, I've just got to factor that into my thinking...'

'No need.'

Zweil paused, scratched his head, and then scooped the skirts of his ayatani robe up out of the water and wrung them out. He kept doing that. Domor wasn't sure why. As soon as he'd wrung them out, Zweil would simply drop them back into the water and keep going.

'Well,' said Zweil. 'That's what I think. The darkness follows the light, you see? Like a... like it can smell it.'

'Uh huh.'

'Opposites, light and dark, each needing the other to survive. To exist.'

'Right.'

'Can't have one without the other. They can't be separated.'

'I've often thought that,' said Domor, not really listening.

'So we're in this shit,' said the old man, 'we're in this awful, awful shitty shit-balls mess, because she's here.'

'Who?'

'Haven't you been listening? *Her*. The Saint. My beloved Beati.'

'Oh.' Domor paused. 'I thought you meant Yoncy.'

'Yoncy?' The old man asked, puzzled. 'Why would I mean Yoncy?'

Domor shrugged.

'Well, Shoggy? Why did you think I meant her?'

Domor shook his head. 'Yoncy's odd,' he said. 'Odd follows her around. Haven't you ever noticed that? And this thing we keep hearing, it sounds like whatever it was came for her at Low Keen. I heard it, father. It sounds the same.'

'I dunno, Shoggy,' said Zweil. 'That's a terrible thing to think about a little girl.'

'She's not a little girl,' said Domor. 'She's... look, I love Kolea. He's my brother. Dalin's a good boy. Solid and brave. And Tona, well, she's done a hell of a thing, raising them. But Yoncy... I'm not the only one to think it. Elodie, she gets freaked out by her. Even Gol.'

Zweil thought about this for a moment, then started to laugh loudly.

'Shhh!' said Domor, in alarm.

'You think Yoncy's coming for us?' Zweil laughed.

'No, I don't.'

'Yoncy. Hnnh! Yoncy? I've heard some notions in my time-'

'Well, you just said it was the Saint.'

'No, I didn't!' said Zweil sharply. 'I said the darkness is here because of her. She's light, Domor. The light of the Throne. Just *so* magnificent. And the darkness is drawn to that. The shadow of the warp, you see? She's the candle-'

'I get it.'

'-and the warp, see, that's the-'

'I get it. The Archenemy, the Ruinous Powers, they're here tonight because she's here.'

'In the palace,' Zweil nodded. 'I can feel her presence, calling to me.'

'So we're not the targets?' asked Domor. 'We're just in the way?'

'I suppose so. The darkness has come for her. She's strong, and she'll fend it off, but I hope she's got loyal soldiers at her side.'

'She might not even be here yet,' said Domor, sloshing forward. 'There was no announcement. No ceremonial welcome-'

'Oh, she's here. I told you, I can feel her-'

Zweil fell silent.

'Father?'

Domor looked around. Zweil had stopped, deeply pensive.

'What's the matter?'

'I can feel her,' said Zweil. 'I can feel her close by.'

'So you said.'

'No, Shoggy. Think about it. I can feel her. And I thought, well, that's nice and reassuring. A comfort. But I can *feel* her. Like a lodestone feels true north.'

'What?'

Zweil turned abruptly and began splashing off the way they'd come.

'Father? Father!'

'Come on, Shoggy!' Zweil called back. 'I was stupid, is what it is! It was right before my eyes and I missed it.'

'What was?'

'I can feel her call,' Zweil said emphatically. 'Goodness, Domor. Don't you listen? Keep up. She can lead us out of here. I only have to listen, to let myself feel. Then follow. Be her pilgrim, her imhava, just as I've done my whole life. Follow her path. Go to her, wherever she's calling from. Let her guide me out of the darkness and up into the light. You too, of course.'

'We've been that way,' Domor protested.

'We've been every which way,' Zweil replied. 'There's no sense to this place any more. The warp's seen to that. We just follow the light. What?'

Domor was smiling. 'That makes as much sense as anything I've heard today, father,' he said.

Zweil nodded. 'Miracles wear disguises, my boy. Like, you know, moustaches and hats and those sash things with the pom-poms on them. Also, masks. The point is, you don't always recognise them at first, even when your mind is a highly tuned spiritual organ like mine. The Emperor protects, Shoggy Domor, and today he is protecting us through the sanctity of his Beati. We were just too scared and bothered and worked up to see that before. But I see it now, oh yes! A revelation. The scales have fallen from my eyes, and I behold the path of salvation–'

There was an awful, blood-chilling screech and something black sawed out of the darkness right at them. Zweil cried out and fell over in a huge splash of flood water. Domor recoiled. Terror seized him again.

This was it. This was it. This was fething it–

He felt claws slice into his cheek, hot blood pouring down his face.

The darkness was still shrieking at him.

'Shoggy? Shoggy?'

The shrieking stopped.

'Father?'

'Oh,' said Zweil. He got up, soaked through, wiping his face, and peered at Domor. 'It got you a good one. Gashed your cheek.'

'What the feth–?' Domor stammered.

Zweil splashed past him, and scooped a bedraggled mass out of the water, a large, tattered shape that had been thrashing around where it landed.

'Oh, hush now, you poor little bugger,' Zweil cooed.

It was the regimental mascot.

'Shit,' said Domor.

'You see?' said Zweil. 'It's Quil. Poor little bugger.'

'Quil?'

'I named it. Because it didn't have a name. It's short for–'

'Whatever,' said Domor.

The psyber-eagle had been damaged and wounded. Feathers were mangled, and it was matted with blood. One of its heads had been sliced off.

'Poor old bastard,' said Zweil, clutching the surprisingly large and heavy creature in his arms as best he could manage. 'It's lost a head.'

'So I see.'

'Like a... what's the word? What do you call a two-headed eagle that's missing a head?'

'An... eagle?'

Zweil shrugged. 'I suppose.'

The psyber-eagle started to thrash wildly in his arms, raking the air with its wings.

'Steady! Steady!' Zweil cried. He was forced to let it go. It flew back up the hallway away from them, feather filaments drifting in its wake.

'See?' said Zweil.

'What?'

'It's going the same way. The way I was going. It can hear her too. Birds are very cunning. Hunters, you see? It's attuned. It's following her call. Saints can do that, you know? They can call animals and creatures of the wild to their side. The grazing beasts of the farm and the hunters of the woods alike, they come flocking. I'll bet it can hear her better than I can. The sharp sense of the untamed, you see, untrammelled by conscious thought. Running on instinct.'

'You're saying we should follow it?'

'Yes. It'll take us to her. It'll take us out of the shadows.'

'Right,' said Domor.

Dalin stopped, and leaned heavily against the stone wall.

'Dal?' Kolea asked, turning to look at him. Dalin was pale, and sweat was leaving blanched trickles in the dirt on his face.

'Give me a moment,' said Dalin.

'Are you sick?'

'I feel...' Dalin swallowed hard. 'My head hurts. My ears. You feel that? Like a buzzing? A scratching?'

Kolea nodded. 'That's been going on since before the lights failed.'

'What is it?'

'Some manifestation,' Kolea said. 'A harmonic, a vibration. I don't know. It's the background noise of this bad shadow.'

'It's making me feel ill,' Dalin said. 'My head, my gut. Like a fever–'

Kolea pressed the back of his hand to Dalin's forehead. Dalin jerked back in surprise.

'What are you doing?'

'Checking your temperature. There's no fever.'

'What are you, my dad?'

Neither of them spoke for a moment.

'Yes,' said Kolea.

Tears welled in Dalin's eyes. He wiped them away, hurriedly.

'I'll tell you what it is,' said Kolea. 'It's just anxiety. I feel it too. We're both worried sick about Yonce.'

'I suppose.'

'We're going to find her, Dal.'

'I know.'

'No, I mean it.' Kolea sighed. 'I made an oath, you see? Swore I'd protect the both of you.'

'When was this?'

'Oh, when you were born. That was the first time. But it was after the Aigor drop. That's when I made it, out loud. Spoke it. To myself, and to the Emperor, who I hope was listening.'

'We could die down here,' said Dalin. 'I think we probably will die down here.'

'No, that's the thing,' said Kolea. 'It wasn't a whim. It was an oath. Solemn in intent. A Kolea oath, you see? The Kolea family has a strong and proud tradition. The universe respects a Kolea oath like, Throne yes. Knows not to go breaking it.'

'Gol–'

'I'm serious, Dal. Even the fething Ruinous Powers know better than to try and defy an oath like that. I will stand with you, you and Yoncy, even in the darkness. I'll stand between you and hell–'

'Gol.'

'What?'

'I know you mean well. I appreciate the effort. You're just pretty new at this father business, aren't you?'

Kolea shrugged. 'Not had much practice over the years,' he said.

'I know,' said Dalin. 'I appreciate it. But it's weird. Let's just find her.'

Kolea nodded. 'I was trying too hard?' he asked.

Dalin smiled. 'Just a bit.'

Kolea turned and hefted his weapon up.

'All right, Trooper Dalin,' he said. 'Let's head that way. To the left.'

He let his voice trial off. He raised his right fist and flicked the signal for 'noise.'

Dalin raised his weapon, instantly alert.

Somewhere, not close, but still in the undercroft, there was a sawing howl.

Then, nearby, a splash.

They both wheeled.

'Show yourself!' Kolea growled.

'Gol?'

'Bask?'

Baskevyl and his squad appeared. They lowered their weapons and sloshed towards Kolea and Dalin.

Kolea and Baskevyl embraced.

'Thank the Throne!' Bask said.

'You all right?' Kolea asked.

'Just lost,' said Baskevyl.

'And scared,' Osket said.

'What's up with him?' Kolea asked, looking over at Blenner. The commissar was leaning against the wall, his eyes closed.

'This is getting to him,' said Baskevyl quietly. 'The tension's making people sick.'

Kolea nodded. 'It's not just tension,' he replied. 'I think the warp is acting on us all. Dalin's sick too.'

'At least you found him,' said Baskevyl.

'Yeah. And Yoncy's around here somewhere too.'

'All right, let's stay together and find her. We ran into Meryn's team a while back, but divided again. That was a mistake.'

'Safety in numbers?' asked Kolea.

'Right,' said Baskevyl. 'And firepower. Whatever this is, I think we're going to need to put it down hard. It makes a real mess of people.'

'It's killing?' asked Kolea.

'Yes, whatever it is. It's trapped us in here and it's killing. You seen anybody?'

'No,' said Kolea. 'This gakking place is playing mind-games. I was with Erish and that lot, then lost them. The walls moved. I haven't seen anybody except Dal and Yonce. And that's weird, because there were a lot of people down here. I don't know where they've all gone.'

'Bonin was leading them out,' said trooper Ells. 'But, I dunno...'

'Maybe it's eaten them all,' said Osket.

Kolea and Baskevyl looked at him.

'You're a fething ray of sunshine, Osket,' said Baskevyl.

'Sorry, sir.'

'Let's move forward,' Baskevyl said. 'Eyes open for Kolea's girl, all right?'

'Stay close to Dalin for me,' Kolea whispered to Baskevyl.

'Sure. Why?'

'I think I got a little heavy-handed. Tried to do the whole caring father thing and did not pull it off. He needs a comrade and an officer.'

Baskevyl nodded. 'No problem.'

'And I'll see if I can get Blenner to pull his wits together,' Kolea said.

'Good,' Baskevyl whispered back. 'He's spooked badly, Gol. I think... I think he might be on something.'

'Pharms?'

'I don't know. But I think he keeps taking something. If he's wired, he's a liability. I mean, I feel sorry for him. Fear is a bitch, and I know it bites us all in different ways. But he's been a useless sack of shit since this whole thing started.'

'You mean since he joined the regiment?' asked Kolea.

Baskevyl snorted.

'Don't be unkind,' said Baskevyl. 'He's had his moments. But down here today? I think he might have been more rattled over the Ezra business than we thought.'

'What, executing Wilder?'

'I know, I know. It was the right call after what that shit did. But I think our dear Vaynom might be struggling with it. Killing a foe in battle is one thing. Sanctioning one of your own...'

'He's a commissar, Bask.'

'Yeah. But as you point out, not a very good one. I wonder if he's ever had to do that before. I mean, carry out a summary sentence that way. I think it's shaken him.'

'He almost said as much to me,' said Kolea.

'Right. Now this, plus maybe pharms. It might be a good idea to get his weapon off him. If this goes balls-up and turns into a close-quarter fire-fight, he could be an utter liability.'

'Got it,' said Kolea.

'Right!' Baskevyl announced, raising his voice again. 'Let's roll out. Head down to the left.'

'All right there, Vaynom?' Kolea asked, falling in beside Blenner.

'Oh yes, fine and dandy,' Blenner said. He was unconvincingly chipper. Kolea could smell the stink of his fear even above the rank odour of the flood water.

'This is a bad deal,' Kolea said, trying to sound reassuring. 'But we've got each other's backs. I've got your back, all right?'

Blenner nodded. He adjusted his cap and hoped that, in the gloom, Kolea couldn't see that he'd begun to cry.

The Saint led them to the bottom of the steps.

'I didn't know the undercroft was this far down,' said Gaunt quietly.

'It wasn't,' replied Hark.

Gaunt tightened his grip on his sword. He glanced at Curth.

'I would prefer it if you went back up, Ana,' he said.

Curth shook her head.

'There may be wounded, Lord Executor. You need a medic,' she said simply.

'While we're on the subject of staying out of harm's way, sir,' Sancto began.

'Don't even try it, Scion,' said Gaunt.

'Yes, my lord.'

All the lights were out, but the undercroft was lit by a dull glow, as if unhealthy light was oozing out of the stones. The Beati led the way down, flanked by her two alert officers, then came Gaunt, Hark and Curth and the four Scions. Behind them were Daur, Beltayn, Trooper Perday and the inquisitor. Gaunt had sent Grae to find aid for Onabel and direct the reinforcements Gaunt hoped to Throne were on their way from Van Voytz.

The long flight of stone steps ended in an archway that seemed too big and broad for even a palace wine cellar.

The air scratched at their ears and the insides of their heads. It was like a buzzing of flies or the restless boring of maggots, as though everyone in the party was already dead and decomposing. There was a smell in the air of waste and rot.

Beyond the arch lay a vast chamber. Gaunt could see its impossibility in an instant. No deep cellar in a massive stone edifice like the Urdeshic Palace could be so wide and low without the need for pillars or column supports. The walls were whitewashed, but that looked sallow yellow in the ugly light.

The floor was black.

They advanced slowly, weapons raised, covering each other.

'This wasn't here,' said Hark softly. 'It was a hallway, then barrack chambers off the side. Not this place.'

'It's getting stronger,' said Laksheema. She adjusted the setting on the archeotech weapons built into her sleek golden cuff. 'If it's feeding, and growing... its ability to manipulate and warp reality is increasing.'

'Agreed,' said the Beati gently.

'Woe machines were mechanical engines,' said Curth. 'They couldn't–'

'Heritor Asphodel, may the Throne curse him, was a genius,' said Laksheema. 'I fear we continue to underestimate what his vile imagination could make and unleash.'

Hark stood on something that broke with a crack. He looked down.

'Oh Throne,' he murmured. He could barely see it because it was as black as the floor. Curth bent down with him.

It was part of a human jawbone, with three molars still embedded in it.

It was black because it was covered in blood, and in the odd light, the redness of the blood appeared black.

They realised what they were looking at. The whole floor of the chamber was soaked in blood, and littered with the physical debris of dozens of people. Scraps of bone, odd ribs, hunks of meat and muscle, no piece so big it couldn't sit on a man's palm.

'It's fed,' said Laksheema.

Daur began to tremble. He fought to keep it in, but a terrible groan of anguish broke through his gritted teeth. Beltayn grabbed him and held him tight with both arms to stop him falling. Curth and Gaunt went to him.

'Ban?' Gaunt said.

Daur couldn't speak.

'Ban? Go back,' said Gaunt. 'Go back up. You don't need to be here. I'll finish this. You have my word.'

'No,' Daur managed to answer. His voice was tight and small as if it was being crushed by a high gravity field. 'I need to be here now.'

Gaunt nodded.

'Keep with him,' he said to Curth.

They moved forwards again. The far end of the vast charnel hall became visible in the gloom. Eight doorways, forking off in different directions.

'Don't tell me,' said Gaunt. 'Not like this before?'

Hark shook his head.

'It's playing with us,' said Laksheema. 'It senses us. Senses her, I think.'

She nodded towards the Beati. The Saint was facing the doorways, her sword raised.

'It wants to divide us,' said Laksheema. 'Trap us, make us lost in its little pocket maze.'

'You seem to know a lot,' said Sariadzi.

'I've seen a lot,' said Laksheema. She paused. 'Nothing on this scale.'

The Beati stepped towards the doors. Auerben and Sariadzi hurried to flank her, but she held up a hand to keep them back.

'I won't play its games,' she said. 'Just so it knows, I'm saying that out loud. I won't play these games.'

The whine of a bone saw echoed from one of the eight doorways, followed by silence. Then there was a scrape of stone against stone. The end wall was slowly shifting in front of them. They could see the stonework moving, grating edge against edge as it realigned. Seven of the doorways vanished, becoming solid wall. Only one remained.

'It heard you,' said Laksheema.

'Or it's playing another game,' said Hark.

The Beati raised her sword and approached the doorway. They formed up behind her, following tight. After a few steps, they realised they were stepping into floodwater several centimetres deep. Lights blinked on, the old lumen lamps of the undercroft in their rusted wire frames, illuminating the white-washed walls ahead of them.

'This... this is how it was,' said Hark. 'The main hall. There should be a doorway ahead to the right. The first billet.'

There was. The old wooden doors had been pushed shut but not quite closed. They looked as though someone had taken a circular saw to them repeatedly.

Gaunt moved in beside the Saint, and they approached the doors together.

'My lord!' Sancto hissed.

'Shut up.'

Gaunt looked at the Saint. She nodded.

They kicked the doors open together.

The man stood facing them, just a few metres inside. He fired his lasrifle at them repeatedly. It made a dry, clacking sound. Its powercell was long since exhausted.

The man dropped it, his arms limp and heavy, and drew his straight silver. He took a step forward, then halted.

He stared at their faces, bewildered, as though he didn't properly recognise them.

He was covered in dried blood.

'M-my lord,' he said.

'Mach,' said Gaunt.

Exhausted and traumatised beyond measure, Bonin flopped to his knees at Gaunt's feet.

'I tried,' he whispered. 'I tried. I tried to keep them safe. As many as I could. It came from everywhere. Every shadow.'

Gaunt bent down. 'Easy, Mach,' he said, holding the man by the shoulders. 'Ana? Here, please.'

Gaunt looked past Bonin. Another man was nearby. He stepped out of the shadows, a chair leg in his hand ready to use as a club. He too was caked in blood, and swayed wordlessly on his feet.

It was Yerolemew. The Saint went forwards to support him.

'Sit,' she said. 'Sit down.'

'We... we have to keep going. Keep the doors shut...' the old bandmaster murmured.

There were others. Trooper Luhan crawled out of cover, put down his rifle and started to cry. Sobs and murmurs spread through the darkness behind him. Shapes stirred. Gaunt saw the terrified faces of women and a few children, all members of the retinue.

'How many did you save, Mach?' he asked.

Bonin shook his head, his eyes lifeless.

'Twenty... maybe thirty...' he said. 'Any we could.'

Gaunt squeezed his shoulder.

He rose and faced the cowering survivors.

'The Saint's here,' he said. 'The darkness is going to end. We've come to get you out.'

'There are no stairs...' Yerolemew mumbled.

'There are now,' the Beati assured him. 'Stairs, a door, and light above. You have endured great horror, but you have remained strong. The Emperor has protected you.'

'Not enough,' said Bonin. 'Not nearly enough. We tried, but...'

'I need these people led up out of here,' said Gaunt. 'Fast. Now. Sancto?'

The Scion frowned. 'I will serve your word without question, my Lord Executor,' he said, 'except in this one way. My primary oath is to protect you. I will not leave your side.'

Gaunt looked him in the eye. Sancto did not flinch. Gaunt didn't like him, but he had to admire the man's steel discipline and devotion.

'Can they all walk?' he asked. 'Can you all walk?'

He was answered by moans and weak affirmative noises.

'All right,' said Gaunt. 'Perday, Beltayn? Lead them out and up the stairs. Have them link hands. Take them all, one of you at the front, one at the rear. Yes, like children, Bel. Get them out and get them to the nearest medicae hall.'

'Level three,' said Hark.

'Now, while the walls stay where they are,' said Gaunt.

'Mach? Sergeant major? Luhan?' Gaunt looked at the three shell-shocked Ghosts. 'Bel's in charge. Just follow him. No arguments. Follow him, and do as he tells you. You're walking wounded. You're also brave as feth.'

Bonin nodded dumbly.

Beltayn took his hand and began to lead the line of shuffling, blank-eyed survivors out.

Daur looked at Bonin as he passed.

'Elodie?' he asked.

'She... she was on the stairs,' said Bonin in an empty voice. 'I didn't see her after that.'

The long line of survivors snaked out. Sancto's team covered them until they had cleared the hallway.

'It didn't get them all,' said Lakshecma. 'It's still hungry, then.'

'Agreed,' said the Beati.

They waited until the survivors had walked clear, then exited the chamber where Bonin and the others had concealed and protected them, following the hall deeper into the undercroft. Blood stains flecked the whitewash in places, bloody hand prints smeared across the stonework.

The hall narrowed and dropped down by way of six stone steps. Flood water lapped at the steps, knee deep. The saint didn't hesitate. They waded after her through the chill water and through an arch into another large billet. This one was vaulted, with stone pillars supporting the bowed ceiling. Pieces of bedding and splinters of wood floated on the gently rocking surface of the flood. An empty mess tin. A child's toy.

'It's close by,' said Laksheema.

The scratching and buzzing had grown louder. Curth looked down at the water around her legs, and saw that the surface was trembling as if subject to microvibration interference patterns.

They fanned out, weapons ready, leaving little frothing wakes behind them. Curth stayed with Daur.

Sancto suddenly swept his weapon around, aiming.

Yoncy was standing ahead of them, several metres away. She stared at them with big, frightened eyes. The water came up to her thighs and she was soaked, her clothes clinging to her. She hugged herself for warmth, her flesh pink with cold.

'Papa Gaunt?' she said.

Gaunt pushed Sancto's aim up.

He stepped towards Yoncy.

'Yoncy? Are you all right? Are you alone here?'

Yoncy nodded, her teeth chattering.

'I got lost,' she said. 'The bad shadow was here.'

Curth splashed over to join Gaunt. They approached Yoncy together.

'How is she still alive?' Laksheema called out.

'Same way as Bonin and the others,' snapped Hark.

'Alone?' asked Laksheema.

Gaunt waded towards Yoncy, who held out her hands to be picked up.

Curth caught his arm.

'She was giggling. We heard her,' she said.

'So?' he asked.

'*The offspring of the Great Master,*' said Curth. 'What Laksheema said. A daughter. Born on Verghast.'

Gaunt looked at her, and then back at the child stretching out its arms to him.

'This is Major Kolea's child?' asked Laksheema suddenly.

'Yes,' said Hark.

'It is possible the signal may be interpreted in a number of ways,' said Laksheema. She strode forwards, the water rippling around her long gown. 'Lord Executor–'

'Yoncy,' said Gaunt. 'Listen to me, Yonce. Why were you laughing? What made you laugh?'

'Because it's time, silly,' she said. 'Papa says it's time. I didn't want it to be, but he says it is. The bad shadow won't wait any longer.'

A low whine began, like a bone saw cycling up to full power. Violent ripples radiated out across the water from Yoncy Kolea, and out through the air around her as subspace membranes cracked and buckled.

Curth screamed. Gaunt just put himself in front of her.

Yoncy was no longer Yoncy. A stifling darkness whirled out of her as though a dead star had blinked anti-light. She fractured and rearranged in a neat but complex fractal fashion, folding like some intricate, hinged puzzle. Her smile was the last thing to disappear.

What took her place was still her. It was also the most abominable thing any of them would ever see.

FOURTEEN

TRUTH AND OTHER LIES

'This is grim, there's no way to pretend it isn't,' said Kolea as they waded along.

'Your little girl, she'll be all right,' said Blenner beside him. 'I'm sure of it, major.'

He didn't sound convinced. In the half-light, Kolea could see Blenner's stressed body-language, as if he was trying to flee into himself because there was nowhere else left to go.

'I appreciate you trying to sound encouraging, Vaynom,' he said.

'Well, that's what commissars are for,' said Blenner, his laugh empty.

'That and other things.'

Blenner sighed. His breathing had sped up. 'Comes with the territory,' he said.

'Must be hard though, that first time?'

'I don't want to think about it,' said Blenner.

'Sorry,' said Kolea. 'We should keep our chins up.'

Blenner nodded. 'I'm... I'm finding that hard these days, major,' he replied.

'Sometimes you just need someone to talk to,' said Kolea. 'A friend. You know? Otherwise, those things can build up inside. Lock a man's mind down. Make him do stupid things.'

'Things?'

'I've known men fall apart,' said Kolea. 'Turn to drink. Or abuse pharms. Just to keep the daemons inside.'

'Pharms?'

'There's always a way back, Vaynom. You just have to open up and talk.'

'I wish–' Blenner began.

'What?'

'I wish you hadn't just said "daemons",' he said.

Kolea smiled. 'Vaynom?

'Yes?'

'Earlier on... you remember? When I first came down into the billet. You were going to tell me something.'

'Was I?' asked Blenner. 'I don't recall.'

'I do,' said Kolea. 'If I ever saw a man who was going to lift a burden off his shoulders, it was you then. What was it?'

Blenner didn't reply for a moment. Then a little crushed squeak came out of him.

'I can't do it,' he said. Kolea could barely hear him. 'The guilt. It's the guilt, you see? Just *on* me, on me all the time.'

'Talk to me, Vaynom.' Kolea had dropped his voice to a low hiss. They had slowed down, and the rest of Baskevyl's squad was pulling ahead slightly.

Blenner looked at Kolea. His eyes were puffy and red. A little tic was making his left cheek twitch.

'Low Keen,' he said. 'It was stupid. So stupid. I... I was just trying to hold it together. They had their claws on me. I mean, I was properly screwed. They had dirt on me that would have... it would have been the end.'

'Who?'

Blenner gulped, and wiped his eyes.

'None of it matters now,' he said. 'It all seemed so important then, but now? Here? Feth! It's so ridiculous! The horror here, our lives... death coming for us, and no way out.'

'Tell me,' said Kolea.

'What?' Blenner uttered an empty laugh. 'A death bed confession?'

'Think of it as absolution,' said Kolea. 'If this is going to be the end of us down here, then how do you want it to go? Don't you want to pass from this duty into the next life with a clear conscience?'

'Only in death, eh?'

'That's where they say it ends. Duty, that is. I don't know about guilt.'

Blenner hesitated.

'I can't remember whose idea it was,' he said softly. 'Gendler, maybe? Wilder jumped at it, and they pulled me in because they knew, they *knew*, they could blackmail me into assisting. It was just money, major. Just money. Gaunt's boy had so much, I mean, *so* much. Access to House Chass accounts. We didn't know, not then. We didn't know that the boy was... not a boy.'

'And?'

'Gendler was supposed to jump him in the showers. Put the scares on him, and force him to transfer a little funding our way. That's all it was supposed to be. But Gendler, that feth Didi Gendler, he was heavy-handed. Knocked the boy down. That's when we came in. That's when we realised that the son was actually a fething daughter. Then Gendler fething improvised. Decided she couldn't talk if she was dead.'

He looked up at Kolea.

'Ezra found them. I think he was watching Merity, shadowing her. He went in and he killed Gendler. Wounded Wilder. Then we came in and pretended to help him, though we'd been in on it all along. He killed Ezra. Said we could say that Wilder had done it. And that I'd found them and executed Wilder on the spot. No loose ends, you see? You see how that worked? He made me kill him, Gol. He made me shoot Wilder. Wilder was begging me not to, and I just–'

'Vaynom? Vaynom, listen. Who made you? Who was the other man in your group?'

'Meryn,' said Blenner.

Kolea clenched his jaw tight.

'That little shit,' he whispered. 'It was him? He killed Ezra?'

Blenner nodded. Kolea wanted to punch him in the face and then keep punching. But he held his rage back.

'You've done the right thing, Vaynom,' he managed to say. 'The brave thing. You feel better now, right?'

Blenner nodded again.

'Good. All right. Let's deal with this, and if we survive it, we can deal with Meryn. You've done the right thing.'

'I just couldn't do it any more,' said Blenner.

'Vaynom, I need you to give me your weapon now. Your sidearm. Can you do that?'

'Yes,' said Blenner, and handed his pistol to Kolea.

'Good. I–'

'Gol!' Baskevyl's voice echoed back down the hallway. 'Problem?'

'No!' Kolea called back.

'Close it up! We don't want to lose the pair of you!'

'All right!' called Kolea.

He took hold of Blenner's arm and began to move him along the hall. There'd be time for anger later. He couldn't let it weaken him now. He couldn't let it break his concentration. There was too much at stake.

They had just caught up with the others when the bone saw started shrieking. It sounded very close, as though it was just on the other side of the thick and unending stone wall.

'Oh Throne!' Baskevyl cried. He raised his weapon.

'Move!' he said. 'Move! With me, now!'

Luna Fazekiel started to tremble uncontrollably when she heard the bone saw howling again. It was very close, and persistent this time. The long, drawn-out shrieks of destructive wrath echoed down the hallways.

She shoved her pistol into her belt to stop herself dropping it, and then clenched one hand around the other in an effort to control the trembling.

Meryn looked up in fear, twitching with every echoing shriek.

'Feth,' he whispered. 'We're so fething done. Just done. You know what? Feth him. Damn him. Screw him to hell! Fething God-Emperor, he does this to us?'

'Captain,' Merity said, trying to hold her own terror back.

'What?' he snapped, rounding on her. 'It's true! It's true, you stupid little high-hive bitch! We serve him, serve him all our days, following his fething light, because he's the way and the truth and all that bullshit! And for what? This? This shit? If we are his children, and he's our god, then he's a fething monster!'

'That's enough,' Fazekiel said, her voice not much more than a stammer.

Meryn sneered at her. For a notably handsome man, his face had twisted in an ugly way. 'What? That blasphemy, is it? Not the sort of thing a Guardsman should say in earshot of his Prefectus stooge? I don't care. Feth you. You know it's true as well. It's a joke. It's a farce. We give our lives every day, year-on-year, just to serve his great and inscrutable scheme. I have marched every bloody step from Tanith to this. There's never been any hope. There's never been anything but the most fleeting respite. And I've seen horrors. Horrors no one should see. And this is the reward. Trapped in a pit with some daemon fiend. Feth Terra. Feth the God-Emperor–'

'I said that's enough, captain,' said Fazekiel.

Meryn looked away. 'What's he going to do?' he murmured. 'Damn me? Curse me? There's no curse worse than this.'

He closed his eyes and clasped his hands to his forehead.

'There's never a way out,' he whispered. 'Never.'

Fazekiel swallowed hard and took a step towards him gingerly. She reached out one trembling hand in a futile gesture of consolation.

Something black and thrashing landed on the ground between them, shrieking. They both leapt back.

Meryn lowered his warknife.

'It's the fething mascot,' he said. He started to laugh. Somehow, Merity felt his empty, cold laughter was worse than the echoing daemon-shriek.

She looked down at the wounded eagle. It was shuddering, its plumage a mess. Its remaining head jerked from side to side, regarding them with wild incomprehension.

'There it is! You see? There–'

The old ayatani and Shoggy Domor appeared from a hallway beside them. They came to a halt and stared.

'Throne,' said Domor, 'I never thought we'd see another living soul again.'

'Shoggy,' Meryn said in disbelief.

'Are the three of you all right?' Zweil asked.

'Yes, father,' said Merity. 'Glad of company.'

Zweil looked at Fazekiel, then went over to her and hugged her tightly, pressing her head against his shoulder.

'There, there,' he said as she wept into the folds of his robe. 'It's all been a bit much. But we're coming through it now. The Emperor protects. He really does.'

'No, he doesn't,' said Meryn. 'You hear that, right? That's the sound of death coming for us.'

'Come on, Flyn,' said Domor. 'Father Zweil is–'

'What's he going to do?' asked Meryn. 'You know we're all fethed.'

'I don't like your tone, young man,' said Zweil, releasing Fazekiel from his embrace. He looked at Merity with a sad smile, and squeezed her hand.

'Your father will be proud,' he said. 'You've kept your reserve. Must run in the blood, eh?'

'I think my courage is about gone,' Merity said.

'Courage is transient,' said Zweil. 'Like flowers and pain and also soft cheeses. The things that matter are the things that last. Faith. Belief. And hope is surprisingly durable.'

'I don't believe in anything,' muttered Meryn.

'That would explain a lot about you,' said Zweil. 'I myself have belief to spare. I believe we're getting out. I believe we'll live.'

'You mad old bastard,' said Meryn.

'Father Zweil may be mad—' Domor began.

'It's been said,' Zweil agreed with a chuckle. He had stooped down to comfort the eagle, cooing at it and stroking its feathers.

'But I trust him,' said Domor. 'He's got me this far.'

'I'd hate to think what sort of shit you were in before, then,' said Meryn.

'Are you going to stay here, or are you going to follow us?' Domor asked.

'Where to?' asked Meryn.

The bird shook out its wings, squawked, and took off again.

'That way,' said Zweil, pointing to it as it flew off.

'You're following the fething bird?' asked Meryn.

'We're going to the light,' said Zweil. 'Come on.' He took Merity by the hand.

Meryn just shook his head in despair.

'He's not wrong,' said Domor. They all looked at him, even Zweil.

'I'm not?' he asked.

Domor adjusted his optics.

'I'm reading light down there. Right where the bird flew. Outside light. Throne, it can smell fresh air.'

'Are you joking?' asked Fazekiel.

'No,' said Domor. He set off, striding urgently down the hallway. They followed him.

'See?' he called back. 'Do you see this?'

There was light ahead. A pale shaft of light slanting down.

'It's the steps!' Domor yelled. 'It's the fething steps.'

They caught up with him. There was no sign of the eagle, but ahead was a broad flight of stone steps. It was, without doubt, the entry steps that connected the undercroft with the upper levels. Thin light shone down from above.

Domor grinned at them, then gave Zweil a hug.

'Come on,' he said. 'The Emperor was watching us after all.'

'A little faith, Shoggy,' said Zweil, leading Fazekiel up the steps after Domor. 'I told you, boy. A little faith, I said.'

Merity glanced at Meryn.

'I hope he wasn't watching you,' she said.

'Movement, sir!' the Urdeshi trooper called out. 'More survivors coming up!'

Grae pushed his way to the front of the Urdeshi detachment covering the undercroft door. Domor appeared, leading the others the last of the way.

They looked around, blinking in the light, staring at the armed and armoured soldiers surrounding them. Power was still out in the entire palace, but Grae had set up portable light rigs with battery cells to bathe the doorway area.

'How many of you?' asked Grae.

'Five, sir,' Domor replied.

'Tanith?' Grae asked.

'Yes.'

'Trooper Zent?' Grae said to a subordinate. 'Get their names then escort them to the medicae area.'

He looked back at Domor's bedraggled party.

'Did you see anybody else down there. Anything?'

'It's a warp incursion, sir,' said Fazekiel. 'Something's loose.'

'We are aware of that, commissar,' replied Grae. 'Are you Fazekiel? It was your amber alert that got us mobilised in the first place.'

'What's happening up here, sir?' asked Domor.

'Power's down,' said Grae. 'We think it's a result of the incursion. Come on, let's move you clear and get you seen to.'

'How many others got out?' asked Merity.

Grae looked at her.

'Are you Merity Chass?'

'Yes,' she said.

'That's a blessing at least,' said Grae. 'How did you find your way out?'

'We stuck together,' said Meryn. 'Just saw it through and looked for an exit.'

Merity glared at him. She was too tired to qualify his reply.

'Good job, captain,' said Grae. 'I'm sure the Lord Executor will commend you for seeing his daughter safe.'

'I asked how many got out,' Merity said.

'About thirty so far,' said Grae. 'Mainly retinue, badly traumatised. I hear it's grim down there.'

'Grim as hell, sir,' said Meryn.

'Where is my father?' asked Merity.

Grae glanced at the doorway.

'He's gone in to eradicate the threat,' he replied. 'The Beati is with him.'

'That's a mistake,' said Merity. 'It's... you have no idea. It's a horrifying destructive force. You should be closing the area off and purging it. Or sending in a battalion strength of heavy troops.'

'Our resources are limited,' said Grae. 'The palace is defenceless. All systems are down and the Archenemy is striking at the city. As soon as you're checked out, you'll be joining the evacuation.'

'I'd prefer to stay, sir,' said Merity.

'Not a choice you get to make,' said Grae. 'Even the Warmaster is being moved clear.'

They were led up two floors, through palace hallways lit only by emergency lanterns. In the night outside, heavy rain beat against the windows. It was strange not to be able to hear the constant fizzle of the palace void shields.

A prayer chapel had been converted into a medical post. By lamplight, medicae staff were checking all survivors brought in. Most of the survivors were sitting in the chapel pews, silent and huddled, staring and exhausted. Merity saw women from the retinue and a few children. Their clothes were dark with dried bloodstains. Nearby, Beltayn and Trooper Perday stood with Bonin, Yerolemew and Luhan, waiting for news. Domor and Zweil went over to them immediately. Merity saw Domor and Beltayn talking with animated urgency. Bonin, Luhan and the sergeant major moved with the dull, blank stupor of the profoundly combat-shocked.

Urdeshi corpsmen led Merity and Fazekiel aside for examination. Meryn just sat down on a pew, refusing attention.

The corpsman with Merity went to take her carbine away. She shook her head.

'I want to keep it,' she said.

She sat patiently on a metal stool while a palace medicae checked her eyes with a light and took her pulse. An eerie calm settled her, the empty void that followed protracted stress. Her hearing became muffled and everything seemed like a dream: the hollow faces of the silent survivors, the low murmur of voices, the clink of medical equipment in chrome trays, the flutter of candles, the wink of light on the gold leaf adorning the old frescoes on the chapel ceiling.

'Thank you,' she said quietly.

Fazekiel was sitting on a stool beside her while an orderly took her resting pulse.

'What?' she said.

'You got me out of there,' said Merity.

'Not really,' said Fazekiel. 'Father Zweil was right. You kept it together.'

'I just... I didn't want to die,' said Merity.

She glanced at Fazekiel. The commissar was letting the orderly remove her coat.

'You kept it together better than me,' Fazekiel said. 'That thing, that noise... it's haunted me since Low Keen. I can't explain. Domor and I, Blenner too. We all heard it there and I think it made us-'

'What?'

'Vulnerable. More susceptible to fear. I don't know. I know I've never been that scared before. I know I shouldn't have been that scared. That lost. I-'

'It doesn't matter,' said Merity. 'You didn't break like that bastard Meryn.'

They looked across the chapel at Meryn, sitting alone, a brooding look on his face as he stared at nothing.

'I think he saw more than us,' said Fazekiel.

'Maybe,' Merity said.

She looked at Fazekiel.

'It's not important now. Throne knows, it's trivial. But when this is done, you need to talk to him,' she said.

'To Meryn?'

Merity shrugged. 'About the incident. I couldn't say down there because he was with you. You kept asking. But that's why I came to find you. I remembered hearing him speaking to Dalin just outside the shower block. Just before it happened.'

'You think Meryn was involved?'

'Yes,' said Merity. 'He almost admitted it to me in the undercroft. He warned me to keep my mouth shut.'

Fazekiel nodded.

'I'll break him,' she said. 'I'll end his career. Once he's confessed, it'll be sanction for him.'

Meryn sat alone. On the far side of the chapel, Merity Chass sat with Fazekiel, orderlies bustling around them. They were talking.

That's how you get treated, he thought. That's the privilege right there. The daughter of the Lord Executor. So fething special. People give thanks to see she's survived.

She was nothing. Just a high-hive aristo bitch, born into wealth and power. She knew nothing about real life, and certainly nothing about soldiering.

Meryn did. He'd been a Ghost since Tanith. He'd come all that way, watching his own back because no other bastard would. He had the skills. He'd learned them along the way. How to fight to survive. How to defeat an enemy that was going to kill you. How to use a blade.

And, thanks to the damaged bastards they'd brought in after Vervunhive, how to read lips.

He watched them. Merity Chass and Luna Fazekiel.

He watched them talk.

Gaunt held on to Curth's arm and dragged her through the darkness. The air was freezing and howling around them, and the water in the chamber was thrashing, like waves driven by an ocean gale.

They could hardly see. The bad shadow was everywhere, lashing out tendrils of hideous fractal darkness, folding light into void-blackness along sharp, straight edges.

Gaunt hauled her against one of the chamber's stone columns and lashed out into the elemental fury. Whatever his power blade struck, it caused a huge spray of sparks, as though he had shoved the sword of Hieronymo Sondar into a grinding lathe.

There were flashes in the churning darkness. Weapons discharging. Over the shriek of the bone saw, Gaunt heard the rasp of Hark's plasma gun, and the rapid snap-roar of hellguns. The Scions.

'Yoncy!' Curth yelled in disbelief. 'Yoncy!'

'Hold on!' Gaunt yelled back over the tumult.

Sariadzi suddenly appeared, staggering through the crashing waves. His upper body had been slashed in a dozen places and all his fingers were missing. He tried to cling to them. Curth attempted to hold on to him and pull him close. He looked at them in desperation, pleading in his eyes, no words coming from his gaping mouth.

The sharp edges of the darkness seized him from behind, jagged and piercing like negative lightning. It ripped him away from them. In the split second before he vanished from sight in the lofting spray, he disintegrated as though his entire body had been pushed through a mincer.

Light suddenly bloomed through the chamber, a fierce golden glow that began in the heart of the place and flowed outwards. The tendrils of shadow retreated swiftly with an angry crackle.

The surging water calmed to rocking waves.

Gaunt looked around. He saw Hark two pillars away, leaning against the stone column for support. His leather coat was shredded, and his cap was gone. His augmetic arm had been torn off, leaving only a stump of sparking, torn biomech. With his one good arm, he clung onto Inquisitor Laksheema. She was limp and drenched in blood, and her augmetics, even her beautiful gold mask, were crazed and scratched as though they had been sand-blasted. Smoke was billowing from the golden cuff on her left wrist where intricate and powerful digital weapons had overloaded and burned out.

There was no sign of Auerben or Daur, or any of the Scions, except Sancto, who was on his knees, the water up to his sternum. He was clutching his torso, bloody spittle drooling from his agonised mouth.

The Saint was in the centre of the chamber, at the very heart of the light. It shone out of her. All around her, the frothing churning water had smoothed to a mirror stillness.

She was locked in combat, her sword flashing as she swung two-handed into the beast attacking her.

The woe machine.

It was a shadow mass three times her size, a focus of darkness penned in by her radiance, but still lashing and rending with razor tendrils. It was hard to look at, and harder still to define: a cloud of knife-edged shadow that shifted and swam in supple, geometric patterns. It had a constantly changing texture, like rippling mirror scales, part absolute void, part iridescent black, like the wing-cases of some daemonic beetle. It was a storm of whirling, midnight-black thorns surrounding a super-dense core of immaterium darkness.

But the worst part wasn't the look of it, the churning, abstract nightmare. It was the feel of it. The intense quality of primal horror that radiated from it. The eager, inhuman malice of pure annihilation.

It was Asphodel's perfect vengeance weapon.

It was the Anti-Saint.

The Beati was covered in lacerations, blood streaming from a thousand knife cuts. Her clothing was shredded, and her breastplate and armour pitted and scoured. Her sword whirled in her hand, deflecting the oil-thick darkness that lashed and tore at her. Her sword was not especially large, nor was it particularly extraordinary. Just a standard, bulk-issue officer's weapon.

It was the force she imbued it with that counted. A crisp, green aura shone around the blade, and where it struck, the darkness burned. She was drawing on all her power, channelling from a distant and almighty source. The divine light pouring out of her had caged and contained the woe machine, at least temporarily. She thrust and stabbed to end its existence. A phantom shadow of wings, huge and made of emerald light, had sprouted from her back. A halo of bright light surrounded her head.

'We have to help her,' said Daur, appearing at Gaunt's side. He was soaked to the skin, his uniform torn. He was covered in small wounds.

Gaunt nodded.

'She has it pinned,' he said. 'She's contained its power.'

He and Gaunt moved forward together.

'Don't be fething idiots!' Curth yelled after them.

Sancto saw them moving forward. He got up with a raw growl, clutching his hellgun with one hand and a terrible belly-wound with the other. Something had slashed clean through his body armour and almost gutted him.

All three of them fired into the shadow assaulting the saint. It barely seemed to notice Daur's shots or the blasts from Sancto's weapon, but the explosive round from Gaunt's bolt pistol blew a hole in it. Thorns spiralled away, like a swarm of insects driven from a nest.

In seconds, the damage had re-formed, and the thorns had re-joined the main, whirling mass.

They all fired again, repeated shots. Auerben stumbled up to join them, her hair matted with blood. She added her own shots to the fusillade.

'It won't die!' she wailed.

'It's gonna die,' Sancto snarled. 'It took all my men. Took 'em all and shredded them!'

The woe machine dropped back, still whirling and keening. The water under it rippled and seethed.

The Saint stood her ground, panting. Her ghost wings were fading and flickering, as if the power sustaining them was ebbing. Blood dripped off her armour. They went to her side, but she flung a hand to warn them back.

'It's still strong,' she gasped. 'Impossibly strong. But it's still not full-grown. It wants my power. It wants to feed on me, so it can fully form and then–'

'Then?' asked Sancto, fighting back his pain. 'Then what?'

'Then it will do the Anarch's bidding and raze this city and everything in it,' said the Beati.

She took a step forwards.

'I won't let that happen,' she said.

'Wait!' Auerben yelped.

'You're hurt,' said Gaunt.

'That hardly matters,' she said. 'The Emperor is with me.'

She took another step. The pitch of the woe machine's keening intensified again, the sawing shriek filling the air. Its intricate, churning patterns of leaden darkness and polished black grew more fierce. It surged to meet her.

A storm of heavy las-fire blocked it. Multiple weapons unloaded into it at full auto.

Gaunt turned. Baskevyl and Kolea were advancing across the chamber, flanked by Dalin and the men from Baskevyl's search squad. All of them were unleashing heavy, accurate suppression fire. Squad drill, close focus fire-team pattern. Twelve lasrifles emptying sustained destructive force into the abomination.

The woe machine roiled backwards like an angry mass of flies. Baskevyl's men were reloading as they came, switching out dead cells for fresh ones as they ran dry, maintaining the punishing fusillade.

The woe machine retreated further. Darkness and fluid shadows spread out around the walls. Its thousands of individual, razor-sharp cutting

teeth chipped and rattled against the ancient stone walls. The temperature dropped. They heard stone blocks scrape and grind as it threatened to
warp the undercroft reality again.

'Is it hurt?' Gaunt asked.

The Beati nodded.

'Hold fire!' Gaunt yelled to Baskevyl. 'Let's get in close. Save whatever
you have left until we–'

'What is it?' Kolea asked.

Gaunt looked at him. 'I–'

'Sir?'

'I was wrong,' Gaunt said to him. 'I was wrong, Gol. I'm so sorry. It's a woe
machine. We brought it with us all the way from Vervunhive.'

He could see Gol Kolea's face twitch as he fought to control his reaction.

'Yoncy?' he asked very quietly.

'It never was her, Gol,' said the Beati. 'She was never real.'

Dalin uttered a slow moan of anguish. He dropped his rifle and fell to
his knees in the flood.

'That can't be true,' he mumbled. 'That can't be true. It can't.'

'That's Yoncy?' Kolea asked, his voice dull.

'Oh, throne, Gol...' Bask exclaimed, heartbroken.

'That?' Kolea said. He stepped forwards. Baskevyl tried to hold him back,
but he shook his dear friend's hand away.

'The warp has tricked us all,' said the Beati. 'Lies are its first weapon–'

'Feth that,' said Kolea, staring at the seething mass of darkness. 'I had a
child. A child. I swore I'd–'

He stepped closer.

'I loved you, Yoncy,' he said. 'I would have done anything to... to...'

The howl of the saw barked at him.

'Yeah. You know me,' said Kolea. 'You were human long enough. You
know me. Can you kill me? Your papa? Eh? I think the warp made you too
human. There's too much human in you still.'

The razor storm shivered. Its frenzy decreased.

'Yoncy?' Kolea called. He held out his hand. 'You come back now, you
hear? Come back to me. Come back to papa.'

The darkness shifted. Shadows folded, shearing and twisting into new
patterns of darkness. A smaller shape formed. A vague human shape inside
the buzzing cloud of thorns.

'Yeah, that's right,' said Kolea. 'That's good.'

He looked at the Beati. When he spoke, just the one word, there was a
tiny break in his voice.

'Now,' he said.

The Saint's green wings reignited with power, brighter than before, and
she plunged her blade into the shadow.

The darkness exploded.

Deaf, blind, dumb, insensible, they were all hurled backwards into the
consuming void.

FIFTEEN

INTO FIRE

Zhukova gestured, and Criid moved the fire teams forwards. The air in the vent stank of sulphur and it was so warm and close, it made their lungs tight. All of them were streaming with sweat.

The entire environment felt toxic in the worst way. Every now and then, a rank breath of air would rumble along the duct from far below. Criid kept expecting a super-hot vent of gas to come boiling up and roast them where they stood.

'Down from here,' Zhukova said. A wide vertical duct connected to the horizontal one they had been following. Rusted grip rails ran down one side, for use by servitor work crews. The drop glowed with bioluminescent algae.

'You sure?' asked Obel.

Zhukova had been tracing the pattern on her palm with her index finger. She coughed and nodded.

Maggs peered down the drop.

'Straight down?' he asked.

'Yes,' said Zhukova. 'Fifty metres or so. It meets the main thermal out-flow. We can intercept the hostiles.'

'How do we get the support weapons and flamers down that?' asked Ifvan.

'Carefully,' said Criid.

She swung over the lip, got her feet on the first grip rail and looked at them.

'Come on,' she said.

Pasha stopped pacing. She looked over at Spetnin at the arcade hatch.

'It's getting quieter out there,' he said. 'No more assaults in the last few minutes.'

Pasha nodded. 'We've given them long enough. Ready up. We're taking that Gnosis Repository.'

Her squads prepped weapons. Pasha re-checked the antique sleetgun she had spent the last few minutes examining. She was confident that she understood its function. She'd taken a satchel of shells from one of the skitarii corpses. She was going to need decent stopping power.

At the compression hatch, Mora's squad was ready, lined up for fast assault. At her nod, Ludd punched the hatch key.

The compression hatch sighed on its hydraulics and opened.

The Gnosis Repository was quiet. The bodies of their dead lay where they had fallen. Mora's team led the way, moving quickly, weapons hunting for movement. Elam's first squad followed, with Ludd. Pasha led the third assault element inside.

Nothing moved. No fire came their way from the ducting network at the far end.

Ludd glanced into the open crypt-safe.

'Etriun,' he said.

Pasha glanced in at the versenginseer's corpse, face up on the crypt floor. Her brow crinkled with distaste.

'Keep moving,' she instructed.

Mora's squad approached the Repository's far end. Steam guttered from several sub-ducts that had been forced to release pressure. The heavy lid of the main down-duct had been forced, and lay on the deck. Broken locking bolts were scattered on the ground around it.

Pasha pushed forwards and leaned over to peer down the duct.

'Feth's sake,' said Elam. 'Don't just go sticking your head in there!'

She regarded him sarcastically.

'Head still attached,' she told him, gesturing to her neck. 'The enemy is in there, and running. I pray to Throne that Tona and Lunny have got their strength down in front of them. We box them in like rats in a pipe. So, Asa, I am going to stick more than just my head in there.'

She heaved herself out onto the duct's access ladder, a metal frame that ran down into the darkness below.

'You coming,' she asked, 'or have I got to do this alone?'

A light rain had started to fall out of the low, ink-black sky. Behind them, the last crackle of exchanged fire with the insurgents echoed from the end of the approach road.

Bray signalled, and the first of the squads moved out, running low and quiet across the rockcrete apron towards the gatehouse. Chiria and Haller brought up the rear, lugging a .20 and ammo box between them, moving at a shuffling trot.

Bray threw a stop signal, and tossed a rock towards the gatehouse. It clattered across the open yard, in range of the gatehouse sensor net.

Nothing stirred. No lights kicked in, no hum of auto-aiming weapons. The place was dead.

Bray let his breath out. If the gatehouse had been live, it would have probably stopped them cold. Cracking that kind of bunker was tread-work. Besides, if the gatehouse had opened up, the slaved weapons in its embrasures would easily have had enough reach to hit the bomb truck they pushed up out of range of the insurgents behind the highway rise.

They moved in. Bray waited, edgy, as Mkoyn burned through the outer door's lock with a cutting torch. He toed open the heavy door, the lock mechanism still glowing and dripping gobs of molten steel.

The Ghosts made entry, clearance style.

Gatehouse command was dead, and so were the two Urdeshi Steelsiders in it. The whole place was torn apart by intense gunfire. The walls were peppered with blast holes, and the floor was covered in drifts of spent brass. Smoke fumed the air. Monitor screens hung, shattered and crazed. Those still linked and functional displayed dead-air feeds. A noxious smell wafted from dead things caged in each of the bunker's gun embrasures.

They checked the bodies. Both Steelsiders had been riddled with bullets at close range. The smashed ruin of a gun-servitor lay near the door. One of the dead automata's cyclic cannons was still rotating, a dry, grinding whirr. It had emptied its entire munition canisters.

Chiria set down the heavy .20 and relieved one of the dead Urdeshi of his .30 short-snout, strapping the hip-mounted onto a gyro-stable body-frame.

'Easier to carry,' she said. Haller nodded, and secured the other short-snout. They straightened out the fat, armoured feed belts. The slaved auto-hoppers were dead too, but Chiria found the release catches and lifted the hoppers from their mountings. They were heavy, but she and Haller hefted them up like buckets.

Bray moved through the inner door and entered the walkway across the ditches. Rain pattered down, jingling the chain mesh. He led the fire team advance. There was a caged inner run beyond the ditches. The meshing here had been torn down.

'Something was penned here,' said Mkeller.

Bray nodded. Whatever it was, it was loose.

Trooper Armin called to Bray there was something on the ground near the door to the main wall. It looked like a large dog. They approached carefully.

It was a bio-mech thing, a quadruped defence servitor of canine build. What organics it possessed had originally been human. The sight of it disgusted them both.

It was sprawled on its side. They could tell it was still alive, though its vitals were collapsing.

'Shot?' Armin asked.

Bray shook his head. Thick black mucus was welling from the creature's steel jaws, and films of it crusted the thing's eyes. Its systems had crashed. It had been compromised and corrupted, and that corruption was now killing it.

Bray keyed his bead.

'Bray to Kolosim.'

'Go.'

'We've reached the inner gate. The place is dead. No contacts. Can confirm signs that the Mechanicus elements turned. Probably some kind of mechanical infection. I don't know the right word, but it got in their system, drove them mad, and then shut them down.'

'Dead?'

'Looks like it, sir. Burned them out really fast, but they went down feral. No signs of gunfire from inside.'

'How long to main entry?'

Bray and Armin tried the massive blast door. It was sealed tight.

'Three, maybe four minutes to cut an entry.'

'Copy that. Get it done.'

* * *

Behind the transports on the approach road, Kolosim looked at the men behind him ready to deploy.

'Move up,' he said. 'Bray's about to let us into the place. It's gone quiet, but stay sharp.'

He turned to look at EM 14.

'Let's go,' he ordered.

Behind him, two full companies of Ghosts began to advance on the gatehouse.

Eli Rawne's plans always erred towards the simple. Life had taught him that much. The more moving parts, the more chance there was for something to go very wrong. He liked lean plans that were supple enough to absorb nasty surprises.

His plan for Camp Xenos had been so lean, there wasn't a scrap of body-fat on it. Get in, grab Mabbon, get out. But life, or some great external power that Rawne didn't choose to believe in, was laughing at him from the void. It had other ideas.

He'd been anticipating Sekkite insurgents or, at the very worst, packson units. He'd chosen to move light, with just one section, to make the most of speed.

The things he was facing instead – 'Qimurah', the pheguth had called them – were the sort of freaks that made that Great External Power In The Void positively hoot with glee. The Great External Power In The Void wasn't something Rawne had any plans to get to know on a personal level. For a start, the Great External Power probably had a face like a grox's puckered arse. But sometimes – times like this – Rawne felt a burning desire, like an ingot of foundry-fresh steel sinking deep down in his gut, to meet that laughing fether face to face and have words.

Strong words. Strong words punctuated by straight silver every time Rawne made a salient point.

With Varl and Brostin in tow, he'd barely got Mabbon into the main guard-house when the yard-front area lit up. Cardass called out four shooters, minimum. They were pinned down. Their transport was sitting in the yard, near the gate block. Just thirty metres, but the rockcrete yard was wide open all the way. It might as well have been parked on Balhaut.

Rawne reviewed his situation fast. Most of the Camp Xenos garrison had been dead by the time he'd arrived. He'd lost several good men of his own just getting inside. In the time it had taken him to secure Mabbon, Troopers Okel and Mkfareg had been butchered too. Oysten, his adjutant, had also taken a hit. She'd survived, but the las-bolt had destroyed her vox-caster set.

That meant no warning was getting out. No message to Pasha that the frighteningly resilient things currently killing his men were also probably coming for her. In larger numbers.

It also meant there would be no calling for help. Oysten was pissed off about it. If there had been time, Rawne would have enjoyed seeing his normally meek and precise adjutant getting riled.

'I'd just got that fether tuned up!' she snarled. He helped her pull the smashed vox-caster unit off her back. More shots ripped in through the windows and outer door.

'It seems your exit route is blocked?' Mabbon asked.

Rawne glared at him.

'Strangely enough, prisons aren't built with multiple exits,' he replied.

He signalled Brostin forward to join the Ghosts defending the front of the guardhouse. Varl was sticking tight beside the pheguth.

'We could do with another shooter, you know?' Varl said to Mabbon.

'I don't want a gun,' Mabbon replied.

'Not really your choice,' said Rawne, snatching fire through a window slit.

'Oddly, it is,' said Mabbon. 'I've been a prisoner for too long. Colonel, how many years has it been now? And every day, you and your Ghosts actively preventing me from having anything, anything at all, that could remotely be used as a weapon?'

'I let you keep your mouth, didn't I?' Rawne spat.

Trooper Kaellin uttered a grunt as a well-placed las-round found his forehead and threw him back from the window slot. He was dead before he hit the floor.

Rawne cursed. The Archenemy were incredibly effective, and his team were penned in a target building that was being demolished around them one las-bolt at a time. The Suicide Kings, his fine first section, had been reduced to eight: him, Oysten, Varl, Bellevyl, Brostin, Cardass, Laydly and LaHurf.

End of an era. End of the infamous Kings. He was damned if this was how he was going to go out.

Then again, he reflected, I'm probably long since damned anyway.

'I told Sergeant Varl this, and I'll tell you too, colonel,' said Mabbon. 'It's me they want. They don't care about you, except to kill you on their way to me. Let them have me and spare–'

'No.'

'Rawne–'

'No, Mabbon,' said Rawne. 'I've got orders. A duty. And duty only has two endings. Accomplishing it or–'

'I know the other one,' said Mabbon.

Rawne got in beside Laydly, who was burning through his ammo at another of the window slots.

'Cardass says four,' said Rawne.

'That's what I count, sir,' said Laydly. 'One on the roof of that bunker there. Two in the blockhouse beside it, the other one up by the gate–'

A burst of las bracketed the slot. Laydly stopped pointing, and he and Rawne ducked. Rockcrete chippings and metal fragments rained down on them.

'You'll have to take my word on the last one,' Laydly said.

'What did that bunker look like to you?' Rawne asked.

Laydly shrugged. 'A silo, maybe?'

'That's what I thought,' he replied. Xenos was a prison, not a fortress. It wasn't designed to keep attackers out, it was designed to keep people in.

Vital elements, like the guardhouse and any garrison areas or arsenals would be securely distanced from the cell block compound.

'Bellevyl!' Rawne called out.

Trooper Bellevyl was holding another window slot several metres left of Rawne.

'Sir?' the Belladon called back.

'Think you can lob one onto that bunker?'

Bellevyl pulled a face, assessing his very limited angle of fire.

'Dunno, sir,' he said.

'Let me re-phrase,' said Rawne. 'Lob one onto the bunker, Bellevyl.'

Bellevyl nodded. First section, B Company – the Suicide Kings – were Rawne's personal squad. Every Ghost in it had been hand-picked by him. In the early days, they'd all been Tanith, because Rawne had nursed an antipathy to any new influx from Verghast or Belladon. But he had mellowed. Skill-sets and raw talent mattered more to him than some notion of loyalty to a world that no longer existed. That, and the fact that so many of the original Tanith in first section had been smoked over the years he'd needed replacements.

Like the First's scout cadre, B Company first section followed its own rules. It was part of the privilege of membership. Rawne allowed greater discretion in weapon choice. He liked the idiosyncratic adaptability of variety. The Suicide Kings went to work packing a range of firepower normally found in elite storm troop platoons. Okel, Throne rest him, had carried a large calibre autogun that chambered armour-piercing rounds. Conglan, now dead out on the yard somewhere, had favoured a hellgun. Oysten, along with her vox-caster, lugged a stock-less riot gun and a bag of breaching shells. Cardass carried a box-fed .20 stubber with a pump shotgun cut-down bolted under the primary barrel.

LaHurf and Bellevyl had standard pattern lasrifles like Varl's, but both had increased the carry-weight by a third through the addition of under-barrel grenade launchers.

Bellevyl slotted in a chunky krak grenade and lined up at the slot, scooting around for the best angle. Heavy enemy fire kept licking at his position, making him duck.

'Take your time,' Varl said. 'No fething rush.'

The ceiling collapsed.

A Qimurah dropped down onto them in a shower of flakboard and masonry debris. He landed on LaHurf, breaking both of the man's legs. LaHurf was still screaming when the Qimurah struck him with a fist-full of talons. The blow lifted LaHurf off the ground, spinning him in mid-air, blood jetting in all directions from his torn throat. He landed hard.

The Qimurah reached for LaHurf's weapon.

Ignoring the tight confines, Cardass opened up across the room with his .20. The deafening hard-round burst tore chunks out of the Qimurah's chest and shoulder, and threw him against the guardhouse wall. Despite severe wounds that would have killed a standard human instantly, the Qimurah lurched forward again with a roar, neon blood pouring from his injuries, and opened fire with LaHurf's weapon. Bellevyl was killed at his window slot. Oysten was winged. Cardass was hit in the left hip, and overbalanced.

Brostin hit the Qimurah in the side of the head. He was using one of his flamer tanks as a club. Two blows knocked the creature down, and Brostin kept beating, slamming the heavy metal cylinder into its skull over and over again.

'There,' he said, finally tossing the tank aside. It was slick with neon blood. The Qimurah had nothing left above the neck except a spatter of yellow paste and bone shards. 'Knew there'd be more than one way to kill these bastards with a flamer.'

Oysten was already up, blood oozing from her shoulder. She and Rawne ran to Cardass.

'I'm all right,' Cardass said. He wasn't. His hip was a ragged mess. Oysten reached for field dressings, but Cardass told her where she could stick them. He heaved himself back to his window slot and started to fire his stubber again.

Varl had dashed across to Bellevyl's position.

'Sorry,' he said to Bellevyl's corpse. Varl felt bad about it. No man deserved to be mocked the instant before his death. Varl set down his own rifle, and hoisted Bellevyl's. He checked the grenade was still set in the tube launcher.

'Call it! Bunker?' he asked, peering out of the slot.

'Would you?' Rawne shouted back. Prolonged bursts of fire were striking the guardhouse facade.

Varl angled the gun and fired the underbarrel. It launched the grenade with a sound like an ogryn hawking into a tin spitoon. The grenade sailed up and out, described an arc across the contested yard, and landed on the bunker roof.

It exploded with a fierce sheet of flame that was entirely consumed a second later by the detonation of the bunker itself.

Rawne had been right. Camp Xenos kept its munition store away from the main buildings.

The blast was considerable. It battered the gate area, swallowed their transport in a shock of expanding flame, and blew out the blockhouse beside the bunker. A cone of fire lifted off the bunker site, blooming out into the night sky like a mushroom cap. Debris rained down. They could hear secondary pops and bangs as stored munitions and power cells caught and cooked.

Something landed in the yard along with the debris from the blockhouse. The Qimurah, one of the shooters using the blockhouse as cover, had been cut in two. He was scorched and dripping yellow fluid. His head lolled, and he began to drag his upper half across the yard towards the guardhouse with his spasming hands.

'Kill it!' Rawne told Cardass.

'He's been cut in half–'

'Does he look dead?' Rawne asked. 'He doesn't look dead to me.'

Cardass angled his .20 down and raked the clawing mass with stubber fire until it stopped moving.

'Move!' Rawne yelled. 'We're out now!' The blast had killed one for certain. Maybe more. Whatever their losses, the Qimurah squad had been blinded and rocked. They had a moment of opportunity.

Varl grabbed Mabbon. 'Truck?' he said.

'That's gone,' Rawne replied. 'Head for the wire and out.'

Varl bundled Mabbon through the door. Laydly followed, then Oysten. Brostin grabbed Okel's big autogun and ran out after them.

Rawne looked at Cardass.

'Judd! Now!' he barked.

Cardass smiled.

'You need covering fire, sir,' he said. He locked eyes with the colonel. Rawne knew what he actually meant was *I can't walk. Hip's gone. I'm bleeding out and there aren't enough of you to carry me and stay functional. This is where you ditch me.*

'Cardass–'

Cardass ignored him, lining up his .20.

'Covering fire in three,' he said. 'Two...'

Suicide Kings, Rawne thought. Like the old card game. It had seemed like a clever name once.

He ran out across the yard after the others, his head low. There was burning debris everywhere. Cardass' heavy fire ripped from the guardhouse window slot and punished the gate and the front of the blazing blockhouse.

Varl had reached the fence. High chain wire and a ditch separated the prison's front yard from the perimeter of the neighbouring vapour mill. The mill loomed, pale in the night, exhaling huge, crawling plumes of white steam from its stacks.

The night was cold. They had the heat of the flames behind them and the night breeze in their faces. The bunker blast had taken down several sections of the security fence. Varl led the way, scrambling over the flattened fencing.

Rawne was last to arrive. Las-bolts whipped around him as he ran. He fell.

He tried to get up. Behind him, a Qimurah was walking slowly out of the inferno of the blockhouse. His blistered form was still on fire, and a splinter of roof spar had impaled his chest. He was firing his lasrifle from the hip, as if that was the highest he could raise it.

Rawne heard the rattle of Cardass' stubber. A sustained burst of fire knocked the Qimurah back into the flames.

Brostin grabbed Rawne's arm and dragged him to his feet.

'Come on, chief,' he yelled.

'All right,' said Rawne.

'You sure?' Brostin asked.

'Yes,' said Rawne. He decided not to mention the las-round that had gone through his abdomen. He could feel the blood running down his thigh and into his groin.

They headed for the fence.

Behind them, Cardass' weapon fell silent. Gunfire from the remaining Qimurah warriors chased them into the night.

* * *

'This isn't a rescue,' said Mkoll as the third stasis tank finished draining.

Milo nodded.

'I understand,' he said.

'What is it then?' asked Mazho.

'An opportunity,' said Mkoll.

Colonel Mazho was the first prisoner Milo had insisted on releasing. He was a stocky, middle-aged officer from the Urdeshi Fourth Light 'Cinder Storm' who had been assigned to the Saint as military liaison by high command after her arrival on the forge world. He'd served with her ever since, which made him enkil vahakan. He and Milo had been captured together.

'How did that happen?' Mkoll had asked.

'Oureppan,' Milo had told him. 'The Saint had achieved a miracle at Ghereppan. The Archenemy was reeling. She became convinced that Sek was located nearby. Oureppan. A place called Pinnacle Spire. So we went in fast, so as not to lose momentum. It was a trap.'

'A trap?' Mkoll had asked.

'For her. A warp vortex. He wasn't really there, you see? He was projecting himself using psykers. Well, the trap failed. She survived. The vortex destabilised. The blow-back hurt Sek, I think. Hurt him badly. And we were too close. We were pulled through to his side. Blink of an eye, and we were aboard his ship.'

The last of the nutrient suspension flushed from the third tank. Mazho was sitting on the rusted deck trying to shake off the raw ache of stasis shock. He was peering around, half-blind and dazed. He finally reached into his tunic pocket and pulled out a pair of rimless spectacles. One lens was cracked. He'd lost just about everything except his ragged Urdeshi fatigues, but somehow his spectacles had survived.

He got up to help them as Mkoll opened the third tank's hatch. It took all three of them to drag out the body inside. It was a massively heavy dead weight. They laid the body on the deck, and Milo pulled the vox-plugs out of its temples.

'Pain goads,' said Mkoll. 'They weren't going to take any chances.'

They looked down at the body. Kater Holofurnace, of the Adeptus Astartes Iron Snakes, had been stripped of his plate armour and left in its ragged underskin, a tight mesh bodyglove. The armour had not been removed efficiently, and many of the inter-cutaneous plugs and anchor points had been damaged. The Snake's body had been studded with steel spikes, each one staked into a major muscle group or joint. The spikes were pain goads designed to paralyse and incapacitate. Each one had a small rune glowing on its head.

Holofurnace moved his head and uttered a low groan. Fluid ran from his mouth, and his eyes blinked open, glassy.

'He's immobilised,' said Mkoll. He drew his skzerret.

'You going to end his pain?' Mazho asked.

'Of course he isn't,' said Milo.

Holding the serrated edge of the blade flat, Mkoll began to lever the goads out of Holofurnace's flesh. As each one came free, a shudder of pain ran through the Space Marine. Blood and other bio-liquids dribbled from each wound. They reminded Mkoll of the stigmata he'd heard some sacred beings displayed.

It was going to take a while. It took effort to dig each goad free and pull it out. Mkoll took the laspistol from his waistband and handed it to Milo.

'Watch the hatch,' he said.

'How long do we have?' asked Mazho.

Mkoll didn't reply. Mazho limped around the chamber and peered into the other tanks. Two of the other prisoners were comrades from Oureppan, both men from Mazho's command. They hadn't survived the vortex intact. It was not possible to free them from suspension. Mazho turned away and closed his eyes.

'Who are you?' Mazho asked.

'That's Mkoll,' whispered Milo from the doorway.

'The Ghost?' Mazho looked intrigued. 'Brin's told stories about you.'

'They were all true,' whispered Milo.

'So how many of you are there aboard?' Mazho asked.

'I told you this wasn't a rescue,' said Mkoll, plucking out another goad.

'How many?'

Mkoll looked at him. Something in his eyes made Colonel Mazho recoil slightly.

'Just me.'

'How did you get here?' Mazho asked.

'Pure blind chance and an obstinate nature,' said Mkoll.

'I'll bet,' whispered Milo.

'Do they know you're here?' Mazho asked. 'Are they looking for you?'

'Stop with the questions,' Holofurnace growled. He opened his eyes and looked up.

'Mkoll,' he said in a low voice.

'War brother,' replied Mkoll, nodding.

'Come to kill me?' asked Holofurnace.

'You'd be dead,' said Mkoll, yanking the last goad out of the Space Marine's torso.

Holofurnace laughed, but the laugh turned into a wince.

'Pain goads,' said Mkoll, moving down to the legs. 'I'll have the last of them out in a few minutes. Then some feeling might return.'

'I'm not sure I want it to,' said the Iron Snake. He sat up.

'Already?' said Mazho, amazed.

'Pain focuses the mind,' said Holofurnace, flexing his hands.

'Doesn't it just?' replied Mkoll.

Holofurnace held out a huge hand to Mkoll.

'Give me that,' he said. 'I'll finish it.'

Mkoll handed him the dagger. Holofurnace leaned forwards with a grunt and started to hook the goads out of his paralysed legs.

Mkoll rose.

'What did you mean when you said opportunity?' Mazho asked, rising too.

'I'm here by blind luck. You're here by bad luck. Luck alone led me to you,' replied Mkoll.

'Not sure it was luck,' whispered Milo. 'The influence of the Beati flows–'

'Not here it doesn't,' said Mkoll.

Milo looked at him.

'This ship is sitting at the heart of the Archenemy's primary stronghold on Urdesh,' said Mkoll. 'The enemy is here in brigade strengths, all around us. The nearest Imperial force is ninety plus kilometres from here, and no one on our side knows of this location.'

'So we're behind enemy lines, cut off, without support?' asked Holofurnace, yanking a goad out of his knee. 'In the heart of a nest of devils?'

'The odds are not in our favour,' said Mkoll.

'Is there a way out?' asked Mazho.

'No,' said Mkoll simply.

'So all that matters is what we do while we're here?' asked Milo. 'What we accomplish before they find us and take us out?'

'Yes,' said Mkoll.

'And you've already decided what that could be, I'm guessing?' said Holofurnace.

'Yes,' said Mkoll.

The Iron Snake pulled out the last of the goads, and hauled himself to his feet. He grimaced as locked muscles eased and flexed. He got upright, then immediately slumped, leaning hard on the hatch door of his tank. Mkoll darted to support him and stop him toppling.

'Thank you, brother,' said Holofurnace, his voice laced with pain. 'I'll be myself again in a moment, I promise.'

'Lean on something,' growled Mkoll through gritted teeth. 'You're too fething heavy to hold upright.'

Holofurnace chuckled, and shifted his weight, getting a better grip on the rim of the heavy hatch. Mkoll straightened up.

'So tell me,' Holofurnace said.

Mkoll frowned thoughtfully.

'We have three choices,' he said. 'One is to try and annihilate this stronghold from inside. I think finding the means to do that will be near impossible. The second is more viable. We try to commandeer a communications station or similar. Get a message out. Alert crusade command to this location in the hope that air strikes or orbital bombardment can level it.'

'That works,' said Holofurnace. 'Astartes code can verify us and emphasise the significance of our signal. If high command isn't asleep at the helm, fleet elements could have this site triangulated and locked in seven or eight minutes.'

'Loss of this stronghold would cripple Sek's efforts on Urdesh,' Mkoll agreed. 'So that strategy has a lot going for it.'

'What's the third idea?' asked Mazho.

'Sek,' said Mkoll. 'He's the key. Whatever damage the crusade does to his armies, they will continue to be a threat all the while he's alive. And he's here. On this vessel.'

'But a fleet strike–' Mazho began.

'There's always a chance he could escape,' said Holofurnace.

'He can't escape if he's dead,' said Milo.

'So if we can only attempt one thing, and we want it to have the maximum effect...' said Mkoll. He let the rest hang, unsaid.

No one spoke for a moment.

'Whichever we chose,' said Mazho, 'we're dead.'

Mkoll looked at him.

'You need to grasp, sir,' he said, 'that we're dead already.'

SIXTEEN

CLOSE QUARTERS

Mkoll buckled the sirdar's helmet back on. He glanced at the other three, made the Tanith hand-sign for *mute*, and walked off along the brig.

The interrogation he had observed on his way in was finished, and the cell door locked. He wondered if the Urdeshi colonel inside was still alive.

He hoped to the Throne he was not.

The two packson watchmen were still on duty in the security post. One opened the inner cage to let him through. The other stood leaning on the back grip of the sentry gun.

The packson with the key remarked that the sirdar had been a long time. Mkoll replied that the best work often took a long time.

'Harneth den voi?' the packson asked. *So you got what you wanted?*

'Den harnek teht,' Mkoll replied. *Everything it was possible to get.*

With an open palm slap, he rammed the pain goad into the key-holder's solar plexus. The man's entire system shut down. His mouth opened to voice the unthinkable agony that was screaming through his nervous system, but his vocal chords and lungs no longer worked.

He buckled to the deck. The other watchman turned from the sentry gun in surprise as his comrade collapsed. Mkoll was already on him. The skzerret went in between his ribs.

Two kills, three seconds. No sound.

Mkoll used the watchman's key to reopen the inner cage and dragged both bodies through. He stood in plain sight at the end of the brig corridor and made the hand-sign for *clear*.

Milo and Mazho hurried down to him. Holofurnace followed, limping.

'Uniforms,' Mkoll said.

Milo and the colonel stripped the packsons of their kit and pulled it on. The fit was poor, but it would have to do. Mkoll went back into the security post, and searched the area. Both packsons had been armed with old Fleet-pattern lascarbines, which were hooked on a wall rack. Mkoll took them down and checked them. Decent weapons, short-pattern for use in shipboard environments. The packsons had kept them clean and in good order. The more disciplined, Astra Militarum-style regimen observed by both Sekkite packs and the Blood Pact had some benefits. Milo and Mazho would have spare clips in the over-rigs of the uniforms they were acquiring, as well as ritual daggers. As they entered the cage in uniform, Mkoll tossed a carbine to each man.

'Carry them down, over the crook of the arm,' he said. 'Packsons don't shoulder weapons.'

Milo nodded.

Holofurnace appeared.

'No disguising me,' he said.

Mkoll knew there wouldn't be. Most of what would follow was going to be improvisation, though Mkoll had talked them through a few basic plays.

Holofurnace took the big Urdeshi sentry gun off its tripod. It looked like a regular autogun in his paws. He picked up the ammo box and made sure the belt between box and weapon was slack enough not to jam with any sudden movement.

Mkoll opened the outer cage.

'Someone will soon spot that the brig watch is unmanned,' said Mazho. He was having difficulty getting his spectacles to sit comfortably inside the stolen helmet and its ghastly mouth-guard.

'The plan isn't perfect,' Mkoll replied. 'Sooner or later, someone is going to spot that not everything on board is the way it should be.'

They moved through the ship, rising to deck seven and then six. Mkoll led the way, and every time he heard movement or spotted personnel approaching, he signed to the men behind him, and Holofurnace pulled himself into cover: a bulkhead, a through-deck well, or an inspection bay. As soon as the contact passed, Mkoll moved them on.

At a junction on deck six they had to wait for almost fifteen minutes while work crews and servitor gangs moved machine parts through on trucks. Once it was clear, they hurried on, through a compartment airgate, and followed a shadowed walkway that ran along the side of a large processing bay. In the harshly lit space below them, they saw gun-crew servitors loading huge munition shells into the bare-metal clamps of conveyer trains. Tall figures in dappled golden gowns supervised the labour, shouting instructions through hand-held vox-horns. As each half-tonne shell loaded, the automated track rattled forwards and lowered them into deck shafts where they descended on hydraulic rotators into the autoloader magazines on the battery deck.

Mkoll and the others watched for a moment from the shadow of the rail. The enemy warship still had fight in it.

Mazho looked at Mkoll with one eyebrow raised. Mkoll shook his head. Due to their sheer size and power, shiftship munitions were remarkably stable and inert until selected for use. They could waste hours trying to force a shell to detonate, and even then there was no guarantee of a cascade in the magazines.

And they didn't have hours.

On deck five, they waited as an excubitor strode past with two lekt psykers hobbling in his wake, then almost ran into a damogaur and squad of six packsons. Mkoll didn't even have time to signal, but he knew Holofurnace must have slipped out of sight behind him because the damogaur started to question Mkoll and his two packsons about the location of an etogaur called Karane.

'I haven't seen him, damogaur,' Mkoll replied. 'Perhaps he is on the bridge with He whose voice commands the stars.'

The damogaur looked at him, annoyed.

'The Holy Magister's not on the bridge, you shit-stain,' he snapped. 'When was the Holy Magister last on the bridge?'

'Apologies, damogaur, of course not,' said Mkoll quickly. 'I misspoke. I meant–'

'No, I've tried there too,' the damogaur replied. 'The Oratory is closed to all at the moment. Karane must be ashore, then.'

He cursed.

'What's your name, sirdar?' he asked.

'Eloth, my magir.'

'If you see Magir Karane, Sirdar Eloth, tell him the shipmaster needs those manifest orders by dawn. Dawn, you understand?'

'Yes, my magir.'

The damogaur snapped his fingers, and his pack followed him away down the hall.

'What was that?' whispered Mazho.

'Our objective's no longer the bridge,' Mkoll replied.

'So where?' asked Milo.

'The Oratory.'

'And where's that?' asked Mazho.

'I have no fething idea,' replied Mkoll.

They reached deck three, and almost immediately entered a large section that was undergoing heavy repairs. Work crews of industrial servitors were fitting new armour lining along a section of hull panel that ran for about sixty metres. Welding arrays sparked furiously. Slave gangs were wheeling out tubs laden with fused scrap metal and lumps of slag that had been stripped out from the failed lining.

Mkoll got his little squad in temporary cover, and then walked on through the repair zone alone. He spotted an open compartment where two provision officers in filthy golden robes were arguing about puncture sealant. The compartment was being used as a supervision post for the work. It was stacked with tools and rebreather sets. There was a small work table covered in junk and requisition dockets.

He strolled up to the provision officers, and as he did so, realised they weren't packsons of the Sekkite host. They were V'heduak, companions of a different tribal order that served as the equivalent of Navy personnel for the Archonate Fleet. They were tall men, larger than Mkoll had realised when he first approached, their big-boned mass and heavy muscle speaking of many family generations serving in high gravity shift operations. He had encountered the V'heduak's brutal tech-cannibal shock troops before, but not the ruling class. Their heads were shaved except for long, square beards, and they had dented blast visors lowered to their chests. Their faces were fetishistically covered in piercings, so many in the ears that the flesh was stretched. Their scalps were covered in complex tattoo work. Starmaps, Mkoll guessed. The realms and worlds they had made shift between.

They turned to look at him with augmetic eyes.

'What do you want, soldier?' one spat using a formal construction that emphasised disdain.

'That his voice may never fade, I apologise, my magirs,' he replied, throwing the Sekkite salute.

They returned it, grudgingly, glaring down at him.

'My magirs, Etogaur Karane extends his respects,' said Mkoll, trying to use the awkward construction of formal deference. He began to sweat. This had been a bad idea. His command of the Sekkite tongue was nothing like fluent enough to handle a strange accent and odd word-orders of the V'heduak sub-dialect. 'Etogaur Karane wishes to express his concerns that the strenuous work here may disturb the Oratory.'

'How?' asked one.

'We would not risk disturbing the Magir-Who-Speaks!' the other exclaimed.

'I merely express the concern, my magirs,' Mkoll said. 'The noise and commotion-'

One of the V'heduak sneered at him.

'The Oratory is two decks hence, soldier,' he said. 'It would not be possible for us to interrupt the solace of the Magir-Who-Speaks.'

Two decks in which direction, Mkoll wondered.

'Begone,' said one of the V'heduak. 'And tell your etogaur he is a weeping sore.'

'I will at once, my magirs,' said Mkoll, backing away.

He retraced his steps through the work area. The V'heduak had given him little, but the risk had been worth it. He had spotted something over their shoulders while they had been insulting him.

He passed a row of spoil bins that were packed with scrap plate and insulation materials. Without breaking stride, he dropped one of the grenades from the sirdar's weapon's belt into it. Red dot. He hoped that meant smoke.

It did.

In seconds, thick red signal smoke was pouring out of the spoil bin.

He hurried back to the V'heduak.

'What now, you ulcer?' one roared.

'My magirs!' Mkoll said, pointing. 'A fire! In the waste tubs! Something has caught alight!'

Snorting with anger and surprise, the V'heduak pushed past him. Smoke was now clogging the back of the work space. He heard them shout for extinguishers, and begin to reprimand the servitors for using their fusing torches too close to scrap insulate.

With their backs turned, Mkoll stepped into the supervision post, snatched up the folded sheet of schematics he had seen lying on the table, and vanished entirely into the shadows.

'What did you get?' asked Milo.

Mkoll took out the thick fold of paper, and they opened it out.

'Deck plans,' he said. They were hand-drawn, a top plan and side elevation, and the work had been done with great skill. The ghostly traceries of the penmanship even revealed the intricate lines of principal power relays and coolant systems.

'They were using it to supervise the repair work,' he said.

'No cogitators? No data-slates?' Mazho asked.

'They don't trust digital records,' Mkoll replied.

'I think we can put it to better use,' said Milo, and began to study it carefully.

'I have a question first,' said Mkoll. 'Where the feth is Holofurnace?'

The hot, dark confines of the duct opened out into a long rockcrete gallery. It was a hundred and sixty metres long and thirty wide, an artificial ravine lit by the lambent glow of thick biolume algae. Steeply sloped rockcrete walls splayed out from the central channel, to form high and narrow overlook ledges that could be used as inspection walkways. By the phosphorescent light, Obel noted the large and heat-eroded stencil HALL 7816 on one of the rockcrete revetments. The channel bed running between the high, sloped banks was a mess of fused magmatic spoil through which ran a trickle of foul, liquefied waste. The air stank.

'This is a better site for an ambush,' Zhukova remarked.

Obel nodded. Meeting the Archenemy in the geotherm duct would have been a slaughter. The duct was only wide enough for two people, side by side. They needed room to deploy so they could bring more of their force to bear against a physically superior enemy.

Criid assessed the chamber quickly. It had clearly once served as an overpressure gallery to regulate geothermic flow at times of peak output. The remnants of huge ceramite gates stood halfway down the gallery. They had long since fused to immobility, but their purpose had been to stem or even shut off magmatic flow and geothermal pressure. Urdesh's geothermic system was thousands of years old. Long ago, it had been a subtle system, expertly managed and regulated by dynast technicians who could acutely gauge, direct and govern the natural power.

Those delicate archeotech mechanisms had long since fallen into disuse. Now Urdesh's power grid was an open network of tunnels that either fed or did not. Power modulation was done by the individual sites – the forces and facilities like EM 14 – that tapped into it.

But this now-defunct gallery had advantages. More space, more range. There was cover at their end, and further cover and firing positions provided by the open gates and the high rockcrete ledges. Criid could see the open mouth of the duct at the opposite end. That's where they'd be coming from. It was the only vent out of the duct network serving the Gnosis Repository area.

That is, she hoped it was. If the adepts had lied to Pasha, if Zhukova had read the plan wrong, if there was another, redundant and disused spur they didn't know about...

'They've got to be close,' she said to Obel. 'Let's make it here. It's the best option we've seen.'

'The only option,' said Larkin.

Obel threw quick hand signs – *defensive positions, here.* The Ghost squads behind them began to fan out into the gallery, taking up firing positions around the duct mouth using the ends of the rockcrete revetments as cover. Mkhet and Boaz set up the .20. Lugging the support weapon and its firing stand all the way from the Turbine Hall had left them almost dead on their feet from heat exhaustion. Other squad members had carried the ammo boxes. Falkerin and Cleb prepped the two satchels of tube charges, and Ifvan handed the primed sticks out. In the tight confines of the chamber, explosives would be a last resort, and Criid made sure everyone understood that.

Lubba checked his flamer.

'Keep it tight in here,' Obel advised. 'Backwash could cook our own people, especially if they're up on the overlooks.'

Lubba nodded. He lacked Aongus Brostin's gleeful love of fire, but he understood flames and flamers. He'd been a flame-trooper since he joined the regiment, and Larkin had once described him as 'Brostin without the, y'know, nutso pyro aspects.'

Jed Lubba was a big man. Most flame troopers were. It took bulk and core strength to heft a full-size flamer-unit around all day. He was sweating profusely, his jacket off, his vest dark with sweat.

'Nice and tight, sir,' he promised.

Larkin and Okain clambered up the moulded foot-holds at the end of the revetments to reach the inspection walk, one on each side.

'Feth, it's high,' Larkin complained once he was up.

'Quiet,' said Criid.

'And narrow,' Larkin added. He eased his way along, carrying his precious long-las carefully, and took up position at the top of the left hand gate, in among the rusted gears that had once opened and closed it. Okain had already set up on top of the right hand gate. Other Ghosts clambered up after them, taking up precarious firing positions along the ledges, some on their bellies. Obel wanted to maximise the number of guns they could bring to bear. Maggs and Zhukova picked their way along the channel, heading down to scout the remainder of the gallery and listen at the far-end duct.

'This is recovery?' Obel said quietly to Criid.

'This is stopping them,' she replied.

'But they're carrying the things,' said Obel. 'Gaunt wants the things, right?'

She nodded. 'But he doesn't want the bastards to have them. So if it comes to a choice, better no one gets them than they do.'

Lunny Obel didn't look sure.

'Pasha didn't specify,' he said.

'I don't think she knows either,' said Criid. 'Our orders were to secure and recover. That idea went up the wall. So now it's recover or deny. Look–'

She dropped her voice low, and turned him aside.

'Honest to Throne, I don't rate our chances here. Just thirty-one of us, no support? These hostiles were cutting through skitarii fifteen minutes ago. We'll be lucky to hold them. If we're really lucky, we smoke them. Just pour it on. If there's anything to recover after that, hooray for us. Bottom line, they don't get past us with the stuff unless we're all dead.'

'These things are important, aren't they?' Obel said. 'These eagle stone things?'

'Feth knows why,' she replied. 'But yes. Clearly. They've sent in elites to get them. So if we have to destroy them to stop them taking them, so be it.'

Obel shook his head.

'Hey,' she said, nudging him. 'Come on. Lunny? They've sent in elites, Gaunt's sent us. The Lord Executor, no less. So what does that make us?'

'Elites?' Obel asked with a tired grin.

'No,' she said. 'It makes us suckers and las-bait. But at least I made you smile.'

'Feth you, Tona,' he chuckled.

'Sir!' Sergeant Ifvan hissed.

Okain was hand signing from his position.

Maggs and Zhukova were returning down the channel. They were moving fast, dodging and sprinting along the dirty, uneven bed of the gulley.

Primary order, Obel signed.

Corrod raised his hand and the Qimurah halted. He peered ahead at a pale disc that showed where the duct opened into some grander chamber.

He looked at the detailed plans Ordinate Jan Jerik had given him.

Hacklaw glanced at him.

'Damogaur?'

'We're approaching the gallery,' he said. Hacklaw nodded. He remembered it from the way in.

'If they're smart and diligent, this is where they'll try to stop us.'

'Yes?'

'It's the point I'd choose,' Corrod said. He looked at the chart again. 'Wide enough to deploy, tight enough to defend.'

'I doubt our Imperial foe has the wit or ability to get a force down here fast enough,' said Hacklaw.

'And that is why we have been at war with them for ever,' said Corrod. 'That sort of thinking. We underestimate them. Our foe *is* smart and diligent. They sent soldiers to recover the stones. They wouldn't have sent just anybody. Special troops. Trustworthy elites.'

Hacklaw nodded, chastised.

Corrod looked back at the duct mouth. He squinted, his neon-bright eyes searching. The vents were dulling his reworked senses badly. The mucosal resin excreted to protect his lungs from heat burn was clogging his normally hyper-sharp gifts of smell and taste, and the general heat elevation was making it hard for his eyes to detect human heat tracks.

But he could hear. The soft but urgent drumming of human hearts, elevated with tension. The skitter of loose stones. The clink of metal as clips were gently slotted into receivers.

'They are there,' he said.

'We cannot go back,' said Ulraw. 'They will have secured the other end by now.'

'I said nothing about going back,' replied Corrod. 'We are Qimurah, brothers. We ascend always. We follow the song of his voice.'

'We rush them?' asked Hacklaw.

'Yes,' said Corrod. 'We will lose some. That is the price. But they will not be prepared for our speed or our fortitude. Remember why our magir wrought us thus?'

Hacklaw nodded. The Imperial preference for energy weapons, especially the las-form, had influenced the ritual evolution of the Qimurah. The ingeniants of the Heritor College had given earlier generations of their kind the ability to grow hardshell plates to absorb solid kinetic munitions. That had been back in the dim times of the First Human Wars. Now Qimurah were made to exude the resin coat that sloughed away energy fire. The ingeniants had developed the idea from the study of loxatl biomechanics.

Lasweapons were excellent tools against human flesh. But the Qimurah, while not invulnerable, were far more than that.

'You remember the plan of the chamber?' he asked.

The Qimurah nodded.

'Hacklaw, take your warriors and scale the left side. Gehrent, yours to the right. Ekheer, charge the gulley.'

All the Qimurah hissed assent. They waited for a moment, neon light crisping in their eyes, as what once had been their sweat glands released more mucus to thicken the glistening coating of their flesh. Hacklaw, Gehrent and the warriors who would accompany them took off their boots. They focused with grimacing concentration, ignoring the pain, as they reworked to lengthen the talons on their fingers and toes. The chitin sprouted, cracking and growing, becoming ugly grey hooks.

Corrod settled the old, Guard-issue musette bag on his shoulder. It contained four of the stones. Ulraw had the other four secure in his satchel.

'These get through,' said Corrod. 'That is all that matters. If I fall, if Ulraw falls, someone takes up the burden.'

'Yes, magir,' they whispered.

'Now let us show this human filth how Qimurah fight,' said Corrod. 'For the Anarch, who is Sek, whose voice drowns out all others.'

It had been still and quiet for several minutes. The waiting tugged at Larkin's nerves. He kept his eyes on the mouth of the duct, but had sighted his long-las at a rock in the channel bed some thirty metres in. That was a point nothing would cross without taking a headshot. His musette bag was open at his hip, restocks of over-charged cells ready to grab.

Come on then, let's be having you...

Criid glanced at Obel. Sweat was running down his cheeks and neck, and it wasn't just the merciless heat of the vent system.

'Movement!' Zhukova hissed.

Silently, without battle cry or howl, the Qimurah burst from the duct and came at them. The first glimpse of their enemy made the Ghosts flinch. They were inhuman. Tall as ogryn, thin as corpses, sprinting from the duct with astonishing stride-length, almost springing like bipedal gamebucks.

Their speed was the second shock. How could anything move so fast?

Criid felt fear flood through her. The enemy had flung themselves forwards to attack. They had known it was an ambush, a prepared position. Yet still they had charged.

The Qimurah bore in like a tide, like a cavalry charge, flowing down the channel, firing their lasweapons from the shoulder.

The first shots, the cracks echoing around the enclosed space, grazed and chipped the shoulders of the rockcrete revetment. Then the first two Ghosts dropped, knocked off their feet by inconceivably accurate strikes.

'Fire!' Obel yelled.

The Tanith guns began to blaze. A blizzard of las-fire ripped down the rockcrete ravine, countercut by fire from the overlooking ledges. Boaz opened up with the .20, pumping streams of rounds down the channel. The noise was painful.

The leading Qimurah buckled and fell. Those behind leapt over the fallen, firing. Some of the creatures struck down got up and began to run again.

'Feth this,' whispered Larkin. They'd outrun his pre-set sighting point before he'd even squeezed off a shot.

What the feth were they?

He fired, and the long-las barked. A Qimurah toppled as his skull exploded. His forward momentum kept his corpse tumbling and cartwheeling for several metres.

Larkin didn't stop to enjoy his kill. He slammed in another cell and put a second hotshot into the face of another of the neon-eyed fiends. Okain had opened up too. The two snipers had dropped five of the creatures before the front of the charge had reached the rusted gates. The over-charged hotshots had true stopping power. Not even Qimurah bio-defences could block or soak up that kind of energy force.

The .20 was also taking a toll. The streams of heavy hard rounds were shattering limbs and shearing bodies apart.

They can't get past this, Obel thought. *Doesn't matter what they are, doesn't matter how fast they are, they can't run this killbox. None of them are going to make it to us alive.*

But the bulk of the Tanith firepower wasn't the heavy crew-served or the two long-las weapons. It was standard lasrifles. Hits from them made Qimurah stumble and falter. Some fell, others took visible damage.

But they kept going. They soaked it up. Obel wondered how many times he'd have to hit the same target spot before he did any lethal damage.

The Qimurah came on. Their weapons were basic, but their supple, strong bodies allowed them to fire on the move with great accuracy.

And lasweapons were excellent tools against human flesh.

Four Ghosts were down. Five. Six. Boaz was hit in the throat and arm, and flopped back from the .20, which chattered into silence. Ifvan leapt in to take over, but the .20 had feed-jammed when Boaz lurched away from the tripod. He fought to unblock the receiver.

'Clear it! Clear it!' Obel yelled.

* * *

Larkin heard Okain scream out. Two more groups of the enemy were pouring up the revetments onto the ledge. They didn't have to balance. Hooked claws on their feet and hands bit into the crumbling 'crete like pitons. Some were almost running along the wall on all fours like human spiders.

Larkin and Okain switched aim. They no longer had time to fire at the charging tide below. They began sighting over the gate mechanisms to fend off the horrors that were racing along the walls at their level.

Okain hit one, and the kill-shot hurled the scurrying scarecrow shape off the ledge, spinning and flailing. Larkin blew the head off the first one coming at him, then reloaded to greet the second.

On the far side, Okain missed with his third shot. Hacklaw vaulted over the corroded gears of the gate, and decapitated Okain with a slash of his fore-claws.

Down below, Maggs saw Okain perish.

'On the walls! They're up on the walls!' he yelled. Several of the Ghosts at the duct mouth tried to angle up and fire at the Qimurah advancing along the edges. This further reduced the firepower concentrating on the main charge.

Hacklaw and two others had swept past Okain's station, sending his corpse tumbling down the revetment, and fell into the Ghosts positioned on the ledge. The Ghosts tried to fight back, shooting point-blank at the unexpected attack, or trying to fend off the Qimurah with rifle butts or blades. The Qimurah killed some outright with their meat-hook claws, or simply threw the troopers off the ledge into the channel below, a drop that either killed or crippled them as they hit the rockcrete gulley below.

Ifvan got the .20 cleared, but the front end of the charge was already on them.

The Qimurah had left many of their kin dead and mangled in the rockcrete channel behind them. But with undimmed fury and unfaltering speed, the remainder of the reworked warriors swept into the Ghosts' fragile line.

SEVENTEEN

FLESH IS WEAK

There was no quarter, no room to move, no time to think. The twilit gallery shook with gunfire, stray las-rounds spitting through the fug of accumulated smoke. The leading Qimurah hit the line, taking shots point blank, shredding and dying, and soaking up damage for the warriors behind them. The Ghosts had fixed silver, and resorted to stabbing and thrusting as the Qimurah swept into them. Most were simply bowled backwards by the superior power and force of the Archenemy creatures. Even with bayonets driven deep into blistered neon flesh, they were carried over or dragged backwards.

Some were crushed underfoot, others fell to raking claws or sprays of shot. Corrod was in the thick of it, tearing his way forwards. He had known since setting out that many of his kind would not return from the mission. One did not enter the heartland of the enemy and expect to survive unscathed. The holy work was all that mattered. The orders of the voice. The Qimurah could be remade. New and worthy sons could be blessed and reworked to replace the fallen. They would all share the same, eternal purpose: to prevail, even to the last of them.

And they would prevail. They would break all opposition and bear the keys of victory to his side, and lay them at his feet. Even if they were reduced to just a handful. To just one.

Never had so many of the Qimurah been deployed together, and never had so many perished in the same action. It was a mark of honour. A mark of trust. Their very losses, unthinkable in extent, proved the magnitude of their task. Victory, no more, no less. Ultimate victory in the Sabbat War. A few metres of filthy ground in a rockcrete channel. A few outclassed enemy soldiers in their path.

That was all that stood in the Anarch's way.

A few metres. A few bags of human meat. The Qimurah could conquer that. The Imperials had fought well. Where they lacked strength, they had compensated with wit and diligence. They had executed to effect. They had shown courage and resolve, and tactical skill.

And now they would die because their unworked bodies were too fragile to sustain the effort, their weapons too weak. At the last moment, which was always the only moment that truly mattered, their strength could not match their determination.

He could see the looming mouth of the duct behind them.

'Flamer!' Obel yelled into the carnage. The .20 was overrun. Everything was just smoke and blood and jarring impacts and crashing bodies.

Lubba stood his ground, and sent a lance of sucking, roaring white heat into the first of the Qimurah, searing flesh from bone. The superheated stream annihilated one entirely, scattering fused and burning fragments of bone. Another managed to stagger a few steps, skinless and ablaze, before falling.

Criid and Obel tossed their rifles aside and pulled the adept wardens' staves out of their shoulder packs. They stood their ground and fired.

The air distorted as grav-pulses blasted from the ends of the staves. The next two Qimurah fell back, their skulls crushed like eggs. Criid and Obel tried to fire again, but the Mechanicus weapons took a moment to cycle.

And there were no more moments.

'Lunny!' Criid yelled.

'Charges now!' Obel roared.

On the ledge, Larkin heard Obel's distant order as he scrambled back from the gate. A Qimurah bounded over it, dropping onto him. For a second, he locked eyes with the thing's neon gaze. Then he met it with his silver.

The Qimurah landed and impaled itself on the Tanith blade locked to the end of Larkin's long-las.

It writhed, pulling on the long gun, threatening to wrench it out of the old marksman's hands or roll them both off the ledge.

Larkin pulled the trigger. The hot shot blew the Qimurah in half and hurled the sectioned creature off his blade. Another Qimurah came over the gate gears behind it. Larkin reached for his reload bag, but quick as he was, there wasn't going to be enough time.

Hands grabbed him from behind and shoved him down onto his face. Wes Maggs was kneeling on his back, hosing rapid fire at the oncoming Qimurah. Trooper Galashia was behind him, lighting it up over Maggs' head. The combined fire swatted the Qimurah off the ledge. It plunged towards the channel below just as the Ghosts' explosives began to go off.

Tube charges and grenades were the only things they had left. The dwindling line of Ghosts was being crushed back into the mouth of the gallery. At Obel's order, they had frantically hurled their tube charges and whatever grenades they were carrying.

The staggered blasts lit up along the Ghosts' end of the chamber, filling the artificial ravine with a sudden forest of explosions. It was a desperate choice. A final choice. Many of the Qimurah were blown apart instantly, but the blast pressure was trapped and channelled. The rockcrete ravine cupped and focused the over-shock and drove it up and out.

The Ghosts defending the duct mouth were hurled off their feet by the hammering wave, rolling and tumbling, deaf, dazed and blind.

The over-pressure scorched up the revetments too. It swept Maggs off the ledge. Larkin and Galashia managed to grab him before he fell, and clung on desperately as he tried to drag himself up again, his feet swinging over the drop.

Smoke and flames boiled down the gulley, dense and caustic. Criid tried to rise. She saw a Qimurah almost on her, and fired her stave. The gravity round hammered him back into the revetment wall and split his torso like a ripe ploin. The Qimurah had a guard-issue satchel over one shoulder. It slumped along with his corpse into the filth of the channel bed.

Corrod saw Ulraw die.

'Take it up! Take it up!' he yelled.

He saw Drehek stumble out of the swirling, spark-filled smoke, casting aside an Imperial he'd just gutted with his claws. Drehek saw the fallen treasure, and ran for it. He pulled it off Ulraw's corpse and turned. A javelin of white-hot fire raked him and torched him. The Qimurah and the satchel collapsed in a consuming ball of flame.

Corrod howled. There was no time to go back. No time to recover what was lost. He still had four of the stones.

He threw himself on, the duct ahead.

An Imperial blocked his path. He smashed the man aside, snapping his neck and removing half of his face.

Zhukova, deafened by the bombs, saw the monster kill Gansky. She fired full auto, cutting Corrod off his feet with a hail of las. Corrod rose, his skin blistered and smouldering. She hit him with another burst. He fell, then came at her.

She hit him again, and saw neon blood spurt and spatter.

He was centimetres from her when his head wrenched sideways. The side of his skull caved in and burst.

Corrod fell.

Lunny Obel lowered the stave.

'These fethers just don't know when to die, do they?' he asked.

A hunched, stumbling figure slammed into Obel from behind and knocked him aside. Hacklaw, wounded and disfigured and perhaps the last Qimurah left alive, was still going. His claws tore the musette bag from his damogaur's corpse.

Clutching it to his chest, he plunged on into the duct.

Chiria offered Kolosim the detonator casually, the way a trooper might offer a comrade a pack of lho-sticks.

'You wired it,' Ferdy Kolosim replied. 'You do the honours.'

Chiria shrugged. The scars on her face crinkled with a grin of relish.

'Ghosts, Ghosts,' she said into her bead. 'Stand by for det. Brace and ease.'

It had just begun to rain again. Fine sheets of drizzle washed across the approach to EM 14. The Ghosts huddled in the darkness, braced, and opened their mouths to prevent burst eardrums.

Chiria flipped off the switch-guard and pressed the detonator stud.

There was a light-flash, and then a shock that they all felt in their lungs and bones.

Then a boom split the night in half.

A sheet of flame ripped across the front of the Mechanicore fortress. Huge chunks of rockcrete and ouslite came tumbling out, crunching like a landslip across the apron. The blast shock flattened the security fences, tearing the chain link apart, and blew in the back of the guardhouse.

As the concussion dropped, pebbles, grit and flecks of stone began to fall with the rain.

'Get into it!' Kolosim ordered. The chosen tactical squads hurried from cover, weapons ready. Debris was still fluttering down. Smoke blanketed the site, and numerous fires were burning. The Mechanicore's main gate zone was a mass of broken slag and buckled rebar.

The huge blast doors themselves were still entirely intact. They were simply lying on the ground.

'Nice job,' Kolosim commented as he clambered over the rubble on the heels of the point team. Chiria followed, lugging her short-snout rig and ammo hopper.

'I knew a truck load of hi-ex would have its uses, sir,' she replied.

Needs must, Kolosim thought. Bray and Armin had spent almost twenty minutes trying to cut an entry in the main doors. The Cult Mechanicus built things to last, and on top of that, EM 14's systems had suffered a catastrophic collapse, so there had been no joy trying to rewire the circuits either.

Kolosim had been urgently considering other potential entry points when Chiria had tapped him on the shoulder and simply pointed to the bomb truck that the Sekkites had tried to drive into their lines.

He had said, 'Oh, what the feth. Breach it.'

The point teams slithered and climbed in over the rubble, moving through the heavy haze of smoke and dust with weapons up and sweeping. Primary lights and environment were down, but self-powered auxiliary lumen banks had come on, illuminating the interior hall with a soft, blue glow.

Bray had tac lead. He threw hand signs, fanning his entry team wide. They left the edge of the rubble and the blast area, and crossed a marble floor covered with in-blown grit and lumps of rockcrete. The Ghosts moved from pillar to pillar, bounding cover. Vadim's squad moved in at their heels, then Kolosim with the heavier weapons. Kolosim signalled his own squad wide, then moved up to join Bray and Caober.

The hall ahead was large and silent, a long chamber like the nave of a temple. Back-washed smoke from the entry blast was collecting in the high ceiling space. Kolosim looked around.

A fight had torn through here in the last hour or so. The walls and floor were scarred with bullet and las strikes. He saw several Mechanicus weapons servitors, dead and blown out, plus the bodies of half a dozen Tanith troopers.

It must have been hell, trapped in here when the machines turned.

Caober pointed. Several of the automata had been shot out and wrecked, but several others seemed intact. They had just shut down and died. Kolosim edged close to one and inspected it. Black goo, like treacle, was seeping out of its casing. It had burned out from within, its cogitator and biomech processors dissolving into mush.

'Like the thing outside,' Bray remarked.

'Same here, sir,' called Vadim. He was examining systems built into a wall – a data duct and a row of monitor screens. Tarry black slime oozed from all of them.

'Kolosim to Arcuda,' Kolosim said into his bead. 'Entry achieved.'

'Copy,' Arcuda's voice replied. *'I thought I heard you knock.'*

Arcuda had taken charge of the companies inside the Mechanicore. Pasha and Elam had already descended into the ducts and, like Obel and Criid's hunter squads, they were out of comm range. Word was, Theiss was dead, and he'd died in the first few minutes. Kolosim had warned Arcuda once it had become clear he was only going to force entry by unsubtle means. Arcuda had pulled all Ghost forces clear of the entry hall.

'Moving in by squad,' Kolosim said. 'You still got actives?'

'It's quietened down a lot,' said Arcuda. *'A few bursts, so watch yourself. But the frenzy is done. I think they're all dead, or dying.'*

'It true about Theiss?'

'Yeah. We've taken a beating. Big purse.'

Kolosim winced. *Big purse.* The euphemism stung. The Militarum had bastardised it from Munitorum jargon, an assessment term used in action reports and logistical summaries. *Big purse* was actually 'big perc', the cover-sheet abbreviation for 'big percentage casualty rate', indicating forty-five per cent losses or higher. To Kolosim it always sounded like some thieving bastard had got away after a brutal mugging.

'We're going to need medicae and med-vac soon as,' Arcuda reported.

'Working on that,' Kolosim replied. 'Links to high command and Eltath Operations are still down.'

'Another big hit?' Arcuda asked.

'Can't say. Hoping it's just technical feth. But shit's kicking off all over town.'

'No way the palace has been hit,' said Arcuda.

'You'd think,' Kolosim agreed.

The teams moved forwards again. Kolosim stuck tight with Vadim and Caober.

'What's the plan,' Kolosim asked into his bead. 'Do we start extraction?'

'Cas-vac yes, soon as you can,' Arcuda replied. *'But otherwise we secure the feth out of this place. The operation's still live down in the ducts. No signal yet, but we need to be ready to support. Or block anything that tries to come out.'*

'Copy that. Key me in.'

'We've covered all the possible duct exits,' replied Arcuda, *'but we haven't reached Turbine Hall One yet. That's where Criid and Lunny went in. That's closer to you.'*

'On it,' said Kolosim. 'We'll lock that up.'

He followed the advance in. More automata wrecks. Dead tech-priests and adepts, some of whom had been shot apart or torn limb-from-limb. The Mechanicus had turned on itself as well as its guests. Black slime spattered the floor and was sprayed up some walls. Most of it leaked from the machine dead, but some of it was oozing and dripping from the building itself.

There were more dead Ghosts too. Men and women Kolosim knew well, lying where they had fallen, buckled and twisted. Some had died instantly from massive wound trauma. Others had died slowly, alone and in pain, caught in the open. Blood trails demonstrated that.

'Feth this,' Vadim muttered.

'How do we know they're dead?' Bray asked.

'Throne, look at them!' Kolosim replied.

'Not ours, sir,' said Bray. 'The Cult Mech.'

Kolosim hesitated. Feth of a time to think *that* thought. They looked dead. Servitors and priests, cold and still, leaking black shit onto the floor.

They'd been infected by something.

But they had never been alive in the first place, not in ways Kolosim or his Ghosts understood. Cult Mechanicus were pretty cold and still at the best of times. How could he tell? The shot-up ones, sure, but the others? They knew a frenzy had overtaken them, a killing bloodlust. Then they'd shut down and dropped, spewing the black goop everywhere. Was that death? Or was it just another phase? Inertia? A dormant state while the infection progressed to the next stage?

Kolosim looked around and swallowed nervously. There were hundreds of dead Cult Mech personnel and servitors littering the halls and arcades. He could see forty alone from where he was standing.

What if they were about to come back? Switch the feth back on? Wake up and resume their kill-frenzy?

He'd just walked two full companies in amongst them.

'Feth,' he breathed.

'What?' Caober asked.

Kolosim fumbled for his bead.

'Kolosim to all entry teams. I want confirm taps on every Mech body you see. Repeat. Kill-confirm every potential hostile. No exceptions.'

His team leaders voxed affirmative. The shots started. The men around him spread out, aiming down at the heads or central processors of every dead adept, priest and servitor, and firing a point-blank round to destroy them.

It was grim work. It was vital work. The Mechanicus kept its mysteries and secrets to itself. If there was even a slim chance any of them would revive, it had to be erased.

Obel clambered to his feet and stumbled towards the duct. Criid and Zhukova had already taken off into the vent in pursuit of the fleeing Qimurah.

'Tona!' he yelled.

There was no reply. He felt woozy, his lungs tight from the heat. The thing had hit him hard, and he was pretty sure he was carrying broken ribs or worse. But the adrenaline surge of the savage fight was still pumping through him.

He glanced back at the devastation behind him. Smoke virtually filled the gallery's rockcrete ravine, and fires were burning where both bodies and the chemical silt in the channel bed had caught. The enemy dead choked the gulley mouth, and the Tanith dead and injured were all around him.

'Sergeant!' he yelled.

Ifvan limped to him, gashes on his face. 'Sir?'

'Check the dead. The enemy dead. None of these bastards can be alive, you understand?'

'Yes, sir.'

'Then see to our wounded. Come on, Ifvan! Rally whoever's left!'

Ifvan nodded.

'Where – where will you be, sir?' he asked.

Obel was already hurrying towards the vent.

Tona Criid was a strong runner, but Zhukova was staying with her. The heat in the close confines of the vent was intense. Criid wasn't sure how much longer either of them would last before dehydration shock or the stifling air overcame them.

She wasn't going to let the bastard go.

And there were very few places he *could* go. This was the main vent spur, the route they'd followed to get in. It ran all the way out beyond the limits of the EM 14 site, and eventually joined the main geotherm shaft. No divisions, no sub-tunnels. At least that was what the chart had seemed to show. Two kilometres out to the main magmatic pipeway.

The heat was bad enough. The noxious volcanic gases were burning her throat and binding her chest, as though her respiratory system was corroding. The duct was a tube, and the base was littered with magmatic residue and liquid spoil, making it treacherous under foot. She twisted her ankle twice, and then stumbled so badly she fell and slammed painfully into the curved wall of the duct.

Zhukova pulled her up.

'We can't–' Zhukova began.

'We can,' Criid insisted.

It had been easier coming in, despite the weight of gear. They'd moved steadily, picking their way. Nothing like this blind, headlong rush. Chasing down a pipe into hell after one of its daemons.

They started to run again. Zhukova had strapped her rifle over her back. Criid's rifle was back in the gallery, but she still had the Mechanicus stave.

'He was hurt–' Zhukova said, coughing.

'So are we.'

'No, he was wounded. I don't care how inhuman he was, he was damaged!'

Criid knew she was right. She'd seen the Qimurah go past her, torso and arm torn and blistered from weapons-fire. She'd seen splashes of yellow fluid on the wall of the duct as they rushed into it. Maybe that was their only edge. Maybe they could overtake him, despite his speed, because he'd start to flag as his wounds slowed him.

She saw a vertical beam of pale light ahead. It was the down-duct that led back to Turbine Hall One, the one they'd lugged the support weapons and ammo down, rung by rung.

She ran straight under the opening and kept going.

'Tona!' Zhukova called.

Criid looked back. 'Not that way!'

'He might have–'

'No! He's gone out the same way he went in! Right down to the main thermal line, Zhukova! That just goes back up into the Mechanicore!'

'But–'

'Come on!' Criid turned and started running again.

'Captain Criid!' Zhukova yelled.

Criid cursed and swung back around.

'What?' Zhukova was standing under the ceiling duct, looking up.

'What, Zhukova?'

'He would have gone up,' Zhukova said, 'if it was the easy way.'

Criid stumbled back to her, panting.

'What?' she asked.

'If he was wounded,' said Zhukova. 'Desperate. Knew he couldn't make it all the way to the main line. Decided to hide.'

Criid looked at her. 'Is that a guess? Are you guessing?'

'I'm trying to think as he might think,' Zhukova replied. 'I don't think I can go much further. Not all the way along. And then how many more kilometres to get out of the city, the clave zones, back to enemy lines? If I was hurt, I'd hide. And this is the only hiding place. The only one.'

Criid glared at her.

Zhukova reached up and grabbed the lowest rung of the service ladder. She hauled her way up a short distance into the base of the down-shaft.

She paused, and dragged her hand along the next rung up, then looked down at Criid and showed her palm.

It was smeared with yellow fluid.

'The bastard went up,' she said.

'Feth,' Criid growled. 'Jump down! Jump the feth down, Ornella!'

Zhukova landed beside her. Criid raised the stave, aimed it up the down-shaft, and loosed a pulse of rippling gravitron force.

They heard it strike something in the darkness far above. A dull metallic thump. Dust, pebbles and flakes of rusted metal showered down on them.

Criid pushed the stave into her pack and grabbed the lower rungs, heaving herself up.

Obel ran up, panting and coughing, from the duct behind them.

'Criid? Where the feth are you going?' he gasped.

'Up!' Criid yelled, disappearing from view.

Zhukova looked at Obel.

'Because he did,' she said.

'Is it dead?' he asked.

The Beati Sabbat sighed. Gaunt had never seen her look so exhausted. Even the soft, inner light she seemed to generate had dimmed.

'Yes,' she said.

The billet hall of the undercroft was just a billet hall. All the reality distortions had vanished like dreams. The flood water had drained away swiftly, leaving only foul puddles and debris on the flagstones. Baskevyl's men were lighting lamps so there was a little light at least.

Gaunt slowly looked around. Just a cellar now: cold, damp, damaged, old. Just a place, a solid, ordinary reality, a set of deep chambers no one cared about. The malice that had infused the stones had fled with the woe machine's death-shock. The undercroft had realigned with reality and returned to what it had always been.

Gaunt checked himself. No, the place had changed forever. No one would come here now. It ought to be sealed, not because there was some lingering trace of immaterial evil, but because of what it was. A tomb. A scene of murder. A site so burdened with grief and loss it was hard to even stand there.

The dead littered the ground between waste-water puddles and broken cots. Sancto's men. Osket was moving from body to body, checking for life, though it was just a formality. They had been cut to ribbons. Sariadzi had been destroyed so completely, no trace of him remained.

Gaunt wondered how many others had died here. Ghosts, men and women of the retinue, so devoured by the darkness that nothing had survived to show they had ever existed.

Daur sat in a corner, his back to the wall. This loss, this slaughter, had scarred them all. Gaunt doubted he would ever see Ban Daur flash his eager smile again.

And then there was Gol.

Kolea was sitting on the ground, staring at the spot where Yoncy had been. Only a few fused black thorns remained, like a scatter of dead leaves. There was no expression on his face. Gaunt couldn't begin to know what Gol Kolea was feeling.

Except that part of him was afraid he could. Merity had been down here. She'd been caught in this. Gaunt barely knew her, and what little he did know was lies. In truth, he hadn't known his daughter any better than Gol had known his. But the damage was primal. It defied rationalisation. A child was a child, no matter how estranged, no matter how false.

Dalin Criid stood apart from the rest, leaning against a wall, staring at the whitewashed stones. His weeping had stopped, and his anguished denials had trailed into silence. Gaunt knew Dalin felt this more bitterly than anyone. Even more than Gol, he had been close to the girl. The conflict had broken him. Grief for the loss of a sister, rage at the sheer depth of the betrayal.

Yoncy had never been Yoncy, but that hadn't stopped them from believing she was real. For years, she had been part of them, part of the Tanith company, a survivor, a cheerful, quirky girl who had often been a welcome antidote to the grind of war. Caring for her, laughing with her, protecting her, amusing her... that had been part of their lives, simple human interactions that had allowed them to forget, once in a while, the struggle they were committed to.

Except she had been the war all along. The war had been dwelling with them, within their ranks, inside their trust, inside their minds and their hearts, waiting to reveal its true nature.

This was the greatest wound the Ghosts had ever suffered. It had cut the heart of them out, from the inside, striking from the single place that seemed safe. Gaunt had never doubted the devotion of his duty. He had never questioned his belief that man should fight against the Ruinous Powers with every fibre of his soul. Yesterday, he'd wanted the Anarch dead and defeated, just as he had the week before that, and the year before that.

But this? Sek would die, not because it was Gaunt's duty, not because it was the right thing, not because it was the Emperor's will, and not because his death would protect mankind.

Sek would die because of this.

Stablights bobbed in the archway behind him. Colonel Grae appeared, leading a team of Urdeshi troops and palace staff.

'My lord?'

'See to the survivors,' Gaunt said. 'Get them out of here.'

Grae nodded, and his men moved forward, gathering up Sancto, who was bleeding out and could no longer stand or speak, and assisting Hark, who was still supporting the wounded Laksheema.

Laksheema looked at Gaunt.

'This area must be purged and sealed, sir,' she said, her voice frail. 'The entire level.'

'It will be.'

'I will assign ordo staff to undertake the purification rituals.'

Gaunt nodded. Laksheema turned and allowed Hark to help her limp away.

'What is the situation?' Gaunt asked Grae.

'All power and systems in the palace are out, my lord,' Grae replied. 'Defences are down, and all comms are non-functional.'

'So no word from Rawne?'

'None, sir. There are reports of attacks throughout Eltath. The enemy has made a play.'

'I'll be up directly. Does Van Voytz have command?'

'He does, sir,' said Grae. 'He began evacuation, but then the power crashed. I believe he is working to restore the palace and war room to combat function as quickly as possible.'

'We need it.'

Grae nodded. He saluted, and turned to go, then looked at Gaunt again.

'My lord,' he said, 'your daughter is safe. I had her taken to a medicae station just twenty minutes ago.'

Gaunt found he could not reply.

'She was shaken, sir, but essentially unharmed. I'll request further reports. I would say she acquitted herself well. Braved the ordeal with great composure.'

'Thank you, colonel,' said Gaunt. Grae made the sign of the aquila, and hurried off to oversee the recovery efforts.

Gaunt had never, in his entire life, felt more like weeping. He looked at Gol, seated, silent, staring, and registered a stab of guilt at his own, selfish relief.

'Are you all right?' asked Curth.

'Yes,' he said.

'Ibram,' she said in a low voice. 'This is something... this is... Throne, I don't know. None of us will just walk away from this. It won't just heal like a battle wound. And even when it does, it won't be a scar any of us wear with any pride. And Gol, and Ban and poor Dalin–'

'I know,' he said. He hugged her quickly, to her surprise, then let her go. 'I wonder,' he said. 'Ana, I was thinking... I might be forced to step down.'

'As Lord Executor?' she asked.

He nodded.

'No one would question it,' she said. 'This trauma, it would break any–'

'No,' he said. 'I think I might step down because Macaroth will never permit his Lord Executor to lead a vengeance strike in person.'

'Against Sek?'

'Wherever he is. Yes. He dies for this. For this, above and beyond any part of his heinous catalogue of crimes.'

'Don't be rash,' she said. 'Bram? Bram, listen. You can do more against him as Lord Executor than as an avenger. This is what he wants. It's the spite he uses to snap us. He weakens us by striking at our souls. He wants to break you, and if you step down, he will have succeeded.'

She gripped his arm and stared into his eyes. Only she, it seemed, was not afraid to look into his eyes.

'Sek doesn't feel,' she said. 'He has no humanity. That's why he can do this to us. Don't let him turn your humanity against you. Feel this, and use it to help you prosecute this war to victory. Don't squander it on some doomed gesture. You're the Lord Executor. Worlds depend on you. And Sek should be fething afraid.'

'Afraid?'

'He's made a mortal enemy even stronger.'

There was a clatter. The Beati's sword, scorched and buckled, had slipped from her hand. Auerben rushed to steady her.

'She's passed out,' Auerben cried out, her fire-scarred voice even more of a rasp than usual. 'Help me here!'

Curth and Gaunt rushed to the Saint's side.

'Just exhaustion,' said Curth, examining her.

Gaunt nodded. The Saint had come straight from days of battle at Gherep-pan and Oureppan. Her divine strength had already been depleted before they'd even begun. These superhuman efforts in the undercroft had drained all the reserves she had left.

'I see no major wounds,' said Curth. 'But then, I don't begin to know how the warp may have wounded her in that fight.'

'She is so pale,' said Auerben. 'Her light is gone–'

'Get her up!' Curth yelled. 'Help me! Osket!'

The Ghosts from Baskevyl's team rushed to her, and lifted the Beati's limp form between them.

'There's no weight to her!' Osket exclaimed.

'This way!' Curth urged them, leading the men towards the exit.

The Ghosts, in black, with their fragile pale burden, reminded Gaunt of pall bearers.

'Ana?' he called out.

Curth looked back at him and simply nodded. The look in her eyes told him everything he needed to know. It was the same uncompromising determination he'd seen every time Medicae Curth had fought to save a wounded soul on the fields of war they had crossed together.

There were very few of them left in the undercroft now. Daur, Kolea and Dalin lost in their own pain, Blenner lurking by the door, anxious, as if he was waiting for something. Gaunt was heartened a little to see Blenner show a simple, human response of sympathy for once.

Baskevyl glanced at Gaunt. Shock was etched on his face too.

'Should we try to move them?' he asked Gaunt.

Gaunt nodded. 'Gently,' he said. 'They should mourn as long as they need to, but this place is–'

'I know, sir,' Baskevyl replied. Gaunt took a step towards Kolea, but Baskevyl stopped him. Bask and Gol were best friends. Bask would be a more welcome comfort.

Gaunt crossed to Daur instead.

'Let's go upstairs, Ban,' he said.

Daur looked up at him. He rose, and brushed off his coat.

'No,' he said.

'No?'

'No, sir.'

'Ban–'

'I haven't found her yet,' he said. 'I'm not leaving until I have.'

'Ban, we can get teams down here, a proper search of all–'

'No,' Daur said fiercely. 'I'll look. Me.'

He walked past Gaunt, and disappeared into the neighbouring chamber. Gaunt heard Daur calling her name.

Haller cut loose with a long burst from the short-snout rigged around his body. The link-belt from the hopper at his feet clattered as it fed out. Harsh flowers of muzzle flash flickered around the cannon's wide barrel, and spent brass fluttered into the air.

The automata, limping and drooling black ooze, punctured in fifty places. Its casing disintegrated, flayed off it by the hail of shells, and it slumped, burning from the core, black fluid pouring from its ruptured innards.

'Still one or two of them active,' Haller remarked.

'Stay sharp,' Kolosim said. He looked at Bray. The sergeant was trying to force the hatch into Turbine Hall One. Caober was working with him.

'Any luck?' Kolosim called out.

'Stand by,' said Bray.

'Are we gonna need more shit from that truck?' Kolosim asked.

'No, I've got it,' said Bray, working intently. 'It's just locked from inside.'

Criid and Zhukova clambered out of the open duct, weapons ready. Obel limped out behind them. Turbine Hall One was just as they'd left it. The huge vapour engines had slowed down to an impotent wheeze. The bodies of the dead – Ghost and Mechanicus alike – lay where they had fallen.

'You were wrong,' said Criid.

'No,' replied Zhukova with a firm shake of her head.

'Then where is he?'

Criid edged out across the floorspace, picking her way over bodies, watching for any sign of movement. There were plenty of hiding places. So much pipework, bulk machines, consoles. The hostile could have concealed himself. Criid wasn't sure if he'd had a weapon, but if he did, he could be lining up a shot.

She crossed to the hatch. It was still locked tight, internal setting, just the way Zhukova had sealed it before they had entered the ducts. No one could have exited and locked it again from the inside.

'We went the wrong way,' she said. She was dizzy from the fumes of the duct, dead on her feet from running and climbing. 'He didn't come this way.'

'He did,' Zhukova said.

'Then where is he?' Criid asked. 'Fething where?'

'Somewhere,' said Zhukova. She prowled across the chamber. 'He's in here.'

'I'll tell you where he is,' snapped Criid. 'He's two kilometres away heading out into the main thermal pipe. He's home free. We went the wrong fething way.'

'It was just a call, Tona,' said Obel, sitting down and trying to collect his breath. He was wheezing badly. 'We made a call. It was just the wrong one.'

'It wasn't,' said Zhukova.

'Then where is he?' Criid snarled.

'Hiding,' said Zhukova. She started to slam open storage lockers along the west wall, aiming her weapon into each one as she threw the doors open. Just machine spares. Clusters of cables. Pipework.

'They won,' said Criid. 'They fething won. They got the stones.'

The main hatch let out a bang of auto-bolts and then slid open with a slow pneumatic hiss. Criid, Obel and Zhukova turned, weapons aimed.

'Hold fire! Hold fire!' Bray yelled as he saw them. The Ghosts around him lowered their aim, and fanned out into the hall.

'What happened?' asked Kolosim.

Criid just shook her head, exhausted.

'We met them coming out,' said Obel. 'Held them. Fething mess of a fire-fight. Unreal. They weren't human and they kept coming. Just savage. Big purse. But one got past us.'

'Just one,' said Zhukova.

'Fething bastard had a bag. Had the stones,' said Obel. 'We went after him, but he got out through the geotherm system.'

'Oh feth,' said Kolosim.

'He didn't go that way,' Zhukova insisted. She turned back to her search. 'He came this way.'

'Then where?' asked Criid.

'I told you,' said Zhukova. 'He's hiding. In here somewhere. There's nowhere else. That's the first time that hatch has opened. He's in this chamber right now.'

'Search! Top to bottom!' Kolosim yelled. Squads of Ghosts fanned out, hunting in every alcove, checking the service walks behind machines. Some climbed up onto the inspection gantries. Others stood in a mob by the hatchway, gazing dismally at the dead.

'No sign!' Bray called. Other Ghosts sang out negatives.

'See?' said Criid.

'I'll try and patch through to Pasha,' said Kolosim. 'Tell her the word.'

Zhukova was still searching. She ducked down to look behind the hall's control desks. Trooper Etzen's corpse was sprawled under the console.

He'd been felled by one of the adept wardens' grav pulses. The energy had crushed and mangled him.

Zhukova frowned. The graviton force was powerful, but it would not have removed Etzen's jacket and cape.

She rose.

'Shit,' she said.

'What?' asked Obel.

'Etzen. No cape. No–'

Criid and Zhukova turned. The bodies of four Ghosts had been lying on the floor between the consoles and the hatch. Now there were only three.

Criid and Zhukova sprang forwards, Obel staggering after them.

'What the feth, Tona?' Kolosim exclaimed as Criid pushed past him.

'He's just walking out!' she yelled. She had no idea how a rail-thin, two-metre tall spectre could just walk out, but she knew it had. She and Zhukova pushed through the bewildered Ghosts standing in the doorway.

'Move!' Criid yelled at them. 'Move!'

One Ghost had detached himself from the back of the group. Draped in his camo cloak, he was limping away across the wide arcade outside, heading for the main exit. He was just walking past the Ghost squads stationed in the arcade area.

It wasn't her quarry. This man was short, small. He looked old and frail, the cape pulled tight around him.

But Criid knew it wasn't any Ghost she knew.

'You!' She yelled. 'You! Halt!'

The Ghost kept walking.

'Last warning!' Criid yelled.

The man paused. He stopped limping, he glanced back at her over his shoulder.

He was an old man, weathered and skinny. He looked like one of the scrawny ayatani priests that had been flooding into the city.

He looked straight at her for a second, then turned and kept on going, limping on towards the door.

In that one second, Criid had seen the neon glint in his pupils.

She fired her stave. The grav pulse thumped out of the projector end. Ghosts scattered and recoiled as the seething mass of distorted air bubbled across the concourse.

It hit the limping man in the back, crushing his spine and ribcage, and pulping his internal organs.

Hacklaw fell. He died as he had entered the world, his blessed reworking hidden from view.

Criid and Zhukova reached the corpse. Criid turned it over gingerly with her foot. Just a dead old man, wrapped in a Tanith combat cloak.

Zhukova knelt down, and pulled the dirty musette bag out of his dead hands.

She opened it, and gently lifted out one of the four eagle stones.

'I take it back,' Criid said. 'You were right. Fether came this way.'

They ran through the rain into the drab rockrete compounds of the vapour mill beside Camp Xenos. Snapshots of las whined after them.

'Keep moving,' Rawne said.

'There's no fething cover, sir,' said Laydly, glancing around. The trooper was right, and Rawne knew it. The Plade Parish vapour mill was a large site generating power for an entire district of the city. Open-air yards and service-ways ran between the rows of blank work-sheds and machine-shops. The main stacks and primary hall of the mill were ahead.

It was an automated facility. There was no one around, and every door or hatch they tried was sealed. Wartime. Blackout protocols. The mill had been locked down.

Overhead, masses of white steam oozed from the huge stacks and flowed like a glacier into the night's black sky. Full dark. Rain was blowing in off the wastelands beyond the mill perimeter. It smelled of the fycelene lifted by the munition store explosion.

'Just go,' Mabbon said. 'Leave me. I will face them. It will all end then.'

Rawne wanted to slap him, but the pain in his gut was getting worse. He gritted his teeth to stop himself from making a sound.

'Shut the feth up,' Varl said to Mabbon. 'Just shut up. We lost good people getting you out–'

'I never asked for that–' Mabbon replied.

'I won't let them be dead for no reason,' said Varl. He sniffed, breathing fast. 'I just won't. I just fething won't. So shut up about leaving you. Shut up.'

Mabbon looked away.

'How many left?' asked Oysten.

'Three,' said Laydly. 'Three, I think.'

'What have we got that will put them down?' asked Rawne, finally managing to speak without screaming.

'Launcher, grenades,' said Varl, brandishing Bellevyl's weapon.

'Maybe this?' said Brostin, indicating the big autogun he'd taken off Oken. 'AP rounds. Not much ammo though.'

'Hard rounds are better than energy weapons,' said Mabbon.

'I'll take anything at this point,' said Rawne.

Two las bolts shrieked around a blockhouse nearby.

Rawne bundled them forward. Varl ran with Mabbon, driving him on, the others following, covering the group's six with weapons levelled.

'What can we do that they won't expect?' Varl asked.

'Turn,' said Brostin. 'Turn on them. Meet them.'

'Feth off,' said Oysten.

'No, he's right,' said Laydly. They got in against the wall of a work-barn and he pointed at the sheds and service buildings around them. 'Someone in there, by the steps. Another there. You see, by those tanks? You could get in under the pipework right there. They come through there, the yard, you'd have a killing ground. Rake 'em.'

'No,' said Rawne. 'Suicide.'

'Suicide Kings, sir,' said Laydly.

Rawne glowered at him.

Oysten grabbed Rawne's arm. 'Sir!'

The pull on his arm made Rawne grunt with pain.

She looked at him.

'You all right?'

'Yes, Oysten.'

'Sir, are you hit?'

'No. What did you want?'

She studied his face for a second, questioning, then turned and pointed. About half a kilometre away, on the other side of the mill compound, there was a small light. Oysten handed Rawne the scope, and he took a look.

'Night watchman's station,' he said. It made sense. The mill would leave a supervisor on site overnight, even in raid conditions.

'In case something goes wrong?' Oysten said. 'A fault in the mill? Then what would he do?'

Rawne glanced at her.

'Call it in,' he said. 'Call in for service support.'

She nodded. 'He'll have a vox, that one,' she said.

'We'd... we'd need the Militarum code channels,' said Rawne.

'I know them by heart, sir,' said Oysten. 'Learn them off pat every morning.'

Rawne took her by the face with both hands and smacked a kiss on her brow.

'Go,' he said. 'Go fast as feth. Think you can make it?'

'Absolutely.'

'Call in the fething cavalry, Oysten,' he said. 'We'll dig in and slow these bastards down.'

She nodded, then surprised him by throwing a formal salute.

'It's been an honour, sir,' she said.

'It will be again, you silly bastard. Run!'

She took off into the darkness.

'Right,' said Rawne. 'Let's slow these fethers down.' He looked back at the yard.

'All right,' he said. He was having trouble breathing.

'You all right? Eli?' Varl asked.

'Fething fantastic,' Rawne replied. 'Varl? Keep going. Keep moving Mabbon that way. Just stay with him. Keep him alive.'

He looked at Laydly and Brostin.

'Let's fething do this,' he said. 'Just like Laydly set it out.'

'Only two decent firing positions,' said Brostin.

'I can get in there,' said Rawne, pointing. 'Down by that vent.'

'That's shit-all cover, sir,' said Brostin. 'Go with Varl. Two of you are better than one. Keep that fether safe, all right?'

'I think I'm in charge here,' said Rawne.

'I think we play to our strengths,' said Laydly. 'Suicide Kings. Picture cards are high, and you keep your kings back in case you need them late in the game.'

'I should never have taught you to play,' said Rawne.

'I should never have joined the Imperial Guard,' replied Laydly.

'We had a choice?' asked Brostin.

Rawne looked at them both.

'Live forever,' he said.

They nodded. Brostin lumbered away to the steps of the service shed. Laydly sprinted low across to the heavy feeder tanks. They vanished into the deep shadows, just ghosts, then gone.

Rawne stood for a moment, then turned and hurried after Varl and Mabbon. He was limping. Every step was a jolt of pain.

Hadrel sniffed the rain. He looked at the others. Sekran. Jaghar. Just the three of them. More than enough.

'They're close,' he said. They'd stripped the resin from their snouts so their acute senses were as sharp as possible.

Jaghar nodded. 'I smell blood, sirdar.'

'At least one is wounded,' Sekran agreed.

Hadrel eyed them. The fight had been fierce. He and Sekran were intact apart from some las burns. Jaghar had been hurt in the blast. Swollen crusts of mucus covered part of his face, throat and shoulder.

'We're low on munitions,' Hadrel said. 'They have run us quite a game. So conserve. The pheguth is the one that counts. Bite out his throat if you have to.'

'Kha, magir,' they responded.

'He dies,' said Hadrel.

'He dies,' they echoed.

Hadrel gestured, and they moved forwards.

'He will regret the day he left us,' he said.

Nade Oysten ran through the darkness, following shadows, darting between blank anonymous sheds and silent service huts.

The mill compound was larger than it had seemed. The night watch post still looked a million kilometres away, and every shadow made her jump. She kept expecting one of those things, those Qimurah, to loom up, to spring out of the darkness.

She had her weapon ready, her cut-down riot gun and its bag of breaching shells. Let's see how they like that, she thought. Let's see how they like a face-full of wound titanium shot-wire.

Oysten touched her face where Rawne had seized her with both hands to kiss her. There was blood on her fingers.

She'd known. Just the way he had been moving, holding himself. Always a lying bastard. That look he'd shot her.

Say nothing.

She turned towards the distant light and started running as fast as she could.

There was no sound except the hiss and spatter of the rain. Laydly had his weapon up, covering the middle of the yard. They had to come through here. He had switched to full auto, last cell locked in the receiver.

He couldn't see Brostin, but he could see the steps of the service shed. Good bit of shadow. Nice angle for that big autogun. Brostin would be the hitter on this one. That thing, at short range, with those armour-piercing shells Okel had prized, would make a hole in anything.

A waiting game now. Patience. Waiting for the deal. Waiting for the cards to land. Those things moved as quietly as any Ghost, but there was an open killbox waiting.

Laydly took aim, nice and loose, ready for the snap.

Sekran's claws closed around his throat. The Qimurah hoisted him off the ground. Laydly tried to scream, but the vicing grip had crushed his throat. Sekran kept squeezing until he'd wrung and snapped the human's neck. As he died, Laydly squeezed the trigger. Full auto, aimed at nothing, sprayed out of the swinging gun, tearing into the rockcrete ground of the yard, pinging off the tanks, stitching up the wall.

Brostin saw the wild burst, saw two figures strobe-lit by the muzzle flash. One lifting the other by the throat.

He yelled Laydly's name, then opened fire. The autogun's big rounds smacked into the feeder tanks. The Qimurah tossed Laydly's body aside and ran at Brostin, bringing up his lasrifle to fire.

'Yeah, you fething come at me,' Brostin snarled.

He put the first armour piercing hard round through Sekran's face, the second and third through his torso. By then, there was very little left of him above the sternum or between the shoulders. The Qimurah folded and collapsed in the middle of the open yard.

Brostin switched around, looking for the others. He saw movement and banged off two more shots.

On the roof of the machine shop opposite, Hadrel noted the muzzle flashes. He took the grenade out of his jacket pocket and weighed it in his hand. They'd picked over the bodies of the Imperial dead, and found a few useful items.

He threw it.

Brostin heard it strike the gutter above him. He knew the sound of an anti-personnel bomb whacking against metal. He threw himself forward.

The grenade splintered the front of the service shed and obliterated the steps. The blast rolled Brostin hard across the rockcrete, and shrapnel whickered into his flesh.

He lay for a moment, deaf and dazed. Then he tried to rise.

My turn again, you fethers–

The front wall of the wrecked service shed collapsed, and the entire roof gave way. An avalanche of slabs and rockcrete roof tiles buried Aongus Brostin.

Dust billowed off the heap of rubble. It was piled up like the rocks of a tribal grave on some lonely hillside. Just one hand protruded, caked in dirt.

Hadrel leapt down from the roof and landed on his feet. Jaghar emerged from cover and walked to join him.

They clutched their lasrifles and advanced side by side.

'Just the last of them now,' said Hadrel.

'Gol? We have to go up now,' Baskevyl said gently. 'Can't stay down here all night.'

Kolea didn't reply. He was staring at the burned thorns.

'Gol?'

'I made a promise,' Kolea said at last. 'Swore it, Bask.'

'It was a promise you couldn't keep,' said Baskevyl. 'They don't count.'

'I should have known.'

'None of us knew, Gol.'

Kolea looked at him.

'I did, though,' he said. 'I thought it. I considered it. I even... I even took it to Gaunt. I told him what I feared.'

'I'm sure he–' Baskevyl began.

'He reassured me,' said Kolea. 'He talked me down, said it was a mistake.'

'Nobody could have known the truth,' Baskevyl said. He glanced over his shoulder. Gaunt and Blenner were standing a few yards away, watching them. He could see the expression on Gaunt's face. Guilt. Guilt for brushing Kolea's fears aside.

They all felt the guilt. Baskevyl certainly did. Odd nagging doubts that he'd cast aside as stupid. Then the things Elodie had said to him–

He clenched his eyes tight shut. She'd known, but just like Gaunt had done with Kolea, Baskevyl had allayed her fears. Because it just *couldn't* have been true.

Now she was dead. Now so many were dead. Nobody had listened. Daur's wife was dead because Baskevyl hadn't taken her seriously.

Kolea got up suddenly.

'Gol?' Baskevyl rose, and put his hand on Kolea's arm.

'I've still got a son,' Kolea said, and pulled his arm away. He walked over to Dalin, who was hunched against the wall.

Baskevyl joined Blenner and Gaunt. They watched Kolea approach the boy.

'He just needs time,' Baskevyl said quietly. Gaunt nodded.

'What did he say?' asked Blenner.

'What do you think?' Baskevyl replied.

'I don't know. I was just wondering.'

'He can't believe it, even now it's happened,' said Baskevyl. 'He blames himself. He blames everybody. That part'll go. But he'll never stop blaming himself. He's not making much sense at all, to be honest.'

'Well, he wouldn't,' Blenner nodded. 'I mean, a shock like that. A tragedy. It'd shake a man to his core. It's shaken all of us. I doubt an ounce of sense will come out of him. Just... just a lot of old nonsense.'

'What?' asked Baskevyl.

'I just meant,' said Blenner, awkwardly, 'we can't expect him to make any sense. Not at a time like this. He'll probably say all sorts of things, rant and rave, you know, until that pain eases. A trauma like this, that could take years.'

Baskevyl stared at him.

'Are you trying to make some kind of point?' he asked.

'N-no,' said Blenner.

As they watched, Kolea knelt down facing Dalin. He reached out and put his trembling hands on the young man's shoulders.

'Dal.'

'Leave me alone,' said Dalin.

'I don't know what to say, Dal,' Kolea said. 'I don't think there's anything anyone can say–'

'She said plenty,' said Dalin quietly. 'All those weird things. She was always so strange. But she was my sister.'

He paused.

'I thought she was,' he added.

'Dalin, let's go up. Get out of here, eh?' Kolea said.

'She was always so strange,' Dalin said, staring at Gol. 'Growing up, all her games. All her stories. I used to love them. Now I remember every one of them and I see how creepy they were.'

'Come on, now.'

'Then the things she said tonight. When I found her. The things she said. They didn't make any sense. But then her stories about bad shadows didn't make any sense either, and they were true. She told me there was a woe machine. That was true. What if all the things she said were true?'

'Like what?' Kolea asked.

Dalin shook his head.

'Look, son, none of us could have known–' said Kolea.

'I'm not your son.'

'Dal, listen. None of us could have known. Not me, not you, not–'

He stopped. There was still a burning anger inside him. He hated himself for it, but the anger was directed at Ibram Gaunt. Kolea had laid it all out, exposed everything that had plagued him, and Gaunt had just talked him out of it. He'd brushed all the fears away, found ways to account for every strange detail, and swept it all out of sight.

If he'd *listened*–

But no. He'd had an answer for everything. Your mind's *confused*, Gol. The Ruinous Powers play games. Even the Archenemy wouldn't lay a plan *that* elaborate. They couldn't see the future and be *that* many steps ahead.

A brother would know his sister.

Kolea looked at Dalin.

That had been the clincher. The one that had really changed Gol's mind.
A brother would know his sister.

'What did she say to you, Dalin?' he asked.

Dalin shook his head again, lips pursed, fighting back tears and daring
not to speak.

'Dal? Dalin? What did she say to you?'

'It was all true, wasn't it?' Dalin sobbed. 'It was all true and I didn't know.'

Kolea pulled him close and wrapped his arms around him. Dalin wept
against his chest.

'Easy, Dal, easy,' he murmured. 'What was it she said to you?'

Dalin whimpered a response that Kolea couldn't hear with the boy's face
buried in his chest. He eased Dalin back, wiped the tears from his cheeks,
and looked him in the eyes.

'I'm here,' he said. 'You can tell me. I'll protect you.'

'You can't,' whispered Dalin.

'Of course I can. I made that oath, remember? The Kolea oath? Walk into
hell to protect you.'

'You couldn't protect Yonce.'

'Well, I couldn't. Because she wasn't mine, was she? But you. You are.
You're my son.'

'Not really. I'm not really.'

'Ah, so our road through life's been an odd one. So what? That's all right.
Blood is blood. So come on, what did she say that upset you so much?'

Dalin stared at him.

'She said there were two of them, papa,' said Dalin.

EIGHTEEN

IN THE SLOW HOURS

As a younger man, a mere colonel in the Calahad Brigade, Barthol Van Voytz had acquired a distrust of the night that had never left him. He was not afraid of the dark, and like any good soldier he knew that darkness could be an ally and a weapon. And back then, there had been a concrete reason. During the gruelling campaign through the Fenlock Forest, night had been the most dangerous time. The Drukhari butchers had always struck between sunset and sunrise. Ninety per cent of Calahad casualties had been taken after dark.

But it was the night itself. A part of it, specifically. Past middle night, there was always a period of particular blackness, with dawn just a hope. It was the worst time. He called it the slow hours. It was a time when a man might feel most lost, his very mortality at its most vulnerable. A man, say a young colonel, might fret away those creeping hours, awaiting almost certain attack, knowing his men were at their coldest and slowest ebb, aching for the dawn. A man might dwell upon the darkness, knowing it promised only ill. A man might have far too long to contemplate his own small soul, his human weakness, and the meaningless measure of his little life.

Standing in the war room of the Urdeshic Palace, that young colonel now just an old pict in a regimental archive, Van Voytz knew the slow hours were upon him again. The power had been down for over an hour. Fear clung to every surface. The palace, perhaps the most impregnable stronghold on Urdesh, was wide open. Eltath was under attack, and there was some unknown danger here, even here, inside the fortress.

And no solid data. They were blind, deaf and dumb. The shields had fallen. A grave moment for any commander to handle, but fate had decreed it should happen now. Past middle night, with sunrise still too far away: that particular heavy, slow and silent chapter of the night that took too long and was no friend of man.

He'd never checked – he was sure some rubricator or archivist could compile the data if he asked – but Van Voytz was sure that the Astra Militarum had lost more battles in the slow hours than at any other point in the diurnal cycle.

Lamps had been lit in the five storey chamber, candles in tin boxes. For all their sophistication, they had been reduced to candles in boxes. Personnel moved with stablights, conversing in low voices, working at repairs. The hall's great windows were just paler blocks of darkness.

'Any word?' he said to Kazader.

'Nothing from below, my lord,' Kazader replied. 'Last I heard, the Lord Executor, via Colonel Grae, requested full troop support to the undercroft.'

'Which I approved,' said Van Voytz.

'Indeed, my lord,' said Kazader, 'but there is conflict. To maintain effective watch-security on the palace and precinct, we cannot afford to move companies from the walls or–'

'Dammit, man. What about the evacuation?'

'It continues as best we are able. Again, it is slow, of course, in these conditions.'

'The Warmaster?'

'I have not had word, my lord.'

'Has Urienz got him off-site or not?' Van Voytz asked.

'I'll despatch a runner to find out.'

'Do that. Kazader?'

'Sir?'

'Has *any* support been sent to the Lord Executor?'

'Orders have been posted, my lord. With respect, I stress again that under these circumstances, it takes a while for men to be redeployed, and sufficient cover maintained along the bastion–'

'How much has been sent?'

'I believe Colonel Grae has three platoons of Urdeshi with him, sir.'

'That all? I gave the damn order almost an hour ago, Kazader.'

'My lord, as I explained–'

'Screw your excuses,' Van Voytz growled. 'I'm a lord militant general, Kazader. I have theatre command here! I give an order, I expect–'

He fell silent. He could see Kazader's expression in the candlelight. It was contrite, attentive. But it said *Look around, you old fool, you have command over shit*.

'My lord?' an adept called out.

'Yes?'

'We're ready to test again.'

'Do it.'

Van Voytz heard orders being relayed, and the clatter of main connectors locking into place. There was a pause, then a deep, bass-note thump of power engaging.

The glass tables of the strategium stations underlit with a flicker. The light throbbed, as unsteady as the candle flames, then stations lit up, followed by the main monitors, repeater screens and sub-consoles. The war room lights came back on at emergency levels. Cogitators began to chatter as operative systems refreshed and rebooted, and backed-up data began to scroll up the screens at an alarming rate, as though some information dam had broken.

There was a ragged cheer and some small applause from the war room staff.

'Decorum! To your stations!' Van Voytz yelled. 'City reports to me in two minutes! I want an active read of Eltath security, and tactical appraisals in five. Vox?'

'Systems up but limited, my lord.'

'Live links to all company and division HQs in the Eltath theatre as soon as possible,' Van Voytz demanded. 'I want Zarakppan too, priority, and get me the fleet!'

The vox station coordinators hurried to obey.

'Eltath overview on strategium one, please!' Van Voytz ordered.

'Compiling data composite now, sir.'

'Shield status?'

'We have power to the war room and battery defences, my lord,' replied an adept. 'Power supply will be restored to the rest of the palace in twenty minutes, barring further interrupts. Estimate void shields to power in forty-seven minutes.'

'Make it thirty,' snapped Van Voytz. He cracked his knuckles. Now they were in the game again.

'Circulate the formal evacuation order,' he said. 'All stations.' The power-break had gagged the order digitally. So far, he'd only been able to have it circulated by word of mouth and paper flimsy. 'I want a progress report in three.'

He paused, and scratched his cheek, thinking.

'Request you confirm that,' said Marshal Tzara. 'You wish evacuation to proceed?'

'Yes,' said Van Voytz.

'Then you still believe the situation in the undercroft—'

'The power died for a reason, Marshal,' he replied. 'It wasn't a random bloody fault.'

'We don't know anything,' she said calmly.

'Exactly,' he replied. 'Except we do, because Gaunt told us that shit was happening.'

He glanced at Kazader, and then back to the Keyzon Marshal.

'Marshal Tzara?'

'My lord general?'

'I'm committing theatre control to you as of now. You have my orders and my objectives. Follow them.'

'With discretion?' asked Tzara.

'With the dedication of a Throne-damn bloodhound,' he replied. Then he nodded. 'You have discretion, of course, Tzara,' he said, 'but use it sparingly. Are we understood?'

'Perfectly, lord general.'

He straightened formally, and made the sign of the aquila.

'I commit theatre command to you at this time,' he said. 'Let it be so recorded.'

She returned the salute.

'I accept and receive this duty,' she replied. 'Let it be so recorded.'

Van Voytz turned to Kazader.

'Get your storm troops, colonel,' he said. 'You're with me. And find me a damn gun.'

'Is that lights?' asked Hark.

The wardroom they had been taken to was lit with small lamps and candles, but its large windows looked out across the Hexagonal Court towards the main keep.

Inquisitor Laksheema was standing at the windows, staring out. She was a tall, slender phantom in the twilight.

'I believe so,' she replied. 'It looks as though they have restored power to the main keep.'

'That's something, then,' he replied. 'Felt like we were sitting here with our pants down.'

'Something you often do, Commissar Hark?' she asked.

'I'm a soldier, mam,' he replied. 'We get up to all sorts.'

Hark was lying back on a couch. A Keyzon corpsman had just finished swabbing and stitching the gashes on his throat and face, and now had turned to the stump of his augmetic and was sealing the shredded wires with a fusing wand.

Laksheema had refused any treatment. Her robes were torn, and the burnished, ornate augmetics of her face and body were grazed and scratched. When the orderlies had come to her, she told them that she was not in any pain and they should attend those who were.

Hark wondered if she had any significant organic parts, anything that could feel pain. Feel anything.

She was pacing before the windows. The digital weapons inlaid in the golden cuff of her left wrist had been destroyed in the ordeal. She kept adjusting the still-functional ones built over her right wrist like an elaborate golden bangle.

She crossed to the doorway of the adjoining room and watched the Urdeshi surgeons working by candlelight to repair the grievous wounds Sancto had received. The Scion had long since slipped from consciousness. He'd been laid out on a dining table, and the floor around it was littered with parts of his body gear and blood-soaked surgical towels.

She observed impassively for a moment, then walked back through the wardroom and stepped out into the corridor.

Hark glanced at the corpsman.

'Enough,' he said.

'Sir?'

'You gonna re-fit me with an arm tonight?'

'Sir, I'm just a–'

'Thought so,' said Hark. He got up off the couch, and tossed aside the surgical smock that had been draped across him. 'Thanks for your duty,' he said to the corpsman.

Hark walked out into the hall. He was sore as hell. Every joint. He couldn't have been more thoroughly bruised if Brostin had come at him with a mallet. The arm he didn't mourn. The augmeticists would fix him a new one. His plasma pistol, though. It had been a beauty. He'd miss that.

He sighed. There were many more important things to miss and mourn.

The corridor was wood-panelled and grand. Old paintings hung in gilt frames, though it was impossible to see what they depicted. Layers of age-darkened varnish and the weak glow of the lamps in the hall conspired to make them impenetrable. There was almost a warmth to the hall with its dark wood and dim yellow light. The Urdeshic Palace had been a fine, grand place once. He would not, he felt, remember it fondly.

Several doors along was the entrance to the prayer chapel where most of the Tanith survivors were being ministered to. He could hear Zweil, leading them in a deliverance blessing.

Not quite Hark's cup of caffeine.

Down by the chapel door, in the shadows, he saw the orange coal of a lho-stick. Hark squinted. It was Meryn, leaning against the wall, smoking. The old ayatani's blessings were clearly not his cup of caffeine either.

Hark began to walk in Meryn's direction. He was a cigar man, himself, but a shared smoke with a Guardsman was a bonding thing that often helped after a nasty go-around.

But he stopped. Flyn Meryn wasn't good company at the best of times. Hark walked the other way instead.

Something stirred in the shadows above him and rasped. He glanced up, and saw the regiment's mascot peering down at him. It was perched on a game trophy, the mounted skull of a creature that possessed the broadest and largest antlers he'd ever seen.

'Rough night, bird,' he said to the half-hidden eagle. It clacked its beak angrily. 'I hear you,' he replied, and wandered on. He flexed his hand. His one remaining hand. The bird had made him jump. He had reached instinctively for his weapon, but the arm he had reached with was just a phantom, and the holster empty. With his good hand, he felt under his coat to the back of his waistband, and found his hold-out weapon, a snub-nose laspistol in a leather buckle-on pouch. At least that was still there.

Laksheema was standing at a doorway just ahead, staring in. He joined her.

Through the open door, he saw Curth and several medicae aides attending to the Beati. She was laid out on a bed, straight and still, like a body ready for viewing.

Captain Auerben was watching Curth work. She noticed Hark and the inquisitor at the door and came out to them.

'She has not regained consciousness,' she said. Her voice was just a croak. Hark had been told that Auerben had been hurt by a pyrochemical burst during the last Morlond campaign. It had scarred her face and burned her throat. Auerben paused, took an inhaler bulb from her pocket, and puffed it into her mouth to moisten her throat.

'Excuse me,' she said.

Hark shrugged. 'Ana Curth knows what she's doing,' he said.

'I'm sure she does,' said Auerben. 'There are no significant injuries. It is extreme fatigue. A sapping of her will. I told her she was pushing too hard.'

Auerben took another puff from the inhaler.

'But the woe machine,' she said. 'It was a focus of ruinous power. It sapped her, and fed on her light. I fear it may take a long time for her to recover strength.'

'We repair. We recharge,' said Laksheema.

'She means we heal,' said Hark with a smile. 'The Emperor protects. His grace will flow back into the Beati in time. She will be restored as she once was.'

Auerben nodded. She went back into the room and resumed her vigil at the bedside.

'The machine was a grim device,' said Laksheema. 'I am ever horrified by the limitless ingenuity of the Archenemy.'

Hark nodded in agreement. 'It may have been the worst thing I have ever encountered,' he said. 'You?'

'I have faced daemons, commissar,' she replied.

'Oh, we've all faced daemons, inquisitor,' he replied.

She looked at him with a questioning frown.

Hark grinned. 'I don't know,' he said. 'I've faced more powerful things, more dangerous things, though Throne knows that was hell. Without the Saint, we'd all be dead. The palace too.'

'Indeed,' said Laksheema. 'It was young. Not fully grown. But already a threat we could scarcely combat. Without her, it would have been enough. The palace lost, Eltath, Urdesh itself. The Anarch had victory there, for a moment. Total victory. If the woe machine hadn't been checked, the crusade would have been crippled beyond recovery. The Sabbat Worlds would have fallen, and all our years of gain lost. Anakwanar Sek almost won tonight. Not just the battle, the war.'

'It wasn't just its power or its fury,' said Hark. 'It was the very feel of it. The shadow of the warp was in it, as strong as any warp spawn. It radiated fear, that's the thing. It didn't just inspire fear because of what it was. It generated it. It amplified it within us.'

'Part of its arsenal,' said Laksheema. 'Woe machines are essentially mechanical instruments, but the heritor ingeniants have found the means to bind other elements. The warp. The human soul. Asphodel was a genius, you know? To take a killing machine and construct it with such intricate care it fitted inside a human shell. They call it reworking.'

'Who do?' asked Hark.

'The Heritors of the Archonate. Alloying human and warp and machine into one material. Fusing them, and giving them the capacity of shift.'

'Like a ship?' he asked.

'No, like a lycanthrope, Hark. A shape-changer, the transmutation of form. Deceit and guile and disguise, they are weapons of warfare we utilise. And such things are second nature to the warp. But the reworked take that to an obscene level. Of course, change is a primary aspect of the Four, a fundamental property of the Way-Changer, the dark un-god of sorcerous transition.'

'You're very knowledgeable,' he remarked.

'Years of study,' she replied.

'How many years?'

Laksheema favoured him with her cold smile.

'It is impolite to ask a lady her age,' she said.

'You're no lady,' he said.

'Also impolite.'

'I mean you're beyond human, inquisitor. Reworked – is that the word? – in your own way. Like me. Though I am crudely wrought compared to you. How old do you feel?'

'Viktor,' she replied, 'I barely feel at all, and I haven't for a very long time.'

He was about to reply when a wind blew down the hallway, fluttering all the candles and lamps.

They turned.

'What was that?' he asked. She didn't answer. A second later, they heard a scream. It came from far away, deep in the core of the palace, but it was so loud and piercing that it made the walls tremble.

It wasn't a human scream.

Hark found he had his hold-out weapon in his hand. The fear had returned. The fear that had drowned him in the undercroft had soaked him again in a heartbeat.

'Feth,' he said. 'What was that?'

Laksheema looked at him.

'Do you feel that?' she asked.

He nodded. 'Right through the heart of me,' he said. 'Just–'

'Terror,' she said. 'There is another one. There is another woe machine here.'

Light shuddered. Shadows twisted. Gol Kolea looked at his son in surprise. That scream he had uttered...

Dalin Criid looked back at him, blinking fast.

'Dalin?' said Gol.

'No. No. No no no–' Dalin moaned.

'Dalin!'

'How could I not know this?' Dalin asked. 'Never. Never knew.'

Gol let go of Dalin's shoulders. 'Oh no,' he whispered. 'Oh no.'

'She *was* my sister,' said Dalin.

Dalin Criid hinged open. His flesh peeled and folded like the rind of a fruit, his bones twisting like weeds. A subspace lattice bulged, stripping organics back into the immaterium and folding sentient inorganics out into real space in their place. He split down a centre line from the crown of his head and turned inside out with a snap like a switchblade.

He became a cloud of interlacing knives, each one vibrating and slicing as it moved. The blades, all black metal, moved in flawless formation, cycling and shifting in intricate, synchronised patterns, first a rippling figure of eight, then more complex hyperbolic formations obscenely alien to Euclidian geometry. The whirring blades flashed in abstract conic orbits around a central hub of dazzling yellow neon light, like a miniature sun.

Gaunt stared in disbelief. He reached for his bolt pistol, his hand shaking.

Vaynom Blenner stumbled backwards with eyes like saucers, and fell down hard.

'Oh, Throne,' gasped Baskevyl. 'Gol! Gol!'

Still on his knees, Gol Kolea looked up at the whirring cloud of blades. His hands came up in front of his face instinctively to ward it off, then he lowered them. He stared directly into the neon light.

'Dalin,' he said, as if calling a child home after dark. 'I won't let you go alone. I'll walk into hell–'

The cycling blades slowed, as if confused. They stopped, hanging still for a second, then slowly began to cycle in the opposite direction. Their pattern altered, returning to the simple, lemniscate orbit.

Then the figure-eight ploughed forward, and Gol Kolea was gone.

Baskevyl screamed his friend's name, but there was nothing left to answer him except a billowing mist of blood.

Gaunt's bolt pistol boomed. Explosive rounds tore into the glowing cloud of blades. Blade teeth shattered like glass as the rounds detonated like solar flares around the little burning neon sun. Fresh blades slid out of subspace to replace the broken ones, joining the perfect, rushing synchronicity of the revolving pattern.

The woe machine rose up, and turned towards them. Its neon sun-heart was throbbing hatred. Its noise was the whoosh of sword-strikes, the shearing snip of scissors, the steel-on-stone wail of a sharpening wheel. Terror radiated from it like heat.

Blenner was thrashing and twisting in a paroxysm of fear, shrieking and clutching his head.

'Get back, Bask,' Gaunt warned.

The woe machine drifted towards them. It elongated vertically, its rushing figure-eight extending taller and thinner, its inner sun stretching into an oval.

Gaunt faced it, forcing the lid down on his terror. He couldn't fight it. There was nowhere to run. The wind whipping from it tugged at his coat. It smelled of hot metal and burned blood.

Gol's words, Gol's last words, had made it hesitate. Something human was still in it. Something that had been unwittingly human for so long, it couldn't shed the habit as easily as it had shed its disguise.

'Trooper Dalin!' Gaunt yelled. 'Trooper Dalin, stand easy!'

The rotation speed slowed and became irregular. The pattern deformed, some blades drifting out of alignment. The light of the neon sun dimmed slightly, wavering in intensity.

'That's an order, Trooper Dalin!' Gaunt barked.

The figure-eight collapsed. All the blades re-formed into a simple pattern, a single circle orbiting the sun-heart. Gaunt could feel it struggling. The waves of fear were overlapping waves of confusion and panic. It was fighting with itself. The very ingenuity of its design, human fused with warp-machine, was battling with itself.

'Trooper Dalin!' Gaunt cried again.

The circle of spinning blades shifted position, rotating in a plane around the little sun until all the tips were pointing away from the three men and directly up at the ceiling. The blades sat like a spiked crown around their neon heart.

Then their rate-of-cycle increased dramatically. The woe machine rose and ripped into the ceiling, slicing through the ancient stone as though it was soft fat. The wailing woe machine gouged up into the ceiling, and vanished from view.

Dislodged blocks tumbled onto the chamber floor. The undercroft ceiling began to split and collapse, the integrity of its ancient vault sheared through.

'Out! Out!' Gaunt yelled to Baskevyl. The path to the exit and the stairs was no longer blocked. They grabbed the screaming Blenner and stumbled towards the door as the ceiling crashed in behind them.

The palace was shaking. All around, men and women called out in alarm and panic. Candle flames jerked and fluttered. Some went out in wafts of grey smoke. The lamps rattled on their hooks. Old paintings quivered in their frames. The psyber-eagle squawked as dust sifted from the jittering antlers it had settled on.

Objects on table tops trembled and shifted position. Glasses smashed. Medical trays skipped, dislodged and spilled to the floor. Cracks and splits appeared in the ancient floor tiles.

Hark and Laksheema rushed back into the wardroom where they had been treated. The Keyzon corpsman was staring out of the tall windows in amazement. They joined him, gazing down into the broad yard of the Hexagonal Court. The space was torchlit – burning tapers fixed in iron brackets. A company of Helixid troopers were loading packs into two Valkyrie carriers that had set down as part of the evacuation effort.

Hark and Laksheema could hear the men shouting, looking around frantically in an effort to comprehend the source of the shaking.

'Is... is it an earthquake?' asked the corpsman. 'Is it the volcanics?'

'No,' said Hark. He could hear the wailing. The high-pitched metal squeal was getting louder by the second.

The woe machine reached ground level. Its whirring blades erupted through the flagstones of the Hexagonal Court, spitting splinters of stone in all directions. Some of the Helixid troops died immediately, cut down by the whizzing slivers.

Others were caught in the cloud of blades as it rose from the ruptured stone floor and expanded, blades flattening into a horizontal dish around the burning heart. The men vanished in puffs of blood vapour, or fell like parts of a broken puzzle, cut in sections.

The tail boom of one Valkyrie was lopped clean off, leaving bare metal stumps and sparking cables. The severed tail fins were hurled like a toy across the court, and punched in the wall and windows of a ground floor chamber. The other carrier, its ramp still down, tried to throttle up and lift clear. The blades shredded one side of it clean away, leaving the Valkyrie excised in cross-section. Its straining engines ignited, and it exploded in a savage fireball.

Hark slammed Laksheema down and away from the windows as the concussion blast blew them in. A blizzard of broken glass burst across the room.
The corpsman stayed standing for almost ten seconds, blinded, flayed back
to the bone from the thighs up. He fell sideways like a discarded kit-bag.

Down below, the woe machine had formed a new shape – a war shape,
a woe shape, an octahedron four metres across made of sliding, slither-
ing blades, the neon light glowing inside the lattice shell. The few Helixid
troopers who hadn't died or fled fired on it. The woe machine rushed at
them, las-rounds pinging off its blades, one tip dilating to form a spinning,
sucking maw.

Hark got up, broken glass cascading off him, and rushed to the door.
Behind him, Laksheema struggled to her feet.

'Out!' Hark bellowed into the hallway. 'Out now! Woe machine!'

Terrified staff and personnel began to scramble from the rooms all along
the hall. The air itself was vibrating. An ancient painting of Throne-alone-
knows-what fell off the wall with a crash as its ancient string snapped. Its
gilt frame shattered.

Auerben appeared, people shoving past her. She looked at Hark.

'We can't move her,' she said. 'We can't.'

By the chapel door, Meryn shrank back against the old wood panels as
though he was willing the palace wall to swallow him up.

He could hear the killing, the screams. He could smell the blood.

There was going to be another slaughter. And it was going to make the
first one pale into insignificance.

He started to laugh, unable to stop himself, because there was nothing
funny left in the world.

NINETEEN

WHOSE VOICE DROWNS OUT ALL OTHERS

The hooded V'heduak magir strode down the companionway straight towards them.

'Shit,' Mkoll whispered to Brin and Mazho. 'Let me do the talking.'

He turned to face the magir, trying to frame the formal constructions of the Blood-fare caste.

The V'heduak grinned down at him.

'You bastard,' Mkoll murmured.

'I acquired a disguise,' said Kater Holofurnace.

'Clever,' said Mkoll.

'I was slowing you down,' said the Snake. 'Now we can move freely.'

'Where did you–?' Mazho began.

Holofurnace shook his head. 'One of them was fool enough to walk away alone. They won't find his corpse.' He parted the edge of the robes slightly, and let them see the belt-fed .20.

'We know where to go,' said Milo. He had the fold of deck plans.

Holofurnace nodded. 'That show any weapons lockers?' he asked.

'Yes,' said Mkoll. 'But they're secure and we–'

Holofurnace held up a ring of notched metal bars.

'The Blood-fare had keys,' he said with a smile.

Three packsons were guarding the strong room. They saluted, hands to mouths, as the V'heduak strode past them. He slotted his keys into the heavy door's lock without comment.

The packsons watched him for a moment.

'Magir,' said one tentatively. 'The orders are to leave all weapon rooms locked and secure while–'

Mkoll glared at them.

'You question the magir's authority, stool-worm?' he asked.

'No, sirdar. No. Your pardon.'

Holofurnace pushed open the hefty door, and they went inside, pulling it shut behind them. The locker was small, the walls shelved and racked. A small metal bench stood in the centre of the room. The plans had showed there was a locker like it on almost every deck, stocked for the quick distribution of arms to the ship's crew in the event of a boarding action.

'Not much,' murmured Holofurnace, glancing around. 'It's crude stuff. I was hoping for something with some punch. Plasma or cyclic.'

'It's just crew-issue small-arms,' said Mazho. He stared at a rack of boarding hatchets.

'Be selective,' said Milo. 'There's reloads at least. Pack your pockets with cells.'

'Think small and useful,' said Mkoll. 'Concealable.'

'If we're going to kill the devil in his own lair,' said Holofurnace, 'we need power.' He looked at them. 'He's a magister. He won't be human now, if he ever was.'

'We don't know what he is,' said Mkoll.

'I saw his face,' said Milo quietly. 'In the vortex. I saw his face.'

Mazho shivered. He'd glimpsed it too.

'He's definitely not human,' said Milo.

'So he won't die like one, which is my point,' said Holofurnace. 'Carbines? Blades? Even this?'

He put the heavy sentry gun down on the table.

'I have grenades,' said Mkoll.

'How many?' asked the Iron Snake.

'Two,' said Mkoll. 'One smoke, one anti-personnel.'

'Two,' sighed Mazho.

Holofurnace looked at Mkoll. 'Oh, my brother,' he said with a smile. 'Scout and hunter. Best of both. You move light but you think small. You can hunt this prey, I don't doubt that, but can you kill him when you run him to ground? Straight silver won't be enough here.'

'This might help,' said Milo. He'd spotted a battered crate on a lower shelf, and dragged it out. It was heavy, but he lifted it clean to the table. Mkoll watched him. Milo wasn't the boy piper any more. He was strong, and he was tall. He handled weapons with complete familiarity. He had become a seasoned warrior in the years after the Ghosts. And that had been more years than Mkoll could accept. Thanks to the warp incident that had broken the *Armaduke*'s return voyage to Urdesh, Milo was ten years older, relative. That made him over thirty standard. Mkoll knew he had to stop thinking of Milo as some boy, some eager but harmless adolescent lasman like Dalin Criid, or the Belladon bandsman Arradin. He wondered if that, in part, was why the regiment had welcomed Dalin when he became old enough to pledge in. A little of Boy Milo about him. A return to the early days.

He wondered where they were now, how they were faring. Had they held the batteries that night? Was the retinue safe in a new billet? He hoped Dalin was safe. He'd grown fond of him. A brave lad. Just like Milo had been.

All those years, he'd thought of Milo often, and prayed he was safe at the Saint's side. He'd never pictured him as a grown man.

Milo unlatched the crate.

Anchor mines, wrapped in wax paper, packed in plastek beads. Imperial issue, salvaged by the Sons from some overrun depot. Each one was the size of a ration tin. They packed a fyceline/D60 mix that could blow a hole through a ceramite bulkhead.

Milo took them out, handling them with care and expertise.

'Mechanical timer,' he said. 'Contact-fusion anchor pad on the flat side.'

'I know bombs, lad,' Mazho snapped, picking one up.

'Good,' said Milo. 'Then you'll know to treat them gently. Not to snatch or shake them. They're volatile.'

'I know that,' said Mazho. He put the mine down again carefully.

'Two each,' said Mkoll.

'Three if we carry fewer cells,' said Milo.

'Heavy pockets,' said Mkoll.

'Bigger punch,' said Holofurnace.

'Because straight silver won't be enough,' Mkoll nodded, conceding.

Holofurnace found a musette bag and emptied out the hard round clips it contained. 'I can take four. Maybe five.'

'Load up,' said Mkoll.

They stepped out of the locker, and the V'heduak sealed the door with his keys.

'Everything's in order,' Mkoll said to the packsons. 'Lucky for you.'

They followed the main spinal towards the Oratory, Brin, Mkoll and Mazho forming an honour guard escort behind the cowled Iron Snake. The whispering buzz of voices was getting louder. It vibrated their ears and made their skin crawl.

The hallways were busier in this part of the ship. Crowds seemed to be gathering: packsons, Sekkite officers, even other V'heduak magirs.

'What is this?' Mazho whispered.

Mkoll listened, catching snatches of conversation from the crew they passed.

'A summoning,' he told them. 'The Anarch is calling them. He's going to speak.'

'He's speaking all the time,' Mazho whispered.

'No, this is a formal declaration,' said Mkoll.

'Of what?' asked Milo.

Mkoll kept listening.

'Of victory,' he said.

The Oratory was a spherical chamber that occupied a socket through three deck levels. The exterior was ribbed with iron-plate armour, and wrought from a pale brown, polished material.

As they came closer, Mkoll realised it was human bone. Thousands upon thousands of gleaming skull caps bonded together. The entrance was a huge doorway accessed via the middle deck. Two rows of abominable excubitors with power lances stood guard outside, forming an avenue that channelled the gathering officers inside. The low murmur of the gathering was drowned out by the rasping whisper in the air.

'Once we're in there, there's no coming back out,' whispered Holofurnace as they watched from a distance.

'Agreed,' said Mkoll. 'But we knew that.'

'Yes,' said Mazho, clearing his throat. Mkoll could see the colonel was sweating behind his leather mouth guard. Mazho was a brave man who had served the Fourth Light 'Cinder Storm' with distinction. But this was no battlefield. This required another type of courage.

'We can do this,' Milo said to the colonel. 'For your world. That's all you've ever fought for.'

Mazho nodded. 'I know,' he said. 'I'm not afraid. Not of death. Just centring my mind.'

'You do it for Urdesh,' Holofurnace said.

'I do it for all worlds, sir,' Mazho replied. 'Fourth Light. Cinder Storm. Light on the breeze, then burning all around you.'

'Cinder Storm,' nodded Holofurnace.

Milo looked at the Oratory sphere again.

'It's a shame we can't–' he began.

'I was thinking that,' said Mkoll. 'We might have time. It's going to take a while for them to file inside.'

He looked at Holofurnace.

'Give me the bag,' he said.

Holofurnace handed it over.

'Stay here,' said Milo. 'You and Mazho. Stay right here.'

'We could all–' Holofurnace began.

'No, leave this to us,' said Milo. 'We're Ghosts.'

They dropped a deck, keeping to the shadows, and skirted around the vast base of the bone sphere. Brin Milo hadn't forgotten the old Tanith craft. He was silent, a shadow in the shadows.

They paused under a stanchion arch, and waited as a Sekkite platoon passed by. Mkoll opened the bag. Holofurnace had packed six mines inside it.

'All of them?' Milo asked.

Mkoll nodded. 'And one from your pockets. Keep two back. We'll see if we can set them inside, along with the ones Mazho's lugging.'

'Long timer?'

'What'll that give us?'

'Thirty minutes. Give or take. They're not accurate, or reliable.'

'Longest mark, then. Go.'

They darted low between pools of shadow, running side by side, and slithered in under the curve of the sphere. The Oratory sat on huge shock gimbals, and thick trunks of cable sheaves and power ducting sprouted from its south pole into the deck.

Milo placed the first charge, using the fusion anchor to fix it to the bone. He removed the steel pin, and flipped the activator. They ran on a few metres, then fixed the second, trying to space the mines fairly evenly on a line of latitude near the sphere's base. The fifth one wouldn't stick, its anchor plate too old and corroded. Mkoll switched it for one of the mines in his coat pockets.

'Hurry,' Milo whispered.

'I'm hurrying gently,' Mkoll replied.

'What's taking so long?' Mazho whispered. The procession of Sekkite seniors had almost finished filing into the Oratory, and the excubitor vanguard was preparing to unhook the doors and swing them shut.

'They're coming,' Holofurnace assured him.

'What if they've been taken?' Mazho asked.

Holofurnace looked grim. 'Then it's down to us,' he said. He beckoned Mazho, and they stepped out of the shadows and joined the last of the officers gathering before the doors.

They fell into line, the queue advancing slowly. Mazho kept looking back. He couldn't see anyone behind them except enemy staff officers and V'heduak magirs.

'Stop doing that,' Holofurnace whispered to him. 'If they're not coming, they're not coming.'

The whispering was getting louder, buzzing from the entrance like the sizzle of churning blow-flies.

They stepped through the doorway.

Eight Sons of Sek moved a slave gang along the walkway, then herded them through a hatch onto the main spinal.

Mkoll and Milo waited until they were out of sight, then moved out of cover and set to work attaching the last of the mines.

'We've taken too long,' Milo said.

Mkoll didn't reply. The timer mechanism was refusing to set.

'I need to be in there,' Milo said.

Mkoll glanced at him.

'You know duty, Oan,' Milo said. 'Better than most. This is mine.'

'Yours?'

'Sek,' said Milo.

'This is an opportunity, that's all.'

Milo shook his head. 'I've seen things,' he said. 'I've walked at her side and seen the galaxy the way she sees it. Learned to a little, at least. There's chaos, but there's order. An order driven by will. A grace that holds the chaos at bay.'

'We all believe that,' said Mkoll. He cleared the timer and tried to rewind it.

'No,' said Milo. 'We believe it. But I've seen it. I thought they were coincidences at first. Just quirks. Chances. But I see a pattern now. She showed me that. Taught me to notice it. An orchestration. A determined force, vastly outnumbered by the immaterium, but holding it in check. Out-playing it, move-for-move, like a game of regicide. It doesn't always win, but it moves the pieces it has, and places them where it can for the best effect.'

'I prefer cards,' said Mkoll. He took the mine off and blew into its corroded timer. 'Suicide Kings...'

'I'm serious.'

'I know. You're talking about fate.'

'That's one word. Call it what you will. I think it's why I made it off Tanith with the First, why we found Sanian, why we... It's why she chose me. She knew... she understood, that one day I would be here.'

Mkoll smiled. 'To kill Sek?'

'Are you mocking me?'

'No, Brin. If you believe that's why you're here, as a chosen instrument, a weapon selected and deployed by... I don't know... destiny, then Throne bless you. That's the strength that drives you. Use it.'

He looked at Milo. He could believe it. There was a purity of purpose in Brin's eyes. Not the blind fanaticism of the zealot or the pilgrim-radical, nor the howling and unquestioning fealty of the warp-corrupted Archenemy. A true faith, a certainty. He could see that long years in the company of a creature as gnomic as the Beati could do that to a man. It could affirm his purpose, give him a sense of calling that would carry him through the darkest and most hellish events. The boy piper had truly long gone. Milo had become a warrior of the Throne, as sure and committed to his function as any Astartes.

'Don't you feel it?' Milo asked. 'Aren't you the same? You, and the Ghosts? I was there in the early years. I saw what was accomplished. And I've read the reports since. The deeds, the achievements. Gaunt, the regiment, you. That doesn't just happen. That isn't just luck. I think we've all been guided by that grace, all along, whether we like it or not. Whether we *know* it or not. It's taken us to the places we've needed to be so that we could do the things it's needed us to do. You must feel that too.'

Mkoll shrugged.

'I don't think on it, Brin,' he said. 'I suppose I only ever consider the immediate. The shadows around me, the foe ahead. I haven't had the opportunity to see things the way you have, at her side. You're a weapon. I don't doubt that, I really don't. We're all weapons. I trust in the providence of the Golden Throne, but I don't have the vision to see any great plan at work. I'm just Guard, Brin. Just Guard. I go where I go and I do my damnedest when I'm told to march or fight. I tell you this much, though... I find it hard to swallow that fate has any great plan spun out across the years. Our side *or* theirs. Reading the variables across a thousand worlds? Planning moves decades in advance? Plotting the future and setting players in position to execute some ingenious gambit years down the line? I don't think it works that way, not for us or the Archenemy. I think it's all a brawl. A free-for-all. Just carnage, and you swing when you can. Instinct. Reaction. Opportunity. What is it Hark calls it? Fight time? Shit just happens, the moment's on you, and you just do. Then you see who walks away. That's all there is. No transcendent plan. Just moments, one after the other, bloody and senseless. You do what you do. Duty gets you through, or you're dead.'

He clamped the last mine in place and set it running.

'Guess we'll see which of us is right, eh?' he said.

Mazho stepped into the Oratory, jostled along by the press of bodies passing through the door. Fear was almost strangling him. He could feel his rapid breathing sucking against the hand-strap across his mouth. He looked up.

The Oratory was huge, even bigger than the exterior shell had suggested. It was a vast, circular theatre. Rings of tiered stalls, each level fringed by a rail, stepped down the lower half of the sphere to a large dais in the centre of the floor. They were entering through the main doors at the equator of the sphere, around which ran a wide, railed walkway. Steep flights of steps ran down between the banks of stalls to the dais below. The place was packed. Sekkite officers, the magirs of the vessel, tribal dignitaries and arbitors of the warp-faith were filling the stalls, finding places to stand, talking and greeting and exchanging the hand-to-the-mouth salutes. Hundreds of them. Bloody hundreds of them. The weight of the mines packed in his pockets felt like they'd give him away. His mind raced. He was just a packson. All around him were seniors of the Anarch's host. They would know he was too lowly to be present. They would *know*.

The press of bodies carried him forwards. He was forced onto the steps, descending from the equatorial ring into the tiers of stalls. Voices were all around him. Whispers in his ears. He'd lost sight of Holofurnace. The flow of the crowd had separated them. He shot anxious glances, trying not to look jumpy, scanning the stalls around him as they filled. Where was the Space Marine? He saw robed V'heduak giants. Each one was cowled. Was that the Snake there? Was that one?

The air stank of dry dust. Sweat was running down his spine. The whole auditorium was made of human bone: the floor, the steps, the platforms of the tiers. The handrails dividing each ring of stalls were fused from polished human long bones, fashioned not crudely but with precise craftsmanship. He glanced up. The dome above, hazed in the golden candlelight, was a mosaic of skulls. Thousands of them, fixed side by side on concentric shelves, staring out blindly, like some vast ossuary, a catacomb's bone house displaying the relics of the dead. So many staring sockets. So many gaping jaws. The whole ceiling, the whole dome, was solid with yellowed skulls.

He was forced into one of the stalls halfway down the tiered bowl. The Sekkites around him spoke to each other, nudged him impatiently to move along and make room. He ran out of space, boxed in by packson damogaurs and V'heduak giants. He got a place at the rail, gripped it to steady himself, then took his hands away. Bone. He didn't want to hang on to bone.

Below him, the dais was a platform raised on a scaffold of bones, turned, shaped and jointed like the work of the finest cabinet maker: interlocked femurs, some laminated to form thick post uprights, the cross-braces secured with shoulder blades and sacral plates, inlays of carved finger-bones. The railing around the edge of the dais was a basketwork of ribcages supporting a top-rail made of vertebrae carefully matched for size, and fitted together to make one long, continuous spine. The joinery had been done with experienced precision. Everything was polished, and delicately carved and veneered, like an exquisite ivory sculpture. It gleamed, a warm glow.

It was the most appalling thing Mazho had ever seen.

The dais faced the main doors. Behind it, the lower stalls were a reserved quire, the curved bench seats were packed with lekts, the Sekkites' macabre psyker caste. They chattered and gibbered, their mouths covered by hand-print brands. Many were veiled. Mazho could feel the scalding throb of their minds, amplifying the whispers that buzzed and crackled in his ears.

He tried to control his frantic breathing. Iron bars of terror were locking him rigid.

A loud boom caused a temporary hush. The towering excubitors had closed and barred the doors. They took their places amongst the crowds on the equatorial walkway, gazing down, their power lances held upright.

· He was in now. The only way out was shut. It had become a dream that didn't belong to him.

A figure stepped up onto the dais. Mazho had no idea where it had come from. It had just emerged from the crowd packing the auditorium.

It was the Anarch. It was Sek.

Holofurnace found a place to stand at the bone-railing of the equatorial walk. He'd lost Mazho. From under his cowl, he surveyed the tiers below, his acute, post-human eyesight searching for detail. Where was he? Where–

There. Off to the right and down in the thick of it. A tiny figure, packed into an overcrowded stall. The poor damn bastard.

The excubitors were preparing to shut the doors. What of Mkoll and the Saint's man? Had they come back in time? He studied the crowd again. Damogaurs, etogaurs, packson tribunes with tribal standards, a quire of cackling lekts, excubitors, cult shamen, Blood-fare officers and steersmen. The host was still taking its places, thronging the staircases, shuffling into stalls, milling around the base of the obscene dais.

'D'har voi vehen kha,' the V'heduak beside him said, and laughed.

Holofurnace nodded. He knew none of the words. He made a laughing sound and hoped it would be enough.

There. There was Milo. He was moving down one of the staircases, slipping through the crowd. Holofurnace watched. Unnoticed by those around him, Milo paused to re-strap his boot. Just a feint. Holofurnace saw him quickly, furtively slide a small object under the lip of the stall. A mine. Milo rose again. He threaded his way on down the steps.

Good boy.

The Snake scanned the throng. There. And there was Mkoll. Down on the floor beside the dais, moving through the gathering, pausing, looking out into the Oratory as he fished a hand behind his back and anchored a mine to a dais post. Right in plain sight, but no one saw. Mkoll moved with confidence, as if he was supposed to be there.

Mkoll looked up. He'd spotted Holofurnace across the packed chamber. A hunter's sharp eyes. No chance to sign or signal. Just an exchanged nod.

'Voi vehtah sahk!' the V'heduak beside him exclaimed, nudging him.

'Kha,' Holofurnace said.

He'd lost sight of Mkoll. There was Milo again, though. Three-quarters of the way down the stairs. Another casual stoop to adjust his boot. A quick pass, sleight-of-hand. Another mine set, locked in the shadows of a stair riser. Milo rose again. Holofurnace tracked him as he edged into a lower stall. There was Mkoll too. They jostled through the press until they were side by side.

The main doors shut. The excubitor guards stepped to the rail. One pushed in just metres from Holofurnace, a terrible ghoul with stub-horns, taller than any Adeptus Astartes, his ornate lance held proud and straight.

There was a figure on the dais suddenly. The buzzing whispers grew louder.

Sek was here.

A hush fell. They watched him take his place.

'Oh, Throne,' Milo whispered.

Mkoll said nothing.

Fifty metres from them, and higher up, Mazho gazed in silent horror. This wasn't the thing he had glimpsed through the madness of the vortex at Oureppan. It was worse.

A skeletal giant, its skin a mummified and flaking brown stretched taut and paper-thin around its bones. A ragged robe, decayed from centuries in a tomb. A crown of iron spikes. No lower jaw, just a yawning void.

Mazho sank deeper into the numb depths of terror. He tried to mumble a penitential prayer, but he couldn't remember any of the words.

Holofurnace watched too. From the high rail, he saw his enemy in person for the first time. He considered the sheer bulk of the Anarch, the ungodly mass, a lumbering daemon that hauled itself into place. It was female in aspect, throat, shoulders and hunched back fledged in iridescent plumage. A carrion bird's beak, big as a power-claw, snapped and yawned to reveal the blue, rasping dagger of its tongue. A spiked silver crown formed a band above its dozens of glittering eyes. Neon-yellow pupils flashed and shone. It spread its arms, its daemon wings. It possessed a terrible beauty that speared Holofurnace's heart like a cold blade.

He could not look away.

Brin Milo shivered as he watched the magister take his place. Sek was just as he had seen him, the glaring demiurge that had haunted his dreams since the vortex. Upright, strong, with the power and build of an Astartes warrior, clad in black and yellow silks. His head was a bald mass of scar tissue. Black thorns grew from the gnarled flesh of his scalp, surrounding the top of his head like a spiked crown. The tubes and pipes of augmetic support systems knotted the back of his head and neck like vines. His face was a steel mask, sutured in place, a visage of cruel angles and sharp lines. Filthy light shone from the eye slits and the yawning, down-turned mouth. A chrome vox-mic, the tannoy speaker from some battle-engine, was fixed to his chest-plate and positioned so that the caged disc was set in front of his mouth.

Sek was about to speak.

Mkoll gazed, eyes narrowed, his gorge rising. This was the foe at last, barely six metres away. All that power, all that authority, invested in such a wretched thing. It came as little surprise. Mkoll thought of Macaroth. For all that great Macaroth was Warmaster, commander of crusading hosts, they said he was just a man too, an ordinary man of flesh and blood, of weaknesses and flaws, just another mortal who happened to wield the greatest authority in the sector.

Anakwanar Sek was just a man. An old man, run to fat, of average height and sloping build. His robes were filthy and lacquered with grease. His hands were cased in shining silver gauntlets, clawed and segmented master-pieces of antique armour that he had stolen from some corpse, and wore to boast he was a figure of great importance. He looked like a gutter-gang vaga-bond who had chosen to wear ill-fitting, polished, regal boots he'd looted from the body of a high-hive noble. His body twitched with a palsy. His skin was scabbed and diseased. Mkoll couldn't see his face because Sek, with one ostentatiously gloved hand, was holding up a cracked porcelain mask on a slender stick. The top of the stick was fashioned into a golden hand that wrapped across the mask's mouth. Some twitching darkness lurked behind the serene mask.

Just a man. Just a vile old man. Mkoll could kill that.

The ceaseless chattering of the lekt quire increased. A buffet of psyker force welling out across the Oratory. Everyone winced, all of the Sekkite seniors and four Imperial interlopers lurking amongst them.

'Let my voice drown out all others,' the lekts hissed in unison. Now the constant, scratching whispers wove together into one set of words.

'Anarch I am. Anarch of all,' the lekts sang.

The host roared, shaking their fists, saluting, fingers to their lips.

'All that was set in place has come to its conclusion,' the quire hissed as the roars died back. 'This night and the next day. My hours. My awaited moment, long foreseen. Those who hold the key of victory will pass to me what has always been mine.'

'He's saying,' Mkoll whispered, '...he's saying the enkil vahakan, "those who hold the key of victory"...'

'I understand,' Milo whispered back, unable to tear his gaze from the dais. 'I understand what he's saying.'

'But he's speaking in the Sekkite tongue...' Mkoll hissed.

'No, he's not.' Milo replied. 'I understand every word. He's declaring victory.'

The unclean voices of lekts swelled in exultation.

'I have sent the blessed reworked,' they announced.

The host roared again. 'Qimurah! Qimurah! Qimurah!'

'The blessed reworked, all eight times eight, have slipped like a skzerret's blade into the heart of the foe,' the lekts chorused. 'By dawn, they will be returned to the sound of my voice. They will bring the Enkil Vehk, the key that was shamelessly stolen from me. This will be the victory I have pur-sued. The key will open the way. The key will sunder the stars. No one, no corpse-emperor, no Throne warrior, no false angel, no... not even any bold magir or preening Gaur... will stand in the fury of my wrath. The Archonate will prevail, reworked in glory. Anarch I am.'

The host roared again. A chant began. 'Sek! Sek! Sek! Sek!'

Mazho saw the mummified titan raise a tattered hand for silence. Holofurnace saw an ethereal wing sweep for order. Milo flinched as the demiurge lifted his fist, compelling attention. Mkoll saw a silver gauntlet gesture, bidding them to indulge him a moment more.

'For the plague of Terra is beheaded this night,' the lekts proclaimed. 'While the blessed reworked perform their holy ministry, I have unleashed woe upon the place called Eltath. The Herit ver Tenebal Mor. The Heritor's bad shadow falls across the ground. The enkil vahakan will perish, all. All their chieftains. All their warlords. The crusaders of the corpse-prophet, so long a plague upon our realm, will be emasculated. Their order lost. Their authority annihilated. By dawn, this will be finished. The plague of Terra will break, as a fever breaks, lost and leaderless, and from tomorrow they will scatter, hopeless and afeared, into the farthest stars, and we will drive them before us, shattered, humiliated and put to rout.'

The host howled. The Sekkite Sons drummed on the handrails. They turned to one another in raptures, clasping hands and embracing.

Mazho gasped as the damogaur beside him turned, yelling, and hugged him.

'Dahak enkil voi sahh, magir!' the officer shouted in his ear. Mazho could smell his sweat, the stink of his breath.

'Dahak enkil?' the man asked, breaking the embrace and looking at Mazho, puzzled. 'Dahak enkil voi?' Mazho could barely hear him over the chanting. He didn't understand the words anyway. He turned aside, pretending he was eager to congratulate the man to his left.

The damogaur seized him by the shoulder and turned him back. He gripped Mazho by the chin-strap and tilted his head, peering in under the helmet's brim at Mazho's eyes.

'Sp-ecta-kles?' he said, not understanding.

Up at the high rail, Holofurnace was trying to keep Colonel Mazho in sight through the forest of pumping fists and swaying banners. He glimpsed Mazho turning, a damogaur grabbing him by the face.

It was time. He threw back the folds of his borrowed robes.

'Sp-ecta-kles?' the damogaur hissed into Mazho's face. Angry understanding flushed his face.

'Pheguth!' he snarled.

'Fourth Light Cinder Storm!' Mazho replied, and punched his skzerret into the damogaur's chest. For a moment, no one around him realised anything was wrong. The cheering was too intense. The damogaur slumped, held upright by the tight-packed bodies.

Then gunfire ripped down from the equatorial walk.

Holofurnace had swept out the heavy sentry gun and opened fire, feeding the belt with his left hand. Hot shell cases bounced off the startled Sekkites at the rail beside him. The shots raked down the steep tiered bank of the

Oratory, the first bursts killing cheering Sons in the front two rows. The .20 was not a sophisticated gun and, despite his strength, Holofurnace was not assisted by the automatic balancing, levelling and aiming systems of his Astartes armour.

He corrected by eye. His second and third bursts ripped across the dais.

He saw the winged daemon stagger, its golden armour puncturing. Scraps of white feather billowed into the air. Parts of the guard rail and dais platform splintered in showers of bone shards.

The massed cheering swelled and changed as one noise, becoming panic and howls of astonished horror.

Milo saw the towering demiurge shudder and reel, blood bursting from his black and yellow robes. He swung up his carbine, and blasted point blank into the Sekkites to his right, brutally clearing a space in the stall, then turned and blazed on full auto at the dais.

Mkoll vaulted the guardrail, the sirdar's long-nosed autopistol in his hand, and landed on the bone steps. Men were already bolting from the stalls all around him in blind panic. He kicked a packson out of his way, sending the Sekkite tumbling down the stairs, and gunned down another two who came clawing for him. Then he ran down the steps towards the Oratory floor, firing as he went, zipping hard rounds across the ducking bodies in the stalls. He saw them hit. He saw the old man jerk as bullets smacked into his greasy robes. He saw blood. The porcelain mask slipped down. Mkoll glimpsed some vast and writhing maw where the old man's face should have been. It yawned in pain and shock.

Mazho tried to get his carbine raised clear. Everyone was shouting and screaming. The lekt quire screeched in agony.

'For Urdesh!' he yelled. 'For Urdesh! Cinder Storm!'

He tried to aim. The Sekkites in the stall fell on him from all sides, clawing and grappling. Mazho went down under the weight of them. A raging V'heduak wrenched the weapon from his hands. A packson hit him across the face so hard it broke his cheekbone and knocked his helmet askew. He lost his spectacles. The world became a blur of raining fists and screaming faces.

He disappeared beneath the berserk mob. His bones cracked and snapped as they kicked at him, and stamped on his helpless form.

The vicious, murderous beating jolted one of the ageing anchor mines. It went off, tripping the other two simultaneously.

The combined blast tore out the mid-section of the stalls, billowing out in a fierce, searing firestorm. Those closest to Mazho, including his frenzied tormentors, were vaporised instantly. Others were thrown headlong into the air, tumbling and falling on the rows below. Chunks of cracked ivory scattered like kindling.

The blast shook the entire Oratory. It rocked Holofurnace back. He had hosed almost all his ammunition at the dais. The feathered witch-thing had fallen to its knees, writhing, soaked in blood. Some of the quire were dead too, mown down in their seats by overshot.

The crowd around him grabbed at him, tearing his robes. He shook them off. He swung a fist that broke a packson's neck. He grabbed a clawing V'heduak chieftain by the throat and hurled him over the rail.

'Ithaka!' he roared, using the name of his homeworld as a curse of defiance. An excubitor lunged at him, swinging his power lance. Holofurnace jerked clear, and the lance's long blade splintered the bone guardrail. He put the rest of his ammunition through the excubitor's face, blowing the fiend's skull apart.

The belt was out. He brandished the sentry gun like a cudgel, cracking skulls and knocking Sekkites into the stalls below. Several las-rounds hit him in the lower back, shunting him forwards.

Milo's first mine went off, annihilating a section of staircase in a blizzard of fire and bone shrapnel. The second mine detonated an instant later, obliterating another section of the staircase further down, and rippling flames along two blocks of stalls. Sekkites staggered, blundering, blinded, their clothing on fire.

The mine Mkoll had fixed to the dais fired, destroying half the spine railing and causing the entire platform to slump sideways. Upwashed flame boiled across the Anarch's flailing figure.

Mkoll was near the bottom of the staircase. The blast shock knocked him off his feet. A body fell across him. He struggled to get the dead weight off his legs.

Milo saw Mkoll go down. He wanted to rain more fire at the Anarch, but Sekkites were rushing him from all sides. He switched furiously from target to target, chopping each one down as they came at him. Cinders and burning ash drifted around him like snow.

The exterior mines went off in a quick, staggered, uneven series of muffled roars. The Oratory rattled in its socket. Men sprawled off their feet. Dislodged skulls rained down from the dome, shattering like pottery on the floor and stalls beneath. Flames surged up in a dozen places around the dais and the lower stalls.

Gripping the rail, the Anarch hauled himself upright, braced against the drunken slope of the damaged dais. His maw uttered a roar of rage, and the remaining lekts echoed it in shrill chorus.

He had been betrayed. Deceived. Wounded in his own sanctum. His victory would only matter if he survived to see it.

Sek howled again. The uncouth noise of his voice drowned out everything around him. Some Sekkites simply fell dead, ears and brains pulped by the volume of his wrath.

He tore off his silver gauntlets and bared his hands. He focused his magisterial powers, invoking the dark eminences of the outer warp that he served. The quire took up his supplication, chanting words and conjurations that pre-dated mankind. The Saint had wounded him at Oureppan, and drained his psykomantic potency. He channelled all he had left to preserve himself.

The immaterium flexed, splitting the air around him. Foul winds sucked and screeched. Tendrils of yellow lightning flickered around his gesturing hands.

He was opening a gate to flee. He was folding the curtain of the warp aside through willpower alone, gouging through the subspace membranes, and throwing wide a door to step through into safety.

Milo saw reality bending around the demiurge. Another vortex. Smaller than the one at Oureppan that Sek had opened to destroy the Beati, less controlled, less stable. But a doorway all the same. A way out.

Milo yelled out, rushing forwards, hands grabbing at him from all sides, pulling him down.

Mkoll ran towards the burning dais, emptying the last of his autopistol's clip into the Anarch's back. They had to stop him. That had been the point of everything. They had to kill him here, now, before he slipped away and became invisible and untraceable for another decade or more.

Holofurnace punched a raving etogaur aside and grabbed the dead excubitor's fallen power lance. Other excubitors were rushing at him, lances raised to strike.

The lance was long and heavy, more a halberd than a spear. Its blade tip was as wide as a cleaver and as long as a tactical gladius. Its weight and balance were poor.

But it was not so different from the wyrm-spears he had learned to handle back on Ithaka.

He pulled it back, right arm crooked, left extended before him, the lance horizontal beside his face. He saw Mkoll, far below, skzerret in hand, clambering onto the dais to grab at the fleeing magister.

The Tanith huntsman had been right. It had come down to straight silver at the last.

To bare blades.

Holofurnace let his fly. The cast was good. The shaft flew as true as a sea-lance. He saw it strike, slicing into the Anarch's back, driving deep, cutting through, transfixing the daemon's feathered torso.

He saw the daemon stumble forwards. He saw the subspace gate shatter, unfurl and then collapse in a wash of obscene light.

The excubitors fell on him, striking him down with hacking, butchering blows. He fought at them, clawing and punching. Their hands were on him, inhumanly strong, pinning him, gripping him. He could not break free.

Holofurnace looked up, blood streaming down his face, and met the eyes of the excubitor who would end him.

'Vahooth voi sehn!' the excubitor screamed as he brought the lance blade down.

'Ithaka!' Holofurnace replied with the last breath he would ever take.

TWENTY

BLOOD FOR BLOOD

Gaunt and Baskevyl bounded up the undercroft steps with Blenner trailing behind them.

'Grae!' Gaunt yelled.

Colonel Grae and his complement of Urdeshi field troops were milling in the lamplit hallway, clutching their weapons and looking up in dismay at the sounds of destruction rumbling through the palace above them.

'What is this, my lord?' Grae asked.

'Another one,' said Gaunt. 'Another woe machine. Stronger than the first. Is the palace evacuated?'

Grae shook his head.

'We'd barely begun,' he said. 'The power has only just been restor-'

Gaunt pushed past him. 'Where's the Warmaster?'

'I don't know,' Grae called, hurrying after him. 'I think, still on site.'

'Dammit, Barthol,' Gaunt murmured. He looked at Grae. 'And the Beati?'

'Taken above,' said Grae. 'The medicae have her-'

'It's loose in the palace,' said Gaunt. 'Up there. Hunting for every target it can find. It'll be seeking out Macaroth, the Saint... that's its purpose.'

'How do we stop it, my lord?' Grae asked.

Gaunt was already running up the steps into the main hall of the wing.

'I don't know if we do,' he said. 'I've seen it.'

'It's an abomination,' Baskevyl said to Grae. He shrugged at the intelligence officer. 'This night has been long enough, I think.'

'Don't go up there!' Blenner wailed from behind them. 'Fething hide!'

'The best we can hope is to slow it down,' Gaunt told Grae. 'Buy any time we can to get Macaroth and the Beati clear.'

'And *you*, sir, surely?' said Grae.

'Where did my daughter go?' Gaunt asked.

'Quartered with the Saint,' said Grae. 'The chapel. That's where she was taken. All the survivors-'

Gaunt looked down the steps at the Urdeshi troops.

'All of you, with me,' he said.

'You heard the Lord Executor!' Baskevyl yelled.

They swept into the main hallway, Baskevyl forming the Urdeshi into firing lines at Gaunt's heels. Grae and Blenner ran after them. Broken glass littered the floor. Gaunt could smell burning. He could hear the rip and chatter of gunfire, and then the answering wail of a blade on a whetting wheel.

Palace staff stumbled past in the opposite direction, fleeing, panicked. Some were injured and bleeding.

'Don't go that way!' one man yelled.

'Get clear! Get out!' Gaunt told him as he ran past. Gaunt didn't break stride. Sword in one hand, bolt pistol in the other, he stormed down the long hall towards the source of the uproar.

He slowed as he felt the ground beginning to shake.

The wall ahead disintegrated in a shower of stone and dust. The woe machine revealed itself, a floating octahedron of grating, sliding blades locked around an inner glow.

It came towards them slowly, shrieking its metal-on-metal cry.

Three of the Urdeshi dropped their weapons and fled.

'Line! Line!' Gaunt yelled.

'Keep that line!' Baskevyl bawled at the Urdeshi. The troops formed up, clattering their weapons to their shoulders, aiming.

'Grenades ready!' Gaunt yelled.

He heard the troopers slot and lock their under-barrel launchers.

'Hold!' Gaunt ordered.

The woe machine purred closer. The blades at the tip of its form began to spin and open out, blooming like a barbed flower, yellow light shining out of it.

'Dalin!' Gaunt called out. He hoped there'd be a response, some vestigial flicker of recognition as there had been before.

But he doubted it.

And none came. The wailing note simply began to rise into a squeal of wet fingers on glass.

'Commence fire!' Gaunt ordered. Eyes narrowed, he began to blast at the cloud of whirling blades with his bolt pistol. Either side of him, the Urdeshi opened up, training rapid, accurate fire from their lasrifles. Baskevyl ripped bursts of full auto from his own rifle, and Grae blazed with his service pistol. Blenner, a few steps behind him, stood empty-handed, gazing at the advancing horror.

The sustained fire flickered and danced across the woe machine: the fiery bursts of Gaunt's heavy shots, the flash and spark of the assault weapon barrage. Spinning black blades shattered, and were instantly replaced.

The woe machine started to spit blades. The razored darts pulsed from its rotating central mass almost silently. An Urdeshi screamed and dropped, a blade skewering his thigh. Another toppled back with a blade transfixing his head. Grae grunted and slammed against the wall, a leaf of black metal embedded in his shoulder. Gaunt felt one slice through the meat of his upper arm as it whizzed past. He put three more bolt-rounds into the thing's cycling maw.

'Fall back, slow!' Gaunt ordered. 'Draw it this way! Maintain fire!'

They took a step back, then two, weapons blazing. The woe machine stirred forwards. In unison, all the blades on the front half of its form scissored around to point at them. It was about to loose them en masse in a pelting hail of knives that would murder the entire squad line.

Gaunt saw figures moving behind the woe machine at the far end of the hall. He heard a firm, clear voice calling for squad discipline.

Van Voytz. Kazader. A damn company of Urdesh Heavy Infantry. Storm troops. The notorious 17th.

Gaunt's micro-bead crackled.

'Get your arses out of the line of fire if you please, Lord Executor,' Van Voytz said.

'Cover, now!' Gaunt yelled. His men scattered, heading for doorways and side rooms. Two of them dragged the trooper with the skewered leg clear. Baskevyl had to grab Blenner and almost lift him out of the way.

The storm troops began their blitz. Their methods were not subtle. Hellgun fire. Rotator cannons. Support las on man-portable rigs. The heavily armoured shock troops advanced down the long hall, demolishing the floor, the ceiling, the plasterwork, the panelling; pinning the woe machine in a kill-storm of destruction, a focused barrage that had seen the 17th drive through Arch-enemy lines, fortified positions, and even light armour opposition.

Churning black blades broke and shattered. The light inside the woe machine flickered, straining. It recoiled, stung hard, and with one rushing clatter, the sound of a thousand swords being drawn at once, it switched the angle of all its blades to face the steadily advancing Urdeshi.

'Heard you needed some support,' Gaunt heard Van Voytz chuckle over the link.

'Appreciated, lord general,' he replied.

'Down payment on my debt, Bram,' said Van Voytz. *'For Jago–'*

'Just kill it, Barthol,' said Gaunt.

The woe machine began to spur forwards to meet the oncoming storm troops. The Urdeshi didn't waver. One step after another, resolute, they marched at it, burning through their ammunition to blow it apart.

'Grenades!' Gaunt called out. 'Give it grenades while its focus is drawn!'

Grae's Urdeshi Light swung out of their meagre cover. Their under-barrel launchers popped with hollow thumps. Krak grenades, arced in with prac-tised skill, dropped on and around the Heritor's weapon.

The blasts came rapidly, an overlapping ripple of hard concussions. Troopers at both ends of the long hall rocked back as the shockwaves pum-melled them. A cluster of fireballs pounded through the space occupied by the woe machine, choking the hall with surging flames.

The woe machine shrieked. Its geometric rotations disintegrated, cohe-sion lost. Blades whirled out of alignment, crossing, colliding, snapping against one another.

The pattern broke. Black metal fragments spun out of the fire-wash like the vanes of a rupturing turbine engine. Stray blades augured into the walls, the floor and straight up into the ceiling. Most stuck fast, buried like arrows in the stone.

The woe machine had become unwound, thrown apart by its own cycling motion.

'Again!' Gaunt yelled. The Urdeshi around him re-slotted and locked. They raised their weapons to fire and deliver extinction.

But the woe machine was not dead. Its circling ribbon of blades, some broken or chipped, rose out of the flames in a strained and elongated figure-eight noose, looping out wide like a thrown lasso.

It was enraged. It was hurt. It wanted to flee.

It took the shortest route.

It went through the storm troops.

Baskevyl gazed in horror as the armoured men began to drop. Like wooden skittles slammed down in one strike, they rocked and fell, every one of them cut through a dozen times. Blood squirted from deep, scalpel-clean wounds, or poured out between the joints of their ballistic plate.

Screaming, its circling blades wide-spaced and overtaxed, the woe machine cut a hole through the end of the long hall and vanished.

Gaunt, Baskevyl and some of Grae's Urdeshi hurried through the long stretch of scorched and burning devastation to reach the 17th's half of the hall.

The storm troops lay in a carpet of bodies across the wide floor. Few of them were intact. Gaunt stepped over severed limbs and heavy weapons cut cleanly in two. There was blood underfoot, a broad pool of it, and speckles of blood-spatter covered the white-washed walls on either side.

Kazader was dead, his left arm split at the wrist and bicep. Half of his face was simply missing.

Van Voytz was still alive when Gaunt reached him.

He was on his back, staring at the ceiling. Gaunt could see his wounds were not survivable. Van Voytz was aspirating blood, bright red drops that dappled his cheeks and chin like a freckled birth mark.

Gaunt knelt down.

'Barthol–'

Van Voytz blinked, unable to focus. He groaned, blood gurgling in his throat like phlegm.

'Am I dead, Bram?' he mumbled.

'You are, my lord.'

'Well… shit,' Van Voytz said, his voice drowning and bubbling. 'That's payment in full, then. Eh? Blood for blood.'

'Stay still, Barthol. We'll fetch a chaplain. An ayatani or–'

'I don't need absolution, Gaunt,' Van Voytz gurgled. He was still staring blindly at the ceiling. 'Made my peace, long since. Just loyalty to prove, if late in the day.'

'You had nothing to prove, lord general.'

'Hnh. Late in the day. Always so dark at this hour. I knew, when it came for me, it would come in the slow hours–'

A slackness softened his face and body, the rigidity of pain released by the oblivion.

He was gone.

The night was wretchedly black.

In the small watch room of the Plade Parish vapour mill, the night watchman dozed across his console, stirring every now and then to wipe drool from his mouth. A single lamp burned, his only comfort. Rain beat against the room's broad window ports, a blur of streaming water.

Nade Oysten appeared at the window, soaked through and out of breath. She yelled at him. He didn't stir. The watch room was sealed and soundproof against the thunder of the mill when its turbines cycled every two hours.

She beat on the glass, yelling, hands flat and frantic. Her mouth moved silently. The thick glass just flexed slightly in its frame.

The watchman dreamed on.

Oysten tried the door, yanking at it, screaming silent profanities. It was locked.

She stepped back, defeated, and stared through the windows for a moment at the slumbering man. The rain had washed Rawne's blood off her face.

She raised her cut-down riot gun, reached into her bag of shells, and loaded a breaching round. She stepped back, almost vanishing from view.

The big flash was silent.

The damage was not. The window in the door blew in with a smash like a dozen lead-crystal decanters hitting a stone floor. The metal door ruptured in its frame, and buckled, its handle and lock torn out in one lump that sailed clear across the room.

The watchman hurtled awake, yelping, blinking and confused.

Oysten kicked open the ruined door and stepped in out of the rain.

She glared at him.

'Wha– wha–' he stammered.

'You have a fething vox somewhere, you idle fething ball-bag,' she said. 'Where the feth is it?'

The sun had risen thirty minutes ago, though it was still an hour before dawn half a world away in Eltath.

Orchidel Island, a flat rock of wind-swept salt-scrub and gritty beaches, lay at the southern end of the Faroppan archipelago. Few came there. It was a long way from the volcanic systems that fired Urdesh's precious forges.

Once in a while, agriboats passed by, heading for the rich, offshore blooms in the southern ocean during the late summer algae season.

It was not late summer. No boat had passed by in six months.

The sky was clear, a soft grey-green. No cloud. Visibility out ten kilometres across the breakwaters. The waves rolled in along the broad shingle beach, hushing on the stones as it had done since the world was born.

Ten metres from the shore, the air blistered with a noise like spitting fat. For a few seconds, reality wrenched open and debris crashed out into the shallows. Smoke billowed with it. The scent of burning bone that the wind swiftly carried away. For a moment, the beach rang with the echoes of a distant, shrieking quire.

Then space closed again with a sledgehammer thump, an implosion of pressure so fierce, the sea beneath withdrew briefly, baring its bed of silt and algae-crusted stones.

Then rushed back in, and all was as it had been before.

A ragged figure stirred, half-swamped in the rolling waves. He crawled and clawed his way up the beach, the waves breaking around him in crossing plumes of foam.

Sek paused, panting, on his hands and knees, his feet in the water, blood trailing from his wheezing mouth onto the shingle. He was soaked through, engulfed in the pain of his wounds, and maimed by the violence of the translation. His power was reduced to an ember. It had taken everything to break away and escape to this remote and unregarded spot.

He crawled on, the shingle crunching and scattering under his hands. Clear of the water, he rose to his knees, reached back, and slowly drew out the power lance that skewered his torso. He gasped with the effort, and dropped the weapon on the beach beside him.

Out in the breakers, metres from the beach, Mkoll floated, rocked by the surging waves. He was gazing up at the sky. Daylight. A dawn. He knew he should move. That he *had* to move. He knew he had come there to finish something.

But his memory was vacant. He couldn't remember anything. He had no idea why he was floating on his back in a cold sea, or how he had come to be there. His body was numb from the savage trauma of subspace bilocation, a process few mortals would ever choose to endure, even when armoured or cushioned by protective invocations.

He let the sea lift him and drop him, over-and-over, the soothing motion of the breakers.

Someone waded past him, staggering and splashing. A shadow blotted out the sky.

Milo reached down and clawed at Mkoll's jacket, searching his pockets. He found the two grenades. One smoke, which he tossed aside.

One anti-personnel.

He gripped it, and waded ashore, teeth clenched, dazed and staggering. The Anarch was just ahead of him, crawling on his hands and knees. No demiurge now, no towering god. An old man in tattered robes, wounded in a dozen places, blood spotting the grey and green pebbles in a trail behind him.

Panting, unsteady, Milo reached him.

He grabbed Sek by the shoulder and threw him over, rolling him onto his back. The Anarch whined, and winced in pain.

He looked up at Brin Milo.

Milo stared down.

The old man had no face. Small eye sockets gazed up at the Tanith soldier. Beneath them, the rest of his face was a gaping hole. It was fringed with writhing, jointed claws like tiny human fingers. They twitched, holding the gaping mouth wide. Inside the maw was an endless blackness that the morning light could not illuminate. There was nothing in the blackness except the voice.

Enkil vahakan, it said.

The words buzzed at Milo's ears, making him flinch.

'You've said enough,' Milo whispered. 'You've spoken all you have to speak. It's time for silence.'

He dropped astride the old man's chest, pinning him to the loose shingle. Sek tried to fend him off, beating at him with his bare hands.

Milo fended the blows away. He clenched his fist around the grenade, thumbed out the pin, and stuffed his hand into the yawning maw.

Sek thrashed, choking. Milo held on, shoving his hand deeper.

Sek refused to submit. A surge of neon light lit his empty sockets. He hurled Milo off him.

Milo landed badly, rolling, spraying pebbles. The grenade flew out of his hand, and bounced across the shingle. He tried to scramble clear.

The grenade detonated. It threw up a cone of flame and rained shingle in all directions. Milo was half caught by the blast and flung across the beach, dazed and limp.

He tried to rise, his ears ringing, his head spinning. He slumped down on his side.

Anakwanar Sek rose to his feet slowly. It took effort to get up. He clutched at his wounds, blood dribbling from the damage his foes had inflicted.

His maw-fingers twitched and fidgeted.

He had picked up the power lance. For a moment, he leaned on it, panting, using it like a staff to support his weary weight. He stared at the fallen warrior who had almost killed him. Milo wasn't moving.

Sek stood up straight. He raised the lance, and spun it slowly with both hands in a skilled figure around his body that betrayed the weapon skills of his early years as a damogaur in the Archon's host, four centuries past.

He brought the lance to his shoulder, haft up and back behind his head, blade tipped down, hands clasped and spaced for an expert down-strike.

This man would die first. He would be the first mark of Sek's vengeance. Others would follow, one-by-one, then scores, then hundreds, then thousands, then millions.

He would make them pay for his defeat. He would make the corpse-prophet's minions pay, until they wished that he had won at Urdesh so that suffering would not be multiplied a thousandfold upon their defiant kind.

He thrust.

A boot drove into his ribs, knocking him sideways and making him gasp with pain.

Another man had come.

Then *two* would die first.

Sek steadied himself and swung the lance.

Mkoll leapt back. The shingle squirmed under his boots. The lance blade lopped the air. Sek twisted and re-addressed, feet braced, looping the lance around to jab.

Mkoll danced clear. He dodged the next swing. He hunched low, a fighting stance, the skzerret in his hand. Not straight silver, but it would do.

Sek stamped forwards, scything the blade. He had speed and finesse for a wounded old man. He had strength.

Mkoll sidestepped. As Sek passed him, he slashed with the knife, and tore a deep gash along Sek's upper arm.

Sek snarled. Mkoll felt the buzzing swarm into his ears. The Anarch lost the grip of one hand, blood weeping down his arm, but he kept his footing, and rotated the lance with frightening skill, spinning it in his right hand.

He lunged, then lunged again, forcing Mkoll backwards up the beach away from Milo's prone form. He returned to a double-grip, blood-wet hands sliding on the lance's haft. He speared at Mkoll.

Mkoll feinted right, avoiding the lethal strike. He punched in low with his left fist, cracking ribs, and as Sek hunched, followed with his right and slammed the dagger into the Anarch's chest.

Sek flailed backwards. He dropped the lance. The air throbbed with the buzzing whisper of his cries. Mkoll came on, relentless, stabbing twice more with the serrated blade. Blood stippled his face as he pulled the blade out with each strike, ready to repeat it.

Sek fell on his back.

Swaying, Mkoll knelt down to finish the kill.

He ran the blade in where the heart should be. Sek shivered and convulsed.

His right hand snatched up, scattering pebbles, and clamped around Mkoll's throat. Mkoll gasped, his air cut off. The Anarch squeezed. Frail neon light blazed in his dark orbits.

Sek would not die. *He would not die.*

Kater Holofurnace had been right all along.

Blades were never going to be enough. Anarch Sek was a magister. A man like Oan Mkoll, just a mortal man, was never going to carry enough punch to finish a monster like the Anarch.

Mkoll's vision dimmed. Blood pounded in his head. The strangling grip around his throat tightened. His wet clothes clung to him. He felt a dead weight in his jacket pocket.

Unable to break the grip that was killing him, Mkoll let go of the knife and pulled the anchor mine out of his coat.

It was the last one remaining, the one they hadn't used because its anchor pad was broken and refused to grip.

Mkoll had seen what Milo had tried to do. He rammed the anchor mine into Sek's hissing maw.

Sek gagged. He let go. Mkoll scrambled backwards, kicking up stones, retching and gasping.

Sek writhed, choking, trying to disgorge the mine from his mouth. He sat up, and rolled onto his knees, kneeling for a moment, clawing at his mouth.

The mine went off.

Foul tissue and liquid sheeted in all directions.

Mkoll sat up, blinking away the blood in his eyes. Gore plastered him and the shingle in a two metre radius around the Anarch's body.

Sek was still kneeling. His hands had flopped in his lap. He was gone from the shoulders up, smoke fuming from the massive blackened wound and a charred stump of protruding spine.

Mkoll raised his fingers to his lips and blew a goodbye kiss to mock the Sekkite salute.

The whispering had stopped.

TWENTY-ONE

MANY, MANY ARE THE DEAD

People fled past the chapel door in terror. The sounds of battle and destruction from the floors below were like an approaching nightmare.

Hark looked in through the door as people hurried by behind him.

'Clear out!' he yelled. 'Come on! It's coming this way! Head to the west exit. There are destriers on the landing field! Move, now! This is a full evacuation! If you can't make the carriers, get out of the building and hide!'

'You heard him!' Beltayn shouted. 'Don't dawdle now!'

Most of the retinue and the other survivors who had packed into the chapel had already fled. The remainder were too badly wounded, or still too deep in shock to understand what was happening.

'You have to leave!' Beltayn yelled. 'This thing is killing as it goes! It's just... just blades! Many, many are the dead!'

A few of them struggled to their feet and stumbled blankly towards the door. They had already suffered immeasurably that night. It was hard for them to comprehend that anything could be worse.

Beltayn steered them out.

'Go! go!' he yelled.

'Take her! Bel, take her!' Merity shouted, pointing to an old woman from the retinue who was staring numbly at nothing.

Beltayn ran to the woman, and got her on her feet, gently guiding her by the shoulder and the hand.

'You too, Mam Chass,' he said.

'We're coming,' Merity called back. Two stretcher cases remained, unconscious, and too injured to walk even if they'd been awake.

Merity and Fazekiel crossed to them as Beltayn led the old woman out.

'We can't carry both,' Merity said.

'Then this one first,' said Fazekiel. 'We'll come back for the other one.'

Merity nodded. 'Come back? There's a prospect. All right, take that end.'

'I can help,' said Meryn.

They looked at him. He'd come from nowhere. His face was sallow with fear.

'Get some help, then, captain,' said Fazekiel. 'Another bearer, anyone, and we can carry them both.'

'No,' said Meryn. 'You take that one. I'll shoulder-lift the other. There's no time to be lost.'

'All right,' said Fazekiel, turning to grip the stretcher's handles. 'I appreciate your help.'

Meryn nodded. 'Help,' he muttered. 'That's right. A night like this, it's time to help yourself.'

'What?' Fazekiel snapped.

Meryn ran his straight silver into Fazekiel's back. She gasped, and fell backwards as the blade came out again.

Merity stared at Meryn.

'Oh, feth,' she said.

Beltayn gently escorted the old woman along the panelled hall, passing the wardroom and then the chamber door where Hark stood with Laksheema and Auerben.

'Get her clear, Bel,' said Hark.

'I will, sir.'

'Everybody out?'

'Almost!'

'Then get out yourself. We'll do the rest.'

Beltayn nodded, and hurried on his way. Hark turned to his companions.

'How will we do the rest, do you suggest?' Auerben asked.

Hark grunted. He pushed past them and entered the chamber. The medicae staff had been ordered out, but Curth still tended the Saint. Zweil sat nearby, hands clasped, murmuring a prayer.

The eagle perched on the back of a chair.

'The feth's that doing in here?' Hark asked.

'Not high on my list of priorities,' replied Curth, without looking up from her work.

'The thing's coming, Ana,' he said. 'Coming right for us. We have to move her.'

'Well, we can't,' said Curth. 'She's barely hanging on. I believe she's healing her psychic wounds, or something is, but it's slow and it's uncertain. If we move her, she will die.'

'Then... then we have to leave her,' said Hark.

Zweil shot him a toxic look.

'Absolutely not,' said Curth. 'I'll stay with her.'

'Me too,' said the old priest.

Hark sighed. 'I bloody knew you'd say that,' he said.

'You're not going either, are you?' asked Zweil.

'No,' Hark admitted.

He turned back to the doorway.

'We make a stand here,' he said.

'I was already planning to,' rasped Auerben. She had a lasrifle in her hands.

Hark nodded. He pulled out his hold-out gun.

'We make a stand with that?' Laksheema asked, looking at the small weapon dubiously.

'It's not about size,' said Hark. 'No, I'm lying. Right now, a tank would be good. I feel you've got something effective up your sleeve, inquisitor. And I don't mean that metaphorically.'

Laksheema raised her right wrist. The lamplight glittered off her ornate bangle.

'Antimat disruptor,' she said. 'Xenos manufacture. Very small, but size isn't everything, as you say. I used to believe these could stop anything. But I burned out the other one on the first machine.'

'It's better than nothing,' said Hark.

They took up station in the doorway. The wailing swish of blades was coming closer.

Merity backed away from Meryn very slowly. The candles in the chapel flickered.

'What did you tell her, eh?' he hissed. He glanced down at Fazekiel. 'Don't worry, I know. I'm a Ghost. I read lips for a living.'

'What the hell are you doing?' asked Merity.

'Taking advantage of an opportunity,' Meryn replied. 'You heard Bel. Many, many are the dead, like the old song goes. All cut up to ribbons. Death's everywhere. Who knows what the final body count will be? Who knows what dirty little secrets will die with the dead tonight?'

'Meryn... Flyn...'

'Don't Flyn me,' he said. 'You've got me good. But some secrets are meant to stay secrets, you see.'

'I think you might have gone fething mad, captain,' Merity said.

'I think I'm perfectly sane,' he replied. 'I'll take my chances. I'm quick on my feet. A little straight silver, and my secret's safe. I'll be gone, out there, in a destrier, running clear. What are two more corpses in a bloodbath like this?'

He stepped closer. She backed up. He smiled. Her eyes darted around. Relf's carbine lay on a cot nearby.

He saw where she had looked.

'Don't even,' he said.

Merity faked right then darted left for the cot. Meryn lunged at her, missing by a slim margin.

Merity forward-rolled across the cot, just as she had been taught in the relentless basic training drills aboard the *Armaduke*, back when she'd been a novice trooper called Felyx Chass.

She came up gripping the carbine. She aimed it at him with a grin. Then her face fell.

Meryn was aiming back at her. He'd snatched up Fazekiel's pistol from the medicae cart.

'Drop the carbine,' he said. 'I'd rather do this quietly. People might question gunshot wounds.'

'Let them question,' said Merity. 'You bastard.'

Meryn fired. The gun clacked, empty. *I don't think I can protect you again.* He remembered Fazekiel saying that, down in the undercroft.

The stupid bitch had meant she'd used up all her ammo.

He threw himself at Merity, the war-knife slicing in.

The carbine bucked in her hands. The muzzle flare was intensely bright in the gloomy chapel.

Rapid fire shots tore into Meryn, puncturing his torso six times and shredding off his left arm at the elbow.

The final two went into his face, destroying his look of indignant surprise.

'Gunfire,' murmured Hark.

'Las,' agreed Auerben.

'It was close,' said Hark. 'Sounded close. Throne, it must be nearby now.' He glanced back at Curth and Zweil, vigilant at the Saint's side. He smelled, very faintly, the scent of islumbine. He put it down to his frantic imagination. But the idea reassured him.

'I can hear it wailing,' said Laksheema.

'I told you it was close,' said Hark.

'Very close,' the inquisitor replied. 'So why can't we see it?'

'What are you showing me?' asked Marshal Tzara above the din of a war room seething with activity as it tried to rebuild its strategic overview of the Eltath zone.

'Pict capture,' replied Biota. 'It has just come in. Vox operation received it two minutes ago, so I brought it to you directly.'

'What is it?' she asked. She stared at the on-screen image. It looked like a fuzzy map of an island. Graphic enhancement had compensated for the nocturnal view.

'Well, it could be a breakthrough,' said Biota.

'It is an island, sir,' snapped Tzara. 'An island in a sea. My concern is the Eltath theatre. Bring me data on *that*!'

'Please look,' said Biota. 'These images were captured by the battleship *Naiad Antitor* during a routine orbital sweep ten minutes ago. That's Coltrice Island, a cone atoll west of the Eltath Peninsula, at the southern end of the Sadimay archipelago. It's a dead volcano, hollow inside. Used in ages past as an agri-town and safe harbour, thus sometimes called the Fastness–'

'Your insistence on detail bored me yesterday and it bores me today, tactician,' Tzara warned. She kept glancing at the station chiefs who were holding signals in the air. 'I'm coming!' she cried.

'Observe here,' said Biota, enlarging the image with his fingertip and enhancing the thermal contrast. 'On the last routine sweep, twenty hours ago, the island was cold. No heat read. No human activity. Look at it now, Marshal. We think it was cloaked by some form of masking field or cloak device, which has recently failed.'

'This is heat?' asked Tzara, peering in.

'Indeed, a venting plume.'

'Volcanic?'

'The cone is extinct.'

'So what?'

'We think it's a ship fire, mam,' Biota said. 'An engine fire or significant internal heat damage.'

'A ship...' said Tzara. She frowned and peered again.

'Quiet!' she yelled over her shoulder at the war room bustle. The noise subsided. 'A ship, tactician?' she asked.

'Yes,' said Biota. 'If I enlarge again... like so... you'll see the shadow here. I'll enhance contrast. A shadow, under the projection of the cone lip. That's a shift-ship of considerable tonnage. A fast cruiser.'

'Is it one of ours?' she asked.

'We're waiting for confirmation,' he replied. 'A damaged vessel might have run to cover there and been unable to signal its position. But...'

'But?'

A hand reached in past them, and enlarged a spectrographic code in the side-bar of the main image.

'That plume is venting high levels of iridium matroxon,' said Macaroth.

'My lord,' said Tzara, pulling herself upright.

'You are quite correct, my lord,' said Biota.

'That's fuel burning,' said Macaroth. 'Our ships burn a standard antium-beronel intermix. That's an enemy ship, and it's been hiding as close to Eltath as it can get.'

'Is it him?' Tzara asked.

'We've searched for the bastard everywhere,' said Macaroth, 'and he's cowering on our very doorstep. Marshal?'

'My great lord?'

'Link me to the fleet,' said Macaroth. 'I wish to call in an annihilation strike in the next thirty minutes and wipe that island off the face of Urdesh.'

Merity lifted Fazekiel up, and wiped the blood off her face and out of her mouth.

'Luna? Luna?'

Fazekiel blinked weakly.

'That really hurts,' she whispered.

They heard the wailing rush of blades nearby. It was very close.

'Oh shit,' whispered Merity. 'It heard us. It heard the shots. It's coming.'

'Leave me,' said Fazekiel.

'Balls, I will!' Merity replied. She tried to hoist Fazekiel up, but the woman had blacked out and become a deadweight.

'Come fething *on*!' Merity snarled.

'I came looking for you,' said a voice behind her.

Merity looked around in surprise.

It was Dalin.

'Oh, thank Throne,' she said. 'Please help me, quickly. We don't have much time.'

'Papa's dead,' Dalin said.

Merity laid Fazekiel back down gently and rose to face Dalin. His face was blank with shock. He appeared to be bleeding. She couldn't tell where he had been wounded, but his hands were dripping with blood. Drips spotted the floor around his feet.

'Oh, Dal,' she said. 'Gol? He's dead?'

'Papa's gone,' he said.

'We have to go, Dalin,' she said, stepping towards him.

'There's nowhere *to* go,' he said. 'I don't understand. I don't understand any part of this. It's all just chaos in my head.'

'I think you're in shock, Dalin,' she said. 'You've been through too much. If Gol is... and Yoncy...'

'She was my sister,' said Dalin.

'I know. You believed that for so long. We all–'

'She *was* my sister,' he repeated.

'Let's go, all right? Dalin? Let's go. You're not feeling yourself.'

'I'm not myself,' he said.

'Of course you aren't–'

'I came to find you,' he said, 'because I don't understand anything. I don't know any more. Except I know I trust you. I like you.'

'I like you too,' Merity said.

'I think I might have been in love with you.'

'Oh,' she said. She smiled. '*Might* have been?'

He shrugged, expressionless.

'I want to understand,' he said. 'And *you* know.'

'Know what?'

'You know what it's like,' he said. 'To hide yourself. To hide your *real* self. Hide it inside and look like something else.'

'That?' she said. 'Oh, that was just a game. It was childish, and I regret it.'

'Childish,' Dalin echoed. 'Everything's childish. Just games. Games that Papa makes us play.'

Merity turned to Fazekiel. Dalin grabbed her arm. His grip was strangely hard.

'Ow,' she said in surprise. 'Let me go, Dalin.'

He didn't.

'That hurts. Please, let me go.'

He released his grip.

'I don't want to hurt you,' he said. 'I don't want to hurt anyone. But Papa's dead, and I miss his voice. He'd tell me what to do. He'd explain it all to me.'

'Some things... they can't be explained,' Merity said. 'Life is cruel and hard. It's unfair. You just do what you can.'

He thought for a moment.

'The difference,' he said. 'The difference between you and me. You knew what you were hiding. You did it on purpose. I never knew. I never knew at all. I never knew what I was hiding.'

'I don't understand, Dalin,' she said.

'Papa's dead,' he said. 'He can't explain it. I thought you could. But you can't either.'

He raised his left hand. It was soaked in blood.

The sword sliced through him from behind. Dalin lurched, ripped almost in two. His face remained impassive. Gaunt hacked again, driving the sword of Hieronymo Sondar through the husk of Dalin's body. He struck repeatedly and without mercy, until the Ghost was mangled on the floor.

Merity screamed. 'Oh Throne! Stop! *Stop*! What the feth are you doing? *What the feth are you doing?*'

'Get back,' said Gaunt. 'Get well back. He was vulnerable for a minute. He wanted to talk, so his defences were down.'

'You *killed* him!' she yelled. 'You fething sliced him to *ribbons*–'

'Look!' Gaunt hissed.

She looked.

There was no blood, except the blood that stained Dalin's hands. The deep cuts in his body revealed nothing but odd, dark strips, like thin metal leaves sheaved together. The ends of his fingers on both hands were split, as if they'd ruptured from within. Gleaming points, like the tips of scissor blades, protruded from the frayed skin.

His eyes were still open. A dull yellow light, like a pulse of neon, flickered inside his severed torso.

'Oh, Throne,' Merity whispered.

'Inquisitor?' Gaunt called. Laksheema stepped into the chapel, followed by Hark and Baskevyl. Baskevyl gently drew Merity aside. She gazed at Dalin in utter bafflement.

'That was a risk, my lord,' said Laksheema.

'A chance,' Gaunt replied. 'His guard was down. Please, while he is still dormant. The self-repair is rapid and alarming.'

Laksheema nodded. She aimed her right hand, arm outstretched.

'Look away,' she said.

The disruptor made a high-pitched squeal. A steady, pencil-thin beam of blinding mauve energy lanced from her wrist and scored into Dalin Criid's body.

She kept it burning for almost a minute, until there was nothing left but cinders and flakes of ash, like the soot in an empty grate.

TWENTY-TWO

THE VICTORY

'When were you hit?' asked Mabbon.

'Doesn't matter,' said Rawne.

'You're *hit*?' asked Varl.

'I said it doesn't matter,' said Rawne.

They struggled on through the rain, past the silent rockcrete blocks of the mill.

'It does,' said Mabbon. 'You can barely walk. Let me see.'

'Get off me,' said Rawne.

'Oh feth, Eli,' said Varl. 'Look at you. I don't know how you're standing. Why didn't you say?'

'Because it's something that happened and there's nothing we can do about it,' said Rawne.

He looked at them. His face was pale. He had to lean on the wall just to stay upright.

'You can't even lift that gun,' said Varl quietly.

'I can if I need to.'

'You know they can smell the blood,' said Mabbon.

'I do *now*,' said Rawne.

'Doesn't matter,' said Mabbon. 'They'd have our scent anyway. Sweat, pheromones, fear. But blood is always strongest.'

'We just need to keep moving and lay low,' said Rawne. 'That's all. Oysten will come through. I know she will.' He tried to straighten up, but he couldn't.

'And if we have to fight?' asked Varl.

Rawne held out the lasrifle to Mabbon.

'You take it,' he said.

'No,' said Mabbon.

'For feth's sake!' Rawne growled.

'I won't fight anymore, Rawne,' said Mabbon. 'I've fought for too many sides. Too many causes. None of them have made sense to me. So rather than make an oath to others, I made one to myself. I would fight no more. It's the only pledge I think I can keep.'

'Pardon me, pheguth,' said Rawne. 'You're hardly one to give a lecture on principles. You fething traitor.'

Mabbon looked away.

'But you fought for *us*,' said Varl. 'In the end, you came to us. Crossed the lines.'

'Not to fight,' said Mabbon. 'Even if you had let me.'

'You came to help us win,' said Varl. 'To help us stop the war. That's the same thing!'

'No, that was very different,' said Mabbon.

'Well, I've seen some things,' said Rawne, grimacing. 'Now I've met the only fething pacifist objector in this whole fething galaxy.'

Varl suddenly signalled. *Movement.*

They hurried in against the flank of a work-shed.

'Something,' Varl whispered.

An object hit the wall behind them and bounced onto the floor. The grenade wobbled like an egg as it rolled.

Varl threw himself at Mabbon, driving him aside. Rawne tried to dive the other way.

The blast made a dull and hollow crump in the driving rain.

Rawne found himself lying on his side, his cheek against the wet ground. He couldn't move. It had been almost an hour since he'd taken the hit in the yard of Camp Xenos. He'd been bleeding ever since, and he knew the loss was severe. He was too weak. Too weak for anything. His will was strong, but his body had given up.

He felt himself slipping into the dark place he'd spent his life fighting to avoid.

Mabbon stirred, and got to his feet. Small flecks of shrapnel had cut his face.

Rawne was down, curled on his side to Mabbon's left. Varl lay to his right. The sergeant had shielded Mabbon with his own body. Mabbon saw the bloody shrapnel wounds and scorched clothes on Varl's back and legs. He was face down, and still breathing, but the blast had thrown him into the wall and rendered him unconscious.

Mabbon saw the two figures approaching out of the rain. They were walking side by side, with no sense of haste. One carried a lasrifle, the other was empty-handed.

Mabbon sighed. He reached over and picked up Varl's weapon, then stepped out to meet them.

Rawne saw the three figures. He couldn't speak. He saw them side-on, the world turned on its edge. He tried to move. No part of his body responded.

But he could hear them speak. Like Oan Mkoll, he hadn't survived a year on Gereon without learning the enemy tongue.

Mabbon faced the two Qimurah, rain streaming down his face. He held the weapon low, down at his hip, covering them.

'Hadrel. Jaghar.'

'Pheguth,' said Hadrel.

'No more grenades?' Mabbon asked.

Hadrel shrugged, his hands empty.

'Resources are limited,' he said. His eyes flashed yellow and his talons crackled as they elongated into hooks. 'But we don't need munitions.'

'You'd fight us now?' asked Jaghar, his rifle raised.

'I'd rather not,' said Mabbon. 'I've had enough. If it had been down to me, I would have submitted to you at the very start. But you threaten these men, and I will not let you kill them.'

'What are they to you?' Jaghar sneered.

'Nothing,' said Mabbon. 'Not even friends. But they have protected me with their lives. I owe them as much. Let them live and I'll come with you.'

'All right,' said Hadrel.

'You lie so easily, Hadrel,' said Mabbon.

'I know,' Hadrel replied. 'But you know lies better than I do.'

He took a step forwards.

Mabbon raised Varl's rifle in a quick warning gesture, adjusting the under-barrel tube.

'No closer,' he said. 'You have a rifle, and you have claws. I have a grenade tube. The reworked are blessed and they are mighty, but this will make a mess of you both at close range.'

'Indeed,' grinned Jaghar. 'If it was working.' He eyed Mabbon's gun. 'I can see from here the mechanism is jammed.'

Mabbon was well aware of that. The launcher tube had been buckled when the blast slammed it against the wall. He'd noticed that the moment he'd picked it up.

'Well,' he said. 'A bluff might have worked.' He tossed the rifle aside.

'I wanted to know why,' said Hadrel.

'All of us did,' said Jaghar.

'Why did you turn, Mabbon?' Hadrel asked.

Mabbon laughed. 'I am tired of explaining. I don't owe you any answer, not you or anyone. I am done with war.'

'But you sided with *them*,' said Hadrel.

'For the stones, nothing more,' said Mabbon.

'But they are everything,' said Hadrel. 'The Anarch has told us so. Enkil Vehk. A certain victory, and you brought it to them.'

'The eagle stone key is an abomination,' said Mabbon. 'You know what it does. I am done with war, and it is the greatest monstrosity war has built. I cannot stop this crusade, this endless bloodshed, but I thought perhaps I could stop that.'

'By giving it to them?' asked Jaghar. 'To the corpse-prophet's chieftains? How is that not taking sides?'

'The Anarch knows what the key does,' said Mabbon. 'He knows where to take it and how it works. But the men of the Throne, they know nothing. Except that the key is valuable, and must be kept from you. If they possessed it, they would guard it. Remove it from the Sabbat Worlds. Keep it from you, so that it could never be used.'

'They would learn its secrets,' said Hadrel.

'I doubt it. A thing that old, that vergoht? They would never puzzle it out.' He looked at them both. 'They would not know how to use it, but they could keep it safe so Sek could never use it.'

'The great magir will have the key by dawn,' said Jaghar.

'When his voice next speaks, it will be to tell us that the key is recovered,' said Hadrel. 'Corrod has been sent.'

Mabbon sagged. 'Then it was all for nothing,' he murmured.

The rain pattered around them.

'It was all for victory,' said Hadrel. 'That was a thing you once rejoiced in. Why did that change?'

'It changed because I was good at it,' said Mabbon. 'As sirdar, as damogaur, as etogaur. I rose and I conquered. I burned worlds. I was a champion of the Sekkite host, inculcated to the truths of the Anarch.'

He looked down at the ground and watched the raindrops dance around his feet.

'He was pleased with my service. So pleased to turn a man from one side and make him its unflinching foe. So he rewarded me. He bestowed upon me the highest honour, as a favour for my service.'

'A blessing,' said Jaghar.

'A curse,' said Mabbon. 'It let me see the truth. The deranged hell of the immaterium and those gods which dwell within it. I saw them all. I saw myself. I saw how he had changed me. I saw what he had made me. It was enough. I turned my back on war forever.'

He looked at them levelly.

'Walk away,' he said. 'This does not have to happen.'

'We will not,' said Hadrel. 'You are pheguth, and you will die. You and those who shelter you.'

Mabbon exhaled, a long slow breath.

'I will not let you harm them, even if that means breaking my oath. I've broken many, so I suppose that doesn't matter in the end. Last chance, sirdar magir. Walk away, and I'll let you live.'

Jaghar fired. The las-rounds tore into Mabbon's side and rocked him backwards. He ploughed forwards anyway, rushing into the hail of shots, flinching with each impact.

He tore the rifle from Jaghar's hands, and sent the Qimurah flying with a fist. As Hadrel came at him, Mabbon swung and smashed the rifle across Hadrel's face.

Jaghar bounded at him. Mabbon tossed the broken rifle away and met Jaghar's attack with a punch that cracked teeth. Jaghar tumbled back.

Mabbon lunged after him. The pheguth's clothing was torn, shredded by the las-fire. The flesh of his chest bubbled and dripped with yellow gore.

Neon heat welled in his tired, empty eyes. His fingers bulged. Bone snapped. The flesh broke and sprouted talons.

He smashed Jaghar down with a blow that snapped the Qimurah's head aside and sprayed yellow gore into the air. Hadrel smashed into him, raking claws deep into Mabbon's chest and back. Yellow plasma gushed from the wounds.

Mabbon grappled with Hadrel, strength to strength, limbs locked. He forced the sirdar backwards, their arms entangled. Jaghar crashed into them, gouging his claws and teeth into Mabbon's flank.

Mabbon swung, hurling Hadrel away. He smacked Jaghar aside with a backhand, then ripped his talons through the Qimurah's throat. Jaghar fell to his knees, clutching at the frothing yellow liquid pouring from his opened neck.

Mabbon grabbed his head with both hands, twisted, and wrenched it off. Jaghar's corpse fell forward.

Mabbon staggered, mauled and bleeding. He swayed. Hadrel was on his feet again.

'You were always the best of us, Mabbon,' he hissed. 'So very blessed.'

'I never asked for it,' said Mabbon. He spat yellow blood, his eyes neon fire. 'I never wanted it. But he blessed me *anyway.*'

They clashed like charging bulls, talons tearing and rending, and tore away each other's flesh with the fury of daemons.

His vision greying back to nothing, Rawne watched as they both fell in the rain, tangled and torn apart, locked together in a final embrace.

Neither of them rose again.

His vision failed.

When it returned, for a brief moment, the cold of eternity was in his bones. He glimpsed lights, dazzlingly bright in the rain, pulsing green and red. He heard the scream of lifter jets. He heard Oysten's voice calling his name.

Calling him back.

And that was all.

EPILOGUES

ONE WEEK LATER

Cold daylight streamed in through the preceptory windows. Hark entered the room, the empty sleeve of his leather coat neatly pinned up. Onabel held the door open for him. He nodded his thanks, and she turned and limped away very slowly with the aid of a walking stick. Her injuries had not been physical, but they would take a long time to heal.

'Commissar,' said Laksheema. She had been waiting. Her gown was clean and fresh, but he noticed she hadn't had her golden augmetics repaired. The polished surfaces of her face and body were crazed and scoured. Perhaps she hadn't had time, he thought, or perhaps she had chosen to leave the scars as they were.

One could only repair one's self so many times.

'Are you well?' he asked.

'Well enough,' she said. 'And you?'

Hark nodded. There was a silence.

'Neither one of us is good at small talk,' he remarked. She tilted her head, agreeing.

'You've come to receive my report,' she said.

'The Lord Executor awaits it with interest.'

She lifted an actuator wand, and a screen lit. It displayed detailed picts of four eagle stones, side by side.

'Your Major–' Laksheema paused and consulted her data-slate. 'Petrushkevskaya–'

'Pasha,' he said.

'She delivered the recovered stones to the palace under guard,' said Laksheema. 'They were received by the ordos. Four had been retrieved intact.'

She flashed up another image. This showed four other shapes, broken into fragments, scorched and cracked, their ancient patterns barely visible.

'Four other stones were recovered by a Sergeant... Ifvan. They had been subjected to intense burning. A flamer, I understand. They were severely damaged and incomplete, and much detail lost. These were also delivered, and savants are now working on restoration and reconstruction.'

'Will that be possible?' asked Hark.

'Hard to say,' she replied. 'It is hard to reconstruct something when you don't know what it is. Also, all the scanned details and analysis studies made after the original recovery were lost when Mechanicore Fourteen was razed. The EM Fourteen facility had the only copies of the data because it was considered so sensitive. The machine plague – *Berserker* – devoured it all.'

'So... it's all pending?' Hark said. 'I thought it might be. The Lord Executor will be particularly keen to know the stones are secure.'

'They are in the central vault of the capital ship *Deluge*,' she replied, 'and that information, by the way, carries a vermilion classification. As per the Lord Executor's instruction, the security and examination of the Glyptothek is in the hands of the ordos. The Cult Mechanicus will not be involved.'

'As I understand, it was hardly their fault,' said Hark.

'The adepts failed,' said Laksheema bluntly. 'Their security was insufficient. We have received several formal petitions from the Mechanicus, requesting that we release the objects to them, or at least permit their full participation in their analysis. They wish, I think, to know what could be so valuable it cost an entire Mechanicore station. These petitions have been denied. That can be reviewed. It's not my choice.'

Hark sat back and gazed at the images.

'We knew they were important,' said Laksheema. 'Precious to the Archenemy, at least. I had favoured the explanation that they were of ritual or cult significance, but Sek committed everything he had to their recovery. To me, that suggests the stones have a more strategic function.'

Hark nodded. 'We have hearsay evidence to support that,' he said. 'A report from the field that night. Archenemy combatants discussing the purpose of the stones. It's not much, but it would appear they are a weapon, or the key to a weapon. A xenos device. Something so monstrous that even they were in awe of it. But something *either* side could use.'

'Xenos?'

'That's our reading. The word used was "vergoht". Forgive my pronunciation. I'm told it means *alien, forbidden,* or *against natural order.*'

'Is that all?' she asked.

'Yes,' he said. 'It's a start. It points us in a direction at least.'

'But this field evidence, is it reliable?' Laksheema asked.

'The source is beyond reproach,' Hark replied.

Laksheema deactivated the display. They both rose.

'I'll convey your report to the Lord Executor,' he said.

'I am at his call if anything further is needed,' she replied, 'and will contact his office at once if anything new emerges.'

She walked him to the door.

'Express my regards to him,' she said. 'I also wish to convey my sympathies for your regiment's losses.'

'Do you?' he asked.

'Of course.'

'Just abstract platitudes, I'm sure,' he said. 'You told me you don't feel, and I believe that.'

'I am not entirely without feeling, Viktor,' she said. 'Not yet at least.'

'Then I will convey them,' he replied. 'I have a feeling that, from here, we will be working in close collaboration for a while to come.'

'I look forward to it,' she said. 'Despite all that occurred, I enjoyed our relationship.'

'Our working relationship?' he asked.

'Is there another kind?' she replied.

'Not that I'm aware of,' said Hark. He smiled. 'Good day to you, inquisitor.'

Ban Daur moved the lamp. This time there had been no mistake about it. He could hear sobbing. A woman weeping.

He got up, leaving his water bottle and food-pack on the floor, and walked along the hallway, holding the lamp high. The undercroft was empty and silent.

He didn't dare call her name.

He heard the sobbing again. His heart began to race. Behind the wall? The walls had moved once, though now they seemed dead and solid and inert.

He followed the sound.

He found her in the hall that had served as the central billet. She was perched on the pile of rubble and stone blocks where the vaulted roof had fallen in. A narrow shaft of daylight shone down on her, spearing through the hole in the Hexagonal Court above.

His heart sank.

He clambered up beside her and sat down, setting the lamp next to his feet.

She glanced at him. He was filthy. He hadn't washed for days. He hadn't emerged from the undercroft, despite direct orders. He'd only eaten because Haller and Baskevyl had brought him rations.

Tona Criid's dress uniform was immaculate.

'I didn't mean to disturb you,' Criid said, wiping her eyes. 'This is just the first chance I've had to come down here. To see.'

Daur nodded.

'This was the room, wasn't it?' she asked.

'Yes,' he said.

People had died in every chamber of the old undercroft. Every single one. They'd died in droves in the Urdeshic Palace above, too. But here, in this room, Gol Kolea had died, and Yoncy had perished, and Dalin had –

– had ceased to be Dalin.

'I just had to see it,' she said.

'I understand.'

'I am at a loss,' said Criid. 'They were mine for so long. I took them out of certain death. I never... I never for a moment suspected that–'

'Of course you didn't,' said Daur. 'He was clever and he made clever things. Ingenious tricks that fooled everyone. We learned that at Vervunhive. None of us could have guessed how elaborate they could be.'

'They weren't tricks to me,' she said. She let out a slow, calming breath. 'I don't know what I'm going to do without–'

She stopped herself and shot a look at him, ashamed.

'I'm sorry,' she said. 'Feth, I'm sorry, Ban. That was a stupid thing to say.'

He shook his head.

'It was honest,' Daur replied. 'I'm sorry this has happened to you.'

'Is there...' she asked. 'Have you found any trace at all?'

'No,' he said. 'Nothing. I thought I might find something that could... could stop me searching. But there's nothing to find. I just can't let go of the idea that she's still here. Behind a wall somewhere. Just shut away by a fold of reality. Trapped on the other side, but alive and whole and waiting. And all I've got to do is look hard enough.'

He fell silent.

'I'm fooling myself, I know,' he said quietly. 'It's just something to cling to.'

He looked at her.

'Why are you so dressed up?' he asked.

Tona glanced down at her formal braid and pressed lines.

'There's a parade,' she said.

'Feth.'

'I know. A fething parade. Apparently it's the right thing to do. A show of respect and thanks. To the living and the dead alike. I'm supposed to be there. And I'm going to be late.'

'And you don't care?'

'Feth, no.'

She looked around at the dark walls. The shadows that were just shadows.

'This is my parade,' she said.

She looked at him.

'Will you ever come out of here?' she asked.

'They may have to drag me out,' said Daur. 'I don't think I can ever leave.'

'Ban, I think there are only ghosts here now,' she said. 'You can't live out your life with only ghosts for company.'

He looked at her and almost smiled.

'Yes, I just heard myself,' Criid said. 'Feth, I can only say stupid things today, right?'

He took her hand and held it tight.

They were waiting for him outside his quarters, wearing their dress blacks, but he walked right past them when he came out. His Scion guard, all new appointees unaccustomed to his habits, jumped to follow him.

'My lord?' Baskevyl called. He and Pasha scooped up their dress swords and ran to catch him up. 'My lord, it's about to start,' Baskevyl called out.

'I know,' said Gaunt, still striding. His own dress uniform, though very plain, was quite imposing. 'I have to make a visit first.'

He stopped suddenly, and turned to face them. The Scions skidded to a halt.

'They expect me to write a speech,' he said to the two company officers. 'An address. What the feth do you say? After that?'

Baskevyl shrugged.

'Not much to say,' Pasha agreed.

'I know,' said Gaunt. 'We won. We survived. Too many didn't. Thank you for coming. There are drinks on the terrace.'

'That should do the trick,' said Baskevyl.

'Van Voytz was good at this,' said Gaunt. 'He could spin a rousing address. Like a bastard.' He fell silent and stared at the floor.

'Sir–' Baskevyl began.

Gaunt looked up.

'Yes, you came to find me,' he said. 'What did you want?'

'We came to *fetch* you,' said Baskevyl.

'The big hoo-hah is now,' said Pasha. 'You are, mmmmm, maybe *late*?'

'Consider me fetched,' said Gaunt. 'Tell them I'm coming.'

They saluted.

He turned, then swung back to them.

'Screw the parade,' he said. 'That's all for show, and the dead can't hear any of it. I want to commend you both, here and now. Face to face, not across a parade ground. The Tanith First excelled. You were both unflinching in the face of... of... *feth*! My thanks. I want you to convey my gratitude and admiration to all in the regiment. Do this personally. Express my highest regard.'

'Yes, my lord,' Baskevyl nodded.

'The process is very slow,' Gaunt added, 'because of all the red tape and paperwork, but there will be decorations to follow. Citations for honour and valour. A surprising number. You know who. I may be able to speed that process. It should be easier to issue commendations now the Tanith First is the formal escort brigade of the Lord Executor.'

'It is?' asked Baskevyl.

'Macaroth agreed to it this morning' said Gaunt. 'You'll be the core I build my army group upon, Bask. Your duties will change. It may get very ceremonial from now on.'

'Ceremonial is nice. Is very restful,' said Pasha.

'There'll be a new pin to wear,' Gaunt said, gesturing to his collar. 'I don't know what else. We'll work out the details. Now let me run this errand and I'll join you on the field.'

He made the sign of the aquila and strode away.

The infirmary, its walls and floor painted a pale, gloss green, filled one whole wing of the palace compound. Gaunt strode in with the Scions behind him, and consciously slowed his pace to suit the quiet calm of his surroundings.

'Stay here,' he told his bodyguard. They obeyed. Scion Cleeve had not yet found the pluck to argue with him the way Sancto had. Gaunt wondered if Sancto would ever be fit to return to duty.

He wondered if he'd ever want to.

He walked past rooms where medicae staff tended the injured from the retinue, the Tanith, and from all the other regiments and support divisions affected by the onslaught. So many people, yet a fraction of the number killed. There were more trays occupied in the morgue than there were beds filled in the infirmary.

He reached the door of a guarded room. Troopers of the Jovani Vanguard clad in polished chrome armour snapped to attention.

The room was quiet. There was a smell of counterseptic and floor wax, and a very slight trace of islumbine.

Ana Curth saw him, and crossed the room to meet him.

'Any news?' he asked.

'She sleeps still,' said Curth.

They looked over at the bed where the Beati lay, shrouded by a tent of gauze.

'Is that normal?' he asked.

'Nothing about her is normal,' Curth replied. 'Her vitals are improving. There's colour in her cheeks, steady rhythms. Perhaps a few more days.'

He nodded.

'She was exhausted before she arrived,' said Curth. 'After Oureppan. More drained than she wanted to admit. And then I think she used every spark of power she had left to kill the first woe machine. No thought for herself. We are lucky to still have her.'

'Well, keep me advised,' said Gaunt. 'Macaroth has expressed his concerns.'

'Of course,' Curth said. 'Don't you have a ridiculous parade to attend or something?'

'Yes,' Gaunt said. 'But I heard he was awake at last.'

'Earlier this morning,' she said.

'I wanted to see him first.'

'Room at the far end,' she said.

He looked at her. 'Well,' he said.

'You saved my life, you know,' Curth said. 'In the undercroft. Not for the first time.'

'You've saved mine, and more than once.'

'It's not a competition,' she said. 'Though if it was, I'd be winning.'

'Your continued duty can never be repaid enough,' Gaunt replied.

'Is that a line from your speech?'

'Yes,' he admitted.

'Bit rubbish,' she said.

'I felt that,' he said.

Curth smiled. 'I do what I do because it needs to be done,' she said.

'People *keep* saying that,' said Gaunt.

'Do they? Who?'

'Just the people who matter most,' he replied.

'And there,' she said, 'I thought you just wanted me for my duty.'

They paused. He glanced around awkwardly.

'So,' he said.

'Indeed,' she replied.

'I'll go and–'

'You should,' she said.

He took off his cap, stepped forwards, and kissed her cheek. She stayed very still.

He stood back, and re-set his cap.

'I'm going now,' he said.

'I see that.'

He turned.

She smiled slightly as he walked away.

* * *

Zweil was doing his rounds in a nearby ward as Gaunt strode past.

'He looks busy,' the old priest remarked to Blenner, who had agreed to accompany Zweil on the infirmary visit.

'He does,' said Blenner. 'Good old Lord Ibram.'

'Well, they all seem to be coping in here,' said Zweil. 'Let's move along to the next ward, shall we?'

Blenner escorted him out into the hall, moving slowly so he didn't leave the old, shuffling man behind.

'They won't let me bring the bird in,' Zweil said.

'So you said, father.'

'I thought it might cheer people up. But *oh* no, they say it's unsanitary. Just because it craps on the floor. I called it Quil, you know?'

'Also information I already have at my disposal, father,' said Blenner.

He stopped and turned to Zweil. They were alone in the pale green corridor.

'Can I ask you something, father?' Blenner said.

'Depends on the area,' replied Zweil with a frown. 'I'm good on some topics. Like boats. Also, weaving, which I once liked to do. Other subjects, it's more hit and miss, if I'm honest.'

'Guilt?'

'Oh, yes, my my. That's priesting work. Out with it.'

'It's a–' Blenner cleared his throat. 'Purely hypothetical, of course. An ethical debate I was having.'

'With?' asked Zweil.

'Sorry?'

'Who was this ethical debate with?'

'Oh, uhm... a friend.'

'Ah yes,' Zweil said, nodding sagely and tapping the side of his nose with a bony finger. 'Know him well.'

'So,' said Blenner, 'let's say a man has done a... a questionable thing. A bad thing. He confesses, to seek absolution.'

'That'd be the way to go,' said Zweil, nodding along.

'But his confessor dies,' said Blenner. 'Soon after. Does... does the absolution stand? Is the man still forgiven, or does the burden remain upon him?'

'Hmmm,' said Zweil, pondering. 'That's a knotty one. Bit of a murky area, philosophically speaking. Here's what I'd tell this friend of yours, Vaynom. He's *probably* all right. In the clear. His conscience all shiny and clean. Because he made confession of his sins, you see? But just to be on the safe side, you know, he should try to be the best fething person he can possibly be for the rest of his born days. See? Just to hedge his bets? In case the absolution didn't take.'

'I see,' said Blenner.

'Can he do that, do you think? This friend?'

'I think he can try,' said Blenner.

'Good,' said Zweil, and started to shuffle on his way again. 'Because, tell him from me, guilt's a little shit who will bite you on the fething arse and kill you stone dead. No doubt about it.'

Blenner nodded. He wiped his mouth on the back of his trembling hand.

'Are you coming, Blenner?' Zweil called. 'They should have let me bring the bird instead of you, you know? The bird cheers people up. I'm teaching it tricks. You, you're as much fun as a fart in a dreadnought.'

Merity Chass also saw Gaunt stride past. She was sitting at Fazekiel's bedside.

'Do you want to go and talk to him?' Fazekiel asked.

'He's busy,' said Merity. 'There'll be time later.'

Luna Fazekiel nodded. 'Well, I appreciate the visit,' she said, 'but I'm no company. I'm very tired. At least it's clean in here. Very clean. Very neat.'

She saw that Merity was still staring at the door.

'Are you sure you don't want to go and talk to him?' Fazekiel asked. 'He *is* your father.'

'That's a work in progress,' said Merity.

'You're awake, then?' said Gaunt. He took off his cap and sat down at the bedside.

'Yes, that was a mistake,' said Rawne. 'It didn't hurt when I was unconscious.'

'I wanted to stop by,' said Gaunt.

'I'm honoured,' said Rawne. He was bandaged from throat to groin, and drips fed into his arms. He looked anaemic, with dark circles around his eyes. 'I suppose you want to quiz me about the report I gave to Hark this morning?'

'I read it,' said Gaunt. 'Some interesting details. I presume you're sure about the language used?'

'I am.'

'And it wasn't a hallucination?'

'Wish I could say it was,' said Rawne.

'It provides a lead,' said Gaunt, 'and sets up some interesting questions. Regarding the stones, I mean. As for Mabbon, we know more about him now he's dead than we did when he was alive.'

'He fought for me, that's all I know,' said Rawne. 'For me and for Varl. Out of honour. Like a daemon.'

'So I understand,' said Gaunt.

'No, *literally* like a daemon.'

Rawne lay back.

'I hear it got interesting,' he said. 'Hark was filling me in. Close to the wire here, and with Pasha's mob too.'

'As close as it got with you,' said Gaunt.

'Hark says the battlefleet annihilated some island. Took out Sek's flagship. Is the fether dead now?'

'That's the presumption,' Gaunt replied. 'His gambits failed. Except with Mabbon. The Sekkite host collapsed almost overnight. Those that survive are fleeing the system. Urdesh is won. This is a victory.'

'So *that's* what it feels like,' said Rawne.

He looked at Gaunt.

'Is it true what I heard? Kolea?'

Gaunt nodded.

'And the lad Dalin, and–'

'We lost a lot. It's hard to take in.'

'It always is,' said Rawne.

Beltayn appeared at the doorway.

'My lord,' he said.

'I know, I know,' said Gaunt, getting up, 'I'm late.'

'No, sir, you need to read this.' Beltayn held out a signal sheet. 'It was just received. I brought it to you at once.'

Gaunt took the sheet and read it. Then he held it up so Rawne could read it too.

'Well,' said Rawne. 'There's your confirmation. An unequivocal victory. What does this part mean, the bottom here? 'Execution undertaken by unidentified Astra Militarum personnel'?'

A Munitorum aide directed him to the new Tanith billet as soon as he stepped off the landing field.

It was a fine set of chambers, just off the palace's Circular Court. Sunlight at the windows, rows of clean cots, a scrubbed floor.

The place was empty. He walked in, in his clean but borrowed clothes, down the length of the first chamber, between the lines of cots, each one laundered and made-up with precision.

A man, the only person around, sat on a cot at the end of the long line, buttoning the jacket of his dress blacks. He looked up.

He barely reacted. Just a flicker of surprise. Mach Bonin rose to his feet, smoothing out the front of his dress uniform.

'There you are,' he said, as if Mkoll had only stepped outside for a smoke. 'There's a parade about to start. I'm late as it is.'

He reached down and slid an old kitbag out from under his cot. He dumped it on the next cot along.

'I was holding this for you,' Bonin said, matter-of-factly. 'That cot's free, so you can have that.'

Mkoll nodded. 'We'll need another bed,' he said.

'Yeah?' asked Bonin.

Mkoll pointed down the hall. Brin Milo was standing in the doorway. He looked reluctant to step inside.

'Where did you find him?' Bonin asked.

'Long story,' said Mkoll.

A strong wind was blowing in across the High Parade behind the palace. A hard sun burned high in the sky. The pale skies of Eltath were clear of smoke for the first time in months.

Years, probably.

Ibram Gaunt, Lord Executor, walked out onto the field, his camo cloak billowing behind him. Drill officers barked, and the assembled companies snapped to attention. Brigades of Jovani, Helixid, Narmenian, Vitrian, Keyzon and a host of gleaming Urdeshi regiments. To one side, the small formation of Tanith, in perfect order. A row of field guns stood ready to fire the salute.

Gaunt stepped up onto the podium. An Imperial flag had been draped over the lectern. Overhead, huge standard banners swayed and cracked in the wind.

He nodded to the honour guard as he walked past them, and to the seniors of high command in attendance: Urienz, Blackwood, Cybon, Tzara and Grizmund, each one of them regal in their ceremonial uniforms.

Gaunt stepped to the lectern. He took out a sheaf of papers. He looked out at the assembled regiments, then down at his notes. He paused, and gestured to Ludd, who was leading the honour guard. Ludd hurried forwards.

'My lord?' Ludd whispered.

'Take these, Ludd,' Gaunt said. 'I won't need them.'

Ludd took the sheaf of papers, careful not to let any of them blow away in the wind.

'Isn't this your speech, sir?' he asked nervously.

'It's someone's speech,' said Gaunt. 'Not mine.'

Ludd stepped back into line, stuffing the papers into his coat pocket. The lords militant and high officers looked at each other, baffled.

'Astra Militarum,' said Gaunt, speaking into the vox mic. His words boomed out across the field. 'Guardsmen. Lasmen. I have been asked to address you today. To deliver thanks for the struggles we have all endured together on Urdesh Forge World, and to celebrate our accomplishments here. Death is a part of those struggles, and that makes it hard to celebrate, even in a time of triumph. I wrote a speech. It was shit, so let's draw a veil over that.'

A murmur rippled across the field.

'It was just words,' Gaunt went on. 'They rang false to me, so I know for sure they'll ring false to you too. I've heard enough generals speak in my time. It usually means nothing except that they like the sound of their own voices. You all know what you've done.'

He paused. He reached into his pocket and took out the signal paper Beltayn had handed to him. He began to unfold it.

'A few minutes ago,' Gaunt said into the vox, 'I was passed a signal. Information that has just been received. I want to share the contents of that signal with you, because it will mean more to you than any glowing words I can muster.'

He cleared his throat, reading off the thin paper, which fluttered and flapped in his gloved hands.

'Just before noon today, the Astra Militarum Intelligence Service confirmed a report received yesterday from an Aeronautica Imperialis patrol in the Southern Oceanic Zone. The report, which has been verified, declares that seven days ago, on an island called Orchidel, in the Faroppan archipelago, the Archenemy Anarch, known as Sek, was apprehended and terminated by Astra Militarum troops.'

He looked up. The wind blew across the field. The banners whipped and cracked.

'I repeat,' he said, 'the identity is verified and the termination is confirmed. The Anarch is dead. Today, we have achieved a victory that has not been paralleled since Balhaut. Perhaps, *the* victory of this crusade. I feel that's the only thing you need to hear from me today.'

He stepped back from the lectern. Despite the wind, he could hear that the applause and cheering had already begun to spread through the lines.

He turned, and beckoned Trooper Perday forward from the honour squad. She looked so nervous and afraid he thought she might faint. In her arms, she clutched the battered old set of Tanith pipes he'd given her three days before, and which she'd been practising on ever since, enough to master the basic skills. The boy was never coming back, but Gaunt felt that the original Tanith traditions ought to be respected.

'Trooper Perday?'

'Yes, my lord,' Ree Perday replied, swallowing hard.

'Now you can play something,' he said.

THIS IS WHAT VICTORY FEELS LIKE (FOREVER THE SAME)

They were burning the dead again. Third day running.

Viktor Hark managed to ignore the smell for a while. He was hardened to the dispiriting odours of the battlefield. Career Militarum, you learned to just block them out and get on with your business.

And he had business aplenty to get on with. He adjusted his chair, picked up his stylus, and returned his attention to page seventy-six of the Munitorum requisition briefing.

'Feth it,' he said. He put the stylus down, and got to his feet. The smell was truly foul. He stomped to the window of his large tower office. It was a fine day; that's why he'd left the window open. The mass cremations were underway about six kilometres away, but the coastal wind was driving the smoke, and the stench, across the Great Hill and into the precincts of the Urdeshic Palace. He leant out to close the window. Fair enough to endure the reek on the battlefield, but this wasn't the battlefield. Not any more. This was liberated Urdesh, the hour of triumph, and this was not what the world was supposed to smell like.

It was not what victory was supposed to smell like.

The window was small and old, and he was large and formidable, but it fought back anyway. Hark muttered 'Feth it' again, twice, followed by a 'Feth this', and a testy 'Feth it all', before the window finally submitted to the authority of the Prefectus and the power of his augmetic arm.

He returned to his desk and resumed his seat. The stink still hung in the room, permeating the limewash and the filing crates and the unfathomable oil paintings left behind by his predecessor. Permeating his clothes.

'Fething feth it,' he said. He wondered if the mess was open yet.

There was a knock at the door.

'Open!' he barked, not looking up, expecting Ludd with more papers. It wasn't. It was Baskevyl.

'A moment?' Baskevyl asked.

'Of course, of course,' replied Hark, beckoning enthusiastically as he made a quick margin note on the requisition briefing. Then he suddenly leapt to his feet and stood to attention.

'What... are you doing?' asked Baskevyl, cautiously.

'Standing up. *Sir.*'

'Because...?'

'Guardsmen of all rank, from file to senior, will stand attentive when the commanding officer enters the room. My sincere apologies. That was absolutely inexcusable.'

Baskevyl narrowed his eyes slightly and regarded the rigidly upright commissar with great wariness.

'Is this some kind of...' he said. 'Are you taking the piss, Viktor?'

'Sir. No, sir.'

'Oh, for Throne's sake... Viktor...'

'I am senior Prefectus officer of the Tanith First, and you are the regiment's colonel.'

Baskevyl sighed.

'Sit down,' he said.

Hark sat down.

Baskevyl wheeled over another chair and sat facing him.

'Don't be doing that,' Baskevyl said wearily. 'We're friends. I think that allows us a certain degree of informality.'

'It is my responsibility to maintain and exemplify formal protocols,' said Hark, 'and if I don't get in the habit, we can hardly expect any hairy-arsed lasman to-'

'It's a habit I'd prefer we *didn't* get into,' said Baskevyl.

'You *are* colonel.'

'Acting.'

'Even so. We have standards.'

'He will be back.'

Hark nodded. 'Yes. Of course he will. But Ana says Rawne could be out for six months. Six minimum.'

'Well, I tell you this much,' said Baskevyl, 'when he *does* come back, Rawne won't like you doing that any more than I do. Because he doesn't want to be *colonel* any more than I do.'

'Well,' replied Hark philosophically, 'what any of us "want" has never really factored into the scheme of things, has it?'

'In the regiment?'

'In the Astra Militarum.'

Baskevyl nodded. He sagged in his chair.

'It should have been Gol,' he murmured.

Hark wasn't sure how to reply. Before he had to, Baskevyl sat up again and said, 'What *is* that stench?'

'Burning bodies,' said Hark. 'They're using a derelict manufactory site out at Kadish Hill, but the wind's in the wrong direction.'

'Enemy dead?'

'But of course,' said Hark. 'We're not barbarians. Our fallen are being treated with the respect they are due. But mass disposal is necessary. The local population is stringing up Sekkite corpses in the street, so I hear. Pelting rocks at them. All part of the manic festivities. Also disgraceful, and a public health issue. So... the Munitorum is processing.'

'You can't blame the Urdeshi,' said Baskevyl. 'This is a turning point for them. They've suffered under Archonate occupation way too long.'

'They have,' said Hark. 'And, my friend, this is a big moment for us too. This is victory. The greatest since Balhaut. We have delivered the grace of the Throne, and restored the Pax Imperialis. We have made good on pledges sworn on the eve of the crusade to deliver the Sabbat Worlds from the malign grip of the Archenemy–'

'Spare me the propaganda...'

'I'm saying, Bask, this is what victory feels like.'

'Maybe. It's not done yet,' said Baskevyl.

'No,' Hark admitted. 'No. A few years more, perhaps. But the Anarch's dead. The Archon stands alone. We enter the endgame. We should at least celebrate *that*.'

'Well, we could start by you not jumping up like an idiot every time I walk into a room.'

'I... can accommodate that.'

Hark looked across the desk at Baskevyl. The Belladon seemed to be fascinated by a patch of carpet, and Hark couldn't remember the carpet being all that interesting when he took the office over.

'What's on your mind, Bask?' he asked.

Baskevyl roused out of his reverie. He glanced back at Hark, flashed an entirely counterfeit smile, and said, 'A, B, C, E, G, T, and V. I'd like to hear your thoughts. I can't seem to settle on decisions.'

'Ah,' said Hark. 'That. Of course.'

'And I also,' said Baskevyl, 'want you to tell me, to my face, that the effort is worth it, too.'

'Worth it? How do you mean?'

Baskevyl looked at him as though he ought to know. There was a brooding disquiet in his eyes.

'You are a good friend, Viktor,' he said. 'Probably the best I have left–'

'High praise *indeed*,' said Hark, one eyebrow raised.

Baskevyl chuckled. 'You know what I mean. I'd normally talk details like this through with a good friend. See which way the wind is blowing–'

'Easterly, from Kadish Hill,' said Hark. Baskevyl ignored Hark's levity.

'I'd go to Gol with this,' said Baskevyl. 'And I keep forgetting I can't.'

Hark pursed his lips and nodded.

'It was the same after Corbec,' he reflected.

'I can imagine,' Baskevyl replied. 'Except it wasn't. Rawne's fethed up, and this isn't his kind of thing anyway. When Corbec died, Gaunt was still very much hands-on. But he isn't any more. And he *won't* be. And Gol's not here. It's just us scraps and actings and survivors left to sort the details out, and it hardly seems worth it.'

'Because?'

'Because I think the Ghosts are done, Viktor,' said Baskevyl.

'What, because... Gaunt's Lord Executor?' asked Hark. 'Bask, he's not... I mean, he won't be involved at company level again, I realise, but he has assured us several times that the Tanith First will form his personal command detail, the core of his new armies. We get a few months here at Urdesh to recuperate and heal our wounds, not to mention revel in the honours and garlands heaped upon us from every quarter for our role in the victory, then–'

'Then what?' asked Baskevyl. 'We'll never be front line again. Our war is over. We'll get shiny new uniforms, and we'll parade up and down behind the fething band every time Gaunt takes a review, and people will say, "Oh, look at those fine lasmen, with their bright shiny buttons. They were the ones who brought the Anarch down". And that, Viktor, will be the rest of our lives. Honoured veterans. Sitting around in one forsaken palace after another, polishing our medals, waiting for the next ceremony. We will become domesticated. House pets. Tamed and caged by a new kind of duty.'

'Huh,' said Hark. He sank back in his chair. 'My, my. We spend our lives longing for the meat grinder to end, and when it does, we miss it. The curse of the Militarum. Forever the same.'

'What?'

'You know, the old Tanith toast? My point is, Bask… Is a happy ever after and a life of honoured, ceremonial retirement *really* so fething awful? Isn't it what we were fighting for all along?'

Baskevyl shrugged.

'Some people, Viktor,' he said, 'deserved to be here to enjoy it.'

'I'm not arguing that. The *other* curse of Militarum life. Look, I'm senior Prefectus officer, and apart from jumping up and down like jack-on-a-spring when you come through a door, I am also obliged to keep things running so, yes, it *is* worth the effort, and even if it wasn't, we have to do it anyway. Let's get the companies sorted. If we got to pick and choose the jobs we liked, this wouldn't be the Imperial fething Guard, would it?'

'Duty, eh?' said Baskevyl. 'Forever the same?'

'Something like that. Now…'

Hark rose to his feet and brushed down the front of his jacket.

'…First things first, what we really need is a party.'

Baskevyl frowned at him.

'What? Feth, *no*.'

'I'm not talking about some mindless celebration to mark the victory, Bask,' said Hark. 'We'll leave that to the common folk who remain mercifully unaware of the bitter price a victory demands from those who achieve it. I'm talking something small and dignified. A dinner party. Just us and the company seniors. We'll set empty chairs for the missing as a mark of respect, and then, together, we will decide who should fill them.'

'You got a light?' asked Brostin.

'What?' Cant responded. He cleared his throat. His voice was still tight, the garrotte wound that had nearly killed him on the *Armaduke* still healing. Sometimes, in ways he couldn't control, his voice came out like a whisper or a ridiculous squeak. He was about to say 'What?' again, but he saw that the hulking Tanith was wiggling a tatty cigar between his teeth.

'Oh, yeah,' said Cant. He got off the wall, fished out his lucifers, and lit Brostin's smoke. Brostin inhaled contentedly, but kept the cigar clenched between his teeth. He only had one functioning hand, and that had three splinted fingers, so the effort of actually holding a cigar had been abandoned.

'They won't let me have a light,' said Brostin, gazing into the distance.

'I can't imagine why,' replied Cant.

'Eh?'

Callan Cant coughed again, to rid the whisper-squeak from his voice.

'I said,' he repeated, 'I can't imagine why.'

'Oh, you can't, can you, Cant?' asked Brostin, and chuckled to himself.

Cant sighed. Brostin wasn't a good friend by any means, but they were both survivors of B Company's otherwise decimated First platoon, the 'Suicide Kings', so they had looked out for each other during their mandated infirmary stay. Cant had been wounded before the Ghosts had even arrived on Urdesh, so he'd missed everything that had transpired in the past few weeks, including the brutal last stand of the Suicide Kings at Plade Parish. Aongus Brostin had been there for that, at Rawne's side, and had ended up suffering severe crush injuries for his efforts. He'd been trapped under rockcrete rubble for hours.

A fine pair they made, out in the sun on the infirmary's terrace. Cant, skinnier than usual, pale, dark rings under his eyes, a dressing around his throat like a roll-neck collar covering the thin, pink scar-line where an Archonate wire had almost sliced his head off. Brostin, in his invalid chair, strapped to a backboard, both legs and one arm pinned and cast rigid. He looked like a statue that had been taken off its plinth and laid askew across an armchair. No one knew if he'd walk again, or if he did, if he'd ever be able to lug the weight of flamer tanks around.

'Smoke,' remarked Cant. It explained the irritation in his throat. They'd been allowed out onto the terrace to get some fresh air. There was a good view across the courtyards and walls of the Urdeshic Palace, and the city of Eltath beyond, sprawling in a bright sea haze. But smoke was blowing in across the yards from somewhere in the distance.

'Bodies,' said Brostin.

'What?'

'That's dead meat burning,' said Brostin. 'Cremation work. Fething amateurs.'

'What do you mean, "amateurs"?'

Brostin sniffed. 'You can smell it, Cant. They've got the temp too low and nothing like enough fuel. Corpses'll burn like tallow fat. That's the stink, see? They want a fiercer heat. And someone who knows how to work a fething flamer.'

Cant nodded. The immolation of cadavers wasn't quite the topic he wanted to discuss. He had barely spoken to anyone in weeks. He wanted to know about everything that had happened, about the Tulkar Batteries and the fight to hold the city, about the monumental victory that had, apparently, happened while he was in a pharmaceutical haze.

And he wanted to know about the Kings' bloody last stand, and what would happen to them, and to B Company, with Rawne so badly wounded and Gaunt gone. But Brostin was hardly the person to ask. Cant didn't want to stir him up with questions about the events that had put him in traction and left him sitting here in the sun, unable to light his own smoke, with little prospect of an active future.

'Gonna be Lurgoine,' mused Brostin, gazing out at the distant smoke. 'You mark my words. Jo Lurgoine. Now Rawne's out. Lurgoine, or maybe Fergol Wersun. Gotta be a veteran Tanith for B Company senior, and they've both paid their dues, Throne knows, so they're the favourites. Both overdue a promotion. Wersun's a fine lasman. Tough as rockcrete, but Jo's more level-headed, so my money's on him. That's what you were thinking, isn't it?'

'No,' Cant lied.

'It is.'

'It'll just be temporary, though,' said Cant. 'Surely? Once Rawne is–'

'Nah, Rawne's pegged for regimental command if he pulls through. No more company lead for him. It'll be Lurgoine. Or Wersun. Permanent.'

Brostin fell silent, pensively exhaling smoke around his cigar.

'Or Ruri Cown,' he added. 'But a Tanith, definite.'

They heard footsteps behind them. Cant turned. Brostin used his splinted hand awkwardly to back-rotate the left wheel of his chair and swing himself about.

Doctor Kolding had a data-slate in his hand.

'Just came to notify you, Trooper Cant,' he said. 'We've reviewed, and you're fit enough to be discharged. Light duties only, and I want you back here every morning to have the dressing checked.'

'Good. At last,' said Cant.

'Well,' said Kolding. 'Be sensible. Mind how you go.'

Kolding paused, as though there might be other things to say, but he'd never been one for small talk. With a curt nod, he turned and walked away.

'Good for you,' growled Brostin. 'You must be sick of this place.'

Cant nodded. He'd been praying for a release note. Now he felt guilty leaving Brostin alone.

'I can come back and visit you,' he suggested.

'Oh, you can, can you, Cant?'

'Yeah, I *can*.'

Brostin sniffed. His stare had returned to the distant walls and the pall of smoke.

'I'll be fine,' he said quietly. 'Chance to put me feet up. Take life slow and easy. Haven't we all wished for that?'

'Well, can I bring you anything?'

Brostin thought about it. He fished the ratty cigar from his teeth with his bandaged hand.

'I want a drink,' he said.

'A drink?'

'Sacra.'

Cant shrugged. 'I can probably get you some sacra,' he said.

'No,' said Brostin. 'I want *my* sacra. *My* sacra in *my* bottle. It's the good stuff. You can fetch it for me, from me kit.'

'I can do that,' said Cant.

* * *

This was what victory felt like.

The streets of Eltath were shaking. Crowds were choking Princeps Avenue all the way back to Ordinel Place and the Great Hill Road. People cheered as the parade wound through, their cheeks and foreheads painted blue, white and gold, the tricolour emblem of Urdeshi forge world. Pennants danced and flags waved furiously. Temple bells were pealing from every tower and spire. The roar of the crowds almost drowned out the playing of the marching bands, all drilled Urdeshi ceremonial units that were followed by Urdeshi infantry regiments, followed by Keyzon and Helixid formations, followed by processions of fab worker unions and clade guilds, their gilded and tasselled banners high in the sunlight, streamers fluttering overhead. Some of the Urdeshi soldiers broke their perfect marching files to take flowers from the reaching hands of the crowd, or steal cheeky kisses before running back into line. People stood with hands on hearts, singing the battle hymns of the clades. Flowers, everywhere – garlands of islumbine around necks, sprigs of islumbine in waving hands, twists of islumbine tucked into drum straps or epaulettes, wreaths of islumbine around company standards. The flower of the Beati was not native, but suddenly it seemed to be flourishing everywhere.

Between the regimental blocks came columns of esholi, ringing handbells, carrying relics, or shouldering biers on which sat effigies of Saint Sabbat. Street hawkers were selling medallions of the Saint by the handful, and votives of Saint Kiodrus too. Saint Sabbat's illustrious companion, her Lord Executor during the original crusade, was enjoying a popular resurgence now there was a new Lord Executor to idolise.

Arrowhead formations of Thunderbolts soared low over the city, following the route of the march, the howl of their afterburners briefly overwhelming the vast noise below, their fleeting shadows making the crowd look up, and point, and cheer. The Aeronautica birds banked high and wide over the bay, popped tricolour trails of smoke, and turned back to make another pass. Another three circuits, and they would sweep to the carrier decks of the mighty *Naiad Antitor* to refuel, load more smoke canisters, and do it all over again. First Minister Hallemikal and the senior ordinels of the Upper House came out onto the balcony of Convocation House to watch the fly-past and wave to the crowds. From the high docks of the shift-port above the city, in the slope of the Great Hill, berthed ships sounded their sirens and their approach horns, the deep call of void giants resting in their dry-dock silos. Out in the bay, the sea was full of boats and amphibia, of sails and flags, the water strewn with islumbine petals. Later, after dark, there would be feasts and skyrockets long into the night.

It had been the same for three days. It would be the same for another month.

The Ghosts, on a day pass, pushed their way through the seething mob, politely refusing the garlands pressed at them, awkwardly accepting kisses and embraces.

'Feth this,' said Kester Raglon. 'There's no room to move!'

'What?' Wes Maggs yelled, hand cupped to his ear.

'He said there's no room to move!' Jed Lubba yelled back.

'There must be somewhere we can get a quiet drink,' shouted Noa Vadim.

'What?' Maggs bellowed.

'With me,' said Mach Bonin. 'No, thank you,' he added, to a woman who was either eager to kiss the Tanith scout or give him the small infant she was clutching.

'It's a good thing you can't hear this,' Raglon said to Nessa, 'because it's fething deafening!'

He had garlands of islumbine in both hands and he didn't know what to do with them. The planes went over again, low, the noise of them making their diaphragms quake. Nessa Bourah grinned at Raglon, and put her hand to her chest. She could feel the mayhem, and that was enough.

They made their way through the scrum to the rear of the crowd, and squeezed out into a side street. There were people here too, running, laughing, drinking, and the tumult of the main parade echoed behind them, but it was easier to move.

'Feth,' said Maggs. 'I thought I was going to get the life kissed out of me.'

Most action you're going to get, Nessa signed.

Vadim snorted.

'What?' said Maggs. 'What did she say? She said something, I didn't see it.'

'She said we're heroes,' said Bonin. 'Whether we like it or not. So get used to it.'

'Where are we?' Lubba asked. Squealing children scampered past with flowers in their hair and paint on their faces.

'Little Clade Street,' said Werd Caober, bringing up the rear, last out of the crowd. 'Arcuda said there was a decent place around here somewhere.'

'Kolosim says there's a good liquor-house on Zaving Square,' suggested Maggs.

'Well, that's over that way,' said Caober. 'We're not going to fight our way back through those crowds.'

'Shit,' said Raglon, stopping suddenly. 'Look at that.'

On the next street corner, there were three Sons of Sek. They were strung from the bracket of an iron street lamp. Small children were laughing as they milled around and threw stones at the suspended corpses.

'They're doing that a lot, so I hear,' said Vadim.

'Who?' asked Maggs.

'The Urdeshi,' said Caober. 'Street gibbets all over the city. Every corpse they find.'

'Doesn't seem right,' murmured Raglon.

'No more than they deserve,' said Bonin.

'Maybe,' said Raglon.

'They'd do it to us,' said Caober.

'Yeah, but it's not about them,' said Raglon. 'It's what it says about us. We could show some dignity in victory.'

'Feth dignity,' said Maggs. 'I'm thirsty.'

The Ghosts looked at the hanged corpses for a moment. They could smell the bloating and the encroaching decay. The roar of the city nearby seemed to diminish for a moment.

What did they do to their mouths? Nessa signed, but no one noticed.

'This way,' said Caober abruptly. 'Let's get arse-faced.'

'Well, you've got a head start, then,' said Maggs.

The bar on the next street was busy, crowds spilling out into the road.

'Here'll do,' said Vadim.

'I'll buy the first round,' said Raglon, the only officer in the group.

'I don't think you'll need to, Rags,' said Lubba. The patrons at the bar, all locals, had seen them, and were already waving and shouting and clapping.

'Well, it's a dirty job...' Maggs grinned, and led the way forward.

Raglon glanced back. Bonin had been left behind. He was still staring at the makeshift gibbet.

'All right, Mach?' Raglon asked.

'Yeah.'

Raglon wanted to press it. Bonin had been right in the hell of it, down in the Undercroft when the woe machines cut loose. No one really knew how he had survived, or the others with him, or how they'd managed to fight and protect an astonishing number of the regimental retinue from the horror in the dark.

'Something on your mind?' Raglon asked.

'No,' said Bonin. 'Let's get drunk.'

'Ah! Piece of the shit!'

Sergeant Haller came to a halt at the sound of the familiar voice, and backtracked a few paces down the palace hallway until he came level with the half-open door.

'Problem, major?' he asked.

In her quarters, Major Pasha glanced at him. She was sitting on her cot, a uniform jacket in each hand, and more clothes spread across the floor from her kitbag.

'Yes,' she said. 'There is dinner.'

'Dinner?'

'Dinner, yes. Party. Dinner party. More parties, never-ending. Three this week, Haller. *Three.* And more to come. Victory! Huh! Harder gakking work than fighting! And now, Viktor Hark, he says we have another dinner. Formal. Senior staff.'

'I'm sure it will be... very convivial,' said Haller.

Pasha got up.

'As you may have noticed, my dear sergeant, we have fewer officers to go around than usual these days.' Pasha shook her head sadly. 'Laid up hurt, or ... ah, Throne bless the dead. There is too much to do, Haller, and not enough of us to do it. I have four of the meetings today. *Four.* Munitorum. Tactical. Then war room. Then meeting to review memorial services. I have no time for more things.'

'The dinner?'

'Yes, the dinner. Well, not so much the dinner, but it is being dress code. Formal. I wore my dress uniform at function night before last, and some gak-idiot Keyzon spilled the wine down it. It, I cannot wear. So I come to find my spare.'

She held a jacket up for him to see.

'That's... pretty much ruined,' he said.

'Yes! Yes, it is. Piece of the shit. My kit was in Undercroft billet, and Undercroft billet flooded, now everything is ruined piece of the shit. I do not have time to find replacement.'

'Well, I could do that for you.'

'You could?'

'Of course.' 'You have time?'

'I can spare some.'

'Oh, Cin Haller. You are good man. Honest, good Verghastite son. You know tailor?'

'Tailor?'

'Tai-lor,' she said, over-enunciating. 'Gar-ment ma-ker?'

'No, but I thought stores could–'

'Munitorum no good, Haller, no good. Take too long. Request slip, and the authorisation, and then requisition, and then blah blah in triplicate...'

'Then I think I know someone,' said Haller. He held out his hand. 'Leave it with me, major.'

She passed him the ruined jacket. It was damp, and it stank.

'Just like this one?' Haller asked.

Pasha narrowed her eyes. 'You saying I have put on the weight?' she asked.

'No, I meant the styling of it, mam.'

Pasha grunted. 'Yes, like that. Thank you, Haller. You are helping me out a great lot.'

The gymnasium of the Palace barrack wing was a large, cold space. White-washed walls, hardwood floors varnished like glossy caramel, large windows that shone with the high air and the sea light. There was no one in except Chiria when Criid arrived. Chiria was lifting weights on a corner bench. They nodded to each other, but said nothing. That suited Tona Criid. She had nothing to say.

She crossed the big, brown leather floor mat behind the practice cages. They were old machines, immaculately maintained, though no Astartes had used their vicious programs for combat drill in a long time. She had thought about running, her favoured method of burning away energy and anger, but running would mean leaving the Palace compound, and she couldn't face the city. The crowds. The celebration.

Loss and rage wrestled inside her, fighting for supremacy. Whichever of them won, she would still be broken.

She pulled her shirt off over her head, and stood in boots, breeches and vest as she bound her hands with tape. Then she took a breath, bowed her head, and launched the first blow. She rained them hard. The hanging bag, brown leather like the floor mat, shivered on its chain with every muffled slap.

She kept hitting until her knuckles were raw. They were dead. They were all dead, and nothing made sense any more.

She paused, panting, ready to go again, and saw Chiria standing at the edge of the mat. Chiria was a head taller than Criid and her muscled arms twice the size. She was wiping sweat off her neck with a cloth, her weight reps done. There was a look on her famously scarred face, and Criid knew what it was.

'No offence,' Criid said. 'I don't want to talk.'

Chiria nodded.

'I guessed that,' she replied.

'Nothing to say,' said Criid.

'I understand,' said Chiria. She walked over to the wall racks, and took down a pair of focus pads. They were old, brown leather too. She put them on, ducked under the speed ball, and came across the mat to face Criid.

She took a braced stance, and cupped the pads up.

'Not in the mood,' said Criid.

'Better than the bag,' said Chiria. 'More responsive. Do your worst.'

Criid hesitated. She realised Chiria really wasn't going to talk. She knew better than to try, because how do you even start? She wasn't trying to use the opportunity to have a quiet word, or console. She was just standing there with her hands up, waiting to be hit.

Criid slammed punches into the pads. Chiria took them, nodded, and they began to circle. Criid punched some more, harder and with less finesse, and Chiria just soaked up each blow with gentle, corrective back-steps.

'Do your worst,' she urged.

'You don't want that,' said Criid. 'It'd break your hands.'

Chiria grinned, and raised her eyebrows as though to say 'as if'.

Criid let it all go. Fifteen minutes straight, no let up, pounding into the pads that floated and bobbed in front of her, moving around the mat.

Chiria stepped back and lowered the focus pads. Criid was out of breath, sweat dripping off her onto the leather.

'Any more, and you'll break *your* hands,' said Chiria.

Criid nodded.

'I'll be back tomorrow,' said Chiria.

Criid nodded again.

'My form's not good,' she said, breathing hard. 'All over the place.'

'Doesn't matter,' said Chiria. 'Just do it. I don't care what I look like, I just do what needs doing. However long that takes.'

'Yeah,' said Criid.

'Unless you want to stop?' said Chiria.

'No,' said Criid. 'I'll keep going. However long that takes.'

'Tomorrow, then,' said Chiria, and walked away. On her way out of the gymnasium door, she passed Merity Chass coming in.

Criid was stripping off her wraps. Chiria, bless her bones, had had the decency not to even try a conversation. Gaunt's daughter couldn't be trusted to do the same. Criid gritted her teeth. She didn't need this.

'I've been looking for you,' said Merity. Her hair was growing out. Her tunic and breeches looked like the basic uniform of the Tacticae Division.

'Listen, I'm sorry, but I really don't want to talk about anything,' said Criid.

'I understand,' said Merity. 'I don't want to talk about it either. None of it. Dalin. Yoncy. Gol. What the feth is there to say?'

Everything, thought Criid. Nothing. The children had been hers. She had saved them, and raised them. Then it turned out they were Gol's, by some miracle, and she and Gol had worked together to share the responsibility.

Then it turned out that the children weren't children at all. And now they were gone, and there was a hole left where they had been, a gaping wound, a fathomless pit, and Gol, by some cruel and unbearable injustice, had been lost in the same pit, and others with him, like Jessi Banda, and Leyr, and Neskon and Ban Daur's woman Elodie, and General fething Von Voytz, and so many more.

And the greatest injustice of all was that Criid had been spared, so she would have to live with it. She'd never be whole again. None of them would, none of the ones that this had touched. And that meant everyone, because those children had been known and loved by everyone, and Gol Kolea had been the heart of the regiment.

If this was what victory felt like, then Throne help those who lived to see it.

Criid tossed the wrappings into a metal bin, and leaned against the wall, hand splayed, head down, the sweat dripping from her face disguising the tears falling from her eyes.

'How can you miss something so completely and also hate it?' she asked.

'Someone,' said Merity.

'No,' said Criid. 'They were lies. They were weapons.'

'I was with Dalin right at the end,' said Merity. 'He came to find me. I don't think he'd have done that if he'd been a lie. I think that part of him was still there. Enough to slow him down and delay his onslaught.'

Criid looked at her.

'I thought you didn't want to talk about it?' she snapped.

'I didn't. You asked.'

'You miss him?'

'Of course. We were close. He was my friend, until he wasn't.'

'He was my son,' said Criid. She straightened up.

'What do you want?' she asked.

'Not this conversation,' said Merity. 'Neither of us are ready for it. But you made a promise to me. Or rather, to my lifeward.'

'What?'

'That you'd protect me. That's what you told her.'

'Feth sakes, I haven't got time for this,' said Criid.

'You misunderstand me,' said Merity. 'Since I arrived on Urdesh, I've got through two bodyguards. My lifeward. You were there for that. Then they gave me a Scion. Her name was Relf. I didn't know her long. She died in the Undercroft.'

Criid stared at the girl. There was no expression on Merity's face. It was easy to forget quite how much shit she'd been through too. If she'd been able to feel anything, Criid would have pitied her.

'So what?' Criid said. 'You want me to be your lifeward now? Your bodyguard? Because I made some fething promise? You want me to protect you?'

'Oh no,' said Merity. 'I don't want to rely on anybody. I want to protect myself. But someone needs to teach me how. You're a soldier. A good one. I'd trust your lessons.'

'Self-defence?' Criid asked. The request had wrong-footed her.

Merity nodded. 'And firearms. Whatever techniques you've got the patience to teach me. I only ever did basic.'

Criid shook her head wearily.

'There are times,' she said, 'when you remind me of your father.'

'I'll try not to be insulted by that,' said Merity.

Criid reached to her hip and drew her warknife. She held it out, grip first, towards Merity.

'Then we'll start with blades,' she said. 'Straight silver. That's the Ghost trademark, so you'd better learn it.'

Merity took the blade.

'What will you use?' she asked, but Criid had knelt down to pull a blade from a boot sheath. It was stubby, half the length of the warknife, like a baby sister.

'Short silver,' she said. 'A lot of us carry backups. Blade fights are ugly, and the only good ones are the quick ones. There's no finesse. Nothing fancy. You do whatever works. You get in first, and finish it fast. A knife-fight that lasts gets slippery and messy, and you lose grip, or footing. Or you bleed out. So you kill the fether hard before he cuts you. With me so far?'

'Every word,' Merity replied.

'Good. Now come at me.'

With Pasha's mouldering dress jacket under his arm, Haller was crossing the Circular Court when he spotted Ban Daur. His old friend was standing alone, facing the wall.

Haller didn't much want to talk to him, because he didn't know what to say. Daur had just lost his wife in the most horrific circumstances. But no one had seen Daur for days, and now here he was, just staring at a wall.

Haller wondered if he should fetch Hark. Or Curth.

'All right?' he asked.

Daur looked at him. His uniform was grubby. He seemed calm, though he needed a shave.

'Hey, Haller,' he said.

'Something wrong with that wall?' Haller asked.

'No, I just...'

'What?' asked Haller.

'Where are you off to?' Daur asked.

'I'm trying to get Pasha's jacket fixed. There's some dinner, or something. Anyway...'

Daur nodded.

'Probably a good idea, getting in Pasha's good books,' said Daur.

'It's just an errand,' said Haller. 'What do you mean, Ban?'

Daur looked up at the sky. It was bright and hazy. They could hear engines in the distance. Thunderbolt flights, out over the bay.

'Well,' said Daur, 'there are jobs in the offing. Promotions. You'd be in the mix, I should think. I've recommended you before now. I think you've got a good chance this time.'

'You mean... a company senior?' asked Haller.

'Seems there are a few vacancies right now,' said Daur. He said it deadpan, and seemed amused by it. Haller was a little shocked.

'You think I'm... currying favour to get her backing on a promotion?' he asked.

'No,' said Daur. 'It was a joke. Sorry, my sense of humour needs recalibrating.'

Daur looked around suddenly, as if he'd heard something, then turned back to Haller.

'Actually,' said Haller, 'Baskevyl was talking about me filling in for you. Acting senior on D Company. Just for now. Until you're...'

'Better?' asked Daur.

'You know what I mean. You need time.'

Daur nodded.

'Unless you're going to... just carry on,' said Haller.

Daur shrugged.

'No idea,' he said. 'But if it came to it, I'd be happy to see D safe in your hands. Although...'

'What?'

'Acting? Do you just want acting? There are permanents on offer, and you've been on the shortlist for a long time. It'd be you, Derin, maybe Cown.'

'Lurgoine,' said Haller. 'Wersun too.'

'True,' said Daur. 'Well, there are enough spots, may the Emperor protect us. C Company–'

'No,' said Haller quickly.

'No?'

'Not that one.'

'But you're Vervunhive. Makes sense.'

'No. Not Kolea's,' said Haller. 'I won't take it. No one wants it, Ban. No one can follow him.'

'Oh, but you'll take mine off me?'

'Because you're coming back,' said Haller. He wavered. 'Aren't you?'

Daur glanced aside again.

'What's the matter?' asked Haller.

'Nothing,' said Daur. 'C Company would be a good fit for you, Cin. You'd make it your own quick enough.'

'I don't want to make it my own. I wouldn't take it. I don't want people thinking I'm trying to replace Gol.'

'It doesn't matter what people think,' said Daur.

'It does to me,' said Haller. 'Heritage. Respect. Respect for tradition. I don't know. There's a way of doing things. Ceremonial. Like... like wearing the right jacket.'

He looked down at the ruined coat he was carrying.

'Whoever takes C Company should have earned it. They should be bulletproof. Not just the next idiot on a list.'

'Well, E Company, then?' said Daur.

'Oh gak! Seriously? Meryn's mob? The unlucky bastards? The cursed company? No thank you!'

Daur stared at him, and then started to laugh. Haller winced. It didn't seem right Daur laughing. Haller hadn't meant to be amusing.

'I tell you what you are, Cin,' Daur chuckled, 'you're fething picky! Not this one, not that one. Company senior is company senior. It's an honour, and you deserve it. Stop making objections. Respect for tradition, my arse.'

'Oh, I want it,' said Haller. 'But C was Gol, and E was fething Meryn, and it's toxic.'

'Have it your way,' said Daur. 'Go and get that coat mended. And try not to trip up on any heritage or tradition while you're doing it.'

Haller hesitated.

'You be all right out here?' he asked.

'Of course. Why wouldn't I be?'

'Because. Because of what happened to... I'm so sorry, Ban.'

Daur didn't reply.

'Look,' said Haller. 'You keep... you keep looking around. Is there something bothering you?'

Daur shook his head.

'I keep hearing voices,' he said softly. 'Everywhere I go. Even in the quiet corners of this place. Sometimes, it sounds like...'

He stopped. He looked at Haller.

'It sounds like her, sometimes,' he said. 'Like she's just behind a wall, calling out. Don't look at me like that. I'm probably just going mad. I'm going to get Ana to check me out. Of course, if I *am* mad, I'll be relieved of duty, so D Company can be yours full time.'

'Voices?' said Haller.

'Old voices, Haller. You know, ghosts. Corbec. Feygor. Merrt. I swear I heard Bragg laughing in the back quad yesterday. Sometimes it's her. It's just me, Haller. Just my imagination. The good old torments. You know how that gets. Day before last, I was sure I heard Brin Milo in the billet. Even thought I saw him too.'

'Well, you probably did,' said Haller.

'What?'

Haller frowned.

'Didn't anyone tell you?' he asked. 'He came back. Milo came back. He survived. Came back with Mkoll. The KIA report was wrong. You probably *did* hear Milo.'

Daur looked stunned.

'Really?' Daur said. 'He came back? Is he... Is he going to rejoin the regiment?'

Haller shrugged.

'No one knows,' he replied. 'No one's really spoken to him. He's, like, all grown up. Not a boy any more, not at all. And very distant. No one knows what to say to him. It's all a bit awkward, to be honest. But still, he made it, and I'm happy about that.'

'He came back,' Daur murmured. 'Well... that's something.'

'But we're going to get a drink, right?' asked Asa Elam as they walked down the Great Hill into the city.

'Yes, we're going to get a fething drink,' replied Darra Bray. 'Leave off. I just need to make a stop on the way.'

'As long as there's some drinking,' said Elam. 'And some celebrating. And all of that.'

'What stop?' asked Shoggy Domor. Bray sighed, and began to explain it again.

'Cant came to me,' said Bray. 'He's got a problem. He's just got signed off out of the infirmary, and Brostin asked him to fetch his sacra for him.'

'We can get him sacra,' said Domor. 'Osket's got a still and–'

'No,' said Bray. 'Brostin wants his bottle. His own bottle. Bragg gave it to him, years ago. Anyway, Cant checked Brostin's kit, and the bottle's been smashed. I think it was in Brostin's musette bag when that rockcrete fell on him.'

'Oh, shit,' said Domor.

'I know,' said Bray. 'So Cant came to me. Asked where we could get another. And we can't because, you know.... I mean, who's got one of Bragg's actual, original bottles left any more?'

'Larkin?' said Elam.

'Oh, probably,' said Bray, 'but he's not going to give his up, is he? So Cant came to me. He's made this promise. I said I'd help. Look, here it is. I knew I'd seen one. This won't take a moment.'

He ran down some pavement steps to the low parade of a small commercia.

'But we *are* going for a drink?' Elam called after him.

'Oh, feth you!' Bray called back over his shoulder.

'Uh, "Feth you, *captain,*" if you don't mind,' Elam replied as he and Domor followed Bray down the steps.

'So you can't fix it?' said Bray.

The ceramicist's workshop was small, and low, and dark, and smelled of glazes and kiln dust. The ceramicist, an old Urdeshi man, looked down at the bundle that Bray had unfolded on the counter.

'No,' he said.

'Really?' asked Bray.

'It's broken,' said the old man. The shattered pieces of the sacra bottle were spread out on the gun-cloth Bray had wrapped them in.

'Oh,' said Bray. 'I thought you could... put it on your wheel thing?'

'You don't really get how ceramics work, do you, lad?' observed the old man.

Elam leaned in over Bray's shoulder and whispered, 'This is a waste of time.' Bray shushed him. Domor was waiting in the doorway, leaning on the jamb, smoking a lho-stick.

'I thought there was a technique...' Bray said.

'There is,' said the old man, 'I suppose, if you have most of the pieces. I could reassemble it. But it wouldn't hold anything. You couldn't put liquid in it.'

'But it's for sacra,' said Bray.

'I don't know what that is,' said the old man.

'Well, this was a bottle given to my friend by Bragg...'

'I don't know who that is.'

'Doesn't matter. This is a traditional bottle. A traditional style, you see? It's a sacra bottle, from Tanith.'

'I don't know where that is,' said the old man.

'What I'm saying is,' said Bray with such patience Elam was beginning to smile, 'they don't make them any more. Anywhere. So I need to repair this one.'

'Can't you just get a different bottle?' the old man asked. 'I have many.'

'Yeah, but it won't be a sacra bottle from Tanith. It won't be this one. Because this one is special. It was given to my friend by my other friend–'

'I can repair it,' said the old man. 'But I'm telling you, you won't be able to put this sacra stuff in it.'

'Give it up, Darra,' Elam whispered to Bray.

'I'm telling *you*,' said Bray to the old man, 'they don't make these any more–'

'Well, they could,' said the old man, sorting through the pieces. 'I could. It's not a complicated shape.'

'You could?'

'Yes.'

'And it would look like this?' asked Bray.

'Yes.'

'And you could put sacra in it afterwards?'

'Yes.'

Bray looked at Elam. Elam laughed out loud at the earnest, harried look in Bray's eyes.

'Do you think he'd notice it wasn't the same one?' Bray asked Elam.

'I doubt it,' said Domor from the doorway behind them. 'A shed fell on him.'

Nessa finished her drink and slammed the glass upside down on the table. The crowd, filling the liquor-house to capacity and pressed in all around, exploded in wild cheers and laughter. Nessa executed a mocking, modest bow and wiped her lips.

Maggs sat back in his seat, coughing.

'Every time,' said Caober, taking money from those who had wagered.

'You shut up,' said Maggs, blinking hard to clear his vision.

'How many times is that?' Lubba asked, patting Maggs on the back. Nessa grinned and held up seven fingers.

'You shut up,' said Maggs. 'And your fingers too.'

'You don't drink like a scout, Wes,' said Raglon.

'Feth off,' said Maggs.

'Another round?' asked Vadim of the crowd, to shouts of approval.

'I don't think Wes is up to it,' said Lubba.

'I think a real scout should show us how it's done,' said Caober. 'I'll be fethed if the sniper cadre takes recon eight in a row.'

Nessa, watching his lips, laughed.

Mach, she signed. *I'll whip* his *arse too*.

'Right,' said Vadim. 'That's a challenge. Ladies and gentlemen, a new contestant will take on our reigning champion! Wagers, please!'

Raglon glanced around.

'Where *is* Bonin?' he asked.

Night was beginning to fall, and the first of the skyrockets were banging and fizzling above Princeps Avenue. The crowds had not dispersed. Taverns had opened their shutters to the street, and grox were roasting on spits. The festival would last into the small hours.

Mach Bonin kept off the main thoroughfares. He walked through the back lanes of the old quarter, through quieter, narrower streets where the smell of roast meat and woodsmoke hung in the air, and the crowd was a dull background roar, and the light flickered, multicoloured, as fireworks went off overhead.

At Brackett Street, there was another gibbet. Two bodies, both Sekkite troops. They'd been hacked about, mauled before and after death. He stood and looked at them. He looked at the faces. He looked at the mouths.

Same thing. And done recently.

He had to be close.

A long, grim day was coming to an end, but there were still a few hours left to get work finished.

The mortuary was a chilly space of stark white tiles. There was row after row of wheeled metal trolleys. Ana Curth didn't think she'd ever seen a charnel house of quite such capacity. The coloured flash of rockets came and went against the darkening sky in the small, high windows. From below their feet, they could hear the clank and rumble of hatches as Militarum crews wheeled in more bodies from transports in the yard.

'Let's get it done,' she said. She had the data-slate.

Ayatani Zweil nodded.

'No one thinks about this part, do they?' he remarked, toying with a sprig of islumbine.

'How so?'

'Well, this is not an aspect of victory that anyone ever considers. They're all out there, hullabalooing and what have you, because the wretched Anarch is dead, and Urdesh is free, and everyone will live happily ever after. They don't think about the cleaning up. The taking stock. The sober accounting of the price we paid.'

'We do,' said Curth.

'We do, ah yes,' said Zweil. 'The priest and the doctor. Forever the same.'

It was a simple process. They checked each trolley in turn, folding back the shroud sheet to reveal the body. Curth cross-checked the death list, confirmed identity, and sealed the death notice with her medicae authority. As she did, the ayatani blessed each body, murmured a few words, and performed the last rite of benediction.

A last five minutes spent with each of the fallen. The Munitorum would handle the burials. One trolley, then the next. It didn't take long before they found a face they recognised. There would be others. Curth wondered how many more. No one knew the exact figure yet. There would be some impossible to identify, and there would be some, like Gol Kolea or Elodie Dutana-Daur, who weren't there at all.

They worked methodically, row after row, trying to ignore the aching cold of the mortuary air, trying not to react when a shroud folded back to reveal a particularly ghastly mutilation.

'How's the blessed Beati?' Zweil asked after a while.

'Stable,' Curth replied, shifting the cold and heavy flesh of an Urdeshi storm trooper to locate his tags. 'Sleeping still. But I think she'll recover.'

'As much as any of us, eh?'

'Quite.'

'How do *you* think she is?' Curth asked.

'My prognosis, Ana, is much the same as yours,' Zweil replied. 'She is not quite so loud in my dreams these days, not quite so bright. But she has not gone away, not yet. And there is islumbine blooming everywhere, between every cobblestone and in every gutter. I take that as a good sign.'

Curth pulled the shroud back over the waxy face. Zweil had turned to the next cart along.

'Ah,' he said.

She wouldn't have to check the tags. It was Meryn.

They stood and looked at the body for a moment.

'What a vile little feth-wipe that man turned out to be,' said Zweil.

Curth nodded.

'You heard about his exploits, I take it?' Zweil said.

'Oh yes,' she replied. 'Luna Fazekiel told me all about it.'

'Nevertheless,' said Zweil, 'we treat him the same as everyone else. Judgement is not our place. That's the purview of another authority.'

'Of course.'

'I mean the God-Emperor,' said Zweil. 'When I said "another authority", you see? I meant–'

'I know.'

'Oh. Good. Sometimes I wonder if, as a doctor, all you see is the flesh.'

'No, I see the rest. But the flesh is my profession and the spirit is yours.'

Zweil smiled sadly.

'Shall we?' he asked.

'Yes,' she said. She put her seal on the death notice, and they moved to the next cart.

'Sometimes,' said Zweil, 'I think it's a shame that there are no rites for the living.'

'The living?' she asked.

'Yes, Ana. The ones who don't end up in a bag or on a trolley. The ones who survive. Who get to deal with tomorrow. I often think it's harder for them. Harder than death.'

'Harder than death?' Curth frowned at him.

'Of course,' said Zweil, 'I might be barking mad, but that's how it's always struck me. Those who serve the Astra Militarum pay with their lives. All of them. It's just that some do it in one moment, and others do it for the rest of their days.'

'Why bring it to us?' asked Ree Perday.

'Well,' said Haller. He'd laid the ruined jacket out on a table in V Company's gloomy rehearsal room. Some of Perday's fellow band members were looking on. 'Well, because V Company... that is... you're good at this sort of thing. Mending and fixing and sewing on buttons... you're good at costumes...'

Perday fixed him with a glare.

'*Costumes*?' she asked.

'Did I say costumes? I didn't mean costumes,' said Haller rapidly. 'I meant... ceremony. And, uh, tradition.'

'I think the sergeant's suggesting we're not a fighting company,' said Zef Erish, the hulking standard bearer. 'I think he's suggesting that all V Company knows is how to march and play, and maintain regalia, and sit around sewing...'

'I wasn't suggesting that,' said Haller.

'I think you were,' said Migol Gorus from the woodwind section.

'No, you're a fighting company, like all the others,' said Haller. 'I just know that you're good at this kind of thing because it's part of your work.'

'Absolute bloody insult,' said Erish.

Haller exhaled.

'Look, who's in charge?' he asked.

'No one,' said Perday. Haller closed his eyes and nodded. Wilder. Of course, Wilder. And he was dead. V Company, which was principally the colours band and, to many, the laughing stock of the regiment, unwanted and unnecessary, was yet another section lacking a senior officer.

'I'm sorry,' Haller said. 'I didn't mean to come here and insult you. I just seem to have a knack for it. Honestly, I was just trying to get Major Pasha out of a fix. My apologies.'

He picked up the jacket and walked to the door.

Then he stopped and looked back at them.

'You do realise,' he said, 'that you're about to become the most important part of this regiment, don't you? The front line? The vanguard?'

'What do you mean?' asked Erish.

Haller stepped back towards the bandsmen, who regarded him dubiously.

'The Tanith First,' he said, 'is about to be transformed. We're about to become the personal honour guard of the Lord Executor. That probably means we'll never see the field of war again. From here on out, it'll be parades and receptions, reviews and ceremonies, pomp and circumstance. And that'll be down to you. Because I can tell you right now, none of *us* lot know how to do it. Us lasmen don't do ceremonial. Feth, most of the Tanith couldn't march in a straight line if you gave them a map. We're good at many things, *excellent* at a few things, but Holy Throne, we are utter shit at the things we're going to be doing from now on. We'll all be looking to you. You lot know how it works. You know what cap to wear, which foot to start on, how to keep time, how to carry a fething flag. How to turn, in marching ranks, on the spot. I have no *idea* how that shit works. You make it look easy. I'm telling you, your hour has come. From this day forward, the honour of the Tanith First and Only rests on *your* shoulders. We'll all be counting on you. We'll be trying, desperately, to learn how to do what you do. We'll be *begging* you to show us how to do it. All of it. I don't even know what the feth that is.'

He pointed.

'It's a hautserfone,' said Nikodem Kores.

'Right,' said Haller. 'See? Who the feth knew? V Company, your moment of glory is here. *You're* Gaunt's Ghosts now. So buckle up. Anyway... I just wanted to say that. Thanks for your help.'

'Look, we... we *do* know how to mend a jacket,' said Perday. Haller halted in the doorway and looked back. Perday glanced at the other band members. Some were glaring at her.

'Well, we *do*,' she said.

'We do,' said Erish. 'We're always having to fix stuff up.'

'We have to look our best every time,' said Kores. 'Not just special occasions. Every gakking day.'

'Sergeant Major Yerolemew has us for breakfast if there's a stitch out of place,' said little Witt Arradin, the woodwind player, who was no more than eighteen.

'We've got thread machines,' said Perday. 'Spoolers. Stitchers. And boxes of buttons and trim. And bolts of cloth. You can't rely on the Munitorum. Give us that here.'

Haller handed the jacket to Perday. She spread it back out on the table, and the bandsmen gathered to take a look.

'Oh, *that's* ruined,' said Erish.

'It really is,' Perday agreed. 'But we can use it as a pattern. Cut it up. Make another one.'

'I've got some good lining silk,' said Gorus.

'Can we match these buttons?' asked Perday. 'Nikky?'

Kores nodded.

'Who's this for?' enquired Erish. 'Is it the right size?'

'I told you, Major Pasha,' said Haller.

'It can't be,' said Erish. 'The placket's the wrong way around.'

Haller screwed his face up, confused.

'I don't understand,' he said.

'This is a *man's* jacket,' said Perday. 'It buttons left over right. A woman's buttons the other way. See?'

She unbuttoned the top of her own jacket to demonstrate.

'I don't understand,' said Haller with greater emphasis.

'It's just the way it's always been,' said Arradin. 'A tradition.'

'Men dress themselves, women dress each other,' said Perday. 'That's where it comes from. That's what I was always told. This is a man's jacket.'

'Well,' faltered Haller. 'Pasha's never been... I mean, she doesn't make a thing about being a woman. She prefers to be taken on merit, not... you know... Maybe it's a choice, is what I'm saying. Maybe she doesn't want to be seen as different to the male officers.'

Perday shrugged.

'Might be worth checking,' she said. 'When does she need it?'

'Tomorrow night,' said Haller.

'Well, we can get started,' said Perday. 'But you'd better go and check. We can always switch the placket over, but we don't want to be doing that at the last minute.'

'I'll check,' said Haller.

Bonin crossed the old box girder bridge that spanned the Underclade Air Canal, and reached the edge of Vapourial District. The main noise of celebration was behind him, now, back in the old town, but the streets were still busy. Colours flashed from detonations overhead. The fireworks made plosive, popping sounds.

Vapourial had been part of the main fighting zone. The Ghosts had been deployed nearby. Many buildings were shuttered and derelict, and the further he walked, the more the fingerprints of war became clear. Broken windows. Shattered tiles and spills of brick. A burned-out truck.

He was entering ghost streets, where the living, celebrating part of Eltath ended, and the broken zone began – the part that war had dug its fingers into, the part that had been abandoned in a hurry, and to which no one had yet returned.

There were more gibbets here, set up by looters, most likely, or roaming militia patrols. The sorry dead of the Archonate's finest, hanging silent in death, filling the night air with the queasy scent of corruption.

He looked at the faces. The mouths.

Same as before.

He was pretty certain he had the trail. A scent of the wretched living was much more distinct now there were only the dead around.

Haller knocked on the door, and an aide answered. Pasha was in a meeting with six Helixid officers, laboriously running through a sheaf of patrol lists.

'I have a question for Major Petrushkevskaya,' Haller whispered to the aide. 'A question about the placket...'

'Left over right,' Pasha called without even turning her head.

'Gotcha,' said Haller, and stepped back out.

Movement, on an upper floor.

Bonin eased the sagging door open in the darkness. An old fab building, broken down, part of a clade division complex. In the gloom, he could see stained walls, broken glass, brick dust. Enough brick dust to show a scuff mark.

He edged inside. Of course, they'd come into Eltath without weapons. No one carried a lasgun with them on a night out drinking. Not even a side-arm. He drew his straight silver.

Every few seconds, without pattern, rhythm or warning, there came the bang of a firecracker or the fizzling pop of a rocket from a few streets away. At every little detonation, he froze and tensed.

Just fireworks.

He crept up the ragged stairs.

In the Undercroft that night, it had been as though hell had swallowed him. The darkness had been total and choking, stinking of waste-water, pierced only by screams, and a shrill wail like a bonesaw that came and went. He could remember feeling the terrified bodies of the retinue slamming into him, panicking as they tried to find an exit in the dark.

There had been no exit.

He remembered feeling blood splashing his face. He'd fought. Him, and Yerolemew, and Feen Luhan, and a few others. They fought with whatever they had... rifles, handguns, blades, then anything they could grab and wield.

They had fought in the dark, against the dark.

When the light had finally returned, the few of them were far fewer. Mach Bonin would not forget it, and darkness would never quite be the same reliable friend to him again.

But he had survived. And he had learned what desperation meant, and what it did to a person.

He reached the upper floor.

By the strobing light of fireworks, he checked the long, abandoned rooms. There was a stink here. He saw some ragged, filthy blankets, perhaps part of a bedroll. He saw a bottle, and an empty food can that had been hammered open.

The Sons of Sek wore charms, emblems of their foul gods, often around their necks as medallions, the way any soldier of the Astra Militarum might wear a medal of Saint Kiodrus. The Urdeshi, the citizens of Eltath empowered by sheer relief in the hours after victory, had been merciless in their humiliation of the enemy dead. They had killed the few they found wounded, and strung them all up, both the battle-slain and the mob-murdered, their disgrace and defeat displayed as trophies in the streets. They had beaten the corpses, burned some, and pelted others with stones and garbage as they swung in the breeze.

And they had ripped off their charms and made the dead eat them. They had forced the Sekkite corpses to swallow the ugly emblems of their ugly gods. They had stuffed the throats of the enemy slain with the icons they wore, and then sewn their lips shut, so the blasphemy couldn't get out, and so the corpses would tumble into eternity, choking on the very images they worshipped.

Bonin froze. No, just another firecracker, spitting and fizzing.

Someone had been cutting the charms out. Someone, in cover of darkness, had been slipping from gibbet to gibbet, slitting open sewn-up mouths and pulling out the trinkets and the swallowed medals. Someone who was lost and alone and desperate, and trying to find a way out of a hell that engulfed them. Someone trying to gather symbols of power and meaning in the hope that, somehow, they might grant them the ability to reach out to the Ruinous Powers and be heard, or perhaps hear again the voice that no longer spoke to guide them.

Someone who, if they were cutting open stitched lips, was at least armed with a blade.

A rocket banged. Bonin turned with a start, and the packson was on him. He was big and filthy, and every bit as desperate as Bonin expected. A cornered, wounded animal. His lair had been discovered.

Bonin saw the glint of a serrated blade.

He ducked, and twisted. There was no finesse in a knife fight, and the only good ones were the ones you won fast. No hesitation. Cripple the fether hard and fast, and put him down, or you'll be down with him, drowning in your own blood.

Skyrockets went off in series, five streets away. A long, trailing sequence of soft sounds, like paper tearing and wrapped fists pummelling a leather bag.

Bonin slammed the packson back against a rafter, but they were bigger than him, and stronger. The Son lashed out, and the impact threw Bonin across the room. He hit the wall, fell in a shower of dust. He felt hot wetness down his arm where the blade had caught him. He tried to block, but his hand was slippery and wet, and the power of the next attack smashed his straight silver right out of his hand.

Bonin rolled, taking savage kicks in the back and hips. He got up on one knee as the packson lunged to bury the hook-knife in his chest.

Impact.

The packson leaned so heavily on Mach Bonin, he had to brace to hold him up. The Sekkite's legs began to twitch and shudder, and Bonin pushed him away. As the packson fell, Bonin wrenched his short silver out of the enemy's neck.

Outside, firecrackers rippled across the sky in a slow, sustained flurry.

The following night, they were just lighting the lamps in the Circular Court as Baskevyl hurried down the colonnade. He was going to be late. He adjusted the buttons of his dress coat as he strode along, and tugged at the starched collar. He'd never been comfortable in Number One Dress. He reflected that he was probably going to have to get used to it, like a lot of things that made him uncomfortable.

The long, polished table was laid, and the room was softly lit with lumen globes, and silver candelabra. As Baskevyl entered, everyone pushed back their chairs and snapped to their feet.

'Please, stop doing that,' he sighed.

Asa Elam chuckled. Commissar Hark, at the far end of the table, gestured to the empty chair at the opposite end. Everyone was in dress uniform.

'If I sit down, will you do the same?' asked Baskevyl.

* * *

The mood was quiet but genial enough, considering. The food was good, better than they'd had in years. Servitors whirred in and out, bearing plates and trays and tureens. The palace kitchens were eager to serve the very best fare for the senior officers of the Lord Executor's honour company.

They were all present, all the company seniors, all in dress uniform: Major Pasha, Captain Kolosim, Captain Criid, Captain Elam, Captain Obel, Captain Domor, Captain Raglon, Captain Arcuda, Captain Ewler, Captain Mora, Captain Spetnin, and Captain Mklure, along with Hark and Medicae Curth.

There were empty seats too, set in respect. One for Rawne, one for Kolea, one for Meryn, one for Daur, one for Theiss, and one for Wilder. The absence was palpable, even the absence of those who had ended their lives in ignominy.

'I'm pleased to see you here,' Baskevyl said to Criid as the conversation swirled.

She shrugged.

'Where else would I go?' she asked.

'You could have declined the invitation, under the circumstances,' said Baskevyl. 'No one would have blamed you.'

'I see Ban did that,' said Criid, nodding to the empty chair that represented D Company.

'And no one blames him,' said Baskevyl. 'Tona, if you need me to appoint an acting for the duration–'

'I don't,' she said quickly. 'I really don't. I'm broken, Bask. I am so sad, I can't even feel it.' She looked down at her hands. Her knuckles were worked raw. 'But it'll be worse if I stop. So I'm just going to slug it out. Each day as it comes, beat it into submission.'

Baskevyl nodded.

'But if you ever need to stop...' he began.

'I've never stopped yet,' said Tona Criid. 'I don't intend to start.'

'Hear bloody hear!' said Pasha, eavesdropping, and clinking the stem of her glass with her butter knife.

'Perhaps,' said Hark, raising his voice to be heard, 'before the night gets any older, we should discuss the one order of business. Company appointments. Bask has been struggling with that–'

'For shame,' booed Ferdy Kolosim in a deliberately low voice that was probably meant to be an impression of Lord Cybon.

'–so I suggested this dinner in order that we might discuss the possibilities and share our thoughts,' said Hark. 'Right then, Bask is colonel–'

There was a general clinking of glasses. Elam pounded his hand on the table.

'–*and*,' said Hark, 'and he will *be* colonel until Rawne returns. Now, Bask doesn't like it, but he's stuck with it, so tough shit. Right, that one was easy.'

Several present laughed.

'Rawne won't like it either,' Domor called out.

'He really won't,' agreed Curth.

'Well, we'll cross that caustic lake of fire when we come to it,' said Hark.

'Rawne is special man,' said Pasha. 'Very special. He will soon adjust to the idea of being colonel when he realises the alternative is for him to take orders from one of us.'

There was general applause and agreement.

'All right, settle!' Hark called. 'Now, moving around the table. The question of an acting temporary for A Company also seems decided, because Tona has declared herself fit.'

More clapping. Criid stared at her plate, silent. Baskevyl leaned over and patted her on the arm.

'B Company needs an acting while Rawne's indisposed,' said Hark.

'Jo Lurgoine,' said Domor immediately.

'Well, *obviously*,' said Hark. 'I just thought we could pretend this was a discussion, Shoggy.'

'Lurgoine on B Company,' Baskevyl agreed. 'It's well past time he got a command, even if it is temporary.'

'One us better hurry up and die then,' said Pasha. There was a moment's hush.

'What?' she protested. 'I can't be making joke?'

'All right, Lurgoine's decided,' said Hark. He looked down the table at Baskevyl and winked. 'See how easy this is? How fluid and effective?'

'Move on, Viktor,' warned Baskevyl.

'Yes, colonel, sir,' said Hark. 'Right then... C Company.'

He fell silent. The officers around the table went quiet too. No one made eye contact.

'Ah,' said Hark. 'I spoke too soon. This was always going to be a tricky one.'

'Skip it and move on, Viktor,' said Baskevyl, painfully aware how sharply the mood in the room had shifted.

'No, Bask,' said Curth. 'Decide it. Decide it now, or it'll be like a wound that won't heal.'

'Yeah, please,' said Criid softly.

'This is the hardest one,' said Baskevyl. 'This is the one I kept going around and round on, which is why I couldn't decide on any of them.'

'Then this is the reason we're having this dinner,' said Criid, quite fierce. 'So fething do it.'

'It has to be a Verghast,' said Lunny Obel.

'Right,' said Criid. 'Lunny's right.'

'Yes, but who?' asked Baskevyl. 'There are some decent potentials, but those are big boots to fill. I don't think anyone wants the... the honour of it. For fear of fething up.'

He waited for someone to speak. The door behind him burst open instead.

Ban Daur stood there. His dress uniform looked a little wrinkled, as though no one had reminded him to press it.

'I'm late,' he said. 'Sorry, colonel. I nearly didn't... I'm late. That's all. Just late.'

'We're glad to see you, late or not, Ban,' said Baskevyl. 'Have a seat.'

Daur sat.

'You're discussing command appointments, I think?' Daur said. 'I thought I should be here for that.'

'We were discussing C Company, Ban,' said Hark. 'But as you are now present, may I presume a discussion of D Company is no longer necessary?'

Everyone looked at Daur. He took a deep breath.

'Yes,' he said. 'Not necessary. I don't want to vacate. I intend to conduct my duties.'

'Are you sure?' asked Criid, surprised.

Daur nodded.

'Yes,' he said. He looked around the table and the solemn faces watching him. 'Yes. It's that, or sit around waiting. Just waiting. Which helps no one and just makes the time go more slowly. So...'

He looked down at his plate.

'I don't think she's coming back,' he said quietly. 'But she might. So while I wait, I had better make myself useful.'

He looked up again. The candlclight flashed in his eyes.

'You know what?' he said. 'Yesterday, I discovered that Brin Milo has come back.'

Several of them nodded.

'Brin Milo,' said Daur. 'Imagine that. After all these years. Presumed dead. Long gone. Taken from us. But he's back. So there it is. Sometimes people come back when you think they're dead. I think that's the main reason I'm sitting here now.'

Daur glanced around the table. No one spoke.

'So, C Company?' he prompted.

'Gotta be Verghast,' said Obel.

'I was thinking Haller,' said Baskevyl. 'It's about time–'

'No,' said Daur. 'He won't take it. He told me. Cin's a fine man, very loyal. But he won't follow Gol. He doesn't want to step on Gol's legacy.'

'Well, he wouldn't,' said Whyl Ewler.

'No, I don't think he would,' agreed Daur, 'but there you have it. Haller feels the weight of tradition. Heritage, all that. Struggles with it, because he respects it too much. So, not him.'

'What about Fergol Wersun?' asked Raglon. 'Fine soldier.'

'Tanith,' said Obel, with a shrug.

'Even so–' said Raglon.

'Chiria,' said Criid.

They looked at her.

'Kleo Chiria,' she said. 'She's Vervunhive. She's hard as nails. I'd trust her with my life.'

'We all would,' said Kolosim. 'And we all have.'

'And she doesn't care what people think of her,' said Criid. 'She doesn't care what she looks like, she just gets it done. I respect Haller's feelings about C Company. Chiria is not weighed down by that sort of baggage.'

'Seconded,' said Vaklav Mora.

'All right,' said Baskevyl, nodding. 'That's an unexpected and excellent choice.' Knives rattled against glasses.

'So what about E Company?' asked Rade Mklure. 'I mean, now we're making headway?'

'Nobody wants E,' said Matteus Arcuda simply.

'Cursed company,' Kolosim agreed. 'Poison.' There was a general murmur of agreement.

'I learned something about ceramics yesterday,' said Elam, out of nowhere.

'Just how much have you had to drink, Asa?' asked Mklure.

'No, hear me out,' said Elam. 'I watched a man trying to put something back together again. Doesn't matter what. A broken bottle. Anyway. He was trying to help a friend who was trying to help a friend. You were there, Shoggy. This man, he just wouldn't let it go. It was hopeless. It couldn't be done. If he put it back together again, it wouldn't work any more. In the end, he realised he'd have to accept a new one. A replacement. One that looked the same, but was sound and complete.'

He paused. He looked sheepish.

'Go on,' said Pasha. 'This is being marvellously existential.'

Elam grinned.

'E Company is broken,' he said. 'I mean, it's shattered. More losses than any other, even B, and no pride. It's all down to that bastard Meryn. Throwing men away. Wasting lives. I don't think it can be glued back together. I think it has to be remade. From scratch, by someone with the patience to do it. Someone who accepts that sometimes the replacement is as good as the original. Someone who's prepared to... to try again. You know? The way Bragg used to?'

'So?' Hark asked.

'So,' said Elam, 'I nominate Darra Bray. Besides, let's face it, Bray should have been a company senior years ago.'

'About fething time,' said Domor.

Hark looked at Baskevyl. Baskevyl nodded an affirmative. Everyone at the table applauded.

'All right,' said Hark. 'M Company. A replacement for poor Theiss, may the Emperor rest him.'

'Oryn Ifvan,' said Baskevyl without hesitation. 'I'd already decided that one.'

'Good call,' said Criid.

'And the illustrious T Company is also already decided,' said Hark, looking at Nico Spetnin. 'Captain Zhukova was in with a shot there, of course, as acting, but she's bound for the scout cadre, at the chief's request, and she's taken a demotion to do it, so I'm delighted that Nico gets a spot worthy of his abilities.'

'Thank you, sir,' said Spetnin, raising his glass.

'Don't feth it up, Nico,' said Mora, 'or Zhukova will come for your balls.'

'I won't!' Spetnin laughed. 'Or I will wear body armour, day and night!'

'Do both,' Daur advised.

'So, the last,' said Hark. 'A replacement for Wilder at V Company. Colours Company. Which, I know, like C and E, is one that no bastard wants, but not for the same reasons. We treat it as a joke, which is shameful. But, Throne knows, we were a fighting regiment and we never asked for a band. Any suggestions?'

'There are Ghosts who deserve an opportunity,' said Baskevyl, 'even if it is the back-handed compliment of the colours section. It's *still* a section. Wersun's been mentioned. Cown, I think. Hecta Jajjo. Geddy Derin's on the list too. I don't know.'

'Actually,' said Pasha, 'this afternoon, I received request from Sergeant Major Yerolemew. It seems V Company would like to make it known, if it counts for anything, that their choice would be Sergeant Haller. As you say, Ban, he respects tradition and heritage. He respects ceremony. I do not believe Haller would see it as a back-handed compliment. And where we're going, I think ceremony is going to become very important.'

There was a lot of nodding.

'Also,' said Pasha, 'Haller is very good at buttons.'

'How much have *you* had to drink?' asked Mklure.

'Not enough!' Pasha declared, and slapped the table.

'Then let's do that,' said Baskevyl. He got to his feet and raised his glass. 'I'll make notifications tomorrow and get the promotions processed.'

'Do you want to check any of this by Rawne?' asked Hark.

'No,' said Baskevyl. '*I'm* colonel. Now *stand up*.'

They got to their feet.

'To those we have lost and those who are absent,' said Baskevyl.

'The Emperor protects!' came the chorus.

'To our Lord Executor,' said Baskevyl.

'Gaunt!'

'And to his Ghosts,' said Baskevyl, 'may they live forever.'

'First and only!' they replied, and drank.

'What's this?' asked Brostin.

'Your bottle,' said Cant. He coughed, and then tried it again without the squeak. 'Your bottle.'

Brostin was sitting in his chair, out in the pale midday sun on the infirmary terrace.

'Oh,' said Brostin. 'Is it?'

'Yes,' said Cant. He glanced back across the terrace. Darra Bray was standing in the doorway behind him, out of Brostin's eyeline, watching intently. He nodded to Cant encouragingly. He mouthed, 'Go on.'

'Well, give us a sip, then, Cant,' said Brostin. 'I can hardly hold the fething thing now, can I? No, I can't, Cant.'

'Ha ha,' said Cant. He unstoppered the bottle, and tilted it as he brought it to Brostin's mouth. It wasn't very neat, and there was a little spillage, but Brostin smacked his lips.

'Ah, yes,' murmured Brostin. He grinned. 'This is what victory feels like. Say hello to Mister Sacra. Why, *hello*, Mister Sacra.'

'All right?' asked Cant anxiously.

'Yeah.'

'Proper sacra, eh? From your bottle? The one Bragg gave you, all those years ago?'

'Yes,' said Brostin.

'Good,' said Cant. 'Good.'

'Turns out,' muttered Brostin, 'you *can* when you put your mind to it, can't you, Cant?'

'Of course I fething can,' said Cant. He looked back at the doorway, but Bray had gone.

'Give us another sip,' said Brostin.

'Sure,' said Cant, tipping the bottle. 'Is there... is there something wrong?'

Brostin swallowed and licked his lips. 'Nope,' he said.

'Sure?'

'Yes. Why?'

Cant stood for a moment, thinking. He winced and braced himself.

'Look,' he said. He sighed. 'Look, Brostin. Uh, the thing is... this isn't your bottle. The bottle Bragg gave you, it got smashed. This is a replacement. I wasn't going to tell you. I didn't want to annoy you. But I just can't lie about it. It isn't your bottle.'

Brostin nodded, staring into the distance.

'Of course it isn't,' he said. 'You think I couldn't tell?'

'Oh,' said Cant. 'Oh. Well, uh, I had better be going. I'll leave this here.' He put the bottle down.

'I'll come back in a day or two,' he said.

'Hey,' Brostin called after him.

'What?' asked Cant. He cleared his throat.

'What?' he said in a proper voice.

'Give us a light, eh, Callan? Before you go,' said Brostin.

FROM THERE TO HERE

'From there to here' was an Urdeshi pledge. It wasn't formal, just an off-hand phrase that locals muttered as they took a drink. There was no raising of the cup in salute to another when it was spoken, no clinking. The Urdeshi murmured it to themselves, without emphasis and probably unconsciously, as they slugged another shot of amasec or fobraki.

Brin Milo learned it in the liquor-house on Hainehill Street. No one taught it to him, or advised him to say it. He learned it through observation. The other patrons, mostly Urdeshi Militarum or shift workers from the local fab, muttered it casually as they took their drinks, so he started to say it too, mainly so he wouldn't stand out.

He stood out enough as it was. Tall, dark-haired, not local, an off-world Militarum in combat blacks that curiously lacked any rank pins or unit insignia. That marked him out. That, and the fish tattoo over his eye.

That, and the fact that he always came in alone.

The waters of the Holy Balneary in Herodor Civitas are warm, blood-heat. They cure and they heal. They will make everything better. He walks down the steps to the edge of the pool and–

He woke.

'I'd like to see the colonel,' Milo said.

'Do you mean Rawne? That's not possible. He's in the infirmary. Acting Colonel Baskevyl might be available later in the week.'

The commissar's name was Fazekiel. She was carrying a recent wound, and walked with a limp, holding herself stiffly. Her pallor suggested she had left the infirmary too soon, and against medical advice, but Milo knew from experience that commissars were all about duty, and Fazekiel seemed the type who was *all about duty* to the point of clinical obsession.

'I meant, uh, Gaunt,' he said.

She looked at him sharply, as though he had no business speaking the name without an honorific. She'd been briefed, of course. She'd been told Milo was true Tanith, from the old days, from the Founding, returning to the fold, but still, her expression suggested that he had spoken out of turn.

'You mean the Lord Executor?' she said.

'Yes. I'm sorry, I forget he's called that now.'

'There are papers to endorse, Milo,' she said. Fazekiel had a sheaf of them.
'For?'

'For enlistment, essentially,' she replied. 'Re-enlistment, I suppose, is
more correct. I don't have the forms for that. Munitorum paperwork is all
over the place, as you can imagine, but I found these. I'm sure they'll serve.
I'll annotate and authorise any amendments.'

They were basic sign-ups, pro-forma, the commitment dockets a trooper
made his mark on when he enlisted or was drafted. They were for young
men. They were for boys. There were highlighted blocks to fill in, sections
that, at a glance, seemed ridiculous. 'Place of Birth', 'Next of Kin'... did he
have to fill them in if those things didn't exist? There was no blank section for prior service record, because the forms were meant for boys who
had no prior service to write down. He did, but he had no idea how he'd
summarise it, even if there had been a space.

'Why?' he asked.

'Your service history is... ah...' Fazekiel paused. 'Spotty. Admin really
hasn't got a record of you since, ah, Herodor. So this is really just procedural, to get you back in the Militarum system, so you can be assigned and
pay-graded and so forth.'

'No, I mean why...' Milo said. 'Why any of that?'

Fazekiel frowned.

'You're staying with the regiment, aren't you? Transferring back? That's
what Chief Mkoll led me to believe.'

'I'd like to see the colonel,' said Milo. 'The Lord Executor.'

'I don't think that's going to be possible,' she said.

The walls of Brachis City start to fall. He raises the old pipes to his lips, to
triumph them in through the breach and–

He woke.

There were celebrations rolling through Eltath City, day and night. Firecrackers, street parades, feasts in the open air, riotous assemblies of civilians
and service personnel. Milo was told it was like that right across the face
of the planet. Urdesh was free. The nightmare of the Anarch was over. It
was an Imperial victory. Spontaneous rejoicing filled every thoroughfare
and habway. Temple bells rang. Fireworks shivered the skies. It was louder
and more explosive than the final, bleak years of the war. Citizens who had
flinched at every distant blast and fled for shelter at the sound of aircraft
now unleashed skyrockets with manic abandon.

It was in the days following his return from hell that he found the liquor-house.

At the cry, clear and keening, they come up out of the trenches. Eboris has
started to burn, fire all the way along the western ramparts. They start to
run, to charge. He sees her up ahead, sword raised. If he runs faster, he can
catch up with her, and be at her side when–

He woke.

* * *

Urdesh had a long and lauded history. It was a proud world of proud people. It was the beating heartworld of Sabbat industry, a world of forges and fabs, second only to Balhaut in significance. Here had been stamped and pressed half the arms that had made the crusade possible and, as some liked to jibe, half the arms that had made *resistance* to that crusade possible too. Urdeshi weapons and war machines were reliable, well-made, as enduring as the spirit of its people, and ubiquitous. They were stockpiled and used by both sides, because Urdesh had, during its long and lauded history, *been* on both sides.

The Urdeshi were stoic to a degree that Milo found amusing. Their cultural demeanour was fatalistic, their passions phlegmatic, their warriors fierce as a point of principle, their liquor-house songs woeful and bitter. They had endured wars and invasions, they had weathered occupations and purges, they had withstood enslavements and kill-camps. They had known the loss of being conquered and the sacrifice of being liberated, and they had known both of those things several times over. Milo didn't fault them for their indigenous temperament, nor did he believe it was excessive or affected, but still he found it funny.

Lose your whole world, he thought, then play me one of your morose fething woe-songs on your fething fiddle.

Lose your way. Lose your purpose. It had taken him long enough to find that for himself, and now it seemed he had lost it again. Milo wondered why he felt so angry, and he had a nasty feeling it was because, in the final moments, he had failed.

'You did a great work, Brin,' said Captain Auerben.

'Did I?' he asked. They sat together in sunlight, on the stone platforms of the palace battlements. She preferred the air outside, the breeze coming in off the city. She breathed more easily, and used her inhaler bulb less.

Auerben nodded. She'd read the confidential after-action report, of course. All the Beati's staff seniors had.

'You were there at the kill,' she said.

'*For* the kill,' he corrected her. 'I didn't make it.'

Auerben frowned. She was physically small, too small, it always seemed, to bear such a weight of duty and purpose on her shoulders. But then the same could be said of the Beati. Auerben's face was angular, framed by dark hair. He'd long since stopped noticing the burn scars.

'It's not personal,' she said.

'What does that mean?'

'You never struck me as someone looking for medals or recognition,' she said.

'I'm not,' he replied, and meant it.

'Then why do you care? You were there at the kill. You were part of the kill. You helped make it happen.'

But the killing strike was not mine, he wanted to say. He kept his mouth shut, because he knew it would make him sound petulant, like a child. Like a *boy*.

But there it was. He hadn't done it. He'd come close, there on the windswept shingle, but it hadn't been enough.

Milo had foolishly come to think of it as his purpose. No, more than a purpose, a destiny. He had secretly convinced himself it was the reason the Beati had chosen him to walk at her side, as though, through some miraculous intuition, she'd known from the moment they'd met on the dustscapes of Herodor that he'd be the one. That, one day, *he'd* be the man who would kill the Anarch.

So she'd been wrong about that, or he had failed. Neither thought made him comfortable.

'Has she woken?' he asked, changing the subject.

Auerben smoothed a fold out of her mulberry long coat. She still wore the uniform of her old company, the Jovani Vanguard, just as he still wore the black camos of the Tanith. The Beati's staff retinue had no uniform of its own. When you joined, you shed the patches and badges of your old regiment, but kept the uniform. The Beati said that this was a mark of respect to the units she had drawn her followers from, a visible demonstration of the idea that she stood for all and any. But Milo knew it was more to do with meagre resources. The retinue was like a scratch company. You wore what you stood up in. You scavenged and salvaged for kit and clothes. You lived humbly, like an esholi, making do and asking for nothing. He'd kept his pipes, his straight silver, his ghost cloak, but all of those were now gone, lost when he was captured by the Archonate at Oureppan. Mkoll had given him the blacks he was wearing, taken from stores on his return.

'No,' said Auerben. 'No, she has not. She sleeps still. Oureppan, and the fight with the woe machine... they sapped her. Her light faded for a while.'

Milo nodded. 'I'd like to see her,' he said.

Auerben shook her head. 'We are considering...' she began.

'What?'

'Taking her back to Herodor Old Hive,' said Auerben. 'So she can heal in the holy waters.'

'I think that's a good idea,' said Milo.

'It is all but agreed,' said Auerben.

'When do we depart?'

She glanced at him. 'No, the retinue. By "we", I mean the retinue.'

'Am I not part of that any more?' he asked.

'Yes, and always, Brin. But your place is here now.'

'There is no place here–'

'With the Ghosts.'

'No,' he said. 'I left that life behind, and I was never truly part of it. There is no place to come back to.'

'She thinks there is,' said Auerben. 'This is the path you must walk now. She has said as much to me, and to several others.'

'You said she was sleeping still, Auerben,' said Milo. 'How can she have *said* anything?'

The captain looked at him. He abruptly became very aware of her burns. They all carried scars and marks. She'd got hers on Morlond, in a pyro-chemical attack. Milo had always felt that the scars he bore were the loss of Tanith, but suddenly it seemed he was about to get the real wounds he would be obliged to carry for the rest of his life.

A pulse quickened behind his breastbone, the old instinct, harbinger of misfortune.

'You know how,' she said quietly.

He did. He knew the way she spoke to those closest to her. In dreams. He had not dreamt like that since his return from hell. He had thought that the lapse was because she was unconscious, and that the dreams would resume as she recovered.

But, no. The others were still dreaming the dreams of islumbine. None for him.

'Am I cast out because I failed?' he asked.

'I don't know,' said Auerben. 'I don't think so, Brin, because in my eyes, you did not fail. But I think she has another purpose for you now, and it's here, not at her side.'

'Why didn't she tell me herself?'

Auerben shrugged.

'I think she is. I'm sorry it feels cruel.'

He rose to his feet and looked away at the distant haze on the horizon. He would not let Auerben see tears in his eyes. He would not show his hurt, his disappointment. He would not seem like a boy.

'Did you question her choice when you came to walk with her?' Auerben asked.

'No,' he said.

'Then why question it now?'

'I want to see her,' he said.

'She's sleeping, Brin. It's not possible.'

He heard her rise to her feet behind him.

He heard her say, 'It's not personal.'

Siprious, the last day of the assault. Engine-kills ablaze across the field below the bulwarks. A scent of islumbine. He sees her, shining like a star, but he can't reach her. It's too far, and every time he starts to run–

He woke.

'Another,' said the Urdeshi at the bar. 'Another, and one for my friend here.'

I'm not your friend.

The barman poured fobraki into little glass beakers that looked like jars.

'You Militarum?' the Urdeshi asked.

No.

'You look Militarum,' the Urdeshi said, pushing one of the beakers along the bar to him. 'But no unit pins.'

Long lost.

'Yes, Militarum,' said Milo, accepting the drink. It *was* in a jar. A washed and repurposed camo-paint jar. War had left so little intact on Urdesh, they made use of what they could find.

'Forty-Eighth Urdeshi Light, me,' said the man, raising his jar and studying the piss-yellow liquor with dulled eyes. 'Here's to you, and your service, brother.'

He muttered the toast, so off-hand it could barely be made out, and snatched back his drink.

'The Emperor protects,' Milo said, and followed suit.

'Now, *no*, you see?' The Urdeshi said, wiping his mouth on his frayed cuff. 'He *doesn't*. No, sir. You protect *yourself*. You fight for what's yours. Tooth and nail.'

'Of course,' said Milo.

The man pawed at his arm.

'I mean it,' he said. 'That's the way of it. Every Urdesh-born soul learns that early. You fight for what's yours. You're not going to get given anything. If you want it, you fight for it. Tooth and nail. We have lived too long in the halls of war, we don't know another way.'

On that, I agree with you.

'So, which unit? Which unit are you, friend?' the man asked, waving at the barman for another round.

No unit. No nothing.

'I asked you, which unit?'

Say something.

'Uh, Tanith,' said Milo. 'Tanith First.'

The man gripped his arm.

'Are you taking the piss?' he asked, hot liquor-breath in Milo's ear.

'No.'

'You're one of them Tanith? The Big Man's boys?'

No, and not for a long time, and never properly.

'Yes.'

The man slid off the bar stool and raised his hands and his voice to the room.

'Hey! Hey! Shut it!' he bellowed. 'This fellow here, this man with me. No, bloody shut up and listen! He's Tanith! He's one of them Ghosts! Sitting right here, my friend here! One of Gaunt's bloody Ghosts!'

There was a commotion of cheering. The man seized Milo's hand and forced a shake, then pushed on into an unwelcome embrace.

'You were the ones!' he cried. 'You, and your fine High Lord himself! You gave Urdesh back to us!'

No. Not really.

'Let me shake you by the hand, friend.'

You just did.

'You're a saviour, you are. A saviour. I never thought to meet one of you to look in the eye!'

And you still haven't.

'Another drink! Another drink for my fine and brave friend here!'

The barman poured more. Even the barman was flushed and smiling.

'On the house,' he said.

The Urdeshi raised his jar and toasted Milo.

Ask him.

'What is that pledge?'

'What?'

'The thing you say when you drink?' Milo asked. 'I've heard it a lot, but I don't know it.'

'Here's blood in your eyes?'

'No, the other thing.'

'Oh, from there to here? You mean that? *From there to here.* It doesn't mean anything. Just a thing.'

Milo raised his jar.

'From there to here.'

What was the path? It was measured in battles, in passing worlds, one scrap-fight after another. Herodor, of course, the start... Brachis City, the rimwalls of Tenzia, Ashwarati Valley, the Flood Plains, the trench lines of Eboris *and* of Gant Hive, the long winter on Khan III, the Siprious Assault, the ravening of Cygnus City, then Pinnacle Spire in Oureppan.

Others too. Others he had forgotten. Herodor was always the start, as it seemed to him, the start of a life he felt he'd actually chosen and not merely stumbled into. Before Herodor, nothing seemed to matter, not even Tanith. And after Pinnacle Spire, nothing mattered either.

At the Spire, he'd come close, and failed. Afterwards, at Coltrice Fastness, and then at Orchidel Island, he'd merely been present.

He dreamed of them all. They mingled, decomposed, one place decaying into another, like bodies in a shallow grave, obeying dream logic instead of factual sense. His life as an esholi, at her side. From Herodor to Urdesh. His life as an instrument of purpose. From there to here.

He didn't dream of her. He hadn't since Orchidel.

Or if he did, she never spoke.

He woke.

The billet was a fine set of rooms off the Circular Court of the Urdeshic Palace that had been deemed appropriate for the personal brigade of the Lord Executor. It was quiet, a blue gloom of cots in rows. Men slept, a few snoring. The place was half-empty. Several companies had been given furlough, and had gone down into Eltath to enjoy the celebration of the city's liberation. The coloured flash of fireworks blinked at the billet windows now and then.

Milo rose. He didn't know these people. There were far too many new faces, and pitifully few old ones. The Tanith seemed outnumbered by hard-faced Verghastites and coolly professional Belladon. It was the Tanith First, but it wasn't. If you changed the blade and the handle, was it still the same warknife?

Too many old faces had gone. Too much of the past left buried in shallow graves on a multitude of worlds. And the faces he did know didn't seem to know him. Varl, Ifvan, Elam, Raglon... the rest, the long-timers, the survivors... time had passed differently for them. Milo had heard the story. A transit accident on the return from Salvation's Reach. Missing, presumed lost, adrift in the warp-ocean, ten years passing in real time.

Ten years that Milo had lived out. He was as old as them now, older than some. Full-grown, tall, a stranger. Certainly not the boy they had known, the company mascot, the lucky charm, the only civilian survivor of Tanith. He knew their faces, but they didn't know his, and it made them awkward around him, unsure of what to say.

He'd always been a stranger.

Only the fish tattoo over his eye seemed familiar to them.

Milo walked down the row between the cots, silent as a ghost, and opened the billet door. He stepped into the night air.

It wasn't just the separate lives they had led, nor the dislocation of lifetimes, which had returned him to them as a man they didn't know, older than he was supposed to be. It was personal. War bred a comradeship, an intimacy that could not be faked. They had all been through wars, but not the same ones. They could all compare wounds and stories, but they weren't the same wounds and they certainly weren't the same stories. He could tell them of Brachis City and Ashwarati, and all the rest – not that he had much desire to do so – and they would listen, and they would be interested, but they wouldn't *know*. And they, in turn, could tell him of Ancreon Sextus, and Jago, of Salvation's Reach and even of the Tulkar Batteries here in Eltath, and he would be keen to hear, but he wouldn't *know* either.

War was the only life that he and any of them had lived. It was a constant, and it was an inclusive bond. But the respectful fellowship of veteran soldiers was not the same as the blood-bond of comrades in arms who had endured in the same places together. It wasn't a matter of details, or particular specifics, or even private jokes. To go through a battle with others, and trust them with your life, was to be tempered in the same fire. Since Herodor, he and the Ghosts had been forged in different flames. The fires looked the same to outsiders, but they burned differently and left unique patinas on mettle.

It was hard to explain unless you had known war. The experience of a soldier, of a Guardsman, of a common lasman, was universal, but it was also entirely personal. You never, and could not, love someone as much as the souls that had been through the same fire with you.

It was a blood-bond. Stronger than birthplace, stronger than a company banner, stronger than family, like an unspoken and unbreakable oath taken through experience. A bond, a pact. A blood pact.

Milo laughed at where the words in his mind had gone.

'Laughing in the dark. Not the best indicator of sanity.'

He looked around. She'd been there all the time, sitting by a pillar in the dark. He hadn't seen her. He didn't know her either.

'Something amused me,' he said. 'And no, it's not.'

'You're Milo,' she asked, but it wasn't really a question. 'I've heard about you. They talk about you. The boy.'

'Not any more,' he said.

'Clearly.' She got up. Her accent, that was Verghast.

'I hated being called the boy,' he said.

'But you *were* a boy. A child.'

'Yes. But I hated it. And it's the only thing I haven't managed to lose.'

'That's not true,' she said. 'You obviously haven't lost your ability to feel sorry for yourself.'

He blinked. 'What? I'm not– Feth you.'

'Just an observation.'

'Feth you anyway.'

She stepped closer. She was slender and athletic, her black hair tied back. She held out her hand.

'Zhukova,' she said. So this was the infamous Zhukova. He'd heard of her. A Verghast-intake officer who'd accepted a demotion so she could join the scout cadre. First woman they'd let in, and it had been by Mkoll's invitation.

He shook her hand.

'They talk about you too,' he said.

'Oh, they always have,' she replied. She paused. 'Who's "they"?'

He shrugged. 'Mach Bonin. Caober. The chief mentioned you.'

The list was short, now he came to think of it. The only Ghosts he'd had any real conversations with since his return had been the scouts. Mkoll had brought Milo back in, saved him at Coltrice, done the deed when Milo had failed on the beach at Orchidel. Mkoll had brought him back, so the scouts had automatically accepted him, given him a cot, scared him up some kit. But the scouts were all loners at heart, conditioned to silence, so the conversations hadn't been of any real substance. They hadn't questioned him about his time with the Beati. They had just carried on, with him among them, as if he'd never been away. Was that supposed to reassure him, or was it just the detached indifference of the career scout? Mkoll was a great man, but he was hardly the expressive, paternal type.

'In my experience,' Zhukova said, 'self-pity has no value. Self-recrimination, it rots you inside.'

'Why are you telling me that?'

'Because you're feeling sorry for yourself. Because you feel like shit, and you don't know who to blame. Because the world's against you, and you're taking it out on the only person you can. Which is you, by the way.'

'I didn't say anything about–'

'You didn't have to, it's obvious,' she said. She stood beside him and stared out into the midnight gloom of the court. Coloured flashes underlit the streaks of night cloud. 'You lurk about the place like you don't belong. You keep to yourself. You don't smile.'

'You've been watching me?'

'Everyone's been watching you. Most of us because we don't know you, and we've heard the stories. The boy with the second sight. The piper who went to march at the Saint's side. But your friends, the ones who remember you–'

'I don't really have any friends,' he said. 'It's been a long time.'

'They remember you,' she said. 'I've heard them talk. I've talked to them. Larkin and Rafflan. Obel. Bray. Shoggy. They don't know what to say to you. They don't know how to approach you. They want to, but there's a look in your eyes that keeps them at bay.'

'Look, I appreciate you're trying to do something... I don't know what... but you really don't know what you're talking about,' he said.

'There, exactly like that,' she said. She pointed at his face. 'A barrier. And I *do* know what I'm talking about. And what I'm trying to do is steal the chief's straight silver.'

'What?'

'I'm saying, I'm not meddling in your business, you churlish gak. I was out here, doing something, and you walked out, and so I spoke–'

'What?'

'–you interrupted *me*, not the other way around.'

'You're trying to steal his warknife?' he said.

She grinned.

'Oh, that. Yes,' she said.

'What... Why?'

'Mkoll's given me a shot, but everyone expects me to fail. One, I'm a woman. Two, I'm Verghast.' She started to count the strikes off on her fingers. 'Three, I'm an officer, or was. Four, I have no background in recon specialties, and I sure as shit don't have that Tanith tree-magic crap baked into me. Five, I'm a woman–'

'You said that.'

'It bears repeating. They've given me a shot at it, and I'm working my arse off to make the grade, but they are all waiting for me to fail. Even Mkoll. So I'm putting in the extra hours. Like now, Milo, until you interrupted me. One of these nights, I'm going to get in there and lift his straight silver while he's sleeping. That'll wipe the fething smirk off their faces.'

'You won't.'

She sniffed.

'Not you as well,' Zhukova murmured.

'No,' he said, back-tracking fast. 'Because it's Mkoll. None of us could do that.'

'We'll see.'

'Seriously, set yourself an easier challenge.'

'Why?' she asked.

He started to answer, but didn't know what the answer was. It was a genuinely good question.

'Nearly got it, two nights back,' she said. 'He didn't stir. But I couldn't reach the blade. So I left a flower on his bolster instead.'

'A flower?' Milo asked.

'Yes,' she said. She gestured towards the stone planters that framed the courtyard. 'One of those things. I picked one of those and left it.'

'Islumbine,' he said.

'Yeah. It grows everywhere.'

'It does now.'

'What?'

He shrugged.

'He was livid,' Zhukova said, with an involuntary snigger. 'Thought it was some kind of joke or something, which I suppose it was, but he didn't get it. He thought Bonin had done it.'

Milo smiled.

'The knife,' she said. 'Next time. Thought I had a good shot tonight, except you came blundering about.'

It didn't seem to warrant an apology, so he made none.

'What did you mean?' he asked. 'Just now. You said you know what you're talking about?'

'Self-recrimination,' she said. 'That was my vice for a long time. It eats you up, so stay away from it, that's all I'm saying.'

'I've lost a lot,' said Milo.

'I have no doubt.'

'It feels like I've lost everything,' he said, 'except a nickname I despise.'

'Well, loss is often a factor,' Zhukova said, quite matter-of-fact. 'Actual loss, or a feeling that you've lost your way. Or the feeling that you're not good enough. That you're an imposter, and someone's going to call you out any second. That was mine.'

'How did that work?'

'I'm a career soldier, Milo,' she said. 'It's what I wanted to be, what I chose for myself. I'm not bad at it. Got a commission. A mention or two in after-actions. But my whole career, I've been dogged by rumours. By gossip. I only made officer school because I'm a good-looking woman. I only made captain because I'm easy on the eye. I only got a command post because I slept my way through the academy. I only got anything because, I dunno, tits.'

She looked at him.

'Everything I've got, everything I've done... no one ever thinks it's on merit. On ability. Unless banging your senior instructor is considered an ability, which I did not do. I began to believe it. That rots you from the inside. So, there's my advice, free of charge and speaking as one who knows. Don't do it.'

'What changed?' he asked.

'The chief gave me a chance. The first person to actually evaluate me on ability. That's why I resigned my pins and went for it. And that's why I am not going to feth it up.'

'He brought us both back in, then,' said Milo.

'What?'

'Mkoll. Brought us both back in.'

'I guess so. Well, you'd better not feth it up either, then, had you?'

He nodded.

'They're in awe of you, you know?' Zhukova said quietly.

'What? Who are?'

'The Ghosts. Your old friends. You walked with the Beati. Fought at her side. Fought at the chief's side on that fething island and killed the Anarch.

They're in awe of you. That's why they keep their distance. They have no idea how to talk to you.'

'They can talk to me like they used to.'

'Call you "boy"?'

'I don't mean that.'

'No, I know what you mean,' she said. 'You should tell them.'

'I honestly don't know how.'

'Well, you need to find a way. If you're staying.'

'I don't even know that.'

'Wow, boy,' Zhukova said. 'You *are* stubborn. Well, it's been nice meeting you.'

'You too,' he said. But she'd gone. Vanished without a sound into the blue shadows.

He could see why Mkoll had given her a shot.

In Cygnus City, the turret guns are hammering. The next wave of Aeronautica has just gone over, dropping dazzle-flares to paint the redoubts. They'll need to stay in cover when the shockwaves come, then get up and start moving before the smoke clears. He can smell islumbine on the air, but it's not in the air, it's in his head, and so is Cygnus City. It's a memory of the scent of islumbine, a hole that something used to occupy, like the space left in a gun-case when the gun has been removed, but you can still see the fitted depression for it. And the empty memories are just inside a dream anyway, and this is just a fething dream again, and she's not in it, not even a space she used to occupy and–

He woke.

On his fifth or sixth visit, he finally realised why he liked the liquor-house on Hainehill Street. It had certain advantages. Locals drank there, Urdeshi locals, and off-world Militarum didn't venture in.

But most of all, the building was old. Its frame was timber built.

The barman saw him when he entered, and had a jar of fobraki waiting on the wooden bar-top. The bar itself was framed with thick, worked timbers, stained almost black with varnish and smoke and the grease-dirt of years. Posts cut from single tree trunks held up the ceiling, and the rafters had been cut from the same forest.

Not nalwood. He could tell that by the grain. But not local. This timber had been shipped in years before, maybe cadderwood from Taliscant, or Far Halt cedar. Maybe it *was* nalwood. The Tanith mills had traded off-world for centuries, and it had been a long time since he'd walked the forests, perhaps so long that his knowledge of knot pattern and heartwood grain had waned.

But it was wood. It was Great Timber, cut by loggers from an old forest, brought here from there. The warmth of it, the feel of it, it reassured him. And if he squinted, after a few jars, he could imagine the upright posts as trees standing in leaf, and smell the damp musk and leaf-litter of the forest floor, and hear the wind sigh as it stirred the boughs above.

The pulse had never left him. The throb behind his breastbone, beneath the old tattoo he couldn't remember getting. It had been there since his childhood, since the time when he really was just a boy. Instinct, intuition, a warning knot in his gut, call it what you like. Milo didn't call it anything, because he couldn't explain it, and people looked at him warily when he tried to.

She had never questioned it. In fact, the Beati had trusted it, and looked to him when a certain expression crossed his face. It wasn't a curse or a blemish to her. It had been a gift from the Throne, and one to be cherished.

He hadn't felt the pulse since Orchidel Island.

He's on the shingle. The air's cold, a strong wind off a grey, wallowing sea. There's no scent of islumbine, there's just a sense of purpose. The bastard will die. The bastard will die, now and here. This is how it's supposed to end. This is what he's meant to do, no matter how much his ears are ringing from blast concussion, no matter how weak his limbs are, no matter how much his stomach heaves or his head aches from translation sickness. The pulse beats right under the gristle of his breastbone. This is where his path has been leading him. This is where she saw him going. This was why she let him walk at her side, so he could come here and do this.

Everything has led here. From the deep woods of Tanith, from the dust of Herodor, everything, from there to here.

The wet shingle slithers under his feet. Kicked stones skitter. There's the weight of the grenade in his hand. He wants to fall down and vomit and pass out, but he won't. The bastard is right there. Just ahead. A ragged shape on the beach, trying to get up, dirty robes flapped by the inshore wind. The magister doesn't look like anything. He doesn't look like a creature that has dominated the stars, or razed worlds, or united hosts of fanatics with his voice. He looks pathetic, fallen, broken. This, in the end, will be easy to do. An easy kill, quick and–

He woke.

The wood in the Hainehill liquor-house was painted pale blue, the walls white, and the lipped edges of the low tables yellow-gold, the three colours of the Urdeshi banner. Between the thick ceiling posts, most of the liquor-house was given over to seating: low wooden benches around squat wooden tables, no more than a foot off the ground. The tables were oblong, with thick, raised lips around the edges, almost like market pallets. Milo supposed that's what they had once been: market pallets, or ware boards, or maybe dough trays from a bakery, repurposed as tables just like everything else in the place was repurposed. Jars and trays, even the mismatched bottles that were used to store the fobraki, they had all been something else originally. They had been used for a long time, they had served their purpose and, when they were no longer needed, they had been pressed into service in a second life, to serve in a different way.

The paint was so thick, it was hard to see the grain of the wood. The tables and benches were so low, patrons sat hunched, like men around a campfire, except for those who had found benches against the white walls which allowed them to lean back.

Up in the rafters, old, moth-eaten banners had been strung up: the faded flags of long-lost Urdeshi companies and brigades, or the threadbare pennants of local labour guilds and fab worker unions, once paraded through the streets on high days and festivals.

Milo admired the Urdeshi resolve, their steadfast nature, unbowed and dignified after centuries of hardship and war. Where did that come from? Was it some special alloy struck in the alchemy of the forges? Suffering and loss broke some cultures, but not the Urdeshi. It seemed to make them stronger.

But not stronger so they would rise up, renewed, and win. Just stronger to endure the next loss, and the one after that, and the one after that. They expected loss. They expected suffering. Victory seemed like an awkward surprise.

'You Guard?' asked the man in the machinist's smock. 'You Imperial Guard?'

The Sons of Sek were the archenemy. Worse than the Blood Pact, because their feral nature was tempered by a greater discipline. They had harnessed rage and murder like no others.

Milo had been fighting them for a long time, first with the Ghosts and then at the Beati's side. He loathed them, but he also respected them. You had to respect such a capable foe or you'd lose the fight.

And the Sons had lost. They were gone now, broken. Milo had fought them, and he had been their prisoner, and he had hidden in their midst long enough to get some measure of them. Not an understanding, or a sympathy, but enough to get a degree of insight. The devotion to the cause, the certainty of their calling.

The corpses of five of them, mob-killed, were strung from a gibbet at the corner of Hainehill. There were gibbets just like it all across Eltath. The bodies would hang there until decay made suspension impossible. They would be abused, and spat at, and pilloried by every passing citizen, day in, day out, a reminder of someone's victory and someone's defeat. Milo was sure that, when decay finally took its toll, the remains would be dragged to the bastion walls, and skulls put on spikes, and bones in iron cages. The defeated enemy, humiliated and desecrated. The Urdeshi victory would be made to endure too.

At Brachis City, Ashwarati and Siprious, the Sons had displayed Militarum skulls on stakes. Milo remembered it clearly.

What must it feel like to have lost? Milo had no sympathy, but he could imagine. To be so certain. To be so united in one cause and one purpose, unified by a single voice, and for all of that to just disappear. The Sons had lost their voice. They had lost their way.

Better to rot from a gallows-tree than live with that.

* * *

Am I like you, corpse? Am I so different? Loyal, driven by a purpose I believe in with all my heart, fighting for a cause? Answering a voice without hesitation? When our bones hang side by side from a gibbet, or rot side by side in the grave, could anybody see a difference? Duty and faith, honour and belief, those things rot away long before flesh and organs.

You found your way from there to here, and here, for you, is a rope and a crossbar and ignominy. Somewhere, on the road from there, I lost my way.

And all I can do is stand and look up at you. I am breathing, and you are simply swaying in the midday breeze. Beyond that, is there any real difference between us?

'You Guard?' asked the man in the machinist's smock. 'You Imperial Guard?'

Milo nodded. The man sat down on the bench beside him, uninvited. They sat hunched over the blue table, like friends around a firepit on a cold night.

'This is no place for you, lasman,' the man said.

'What?'

'This is an Urdeshi place. Not for your kind.'

'My kind?' Milo turned to look at him.

'Look, I mean no offence,' the man said. He waited as the passing server filled his jar again. 'But others might.'

'I don't know what you're saying,' said Milo.

'Then you're a fool. Urdesh has lived Archonate, and Urdesh has lived Imperial. More years the former. This is just another thing. Urdesh is Urdesh.'

'But we won,' said Milo.

The man in the machinist's smock laughed. He smelled of grease and metal dust, the work-waste of the forge.

'This time,' he said. 'You won, lasman. Urdesh didn't. The cities burn. The land burns. You are just a different master.'

'Is that what you think?'

The man shook his head. 'Not me. Some do. Many do. Urdesh is strong. It survives, no matter what. Archon or Throne, one year or the next, carving their tithes and their tributes, crowing their commands, making promises and never delivering. Urdesh is Urdesh, in the end. Not my sentiments, but out of respect, I wanted to mention it to you. This is no place for you. Coming here, alone. What do you come here for anyway? Praise? Thanks? Deference? Undying gratitude?'

'No.'

The man shrugged.

'What then, lasman?'

Milo didn't know what to say. He couldn't say the reassurance of the old timber, or the solitude, or the anonymity, because those things sounded feeble.

'I like it here,' he said.

'Here, friend, is no place for you.'

There, on Tanith, when he is a child too young to remember it happening, he is given a tattoo over his breastbone. There, in Tanith Magna, when he is just a boy, a pulse of premonition drives him to escape the fire, and allows him to live. There, in the heat of Vincula City, just months later, a tall man in a commissar's uniform unpins his shiny unit badge, and hands it to him to acknowledge his formal entry into the Tanith regiment. There, on Hagia shrine world, the dreams of islumbine begin. There, in the dust of Herodor, the same tall man hands him a straight silver to replace the one he has lost, so he can carry it with him as he walks at the Beati's side.

There, from each there, each step on the path, to here. To the shingle. To the inshore wind flapping the ragged robes. To–

He woke.

To the dirty liquor-house on Hainehill. To the low, blue timber tables. To the creak of a gibbet rope outside as the breeze sways a voiceless corpse. To the jar of fobraki in his hand. A toast, my friend, my friendless friend, my dreamless friend, a pledge.

To Tanith. To Urdesh. To duty. To dreams. Here's to them. Here. From Tanith to Urdesh. From there to here. From–

He woke.

But he did go back. Damn the man in the machinist's smock. Damn his friendly advice.

Another night of fireworks in the skies over Eltath. Music and laughter in the streets. A victory, of sorts, for some. Enough for most to celebrate. Deliverance, from there to here.

Milo walked up the steep streets alone, avoiding the celebrating crowds, the pit-roast grox and the bands, the bunting strung from gutter to gutter, the kegs rolled out and tapped at the kerbside, the liquor-houses and dining halls where the Militarum went off duty to make merry with the locals and wash the war out of their minds with fobraki and amasec, and ale and laughter.

He wandered up Hainehill, into the quieter streets, past the fab and the manufactory row, past the gibbet, creaking and stinking in the night air. Fireworks flashed behind him. The lamps in the liquor-house made a reluctant invitation.

It was subdued. Locals, drinking silently, hunched. A pledge murmured as a jar was lifted towards a mouth. Milo felt he knew what it meant now, the Urdeshi pledge. It was entirely in keeping with their stoic character. A stubborn acknowledgement that here was little different to there, and all that mattered was the persistence in between. A sour, resentful toast to the effort of enduring, a salute to the weary, unending slog of seeing it through.

The barman saw him come in, and wiped the blue, painted wood of the bar with a dirty cloth. He set up a jar, and unstoppered a bottle. No greeting. Grudging eyes on him from all sides.

Milo lifted the jar.

'From there to here,' he said, and knocked it back. He was a lone figure at the bar, an outsider, dressed in unmarked, un-badged black, but the locals had long since decided who he was. Not local, a saviour or just another invader, a stranger with a fish tattoo, at the very least *not them*. Militarum. *Imperial.*

'So this is where you take yourself?'

Milo looked around. There were ghosts in the doorway, dark shadows. They stepped into the lamplight, and were still ghosts.

'What are you doing here?' Milo asked.

'Thought we'd come and join you,' said Mkoll.

'Nice fething arsehole place you've found to crawl into,' said Varl, glancing around in distaste.

'Honestly, what are you doing here?' asked Milo.

'Oh, what? We can't step out for a little laughing juice?' asked Larkin, with a grin.

The three of them surrounded him at the bar.

'What is that stuff?' asked Varl, nodding towards Milo's jar.

'Fobraki.'

'Looks like piss.'

'Tastes like it,' said Milo.

'You really know how to have a good time, don't you?' Larkin chuckled. Mkoll held up three fingers for three more jars. Dubious, the barman set them up and filled them. The three ghosts raised their glasses to Milo.

'From there to here,' said Milo.

'What's that? That's fething stupid,' said Varl with a frown. 'Forever the same.'

'Forever the same,' chorused Mkoll and Larkin. They drank. They made faces. They put down their empty jars, and stifled coughs.

'Let's take a table,' said Mkoll.

Milo took a full bottle from the barman, and left some coins on the counter. He followed the others to a corner table. *Forever the same.* He'd forgotten that. The old Tanith pledge. Milo didn't think he'd heard it since Tanith Magna. Surely, sometime since then? Sharing a flask some night with Bragg and Corbec and Feygor? It was hard to say. But just the sound of it, those three words, was an instant memory, like the smell of nalwood or the musk of a forest floor.

It was an honest pledge. And, just like the morose Urdeshi one, it was a salute to perseverance and endurance, to duty and resolve, to the journey, not the destination. But it didn't seem so mean-spirited or grudging. He guessed that every culture had their own version, expressing the same stalwart sentiment.

Even the silenced Sons.

They sat on blue benches around a blue table that had once been a ware board.

'What's wrong with these seats?' Varl asked. 'Why are they so fething low?'

Milo shrugged. He put the bottle on the table.

'And why is the table so low? And what is that fething filth?'

'We won't be needing it,' Mkoll told Varl. He nodded to Larkin. The old marksman grinned and furtively slid a ceramic flask out of his satchel.

'Proper stuff,' he murmured as he filled their jars with sacra.

'Why are you here?' asked Milo.

'Bored,' said Varl.

'Fancied I'd stretch my legs,' said Mkoll.

'Oh, don't feth with him,' said Larkin. He looked at Milo, showing his bad teeth in a vulpine smile. 'We were worried about you, Brinny boy,' he said. 'You haven't seemed yourself. Not since you got back from all your high and holy adventuring. Thought we'd come and keep you company. Perk you up.'

'I'm fine.'

'Yeah, you are,' said Mkoll. 'So it's probably time you stopped acting like you're not.'

'What?' said Milo, taken aback.

'It's not a good look,' said Larkin.

'Makes you look like a right arsehole,' said Varl.

'I didn't say that,' put in Larkin, 'but it's not a good look, Brinny. It's not you. You're a Ghost, boy, not a–'

'Right arsehole,' said Varl.

'I said we should have rehearsed this,' said Mkoll quietly. 'You two are hopeless.'

'Rehearsed?' Milo echoed.

'She said he was glum,' Larkin said to Mkoll.

'Yeah, she said we should talk to him like normal. Just like we always did, so that's what I'm doing,' said Varl. He looked at Milo. 'Do you feel better yet?' he asked.

'I don't know what's going on,' said Milo.

'Someone told us, on the hush, that you were feeling out of sorts,' said Larkin, 'and that we, and by we I mean everyone, were being a bit stand-offish. Like we didn't know what to say to you.'

'We don't know what to say to you,' said Varl. 'To be fair.'

'We don't,' agreed Larkin, 'but she said we should just talk to you. Settle you down. Say whatever. But that's not easy, because you keep pissing off on your own every night.'

'Who's "she"?' Milo asked, but he knew.

'So here we are,' said Larkin.

'How did you find me?' Milo asked. Mkoll gazed at him steadily.

'*Really*?' he said.

'This is where you go, is it?' asked Varl. 'Why here? Is it the stink of the latrines? The lice? The piss-water?'

'It's the timber,' Milo said.

They all thought about that for a moment.

'I get that,' said Varl. Mkoll raised his jar.

'Forever the same,' he said.

They echoed him, and necked the sacra.

Feth, that was more like it.

They were on their third shot of sacra, and Varl was telling a story about Brostin and a jammed flamer. Varl was gesturing theatrically, but his movements were tight. Like so many of them, he had come out of the Eltath fight wounded, and he was still healing. They all had scars. They all had wounds. Varl was just getting to the punchline when a figure appeared behind Larkin, leaned in, and put something on the table in front of Mkoll.

'What the feth?' said Varl.

'Thought you'd want that back,' said Zhukova to Mkoll.

'What the feth?' Varl repeated.

Mkoll stared at the warknife on the table with remarkable composure. 'That's mine,' he said.

'It is,' she said. 'You boys have a good night, now.'

She walked away towards the door.

'What the feth?' Varl exclaimed.

Mkoll picked up the knife. There was a tiny smile on his face.

'I lost mine at Tulkar Batteries,' he said. 'This is a replacement. Got it out of stores when we came back. I've only had it a few days. Not worked it in yet.'

He held it out to Milo.

'You better take it,' he said. 'I'll get another. You'll need one.'

Milo hesitated.

'You will need one, won't you, Brinny?' asked Larkin.

Milo nodded. He took the knife.

'Fill the jars,' he said to Larkin. 'I'll be back in a minute.'

He caught up with her in the street outside. Rockets and flares over the harbour were lighting the long slope of Hamelhill.

'Wait!' he called.

Zhukova looked back.

'What?' she asked.

'You told them.'

'Obviously.'

'Well, you didn't have to,' he said.

'Clearly, I did,' she said. 'You weren't going to. Or, if you ever got around to it, the God-Emperor would have woken up by then and everything would be over.'

'You don't need to fight my battles, Zhukova,' he said.

'Oh, but that's the point,' she said. 'I do. And you need to fight mine. This life, Milo, it's a group effort. We're a regiment. We count on each other. Otherwise, what's the point? You couldn't do it, so I did. One day, it'll be the other way around. And you'd better not feth up.'

'I won't.'

'That's all right, then,' she said. 'Now go back to your friends, boy. You've got some stories to hear, and some stories to tell.'

She turned, and started to walk away.

'Thanks!' he called.

'It's not about the thanks,' she called in reply, without looking back.

He waited a moment. He decided to watch until she was out of sight, but he lost her in the shadows almost immediately. Showing off, probably.

He turned, and walked back up the hill towards the liquor-house lights.

'You don't listen, do you?' said the man in the machinist's smock. He was standing in Milo's path. In the mauve gloom of the evening street, his friends stepped into view. Six of them. Four big fab workers. Two soldiers. All Urdeshi.

'You have a problem, friend?' asked Milo.

'Not your friend,' the man said. 'Not your friend, "hero". Not your friend, "lasman". I told you to stay away. For your own good.'

'For my own good?'

'That's right. Just a word to the wise, but you didn't listen. You want us to thank you? Buy you drinks and say what a great man you are?'

'No.'

'But you come in every night. Ignored my advice. Urdesh is Urdesh, and you're not Urdesh, arsehole.'

Milo sighed.

'I'm pretty tired of people calling me "arsehole" tonight,' he said.

'Oh, you should be used to it then,' said the man in the machinist's smock. He let a stout chair leg slide into his hand from his sleeve. It was wood, painted blue. Hard wood, repurposed yet again.

'It depends who says it,' said Milo.

'Yeah, when I say it, it's affectionate,' said Varl. He and Mkoll and Larkin were standing behind the men.

'You were gone a while,' said Mkoll. 'Come back and join us.'

Milo nodded.

'I will,' he said. 'And maybe we can stand these fine gentlemen a drink to celebrate victory over the Archenemy.'

'Imperial arseholes,' said the man in the machinist's smock.

'You know what that sounds like?' Varl asked.

'Yeah,' said Mkoll. 'It sounds ungrateful.'

She says, 'The path is what matters, Brin. The path. That alone. Not where it takes you. It's how you get there. It's how you carry yourself. It's how you take the steps.'

'But surely–' he starts to say. The scent of islumbine is very strong. Chief Mkoll was saying almost the same thing last night, over sacra in the liquor-house. But that can't have been last night, because that had been Eltath, on Urdesh forge world, and this was...

...where? Siprious? Gant? Ashwarati?

'Paths shift,' she says. 'They shift all the time. Goals. Opportunities. Possi-bilities. Even destinies. Victory is only part of it. The trick is to find the path. To find it and follow it, and when it shifts, find it again, and follow it again, and never lose your way, no matter how many times it changes. I'm told the Tanith are good at that. Their famous scouts. I know them to be renowned pathfinders.'

He nods, and–

He woke.

The hallway in the Urdeshic Palace was cold, and they were obliged to wait on wooden chairs. When the Prefectus officer appeared, they all stood.

'The commissar will see you,' he said.

'I hope it's Fazekiel,' Varl whispered. 'I can sweet-talk her. Pretty sure.'

'Or Blenner,' Larkin whispered back. 'He's an easy touch.'

'As long as it's not Hark,' Varl murmured.

'Keep quiet,' Mkoll hissed.

'You first,' the Prefectus officer said, pointing to Milo. Milo glanced at the others: Larkin with his black eye, Varl with his split lip, Mkoll with his bandaged knuckles.

'Behave yourselves,' he said. 'I'll take the rap for this.'

He walked into the office alone. The officer closed the door behind him. Milo stood to attention, eyes front, waiting for the dressing down and the list of punishment details.

'Drunken brawling with Urdeshi locals. You put four of them in the infirmary. That's not the responsible behaviour of the Militarum.'

Milo didn't reply. It wasn't any of the commissars he'd expected.

'This isn't the reunion I imagined,' said Gaunt. He was sitting behind the large desk. He put down the incident report, and looked up. He seemed older, yet the same. His eyes were very different. His uniform too: austere, severe, vengefully commanding. Not the garb of a colonel-commissar. Not the uniform Milo had once pressed and repaired and button-polished.

'Anything to say?' asked Gaunt.

'No, my Lord Executor.'

'You sure?'

'I am... surprised to see you. I had been told you were busy. Your new duties. I...'

'I shouldn't be here,' said Gaunt. 'I have seven lords militant waiting for me in the war room, and army lists to review. This is not my job any more. This is so below my duty level, in fact, that Macaroth would scold me if he found me doing it. But Beltayn noticed some names on the overnight watch list, and brought it to my attention. So I asked Commissar Hark to step out for five minutes. He's getting some recaff.'

'Yes, lord.'

'Brawling in the street,' said Gaunt.

'No excuse for it, my Lord Executor. My fault entirely. The others aren't to blame. They just stepped in to protect me.'

'Mkoll, Larkin and Varl?'

'Yes, my lord.'

Gaunt sat back.

'The report says you were defending the honour of the Astra Militarum against local malcontents who were expressing anti-Imperial views.'

'Still no excuse, my lord.'

Gaunt rose to his feet. Milo had grown tall since their last meeting, but he had forgotten how tall Gaunt was.

'I'd wanted to see you,' said Gaunt. 'Intended to, when I heard you were back. I thought you were gone, you see. Dead at Oureppan. The Beati told me so herself. Turns out she was wrong. Even saints are fallible. So I wanted to see you, of course. To welcome you. But things have been so frantic. There's so much work to be done. The next phase...'

His voice trailed off. He looked at Milo with his unfamiliar and unforgiving eyes.

'No excuse for it, though,' he said. 'I should have made it a priority. These are hardly the circumstances I imagined.'

'I don't think I'm a Lord Executor's priority, sir,' Milo said.

'I think you're wrong, Brin. I should have made the time before now. I understand you're rejoining the First.'

'I don't seem to have an option, my lord.'

'Do you want an option?' Gaunt asked.

Milo hesitated.

'No, sir. I don't.'

'Good. Good to hear. Fazekiel's got the paperwork in hand. You'll need to get your kit up to spec. Badges, pins, the rest. Get the Munitorum on it.'

'Yes, sir.'

'I hear...' Gaunt said, then paused. He cleared his throat. 'Chief Mkoll tells me you might feel you'd lost your way. After the Orchidel action, after Sek. A loss of confidence, perhaps. Or regret at your detachment from the Beati's staff. You'd been with them a long time, seen a lot. The Tanith First might seem a backward step.'

'I... felt disconnected, my lord. I felt like I'd failed the task that had been set for me.'

'Failed?'

'I didn't kill Sek,' said Milo.

'No, not single-handedly. But then neither did Mkoll. And neither did I, and neither did any single soldier of the Astra Militarum. What you did do could hardly be regarded as a failure.'

'Yes, my lord. I have had time to reflect on it. And now, I don't see it as a backward step.'

'What changed your mind?'

'A few things. Common sense, mostly. And Chief Mkoll told me that it's about the journey, not the destination.'

Gaunt frowned.

'That's his philosophy?'

'Apparently, my lord.'

'I find it troubling that my head of recon thinks that.'

There was a knock at the internal door. Beltayn looked in.

'Two minutes,' Gaunt said. Beltayn nodded and stepped back out.

Gaunt returned his unblinking gaze to Milo.

'Duty calls,' he said. 'Tell those idiots outside they're cleared. No write-up. Sweating in a hallway is punishment enough. Oh, and I have your pipes. Tell Beltayn to arrange a meeting where I can get them back to you, and where we can have a decent conversation.'

'When might that be, my lord?'

'Feth alone knows. Now, dismissed and on your way.'

Milo saluted and turned.

'No, wait.'

He looked back.

'Do you remember Vincula City?' asked Gaunt. 'Back on Voltemand?'

'Longer ago for me than you, but yes, my lord. I do.'

Gaunt unpinned the Tanith crest from his jacket, and tossed it across the room. Milo caught it neatly.

'Seems only right that I welcome you back in the same fashion,' said Gaunt.

The woods close in. This deep in the heartwood, the trees shift and stir, and paths never stay true for long. The green canopy rustles like a hushing ocean, and the light is emerald. The child is alone, just a boy, alone on the blurring track.

But he's not afraid. The nalwoods murmur and sigh, and the pulse is a reassuring knot behind his breastbone. He can't get lost. He knows where he's going, and if the path fades, he'll find it again. He knows how to get from here to there. It's a talent he was born with, always and forever the same. Someone calls his name and–

He woke.

ABOUT THE AUTHOR

Dan Abnett has written over fifty novels, including *Anarch*, the latest instalment in the acclaimed Gaunt's Ghosts series. He has also written the Ravenor, Eisenhorn and Bequin books, the most recent of which is *Penitent*. For the Horus Heresy, he is the author of the Siege of Terra novel *Saturnine*, as well as *Horus Rising, Legion, The Unremembered Empire, Know No Fear* and *Prospero Burns*, the last two of which were both *New York Times* bestsellers. He also scripted *Macragge's Honour*, the first Horus Heresy graphic novel, as well as numerous Black Library audio dramas. Many of his short stories have been collected into the volume *Lord of the Dark Millennium*. He lives and works in Maidstone, Kent.

YOUR
NEXT READ

KRIEG
by Steve Lyons

The Death Korps of Krieg lay siege to a hive city on the outskirts of Warzone Octarius, desperately trying to prevent untold masses of orks and tyranids spilling out into the Imperium. How far will the ruthless Korpsmen go to achieve victory in a seemingly unwinnable war?